JONATHAN D. LAMBERT

OF GODS AND RUIN

BORNE BY BLOOD
BOOK TWO

CONTENTS

Fullpage image   IV

Fullpage image   V

Fullpage image   VI

Dedication   VII

Prologue   1

Part 1

Interlude   122

Interlude   126

Part 2

Interlude   266

Part 3

Interlude   454

Part 4

Afterword   611

TRETHEFEN
DRUNT
THE WHITE MOUNTAINS
MAST RIVER
BRETHEFEN
THE TRADER'S ROAD
TENNEFEN
THE SOUTHERN SEA
THE PERPETUAL

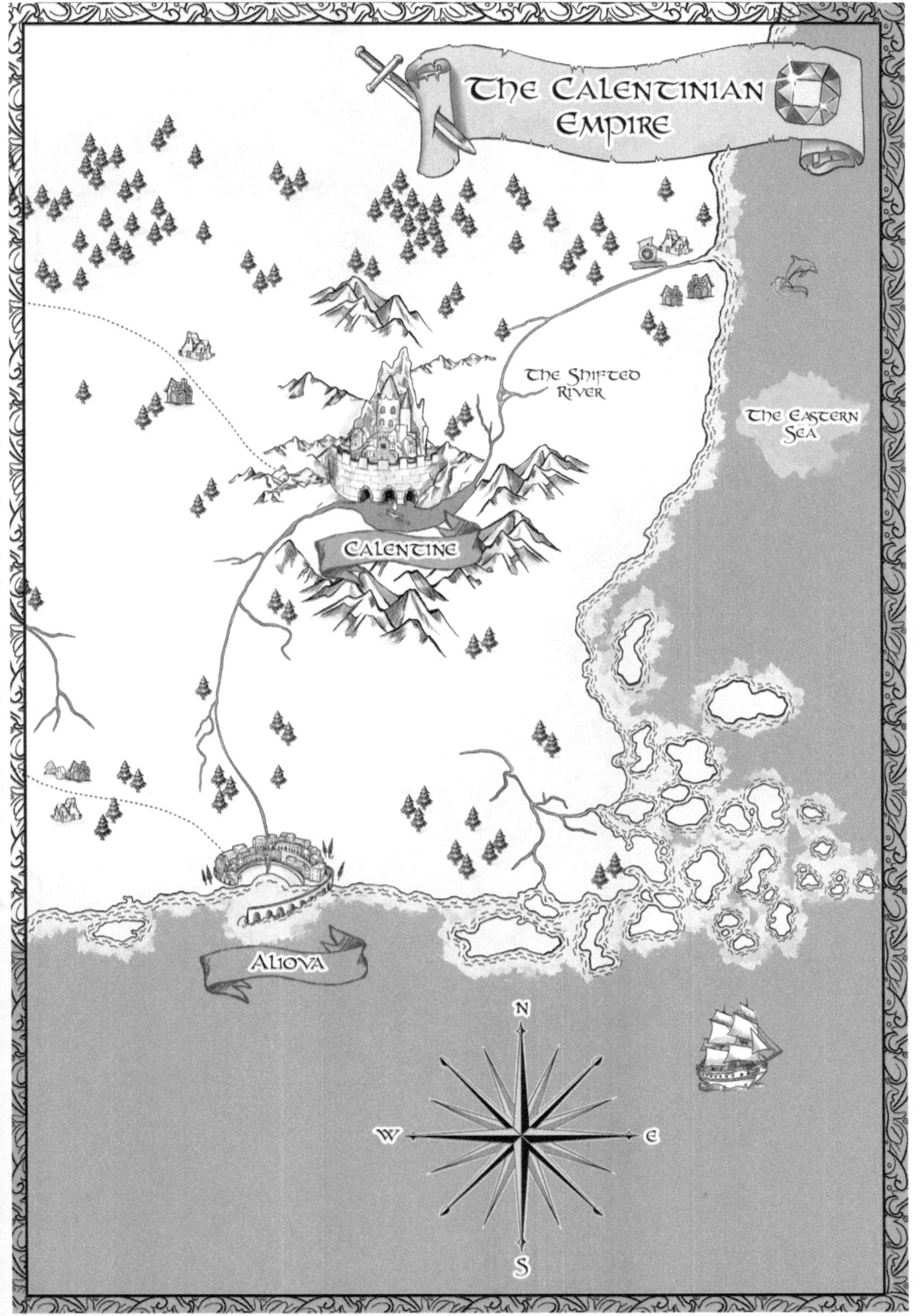

THE CALENTINIAN EMPIRE
THE SHIFTED RIVER
THE EASTERN SEA
CALENTINE
ALIOVA
N
W
E
S

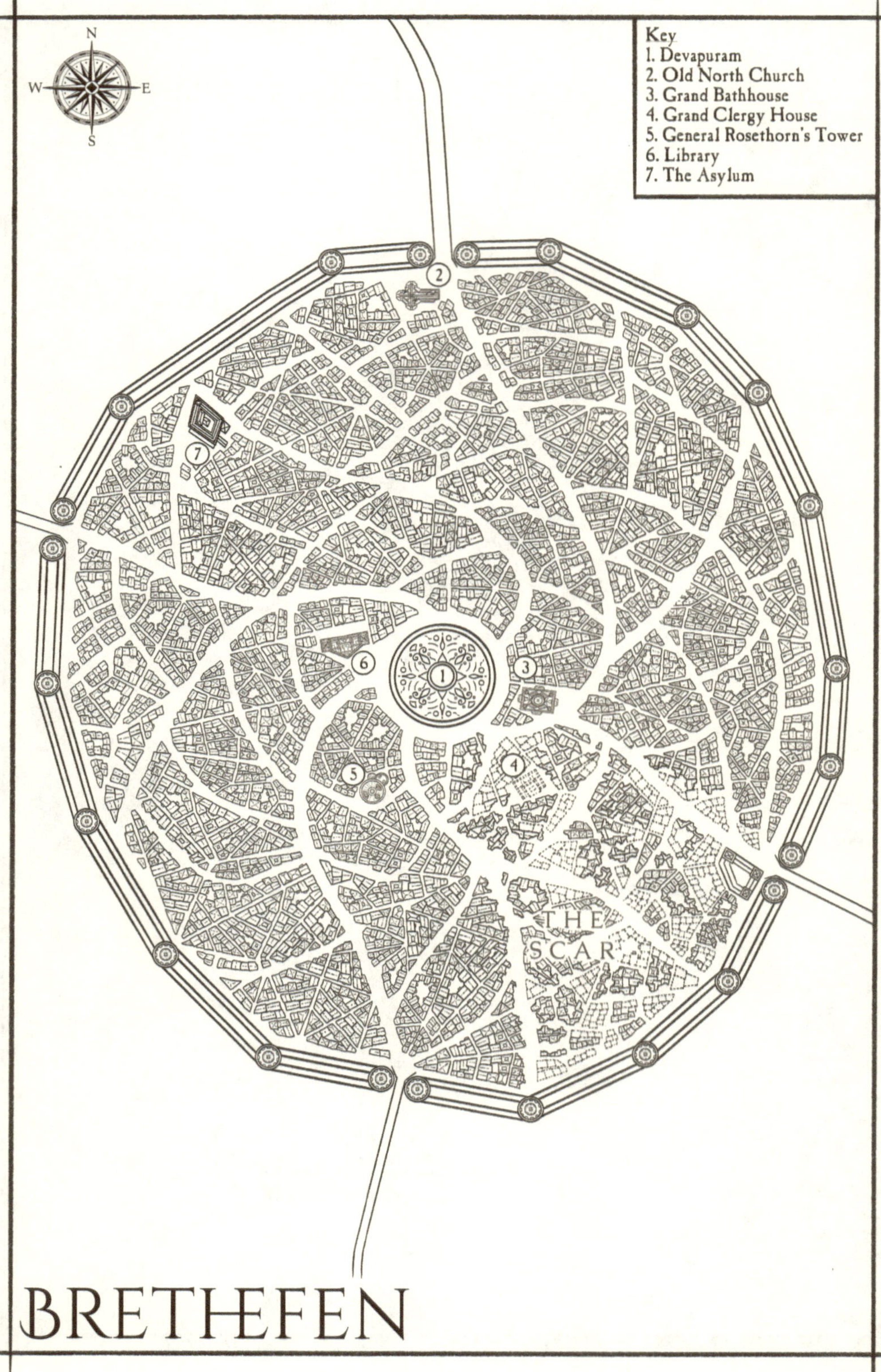

N
W E
S
Key
1. Devapuram
2. Old North Church
3. Grand Bathhouse
4. Grand Clergy House
5. General Rosethorn's Tower
6. Library
7. The Asylum
THE SCAR
BRETHEFEN

To my earliest readers.

Friends, family, and the unexpected fans who stumbled onto these books.

Your eagerness to read these stories encourages me to continue writing them.

Prologue

Desiccated corpses littered the floor. Gaunt, horrified expressions re-mained sculpted onto their faces, the pain endured during their final act unfathomable. It was the aftermath of magic reserved for only the direst situations, dispassionately draining the life from its casters.

Masini maneuvered around them, whistling a tune.

It would have been proper, probably, to be somber and respectful as he worked his way through the remnants of some nine hundred mages. More than a few of them, however, were directly involved in the calculated murder and torture of a dear friend of his, and he found it difficult to resist kicking an occasional familiar face as he crossed the cave's floor.

Dead or not, they deserved worse than an eternity entombed and cut off from the Astral Plane.

Not all of them, of course. There were many among their number who had only done what he intended to do now and protected their home realm from the forces of destruction they'd safely locked away. For them, he felt genuine pity. Also, gratitude, for not being required to be one of the poor bastards.

The ultimate sacrifice in exchange for their realm's security. A steep price that his aspect specialties helped him to avoid. Who else would've been able to create a bubble of the Astral Plane around the chamber? Certainly not any of the other pinnacles. *Definitely* not any of these adhara.

He was supposed to close off the cave now that the ritual was complete, but first, he needed to check on something.

Which brought him to the immense seal. Tall, circular, and standing like a wheel, it filled the entirety of the cave—which was astonishing, considering the sheer girth of what they'd had to drag through here.

The fractals that covered the stone were a complex maze of patterns and endless loops, intended to hold the ethereal souls of those who now littered the floor and use their vidut to hold its charge until long past even their interminable life spans.

Strangely, as he approached the enormous, black slab, the only thing he smelled was the damp of the cavern's seeping water, dripping slowly in the background. The bodies were, for all intents and purposes, mummified.

Rough way to go.

He inspected the seal's fractal lines closely, searching intently. The energy radiating from them was intense, a source that was almost too tantalizing to resist, given the life sentence he was about to serve. A punishment that seemed... excessive. But, given the destruction that had desolated this realm, he couldn't say he would make a different decision in their positions.

Ah, there you are.

His finger ran over the hairline crack in the cadentite. The thick, inlaid stone was still touching, allowing the imposing barrier to function as intended. The seal and what lay beyond would be nearly indestructible, but a good amount of force, concentrated at this spot, and it *would* shatter.

Explosively, he guessed. Best to get someone else to do that if it came to it.

It was a last resort, the backup plan of backup plans. The fact that he was even considering it was madness, and despite his ability to conjure a static entrance to the Astral Plane, he had never gotten far enough in his tutelage to learn how to navigate that horrid place.

Hopefully none of that would matter, and he could go on living in this desert of a realm without worry. It was hard to believe, given some of the others he would need to share it with. It was a big place, maybe he could get far enough from them that it wouldn't matter.

Or, maybe, his worst nightmares would come true, and the people responsible for the murder of someone he deeply cared for would get the idea that they should have what didn't belong to them. Or, worse, they might try to recreate the things that had wreaked this havoc.

People, he found, could have short memories. Especially the ambitious ones. If they were patient as well, then there was a real danger. And there were those in possession of such traits which he couldn't trust.

If only a prison had been built for them, too.

In the meantime, the locals here weren't all that bad. Short-lived, maybe, but more akin to those in the High Realm than many would care to admit. They, at least, weren't colossal giants, or fanged beasts that could out-eat an army.

Yes, there were worse places to be exiled.

Maybe he could open a brothel. Or better yet, a *string* of brothels. The things he could enlighten these primitives to... Well, the few still alive, anyway.

Giving the thin seam a satisfied rap with his knuckle, he turned around and began walking out of the cavernous tunnel, respectfully avoiding a few corpses, stepping on the faces of others. It was time for him to head east.

They had a gate to close, and Protorus *hated* when he was late.

Maybe he had time to stop for a drink?

PART 1
CRUSADES

CHAPTER ONE

Lord General,

The King and this Court bereave Brethefen's tragic devastation—the empire mourns alongside you. Your measures to maintain a sense of structure during this time of turmoil display that our trust in you was well placed, and you may continue knowing you have our express assent. As to your report of the events precipitating this destruction, your directive is to silence these raving fallacies, lest they spread among the populace and nobility alike. Suppress this narrative with immediacy, beginning with the detention of the witnesses not under your direct command.

The white, plastered walls did little to quiet the screaming.

Desnia laid on her cot, squeezing her eyes closed in a vain effort to block out the manic, foreboding, and gut-twisting wails of those sealed behind iron-strapped, wooden doors like the one at the entrance to her tiny cell. They echoed in the barren halls, penetrating not only the door but what felt like her very soul, knocking on hidden fears. Paint flecks peeled from the wall, her cot creaked and groaned with every twist of her body, and the small window and thick adobe walls did less to repel the torrid heat than she'd like.

These concerns were mere drops in an ocean of indignation, however. Her face contorted in a sneer of contempt thinking about the betrayal that had landed her in this makeshift prison—an incarceration that was more a torment to her than she expected anyone to realize.

You always find us the most interesting company, came Masini's sardonic voice in her mind. Her guards had allowed her to keep his ring after the influential arguments of those far above her sewer-dredging station. They'd also been equally threatened about stealing it from her person.

As if that's enough to earn back a semblance of trust, she thought. *Bastard.* "I don't need your shit right now, Masini," Desnia said under her breath. She couldn't afford to be heard talking to herself, lest anyone think she was as insane as the ward's other inhabitants.

And yet, I offer it anyway, he said. *There needs to be a balance of humility and retrospect in your life, Des, and obviously I am the best suited to even these scales of your personal growth. And as long as I am present, forced to listen to the antithesis of the moans I so do love to hear, I am going to remind you of this. Frequently. Perhaps to the point that I, myself, drive you insa—*

"Shut it!" she hissed.

A heavy, gauntleted fist beat on her door. "Quiet in there!" one of her two guards grumbled through the small, barred portal in the door's center.

Asshole, she thought with a shake of her head. *So much for being quiet.*

As I was saying, chirped Masini, *wait, what was I saying? Oh, yes! Couldn't you discuss getting some nicer accommodations with Lord Del—*

"Don't even *speak* his name," Desnia cut in, her words forced through tight lips.

Des, you don't know if he's even the one responsible for our irksome internment. There must be an empty wing in this place, they could at least put us further away from all the Seers.

Desnia flinched at the word. Not for the first time since she'd been confined, she felt an unease, a nagging at the back of her mind that tugged the play strings of her innermost fears. She told herself that her own sanity wasn't affected by the nighttime howls or endless rants, but gods-damn her if it didn't put her even more on edge than normal. Not that the lack of sleep helped.

"He was the one I was going to meet," came her angry whisper, "no one else knew where we were going to be. He doesn't show and I get arrested? He sold me out, Masini." *Just when I thought I could trust someone... Figures.*

The pounding that rattled her door's hinges was accompanied by a face this time, one of malice masking a hint of deviant thirst beneath the steel helm and stubbled face. She was all too familiar with such glares.

"I said quiet!" growled the guard. "Fucking *Eka.* Don't think that because you've got some lords looking out for you, we won't find a way to make your life hell. Disobey me again and I swear you'll be meetin' Strigi's owls in a hurry."

Desnia glared at him. She *should* keep her mouth shut. Antagonizing the man wasn't going to make her situation any better, but she was in no mood to take his berating.

"What the fuck is your problem?!" She stood from her cot and walked to the door, face turning a tinge of red.

"My problem?!" His dark skin didn't betray the flush of his face, but his eyes were gorged with fury. The smell of his breath made her wince. "We lost friends in that fire, you fucking wench, friends who worked at the prison that you burned down. Cousins of mine lived in that area too, we haven't heard from them in the days since *you* torched half the gods-damned city." Tiny sprays of his saliva were assailing her through the door's portal now. "My 'problem' is that whatever punishment the general decides for you isn't going to be enough. But don't you worry, me and the other guards are going to make sure you get your due, fuck what the lords have to say about it."

With that he disappeared from her view, moving back to his post. *I'll let you all die next time instead. Asshole*, she thought, keeping her mouth shut this time. She took the opportunity to get a closer look at the door's lock and handle—a simple enough design, not that she had a means to get past it—before pacing around the room and eventually sitting back down on her cot.

He seems pleasant, said Masini. *Though it was more like an eighth of the city, maybe a quarter.*

Desnia shook her head as she stared at the white-tiled floor. There was little argument to be had over the guard's claims, the thought of the destruction she'd wrought incessantly nagging the back of her mind. The pervasive melancholy that saturated the city was becoming harder and harder for her to ignore.

It's just in my head, nothing more, she thought. Then the buried thoughts clawed their way to the surface. *Maybe I could have done something differently... No. It's done, looking back won't help get me out of here.*

"Fucker was probably rotten *before* the fires," she said quietly. His insults irked her almost as much as her lack of response. She thought about what he said, frustrated. "If he's going to insult me, he should at least use a term I understand. Don't even know what 'Eka' means."

Well, said Masini. She groaned at having unleashed another boring history lesson. *The original meaning has been lost to these people in the bowels of time. The newer, less refined meaning is a curse referring to a pagan god of fire and death, which I suppose is somewhat accurate. I think he's saying he doesn't like you.*

"Wow. How insightful," she said with a heavy layer of sarcasm.

I know, he said. *Where would you be without me? Wait, don't answer that. Anyway, have you worked out a plan to get us out of here yet?*

Desnia shook her head. A normal prison this was not, though it was equally thorough in ensuring cells were bare of anything usable for an escape. Aside from the bars in the windows—which were ruggedly installed—and straps on the door, there was no metal to be found, and her guards were relieved every few hours, but did not leave the door until the new shift arrived. She wore the same white shirt and trousers as the rest of the residents at the Asylum, which offered nothing to aid her.

No one had made an attempt to visit her, not that she expected it. Delvan was obviously too much of a coward to face her after his betrayal, and she didn't expect the brute or short one to give two shits about her. She had no idea where Nerio was; hopefully he'd fled the city or gone into hiding. Jerdine might have vanished through that strange portal of light, but it didn't mean his agents in the city vanished with him. The young priest was the only one she had hoped to see again.

But hope was a poison.

It had infected her caustic pit of emotions. She focused on it, kindled it, because if she didn't the hole in her soul would overflow with dejection. *Had I truly let myself believe?... No. They're like everyone else. Like I need to be—cold, ruthless, heartless.* Her survival was all that mattered, and she needed to look out for herself first and foremost. *Just like they all did.*

"No plan yet," Desnia whispered. "But I'm working on it." She ran her fingers through her sweat-slicked, blonde hair as she cradled her head in thought. Maybe she could get the guard in here and lift a key? Or something to pick the lock? Even then she wasn't sure she could incapacitate two guards while unarmed and cornered. She'd need a distraction. *Sure as hell won't be a fire this time,* she thought.

Ah, said Masini dryly, *well I'm sure you'll think of something. Not like Jerdine and a very powerful, highly motivated ksat-ksat-ksat... Fuck! person are looking to still bring an army over or anything.*

"Yes, I know. You've said this. Repeatedly. I want to find Asta too, remember?" *Though for wildly different reasons.* Her mind wandered back to the cries from down the hall. "How long will it take to get there once I figure out a way out of this place?"

Good question, he replied.

Desnia waited. "Well?!" she said, almost loud enough for the guard to hear. Again.

Hmm? Oh, it's kind of, uh, complicated.

"I'm about to throw you out this fucking window, Masini!"

I don't believe you, as I know you'd miss my eloquent perversity far too much. But, as you're wont to commit... brash acts, I will attempt to explain. Her fingers curled and she took a deep breath. *The entrance to Asta's, huh, weird that I can say that. Maybe because they're not from the Hi-Hi-Hi... eh, never mind. The entrance to their prison is sort of buried.*

"Meaning?" she asked with a furrowed brow.

Landslide. To make sure no one finds it. Problem is, I may or may not remember where I might have done that.

Her head pulled back and hands splayed to the side. "I thought you said it was in the mountains! What the fuck, Masini?!" She heard shuffling from outside her door, eyeing it warily as the guard hit it and repeated his angry, "Shut it," comment. She ignored him.

It is, I know that much. I was the one of the ones who, uh, his tone turned sorrowful, *helped seal it. But, and this is the important part, when I did, I put a flaw in it. In fact, it's probably the reason they can talk to you, along with the other, less temperamental and sane people in this building.*

"Why?" she asked, suspicious and ignoring his gibe.

It's a long story that I probably wouldn't be able to tell anyway. But let's just say that my patriotism was... waning. I love my home, the people there, but the ones in power and the things that they'd done to people that I cared about, just to lock their problems away... It was horrific. Traitorous, even. Asta wouldn't be able to escape, but if I ever needed to, there was a chance I could release them.

A sigh passed through Desnia's lips. Her problems were compounding and becoming seemingly insurmountable.

"Alright," she whispered, "so do you at least have an idea where to look in the mountains?"

Sort of, he said flatly.

I swear to the gods, if he had a crotch I'd punch him in it. "Explain," she growled.

Well, he continued, *it's been a few epochs, and men and Blues alike have fought wars and changed landscape there over the millennia. I have a rough idea, west of here, in what you call the White Mountains.*

Of course, she thought, *gods forbid this be easy.* "That could take longer than my fucking *lifetime* to search, Masini. How am I supposed to explore *thousands* of miles of mountain range?!"

It's not thousands *of miles you need to search, just, you know, a hundred. Maybe.*

A light breeze wafted through her exterior window, lightly grazing over the beads of sweat that covered her skin. It did little to cool her annoyance.

"Ignoring how impossible that still seems," she said, trying not to let the daunting task perpetuate the gloom she was already feeling, "*if* we find the entrance, how do we unseal it?"

Without causing a catastrophic explosion of power? I'm still working that out. Besides, opening the entrance is only half the problem. If we want to release Asta, which is still mildly terrifying to think about, we need to break their chains, remove the, uh, barrier at the entrance, and break the sp-sp-sp... ugh, destroy its cage. Actually, when I say it all like that, it seems like a lot, doesn't it?

"Is this a joke?!" she asked, bolting upright. "We need to narrow this down, Masini! I don't have time for this! I can't end up... Just figure it out. Fast."

You're awfully pushy for a 'Master Thief' that can't pick a lock and slip past two guards, he retorted.

Desnia hissed at him through gritted teeth, "I'm working on it! I've only been here for a few days you—"

The doorway burst open, the guard she'd accosted standing in it, a baton in his hand. "That's it," he said, a malevolent smile tugging at his scowling face, "I'm gonna teach you to listen." The other guard watched closely from the door, his expression equally eager and vengeful.

She glanced at his waist as he approached. As much as she already despised this bitter sewer rat, it appeared he wasn't a *complete* idiot. He'd removed his belt and anything she could grab before entering, speaking to experience with situations such as these.

As he stepped forward, Desnia tried to bolt around him—a futile attempt, but she had little other options. He easily grabbed her and threw her to the floor in a heap.

Wood met her ribs in a painful *whack*, her back arching as she fought for breath. His blows only landed where clothes covered skin—this wasn't their first sadistic outburst, clearly. Desnia curled in a ball on the ground as the baton whistled through the air and struck her back, then her legs. She closed her eyes, waiting for the beating to cease through the agony that pervaded her body.

"Disobey me again," she heard the guard say, "and I won't be so gentle next time, ya' hear? No amount of protection from some privileged little shit is going to stop me from finding out what you got hiding under there." She felt the baton maneuver to catch the bottom of her shirt and pull at it, exposing her beaten stomach. She tensed, sending riving pain through her, as she clutched tightly at the white cloth around her torso.

The guard let out a snort, then she heard him walk out of the room and slam the door shut, leaving her on the floor struggling to move, her breathing labored and muscles spasming.

I need to get out of here, she thought. *And when I do, I hope I get the chance to kill that bastard.*

Chapter Two

Continue your increased collections for the foreseeable future, as the royal treasury estimates the cost of rebuilding to be in the millions of suns. Assets of this magnitude are available only through loans, as much of the crown's funds are currently invested into the southern continent's war. Reimbursing even a minimal interest rate on such extensive lending will be a heavy burden upon the empire, and the beneficiaries of this spending must contribute.

Ale dribbled past the rim of Orne's mug and into the thicket of his beard.

Golden, delicious, inebriating ale. After months of excruciating absence, the gods had delivered it back into his life. He tilted the ceramic back as he chugged one mouthful after another, staring at the wooden beams of the dimly lit ceiling as he drained the entire vessel of its divine elixir. He slammed it down onto the stained tabletop, splattering the puddling wastes of drunken pours that dirtied the surface.

He reached for the pitcher before him, his mind tuning out the background din and focusing on the task at hand. He lifted the handle, finding it light and as absent his much-needed distraction. He let out an annoyed grunt as he put it back onto the table. He glanced at Kolden's mug—which he'd emptied nearly half an hour ago now—and wondered where his brother had scurried off to.

Little shit was supposed to be buying tonight. Gonna make him buy double tomorrow.

He raised the emptied pitcher above his head and shook it as he attempted to make eye contact with the maid standing at the makeshift bar. She was distracted, in deep dalliance with some olive-skinned woman with dark hair. He wagged the pitcher in the air again, his face growing stern, and his mouth parched. Still, the barmaid ignored him.

Didn't anyone know how to do their job around here?

"Hey!" His voice boomed like a tree being felled. The steady rabble quieted for a moment, the twenty or so other patrons turning to look at Orne. He wasn't sure why they looked upset; he was doing everyone a favor. He didn't bother looking at any of them, his eyes staring ahead and holding their focus on the barmaid who finally deigned him with her attention—even if it was in the form of a blank stare followed by a roll of her eyes.

His brow furrowed deeper, and he shook the pitcher above his head for the *third* time. The maid let out a sigh that carried itself across the room and then began pouring another pitcher for Orne from one of the large casks at her back. He lowered the one in his hand back to the table and then caught the dark eyes of the woman whom the barmaid had been bantering with.

The glint of a hilt drew his gaze to the gladius-style sword at her side. *Old design, but a solid one*, he thought with a nod. *Holding a drink in her left hand, probably her sword hand. Same side as the blade, she must quickdraw it.* This woman was clearly not like the other soldiers that were scattered throughout the crowd tonight. This was someone whom he suspected was efficient in the extreme with a blade. Not to mention the fact that its hilt and scabbard were bound in white, muted inanite-dyed leather, leading him to conclude it was darksteel. *Impeccable taste.*

While he was taking in the finer points of her weaponry, she looked at him with a frown, then shook her head and turned her back to him as she took a draft from her own drink. *That's fine, can admire that too*, he thought with a shrug.

The chatter in the cramped space regained its lost momentum, filling the air with something besides the heat and smell of souring ale, along with whatever that strange haze was.

It had only been a week since the encounter with the High Realm mages in the bathhouse and at the gate deep below the city's surface. Not to mention the fire that had ravaged above. Things had changed at a rapid pace in Brethefen afterwards. It only took a few days for taverns like this one—set up in tucked away locations—to begin springing up like carrion birds to a battlefield. Soldiers talked, and it had been easy enough for Orne and Kolden to find their way to one of these establishments each night.

Orne's replenishment landed on his table with a *thud* as the maid—he couldn't remember her name—dropped it off with all the grace of a mule, turning the table's puddles into ponds, much to his dismay. The petite woman grabbed his empty pitcher and held out her hand. "That'll be twelve moons," she said, her posture as stiff as her extended arm.

Orne's jaw nearly dropped to the floor. "Twelve moons! That's outrageous!" Had Kolden been paying that rate all night? He was so inept when it came to money. "I could buy *six* pitchers in Drunt for that much!"

"This ain't Drunt, honey. You have any idea how much it costs to get this stuff brought into the city? What we pay all of *you* to look the other way, especially now? It's twelve moons, take it or leave it." Her hand remained extended before his face.

He groaned, grumbling about how her establishment was still technically illegal under the new city laws and he could have her shut down. He wouldn't, as they had the best ale they'd found in the city so far, but it still seemed beyond extortion to him. *It's a dumb law anyway.*

He pulled the coins from his purse and placed them into the waiting girl's palm, who snapped it closed and left without so much as smile—those were a rare currency in the city as of late. Orne guessed that half the people in here were burning through what little money they had left to drink away their sorrows after the fire's devastation.

As he carefully poured himself another glass, the door to the alley outside opened, two soldiers ducking beneath the low lintel as they entered. The emblems on their shoulders marked them as common infantry, and Orne eyed them as they scanned the cramped tables and maze of chairs in the crowded tavern. As he feared, their gaze landed on the only two empty seats in the establishment—the ones at his table.

He let out a sigh as they made a beeline towards him. He had no interest in fraternizing tonight, or most nights for that matter, and until now he'd been able to fend off everyone who'd considered joining him.

These two did not get the hint.

"Mind if we join you, Sergeant?" said the taller of the two, a boy who'd joined the military as soon as he was able, best Orne could tell.

"Gods-damned feet are killing me," said his friend—another boy about the same age, acne covering his face. He pulled out the chair before Orne could mention it was Kolden's and sat down, placing the back of the chair forward and leaning his chest against it. "Ole Rosethorn's got us pulling twelve-hour shifts now. Feels like we've been on march with how much he's got us running around the city, collecting taxes and breaking up the protestors."

The taller one raised his hand to the bar maid, who Orne noticed was smiling and had become affable as she talked to the woman with the sword again. Orne scowled.

"I'll be right back," the tall one said, "can't seem to find anyone with half a brain to work in these places." Orne's head bobbed with a reserved nod as the boy walked away.

"I don't know about you," said the boy that remained, "but I'm already startin' to miss the principles being in charge. Got spit on twice today, and I swear that if people weren't so damn hungry, they'd be throwing their compost at me."

"At least it isn't rocks," replied Orne in a low voice, taking another sip of his ale.

"Aye. Not yet at least." The boy reached forward to grab the handle of the pitcher on the table. Orne's hand swiftly swung down onto its rim and held it down, a glare to stop an army emanating from his eyes. "I'll, uh, just wait till Ren gets back, then," the boy said shakily. Orne grunted, holding the icy stare.

"But you know what I mean?" he continued. He seemed to be a talker, annoyingly. "People, they're not taking to Rosethorn's martial law too well. You musta seen it? Half my day is scattering the beggars who lost it all in the fire, the other half is collecting money from people who ain't got it. People, they used to look to us soldiers with respect, you know?" *For the whole month you've been one.* "Now, they see us coming and scatter, or sneer, or scream at us. Just doin' my gods-damned job."

Ren returned to the table, pitcher in hand and disgruntled look on his face. "*Ten* moons! Can you believe what they fucking charge here?" he said as he poured himself and the talkative one a glass.

Orne slammed his fist on the table. "That bitch!" he hissed.

"Right?" replied Ren. "Damned extortion if you ask me. I'm already giving half my soldier's pay to my ma'. She's got nothing left after the gods-damned fire, hardly have the moons to get by and now I need to pay a week's rent for a drink. Be paying suns before you know it.

"Never could get ale around here before though, so I intend to drink as much as I can, while I can. I'm Ren, by the way. This here is Trecius."

"Just call me Tre," he said.

"Orne."

"Pleasure, Orne," Ren said. "I feel like I've heard that name somewhere before."

"Not as much as you should have," Orne grumbled under his breath.

"Man," said Tre, "I tell ya', if I could get my hands on whoever started that fire... Gods, the things I would do. Damned merchants are charging double for food, principles kicked out of the city, the general squeezing everyone for coin to rebuild. It's a mess."

"My ma's been coughing ever since," said Ren. "Healers say she's not in bad enough shape to look at over the ones they got in all the burn wards. I'm with ya', I say we find the one responsible and give 'em a taste of their own wrongdoings."

"I hear," said Tre, leaning in over the table, "that they got 'em locked up, hidden away while they figure out what to do to him."

Word gets around fast, thought Orne. He personally agreed with locking Desnia away. Lighting the principle's spire ablaze had been a tremendously *stupid* idea and she should be punished for it. He wasn't sure why Delvan was making such a fuss about it. Putting a scratch in the gate hardly absolved her, and Kolden had been the one to smash the key. He was still yet to thank Orne properly for coming to his rescue, something about having it "all in hand." *He's so full of shit.*

He took another swig of his ale and let out a long, hot breath. He was under strict orders not to discuss anything about that night, which, to his chagrin, meant that almost no one knew about his role in it. Now, instead of receiving accolades and medals, he was forced to sit here and listen to the belligerent ignorance of youth.

"That's not what I heard," replied Ren, "word from the general himself is that Principle Jerdine got too deep into his iguan stash, if you know what I mean, and set the place on fire while he was hallucinatin'. That's why Rosethorn kicked all the principles out and took charge."

Orne stared at the wall in the distance, doing his best to tune out the vapid gossip and not correct the two adolescents, a loathing building his chest that was ready to burst. It was an itch that ate away at him, making him want to scream about the true events and his role in them.

Blessedly, the gentle strum of a lute graced his ears, its dulcet tune smothering the babble of the tavern like a heavy night's snow. A bard sat atop the marred top of the counter, which looked as if it were slapped together with whatever scraps could be found on the street—a stark contrast to the entertainer's finery. He began to hum as his fingers expertly plucked at the strings, the dim light of the room's oil lanterns casting long shadows over his features. With everyone's attention fixed squarely upon him, his hum slowly became a melody, and from his lips escaped a ballad.

> Dark was the night when evil reared
> 'Neath our city it prepared
> to spread and scour our sacred streets

> Tyranny would our people meet
>
> But lo! From distant land
> Saviors came, to make a stand
> Heroine and knight, gold and blue
> against power foul, they were few
>
> Guided by gods their battle raged
> To save us all from death's embrace
> Doom's gate our fair lady broke and
> bade
> With a strike from her blade
>
> Sword's glowing edge her heart did
> meet
> Foiled her assailers did flee
> Owl's talons carry to her judge
> The price paid for peril's plunge
>
> But of this world she was not gone
> By the brave knight, her death undone
> From him poured forth the great gods'
> will
> Her body no longer still
>
> Dark was the night when evil reared
> 'Neath our city hope endeared
> Strong remained our sacred streets
> Blue blessed, gold did gods greet

Some among the crowd clapped and cheered for the song, the entertainer standing atop the bar and bowing deeply. The musician gave his thanks, proclaiming the song title, "Blue and Gold," as he walked around with his hat collecting tips for the performance. Many of the patrons murmured and shared incredulous looks, doubt etched onto their faces. A zealous few stood and called for an encore.

Orne was not among them.

His face burned hot. His shaking hands slammed his empty mug onto the table, rattling the frame and almost toppling the half-finished pitchers. *That isn't even what happened! I was there too, not just Del and the damned thief!*

"That's a hell of a story," said Tre.

"I don't know if I believe the whole 'coming back to life' thing," said Ren, turning back to the table.

"Those Blues man, I tell ya', my gran used to talk about them and the things that they could do. Who's to say they *don't* have the power to bring someone back like that?"

"If they can, then I say it's a waste. Where were they after the fires? Where are they now? The only one I know of is ole Rosethorn," said Ren bitterly.

"Nah, there are others in the city," said Tre. Neither seemed to pay attention to the fact that Orne was nearly ready to rent the table in half. "The one in that there song, there's some priest going around saying he's still in the city. Some noble from Calentine or something. Says that they got the girl hidden away somewhere, won't say why though."

"I'm going to kill that fucking priest," growled Orne.

"What was that, Sergeant?" asked Ren as the bard made his way to their table, his hat held before him.

"Great show," said Tre, tossing a moon into the hat. "Say, you play any-where—"

Orne stood upright so quickly that his chair toppled to the floor behind him. He pointed at the bard, air gushing in and out of his nostrils. "That isn't what *fucking* happened!" he boomed. Heads drew back and eyes went wide as silence once more fell upon the room. "Get your fucking facts straight and... And... Bah! Fuck off!" He wanted to scream, to beat the *proper* lyrics from the bard. But what could he say without defying orders?

Grabbing his pitcher from the table, he took a long draft, tilting the heavy vessel back until every last drop vanished into his gullet. Wiping his beard and tugging his uniform straight, Orne turned and stormed away, leaving a shocked room behind him.

Where the hell is Kolden?! he wondered, deciding it was time to leave.

He strode towards the back door where Kolden had gone to "look into something" almost an hour ago. Hinges rattled as he went through one door, and then another, long halls full of rooms around him and a thickening, sick-ly-smelling haze clogging the air. He checked door after door, finding nothing but people half-conscious behind each of them. Ire and ale still clouded his mind, but he began growing concerned the deeper he went into this maze of milky fog.

Finally, he reached a door that had a guard in front of it. He tried to stand between Orne and his post—unfortunately for him.

With a yank of the man's collar, twist of his body, and well-placed foot, Orne wrenched the man down in a blur, putting his head squarely into the wall with a *crack* before he could draw a weapon. He collapsed to the ground in a heap. Orne turned and kicked the door open, bursting into a room lit by the lacking luster of a few dying lanterns.

Canvas sacks were mounded in the corners, two women working something in a mortar and pestle nearby. Against the back wall a stream of half a dozen men were silently carrying more of the canvas sacks into the room, tossing them into the pile. And in the center sat Kolden, speaking to a group of men that looked to be little more than common thugs. One perhaps was a mercenary, the others had rust all over their hilts and grime that caked their faces and attire.

The *clash* of the door striking the wall drew all eyes to him. The women gave him but a glance and continued working, the laborers in the back letting out a curse in some tongue he didn't recognize, and the people surrounding his brother just gaped in a stupor.

"Kolden!" Orne said, ignoring the room's attention and groaning in the hall. "We're leaving." He didn't have any interest in staying here with that damned bard or terrible barmaid.

The mercenary seemed to regain his senses and drew his blade. The others stood and backed away from the table looking startled and angry.

"You know this soldier?!" one of the men asked Kolden. *Where the hell is Kolden's uniform?*

"What? Oh, no, well," stammered Kolden, "he's, uh, my bodyguard. He gets rather protective; you don't need to worry about him. Let's just settle down and we can talk further about the introductions you mentioned—"

"Nah, I don't like this," said the man. "You never said anything about a bodyguard before, how do I know you're not some army spy, looking to root us out? Huh?"

What was going on here? Orne was getting annoyed that he wasn't on his way to his quarters, his eyes on the dull reflection of the mercenary's sword.

Kolden raised his hands, "Look, gentleman, I already told you what I want, which, by the way, isn't *technically* illegal anyway. So, if we could just continue—"

"We should gut them and be done with it," said the mercenary, taking a step forward, leaning too much on his front foot. Orne drew his own darksteel side sword, listening and aware of the man at the door getting back to his feet. *Gods-damn it, Kolden. Can't leave you alone for a fucking hour without you getting us into shit.*

"That, uh," said Kolden, doing that thing where he thought he was being convincing, "would be a terrible idea. How about we just put the swords away and—"

"No," said the man that appeared to be the leader of this rat's nest. "We're done. Ank, take care of this."

Kolden groaned as the mercenary lunged forward towards Orne, his foot landing too far forward. Orne smacked the blade away with his own, taking advantage of the man's loss of balance and his own sword's momentum to bring its tip in a blurring arc of silvery-black down and through the man's boot. His opponent fell, a screech that sounded as if from a dying animal resonating through the room. *Idiot.*

He heard a noise behind him, the guard from outside having risen to his feet and approaching through the half-ajar door. Orne turned and kicked the wooden panel, sending it wheeling on its hinges and slamming into the guard, knocking him to the ground unconscious once more.

The others Kolden had been speaking to looked on with pale faces, stunned, their hired goon squealing on the ground. The people in the back had set down their burdens and were watching intently, and the women had become motionless. All were silent.

Except Kolden, of course.

"Gods-damn it, Orne!" he shouted. "Can't you see I'm in the middle of something here? What the fuck are you doing?"

"They started it," replied Orne, his fury turning towards his brother.

"They—" Kolden dug his face into his hands. "You charged in here like a bull with a dog biting its balls, Orne! Can't you see that I was busy—"

The wounded man's compatriots seemed to find their courage, drawing the assortment of rusty blades from their sides, their confidence shaky—at best. Orne eyed the workers in the back, grips on knives at their waist, far more competent in appearance than he'd initially assumed.

"No, no." Kolden waved his hand at them. "We'll be seeing ourselves out, don't do something stupid." They glanced at the crying mercenary on the floor, clutching his toeless foot in a pool of blood. None resisted as they left through the door from which Orne had come, stepping over the man on the floor. Thankfully no one attacked or followed them. Orne was sure he could outmatch any of them individually, but when groups of people assailed you, things could get messy. One lucky shot was all it took.

"What the hell were you doing in there?" Orne asked, sheathing his sword as he and Kolden walked, stepping over a few drooling miscreants in the halls.

Kolden didn't answer.

Orne looked at him, seeing a pout on his face. "What?" he asked earnestly.

"What do you mean, '*What*?!'" berated Kolden. He reminded Orne of a badger. "I was finally making progress! Those were dealers that were going to introduce me to their suppliers. At least they *were*, before you burst in for... *What* fucking reason?"

"This bar's terrible, bunch of assholes run the place. We're heading back to our quarters. What were you looking to buy in a place like... Wait, what is this place?" he asked, waving at the smoke in his face.

"I've *told* you this." *No, you didn't.* "I'm trying to buy," he hushed his tone, "cadentite. And this dump is an iguan den, obviously."

Orne's brow dug into his nose. "After everything we just went through, you *want* more of that glowing rock?"

"What we went through is *exactly* why I want more of that 'glowing rock.' You saw the sword that one was wielding."

Orne could hardly forget it. The man had been a master with the weapon, fending off both Orne and Delvan in a match that should have been decidedly in their favor. He was half convinced the man had used some form of magic to aid him—no one could acquire skill such as that in a single lifetime.

"What the hell are you looking for it in here for?" asked Orne.

Kolden sighed in his dramatic way. "I don't know why I bother explaining things sometimes... I heard rumors that iguan was sometimes grown with cadentite mixed into the soil, not sure why. But if anyone is going to have it, it's going to be the people growing the stuff. Those vermin back there were dealers, and they were about to introduce me—"

Orne let out a small chuckle. "Pretty sure the only rodent back there was you, Kolden."

"—to the smugglers that are bringing the iguan into the city," finished Kolden with a glare. "If they could tell me who they were buying it from, then I could reach out to them and try to buy some of their stash. At least, that was the plan, until you *barged* in. The smugglers were there, too..." He groaned and dragged his hand down his face.

"If they were the ones in the back, they didn't seem the type to fuck around with, Kolden."

"Whatever." *Gods forbid you listen to me. He's going to sulk all night.* "Let's just get back to the tavern, you're buying me a drink for screwing everything up."

"We're going home," stated Orne firmly. "I've had enough of this tavern for the night. Besides, your ale's gone."

"Of course it is. Fine, we don't have to go back to that tavern, but I'm getting at least one more drink before we head back. And *you're* buying."

Orne grunted. His brother wasn't about to let this go, and he could be petty. One more drink couldn't hurt.

Chapter Three

The Court shall send a representative posthaste to assess and confirm the extent of the damage, as well as recover the body of Knight Commander Ferrand ce Lione so that he may be buried in the capital among his familial plot. Protect his sapphire as if it were your own in the interim and ensure that his honor is not sullied by these tales of his death. You know as well as I, the testing of our finitude by the masses is a path best avoided. Leave these memories beneath their headstones, for all our sakes'.

Nerio wiped the sweat from his palms onto his robe. The room was sweltering. He felt a chill, despite his perspiration. The gentle chatter of people collecting in the pews of the chapel made his heart race, and as he peeked around the wall to see out into the room tinted by the light of stained glass, his eyes went wide.

No less than *forty* people were gathered here, in the old church at the north end of the city where he and Desnia had once hidden. Its worn, wooden floors were covered in the ceiling's flaking paint, and the sagging, pointed roof was covered in water stains from where the rain easily torrented through cracked tiles. It, however, was not decrepit, merely in need of mending, and the humble abode held itself taller for the assembly gathered in its forgotten hall.

He'd started almost a week ago now, telling their tale of divine intervention to any that would hear it. Now he had a greater abundance of people than he'd ever expected gathering to listen to *him*.

Why the gods had chosen him for this task, he wasn't certain, but he knew it to be his purpose. His holy charge.

That made him stand straighter, confident in his message and the need to spread it. It helped to calm his beating chest, but anxiety's remnants tingled along his skin. As the bells outside began to toll, he took a deep breath and stepped out onto the dais, the murmurs dissipating as he took his place behind the lectern.

Raising his head high while resting his trembling palms on the aging wood before him, Nerio scanned the eyes that now turned their attention in his direction. He recognized a few priests who were becoming regulars at his speaks, and one or two appeared to be soldiers, though they lacked a uniform—these gatherings were not the most appraised of the current ruling caste of Brethefen, but Nerio had no intention of ceasing his efforts. *The truth of the revenant must be told.*

"Th-Thank you all..." he forced out meekly. He clenched his jaw. This was the gods' will, and he wasn't going to fail them as he had himself all those years. "Thank you all for coming. I stand before you today, not in an effort to affront, nor to create some sect that I've heard whispers and rumors of. I am here as a devout follower of Cordism, like all of you. And like all of you, I have spent my life in the shadow of those who would claim ownership over our beliefs and any interpretation of them that they saw as being outside of their own. Those who would outright reject the story I am about to tell you and condemn me as a heretic.

"A week ago, I had an... experience. One that I did not see, until the very end, had been planned and laid out for me by the gods themselves, in all their divine wisdom." He noticed some people shuffling, a few faces angry. Only the principles and King himself were to commune with the gods. Suggesting that he—a young, humble priest bearing the white sash of neutrality—could have been guided by their suggestion and intervention would be seen by many as blasphemy.

Still, he endeavored forward.

"Into my life came their instrument, their deliverance made manifest, in the form of a woman. A friend. I did not know it then, but their web of fate tied us together, and brought us to a head against an evil whose malice went beyond what I could have imagined. A man, a *demon*, whose purpose in this world had been to reap its destruction, building a doorway designed to unleash calamity upon us. He created this malignance under our very noses, and though we remained ignorant of his plots, the gods did not. This man, was Principle Jerdine."

A few audible gasps filled the room's vaults, hands covering astonished mouths. Nerio could feel his heart ramming his chest again, and he wiped his brow with his sleeve. He knew that this was going to be difficult to accept by many; the principle had been the city's leader for longer than Nerio had been alive. *Considerably longer, if what I've been told is true,* he thought. But those, like himself, that knew of the man's darker side would not be surprised by this revelation, and as his gaze wandered through the swarming buzz of confusion, he found several members of the clergy whose faces had turned grave. They understood.

"To aid us in their bid against the uncaging of this evil," he continued, "the gods provided three swords of noble knights, the finest warriors our fair empire has to offer. Together, with these soldiers of fate, we discovered the hidden secrets of the man who dared call himself principle, who dared taint the propriety of that office with his venom, and set off to face him, still unaware of the gods' hands in our lives. We knew, even with the might of those among us, that we may have faced our own deaths that night. But I trusted in the gods, realizing later that they, too, trusted in us.

"Do not be mistaken, however. For I do not mean to imply that I was courageous. I admit," he said, his head hanging with shame, "that I unwittingly played my part in Jerdine's schemes. I lacked the strength that compelled the knights so; a guilt that still shadows me. But thanks to them and their noble sacrifice, we prevailed, delving deep into the caverns beneath the city. And as the fight raged with the threat of our demise and ushering of demons upon us, we were saved by the knife of divinity, their instrument shattering the portal of maleficence with a strike from her blade.

"Our savior was struck down, smote by the blade of the singular demon that managed to claw itself into our world at the beckoning of Jerdine." A tear came to his eye as he remembered seeing that strange, glowing blade thrust into Desnia's heart. He spoke, his voice choked, "And I saw the person whom I care about most pour her hallowed blood across the floor."

The room remained quiet, stares fixed upon him. He worried. Were they angry with him? Did they see this speak as sacrilege? Would this retelling of that fateful night earn him the same end, for no other reason than conveying the truth? *I must continue. It is not about what I want, but what the gods need.*

"Then, their portal destroyed and the fight pressing them back, the demons fled. I thought all was lost. Our city was saved, yes, but despite knowing then that what we'd done had been holy edict, I saw my friend on the ground, lifeless. And I *cursed* the gods for it."

Harsh whispers created a cacophony that rattled the room like the tail of a snake. Nerio swallowed hard. "But then," he nearly had to shout to carry his voice across the echoing space, "a miracle. Through powers unbeknownst to myself or Blue alike, the gods channeled themselves through one of the knights that had fought so selflessly for our safety. Their light poured from him and *healed* our fallen savior.

"The fallen then rose from the dead." A murmur spread through the crowd like dust in the wind.

"I realized then the gravity of my error in misjudging the gods design. That I ever cursed them, it was clear, had been due to lack of my own foresight. A failure most profound. I stand here not only to spread the word of these events, but to beg the forgiveness of the gods for not understanding the breadth of their plans, for how could one such as myself grasp at the inklings of their infinite wisdom?"

Nods of stern faces bobbed throughout the crowd. Were they castigating him and his actions? He again wiped away beads of sweat streaming over his tightly cut hair.

"So, I ask unto you, worshipers of the divine, of Amenesol, Strigifious, Ursorner, and Almedia, who else have they graced such gifts of life to? Who else among us did they crown messiah?"

Whispers and creaking pews consumed the disquiet of the room as people shifted and spoke, their expressions filled with turmoil.

"None, but the King himself," Nerio stated. It was becoming difficult to breathe the thick, heavy air, the pressure he felt in his chest one forged of the fiery gazes of those that sat before him. Each of these speaks brought about risk and danger to his own life as he challenged thousands of years of doctrine. He was not, as he feared they believed, trying to upend the epochs of history that were the foundation of their belief. He was merely writing a new chapter at its end.

"The King remains our Lord," Nerio said, raising his arms to settle the crowd. "But I am here to tell you there is another: not a ruler of kingdoms and men, but a *champion* of them. Her sacrifice cannot be forgotten or locked away! So, I tell you her name now, lest you be told that she does not exist, or that she has perished. Say it aloud, and remember the name: Niallai oc Deste, Night Daughter of the Eighth, Desnia of Calentine city.

"Repeat this name, ink it onto mind and vellum, and know that if not for her we would not be free.

"Many of you have lost everything recently, and I ache for your misfortune," Nerio said, his face grim in the shadows of the cracked stained glass. "I want this new chapter of our doctrine to stand in the forefront of your mind and make all aware that the gods *do* care for you, they *do* hold you in their hearts, so long as you hold them in yours. If you doubt as I did, look to this recounting of their intervention and know that you're not forgotten, and of their designs, you are a part.

"This city was founded on the values of philanthropy, and in this hour most dark we must remember our neighbors and their struggles. Give what you can and may the gods' blessing find you all."

Nerio finished the speak, standing there, swelling with trepidation. Would the people reject him? Argue his word, calling him to be a fraud? He'd never been one to give speaks, projecting words of wisdom and support to the masses, but he'd been to hundreds, possibly thousands of them throughout his life—before and after becoming a member of the clergy—and he'd given his all to emulate even a fraction of the best he'd heard.

Standing there, his eyes darting from face to face in the crowd, Nerio realized that their attention had left him, and had instead found their neighbors, their friends, new acquaintances, and while there were varying expressions among them all, he did not sense the anger he fretted over. *I should stop standing here,* he thought, feeling relief as he stepped away from the lectern and down to the front row where a few priests he'd seen before sat.

"Brother," one of them said, standing and bowing to Nerio.

"No, please, there's no need to bow," said Nerio awkwardly. "I am merely a witness, telling what I've seen and felt."

"But your words, Brother, they inspire," said another of the priests. He was older, with rings climbing to the elbows of his sleeves. Having someone far above his own station speak to him so reverently only stirred Nerio's discomfort. "The people," the man continued, "need such inspiration in a time such as this. The light of your speaks, in times as grim as these, brings hope. And there is nothing this city needs more."

That is all I ever wanted, thought Nerio.

"Yes," agreed the younger priest, "and with such hope, perhaps we can survive this repression. I lost my church in the fires, and many here mourn far greater absences. With the army bearing down upon us, we need speaks such as yours, and this messiah you spoke of, she could be the catalyst this city needs to rise from its ashes."

Nerio repressed a smile, he was not here to feel pride in what he'd said, only to ensure the words were spoken. He opened his mouth to reply but was cut off by the eager young priest.

"I will bring word to the streets of your revelations, Brother. I will gather all I can and bring them to hear your speaks. The gods have shown that this is their will, and the people *need* to hear of this new messiah and know that the sacrifice of their city wasn't for naught."

Nerio's jaw hung agape. He had not expected such enthusiasm for his teachings. In his time pursuing the telling of these events, he'd not stopped to consider what would happen when people *actually* began listening. He wasn't certain what to say.

"I... I would be honored, Brother," he replied, "I would like to—"

There was a pounding on the doors at the far end of the cathedral. Muffled shouts from outside accompanied the *clunks* of metal on wood, and the room was suddenly drowned by fear and worry. Two men, the ones that Nerio had assumed to be soldiers, ran over to Nerio. He braced himself. *If they arrest me, I will find a way to continue. I must.*

They skidded to a stop before him. "Brother," one of them said, a tall man with a shaven head, grey beard and hard, scarred features, "we have to get you out of here, quickly. The general, he means to silence you."

Nerio shook his head in surprise. They meant to help him? Perhaps the gods did still watch over him.

"Um," he replied, dumbfounded, "through the back, there's a small door that leads to the alley."

"Lead the way sir, and hurry," said the other soldier.

"But all of these people!" he said. The pounding grew more harsh and violent, wood cracking and splintering. "We can't simply leave them!"

"Sir," the soldier said with a frightful glance over his shoulder at the door, "they don't have anywhere to put them with the prison burned down. They'll be questioned and released. They want *you,* sir, those are their orders. We need to leave, now!"

His lips tightened into a line as he hesitated, looking at the scrambled confusion of those who'd come to him. After a moment he was spun by the grip of the older soldier, briskly being pulled towards the edge of the large room. His guts twisted in a knot as he thought of all the people. Telling himself that the gruff soldier knew of what he spoke did little to comfort him. It felt as if he were being a coward once again.

He stopped to turn and look back, but a hand pressed against him with a kind urgency and ushered him through the side entry. As he abandoned all who remained inside, he heard the doors to the main hall burst open, a cacophony of panicked shouts and stern orders filling the once tranquil hall.

He hung his head with shame and told himself that this was the gods' plan as he was whisked away.

CHAPTER FOUR

This leads me to a more personal note. As you're assuredly aware, death and the destruction of property follow my son like a loyal hound. He blames these failings on claims of his supposed involvement in wild conspiracies and hidden cabals—which have never been substantiated—rather than accepting responsibility for his own actions. Thus, these should be seen as little more than the fabrications of a petulant, wounded pride. That he has convinced others to corroborate these fantasies is a matter of concern, one that we trust you will quash with efficacy.

The streets were rank with the malodor of Delvan's worst nightmares: ash and death.

Scorched façades and crumbled buildings met his gaze wherever it fell; bleak, irrevocable vestiges of the once jovial and colorful avenues. The moans of the injured, poor, and hungry as inescapable as the sight of their huddled forms. Nearly a quarter of the city's infrastructure had been decimated during their confrontation at the gate, and the homeless now surged to the streets in solemn waves, seeking refuge with desperate hope.

It was a scent that seemed to follow him like a wraith, reminding him of a past that felt impossible to forget even after the modicum of forgiveness he had allowed himself. The difficult truths he'd managed to accept merely calmed the inferno within, leaving remains such as those surrounding him in his heart. And not unlike the littered streets, his mind had become cluttered as of late, despite the burden of guilt that his acceptance had lifted.

Most of his thoughts this past week had been consumed with the processing of his life over the past few months. The beliefs and drive for vengeance that had fueled him during that dark, unremitting time he now knew to be naught but folly, born of his own ignorance. He'd hoped, prayed even, that these revelations would bring from his pain a better understanding, but questions scattered his mind like the refuse beneath his feet. And now, to further occupy his thoughts and twist his loyalties, he'd unwittingly betrayed one of the few people close to him.

Desnia had been arrested—because of *his* testimony.

He kicked a chunk of debris as the morning sun baked its way through his uniform, its hue matching the cloudless sky above and sapphire upon his chest. How unequivocally naïve he'd been to assume that Desnia would be forgiven of the transgressions which occurred during their pursuit of the gate. She was a hero to be lauded, not a criminal to incarcerate. If she was of noble blood and name, like himself, or Kolden and Orne, a parade would have been thrown in her honor. Instead, she was locked away, regardless of her valor. What had happened to the people that begged and pleaded around him was a tragedy, but it was paltry compared to the alternative.

And no amount of letters, requests, or formal propositions had brought him before the general once more to argue her case. *He can't ignore me forever. I'm entitled to an audience,* he thought. *And what she asked me that morning on the Devapuram steps...* He needed to discuss it further with her.

Being forbidden from visiting—let alone knowing where she was being held—made conversation, and atonement, difficult.

Delvan sighed as he walked beyond the edge of the fire's destruction—cutting through its charred boundary was almost unavoidable—and arrived at his third tea shop of the morning. Many of these provided what they prescribed as "healing elixirs" or "herbal remedies," which sounded akin to selling gravel as gold to him, but once you crossed a certain threshold of pain anything seemed worth trying. Not that *he* was in pain, but those he sought? Their mornings had been rough lately, to say the least.

It wasn't hard to spot the hulking figure hunched over a table, seemingly sized for a child compared to his enormity, the cup in his hands like an egg held by a bear. Beside him, forehead buried deep into his palm and face sagging to the sandy pavers, sat the man that appeared a mere dwarf by comparison. He wasn't as short as he seemed, Delvan knew, but his current company effectively made *everyone* seem miniature.

"There you are," said Delvan to Orne and Kolden as he sat down, waving to the shop's owner for his own cup of tea.

"We haven't moved in three hours, Del. Not like we're hard to find," groaned Kolden. "Feel like I've been kicked by one of those damned donkeys."

Orne grunted in agreement.

Kolden, shading his eyes despite the awning above them, squinted at Delvan and asked, "What's *your* excuse for looking so grim?"

Delvan hung his head, fingers fiddling with the specks of ash on them. "I just... had Des on my mind. I can't believe Rosethorn locked her away like that." He shook his head, brown, tangled hair waving before hardened eyes. "I *trusted* him when I told him what happened. I said I could bring Des, *willingly*, to explain the details to him, then he went and arrested her!" Delvan's voice had risen, causing both brothers to wince. "He *can't* ignore me forever. I'll go to the Court if I have to."

"Spoken like the true son of a noble," quipped Kolden with a loud sip from his tea.

"You're both lords, too, Kolden."

"True, just far less pretentious ones."

Normally, he'd have taken offense to such an insult, but coming from Kolden or Orne it always seemed more... grounded. As though they were merely trying to jest the humility into him. He thought back to his final weeks in Calentine and the pointed words of someone who tried to do the same. Strange, how he could come to appreciate the mockery.

"Regardless," continued Delvan, feeling calmer but still frustrated, "he should, by every right, be seeing me. At bare minimum *responding*."

"Look, I don't like that she was locked up either," said Kolden, "but as two people who have *extensive* experience with generals, we can assure you that he really doesn't care that you're angry. But, hey, if you want to let off some steam—figuratively, I mean—you could deign us with your noble-ness at one of the taverns these nights. Might help you forget all about the girl."

Thinking about their offer, Delvan looked at their pale faces, rather confident that the sweat matting their hair contained more ale than it did water. It certainly smelled that way.

"I'm good," said Delvan, despite the part of his brain that itched to join them. "Not sure how you plan on drinking tonight anyway, given that you look like an owl's circling over your head right now."

"This tea works *wonders*," he said with another slurp.

"Mhm," grunted Orne. "Still don't know why they serve hot tea in a fucking dessert. People here are strange."

"It's to make you sweat, obviously. Helps get rid of the hangover," Kolden replied.

"Fucking stupid," Orne grumbled, sipping his tea.

Delvan shook his head. He didn't want to explain to them the truth that'd kept him away from joining their nightly revelry. He'd finally managed to overcome his own guilt about the death of Hilbrun—that shadowy hand that had clutched his heart so possessively over the better part of the last year now dismissed. Or so he'd hoped.

Assuming it behind him after that fateful night, he'd still found, on occasion, the chill of its fingertips gently brushed his spine, waiting for him to welcome it back. Ale had only ever made things worse for him, and the thought of it alone was enough to make his hair stand on end and heart beat faster. Whether it was out of fear, or desire, he couldn't say.

The arrival of his tea pulled him from his trance. Sipping on it in the stagnant heat made him inclined to agree with Orne. He blew on the steaming liquid.

"Don't look so down," said Kolden, wiping a slop of sweat from his brow, "the general is just making a power play while his new martial law gets things under control. Give it a few weeks and he'll probably let her go, you'll see."

"What?" said Orne. "No, they should keep her locked up. Or did you already forget about the chunk of city that she burned to the ground? Got what she deserved."

"She helped us find Kolden, Orne," Delvan said. "Without her, he'd be dead and us along with him, if Jerdine had fully opened the gate. Can't imagine what an army of those... 'warrior-mages' or whatever Ferrand called them, would be like."

Orne's face turned sourer, and he looked away. This wasn't a conversation he was going to continue.

"I had that situation totally under control," said Kolden smugly.

"You were locked in a cage, dumbass," said Orne.

"As a matter of fact, I had gotten out, boulder-brain, and was ready to kill that bastard. Thank you very—"

"Enough," said Delvan just loud enough to make the two flinch. "I'm getting Desnia out, with or without you. We *all* owe her that much."

"After fighting those freaks and the knight commander dying, yeah, why not? What's some mild treason..." muttered Kolden, blinking bloodshot eyes.

That wasn't a length he was willing to go to, but he didn't respond. He was under enough scrutiny as it was and didn't need to give the Court another reason to extend his punishment after what happened in Calentine.

The events of that night showed him there were hidden powers in the world, ones that made his wants feel small and insignificant. It didn't prevent a small part of him from craving redemption, to show his father and all the others that he was worthy of being a knight. It felt childish to consider. His father was an asshole and Delvan knew he shouldn't strive to impress the man, but a lifetime of expectation was difficult to shed. There were greater plights in the world.

They sat silently for a time, the bustle of the flowing crowd mixing with the clatter of chainmail as clusters of guards intermixed with people performing their morning errands. The commotion of the street brought him back to the one in his mind, reminding Delvan of questions that now itched away at him. Questions which had formed anew upon his enlightenment of who Hilbrun had truly been.

His former Senior, his friend and mentor, had been working *with* Jerdine and his "*Magridi*," aiding in their efforts to reopen the gate. And Ferrand, of all people, had been the one working against them, protecting the empire until his dying breath.

How many of Jerdine's machinations had Hilbrun been aware of? He'd always seemed to have had good intentions, and while he may have been misguided, Delvan still struggled to accept that his friend had been corrupted thoroughly enough to turn against his own people.

"Del, I can see your brain working so hard that it's making *mine* hurt," groaned Kolden.

"It's just... I'm having a hard time understanding some things, looking back on them," he said, staring into the distance.

"Do I dare ask, what?"

"The Merchants' Guild, to start. They were holding the key for the principle, presumably because their vault was the most secure place in the empire. Or so they thought. But what were they getting out of that deal? Merchants do *nothing* for free, there must have been something in it for them."

"Lots and lots of money?" asked Kolden, looking as if he already regretted asking the question. "And weren't we just talking about Des? *Why* do we care about the guild?"

"There isn't much more I can do to get Des out right now," grated Delvan. "And we care about *Jerdine*, and the guild is the only connection we have to him." Kolden gave a quiet expression of agreement, the memory of being locked away by the High Realm mages fresh in his mind.

Delvan put a hand to his chin as he thought about Kolden's comment. "The principal probably paid to store the key, I agree, but they had sapphires too."

"You think they were Jerdine's?"

"I don't know," he admitted, "but possessing a gem without being its or-dained bearer? That's a capital offense of the highest degree. Why take that risk unless there was more than just money involved?"

"Cadentite makes you Blues do some strange shit, maybe it was that?" groaned Kolden.

That's a good point, thought Delvan. "There *are* plenty of Blues with ties to the guild. Having stores of cadentite could have granted them access to gifts the rest of us didn't even know we had." Desnia had said the High Realm mage she knew had been the one to tell her about his healing abilities. Maybe Jerdine had done the same for the guild? "And it *still* doesn't explain the sapphires."

"Well, aside from being worth a duchy, the only useful element of a sapphire is making Blues," said Kolden.

Could they have been so bold? "You think they wanted their own private army of Blues?" That was a terrifying thought, one that would test allegiances and oaths alike. "The King wouldn't have it, he's far too protective of them. And it's not as though you can just give someone a sapphire and make them a Blue, they have to have it from before *birth.*

"They would need more than the half-dozen gems in that vault. They would need current, fully-fledged Blues on their side if they planned to stand any chance against the King.

"Hilbrun was aligned with them, but his father's standing in the guild would make dividing his loyalties easier than most. Who's to say others would have joined? The story he told me of the mages from this 'High Realm,' and their supreme power wouldn't have been enough to turn a legion of Blues traitor. Most would've brought it to the Court or King themselves. Hil wanted more, he wanted to be out from under the King's thumb. That takes numbers." *And no small amount of courage. Hil, what were you thinking?*

"Wouldn't be the first time a bunch of Blues defied the King," grumbled Orne. "And who cares? If they want to get themselves strung up in the street, let them. Might leave us all better off. Even the gods-damned tea is two moons a cup now thanks to those merchant bastards doubling or tripling the price of everything."

"Regardless," said Kolden, as he rested his head on the grayed wood of the table. "Jerdine's vanished, along with that sword and the one who wielded it. Compared to that, the guild having a bunch of Blues on the payroll seems pretty insignificant."

Delvan shook his head. "You're missing my point. If Jerdine was using the guild before, what's to stop him from continuing? They could have known what he was plotting, and still helped him regardless, so why not do so while he's in hiding? If we want to find Jerdine, we should start with the guild!"

"I'm more interested in avoiding him than I am in finding him." Kolden raised his head, leaving an imprint of his forehead's sweat on the table. "But personally, I like having my soul *inside* of my body, so I agree that figuring out where the fuckers are is important. In the meantime, *my* priority—second to this pounding head—is figuring out how to fend them off when they come for us, because I'd be willing to bet Orne's halberd that they will."

"Don't touch my halberd," Orne grunted.

"I'm not disagreeing with you," said Delvan. "But I need answers. The guild was in possession of the largest piece of cadentite in the empire for who knows how long. They could know things about it we can't even begin to fathom. And what if that wasn't the only cadentite that they were safe-keeping? There could be more in their vaults that we don't even know about, which Jerdine is probably going to need. There could be some right here, in Brethefen!"

Kolden perked up at that, his foggy eyes becoming keen with interest.

"This seems like a bad idea," said Orne, draining the last of his tea and scowling.

"What's your plan?" asked Kolden. "I can't imagine the guild would welcome you in with open arms after, you know, burning their place down in Calentine. Even with our titles, I'm not sure they'd give Orne and I more than a, 'Hello,' before trying to sell us something and then booting us out."

"Maybe they would if we'd been fucking *promoted*," growled Orne.

"Oh, stop whining," dismissed Kolden. "I'm willing to help, Del, but—"

"You just want more of that gods-damned rock," said Orne.

"And you're just mad because that bard included Del in his song and not you, so shut it," Kolden retorted.

"Wait, what are you talking about? What song?" asked Delvan.

"Some bard apparently wrote a song about you and Desnia fighting gallantly at the gate or some shit. You're getting rather famous among the tavern crowds. Orne, however, wasn't included in said ballad and he's been in a mood ever since."

"Wasn't even a good song," grumbled Orne.

Delvan's face contorted into a mixture of surprise and... shame? It felt strange to have anyone talking about him in a positive light. After what had happened in Calentine, and the ostracizing that followed Hilbrun's death, he'd become accustomed to people talking about him in harsh whispers or odious discourse—Ferrand's preferred method of beratement. To receive praise of any kind felt odd, or undeserved, and left him profoundly uncomfortable.

"Regardless," Kolden said, "if you're right, Del, then we're stuck in a position where the guild has something we need, and we have nothing to offer in return. Even if the three of us went to the bank and withdrew everything we could, they might still tell us to fuck off. Especially if Jerdine still holds influence over them. I hope you have a plan in mind, because I'm failing to see an outcome where we get either the cadentite, Jerdine, or information they might have about either. Not without costing us everything we have."

Delvan leaned back and folded his arms. Kolden was right. The bank wouldn't allow him to pull the sums that the guild would expect from a name as prestigious as his without approval from his father. *And that's* never *going to happen.* This was, of course, assuming the guild would be willing to barter at all. They didn't turn down coin often, but for him they might make an exception. There may be another option, however. Perhaps the information and cadentite didn't have to *both* come from the guild.

"There're the books Desnia stole," Delvan said after a moment.

"The books that none of us can read and inflict excruciating pain when touched?" asked Kolden. "Yes, those definitely seem like a viable option."

"We can grab them easily enough. They're locked away in the barrack's supply depot, and I can probably convince the quartermaster to give them to us." No one liked to argue with a Blue.

"Then what?" asked Kolden. "The only two people who can read the damn things are either locked away or in hiding. Heard the general has a reward set for whoever brings the priest in, been talking too much by the sounds of it."

"And leaving out parts of the story," said Orne with a sneer. Kolden rolled his eyes.

"We can find Nerio, and no, Orne, we're not turning him in," said Delvan. Orne's jaw clenched but he remained silent. "Then we can have him translate. Who knows what's hidden in there? We could even take any evidence we find and present it to the general; if we can find a connection, we could get a writ from him allowing us unfettered access inside the guild. They'd have no choice but to let us in and search the place!"

Additionally, Delvan hoped that somewhere among those encrypted tomes lay an explanation for his newfound gift. How he'd channeled the cadentite to heal Desnia and the others that night still baffled him. It had been spontaneous, an ability that had unlocked itself in a moment of need and shown him a piece of his being that he'd never realized was absent. Now it felt like a limb he could not move, drained of its blood and immobile without the necessary cadentite.

"How, exactly, do we explain to the general how we deciphered the texts?" asked Kolden.

"I'll... figure something out." That earned Delvan a groan from each of them. "Look, we can't just sit around and wait. You said it yourself, Kolden,

Jerdine is not going to forgive us for stopping him. None of us are safe: me, either of you, Des, or Nerio. We need to think about the long term, too. What if he tries again? Builds another gate?"

"If you want to read some books and piss off the guild, that's one thing," said Orne firmly. "But I still think the thief should serve her time."

"I wouldn't sit by and do nothing if either of you were tossed away like common criminals, and I'm not going to stop suing for Desnia's release," Delvan said, his tone resolute, finger digging into the top of the table. Too many times had their paths intertwined. Too many times had their lives depended on the other's. He knew the brothers wouldn't understand, but he felt a kinship with her that was as close as with either of them, despite the relatively short time he and Desnia had spent together. He wouldn't watch her rot away in prison. And what she'd said to him, asked him to help with... It still made his head dizzy.

Dare he say it aloud? It sounded ludicrous, but the things she'd known, confided with him, they had all been true—and far beyond his own understanding. It left a stain in his mind that he couldn't clean, as outlandish as it was.

He bit his tongue. Could he believe she truly needed help finding a *god*?

"Gods-damn it," mumbled Orne. "Why do you two always have to get me into so much shit?"

"Oh, you're no better," retorted Kolden. "And I'm still confident that the general will release her eventually, if he's anything like our father."

"In the meantime, let's get the books," said Delvan. "Then we'll see if we can't find where Nerio is hiding. I'll worry about Des—and the guild—once I get my audience with the general."

"Great," said Kolden, still sounding groggy, "I'm sure nothing can go wrong."

"Let's go, then," said Delvan standing up. "I'm done wasting time."

"This is a stupid idea..." said Orne as the three of them left the comforting shade and stepped into the street's furnace.

The trek to the barracks was not a distant one, but it took a tortuously long time.

Delvan's pace was held to a shuffle as he continuously waited for the afflicted that trailed behind him. Kolden's feet dragged across the dusty pavers, the faintest unevenness causing him to trip and stumble. Orne moved his feet as though on a march, rigid and straight, as had been drilled into him by the army, but Delvan could see that he was as perfunctory as his brother.

Among the throngs, the swaths of homeless lining the street, and refugees of the sun's heat huddled in the shade, Delvan caught eyes that glanced, and heard whispers hushed in awe, treating him as though he were legend incarnate. It made him want to squirm. An urge clawed at the back of his mind telling him to run from the attention, go somewhere that hid him away from the prying eyes.

What made these few idolize him in such a way? The lyrics of a song? *Ridiculous nonsense.*

Much to Delvan's relief, they eventually arrived at the overcrowded barracks. Its passages were tightly packed with freshly arrived soldiers, forcing them to weave their way to the supply depot in the back of the squat, two-story structure. At least, they were until Orne decided to force his way through like a tumbling boulder, Delvan and Kolden close behind.

Since the fire, the general had mustered whatever regiments he could from neighboring cities and towns to help enforce his martial law. New arrivals were entering the gates nearly every hour, and all of the barracks and outposts in the city were being packed to the brims with the relocated soldiers.

He was sure the siblings wouldn't have minded being crammed into a dorm with a dozen other infantrymen, but Delvan had privately rejoiced when they each received a room in the officers' quarters across the street on account of their titles. *Thank the gods.* Elbowing his way through the halls was hard enough for this one excursion—doing it daily would be a nightmare.

They finally reached their destination, passing a heavy, darksteel-plated door and entering the hectic depot. The quartermaster was behind a long counter, rows of storage racks filled with an assortment of weapons, armor, and clothing tucked inaccessibly away behind him. The portly, balding man was currently attending a dozen different soldiers, hurriedly checking their requisition slips before making his best attempt to jog down the different aisles to grab the needed supplies. Delvan braced himself, reciting in his head the words he would say and drumming up the authority he didn't have to dig through the depot.

"Sergeant," Delvan said as he walked up to the counter. Some of the soldiers gave him a wide berth, others looked on in awe. He always forgot how few Blues were in Brethefen, and many still seemed terrified at the legends that surrounded them.

The quartermaster stopped, panting through wide nostrils, sweat dripping down the front of his uniform. "My Lords," he said, dropping a sack of bedding and fresh uniform on the counter. "How can I help ya'?" He grabbed another slip from an infantryman and read it as Delvan spoke, holding his hands behind his back to hide the mild tremor.

"A few days ago, a bag was dropped off. Black, containing a dozen or so books. We need—"

"Listen," the man interrupted, "I don't mean to offend, my Lord, but the number of duties I've got on my plate has buried me asshole-deep to a ten-foot Trethian. If you don't mind, sir, just head out back and grab what you need. I'm not about to decline requests from a knight and I trust ya' know your way around a supply depot."

That was... easier than expected, Delvan thought. He looked back at Orne and Kolden, who shrugged while the quartermaster resumed his former frenzy. *Alright then.*

They walked past the counter, careful to avoid the scrambled path of the sergeant as he rushed to grab a shield from the rack. They began searching the rows, checking every shelf and tucked away corner. There were no closets or doors to speak of aside from the main entrance, as the room was essentially a massive vault. The three of them began pushing aside supplies, opening trunks, and even checking behind piles of pikes leaning against the mud-brick wall, finding nothing all the while.

Where are they?! thought Delvan as he threw a bedroll back onto the shelf with a loud clatter. He delved into another shelf, looking behind saddles and blankets, his hands still annoyingly empty.

Eventually he'd had enough, and while Orne and Kolden bickered about where the books could be hidden, he went back to the manic quartermaster.

"My Lord," the quartermaster said, hardly looking up from the next slip, "you find what you nee—"

"*Where* are the books that were sent here earlier this week?!" Delvan demanded.

"My Lord, honestly I'm not sure what books you're referring to," he said with a sigh, not picking up on Delvan's tone and keeping his eyes on the slip before him. "I work the morning shifts, someone else is here in the afternoons, they musta been here when they got dropped off." He looked up and finally stopped multitasking, his focus now on Delvan's stirring ire.

Delvan took a deep breath, looking at all the soldiers on the other side of the counter staring at him with wide eyes. He needed to maintain a certain level of decorum, his upbringing and training dictated as much. As calmly as he could manage, he said, "You must have logs. Check them and tell me who left here with those books. *Now.*"

The man nodded rapidly, droplets of sweat spraying from his head. He reached under the counter and pulled forth a heavily bound book, slamming it on the table and flipping to the correct page.

"Uhh," he said as his moist finger dragged down the parchment, "says here the books you're looking for were taken yesterday evening by... huh."

"What? What do you mean, 'huh?'"

"Well, sir, the name here's blank."

"Blank? How is that possible?" Anger was fully flushed into his cadence now. Orne and Kolden had moved behind him.

"Well," the quartermaster said shakily, "it means there wasn't a requisition slip to copy from. We collect them through the day, you see, then a scribe comes and transfers all of them into here."

Delvan pinched the bridge of his nose as his eyes squeezed shut in roiling concentration. "Could the general or one of his staff have taken them?" he asked.

"I hope so, my Lord." The man's tanned skin had nearly blanched. "But... well they normally know procedure. They would fill out a slip like everyone else."

Delvan's heart began to feel a chill. He *needed* these books. His mind raced.

"Could the other quartermaster have let someone in, like you did for me?" Delvan asked, his breathing becoming more frantic.

"I suppose," the quartermaster said. "We've been so busy the past week... He could have seen them gone and figured the slip was misplaced or something. Oh, the captain's gonna have our hides for this."

It took everything he had to remain calm, motioning to Orne and Kolden that they were leaving. Their coming discussion wasn't to be had among the common infantry, and he doubted there was more to learn from this quartermaster. It wasn't under his watch the books had been taken.

He charged through the crowded halls, his anger transforming quickly into panic. If it hadn't been the general's aides who had removed the tomes, then who could it have been? Had Jerdine beaten them here, attempting to protect his interests? Delvan hadn't thought the man knew they'd taken the books, but he supposed it was possible.

"What an idiot," said Orne as they emerged onto the sun-lit street.

"How could they have just let someone walk out with those?" asked Kolden, tossing up his hands. "Didn't anyone mention that they're kind of fucking *important?*"

Delvan began pacing back and forth, the sun hot upon his face. "Someone high ranking or with tremendous influence walked in there and took them from under our noses. No one knew they were there, aside from the general, us, Desnia, and—" He groaned. Nerio had been telling the story of that night to the point it'd been immortalized in *song*. Their list of perpetrators could be anyone in the city at this point.

"When we find the priest," said Orne, coming to the same conclusion, "I get to punch him first."

Delvan had a difficult time thinking of an argument against letting Orne do just that.

"We need to focus on the problem at hand," said Delvan, thinking aloud. "Almost no one can read them, aside from Jerdine, Des, and Nerio. So, we have to assume that anyone trying to aide Jerdine is the most likely thief since Desnia's locked away and Nerio is in hiding, not that he likely wants or needs them anyway."

"I don't know, Del, there's a *lot* of people that don't like the general much right now. They could have stolen them just to piss him off," interjected Kolden.

"I know..." said Delvan, flustered, "but we have to work off what is most probable. It's not like we can go knocking on every door in the city.

"We can talk to the other quartermaster, see if he remembers letting any-one into the depot. But if he doesn't know anything, how else could they have been taken?"

"Someone could have broken in during the night," suggested Kolden.

"Maybe," said Delvan, still pacing, "still would've been difficult."

"Bribes," stated Orne as if it were obvious.

Delvan stopped. How had he not considered that? And the principal wasn't the only one who could have provided funding to steal the tomes.

"The guild," Delvan said, even more convinced. If the principle had tran-scribed any of his dealings with them into the journals, then they'd be highly motivated to ensure they never saw the light of day. The general would even-tually find someone who could read the ancient dialect, and if their dealings were revealed, their entire enterprise could be upended.

Kolden rolled his eyes. "Del, I know you and the guild have a blemished history—"

"That's one way to put it," said Orne.

"—and I agree that they're a good place to start looking. I want to find these too, but you can't just go accusing the guild because it's convenient."

Delvan couldn't believe what he was hearing. "They're the most obvious culprit! They've been helping Jerdine for, I don't know, years. Decades!"

"They're the most obvious *to you*," said Kolden. "Could they have them? Yes. Yes, they could. But you don't know who else that sick fuck was working with." He let out a sigh as he looked at Delvan. "All I'm saying is, don't get your hopes up that the guild has them. We might never find these things if the principal was half as resourceful as I suspect he was."

Delvan stood there, speechless. *How can he not see it?*

"He's right, Del," said Orne. Those were words not often spoken regarding his brother.

"They have them, I'm sure of it," repeated Delvan. Kolden's head flopped back as he tossed up his hands. Orne grunted.

"Well," said Kolden, sounding deflated, "we already decided that the guild was the place to start, so I guess we'll find out. Any idea as to how to convince them to hand the books or their cadentite over?"

Delvan was suddenly less confident. Without an initial upper hand, the guild was a predicament, and their whole plan had been routed in a singular act that he kicked himself for not anticipating. *Maybe, if I hadn't spent the past week recovering from the wound of realizing the truth about Hilbrun and Ferrand, I'd have gotten here in time.* He stared at the boot-scuffed ground, deep in thought, until a voice calling to them snagged his attention.

"My Lords," said a young sergeant that marched up to them. He squarely planted his feet and saluted. "You have been summoned by Lord General Rosethorn. You are ordered to attend him at once."

It's about time, thought Delvan. "Thank you, Sergeant, you can tell the general that we will be along presently."

"This is going to be *rough*," said Kolden as he wiped away more ale-filled sweat.

And we have the pleasure of sharing our discovery. When the general finds out he's going to—

A solution blossomed in his mind, taking shape and forming in the briefest of moments. The epiphany, he realized, could mend their situation, assuming he played his hand right.

"No," said Delvan, "this is going to be exactly what we need."

Chapter Five

As to the man who allegedly slew the knight commander, our current theory is that he was one of the Trethish traitors, or possibly one of their descendants. Recover their sapphire if you have not done so already.

The cheap whiskey burned like horrid fire. Smokey air filled the room with a white-blue haze, the hearth's flue choked by layers of filth that rivaled the floor and walls. A peasant's excuse for bedding was crammed in at Jerdine's left and right. The lack of sleep resulting from such impoverished accommodations—as well as scarcity of comforts and arid warmth—further burned his eyes, making them resemble the embers of the dying fire he stared into.

His teeth ached from their ceaseless clenching, his lips only parting for the sneered sips of amber necessity. The blanket draped over his shoulders stank of mildew, further poisoning his mood.

Where has he gone off to? Jerdine wondered between his many vengeful fantasies. *Bastard portaled us into a damned tundra and then vanishes for hours on end, leaving me in the throes of this hellish torture.*

The hours absent his newfound companion were spent ruing the destruction of the gate at the hands of those inferiors. *Centuries uncounted spent planning and preparing; then those wretched Samrans get their leashes tugged into foiling it utterly. Damn you, Masini!*

He gripped the chair's arm tightly, shifting his weight in an uncomfortable motion. The burns that disfigured much of his face and the side of his body had begun scabbing over, cracking and oozing puss that dotted and stained his robe with every miniscule movement. The pain was sharp and agonizing, incessant in its affliction. The healing spell he'd been channeling since the attack would see him to a full recovery, but it took time—and did nothing to dull the suffusing torment.

This would never have been an issue if that bitch hadn't somehow manipulated my Nerio. How dare she or that drunken bastard Masini use him against me?! That whoremonger was supposed to be dead! Jerdine slammed his fist down, flinching from the flare of pain that reflected his fury. When he'd learned that the wench somehow survived the ksatsimtri's vi-blade, it had left him astonished.

And irate.

She and Masini and that tainted shit and his friends and everyone they've ever known will regret this. I will redefine what they know to be torture, all after they watch those closest to them suffer in ways they can't imagine.

He sucked in a quick breath between tight teeth as his body was again needled with acute aches. It would take days before he was able to travel—weeks or months before the sores fully turned into scarring. He shuddered to think about how much longer those would take to fade.

There is *a way to expedite the process...* His eyes wandered to the large, bulky sack that leaned against the hearth, brought here by the ksatsimtri. Its inanite dye prevented him from sensing the wealth of intoxicant within, an inebriate that made the pathetic excuse for whiskey seem like paltry water by comparison.

Such thoughts were dangerous—by all accounts his new associate was short on patience, and even more devoid of leniency. *The boy tries desperately to prove himself, yet if he's inherited a modicum of our matriarch's ruthlessness, it would be best to direct his petulant ambition elsewhere.*

The prospect of rapidly ridding himself of the near-constant torment—even if accelerated by only a few days or weeks—made him weigh his options, however risky they may be.

No, I will just have to trust that this new trove is genuine and await its arrival. The gold he spent on his recent acquisition could purchase a small duchy, though to him it was priceless.

The consideration between whether to send an intermediary or small army to collect his prize had been weighty and incongruous, but eventually he'd settled on the discrete approach. He could not afford the attention such force would inherently acquire. No, best to keep knowledge of his most personal needs in the hands of as few as possible, lest anyone interfere once more. *Where did it come from, though? The timing of such a discovery...*

It was troubling, the possibilities slim. It would have to be a question for another time. By now, Elhurtan should be well on his way to the transaction, then he would meet Jerdine and his new companion on the road. But it had been several days since the man's last pigeon—assuming the ksatsimtri was actually sending and gathering his mail while out on his daily excursions—and disquiet had darkened Jerdine's thoughts as of late. *Once the delivery arrives, I will have to discuss its origin with the adolescent commander. No doubt he will have similar questions and assumptions—or accusations, more like...*

The consequences were worth whatever action he took. He had not survived these millennia isolated on this primitive realm by standing by and waiting for events to unfurl. He *made* his future. In fact, there would be ample quantities to replenish whatever small amount he confiscated to recharge. He eyed the large sack by the hearth once more.

Why shouldn't he take what he needed? He was owed that much, and considerably more after his entrapment.

He sat forward in the chair, the wood creaking as it racked under his shifting weight. The motion was brutal and excruciating, the splitting scabs stinging like a thousand hornets as his arm extended. Fresh fluids stained his robes, tears wetting his cheeks as he fought through the oppressive stabs and pangs. His fingers touched the edge of the rope-synched fabric, curling around it and drawing it near, his muscles straining to support the dense bag and prevent it from tipping over.

This *was* owed to him, but it might be best if his companion were to not discover his... acquisition.

He pulled apart the tightly drawn opening—slightly, enough to fit a few fingers through only, as to not alert anyone. His eyes came alight, glistening in the reflection of the intoxicating wealth that sat before him. *This hoard in his possession, yet he watches me suffer? I swear I will find a means to punish his delinquency—*

There was the crunch of distant snow from beyond the cabin's poorly insulated walls. Jerdine cursed under his breath, attempting to pull the bag tightly closed once more. As the strings tightened, a cluster of objects nestled amongst the coveted wealth caught his eye. Without hesitation—aside from the enervating movements of his disfigured arm—he reached in and withdrew one of the three oblong stones.

Jerdine's eyes went wide as a wry smile cracked his face. The hefty, polished jade fit neatly between his fingertips, the green mineral appearing to those ignorant of its origin as an expertly polished cut of precious stone half the size of his palm, resembling that which you would find upon a shore. *Oh, but what potential you have. What other tricks are hidden up the ksatsimtri's sleeve, I wonder?*

The sounds of footfalls drew nearer. Jerdine hastily slipped the round rock in his robe's pocket, ignoring the pain as he pushed the overweight sack against the cobble fireplace and leaned back into his seated position, muscles twitching from the exertion, the searing agony an inferno crawling over his skin.

The door to their shared room at the vermin-infested inn opened and he was met with a glower. The night's chill crawled into the space, putting his hair on end as Jerdine wondered if the man had perceived the breadth of Jerdine's temerity.

Wood creaked in defiance to the heavy boots that trampled over it, the illusion previously disguising the exquisite, black-scaled armor fading as Jerdine watched from the corner of his eye. *What a waste of vidut,* he thought bitterly. Clearly his compatriot wasn't yet accustomed to the scarcity of the precious essence in this forsaken realm. *And to cover, what, armor of replica custodian hide? Those fake scales will deceive only the ignorant. His effort to impress is merely making him a greater fool.*

"Where have you been? Did I have any messages?" asked Jerdine as his companion dropped a small bag onto one of the dilapidated beds. The response was an ignored silence.

The mage ground his teeth. This insolence was wholly unacceptable. "Damn it, Valander, answer me!" he hissed.

He was not even deigned with a turn of the ksatsimtri's head as he responded. "You shall address me by my title, as is proper for one of your station, else don't address me at all. I would prefer the latter."

Jerdine gripped the chair tighter, pain shooting unrelentingly through his arm and body. "I was fighting wars before you were conceived, you expect me to—"

"What I expect," Valander said, turning to reveal a look of disgust twisting his fractal-covered face, the glowing tattoos accentuating his distaste, "is competency. Your complete lack of which has resulted in the destruction of the gate and delays to the High Council's plans. You were not the one who had to break the news to High Chair, to say that she's irate would be a disservice to her rage."

Jerdine suddenly felt his hand shaking. If he were to be found of little use after such a failure, there was no doubt that Sylvain would have Valander execute him. "I can fix this," Jerdine said, a quiver in his voice. His mind spun with options yet unconsidered, his thoughts these past few days consumed with the anguish of his body and the wrath targeted at those who foiled his plans. "We can build another gate, albeit small, with the amount of—"

"I am not waiting years or decades for you to tinker. No, I have another plan."

One which I must ensure involves me, he thought, his throat tightening and sweat beginning to bead on his forehead.

"I have contacts throughout the empire and beyond," Jerdine quickly spat out. "I-I can provide you with whatever wealth you might seek, with time. Anything you need, it's yours."

Valander turned away and began rummaging through the small bag on the bedding, maintaining his deliberate and irritating silence.

"Do you care to enlighten me to this 'plan?'" asked Jerdine.

Black hair went still as Valander twisted his head slightly, his back still to Jerdine.

"The High Chair's commands are the only reason you yet live, old man," Valander said with derision. *Oh, thank the Greats,* thought Jerdine with a breath of relief. "But do not think I won't cut your throat should you continue to speak to me as though a child." *No, you won't, you're too afraid to upset her, you sniveling brat.* If he had Sylvain's protection, he was safe. He just needed to ensure that his failures never outweighed previous loyalty—a most precarious scale.

"Well, let's hear it then," Jerdine said as he refilled his glass to the brim, holding his breath as he took another gulp.

There was a tense silence, Jerdine could almost feel the disdain of the arrogant youth.

"Children of the Fifth," Valander finally said.

Jerdine nearly spat out his whiskey, his mangled face wincing from the shocked expression plastered upon it. "You intend to use those tainted cattle?! They don't even know how to open a portal! Let alone with any accuracy! They're apes playing with a power they cannot comprehend!"

"With a few seasons of guidance, and a large supply of vidut," said Valander with a nod to the bag by the hearth, "I believe we can succeed. It will be considerably faster than building a new gate, and with the protections we placed on this realm our brethren back home are helpless to aid us."

"Yes, but... *how?* You would need... I'm not sure how many all casting in unison. What makes you think that this is even possible?"

Valander, infuriatingly, refused to face Jerdine. "I've studied my aunt's journals extensively over the years, preparing for our arrival here. You do not give these warriors enough credence. Perhaps, if you had, you would not have been maimed so."

"Your... aunt's? I thought those all destroyed..." Was it possible? *No wonder Sylvain's so eager to come back here.*

It was a realization that twisted Jerdine's stomach. There were secrets here, hidden from even him, that had remained locked away, intended to never be uncovered again—for the better, in his opinion.

Of course that's what she wants. Still seeking to step out from your sister's shadow, Sylvain? Would you dare try to recreate the power that brought us to our knees? The desolation of legions of kin after all these millennia was a nightmare which still awoke him in the dead of sleep, a horror unprecedented. *All this time, focused on returning home, I should have known that she wanted more than to simply conquer. How naïve of me.*

As Jerdine stared into the dwindling fire, the fingers of his left hand tapping the grayed, wooden chair as he delved deep into his thoughts, he failed to notice Valander come to his side. A brief glint of silver caught his eye which preceded a sharp, stabbing pain in his hand.

A scream erupted from his lips as he spat whiskey and dropped the glass to the floor, spilling its contents across the dusty boards. Valander stood beside him in an icy calm, staring down past a jutted chin, cadentite-inked fingers gripping the hilt of a small, steel dagger buried into his hand.

"Pay attention, as I do not intend to repeat myself," said Valander in a flat tone.

"What are you doing?!" cried Jerdine, his breathing heavy and labored, cold sweat running down his temples. He tried moving his hand in defiance, but every motion dug the blade through more flesh.

"My *name* is High Lord Valander Rana, Commander of the Death March Ksatsimtri, Sovereign Governor of the Askarl Realm, and Sword of the High Council. Speak lowly to me again, and the next blade of mine that pierces your skin shall be the last." He rested his hand on the pommel of the vi-blade sheathed at his side, and for a moment Jerdine thought he could hear the screams of all the souls trapped within it.

"Do you expect me to spout such a title's litany during every conversation?!" asked Jerdine as spit flew from trembling lips, free hand clasping the one affixed to the chair.

"Your Grace, my Lord, or Sire shall suffice."

"Fine!" spat Jerdine, the excruciating pain bringing tears to his eyes, blurring his vision. The man remained unmoving, fist wrapped tightly around the dagger's hilt. *This is ridiculous!* Jerdine fumed. He squirmed, but to no avail, the agony too much to bear. "...My Lord," he finally conceded from spittle-covered lips.

The blade was jerked from his hand, soaked in the iridescent purple of his blood. He held the wounded appendage tightly against his chest, trying to staunch the bleeding as the healing spell struggled to mend both his burns and the fresh wound.

As he huddled there, sucking in ragged breaths of the smoky air, Valander returned to his previous task, keeping his back to Jerdine all the while.

"Where can we find a concentration of the Fifth's children?" asked Valander, voice still a chilling calm.

Jerdine shook his head at the absurd proposition before finally answering. "Calentine, the empire's capital. It's where the majority of the tainted bastards are."

A glance from black eyes twisted Jerdine's stomach, causing him to quickly stammer, "Sire."

Valander turned and tossed a chunk of bread and cheese into Jerdine's lap. "Then eat, we have a long journey ahead of us." He dug through the sack and produced another small meal for himself, sitting on the bedding and chewing through it with the voracity of a soldier.

Jerdine's scowl overlapped the wrinkles of agony.

They would be targets during travels. Not only because of recent events, but because they lacked funds. He was—momentarily—broke, still working to collect what coin he could via carriers and third parties from extensive holdings.

But something even more troublesome loomed over this plan.

"How, my Lord," he asked cautiously, fighting off a spike of pain, "do you plan to acquire the aid of so many, directly under the nose of this realm's King? You know what he possesses, do you not? If he hears of what we're doing—"

"Hence why you still live," interrupted Valander.

Ah, he thought with relief, *so I am to be the final architect of your grand design? A feat which I'm sure you will attempt to hoard credit for. To use the tainted knights here, though...*

Valander finished his meal and laid on his back, closing his eyes.

Imbecile. Did he learn nothing from the arrogance of his own father? He'll get us all killed. Jerdine reached down in trepid agony, grabbing the empty glass off the dirty floor and shakily refilling it with the last of the bottle's contents, the blood of his wounded hand smearing over the glass.

He would get nothing else out of his companion tonight, that was clear. He tried to put the suicidal delusions out of his mind, his focus returning to those that had put him into this vile circumstance.

They will pay. They think me without means, but I built that damn city. I know its secrets, where the bones are buried, and who put them there. They will be made aware of the graves soon enough. And I will take back what is mine.

A contemptuous smile tugged at his lips, the whiskey tasting a hint sweeter.

CHAPTER SIX

Although our sleeping enemy has been quiet as of late, we doubt the last century has tempered their ire—not that I need to remind you of this. Reinforcing our outposts in the White Mountains might be warranted.

B lood covered Desnia's hands and arms, dripping in warm, dark globs onto a polished floor. A knife lay at her side, its details difficult to discern through the hazy darkness that filled the air.

It choked her like smoke but was not born from the destructive fires which had followed her life this past year like a haunt in the night. Each breath revealed the truth of the cloud engulfing her, penetrating and suffusing with each interminable moment.

It was regret, abysmal and crippling. It was grief, gushing from the wells of her eyes. And it was agony, shrieking from her lungs.

Its sum was a riving in her chest. Profound and more devastating than any she'd ever experienced.

Desnia realized that she held someone... familiar, in her arms. Their features, like her surroundings, were muddied, as though she stared at them through turbid water. But despite the swirling gloom, she recognized them as a friend, a love, a sibling. Streaming tears failed to wash away the blood drenching her while her body hunched forward, kneeling on the stone.

Over Desnia's cries—which drowned out a raucous background of tyranny clashing with revolution—there was a laugh, cackling and feminine. It pealed with malevolence, but dissipated as a bright, orange light grew from the black fog before her. It burnt away the blood, the ache, and eventually, her body. It took her pain and, in its place, provided salvation.

Then exploded into a ball of blue fire.

Desnia shot upright from the cot, sweat soaking her garbs and the thin pad of stuffed straw beneath. Gulping down huge breaths of air, she wiped her face, attempting to calm her raging heart.

Afternoon sunlight cut through the room from her window, the iron bars leaving lined shadows on the wall. Dust sparkled like gold in the light's beam, a poor imitation to distract her from the otherwise barren, sweltering space. Though the heat was oppressive, she knew it was not what caused the perspiration in her slumber.

You, uh, alright? asked Masini.

She swung her feet to the floor, gripping the edge of the cot. "Great," she said, her voice cutting with an edge. "Just another fucking nightmare."

You want to talk about it? he asked. *Might be helpful, or, you know, potentially insightful.*

"It wasn't," she said tersely. *Just another bump in my sanity's crumbling road.* "Only more meaningless trash." She hoped.

'Meaningless' is a bit inaccurate, Masini said. *Most people just sort of view the As-As-As-fuck! the 'other' place when dreaming. You actually dip a bit of a toe in—*

"Is any of this going to stop the nightmares?"

Well, no, but it will be important once we—

"Then I don't want to hear it."

Masini grumbled, but her head throbbed as pain radiated within. She needed to get out of this place. Every day it seemed the company of the Asylum took its toll on her, chipping away what mind she had left with each ramble of lunacy.

Changing her focus to provide a distraction, she glanced back at the door to her cell. She'd managed the previous night to break a small sliver of wood from the leg of her bed, but the weathered timber proved insufficient in its ability to turn the latch on her door, the audible *crunch* produced as it broke nearly alerting her half-dozed guards.

Hours spent shaping the thing, she thought, glancing at her raw, reddened nail beds, *waiting until the darkest hours of the night, and all for fucking nothing.*

At least the abusive one wasn't on duty. She couldn't so much as cough without that fucker threatening to beat the potential illness out of her. Thankfully she wasn't sick, the idea of coughing enough to make her flinch. She rubbed her hands along ribs that were turning a distinct shade of purple from their previous yellow green.

After a few more breaths, and letting the pain dissipate from her aching side, Desnia noticed a commotion coming from the hallway. Walking quietly along the edges of her feet, she approached the doorway, staying low enough to avoid attention from the sentries at her door.

Among the screams that reverberated along the hall's length, she heard begging, pleads to make the pain stop. Some cried, others whimpered, but regardless of the reaction, the fear that gripped the Seers that shared this level was as absolute as it was maddening.

"I don't remember it being this bad when we came here a few months ago," Desnia whispered.

Me neither, replied Masini. His voice was quieter here, in the Asylum. Either that or he was whispering out of courtesy for the Seers that could hear him as Desnia could. She doubted that was the case. *Something's changed,* he said.

"Could it have been destroying the gate?" she asked.

I wouldn't think so, no. Maybe, if Jerdine did a few things to it, but he barely had the ca-ca-ca-fucking glowing rock to reconstruct it to that shadow of its former self.

"Makes me nervous."

Everything makes you nervous.

"Keeps me alive," Desnia said as she crept back to her cot.

And therefore me, said Masini, *so I guess I shouldn't chide you too much. Does add a sense of urgency to our situation though, I'll give you that. I just hope Jerdine isn't behind it. He's almost as stubborn as you are, and I'm still terrified he's concocted a way to bring more people over. Oh, and also kill you, most likely. He doesn't like people messing with his schemes.*

"All the more reason to get the fuck out of here, and soon." She shook her head. "Have you gotten anywhere with how we're going to find Asta's prison? Or how we're going to set her free?" She couldn't help but think of Asta as a woman since seeing her in that form upon her momentary death. *Though all that's done is change her from a bastard into a bitch,* she thought.

Nope, said Masini. *Still as stumped as a midget being ridden by an ogress. Taking a Blue along would be helpful, if for no other reason than for you to have access to a sapph—"*

"Not fucking happening," she cut in.

Hmm, alright, well in that case I will continue to ponder our precarious predicament.

Her mind wandered back to more present concerns. Mainly that, in the time she'd been imprisoned, no one had come to see her. She was still riled about Delvan and the others but, despite what she'd said to Masini, she'd have liked an explanation as to their treachery—which irked her more than she cared to admit.

Still, to not have anyone come to question her? Nor to issue a sentence of punishment? She'd expected some pompous official or another to come at some point, yet each day the only faces she saw were the guards who delivered her food—two at a time, watching for an attempted escape. *Bastards.*

Perhaps the city was in deeper chaos than she'd imagined? If the fire was all they were going to charge her with, why not be done with it? Not that she was complaining, they could very well execute her for her crimes.

Evidently, she thought, *saving the lives of everyone in the city doesn't balance out the demise of others.* A small pang of guilt for all the lives lost scratched at her again. She buried it deep.

She was alive, even if they weren't, and there was no use in dwelling.

Desnia looked out her small window, staring at the mountains in the distance. The white peaks jutted out of the earth like the serrated edge of a nasty blade, an implication of the dangers of their treacherous slopes. She shook her head. *One insurmountable problem at a time.* Her eyes drifted back to the city.

Strangely, gathering in some of the alleys below, she saw small clusters of people, including a few Hands and priests. *Must be some of the homeless,* she thought dismissively.

She sighed, thinking about what Masini had said, and the last command of the god that crowded her dreams: "Find me."

"There has to be *something*," she said under her breath. "Asta wouldn't have told me to find her if she didn't have a plan. Hell, feels like I've been a pawn in that plan most of my life..."

True, 'she' is the 'mother' of Seers after all. Though not sure if they really identify as one sex or the other. Like an anemone. A very powerful, very scary anemone.

"What do you mean, 'Mother of Seers?'" Desnia asked. He'd never mentioned this before.

Hmm? said Masini. *Haven't we talked about this? I could have sworn—*

"Talk, Masini!"

Wow, rude. Have you ever tried asking nicely? No? Didn't think so. Anyway, 'she' is the master of the pair of abilities that Seers possess. Like Seers, they are the only two powers she wields, but an equal to her capabilities with these forces, I assure you there is not. She sort of views Seers as her 'children' for lack of a better term.

"When were you going to tell me this?!" Desnia blurted, glancing back with wide eyes to check the tempers of her captors. She hushed her voice and continued a moment later. "Don't you think this is important for me to know?

Gods-damn it, Masini!" She closed her eyes and took a deep breath. "How is it that you can talk about this anyway? I thought you couldn't talk about the High Realm or its magic?"

Firstly, I thought I did tell you about it, given that your name literally *translates to 'Daughter of the Eighth.' Not a coincidence, I think. You also seem to get extra annoyed whenever I bring up history, so there's that. Secondly, they're not from the Hi-Hi-Hi... fuck it, you know what I mean. They're not from there. This* is their *home. Besides, I don't think any of this changes our plans.*

"Grr," she growled, wanting to strangle him. Too bad there wasn't anything dyed in inanite here, she could at least put him in his own prison for a while.

Although, as much as she hated to admit it, she wasn't sure how knowing this new information changed what she needed to do. It did, however, raise questions as to *how* Asta could follow through on her word.

"Tell me, what *specifically* can she do?"

Why? he asked with genuine curiosity.

"She... made me a promise." Desnia thought back to their last conversation, the night they'd assaulted the gate and she'd been stabbed through the chest by the High Realm warrior-mage. Her fingers felt at the spot, just above the left breast, that lacked even a faint scar after Delvan's healing.

Would you be so kind as to enlighten me? Masini asked.

"Like you've been sharing with me?"

Look, I apologize. I would offer to kiss your feet in the most platonic of ways, had I a body. But could you please let me know what the immortal demigod promised someone such as yourself?

Did she tell him? Speak her deepest fear out loud? She considered their future and what it held, the obstacles to overcome, and realized that, at the very least, maybe he could tell her if a promise such as the one given could be fulfilled.

"She said that..." The words seemed to catch in her throat. "She said that she could protect my sanity. Stop my mind from breaking like... the others. Do you think that's possible? Is she being honest with me? Or is her only goal to use me like everyone else?"

Huh, I can see why you're so motivated now. Well, um, I'm not sure what I can say...

She slammed her palm against the wall with a loud *smack.*

Wait, just hear me out, Masini said, soundly slightly panicked. That made her smile a little inside. *I can't talk about their abilities, not directly since they're the same types of ma-ma-ma-fuck!* Power *that we utilize. It might be within her capabilities, but it's hard to say since her powers are not commonly practiced among my kind, for obvious reasons.* A groan from down the hall emphasized his point as if on cue. *Unless you're a special combination of talented, bold, and often, stupid, it's as dangerous to us as it is you. We don't have a solution for that ailment, if that's what you're asking. But she is worlds beyond anything we can do, so your guess is as good as mine.*

Shaking her head, Desnia wondered, *Do I have any other options?* "What a twisted being Asta must be to break each of her 'children' like stones under a hammer," she whispered to herself. She rubbed her temples; the headache was turning towards becoming a full-on migraine. The dreams always left her like this, but it seemed to be more frequent and intense lately. But, as she heard the *clap* of sandaled footsteps approaching from down the hall, she realized there may be a solution.

She scurried to the door, putting her face to the small bars in the center of the wooden barrier, ignoring her concerns about her guards for a moment. A member of the white-robed Holy Hands was walking by, a basket in his hand containing a jug of milky-white liquid and ceramic cups. She knew from her previous conversations with Nerio that it was tea mixed with powdered, muted inanite—the one substance she *knew* could provide her with the dreamless sleep she so craved.

"Psst. Hey, Hand," she said. "Can I get a glass of that?"

"Who said you were allowed to talk to anyone, wench?" said one of the guards. It was a different one from her previous assaulter, but he carried himself similarly, and his tone implied an equal level of disdain for her.

"I just want a drink," she said, doing her best to sound innocent, though her words grated along every syllable. "I haven't had anything in hours; this way you don't need to go get it yourself." *You lazy prick.* "You want me to die of dehydration in here?"

The guard, who had turned to face her, squinted at her through the door's opening as his mind processed—poorly, she expected—her request, and determined whether she was attempting something nefarious. After a time, he said, "Fine. Hand, give her a drink, but in a wooden cup only. Can't be havin' any early *incidents* before your trip to the gallows."

"I-I don't have any with me, sir," the young boy, maybe half Desnia's age, said. "Besides, this is medicine for the patients. I can't serve this—"

"No, no it's fine," Desnia interrupted. "I don't mind a little extra flavor, really." Her eyes flicked hungrily to the sloshing liquid in the jug.

"I must return to the kitchen for a wooden vessel anyways, ma'am. I'll bring you back some tea," the boy said. He looked at her with an odd expression, his eyes wide and mouth slightly agape. Was that... awe? It was hard to say, and even more confusing to see directed at *her*. Then, before she could say anything, he scampered away, cautiously glancing at the guards and their swords.

No, you little—Gah! Her nails dug into her palms as she watched the boy—and the one thing that would suppress her dreams—vanish beyond her tiny portal's view.

A valiant attempt, said Masini, *for you at least. Have I mentioned that we need to work on your people skills?*

"Fuck off, Masini." Her splitting head gave her no tolerance for his gabbing at the moment. He seemed to notice this, thankfully, and remained silent. She craned her head and as she stared at the ceiling. A fleck of peeling, white paint fell from its cracked surface and drifted lazily through the currents of the room's heat, tumbling past her face to the floor.

It was then that she recalled something else Nerio had told her once: the medicine wasn't the only thing containing muted inanite in here. A smile of relief graced her lips.

She would make her own medicine.

Chapter Seven

The underground chamber being protected by the runic entrance you described is not out of the realm of possibilities for a Blue to perform, assuming they're privy to knowledge endowed to a select few. Our representative will discuss these details with you, as we dare not document the information on messages which can be intercepted.

Swept pavers and brightly colored walls scrubbed clean of ash elevated the small neighborhood to an oasis of normalcy. It was an illusion to aid affluent locals in forgetting—or ignoring—that not a street away was a pile of fragmented, blackened rubble that once sprouted spires into the sky in grand architectural splendor. The flames had spread their wrath southeast and left this area unblemished, preserving the Devapuram and bathhouse along with the multi-storied building whose stone walls rose high above them, as if the gods themselves had stood before the blaze and guided it away.

Delvan wasn't sure what the original purpose of the structure had been. A place to house visiting dignitaries, perhaps? It provided an impressive view of the domed marvel of Brethefen merely a block away, its pillars and curved, white roof looming over the horizon. Whatever its intended use, it had been quickly commandeered by the Lord General and his closest staff, and they'd spent little time ensuring that anything within line of sight was polished and refreshed, excising the remnants of ruin that had brought the city to its knees.

No homeless either, Delvan noted. *The general didn't waste any time.*

As he, Orne, and Kolden crossed the threshold of the General's towering domain, Delvan began planning his words and points carefully. The thoughts festered like parasites, consuming his mind. The loss of Jerdine's personal journals changed his plans a great deal, including his previously manicured arguments for Desnia's release.

There were ways that he could turn this to his advantage. As their boots fell upon polished stone steps and echoed like tolling bells around him, ideas came to mind, though many were in the form of furious outbursts. Decorum would be required, as the general was himself a lord. A lifetime of training and rigid etiquette prepared him for such encounters, though he found his mind and heart racing without surcease.

Spiraling flights raised them above floor after floor. Tall portals of tinted glass painted everything brightly, including the last few treads which emptied onto the stone-arched top floor. A large wooden door framed in elegantly carved marble stood opposite them. Beside it, a desk attended by a scribe was forced tightly to the wall, the cramped man scratching ceaselessly with his pen. Honor guards stood at silent attention before the entrance, their polished armor reflecting the rainbowed light of artisan glass.

"They must be hot as hell," Delvan heard Kolden whisper under his breath. He tilted his head in thought; he hadn't considered that before. Even he was sweating in the stifling heat of the tower's peak, despite the slight breeze from an open window nearby.

From his seat behind the desk, the scribe—Lieutenant Wellos, if Delvan remembered correctly—shot a quick look at them, his head remaining aimed at his ink-covered parchment. "Names," he drawled, eyes returning to the work before him.

How does he not remember me? I was here not six days ago. "Cadet Delvan ce Saffstar, and Sergeants Orne and Kolden du Traskor," replied Delvan as they approached him.

The scribe glanced at a piece of parchment to his side where Delvan saw his name written. "Yes. The general will see you in a few moments, he's currently in a meeting," the man said insipidly.

Delvan crossed his arms and tapped his foot. *Days waiting for this meeting, and now I'm to wait longer?* Frowning, he looked around, realizing something.

"Where are we to sit?" he asked. He'd been seen more expeditiously on his last visit.

The scribe merely shrugged without pulling his attention from the documents before him, his scrawling the only sound beyond the muffled voices from behind the door. Delvan sighed and paced through the cramped foyer while Orne and Kolden leaned against a nearby wall. He tried to contain his agitation and clear his head—but the memory of his manipulation leading to Desnia's arrest incessantly buoyed to the surface of his thoughts.

I'm tired of being someone else's pawn. His teeth pressed together like grinding stones.

There was a call from within the general's chambers. One of the armored sentinels pulled the door open, an older man dressed in a silk robe exiting with a smug expression on his face. Appearances gave Delvan the impression that the man was a merchant, and he had a sudden desire to wipe the haughty expression from his face.

The soldier holding the door called out, his voice ringing inside of his helm, "The general will see you now."

As Delvan marched with Orne and Kolden through the door, he noticed the stench of sweat and body odor from the honor guard, feeling a sense of pity for the man. The odorant sentry closed the door behind them, and the trio walked to the center of the spacious room.

Its walls were densely decorated with relics of wars and conflicts that would require historians or grandsires of the empire's masses to recall, many patinaed with the ancient stains of battle. Delvan recognized several of them—similar spoils hung in his family's estate in Calentine—but many were foreign, even to him.

They came to attention and saluted the tall, imposing man behind the room's oversized desk.

"King and His grace upon you. You may stand at rest, gentlemen. Thank you for making a timely arrival," said Lord General Rosethorn. He put his hands behind the crisp, light blue uniform, decorated with the same orange trim as Delvan's and cuffed with gold at the sleeves and collar to mark his station and rank. His silver hair was cut to a utilitarian length, his aging face stern and clean-shaven. His eyes gleaned with a sharpness that defied his apparent age, and Delvan knew that, despite the almost spindly form of his limbs and body, stiff with military rigidity, the leader of the Calentinian Empire's western army was not a man to be taken lightly. If the keenness of his wit wasn't enough to avert or subdue, then the gift granted by the faceted sapphire that hung heavily from a silver chain of bear-headed links, sparkling from its crystalline depths in the window's radiance, would be.

The three of them widened their stances, clasping hands behind their back as the general continued. "In an effort to keep this brief, I will get right to the point of your summons. One of your accomplices from the events of the other night, Brother Nerio, has become a problem which can no longer be passed off as a mild inconvenience." Delvan raised a inquisitive eyebrow.

"In case you are not aware," the general continued, "he has been holding speaks in which he describes, in great detail, the events in which you all participated. His preaching is not only creating the beginnings of a rise of insubordination among the peasantry, but it is now in direct violation of the edicts of the Sapphiric Court." The general stabbed at a small, unfurled scroll with his fingers atop his desk. The seal and flowing loops of blue ink upon the pigeon's message were as recognizable to Delvan as the gem around his own neck.

"Furthermore," continued the lord general, "they have reinforced my previous orders, swearing to silence anyone with knowledge pertaining to said catastrophe. You are not to discuss or share this with anyone outside of this room or a member of the Court itself. Am I understood?"

"Yes, sir," they said in unison.

Delvan tried not to cringe as he thought about the whispers and sidelong looks from bystanders on the street—not to mention the song that Orne and Kolden had spoken of. He suspected that this was already far beyond the lord general's ability to silence.

"Excellent, I assumed I could entrust you three with this," the general said with a rigid nod. "But our own obedience does nothing to solve the problem posed by this priest: every speak he performs, each person he tells this story to, erodes our control over the narrative." *At least the general's not completely ignorant to the situation,* Delvan thought. He kept his mouth shut, waiting to speak until he felt the time was right.

"I honestly thought this problem would resolve itself after removing those damned principles," Rosethorn said with a shake of his head, "but rather than staying devout to the King's will and divinity, some have become rather devoted to the young priest. He gains more followers by the day, and I intend to cut off the snake's head before this annoyance becomes some ideal that the masses chose to follow. The boy was a virtual loner, based on our reports, so any insight you may have into his whereabouts would leave the empire indebted to you. All pursuits we've conducted thus far have left us empty-handed."

This is why he brought us here? thought Delvan. *What of Desnia and my petitions?* He could feel pressure building in his chest.

"We don't know where he is, sir," said Delvan. "But perhaps Desnia would? We could talk to her, find out—"

Rosethorn shook his head. "That won't be necessary," he interjected in a cold tone. "I'm aware of the several letters and requests you've made for an audience, Cadet, but the fact remains that your acquaintance is responsible for the arson that has crippled this city. Its rebuilding is going to take years, possibly decades, even with the taxes that we've imposed. It is an infraction which cannot be overlooked, despite her other deeds, and the Court has ratified her incarceration with their own commands.

"Putting that aside. By your own account, she is the singular, living person who knows details about this group that bastard principle was behind, along with the one the Knight Commander was supposedly a part of. We need answers from her. *Honest* ones, which I'm not certain will be given to you. Despite your trust in her, she is still a criminal whose word is worth little. I cannot risk allowing her lying to secure her own release so that she may take immediate flight. Out of respect for your house, and the gem you bear, I have ensured that no harm will befall her before judgement is delivered, and she is relatively comfortable."

Delvan seethed. His face twitched as it resisted the scorn he felt. "Sir, if not for her, the city would be flooded with an army! We'd be under attack! How can we hold her in prison while Jerdine and—"

The general raised his hand to Delvan, a gesture of cessation that he was obliged to follow. He snapped his mouth close, his face fiery.

"I know your story, as does the Court," Rosethorn said, tapping the scroll before him. "They, however, tell me to consider it 'the fabrications of an angry, wounded pride.' They also imply that there are secrets privy to only the Court and King which can explain some of my many questions—we will see if they corroborate your and the girl's words. Though it seems that the Court, given your history, believes that you're spreading falsehoods in order to protect this girl, and that you've convinced Lords Kolden and Orne here to be complicit in your lies. I'm almost inclined to believe them, given that your father wrote such a compelling argument against your accusations."

Delvan's nose flared, gripping his own wrist so tightly it began to go numb. The only thing preventing him from an explosion of anger: a single word. *Almost?*

"Sir, it happened exactly as we described," Orne's voice boomed, a hint of indignance resonating in the large chamber.

The general looked from the scroll back to the three of them, his face difficult to read. "I'm inclined to believe you, Sergeant."

Delvan's eyebrow flicked as he gauged the man before him.

"I'm going to be honest with the three of you, and trust that what I say does not leave this room. I have long been suspect of Jerdine, and we came to a head on more occasions than I can count. For decades, he's managed to somehow wrestle control of the empire's second-largest city and its duchy from the appointed nobility; whether the King allowed it because of the extreme reverence of the city, or some other reason, I can't say. My investigations into how he maintained such a grip left me wanting, and I've always thought there was more to him—beyond his despicable tastes and habits.

"The grim reality is that the fires your accomplice set were the best thing that's happened to this city in many people's lifetime." Despite his restraint, Delvan's head pulled back, his posture wavering. The lord general continued, as to answer their quizzical expressions.

"It allowed nobility to regain control and set that vile pestilence to the wind," Rosethorn explained. "It's presented us with an opportunity to rebuild, in the vision of the King, and recreate the proper order of things. Regardless of what you may think of my stance in this matter, know that the cost is not one I'd have willingly paid. The unfortunate blaze notwithstanding, the loss of a Blue is something I'd hoped to never witness again."

The general turned, looking at a strange, darksteel dagger set upon the mantle behind him. Its blade began wide, curving slightly upward as its edge waved like the tendril of a flame. The long, ornate blade was artistry in its own right, crafted by masterful hands. It was etched with an inscription Delvan didn't recognize, the bizarre language blockish, a pattern emerging from the strange hatching that caught his eye. He wondered as to its origins.

"You will find few, even among knights, who realize what a difficult feat it is to kill a Blue in combat, let alone when outnumbered. Its the type of fight one avoids, and is difficult to forget, as I'm sure you're all aware."

His voice had become solemn, his gaze distant before he turned back towards them, his expression as hard as ever. "Someone who holds power such as this is not something I can 'ignore as fallacy.' The fact that I am being told to dismiss the spilling of violet blood as 'luck' is an insult to the extreme, even from someone as dignified as your father, Lord Delvan." He glared at the note upon the table before grabbing and carelessly tossing it to the far reaches of his desk.

"While I'm sure that more carriers are en route," Rosethorn continued, "for now I have only been instructed to maintain secrecy and ensure the rebuilding of this city. Nothing is mentioned about me investigating the Knight Commander's death.

"I've been to cavern—though we had to carve the stone around the rune-encircled entrance to create another egress. Even with your words of caution, we were woefully unprepared for its destructive protections. Between it and the testimony of the prisoners you pulled from those abominable cages, your telling has merit.

"The representative the Court is sending to feed me some lie about what happened in my city while under my command won't arrive for some three months now, but evidently there is a threat that could transport itself directly back into this city on a whim, assuming it ever left." He shook his silver-topped head. "And I'm to '*dismiss*' it."

It didn't surprise Delvan that the Court had told the general to bury the events of that night in a grave hidden from the public. He did, however, wonder at his father's motivations, which he was certain were as self-centered as they were vague and indeterminable.

"To make myself clear, Lord Delvan," Rosethorn said, his head held high, "my intentions with the girl are first and foremost to become more informed regarding this threat. Beyond that, if the masses knew that we were holding the one responsible for the mess outside, they'd lynch her in the street. My men—the ones I trust—are struggling as it is to enforce this correction in regime, and the legion from Tennefen is still weeks away. We cannot afford rioting.

"For now, I've kept her location—and actions—a state secret. Although with that gods-damn priest out there trying to deify her, it's only a matter of time before word of her location leaks. I need answers from her that I know beyond a doubt are the truth, because without that I cannot protect this city. And if she's able to provide those, I may be inclined to offer a certain leniency to her actions. So, if you wish to protect this girl, Cadet, then you will understand the necessity of finding and *silencing* this priest."

Delvan's could feel his every muscle tightening, his heart a thundering drum. He knew that if he pressed too hard on the issue of Desnia's release then he'd only upset the lord general and would be unable to make his arguments regarding the Merchants' Guild. But she was too important to him to risk losing, and while a promise of leniency was progress, it was not an absolute assurance of her release.

"Sir," Delvan said, trying to drown the harshness in his voice, "if information is what you seek, then let me talk to her. She trusts me," he said. *Or she did, before you stole her away under the guise of my name. She might stab me next time we meet.* "I can get whatever information you desire, possibly even regarding Nerio, *if* we promise her release."

"While I normally appreciate tenacity, Lord Delvan, in this matter I expect your quiet obedience." Delvan's jaw snapped together with a sharp *crack* from his teeth. "I simply cannot trust that she won't use your previous connection to lie to her own ends. Her questioning, therefore, will be overseen by the Inquisition."

Delvan's eyes went wide, his arms pulling away from his posture as they flung to his side. "You're sending a special inquisitor to interrogate her?!" he nearly shouted. "You just said that no harm would come to her! They're as likely to cut off her toes as they are to ask questions!"

"Enough!" barked Rosethorn. "I do not care to repeat myself, Cadet. She won't be harmed, but we need answers. She is no longer your concern."

He subdued a tremor in his hand by squeezing it tightly, his heart beating frantically and forcing even more sweat from his pores. He needed to compose himself and address the general in a manner befitting his title. But thought of the lengths the Inquisition would possibly go to reveal Desnia's secrets...

How can the Lord General promise no harm coming to her, and in the same breath announce she will be interrogated by the party responsible for making the empire's enemies disappear?

Delvan could feel himself growing hot, the air around him shimmering. He took a deep breath as Kolden was forced to take a step farther from his side, calming himself despite the bellows of fury fueling his fire. The general looked at him through narrow, critical eyes until Delvan's external anger fully subsided.

"When you find the priest, bring him back to me," Rosethorn continued, finally pulling his narrowed eyes from Delvan, "and gentlemen, bring him in *alive*."

So you can torture him too? Devan thought. *No, you need him for something, don't you?*

"That will be all, gentlemen," the general said dismissively.

"Sir," said Delvan as he took a step forward. Kolden turned back from the half-step he'd taken towards the exit, looking at him with eyes of curious concern. Orne hadn't budged.

"I have no interest in hearing further arguments, Cadet, and frankly you're moving beyond testing my patience. My decision—"

"That's not what this is about, sir." Delvan tilted his chin up, determined to state his request.

Muscles beneath the general's face became taught. "Speak."

"Sir, after discussion this morning, Lords Orne, Kolden, and myself realized that, as you said, Jerdine still poses a threat to not only your command of this city, but to ourselves as well. As you know from our report, he and this other 'mage' that is with him are capable and deadly enough that we sought to find more information—"

"To the point, Cadet," the lord general said.

"Sir, we went to the barracks to review the books recovered from Jerdine's personal chambers," Delvan continued. He chose his words delicately as the lord general's eyes focused with curious scrutiny. "We wanted to see if there was anything that could provide us with information. The maps had been readable, even if the language was not, and we hoped to find more in an effort to protect ourselves and learn of potential threats."

"The books have already been reviewed, Cadet. What little information was translatable is of little value and they will remain at the barracks for now," said Rosethorn.

About that...

"Sir, the books are missing." Delvan kept his eyes ahead, letting the revelation set in. The general's face flashed into an expressive consternation.

"Explain," Rosethorn demanded.

"The quartermaster has no records of anyone removing them, and the books are no longer in the supply depot."

"Gods-damn it," said Rosethorn, leaning against fists that dug into his desk. "Wellos!" he shouted. The chamber's door opened, and the previously cavalier lieutenant stood at perfect attention on its threshold. "Send someone immediately to find the Chief Inquisitor and tell him to get to the eastern barrack's supply depot. Tell him the principle's journals have been stolen."

"Yes, sir," said Wellos with a salute, ignoring the trio and turning to hastily leave the room, the door shutting heavily behind him.

They're awfully upset about books that 'held little value,' Delvan thought. *Unless...* That's *why he wants Nerio. Asking Des to read the books would give her leverage you can't afford, not while saving face, and you know better than to fully trust anything admitted under duress. You need Nerio to confirm whatever she says.* His eyebrow twitched with realization. *You're more nervous about Jerdine than you claim. Ferrand's death must have struck terror into you.*

This information was powerful, but only as long as he acted on it. It was an opportunity he needed to take advantage of.

"Sir," Delvan said, "I think I have an idea as to who might have taken the journals."

"Let's hear it, then," the general said.

"Sir, I hope that, given the... direction the Court is asking you to take in this matter, you can view some of what I divulged to you in a different light." *The guild and my father may have denied the key being in that vault back in Calentine, but you must be doubting that as you are their most recent commands. Trying to decide who is with or against you in a time like this must have you evaluating everyone, even superiors.*

The politicking of the Court had always seemed a waste of effort during his ignorant youth. However, as he felt sweat slick his palms, he was thankful that the prolonged exposure had inevitably dug the subtle techniques into him. *And brazen accusations are only hindering me...* "Secrets are a currency. Some would say the most valuable one. I would think that any who may have a history of employment by Jerdine would agree, especially by those who make it their trade. They're an asset to be guarded, traded, and even stolen away, should the need arise."

A pensive expression draped the general's face, his knuckle tapping the polished desk in a slow rhythm. His gaze darted between the three of them as silence hung in the stifling air.

"I can see the logic in your argument, Cadet," lingered the general's words, "but given your history I'm disinclined to give it credence. You of all people should understand the consequences of their wrath, and I cannot justify sending you on some vendetta, given the tension the city is already under. Although, you do make a point that is difficult to ignore, reinforced by my previous guest..." He rapped his knuckles again before turning and walking to an open window, eyes drifting to the distance as his back faced the trio.

Delvan tried to wait, tensely holding his breath. *He* must *see it. Why is this garnering a second thought?* He'd assumed that the events in Calentine would make his argument difficult, but it'd still cut him with an edge of umbrage upon hearing his ideas dismissed as merely him seeking retribution. *Even if that is part of what I want, it doesn't change the facts.* He needed Rosethorn to agree to send him into the guild, and as he thought about it, he considered an alternative.

"Sir," Delvan said, the general turning his ear to the side, "you're right. The people are on edge. Those who were in the fire's path lost everything, the Hands cannot collect enough food to feed the hungry, and even those outside the path of the blaze are struggling. Everything is more expensive, the cost of meals has increased tenfold, and after paying the King's taxes, they have nothing left to purchase food, let alone afford housing. It is within the rights of the King and his dukes to moderate price gouging, is it not?"

There was another silence, a breeze fluttering through the window offering a slight reprieve from the heat.

"Perhaps you're not as politically inept as I'd expected," said the general before turning to face them once more. "Despite what your father seems to think, it would seem that you've inherited more than just the family name. Wellos!" he called again. There was a hurried shuffle from outside the chambers before the doors cracked. The scribe once again stepped in and saluted, his mannerisms becoming the epitome of military rigidity, though he was now sweating and breathing heavily.

Must have been a fast climb up and down those stairs, thought Delvan with a hint of satisfaction.

"Yes, Lord General?" the scribe asked.

"Create a writ for Lords Delvan, Orne, and Kolden, presenting my express command to investigate the ledgers of the Merchants' Guild for evidence of price gouging, racketeering, and evasion of the King's taxes."

"Right away, sir," said the sycophant as he saluted again and left.

Delvan couldn't help but smile.

"I can provide you three with two squads of soldiers, along with some scribes and chamberlains to ensure that this looks official. One of my captains will accompany you and head the search as your commanding officer." Rosethorn held up a hand as Delvan opened his mouth. He begrudgingly closed it and let the lord general continue. "I cannot have you, Lord Delvan, of all people, leading a raid into the most affluent and influential guild in the empire. That being said, while everyone else is busy collecting what I expect to be an exorbitant sum of taxes from hidden income, I want you three searching for those missing journals. I'll begin sending carriers now, hopefully my pigeons arrive at the Court before the guild's do, and we stay ahead of the mess this is going to create.

"And allow me to make myself clear. This does not change your obligations in finding the priest. I have other soldiers searching, but you know him better than anyone, as fleeting as your acquaintance might be. Once you finish at the guild, I expect you to begin aiding in the manhunt.

"Lord Delvan, I expect the highest of decorum while conducting your investigation of the guild. Find out what you can but be subtle about it. The only thing that could possibly enrage the guild as much as raiding their coffers is an accusation of stealing from the crown and dealing with that is going to be difficult enough. Lords Orne and Kolden..." He looked at them through narrowed eyes. "You're to remain silent regarding the nature of your task. Search only and allow Lord Delvan to speak to the members of the guild. Consider that an order.

"I'm putting a significant amount of trust in you three. I'm unable to bring too many into the fold of what happened, and since your commitment to the crown is apparent from your actions this past week, I'm hoping that I am not making a grave mistake in assigning something like this to three who have such a... notable history."

Delvan saw Orne and Kolden shift uncomfortably from the corner of his eye.

"Once you finish at the guild," Rosethorn said, "report immediately back to me. That'll be all—"

"Sir," said Orne, taking a step forward. Delvan's stomach turned. Orne and Kolden were no strangers to conversing with authority, but he wasn't sure if Rosethorn would take questioning or interruption as well as their father might—though he admittedly didn't know much about Lord General Traskor.

"Yes?" the lord general said, his voice verging on becoming a drawl.

"Sir, with our previous commanding officer slain and unable to provide one himself, I would like to formally petition for my advancement."

Delvan raised an eyebrow. The general held his stiff posture despite the unorthodox request.

"I will take your request into consideration," said Rosethorn. "Bringing those tomes back into my possession will go a long way, Sergeant. And to be honest, my trust in many of the locals here is weaker than a rear flank. That you," he said, looking at Kolden, "reported a member of the Royal Army was acting on Jerdine's bidding and had access to the chamber is partially the cause for bringing in the legions from Tennefen. Continue to display your loyalty, gentlemen, and perhaps promotions may be arranged. Maybe even advancement towards anointment." Delvan felt his mouth go dry as the general flicked his gaze in his direction.

Even without his father's blessing, the Court could still rule to knight him at the lord general's request, and part of him still yearned for that. He'd begun to assume the title would never be bestowed upon him, despite his younger expectations of being handed the position like all his gem-bearing predecessors.

"Now, I have been delayed long enough by this conversation, as frustratingly enlightening as it has been. Dismissed." The lord general's words were spoken as an express command, and the three of them saluted before turning in unison and marching from the room.

They walked past a few nobles appearing agitated in the unadorned room outside before taking the forms promised from the haughty Wellos, who refused them so much as a glance. Their walk down the stairs was a silent one, all of them waiting to speak until back into the morning air outside, a small breeze dragging abrasive sand across their skin.

"We should get moving, the sooner we get to the guild, the better," Orne said eagerly.

"Oh, shut it," said Kolden dismissively, "you just want your damn promotion. Lieutenants still report to *generals* in case you've forgotten."

"Enough," cut in Delvan. "We will gather the troops promised and head over there. We can't waste time. That meeting was a disaster. What does he think he's doing, bringing the inquisitors in?"

"I think it went well," said Orne, smugly.

"Of course you do..." groaned Kolden. "And I don't trust those black-bag bastards either. I may not be as adamant about her release as you, Del, but I wouldn't wish their dungeons upon my worst enemy, let alone someone who came to my—albeit, unneeded—rescue."

"Well, she shouldn't have burned down half the city, then," argued Orne. Delvan's brow furrowed at the comment, but before he could retort the skewed perspective, Orne took off.

"We're running out of daylight, let's go!" Orne's overly long, muscled legs had him strides ahead of them, not looking back to see if they were following.

Kolden let out a long sigh, then moved at a brisk pace chasing his brother, muttering curses and proclamations of the man's selfishness. Delvan followed close behind, giving the tower one last glance as they walked away. Could he have what he wanted?

Everything he wanted?

Chapter Eight

We've read the accounts you've sent of the recovered children and, given their tortured and dehydrated states at the time, it is clear that their recollection of that night is convoluted at best. The information they've disclosed regarding Principle Jerdine, however—their imprisonment, executions, and his disturbing proclivities—is difficult to refute. We trust in the statements collected by the royal inquisition and have excommunicated him, as well as placed a reward on his capture. To avoid tarnishing the church's image, these specifics must also be held as a state secret.

The fringes of Nerio's robe were darkened with ash stirred on his walk to the speak's gathering place. The former courtyard of a wealthy merchant was destitute, a smear of grey and black among many in the gaping wound of Brethefen's face. Rubble mounded like barrows around him, heaves of jagged edges burying an untold count beneath them.

How I wish we had done things differently, Nerio thought as he lowered his arms, finishing the speak. *But would I be here now if we had? The necessities of the gods are as cruel as they are mysterious.*

In the crowd gathered before him, Nerio recognized many, including additional members of the clergy—some had become regulars at his forums. But beyond the front row of the most fervent devotees were a hundred new faces, heeding the call of family, friends, and loved ones who deciphered in Nerio's words a meaning behind their loss. The greater good had been achieved because of their sacrifice and risen from the destruction was their new messiah.

Nerio stepped off the charred stone block he'd used to raise himself above the crowd, solemnly nodding to those in attendance as he assimilated among them. Some stood, others sat upon the crumbled remains, disregarding the stains upon their robes and clothes. They wept or looked to the sky. Some knelt and prayed.

Smiles were not among them. Nerio understood, for he did scant smiling himself.

What he sensed was a wave of relief, of knowledge that this was the gods' plan. He was happy to provide it for them, but he felt himself straining under the weight of the responsibility he now bore. More than anything, these people needed empathy; could he hope to understand the level of loss they'd experienced? *I only wish there was more I could do. For everyone.*

While he preached of her resurrection, Desnia was still hidden away, taken by the oppressors—or so he assumed—who'd deemed themselves saviors.

They presented themselves as a light of recovery, their tongues of gold and silver forged by the meager coinage stolen from the struggling populace. He'd thought many nights on reaching out to Lord Delvan, possibly even his companions, and imploring them to speak to the general on the people's and Desnia's behalf. But Nerio was all too familiar with how loyalties could obfuscate one's ideals. He wanted to believe they would help the city's inhabitants, Desnia as well, but he could not risk capture himself. His endeavor was too important.

Too many days running, hiding from the masters they serve, to risk such outreach. But was he not obligated to do what he could for these people? *Maybe discussions are warranted—*

His train of thought was interrupted by the cough of a young boy at his side, his mother worriedly holding his boney hand. "Brother," she said, her eyes pleading, "my son is afflicted. I ask, beg of you to call upon the gods and pray for their healing touch once more. I would do anything, *anything*, please."

She pulled the boy's hand forward, the weak steps of his sore-covered legs hobbling him along, his dark, sunken eyes staring down through the ashy soil. Nerio's heart sank, looking at the boy and struggling as he tried to speak. "I am sorry, Sister, I am not but a messenger, the conduit for the gods' will was Lord Delvan, and their blessing of life for another." Tears cut through the black grime on her midnight skin, and Nerio's own pools of sympathy began watering his sight. "We have little to give, but if you find Brother Algus in the triage, he has a few herbs he can spare for the sores. It will help relieve the pain, and I will split my rations with him, if it comes to that."

"Please," she said, her voice cracking and face stricken, "my eldest, he too was afflicted and none of the remedies helped. I cannot lose another child." She wiped her eyes. "If you could speak to the gods on my behalf, Brother, I could convince my friend, a Hand, to help—"

A hand touched at his back, turning his head away from the pleas of the young mother before him. Nerio wiped his own eyes, seeing Brother Yinnenaw—a priest old enough to be his father, and was one of the more common among his crowded speaks—standing there with another, younger priest at his side.

"Principle Nerio," Yinnenaw said, "I am sorry to interrupt, but Brother Meneham here is very eager to meet with you."

"Please, Brother," Nerio said, trying not to sound exasperated, "I must continue to ask you not to call me by such title." He turned back to the mother, anxiously staring at him, hoping beyond his means for aid. "Ma'am, please, go find Brother Algus for what treatment we can provide, I will come and find you to check on your son's prognosis once I have attended to a few things here."

She took a shaken breath, her eyes lowered and then gave a short nod. "Yes... Thank you, Brother. The Messiah and Her grace upon you."

That is a strange twist of the expression, he thought with a tilt of his head. She turned and made her way through the crowd towards a small tent enclosure erected for the sick who had made the pilgrimage to his latest assembly. *How long before we must move them all again?*

Nerio turned back to Brother Yinnenaw. The priest behind him—hardly a few years Nerio's senior—stared at him with the wide eyes of anticipation, the dull light finding a way to glint from his brown eyes. Yinnenaw gave a nod deep enough to be misconstrued as a bow to Nerio, "I will see the young lady and her son to the triage."

"Thank you, Brother," said Nerio as the man left. "Brother Meneham, my sincerest gratitude for coming today. I hope that you have been enlightened to the gods' wills, despite this unfortunate setting."

"Pri-I mean, Brother," he stammered rapidly, "I have been... moved. *Changed* is perhaps the means to describe this shift in my perspective. What you describe is nothing short of miraculous. I'd heard the stories, whispered by so many like legends, but to hear it from the Witness of the divine... It has renewed a faith that I had not realized was faltering—a blasphemous thought, I know. But true, nonetheless. That the gods would intervene in such a way, well, I believe that this changes *everything*." The priest was rubbing his hands together, his head trailing darting eyes all the while.

That Nerio's words were reaching the masses in such a way brought warmth to his heart—what little he'd been able to mend. This was his purpose; he knew it in his soul. Desnia's resurrection had been a revelation to him in his darkest hour, a beacon in the storm. Now it was his responsibility to share it with the world. *That does little to prevent the shame of selfish thoughts.* Was it too much to desire a mending of his own soul? *Not when I turn away the needs of others. Of children...*

"I appreciate your faith, Brother," Nerio said calmly. "Reciting my accounting of that night has been rewarding, with word spreading faster than I would've thought. Truly the gods have blessed my speaks.

"And do not fret over such blasphemies. These are meant to challenge us, to have us assess our faith and renew it more deeply. I, too, have been burdened with profane ideas, some I nearly acted upon."

"And the messiah, she saved you?"

"Indeed," he said with a slight curl of his lip, "though long before she'd been saved herself."

"She truly is a new voice of the gods, then," said Meneham, nodding his head. "A peer to the King even..."

"It may be so, yes. I am sure that He has communed with them, and word of her ascension will reach the lord general soon. Then I can take my words to the Devapuram itself." *Hopefully with Desnia at the altar. Though I'm certain she is not going to be pleased by the hallowing...*

Nerio knew that Desnia was going to loath her appointment by the gods. Reverence shown by the people would probably do little more than draw her ire. He stopped himself from cringing at the thought of her spewing curses filled with acid and sacrilege. *A moot concern if I am unable to locate her...*

"We should be taking to the streets *now*," said Menehem. "The guilds have tripled their fees since the fire, most cannot afford figs from our own orchards, nor grain from our own fields." His words were bitter. "Does the gods' will need wait for permission?

"You are the Witness, Brother, and meeting in seclusion and secrecy is necessary to keep you safe. But you must send others to spread your word on the street, allow it to sway those who would take advantage of us. If not by words, then by whatever divine means the gods' deem sufficient."

Nerio's lips thinned into a pressed line. "While you are not the first to make such a request, you must know that I do not wish for violence, Brother, if that is what you're suggesting." He abhorred the idea that others would be injured from any cause of his own. The people needed time to heal, not to add to their numbers of hurt and hungry.

"Brother, I... Look around you. We come to hear your words, to understand why the gods deemed to gouge their fury through our homes and temples. The hope you have given to all of us has brought light back into our lives, risen—if you will—from the clutches of death. I merely state what many think. These words, they can help more than the few that you can reach in daily speaks. What you've done is clearly aided by the gods, but even they would tell you that you cannot do this alone, Brother."

Meneham dropped to one knee before him, bowing his head. Nerio pulled his head back in confusion. "I wish to be your disciple, Witness, and seek your permission to spread your word on the streets, to whomever may listen."

"Please, stand," Nerio begged, his face turning flush. "I am no principle, Meneham, you nor any other require my permission to spread the gods' will. But I fear that you take a great risk by making such a request."

"No more than you take yourself," he said, still kneeling and looking up at Nerio.

The thought of putting others in jeopardy twisted his insides. *Can I stop him? Defy the gods' will?* he wondered, second-guessing his own words. *No, I must trust they will watch over the deliverers and keep them safe.*

"Before you take these steps, you must know that you could end up imprisoned. Or worse," Nerio cautioned.

"Then I shall preach to prisoners or be welcomed by the gods with their praise."

Nerio's lips pressed tighter, his soul stricken with worry. "Stand, Brother. Please. If you wish to preach Desnia's resurrection, then I would be a hypocrite to deny you otherwise." *Regardless of my own fears.* This was the natural progression, he realized. When he'd first began his recounting of their heroic deeds from that night—now feeling like a lifetime ago, despite little more than a week passing—his intent had been to speak it to as many as would listen, regardless of the cost to himself.

There was a goal for him, one set forth by the gods, but he was not privy to all their designs. What *had* they said to the King? Was Desnia more than His peer? *What if she's...*

He pushed the thought from his mind. It was not his place to judge their duties. He would continue on the path he'd been set upon, and he could see now that enlisting the help of Meneham and others was the next paver in building this road to righteousness.

"You do not require it, but you have my blessing all the same," said Nerio finally.

Only now did Meneham stand, head held high and chest filled with renewed purpose. "Thank you, Brother. I will take to the streets and find others that are willing to spread the word as well. The Messiah and Her grace upon you." He bowed his head deeply before turning and leaving, making his way through the crowd and beyond the limits of the crumbling courtyard.

Nerio rubbed his hands together nervously, watching as the priest disappeared from view. *I must trust that this is what the gods desire,* he consoled to himself. *May they watch over him and the others, as they have myself.*

And may they prevent violence on my behalf.

Meneham was not the only member of the crowd that wished to speak with Nerio, he quickly discovered. With each speak, more and more came forward, offering their help with whatever he may need, telling him of places, such as this courtyard, that could provide a haven for his speaks and the sick that were now flocking to him. His heart shattered like the panes of glass intermingled with the mud and cinder remnants around him with each request for healing. That was not his role, not in the capacity provided to Lord Delvan. His purpose was to enlighten the masses, yet they insisted on calling him by some title or another. He cringed at each utterance. He was a witness, nothing more.

Nerio finished greeting those that wish to speak with him among the dispersing group—more of which seemed to linger after every speak—and made his way to the triage.

The light inside was dim—an attempted comfort for those who groaned and ached among the makeshift cots—and there was a foul scent of illness in the air. He lent aid to those he could, making tea from yertwood root for pain, though it was diluted to the extreme in an effort to meet the ever-increasing demand. He poured a last cup of it and walked over to where the mother he'd met earlier and her son were sitting, their backs to the tent wall, feet crossed as they sat on the scuffed floor—the ash proved difficult to scrub clean.

He rested the cup of tea on the ground by the sleeping boy, his sores covered in pestled herbs and ointment—their supply of which was diminishing quickly.

"Thank you, Brother," the mother said. She seemed to have calmed her earlier hysteria. Nerio felt relief at that, followed by guilt as he knelt before her. *I should not find comfort in such relief.*

"What are your names?" Nerio asked.

"Tilya, and this is Hoffe."

"We will do our best to keep Hoffe comfortable, Tilya," consoled Nerio. "Feel free to stay as long as you need, but I must warn you, we have been forced to move around rather frequently."

Tilya nodded, looking at her sleeping son. "I'm sorry for my actions earlier. I had hoped... I still hope that you can bring the favor of the gods to him."

He wanted to say he would, that the gods would not abandon such a child to the horrors that life often brought upon people. *But they did not protect me, nor the victims of those cages, from the horrific acts of Jerdine.* This had been necessary, he knew, to bring him and the others to that underground hell where Jerdine had done the unspeakable to so many of Nerio's kin.

"The wills of the gods are often inscrutable. We must all simply understand that we fill a necessary role, and the hardships we endure bring us into their light, as much as we often wish it wasn't so." He wasn't sure if that, or anything for that matter, would heal the pain she must be feeling, but he couldn't leave her to commiserate without at least attempting solace, however piddling it may be.

A tear crawled down halfway down her cheek before Tilya wiped it away. "You speak like an elder," she said. "Little wonder the gods chose you as their Witness." After a shaky breath she continued. "There was something I wished to tell you. When I first arrived, I intended to use it as a means to... force you to heal him." Her voice went high as it stammered, tears springing from pools in her eyes—deep brown irises that now looked to Nerio and begged for forgiveness. "Gods forgive me but I have nothing else to barter with. I lost my husband to the fire," she sniveled and wiped her nose, "then we were thrown out of our home when we could no longer afford the rent. Hobbe was sick already and I've been so desperate... Please, beg the gods for forgiveness on our behalf. Don't let them punish my son for my misdeeds."

Nerio rested a hand on the woman's shaking shoulder. He fought back his own tears. He'd known his own pain, different from Tilya, but dark and consuming all the same. "I do not blame you. Perhaps the gods did this to bring you here, to be with us so that we could treat Hobbe."

She nodded, her breathing ragged and shallow. "Thank you, Brother. We are in your debt."

"You are not," he said softly, "I assure you. All are welcome, I expect nothing in return. Now, what did you wish to tell me."

The grimy, soot-stained sleeve smeared a grey line across her dark skin as she tried to calm herself. "A friend of mine, she's a Hand. We were talking about you; about things we'd heard. She's the reason I came here today; it was all I could do not to run here with Hobbe over my shoulder." She fought back more tears, her eyelids pebbles against the tide. "She said her newest assignment had her working somewhere they'd seen you before. Said that all the regulars had good things to say about you. Kind things."

"Where was this?" Nerio asked.

"She called it the 'Asylum,'" she said.

Nerio leaned back, letting out a long breath. It had been too long since his last visit to those tormented souls. He felt at his sash, a piece of stained terracotta tucked away, reminding him of one long lost.

"I am glad for your friend's assignment," he said, pulling back his distant gaze. "The people there are misunderstood, unfortunately. They need kind people to help them."

She shook her head, "That is not what I wished to tell you, Brother."

Nerio's head listed to the side. "Oh, what is it then?"

"My friend, her brother had been to one of your speaks, heard the retelling of what happened. She recognized the description you gave of the Messiah, this *Desnia*. Brother, she's there. They are keeping her in the Asylum."

Nerio fell back, sitting upon the warm stone. His mouth hung open, thoughts racing through his mind. *All this time wondering where she was, and they were hiding her in the last place I'd have expected.* His stomach twisted into a knot, remembering how much Desnia had hated that institution, calling it a prison among other distasteful curses. *And now it has become one...*

"Are you sure of this?" he asked. "You're certain it was her?"

"Unless there is another fair-skinned, blonde foreigner that is worthy of royal guards at her door."

Part of Nerio wanted to be sick, thinking of her locked away in a cell after all they'd gone through. He'd assumed that she'd been taken, refusing to believe that she'd abandoned him. His fear of her leaving had driven him to such a conclusion, and there was relief in discovering that he was correct. But now a concern grew inside of him, a pit of possibilities as to what her captors' intentions might be.

He needed to do something. Find a way to break her free of her incarceration. *The Lord General will never listen to me.* Nerio doubted that Lord Delvan wasn't also attempting to negotiate her release—regardless of his allegiances—and there was little more he could manage that a knight could not. Perhaps, together, they could do something. The benefits now began outweighing the risk of reaching out to the Blue.

While he weighed that in his mind, there was something, at the very least, that he could start with.

"Tilya, could you do something for me?" he asked, his mouth dry.

"There is no need to ask me such a question, Witness. I serve the gods' will, and therefore yours."

He disregarded the strange sense of shame those statements made him feel. If they insisted on calling him something, Witness seemed better than the alternatives. It was a unique title; he would need to try to keep its meaning humble.

"Could you reach out to your friend?" he asked. "I would have a message delivered to Desnia."

Chapter Nine

Keep us apprised of any further transgressions by either members of the church, or Cadet Saffstar. He is rife with personal feuds and is wont to bludgeon his way through anything he sees as opposition.

The awning's shade provided little respite from the hottest day Delvan had yet to experience in the desert city. The afternoon's sun sent shimmering waves of heat through the air, obscuring the streets beyond the intersection where they waited in a watery mirage. The thick, blue-dyed leather and darksteel of his armor only compounded the profuse sweating, the stifling ensemble making the heat unbearable even for him, let alone Orne and Kolden.

Better than going into the guild unprepared. Not again.

"Where are they?" lamented Kolden from a small, overturned crate. Sweat slicked his hair and left a darkened spot on the wall behind him, the leather edges of his hide and darksteel mail armor turning a similarly deepened shade of brown. "Wouldn't think it'd take this gods-damned long to gather two squads..."

Orne snorted derisively, his own hair and beard drenched and dripping. "Our priority is those books, Kolden. We don't get shit if we come up empty handed."

"No, they're *your* priority. I intent to confiscating every ounce of cadentite from the guild's stores I can find. Should be easier than going to all those fucking iguan dens."

Delvan's head spun, his face perplexed. "What were you doing in iguan dens?"

"I wasn't smoking the shit," said Kolden. "Just trying to track down the growers."

Delvan remembered his last visit to a den and recalled Hilbrun mentioning that the drug was sometimes grown with cadentite. "That's actually not a bad idea," he said. "You have any luck?"

"No," Kolden groaned, "not that this lumbering buffoon is helping any."

"I'm not the idiot who nearly got himself killed last night," retorted Orne.

"Because *you* burst in pouting about a gods-damned song!"

"Wasn't pouting," Orne said with a scowl, turning away and looking back down the street.

Delvan ignored their bickering. "I didn't realize there were any iguan dens in Brethefen," he said. He felt at the long-healed rib at his side beneath a black scar on his armor.

"Probably ones in every major city, I expect," replied Kolden. "Been popping up like flies to shit around here recently though. Heard they've been around for a while but with the place going to hell they don't seem to care about being discreet anymore."

"Are you sure it's grown with cadentite?" Delvan asked. The most potent versions of the drug always were, attracting a variety of clientele. Some he'd prefer to forget.

"So they like to boast." Kolden's voice was lethargic, the heat oppressive. "Been trying for days to talk to someone about purchasing some. The bastards are, unsurprisingly, tight-lipped about it. The most I've gotten out of anyone is that it's brought in by smugglers. Was making headway at an introduction last night before Orne decided to make sure some of them only had five toes to count on."

"Probably can't count that high anyway," Orne grumbled.

Delvan folded his arms as he thought about the implications of Kolden's discovery. Could there be someone with access to cadentite aside from the guild? *More importantly, would they be willing to part with it?* He doubted it, but he had more means than most to pay for it. If the guild did have any, it would be a fortuitous bonus. Even a small amount of the mysterious stone could reveal a great deal about his newfound gift. *Probably more if I could speak with Des...*

He would have to worry about her later, for now the general's assurances to keep her from harm would have to be enough. *Hopefully these books have the answers the general is looking for.* He could ensure Desnia's release and get the answers he longed for.

"If you find any, let me know," Delvan said.

Kolden gave a slow salute, his hand flopping to the side afterward. "Hopefully," he replied, "the guild has a bunch of it just, you know, lying around."

"Would that we were so lucky," Delvan muttered.

"Never fucking seem to be," said Kolden.

His memory crawled back into the night at the gate—recent, yet distanced by its profundity. The mystical green light that had surrounded them, emanating from within him. It had healed the hole in Desnia's chest but left one within his own. *What else do I not know?*

"They're here," said Orne.

Delvan turned, seeing his two promised squads of soldiers marching through the hazy veil. He, Orne, and Kolden strode into the blistering sun to greet them.

"Captain Barrol," Delvan said, saluting. This was to be his commanding officer for the raid, and he decided to avoid the argument of asking why it had taken the man two hours to arrive.

"Lord Delvan," said the captain with a nod of deference, "took a while to pull enough men from low priority duties, but managed to scrape together this lot." The gruff man tossed his thumb to the armored group in formation behind him. Three men among them in silk robes, bearing the royal insignia, the apparent chamberlains. Many of the men held themselves similar to Kolden, swaying slightly with glazed eyes in the overbearing heat.

"Might want to get some water for the men, sir," Delvan said.

"Already sent a squire," the captain said. "The guild's only three streets west of here, told him to just meet us there. Don't want to keep our hosts waiting." A smile crept onto the face of one of the more cognizant soldiers. *The guild has upset more than just the peasantry, it would seem,* Delvan thought.

"I trust that your men can handle themselves professionally, Captain?" Delvan asked, his eyes narrowly fixed on the man whose flickering smirk had now vanished.

The captain looked back over his shoulder at the men. Taking a few steps forward, his voice low, he leaned towards Delvan. "Some are eager, I'll admit, but Amenesol himself couldn't find a group of people in this city that wouldn't like to pillage the coffers of the guilds right now. They'll stay in line, and I'll try to make sure they don't enjoy themselves too much, my Lord."

Delvan looked back to Orne and Kolden, who merely shrugged. The captain was right; they all knew it. Enforcement of taxes and tariffs did not preclude one from their pilfering fingers.

Delvan nodded and the captain stepped back, turning to shout a command to the troop. Their rattling steps—with the unison afforded of regimented training—synchronized as they marched, the captain at their head and Delvan falling back to the rear with Orne and Kolden.

The few people in the street parted as they pressed forward, the homeless huddled along its periphery barely turning their heads from their shaded canopies of patched linens and refuse. The headquarters of the local Merchants' Guild appeared from around a corner, the stone edifice rising three stories above the street.

Iron gates surrounded the structure. Expensive panes of colored glass dotted the exterior in true Brethefen fashion, and expertly carved masonry exuded affluence with every relieved lintel and molded arch that surrounded them. Delvan felt his heart jumping into his throat as they approached, his memories of the last visit he'd made to a Merchants' Guild headquarters flickering in his mind like the tendrils of flames, stoking a pain forged in grief of his long-dead senior.

It did not freeze him in mortal terror as it once had, but it remained difficult to dismiss. Delvan tried to pull his attention elsewhere, focusing instead on the guards surrounding the building, a force large enough to make it seem a small fortress—but it was the unexpected sight in the plaza outside that caught his attention.

Beyond the pointed, steel reach of the guards' lances—some beginning to tilt down from their vertical extension into the cloudless blue sky—was a mob of citizens. At their head, voice ringing into the air like one of the city's many bells, was a young priest. Delvan's stomach turned for a second, thinking it was Nerio, but a clear voice full of conviction rang from him which Delvan didn't recognize.

"...all while *we* starve. The gods deemed us worthy of a new messiah, but now she has been locked away and the wealthy deviate from piety to pursue profit! The gods did not deliver this miracle to have its revelation suppressed! We mustn't—"

A loud whistle from the captain pierced the priest's vehement words, heads of the crowd turning and murmuring. Delvan witnessed contemptuous glares that bore through the soldiers before him, a begrudging shift of feet making way for the armed force. Beyond the crowd, leaf-pointed blades resumed their upright position, the stances and grips of the guild's guards relaxing slightly. Delvan's eyes flitted from one set of hands to another, watching for weapons—makeshift or otherwise.

As heads turned from the men onto him, he marked a distinct shift in the throng to his either side, sneers melting like ice. Faces and heads fell, eyes went wide, and lips parted as they turned towards him, whispering invocations that made Delvan shift uneasily in his sweat-stained armor.

"That's enough, everyone!" Captain Barrol said. "Head home before we start making arrests."

There was hesitation in the crowd, a wave of whispers spreading from the captain's announcement. Guild guards stood fast, postures rigid but eyes nervous. The priest that had been speaking met Delvan's eyes, a reverence held in them that he was growing far to accustomed to seeing.

The priest did not reserve his adoration for the captain, his eyes foul and harboring violent ill-will as they set upon the man. *Don't do something stupid,* Delvan thought. He couldn't afford something to go wrong here, giving the guild precious time to bury or hide the stolen tomes or cadentite. Even this stand-off before their offices would provide a cautious guild master with a chance to begin pre-emptive destruction of anything incriminating.

The priest broke his hateful gaze away from the captain and silently walked through the crowd, his shoulder nearly brushing their polished steel. As he passed Delvan, he gave a deep nod, the faint sound of, "Conduit," passing through his lips. Delvan had little time to say anything back, the priest briskly making his way beyond the crowd and down the street from where Delvan and the others had approached.

Their leader gone, the crowd began breaking, quietly shuffling away in differing directions like ants dispersing from the colony. The head of the guild's guard opened the gate and stepped forward, his red-painted armor with gilded edges a contrast to the captain's unornamented steel and chain-mail. "Thank you for the assistance," the guard commander said, "we were concerned for a moment that it might become violent. Gods-damned dregs have been out here near every day in growing numbers, looking more and more agitated by the hour."

And you planned to what, take lance and sword to unarmed civilians? As though Delvan needed another reason to detest the guild.

Captain Barrol pulled a scroll from the pouch at his side, handing it to the imperious guard. "What is this?" the man asked.

"A writ from Lord General Rosethorn," Barrol replied, "allowing us full access to all of the guild's books and assets under suspicion of price-gouging and evasion of the King's taxes. Pull any men you may have inside and have them wait out here."

The guard's brow furrowed down into his nose, scorn cutting deep crevasses on his face. "The general has earned enough from his martial law, wouldn't you say, Captain? Don't make this mistake—"

"If you have a problem then take it up with the Lord General. Men, let's move!" Captain Barrol snatched the writ back and waved his hand through the sweltering air, the squads continuing their march through the gates and towards the ornate wooden door seated atop the steps of the building's entrance. Spikes as hard as darksteel flew from the guards' eyes as Delvan walked by, his fist clenched tightly around his side sword. It wasn't often anyone of lower birth looked at him in such a way, and he had to admit that having Orne and Kolden at his back lent him a sense of security, enough to calm his thundering heart. He kept his face stern, following the rest of the soldiers through the opulent entry.

As he walked between the massive oaken doors, a sensation crawled down his spine, like a cool breeze had brushed the sweat on his back. He shook his head. The lord general wasn't joining them that he knew, and he dismissed the sensation as the heat playing with his mind.

There was a chaos of confusion inside the baroque space, several members of the guild—a few aged faces adorned in silk and luxurious jewelry marking the guild masters among them—having gathered to witness the commotion outside. The elderly patricians were the first to step forward from those gathered, their faces vexed and flush.

"What is the meaning of this?" one of the men asked. He was bald, his remaining hair white and neatly kept, a bulging stomach speaking to gluttonous tendencies.

The captain produced the writ once more and handed it to him, explaining its content. With another wave his men dispersed through the halls, shouting for anyone inside to emerge and gather downstairs, all while expelling the guards stationed indoors.

Delvan watched as the aging merchants made futile gestures and arguments, their tones changing from disconcerted to angry as their demands fell upon deaf ears.

"This is outrageous!" the bald merchant finally shouted. "You come to steal from us *and* disrupt our work?! We have a guild to run, we cannot be having you pull our members from their duties, writ or not!"

"The only one stealing," said the captain, "as I'm sure our chamberlains here will find, is your lot. And I'm not leaving anyone unsupervised so that they can have the opportunity to destroy or modify your accounts before we have time to thoroughly review them. Think of it as a day off, courtesy of the King."

"We both know that the King has nothing to do with this!" the man shouted, the perturbed faces behind him now nodding and appearing equally irate. "We will be speaking with the King, I assure you! The guild will have that scoundrel of a general—"

"I'd choose your next words carefully," interrupted the captain, his hand on the pommel of his sword, "because it sounded to me like you were about to say something *treasonous*."

The merchant huffed, his hands trembling and mouth contorting as he struggled to find words befitting his rage. *What was the guild expecting after charging their enormous fees?* Delvan watched as the last of the royal soldiers divided into the maze of halls, Orne and Kolden eagerly on their heels, leaving only him standing behind the captain.

The merchant's eyes flicked to Delvan as he silently stammered, his expression transforming as he did a double take. "What is *he* doing here?" Spit flew as the elder merchant pointed a shaking hand towards Delvan.

"Lord Delvan is newly under my command and is here to assist. Although I'm sure he can speak for himself." He gave Delvan a nod. "Now, which one of you can lead me and the chamberlains here to your most recent accounting logs?"

"This has turned from an offense to an egregious affront, Captain." The merchant's voice was low, turning into a growl of contempt. "The Court and King will hear of this. Until then, I refuse to be in the same room as this... miscreant. Come with me, I will oversee the royal chamberlains' review personally."

Delvan narrowed his eyes at the merchant, keeping his mouth shut despite the indignation to his title. He could have the man hanged for speaking to him in such a way but, fortunately for him, Delvan needed to keep the group before him as amenable as possible, given the circumstances.

"Lead the way," gestured Barrol, "but if you expect to do more than sit in a corner while we comb through your earnings, you will quickly find that my politeness has limits."

The man huffed once more, then spun in a silken swirl of gold and red and stormed off, the captain and chamberlains following closely.

Delvan looked to the scowling faces before him, the shouting of soldiers distant in the background, searching for one among many that would be the most amicable. He knew that this confrontation was going to be difficult, though he'd underestimated to what degree. He wondered at the source of the perspiration beading on his forehead—the heat, or the memories tormenting him.

I need to put that aside, he thought with difficulty. *What will it take to pull one of these men over the crest of rage they feel for me? What is it that separates businessmen from the rest of society?*

An idea emerged in his mind. The details were lacking, but it was a means to begin a conversation, if nothing else. One he doubted they would be able to resist.

"I'd like to make a deal."

Kolden strode at Orne's side, keenly observing each of the merchants that were ushered from the plethora of offices that filled the gaps between oil landscapes and flattering portraits. Part of him was glad to finally be out of the heat, not that the inside of the guild was much of an improvement. *At least we're not under that gods-damn sun,* he thought as he drew from his waterskin.

As he shoved the cork back in, a telltale sound caught his attention: the rattle of iron as a soldier tugged at a merchant's arm.

"Wait," said Kolden, raising his hand. Orne stopped beside him.

Kolden eyed the man, noting the silk robes that were humbler than some of his brethren, yet masterfully woven and tailored. He was younger than the elders that had been gawking at the front door, perhaps into his fourth decade, and was clean shaven—a rarity among the city's locals—with blue eyes that glinted sharply at Kolden's command.

Most importantly, he carried a set of keys at his waist.

"What's your name, Master?..." asked Kolden.

"Serbinnen," he replied tersely.

"Serbinnen?..."

The man's expression was cut from marble, the only crack formed by the malice carried in his voice. "Serbinnen re Polarne," he finally said through gritted teeth.

"Ah, that's what I thought, Brethish nobility—you *reek* of family money. Think I've been spending too much time with Del. Anyway, Master Serbinnen, do you know what you look like to me? No? Orne, do you know what he looks like?"

"Someone who opens doors," Orne grunted.

"Well said," replied Kolden with a nod. "Tell me, what doors do those keys open?"

Serbinnen stood resolute in stoic silence, his jaw clenched tightly in defiance.

Kolden tugged at his collar, the heat had worn his patience thinner than an over-sharpened dagger. "Listen," he said, exasperated, "we're heading to your vault, wherever the hell it is in here. Bring us there and open it, and everyone's life will be a lot easier. Refuse, and we try to break it down while my brother here tries to break you, and we see who wins. We can be competitive like that, and Orne's a sore fucking loser."

Orne grunted behind him, his inflection saying: *Fuck you, Kolden. You turn everything into a competition, not me. Not that you'd win.*

The master merchant's eyes danced from Kolden to Orne.

"Orne says he's looking forward to it. What do you say?" asked Kolden, crossing his arms and tapping a finger.

Serbinnen took a deep breath before saying, "Fine, follow me. But nothing is to be touched without my supervision. And nothing is to be taken until it can be recorded in our ledgers, so that when we file grievances to the Court—"

"Yes, yes," said Kolden with a sigh. *Not so fun when you're the one being robbed, is it? I'm sure the general is going to give me an earful over this one.* "Shall we?" he asked, gesturing him to lead.

The man spun on his heel and walked down the hall. Kolden sent the soldier that had been escorting Serbinnen to continue gathering members of the guild while he and Orne followed closely behind the spry merchant, their dusted feet leaving tracks on the rich carpets.

The itch in Kolden's brain overpowered even the stagnant air. Running fingers through his slicked hair, his mind raced—considering what he would do with any cadentite held here. Weapons, research, experiments—he needed to know how it all worked. *What kind of knife pulls the* soul *out of someone?* The image of the young boy in his adjacent cage writhing and collapsing to the floor after a markedly brighter knife had emerged from his chest was upon the canvas of his mind. It sent a chill across his skin, raising hairs.

Darksteel was a mere shadow of such a weapon—these "vi-blades" as The Hunter had called them—and Kolden intended to understand his enemy's tools of war to better defend against them. He refused to be caught off-guard again.

He was getting ahead of himself, he knew. He could plan all the experiments in the world, but it wouldn't matter if there was no cadentite in the guild's vault. *How could there not be, though? These rich fucks seem to hoard everything else.*

After twisting through a maze of halls and passages, each turn blending with the previous, they arrived in a windowless, stone room. A few small lanterns hung from the wall, the abandoned space flickering with the yellow hue of flames against limestone blocks.

Opposite them, mounted into the heavy stone, was a solid steel door, taller than Orne and nearly as wide, the great weight of metal sat idly in polished rock. A shadow upon the white stone.

Kolden let out a whistle. "That's a *big* slab of steel. No way that was forged—you guys cheat and get a Blue to transmute it for you? Always wondered if there was any truth to that rumor..." *I'll have to ask Del later.*

"Hurry up and open it," said Orne, his voice gruff. "Don't have all day."

"Watch your tone," grated Serbinnen, "I don't care whose orders you're here on, speak to me like that again and I will see you in the gallows."

That wasn't a great idea, thought Kolden with an eyeroll.

"Shut the fuck up," said Orne. The heat had him in an exceptionally touchy mood. "You're not the one giving fucking orders here, now open the gods-damned door, thief."

The merchant's face broke from his stern expression as he pulled it back in a gasp of aghast shock. "How *dare* you address a lord in such a manner, I'll have your heads—"

"You'd quickly find we have the same rights as you," Kolden said with a sigh. He looked to Orne, his face readable to his brother: *Really?*

Orne looked back to him: *I don't have time for your or this asshole's games. Fuck pleasantries.*

"You two are not of noble blood! I will not stand—"

"Open that fucking door," Orne boomed from his reddened face, "or I take those keys and remove a finger for each one I have to try to get it open."

The man's eyes went wide, his mouth vacant of accused indignations. Kolden stood there, arms crossed and waiting. Orne wouldn't *actually* cut the man's fingers off. *Well, he probably wouldn't. Maybe.*

Serbinnen saw in Orne's eyes the glare that would shake any hardened warrior to their core, swallowed loudly, and after a brief hesitation, took the keys into trembling hands from his waist. Kolden let out a quiet sigh of relief, lacking the desire—let alone energy—to follow through with his threats.

Serbinnen strode to the door, inserting a key into the center of the compass rose that was the guild icon. Turning it with a loud click that resonated through the room, the monolith of metal released from its setting.

Smooth as the polish on the perfect slab of steel, the door opened with a pull of the handle from Orne after pushing the quivering noble to the side. Kolden could hardly contain himself, wanting to jump into the vault beyond. Hopefully his search for cadentite would end here.

Then I can finally get to work.

Delvan closed the office's door, the open window opposite him permitting a small breeze to enter the merchant's chambers. It was a welcome reprieve, no matter how diminutive. It was the other chill—the familiar sense that ran down his spine—which nullified any relief he may have felt. He dismissed it again, the heat clearly playing tricks on his mind. He took another long draft from his waterskin as the aging merchant accompanying him walked behind his desk.

The reaction to Delvan's proposition had been mixed; anger blended with befuddlement in a tumultuous aggregate, but this man—Master Mornath, as he'd introduced himself—had stepped forward, willing to negotiate and speak privately with Delvan, even while his colleagues looked on in gaping betrayal. *No honor among thieves,* he supposed.

"Take a seat, Lord Delvan," Mornath said with a gesture to a chair across from him. "Would you like some wine?"

Delvan's heart skipped a beat as the man grabbed two crystal glasses from the cabinet beside him, pulling a filled decanter of ruby-red wine from behind its glossy doors. Part of his mind was drowned by a craving—whispering wordlessly that if he didn't think or speak his desires aloud, then there would be nothing to protest, nothing to prevent his indulgence of the succulent, velvet liquid. If his own mind didn't object, then how could there be any guilt later? A sip of the seductress which called to him from within the clear chalice would take little more than grasping it in his hand and kissing her lips upon his own; a panacea capable of quenching more than simple thirst...

His arm had begun to extend itself before the thought of Desnia rotting away inside of a cell flashed in his mind. The path before him was one of inaction and self-pity, and he could not stand the thought of Desnia spending another day, week, or month inside that cell while he did nothing to ensure her release.

His arm withdrew, hand snapping closed—much to his heart's dismay. "I thought that wine was illegal in Brethefen?" he asked, taking a seat before the carved desk, its leather top dotted with ink.

Mornath cracked a wrinkled smile, spectacled eyes carefully judging Delvan. "The principles who wrote those archaic laws are no longer here to enforce them, so what's the harm? I thought you might enjoy a taste of home. Calentine is, after all, not abstinent such indulgences."

Delvan shrugged as he took a seat across from the wisps of white hair that grew unkempt from Mornath's face. Of all the merchants that had greeted them at the door, he seemed the least focused on his appearance. *Not that it precludes him from being capable.* One did not become a master merchant among the guild without the aptitude for trade and politics that defined its members. This man warranted caution, and Delvan saw the slight dishevelment as an armor of its own.

"I'm not here to chastise your drink preferences," Delvan said.

"I assumed. Otherwise, half the soldiers in the city would have been arrested by now. I hear there is quite a market for ale and other liquors for hidden taverns and brothels currently."

I'm sure you've more than just 'heard.' One of many profitable ventures, no doubt. "I don't partake," he replied, holding up his hand to prevent the merchant from pouring a glass.

Mornath cocked a wry eyebrow but left the vessel dry. He sat, sipping from his own glass and leaning casually back in his padded chair. "And here I was thinking you'd visited us to experience the best Aliova has to offer. What, then, can I interest you in, my Lord? Surely even a man of your stature has needs that must be filled. Understanding such details is the foundation of any deal, after all."

Delvan licked his chapped lips, taking a moment to choose his words. "I'm looking to do some reading. Specifically on the Ones Before."

"Oh? And was the library unable to find the tomes you needed? It's rather spectacular. Thank the gods it was saved from the fires."

Disappointed that you don't have another avenue for income? mused Delvan. "I was informed that the resources I seek are... elsewhere." *Hopefully, being pulled from your vault or one of these offices right now.*

"Hmm." The merchant seemed deep in thought, his thin, veiny hands bringing the glass back to his lips. "Such heretical documents are, I would imagine, rather expensive. Not that a Saffstar wouldn't be able to procure such means. I'm happy to inquire with my colleagues about such writings, as I'm sure they're certainly a more interesting read than the fiscal accountings your chamberlains are currently pouring through. And with the guild's resources, I expect we could dig up a trove of the knowledge you seek."

He either doubts that I can find them here or believes that I am attempting to hire him to seek them out. Neither option sat well with Delvan. He'd expected the guild members to be more nervous, but he saw none of that in Mornath. Delvan squirmed slightly in his seat, trying to restrain his growing concern. *They* must *be here.*

Mornath smacked his lips as he finished off his glass of wine before continuing, "Coming in here with a writ and collection threats was a bold play, but I must concede that it was a rather well executed one. You'd make a fine businessman yourself, my young Lord Delvan. I imagine you learned quite a bit from Lord Hilbrun in your time with him."

Delvan could suddenly feel his pulse throbbing in his neck, a shadowy hand grazing fingers across his heart. *Of course he knows about Hilbrun, he's trying to throw me off guard.* The story of how the Merchants' Guild headquarters burned down in Calentine had unquestionably made its way to all its senior members. It was an advantage like any other, a card to be played during negotiations. And it was working better than Delvan cared to admit.

"My time with Hil was invaluable," Delvan replied. "I learned a great deal from him. Looking back, it still surprises me just how naïve I was about the world. He shared all manner of things with me, opening my eyes to the workings of the empire, not to mention the guild." One side of Delvan's face turned up into a smile, his eyes fixed on the merchant across from him. It took all his focus to not reveal the twisting of his stomach, nor the blood that rushed from his face.

Age and experience served Mornath well, he was as composed as they came. But through the aloof posture and wrinkled cheeks of a forced smile, it was now his turn to shift in his seat, slight as it might have been.

Delvan continued, trying to push his advantage while suppressing the mild tremor in his voice. "There is a man," *if you can call him that,* "that the lord general and I seek who, despite my and others' efforts, remains alive." There was a slight flash of white as the merchant's eyes went wide for the briefest of moments. *Thought Jerdine was dead, did you?* "He will be found; every soldier in the western half of the empire is currently looking for him. When he's eventually brought in, he will be charged for his crimes, and any that held association with him will be tried to the same level of accountability.

"The information that I seek would not only aid us in finding this villain, but whoever presents it to the lord general would be in his debt—not to mention my own. Maybe enough to forget about whatever evidence may be discovered about other transgressions." *And you only have until Orne and Kolden turn them up to cut a deal.* Delvan expected this to make the man anxious to turn over the journals and cut a deal; instead, he poured himself another glass of wine.

"Even in my many years," Mornath said after another draft, "it is rare to come across such a prosperous deal. Although, while the guild exchanges favors as often as we do coin, in this instance I can confidently say that we'd prefer to locate whatever you may need at a price of, say, whatever taxes the lord general deems we have been 'avoiding.'"

Delvan felt sick to his stomach. *He's not concerned at all. That doesn't make sense, unless... No, it had to be them—*

The chill he'd been avoiding along his back suddenly grew into a warmth that flushed his veins, tearing him from his thoughts. The feeling was as familiar to him as breathing. He'd thought the heat had been playing tricks on him, but there was no question to it now.

Could the Lord General have come to oversee the search? I didn't think he would, but what else—

His memory brought him back to the night in Calentine, the revelation of what had been hidden away there by the guild.

The vault should be open by now, which means... No, they wouldn't be so foolish. Would they?

His head spun back to the master merchant; his eyes calm over the brim of his wine-filled glass. Delvan's thoughts became frantic. If he was right, then by the King's laws they could confiscate everything here, retribution of the guild be damned. His patience for skating around topics had its limits, and the sources of his brethren's gifts was a line he would not allow crossed.

Pretenses aside and brow furrowed, Delvan leaned forward in his chair and asked, "Master Mornath, do you mind telling me why there are sapphires here?"

Gold.

Useless, stupid fucking gold.

The vault was filled with it—suns lined the shelves along the wall in neat rows, with palm-sized bars of tidily stacked ingots reflecting yellow in the lamplight. Emeralds and rubies could be found by the handful; documents and maps were laid out neatly in drawers, and silver moons in an abundance Orne had never seen rose to the ceiling in their stacked containers.

Absolutely nowhere to be found were the gods-damned books they were looking for.

Kolden was frantically ripping out drawers, searching the backs of cabinets for hidden compartments. Orne had already gone through anything large enough to hold the tomes—there were roughly a dozen of them, and they were bulky enough to not be hidden away easily. He hoped that Kolden would find something, but the sting of sweat in his eyes burned through the frayed threads of patience he had remaining.

The pompous merchant was still hovering over them, his chin up and eyes down, looking as condescending as ever. The man's face cringed with each bile-filled curse Kolden spat out, and he winced while trying to stand tall at the sight of drawers and boxes being tossed haphazardly around. Orne glared at him, his fists in tight balls to his either side.

"Would you be careful with that?" asked the merchant spitefully as another drawer went flying. Kolden ignored him as his head disappeared inside of the cabinet's opened front.

Orne removed his dagger and used the pommel to tap against the stone walls, hoping to hear a hollow or find some hidden stash.

"If there is something specific you're looking for, perhaps I could assist instead of you destroying our vault," the merchant said, his voice rising.

We can hear you whine just fine, asshole. "You know what we're looking for," Orne spat.

Why was Delvan the only one allowed to talk to anyone at the guild about the gods-damned books? *Haven't said shit about those mages or what happened at the gate, yet the general still doesn't trust me.* Orne wasn't sure what he'd done to piss off Rosethorn or why the man held a grudge, but he was going to show him here, today, that he was more than worthy of his trust, and a promotion. *But first I need to find these fucking books!*

The base of Orne's dagger smacked the wall hard enough to chip away a corner of the stone, the darksteel hilt vibrating in his hand.

"Do you mind?!" the annoying fuck behind him asked. "I will not stand by while you—"

"Quiet your tongue," said Orne, pointing the dagger at the man's face. "Unless you're going to tell us where the... things we need are, then I don't want to hear another word from you."

There was pounding from inside the cubby that Kolden had crawled into, his brother soon emerging empty-handed and drenched in sweat. "There's nothing fucking here!" Kolden exclaimed. "We need to get Delvan down here, maybe he can sense something that we can't."

Delvan can't sense the fucking books, idiot. Even he knew that. Of course, his brother could probably care less about them, or Orne's promotion. "We're not here for your fucking rocks, Kolden."

"We can be here for *two* fucking things, Orne." He wasn't sure if it was sweat or spit flying from Kolden's mouth. "Go get Del while I keep looking around in here."

"Fuck off," replied Orne. His brother was always trying to give commands. "You go get him."

"Are *you* going to fit inside of these cabinets to search for false backs? No? Then go get Del so we can finish in here and start going through the offices."

Orne's nose flared as he slammed the dagger back into its sheath. He couldn't think of a retort to throw back in his brother's face, and it fueled his already boiling rage. He turned and stormed out of the vault room, going to search for the Blue. *But* not *because Kolden told me to.*

He shouted to a nearby pair of soldiers, calling them over. They marched to him, and he pointed inside the vault, "You two stay here with that asshole and make sure he doesn't do anything stupid."

The face of Serbinnen slowly turned towards Orne and the pair of soldiers, his face a mixture of shock, anger, and indignity. "How *dare* you?!" the merchant hissed. "I swear by the gods, I will—"

"Didn't I tell you to shut up already?" asked Orne. "I wasn't fucking talking about you anyway."

His head still buried, Kolden threw up a rude hand gesture in Orne's direction. He ignored it and stormed down the hall. His brother was right—not that he'd ever admit it, Kolden's ego didn't need inflating—if there was cadentite here, Orne guessed it would be stored wherever they were hiding the books. *Wish it had just been inside the damn vault so we could get out of this plush shithole.*

Everything here felt expensive for no other reason than to display extravagance. There was no utility in it. A sword needed a good edge, a hilt, and a scabbard. Anything more than that was a waste. The one thing his brother did well was forge weapons that did what they needed to do, were excellently crafted—something else he avoided mentioning—and were otherwise plain. *All they need to be.*

He resisted the urge to scuff a carpet with his boot as he turned a corner. After asking a few soldiers, he made his way to the room they'd seen Delvan in—finding it closed, and voices elevated from behind it. *And yet* I'm *the one not allowed to speak,* he seethed.

Orne shoved his way into the chambers—finding another overly ostentatious proclamation of wealth within. Delvan was standing, his finger pointing at the older man opposite him. His voice was raised—not shouting, but not far from it.

"...and if I go down to the vault right now, what am I going to—" Delvan's head snapped to Orne, then back to the calm man sipping wine behind his desk. "Orne," Delvan continued, "convenient timing. Did you find what I think you did down in the vault?"

Not unless you thought it was fucking empty. The smug grin of the man behind the desk made Orne hesitate from announcing his findings out loud—he was already sick of these merchants; he didn't need a reason to make this one any vainer.

He walked to Delvan, leaning low to whisper in his ear. Delvan's face fell as he informed them there was nothing they sought in the vault. He even mentioned that Kolden hadn't been able to find his stupid rocks, for whatever that was worth.

Delvan's eyes darted across the carpet beneath his feet for a moment, his fists clenching tightly, before he threw a last defiant glare at the merchant across from him. With his lips held tight, eyes full of fury that threatened to explode like fiery suns, Delvan tried to peel the smitten smile from the man, but to no avail.

Orne watch as the Blue turned and left, his steps laden with intent. For what, Orne couldn't be certain. *Hopefully he knows somewhere else to look.*

As Orne turned to follow him, doing his best to ignore the arrogant merchant, a cabinet stocked with liquor—the mass of bottles tightly packed like a winter's worth of stacked firewood—caught his eye. Ignoring the trailing gaze of the man behind the desk, he walked over and grabbed one of the bottles, full of an amber liquid that he'd recognize anywhere. He pulled the cork, smelling the faint burn behind layers of caramel and vanilla that were the hallmarks of Drunt whiskey.

This guy's got the really *good shit.*

The merchant held up a finger, opening his mouth to say something Orne didn't particularly care to hear. "That's—"

"Mine," interrupted Orne, popping the cork back in and walking out, bottle in hand, before the merchant had time to say anything further. He shoved the bottle in the satchel around his waist while taking long, hurried strides to catch up to Delvan, who was moving through the halls as if chasing something.

He watched as the Blue turned down one hall, then spun around to go down another, all before looking up at the ceiling and rushing to the nearest staircase. Orne groaned. He was already sweating enough, chasing after the determined knight was beginning to grate his raw nerves.

The thought motivating him, pressing him forward as he closed the distance, was that Delvan had sensed something that could lead him to the books they sought. Part of him hoped that it wasn't cadentite, mostly to foul Kolden's mood. His brother had been especially annoying this week looking for his precious mineral. Orne knew that it was probably in his best interest to help Kolden, but a few more losses would provide him a much-needed humbling.

"Del!" Orne finally shouted as he reached the top of the stairs. Delvan tossed a look back his way, eyes frantic and wide, his jaw set tightly. He didn't wait as he forced his way through another door, Orne now on his heels and letting out an annoyed sigh. He turned from the hall into the room Delvan had burst through, nearly running into the now frozen Blue a mere few steps past the doorway.

Orne sidestepped around him, following his gaze to a pair of high-backed, upholstered chairs centered in a space that was large enough to house a score of soldiers. In one sat another merchant; younger, but still finely dressed, glib as all the others. Across from him was someone that took Orne by surprise, now realizing why Delvan had stopped in his tracks.

Long, black hair swept to either side of a tanned, attractive face above a figure to match. The woman didn't dress in robes fitting a merchant's fashion, instead she wore a rich looking shirt, which Orne thought could have been tailored for a man, but fit her well, and trousers that he thought fit her *very* well. Sitting atop the white silk adorning her chest was a large sapphire, cutting the air with sparkles from its perfect facets.

I swear, she looks familiar. Orne hadn't thought there were any other Blues in the city aside from Delvan and the lord general.

She turned a smiling face from the merchant and looked at Delvan, whose jaw hung nearly to the floor, his shoulders slouching with what Orne thought might be disappointment.

"Wow, I was beginning to think you were ignoring me," she said, her smile turning to more of a sarcastic smirk. "Where have you been?"

"Chasing this idiot," Orne blurted. He snapped his mouth shut, he hadn't meant to say anything.

She looked at him, her smile waning. She stood from her chair and Orne immediately recognized where he knew her from. The darksteel gladius at her side was impossible to forget. *The girl from the tavern last night. What the fuck is she doing here? I didn't know she was a Blue.*

How had he missed *that*? Had she hidden her sapphire?

She looked back at Delvan, grin returning as she gave him a wink. "Don't you know it's impolite to leave a girl waiting?"

CHAPTER TEN

Abetting his fantasies could result in further irreparable harm to not only the empire, but its delicate allegiances and political standings.

Delvan's heart sank.

Part of him was glad to find another Blue in Brethefen; the isolation was unlike any he'd experienced before. There was a connection with other gem-bearers that was difficult to replicate—even Ferrand had had his moments, despite him being... *himself* most of the time. Orne and Kolden helped fill that void—and, somewhat surprisingly, Desnia to an extent—but coming from the sapphire-filled heart of the empire to this desert was a world-shift that he continued to struggle acclimating to.

Still, finding a knight in the guild had not been what he'd expected—or hoped.

The guild in Calentine had illegally held at *least* half a dozen sapphires, not to mention Jerdine's key to the gate. Coming here, he'd anticipated similar lucre, but aside from the singular—presumably legitimate—sapphire before him, he sensed nothing else.

Furthermore, if the vault was empty, as Orne had explained, and the journals weren't in there... *No wonder Mornath was so calm, there's nothing here to find, is there?* He'd become certain, sitting there with Mornath, that the guild had been hiding away sapphires again. It would have been asininity on their part, but he stopped underestimating the arrogance of aristocracy long ago. With grim irony, he now saw his own reflection in their polished image.

The day wasn't over—not yet—and there could still be hidden caches to discover in the building. *I hope.* Hope, however, was doing little to stop him from feeling sickeningly convinced that he might have made an error in his presumed culpability of the guild. *This could all have been a massive waste of time. How could I have been so wrong, again?*

And where the hell are those journals?

"You just going to stand there and gawk, like this creep?" the Blue before him asked from lips that he was having a hard time looking away from.

"Creep?" grumbled Orne.

He blinked and gave his head a hardly perceptible shake, correcting his posture and composing himself as the merchant who'd been sitting with the Blue excused himself from the room, being graced by a smile from the mouth Delvan had been "gawking" at.

"Apologies," Delvan said with half a glance back to Orne. "I thought... I didn't realize there were any Blues in the city aside from myself and the lord general."

"Well, until a few days ago, there weren't," she said. "What's your name?" she asked.

Delvan felt an almost imperceptible swell of power, too faint to be a use of the other Blue's gift. A small spark glimmered in the darkness of his despair, keeping alive hope that there was another sapphire in the building. *I'll deal with that shortly.*

"Sergeant Orne du Traskor," Orne quickly spat out. Delvan raised an eyebrow at the response. It seemed the hulking giant did have a weakness after all.

"Delvan," he replied. "And you are?"

"Bored, mostly. You're really a lord? Wasn't expecting that," she said, looking at Orne.

"Most people don't," Orne replied with a shake of his head.

He narrowed his eyes, frustrated that she wouldn't share her name. *Fine, I can play games too.*

"Am I to just call you Ennui, then?" asked Delvan, crossing his arms.

"Good as any other name," she said with a shrug. "So, your captain mentioned that you're here looking to collect unclaimed taxes or some nonsense. That all you're looking for?"

"Books," said Orne.

Delvan turned his head towards him, his brow furrowed and eyes almost as wide as Orne's. The man's face was one of consternation, and he looked apologetically to Delvan. *What has gotten into him?*

"Maybe you should go help search the offices, Orne," Delvan said, his tone balancing the line between suggestion and command.

Orne snapped his gaping mouth shut and gave a few quick shifts of his eyes from Delvan to the other knight before turning around with a huff and leaving the room. *I can't believe he told her that.*

Despite the inherent instinct to trust a fellow Blue, he hesitated. The fresh wound of learning Hilbrun's true nature—to a limited extent—as well as Ferrand's, had yet to scab over. There were few that he trusted outright anymore, and the fact that he'd found this woman lounging inside of the Merchants' Guild was cause enough for him to be suspicious.

"Don't blame him," Ennui said. "I have that effect on people."

"Clearly," replied Delvan. He looked to the silver chain around her neck, wondering as to which gift she had. The plain, oval links were heavily patinaed, probably handed down over generations. Other than its age, however, it gave Delvan no indication as to her abilities.

"What're you doing here?" he asked.

"What most people do with merchants: business," she said, as if it were the most obvious reason imaginable. "Better question is, what're *you* doing here? My new friend was just telling me that you're the Sparky who burned down the guild in Calentine. You itching for an encore or something?"

Sparky?

The casual insult had his mouth twisting like a snake as he struggled to form words. He was used to banter like this from Orne and Kolden, but to hear it from another Blue had taken him by surprise.

As Ennui walked to a cabinet and pulled out a decanter of amber liquor, filling a short, crystal glass, Delvan forced some diminutive sounds from his mouth.

"Uh," he managed to sound out, "no. I mean, *no*," he repeated more firmly. "I'm here under orders from the lord general."

An eyebrow cocked high onto her forehead, her dark eye looking at him sidelong. "Uh huh," she said, slipping the stopper back into the decanter. "Must be some *really* interesting books for the lord general to send one of the people the guild hates most directly into their nest. When I met with him this morning, he didn't *seem* stupid. Have you considered that maybe he really doesn't like you?"

Rosethorn met with her this morning? Why didn't he say anything? The general obviously wasn't required to share details with him, but telling him of Ennui's arrival would've been polite, if not expected. *Unless he didn't want me to know.*

"If you tell me why you're *actually* here, maybe I'll tell you why the general sent me," he retorted.

"Mhm," she said with a subtle blink of surprise as she pulled the glass from her lips. "I had a feeling you could be snappy. Careful though, I like a challenge and have ways of making you talk." She winked at him again, and Delvan felt his heart skip a beat.

Wait, is she saying—

The sound of breaking glass shattered Delvan's thought, a rock rolling along the floor to his feet. The sounds of clamor from beyond the now-jagged edges of a nearby window deluged into the spacious room.

His hand shot to the hilt of his sword instinctively, relaxing as the immediate surprise passed. He hadn't missed Ennui's hand reflexively doing the same.

Glass crunched underfoot as they both slowly walked to the window, the sun blaring in as a beam highlighted by stirred dust.

The previously dispersed crowd had returned in force, turning the tense air of the city square violently febrile. The mass of shouting, venom-spewing citizens was a wave of odium that swelled against a straining line of lances. The guild's guards stood in formation outside of the gates, the long shafts of their weapons held before them, each end pointed to either side as they attempted to create a barricade, pressing against the wall of rage. More guards stepped forward at the command of their leader—three men now bracing each lance in a desperate bid to force back the onslaught.

Delvan and Ennui watched as the line buckled, guards falling to the stone pavers as the crowd heaved. Men began dragging away their comrades but, to Delvan's dismay, a few of these armored rescuers collapsed of their own accord.

The heat... They're passing out!

"Looks like it's about to get bloody out there," said Ennui, slamming back the remaining whiskey in her glass.

Delvan's eyes were frantic as he watched the riotous crowd, his heart pounding in his ears. He scanned the screaming faces, fists raised into the air, rocks and detritus arcing over the crowd and into the ranks of the guards. His eyes caught a still figure, a stone parting the contemptuous current, staring directly at him. The young priest from earlier—his face calm and eyes smiling—tilted his head in what Delvan felt to be veneration and, after locking eyes once more, turned and worked his way through the back of the crowd, leaving the square and the growing chaos within it.

"We have to get down there and stop this, before it goes any further," Delvan said, trying to hide the panic in his voice.

"Too late," Ennui said with a nod.

Delvan watched with horror as the flanks of the guards' line were broken and overrun. The ranks were forced to pull back into a half-circle around the front gate at the shouted orders of their leader.

Fallen guards were abandoned to be trampled by the throng as rioters flung themselves against the building's perimeter fence to either side of the guild's soldiers, quickly scaling it and streaming towards the building's entrances.

Delvan knew that once the levee of guards broke and the mass flooded through the main gate, the most any inside of the guild could hope for was leaving with their life. The guards' leader shouted out over the crowd, attempting to quell the riot.

He was met with a rock to the face.

Hand covering the gushing wound, he was slow to recover, but after a moment bent over in pain, blood sprayed from his lips as he screamed a command. The lances behind the front line of the barricade of soldiers lowered, the snarled teeth of the cornered predator flashing with glints of silvery steel.

Then the keening of death began.

A distant, skin-crawling scream caused Kolden to jerk his head upright inside of the cabinet he'd crawled into and forcefully whack his forehead into a wooden crossbar. Spitting a curse, he rubbed the aching lump as he pulled himself out and back into the stifling, dim lantern-light of the vault, feeling globs of sweat streaming down his back.

Serbinnen had abandoned his looming sentry at Kolden's feet and was hesitantly peering down the hall from the entrance to the vault's antechamber. Kolden left the vault and walked up beside him, still cringing, his hand held to his forehead.

The sound of shattering glass and icy cries drifted from either end of the long passageway. A pit began to form in Kolden's stomach as he heard the turmoil growing louder.

"What's going on out there?" said a nervous Serbinnen.

"How the fuck should I know?" scolded Kolden. "Whatever it is, it doesn't sound good."

"Well," said the merchant fervently, "aren't you going to go and investigate?!"

"And leave you here alone to stash away whatever you can? No, don't think so." Kolden shook his pounding head. *The nerve of this prick.*

He *was* going to have to go investigate, but this merchant was more obstinate than even Orne, and he refused to let him feel as though he'd won an argument—no matter how small.

"Stash it where?! It's already inside the vault!" Serbinnen exclaimed.

Annoying bastard has a point...

"Fine," he resentfully conceded, "but you're coming with me." He wasn't about to leave the man alone with his precious vault to run off with whatever contents he could carry while he was gone.

"What? Absolutely not! I will not leave the vault open, let alone unattended," said the merchant, crossing his arms.

I don't have time for this. Kolden sighed. "Fine, lock up your gods-damned vault and then give me the keys. Stay here if you want."

There was a loud crash from around the corner, the voices beyond a mayhem of indistinguishable shouting.

The merchant's dark skin paled as his eyes went wide, staring towards the unseen tumult. "Perhaps... I will accompany you," he said shakily.

That's what I thought. "Don't just fucking stand there," Kolden said as the air grew hotter from flared tempers that drew ever nearer, "lock it and let's get the fuck out of here!"

The merchant jumped as he scrambled for his keys, the iron jingling as his quivering fingers sifted for the correct one. He rushed to the vault door and shoved the hulking mass of steel closed with a resounding *thud* that made Kolden wince. He watched the distant hallway corner anxiously, his grip tight on the hilt of his long dagger, until Serbinnen rejoined him at his side.

I need to regroup with one of the squads, figure out what's happening and go from there. He quietly walked out into the hall, waving for the wide-eyed merchant to follow him. He led them away from the nearest sounds of chaos, nearly reaching an intersecting hallway before a shout twisted his and Serbinnen's heads.

A haggard group of four peasants carrying bricks, staves, and other makeshift weapons, had appeared at the corridor's opposite end. They set their sights on the pair, pointing and shouting obscenities before sprinting in their direction.

Oh fuck, thought Kolden as his own eyes went wide and heart hammered rapidly.

"Run!" he shouted, before racing down the hall. He drew his dagger, daring to steal glances behind him as he and the merchant were being pursued. The maze of passages sent them twisting and turning, all while Kolden frantically searched for signs of the other squads.

They rounded another corner, Serbinnen hot on his heels, and Kolden suddenly noticed the edges of his vision blurring in darkness. He shook his head, trying to disband the lightheadedness that had washed over him. He stumbled, realizing in a half daze that they had run right into another group of waiting rioters. One wielded a long wooden shaft as a club and immediately took a swing at Kolden's sweat-drenched head.

Instincts drilled into him over years at the military academy, and his short stature, were all that saved him, ducking as the wooden rod caught the fringes of hair atop his pate. Serbinnen, who'd been looking over his shoulder, lacked similar reflexes. The shaft violently struck the bridge of his nose. All the merchant managed to release was a gurgle and quick spray of blood, his body immediately going limp and dropping to the floor.

Kolden stared for a moment through swimming vision at Serbinnen, the telltale stillness of death in his crumpled form, his mind slow to process what happened.

Instincts flared again, and he spun, his black blade arcing through the air before driving its twin edges into the back of the assailer—resisting with everything he had to not vomit from the nausea-inducing motion. The blade dragged across bone as he drove it into a lung, the staff-bearer dropping to the floor with a silent gasp. Kolden spun, struggling to keep himself upright as his vision whirled, pointing the bloody spike of darksteel at the three gaunt figures that remained before him.

They, too, held makeshift weapons, hesitating as they glanced between Kolden, their dead compatriot, and the keys at Serbinnen's lifeless waist. Every muscle in Kolden's body was tight, adrenaline flooding through him as he swept his dagger left and right, fighting to maintain balance. Shouts grew closer from behind, and just past the three insurgents before him was another bend that he knew led to an exit.

He had to go through them, as dangerous as it was. There was nowhere else to run to.

He braced himself, shifting weight between his feet as he readied himself to pounce. *Just need to take one out, maybe, then sprint past the other two. Assuming I don't pass out...*

Just as he took a step forward, a burly, armored figure bearing a darksteel sword and what appeared to be an ornamental shield—likely pried from one of the walls—marched around the corner behind the men facing Kolden. With three efficient slashes of the inky steel, the men fell, and Kolden was left staring up at his brother as their blood pooled on the floor.

"Took you... long enough..." Kolden panted. He reached down and took the keys from Serbinnen's corpse, puking all over the floor beside him as he did.

"Nice job protecting your ward," chided Orne.

"Should've watched where he was going," said Kolden as he gasped for air, leaning his back against the nearby wall. "What's happening?" He kept his ears attuned to the distant yelling, thankfully not approaching them any longer.

"Mob's trying to break into the guild and sack the place," stated Orne.

"No shit," he retorted. "I meant status. Where're the other soldiers?"

"We repelled them at the east wing, for now. These were some stragglers I was chasing down. Sounds like the west wing is still being hit hard. Was working my way over there next."

Kolden nodded, his eyes pinched closed as he tried to right his spinning head.

"Here," said Orne, handing him a waterskin. "Go to the east wing, reinforce them. You might have time for a breather; you'll be more useless than normal if you pass out from heat stroke."

He gave his brother a sideways glare but didn't argue as he snagged the waterskin and took a long draft.

"Excuse me," came a voice that nearly caused him to spit a mouthful of water. He only now saw that there was an older man with a wispy, white beard that had been hidden behind Orne. "I'll take those, if you wouldn't mind," he said, pointing a frail finger at the keys in Kolden's hand.

Kolden looked at the man—presumably a master merchant, though more disheveled than the others—through narrow eyes, weighing the keys in debate as to what to do. His search of the vault had been fruitless, and Serbinnen hadn't seemed the type to share information. This was probably the best opportunity he'd have to glean information from the guild. *Nothing like a little bit of leverage.*

"Fine," Kolden said breathily, "but I'm going to need something in exchange."

Delvan took a step forward, unable to pull his eyes away as lances reached over the dam of guards and plunged into the crowd, their feet becoming submerged in a flood of crimson as their commander shouted the kill order.

His stomach heaved with revulsion as men and women alike fell to the steeled thrusts, the wails of the mass only agitating it further, driving the guards further back against the gate as their pikes stabbed repeatedly into the crowd.

Turning and rushing from the room, Delvan started shouting commands,

Ennui on his heels. "You!" he said, pointing to the nearest royal army soldier. "Find the captain! Tell him to assemble men at the side entrances, there's a mob trying to break in. Go, NOW!"

The man turned and sprinted away, his armor letting out a *clank* with every hurried step.

"They'll be lucky to last much longer than the guards outside," said Ennui.

"I know," Delvan admitted. He had to calm the crowd, if they *all* managed to break into the guild it would be a slaughter—on both sides. An idea struck him. *More like a desperate gamble...*

"Give me your inanite," he said hurriedly, extending his hand to Ennui.

"What?" she asked.

"Keep a block but I need the rest of it, as much I can get. I'm going to try something," he said direly.

Ennui hesitated for a moment, then pulled a small block of black stone from the pouch at her waist, removing the leather bag and handing it to Delvan.

He snatched it and then sprinted down the hall, reaching the carpeted stairs and launching down them two at time. The stairs spilled onto the main hall, the sound of shouting and ringing steel from the adjacent passageways falling upon his ears. His heavy breathing did little to cover the distant, shrill cries of those that were attempting to penetrate the side egresses.

His continued sprint carried him directly to the front entrance. Soldiers and merchants alike scrambled around him; each making their own desperate attempts to blockade the entrances or beg for protection.

Bursting through the doors and soldiers protecting it, Delvan jumped the short steps and ran to the front gate, ignoring the people climbing the fence to his either side and rushing the forecourt. He skidded to a halt a few paces from the spikes of arched metal that the guards valiantly attempted to hold, the hinged iron now nearly to their backs. The fence and gate did little to separate him from the raucous crowd, and seeing the chaotic, blood-stained mess before him made him realize the throng had taken on a mind of its own, fighting a battle where they felt they had nothing to lose.

He wouldn't allow the destruction that had haunted him these past months to happen again. The people here were suffering enough, and a mass execution could send the city over the edge it already teetered precariously on.

Taking a deep breath, Delvan held his hands in front of his face, palms facing each other. A thick ribbon of swirling fire formed between them as he pulled them apart. He drew from all the inanite on his person, draining and muting every trace of it. His senses then reached outward, searching for more of the abundant mineral in the rock beneath his feet, until it too had nothing left to give.

His face grimaced as his teeth clenched together, the log of twisting orange and white before him a compressed inferno which shook his hands as he struggled to control the glowing mayhem. It demanded release, fighting Delvan like a caged beast as he focused everything he had into the blinding blaze glowing between his hands like the sun itself.

His muscles went taught, straining his every fiber as ligaments threatened to snap. From his belly grew a loud, furious howl as he flung his hands forward at an upward angle, releasing the pent-up fury in a wide and shallow cascading wave, flooding from him like water into a river's delta. It rampaged above the heads of the amassed crowd, spreading to cover the populated square with blazing clouds of roaring tendrils. Gasps of shock and awe followed in the fire's wake before it faded away, exposing the cloudless blue above only after igniting the very air it rested on.

The smell of singed hair, cloth, and leather filled the torrid, hushed air. Delvan stumbled as a knee gave out, barely catching himself as his lungs voraciously sucked in air. His eyes squeezed together tightly as he struggled to catch his breath, his heart hammering against his chest. He managed to tilt his head back up—sweat blurring his vision and stinging his eyes—to see the crowd shuffling, their and the guards' eyes confounded and murmuring as their frightened faces looked from where he'd scorched the sky back to him. The guards' grips remained tight on their lances, heads nervously turning towards different frozen bystanders.

Legs still shaking, Delvan stood straight, calling out over the crowd in the loudest voice he could manage, "Leave! Shed no more blood here today!"

Heaving ragged breaths, he looked over the crowd, watching them as their whispers filled the air like locusts. "Conduit" was the word that spread among them, its cacophony a hiss as the crowd began to slowly step away. The guards cautiously watched, some dropping to their knees in exhaustion while others climbed the amphitheater of bodies to search for fallen comrades.

The guards' commander turned a bloody face towards him, giving a shallow nod as his men began ushering the stragglers away.

Delvan knelt to the ground, unable to stand. The stones beneath the dark-steel knee covers permeated their heat, and he saw that the spikes atop the fence were now bent, disfigured fingers of iron, destroyed in his blaze.

Standing proved impossible, an hour passing before the majority of the square was empty, bodies of those slaughtered being moved outside and stacked in the forecourt behind him. He wanted to check on Orne and Kolden, but an unseen, foreign hand rested its reassuring grasp on his shoulder, a calm relief washing through him, telling him they were alright.

A pair of tall, polished boots and well-fitted leggings stepped up beside him. He was too exhausted to acknowledge Ennui, his muscles weighted like lead.

"At least you kept the fire *outside* this time," she said while chewing loudly on something.

He finally turned his gaze, looking up as she ripped off a piece of jerky, a mischievous smile on her face. He shook his head, ignoring the gibe and looking out at the sun that was nearing the horizon line. The bells would be tolling soon.

"Have anything to share?" he asked, ravenously eyeing the dried meat in her hand.

"Girl's gotta have her secrets, buy me a drink sometime and maybe I'll tell you some," she said with a wink, popping the last of the jerky into her mouth. Delvan sighed as his stomach panged and growled.

"Oh, did you mean food?" she asked with poorly feigned ignorance. "That was the last of it, sorry. Anyway, I've someone I'm looking to meet shortly. See you around, Sparky," she said, grabbing her inanite pouch and walking away until she eventually disappeared beyond the city square.

Was she trying *to be rude?* Such acute use of his gift had left Delvan famished—which Ennui would know.

"Lord Delvan," a familiar voice from behind him called.

He turned to see Master Mornath approaching, his robe stained with splattered blood and face lacking his previously calm, smug demeanor. It was now a visage of exhaustion and mortification. *Yet another mirror,* he begrudged.

He shakily forced himself to his feet, meeting the eyes of the merchant. "Master Mornath," he said, "did you survive this madness unscathed?"

He nodded. "Yes, thanks largely to the tall fellow who's fond of my whiskey."

"Is he alright?" Delvan asked, though he was certain—somehow—that he was. *Kolden as well.*

"Last I saw him, yes." Mornath turned and looked out into the square, the half-circle of bodies just beyond the gate mounded like a breakwall. "So much bloodshed, and for what? The commoners hold us responsible for this inflated market, as though we're to blame. They don't realize we're merely its shepherd," he said grimly.

"I think the mothers watching their children starve in the streets would disagree with you."

The older man gave him a slight shake of his head and sighed. "One day you'll understand. Those in power, such as you and I, always do in the end. Else they succumb." *I'll see it that way about the time you stop seeing people as purses, I expect.* Despite whatever Hilbrun might have been—member of a group capable of unspeakable atrocities—he distinguished himself from the rest of the guild by seeing the humanity in everyone. A lesson Delvan sought to never forget.

"Regardless," the merchant continued, "it would seem that the guild is in your debt, my Lord. Without your show of force, I fear we would have been overrun and strung up in the street."

You still might, if that mob comes back. "I think that your peers in Calentine would disagree with that."

"Mhm," he said with a shrug, "most likely. You saved our lives—most of them—as well as protected our assets. I would say that warrants a level of... transparency on my part."

Delvan raised an eyebrow, waiting silently. He didn't have the energy to riposte with the merchant right now.

"There are no sapphires here, despite what you may think," stated Mornath flatly.

Delvan's shoulders slumped. He wasn't convinced that Mornath was being honest, but he failed to notice the hallmarks of deceit that had previously fluttered from the man's tongue. He could have sworn he'd felt the telltale swell of energy of another nearby sapphire while speaking with Ennui, a mistake he was not wont to make.

"You've held them before," Delvan replied coldly. "In Calentine. Officially they never existed, but I was there. I know what I saw."

"The limits of my gratitude do not extend into admitting high treason, my young Lord," Mornath said. "I speak only to you of the branch that still stands behind us, thanks in large part to you. Ironic that the day you come to take so much from us was the day you gave so much back."

They both stood there in silence for a moment, the bleak scenery bringing a fog of melancholy that hung in the air. There were cries of the few remaining people in the square—wives, husbands, children, all sobbing in grief as they searched the dead. It was an ambiance of misery.

Mornath's voice broke the distant mourning. "We also don't have any cadentite here, which your other friend was rather disappointed to discover. I can provide you with a list of the few contacts I have. I've heard a supplier has been distributing it quietly as of late, so they may have come into possession of some, but any that was here we sold."

"To whom?" Delevan asked, though he suspected he knew the answer.

"Principle Jerdine," the man said, much to Delvan's surprise. He hadn't expected such candidness.

Perhaps there's more I can learn yet. "Did he ever share secrets with you?"

"A fair amount with different guild members, yes. Not that I am privy to all of them. What did you have in mind?"

"Blues. Specifically, our powers."

The merchant tugged at the wisps of his beard, curiously eying Delvan. "No. Not that I've heard at any rate." Delvan's head sunk, his heart heavy. "Do not misunderstand me, my young Lord, just because I am unaware of such knowledge, it does not mean that it was not shared. We are not, perhaps, the hive you think we are. There are many minds within our halls, many with their own schemes and plots and other such ruthlessness they see as profitable."

"Sounds about right," said Delvan derisively.

"While I wish to refute you, today has shown that if, perhaps, we did share more information, we might not have found ourselves in this situation." His voice drifted off as he stared out into the killing field, the rancid smell surrounding them.

"Tell me, what else did you do for the principle?" asked Delvan. "I already know that you held his cadentite key in Calentine."

It was Mornath's turn to look as though a suspicion had been confirmed. "We've had extensive dealings with the man over the years. He's wealthier than I think even the King realizes. Most of it, despite what you might think, was above board."

That's disappointing. Delvan was starving and exhausted yet sickened by the scent of death and gore. Now he added empty-handed to that list. *There's one way to salvage the day.* His eyelids yearned to drape down like curtains over his bloodshot eyes, but he first had to confront the subject that had been prodded earlier yet never stated directly. He had no desire to dance around it any longer.

"Do you have Jerdine's personal journals here?" he asked.

"Not that I'm aware of. Last I knew they were in the possession of the army," Mornath replied. "We'd heard rumors of their recovery, not to mention the events surrounding the fire and his involvement in them. There'd been discussions as to our desire to acquire them—legally, of course. To the right people they would be worth quite the sum. But we ultimately decided against it."

"Why?"

"Because the 'right' people are also very *dangerous* people. Crossing them is a hazard we deemed not worth the profits."

"The Magridi," Delvan said with a sneer.

Mornath's brow rose in surprise. "You're incredibly well informed, Lord Delvan. Though knowledge of that name brings with it a danger to oneself and those close to you. I trust that you understand this?"

Delvan nodded slowly. The memory of death and destruction in the city's heart was oil atop the lake of his mind, ever slicking the surface. "Are they the ones who stole the journals?"

"A likely guess," Mornath said. "But there are others who would seek them out just as fervently. That man's secrets were not as well kept as he might have thought."

What's that supposed to mean? His brain was struggling to keep up with the conversation, his rumbling, cramped stomach painfully begging him for food and stealing his mind's attention. "Who would these other people be?" he asked.

The old man brought back a faint shadow of the smile he'd worn in their earlier meeting. "I'm afraid that isn't my place to say, nor would I have much to discuss, as it were." *Of course not.*

"I need something more, Mornath," Delvan said, his words coming out as a sigh. "All you've done is acquit yourself and tell me what I already knew or suspected. Give me something I can use."

"We're not your enemy, Lord Delvan, despite how much you'd like us to be. As far as what I can give you, I can provide you with the liquid assets of the former principle, which I assure you are quite substantial. I suspect the general will put them to good use and, considering their prior relationship, I expect he'd be rather glad of the donation."

"You'd cross Jerdine, despite his... power?" Delvan asked.

"Gods, no," Mornath said with a shake of his head. "We'll inform him that they were confiscated by the general. A true enough statement, and one that doesn't change the current status quo."

"All in exchange for not collecting unclaimed taxes from the guild, I presume?" Delvan asked. *Always a catch.*

The older man gave a slight smile as he stroked the white strands of his beard. "Sixty-thousand suns, my Lord, is not a sum to dismiss lightly. Several of us had debated whether to continue dealings with the man after the rumors of this recent debacle came to light. I think you'd almost be doing us another favor in wiping the slate clean, as it were. Besides, your chamberlains will not find half as much missing from our payments to the crown, I assure you."

Delvan let out a small snort. *Why am I not surprised.*

"As to your search, perhaps you should question your fellow knight," said Mornath.

Ennui? "What makes you say that? What do you know about her?"

The man shrugged. "Admittedly little. I did not have an opportunity to speak with her, but she garnered the attention of several guild members upon her arrival, I hear by dropping a few names that are as illicit as the ones we've spoken."

Delvan's brow wrinkled as it dug down to his nose. "Can you find out more for me? Ask around?"

"I will try, but alas, it may be some time before you hear from me. The other guild masters and I have decided to leave the city."

Delvan shook his head, eyes wide. The evening bells began tolling in their symphonic rhythm, startling the birds floating atop the waves of heat around them. "What? You'd leave? What about the assets you have here?"

"Locked away and guarded in our absence, with a few staff to ensure everything is in order. Until things calm down here, we're thinking Tennefen is a more... stable residence."

Delvan's jaw hung low. He didn't know what to say, questions raced through his mind. Mornath's responses seemed genuine, which left him... angry. He'd desperately wanted the guild to be responsible, a hangover from his previous vendetta. One that clouded his judgement still, it would seem. *I'm too tired to think straight right now.* He knew the guild was privy to a great many secrets, but that was no different from his own family, or any other noble's for that matter. Someday he would know more about their hidden knowledge, but for now it would seem they could not assist him further.

"I will arrange the funds' transfer before we depart," Mornath said. "Best of luck in your search, my Lord. King and His grace upon you."

"And you," replied Delvan as the man turned and walked back towards the building, its face now scared with broken glass and haunted by the flies and carrion birds swirling around the freshly dead.

Delvan wanted answers. About his newfound ability, about the mysterious Ennui, and about who would have stolen the books that hid a wealth of knowledge he sought. His thoughts drifted to Desnia, the cell she was locked in somewhere unknown to him, and what answers the general was expecting from her—and how. Would Rosethorn *actually* let her go once he had his answers? Delvan doubted it.

He felt the familiar icy hand of shadow once more pick its claws into his chest, emphasizing his failures thus far, paralyzing him. All this effort, and he was left empty handed. He could almost hear the general's admonishments now, keeping him a cadet forever, leaving Desnia imprisoned.

Delvan had reached for everything and yet claimed nothing.

What options were left to him now?

CHAPTER ELEVEN

Lastly, we've received a petition which has been forwarded to you via carrier. This Court had been previously indifferent to the request, but the need for reinforcement of the Trethish border and the necessity to maintain secrecy around recent events have coincidently aligned. It would be in the best interest of the empire for you to acquiesce, and an arrangement may be made to satisfy both needs. King and His grace upon you.

Lord Demrand ce Saffstar
Regent of the King's Sapphiric Court

Morning dew clung to the windowpanes. The tiny prisms scattered a spectrum of colors through the office as they caught the sunlight that would soon steal them away. The bells had not yet rung when they'd been pulled from their quarters, the lord general having sent for them to be seen prior to all other appointments. Delvan felt his stomach growl, the twist of hunger coming despite consuming three full meals the night before. The residual fatigue lingered like the dew on the windows from his display the previous day—hopefully it dissipated just as quickly.

Lord General Rosethorn leaned with palms upon his desk, eyes tracking along inked lines on the thin vellum before him. Delvan, Orne, and Kolden all stood with feet spread and hands clasped behind their back, waiting for the general to speak—the silence turning Delvan's stomach more than the lack of food.

Eyes still on the document before him, Rosethorn broke the silence, "Two royal army soldiers, six members of the guild's personal guard, and thirty-one civilians—all dead. The number of wounded are well over double that. I've seen shorter casualty lists on a battlefield." The general shook his head, still scanning the list. The three of them remained quiet, hearing no question in the general's statement.

Delvan braced himself for what he expected the general's next words to be. Retribution would be called for; punishment to display to the masses and elite alike. He'd become accustomed to being the scapegoat craved by those above him in situations like these.

The general lifted a palm and slammed it down on the desk, rattling it and sending vibrations that Delvan felt through the soles of his boots. *Here it comes,* he thought.

"The impertinence of these people!" Rosethorn said, his lips drawing into a line. Delvan's eyes flashed with brief surprise. "What did they think would happen? Marching on a guild that houses a private army... Lunacy at best, and pure dissidence otherwise.

"They curse the taxes we're using to rebuild *their* city and spread blame like a plague. How long before their temerity turns on the army? Seems any leniency I'd allowed will have to be forgone. It was foolish of me to assume I could permit otherwise." The general shook his head and stood straight, meeting their eyes with his galvanized stare.

Delvan waited. What would it be this time? Removal of his rank? Ostracization to another distant city, perhaps continent? *Would the general be bold enough to try and take my sapphire?* he wondered. It was a rare punishment, but it did happen on occasion. The man would have to have some inclination as to the lengths that Delvan would go to maintain its possession. Attempting its removal would not end well for anyone.

"You three handled yourselves excellently yesterday," Rosethorn finally said.

Delvan blinked. *What?*

Kolden shuffled slightly in his own surprise, and Orne's chest puffed out, his head rising higher.

"Not only did you manage to quell this riot before it became entirely out of hand, but I've been informed that the guild is currently completing the transfer of over sixty thousand suns. Although the conditions of its 'donation' are slightly unorthodox, it was a simple enough arrangement to come to. It fills a very immediate need for funding that will contribute greatly to the rebuilding effort. Well done. I intend to inform your father of these deeds, Lord Delvan. Maybe it will be enough to begin swaying his opinion of you."

You clearly don't know the man.

"Tell me," the general continued, "how fared your other task? Were you fortunate enough to find anything?"

Delvan blinked again, trying to dispel the shock that had caught his tongue in a vice and nearly managed to distract him from his cramped hunger. "Uh," he said, his stomach sinking as he realized he was going to need to share disappointing news. "They did not have the books, Sire. I had thought... I'd been confident that they would, but after lengthy discussions with the guild masters and a thorough search, it would seem that I was... mistaken."

"We ripped that vault apart, Sire," said Kolden. "There was nothing in it that I could tell."

The general narrowed his eyes and rapped his knuckles on the desk after a pause. "An undesirable outcome from such a promising lead. The Chief Inquisitor had similar results as well, unfortunately. I will have him focus on that endeavor for now, but I want you to continue your search for the priest, Lord Delvan. As for the two of you," he said, looking at Kolden and Orne, "I have more that I need to discuss with you. First, I want to say that commendations are in order. You both carried out your duties with exceptional valor yesterday and such efforts are deserving of reward. I am promoting both of you to lieutenant. Congratulations, soldiers."

Orne and Kolden both saluted in unison. "Thank you, sir," they replied. Orne's face beamed, covered with the closest he ever came to a smile. Kolden's shoulders hung lower, his lips a thin line. Delvan knew that he cared more about recognition for his work than he did promotions. It was a step in the right direction at least. *He'll come to see that, eventually.*

"It's the least that I can do and, given the petition that I received today, the most." His face soured, his eyes looking to a thin piece of vellum, freshly unrolled from the limb of a pigeon and held down with weights upon the desk. Delvan saw both brothers' faces blanch.

"Requests of my peers," the general said, "are normally discretionary choices left to me. However, the Court has forced my hand, and it's now a matter of obligation. Lieutenants Orne and Kolden, you're being reassigned to a new post, effective immediately. Your effects are being packed now, and you will leave by midday."

A gaping chasm opened in Delvan's chest, his world spinning as though he were freefalling through its immeasurable depth. *No, no this can't be happening.* The semblance of a life he'd managed to scrounge together from the necrotizing despair he'd felt these past months began crumbling beneath his feet.

"Sir, please, we can send a letter to him—" pleaded Kolden. Orne's face turned scarlet above his thick beard.

"We all follow orders," interrupted Rosethorn, "including myself. I am not in a position to lose soldiers, let alone ones that I trust. But this is not the type of request which can be contested."

Delvan was still reeling, his mouth dry as it hung open. He had to do something, anything. Desperate, he spat out the first words that came to mind. "Sir, I'd like to be transferred with them."

His insides reappeared with a nauseating twist of his stomach. *If I leave, then what will happen to Desnia? She'll rot in that cell for who knows how long.* An instant regret began to rive him. He couldn't abandon her, yet he couldn't imagine a world absent the brothers he'd grown so close to. His heart pounded faster as his torturous specter dug into his chest.

"I appreciate the sentiment, Lord Delvan," said Rosethorn, "but I need you here. Brother Nerio must be located, and you've proven invaluable in helping to maintain the peace. Besides, I won't be sending the Traskors far."

Rosethorn turned to the brothers, their faces grim and doused in turmoil. The urge to vomit began crawling its way into Delvan's throat.

"You are being sent to an outpost two-week ride west of here, in the White Mountains. The Court is concerned that the Trethish are slipping spies past us and want to bolster our defenses. I have no doubt that this is a threat to be taken seriously, our last war with Trethefen was far more gruesome than you'll read of in the histories, but the logic behind their reasoning... I'm not sure what they suggest would be possible with multiple Blues present.

"Cadet Saffstar, I can't see this as a detail that you would've missed, but the man you fought, the one who killed Knight Commander Ferrand, did he bear a sapphire?"

Delvan's head pulled back, his face confused. *I already explained that they weren't Blues. Does he think me a liar regarding the High Realm mages?* "No, sir," Delvan said, eyeing the general, trying to gauge his response. "We're certain that he didn't carry one."

The general's mouth clamped shut and muscles tightened for a moment before giving a satisfied nod. "Very well, I assumed you wouldn't have omitted a detail so crucial but had to ask all the same."

Rosethorn looked back at his desk, tapping the unfurled letter upon it.

"This petition, conveniently, does not state the length of time for your transfer, presenting what some might call a 'political opportunity,'" the general said, looking to Orne and Kolden. "Give me a few months, lieutenants, and I will have you recalled here and given a *real* command. In the meantime, I intend to put these... unnecessary orders to good use.

"I'm concerned that the men at the mountain bastion have grown lax over the years—the Trethish have been quiet for a long time, bastards probably hope us to forget them. Traitors." The general flashed what could only be described as a snarl, as though his words carried bile over his tongue. "I'm going to leave it to you two to get them back into shape. Lieutenant Orne, you will be given command of half the squads currently stationed there, reporting directly to the local captain. Lieutenant Kolden, ensure that the bastion's smiths are capable enough to craft basic armaments and shoe their horses. I've been sending farriers out there on a too-regular basis for long enough."

What a ridiculous waste, thought Delvan as he heard Kolden grinding his teeth. *One of the best fighters in the empire training forgotten security, and an equally talented smith sent to patch armor and shoe horses.* The general's hands were bound, he knew, though it didn't stop him from seething. Did the general realize how far below them this station was? What was the logic behind his father's and the Court's asinine orders? Delvan wanted the brothers here—the general separating them was like a fatal strike, letting him watch as he bled out. *Orne seems to be less upset about it than his brother, though.* It *would* be Orne's first true command. *At least one of us is getting what they wanted...*

"Once things calm down here," the lord general continued, "and you bring the discipline expected of the Royal Army back to the fortress, I can transfer troops to fill in your stations and have you brought back. I think your talents have been squandered long enough."

Orne saluted again. "Thank you, sir."

Delvan thought about the state of the city: the streets crawling with homeless and the hungry, once-bright walls plastered with the dull ash that plumed with each torrid breeze. It was desolation unlike anything he'd seen before, and while his heart prayed for a quick recovery and subsequent return of Orne and Kolden, his mind questioned the general's optimistic timeline. His was a disheartening pessimism, one that sank his shoulders as the cavern inside of him seemed to grow into a canyon, a familiar prick of pins crawling along his left arm and hand.

"Keep up the good work, and Cadet Saffstar, keep me apprised of your progress with finding Brother Nerio. Dismissed," said the general, nodding his head to them.

Orne and Kolden saluted, turning to leave while Delvan stood there, dumb-struck. He was about to be alone—again—and the pain had frozen him in place, his muscles threatening to tear with the slightest motion. *No,* he real-ized, *not entirely alone. There will be Desnia, if I can get her out.* There was also Nerio, who left him feeling conflicted more than anything else. The experi-enced they shared at the gate left a bond forged in death—a chain of steel that pulled at his conscience. What he would do if he discovered the priest was clouded in turbidity. *And there's one other...*

"Sir," Delvan said, his voice meek, "when we were at the guild, there was a woman there. Another Blue." Ennui was an enigma who burned questions into his brain, their number compounded by the comment from Master Mornath. *And she's going to be the only connection I have in this gods-forsaken city that isn't either imprisoned or in hiding. Assuming I can trust her.* Which he was fairly sure he couldn't.

He heard Orne and Kolden stop mid-stride behind him, the lord general looking at him through hesitant, narrowed eyes.

"I suppose it was only a matter of time before you became aware of Lady Mithya," said Rosethorn. Delvan furrowed his brow, wondering as to what her house name was. "I'd sent a request for a Knight Inquisitor, and she was the nearest available. I've asked her to help prove your story of last week's events. I expect this won't become an issue, Lord Delvan?"

...Inquisitor? Delvan's eyes went wide, his face numb and cold despite the sun pressing against it. They weren't planning to torture Desnia—not physically. *They don't realize what they're doing.* The image of Desnia's blood-soaked robe came back into his mind, a detail that Delvan had wanted her to explain to him since he'd seen it. *Now I wish I'd pressed the issue, because if I'm right—about everything—they're going to break her before she can answer anything.*

Delvan parted chapped lips, his dry mouth struggling to form words. "She's... a Truthsayer?"

"And a rather expert one at that," said Rosethorn with a nod. "Don't worry, Cadet, we'll get to the bottom of all of this. If all goes well that knighthood might come early."

Delvan tuned out the general, his mind suddenly consumed with a single, terrifying thought.

Oh, no.

Desnia laid on her side, facing the wall. She wiped away sweat that was threatening to runnel into her eye, her clothes and cot beginning to moisten with the day's first letting of perspiration as the temperature spiked. Her fingernail made a faint scratching noise as it scraped away paint from a small section of wall hidden by the rails of her bedding. The small flakes were collected in her hand, the white chunks finding their way into her mouth with as little motion as possible as to not alert the guards of her actions. Her mouth produced barely enough saliva to wet the chalky substance, and each swallow felt like gravel down her throat.

That, uh, seems healthy, said Masini in his dry, sarcastic tone. His voice had become slightly muffled after ingesting a small handful of flakes.

At least I know it's working, she thought.

"If you know another way for me to get muted inanite," she whispered, "I'm all fucking ears."

I once saw these beasts that had ears bigger than you, you know. Things were tall as a tree, and I swore up and down they had five legs, until someone pointed out that the thing dragging on the ground was—

"Shh!" she hissed as the sound of a door closing echoed through the hall-way outside.

Ugh, moaned Masini, *you're duller than the paint you're eating.*

The place had become eerily quiet since the guards moved the wing's other tenants to a different area the night before. A blessing and a curse—she could clearly hear the guards and their conversations in the hall, but such clarity went both ways.

She ignored Masini, flipping onto her back, eyes drilling through the ceiling as she feigned boredom. She tucked Masini's ring back under her shirt—as much as she despised the act—to keep him from view of the guard on duty. The bastard grew more vicious with each beating, her abdomen now one large, hidden bruise, and she was becoming more paranoid by the day that he'd take whatever she possessed out of mere spite, regardless of the "pro-tections" that had been allotted to her.

From the corner of her eye, she caught sight of her heavy-handed tormen-tor peering into the room through the barred portal, oddly quiet. *He normally has such colorful things to say,* she thought derisively.

"Thank you, gentlemen," came a feminine voice from the hall. "You can go now."

"We're supposed to stay with the prisoner at all times," said the abusive bastard.

"Which is why I have this; seems the general doesn't trust you to hear sensitive information. Can't imagine why." Desnia heard the crinkle of parch-ment from the other side of the door, lifting her head to see if she could catch a glimpse of the new arrival beyond it. "And get me a chair, would you?" the woman continued. "Then feel free to go to the far end of the hall. Only thing you need to hear is me calling for your return. Oh, and I'll take the key."

She'd fully sat up at this point, watching the door through squinted eyes and listening to the grumblings of her guards. *They sent a woman?* she wondered. Either sex was more than capable of the malice Desnia expected from her captors, but it took her by surprise, nonetheless. All the inquisitors she'd seen had been men. With a *clank* of iron on iron, the door unlocked and swung open.

Desnia's heart skipped a beat as she locked eyes with orbs of deep, cascading brown. Dark, lush hair held in a bun sat atop the head of the woman who entered her cell, her olive skin glowing like honey in the window's light. Pants that clung too tightly spoke to an air of nobility—no one from the streets would want to attract the attention garments like those would bring. Her shirt was loose, but cut low, and hanging down from an ancient looking chain of silver was a white, cloth bag, synched tightly around something heavy.

The initial gravity of the woman's appearance wore off as Desnia glanced at the sword at her side, her eyes flicking from it to the smirk that the woman was bestowing upon her. *What the fuck is she smiling at? What games are they playing?* Desnia wondered.

A chair arrived by hand of an annoyed-looking guard, quickly being occupied by the grinning beauty, who casually leaned back in it, eyes fixed on Desnia all the while. Once the door shut behind her, she tugged the cords around the small sack that was around her necklace's end, pulling it off and sending a chill down Desnia's spine. A lustrous sapphire now rested atop golden skin, nestled on her chest like a viper in a breadbasket. Desnia's eyes went wide and her face pallid as she looked back up from the refracted sparkles cut by the stone's azure depths, finding the same grin staring back at her.

"Desnia," the woman said, still leaning back in the chair, "I can't wait to learn more about you."

END PART 1

INTERLUDE

The miasma of Rahere's charred comrades still clung to the scorched surroundings, the sight drawing sweat from his brow and back. The stained, inanite walls swallowed the meager light of his torch, ash from the explosion's remnants indiscernible against the black stone. The cave had nearly collapsed, and the violence unleashed by their actions had been felt for miles around, claiming all within its throat at the time. That cost had reaped reward, however, and a wealth of coin now encumbered his purse.

Suns. Dozens of them. His eyes had never glimpsed such riches, and now the golden coins flowed to him like water from a mountain's peak.

He just needed a *little* more. Then he'd have enough.

His boots scuffed the fine, crumbled gravel—a contrasting white against the ebony stone—along the floor as he delved farther. The remains of the monstrous slab which had stood fast at the end of the craggy passage now littered its length, every step making his heart hammer faster with the passing of the growing detritus.

A dull, foreboding hue birthed itself from the darkness ahead of him, the purple luminescence making his body quiver, shaking the torch that lit his pallid face. The surrounding inanite gradually faded into a profuse, stark white, amplifying the glow in the distance. He rounded a corner, his destination finally before him. And within, his prize.

If he could take it.

Two guards, swords loose in their scabbards and ready to draw from their armored waists, stood on either side of the tunnel's entrance. Its wide mouth—dozens of arm spans across—radiated a low, steady light from within its depths, saturating him in purple as he stood a few paces away. Shaped like a flawless tube, the white stone walls were latticed in a repetitive pattern of thin cadentite along every surface from floor to ceiling. It ended in an impossible absence of light deep in its heart, an amorphous entity shifting and swirling in the distance. The mere sight of it caused Rahere's throat to tighten and ache, making his breath shallow and quick.

The guards turned their eyes to him. "So," the one on the right said, "the gods gave you the red card today, did they?"

Rahere shook his head with an audible gulp. His eyes glanced to his right where a pile of rubble, pushed to the cave's side, was mounded high above an adjacent, smaller stack of glowing cadentite. The valuable stone had been meticulously chipped and carved from the debris of what had once been the slab of muted inanite sealing away this tunnel of morbid intrigue. This was the last of it, waiting to be hauled to a safer hiding place up above.

"The boss says that our supply ain't gonna last forever," Rahere said, hearing the tremor in his own voice. "He told me that if I volunteered, he'd give me a bigger cut. Said he figured me to be the man for the job."

The guards looked at each other without even the flick of an empathetic eyebrow. "Reckon he knows best," said the talkative guard. "One of us is bound to figure out how to carve this cadentite from the tunnel eventually. Hope you're the one to do it, Rahere. Maybe try not to have it blow like the door did, at least while we're down here."

The other guard grunted in nervous agreement.

Rahere tried to steady his breathing as he slid the torch into a ring on the wall. He touched the hammer and darksteel chisel at his side. It was an expensive, but necessary, tool. Several had been damaged beyond repair already; a fresh supply now being delivered monthly. The cadentite was resilient, and the tools wore with each bit quarried from the softer stone that encased it.

This tunnel had proven... difficult, however. Though the same white, muted inanite surrounded the repetitive patterns of glowing purple lines that stretched into that eerie void, every attempted strike ended in sparks and broken tools and the normally soft stone unscathed. They'd delved farther into the tunnel, one man after another, seeking a fault in the cadentite lines similar to the one they'd utilized to shatter the door, to no avail.

And worse, as they traveled deeper, bringing themselves closer to the surreal source of Rahere's fears, every venturer had simply... vanished.

I'll be more careful, he thought. *The others must have missed* something, *I know they did. I'll find it.* Once he prevailed where their incompetence faltered, he'd be rewarded. *Then I'll finally have enough. I'll take my bigger cut, and then... well I can help them sell that, too. Then I'll have enough.*

He stifled his growing anxiety, his body's instincts of survival urging with all its influence to flee. He took a step between the guards, ignoring their visages of emulsified doubt and avarice. They wanted him to succeed as much as he did, for they did not crave to be the next one to enter the illuminated cavern.

"Good luck," the guard said, the other giving a tight nod, nervously fiddling with a loose belt from his armor. Rahere forced himself to stand straight and took a step forward, watching through squinted eyes as his foot fell, waiting for the damp of the cave around him to alter as he laid foot on unknown ground.

Boot uneventfully met stone, and he let out a sigh of relief. He took another cautious step and remained present. Intact. He looked back at the guards—watching him with the intense curiosity of self-preservation—as he drew his hammer and chisel and lightly tapped at a few points along the wall. Sparks flew like fire from a demon as the black metal contacted purple stone, leaving no trace of a scrape or scuff along the flawless patterns of the normally workable rock encapsulating it.

Rahere wiped sweat from his face onto his slick forearm as he took another step down the tunnel, his eyes desperately seeking any minute crack or slivered fracture along the passage's length. Hours seemed to pass as he cautiously scanned the thin lines that traversed the floor, walls, and ceiling, his heart drumming against his chest as he failed to find anything the others had missed, forcing him closer to the blackness that horrified him so.

With the tip of his chisel now marred and dulled, he would soon have to leave for a replacement. But dare he abandon his endeavor without a solution to that which had plagued them? *No. No, best try a little longer. Just a little farther in, that's all. I won't get as close as the others; they weren't careful enough—but I am.*

He glanced over his shoulder once more, seeing the guards watching him with the same, wide leers of trepidation. He took the deepest breath his lungs could manage, and took another step towards the churning darkness, his legs weak and shaken.

And his world went black.

His head twisted frantically in every direction, eyes unable to adjust to the infinite dark as tightness gripped his chest. The tunnel was gone; the guards, his home, all disappearing and instantly replaced by this desolate place. He screamed into the light pricked distance. Nothing answered. He was alone in the void.

Then, a presence. And though he could not see it, he understood it. Knew it.

Primordial and as ancient as its creators, it lacked substance but was able to wrap him completely in its shroud. It was familiar, an emotion distilled, and it engulfed Rahere in its cold embrace—concentrated and abject, it left room for nothing else and wormed its way into him with violent abandon. He tried to claw his way from the abyss, voiceless cries leaving his tear-soaked face as he realized what it was which clutched him firmly in its claws.

Terror.

Unadulterated, penetrating terror in its purest form consumed Rahere, drawing him inescapably into his most malevolent nightmare. It was feeding on his fear, craving and hoarding it to sate its rapacity.

He knew all too well that it would never be enough.

Interlude

W as ale not the greatest gift of the gods?

Red or pale, malted or hopped, there was no version of the divine fluid that didn't hit one's lips like the cool morning breeze before a hot day. It had been only a short time ago that Elhurtan was at the mercy of his employer for a taste of the different variants of alcohol's delectable delight. Running this way or that, meeting one person or another, delivering or receiving items—endless monotony, day after day, for a mere *sip*.

But now, well, it was *everywhere*. Being a patron was far superior to *needing* one.

"That fire was a gods-damned blessing," he said to the dingy tavern's keeper, setting an empty mug down on the shoddy bar top.

The older man raised an eyebrow. "You might be the only one in Brethefen who thinks so. Aside from the smugglers."

"Aren't *they* in the right business, eh? How about another?"

"Need to pay yer tab first."

Elhurtan cracked his most persuasive smile. "I've paid for the rest of the week, Rud, you know I'm good for it."

Rud was unimpressed. *Gods, does nothing turn up this man's frown?*

Not that it deterred Elhurtan. People weren't obstacles, they were opportunities to improve himself, and improvement meant, in this case, further inebriation.

"Rud, my friend, perhaps you and I can work something out here." The man watched in silence, grabbing Elhurtan's mug and rinsing it in the disgusting bucket of greywater behind the poorly lit basement's sad excuse for a counter. "I, as you may know, am a purveyor of the finest finery, greeter to nobility's frivolous futility, and acquaintance to the law's maw. Do you know what that means?"

"That you're a fancy fuckin' errand boy?"

Elhurtan's lip nearly twitched into a sneer, but he managed to hold his feigned grin. "It means, my good sir, that I can get you whatever you want. No price is too high! Tell me, what do you desire?"

"Coin. Moons or suns, don't care much either way. Oh, and mister cheap-as-a-cheat, I want them before I pour you another one of those."

Elhurtan sighed and slumped. The man was as immovable as the Devapuram's pillars. "Oh, *c'mon*! I have a job lined up, I can pay you when I'm back, I swear."

"And when's that gonna be?"

Elhurtan pursed his lips, his brow scrunching together. "Not that long." *A few weeks, maybe? Probably months, assuming I can ever find the damn principle out in the middle of... wherever the fuck he is.*

"Well, then, you can wait 'not that long' to get another pint."

"You're telling me that everyone here is paying you up-front? Give me a *little* credit, Rud, that's all I ask."

"All two dozen of 'em. Don't know where people are findin' the money, but they got it. For now, at least. Maybe you should go ask some of 'em."

Elhurtan rolled his eyes before dropping his head onto his hands, rattling the bar top. A noble's ransom of his precious golden currency sat barreled before him, and he was barred from it. *Just like old times.* No wonder everyone in here looked so glum.

As much as he loathed the journey, he supposed it might be time to make his way to the mountains. Jerdine had fortunately given him the locations of several stashes, the names of those who owed him *sizable* sums—poor bastards—and one small, private bank that held a large cache of gold for the nefarious man.

It had taken no small amount of time nor effort, but Elhurtan had done as he was asked, collecting and reclaiming all the gold and assorted gems which his patron had required of him. *It would've been a lot gods-damned faster if I'd been able to collect most of it from the guild.* He'd let someone else break *that* news to his employer.

Then, as was tradition, he'd used the funds to get belligerently drunk.

He hadn't spent *all* of it, of course—he wasn't even sure that was possible. But he had spent more than he normally dared. He left enough for the transaction, of course—Jerdine was not one to swindle, not unless you wished for the most painful death imaginable—but Elhurtan was an unparalleled negotiator, earning himself discounts that he neglected to disclose to his employer, resulting in a handsome bonus for his efforts.

Normally, that was. You couldn't negotiate with a brick.

It seemed the journey was calling his name—in a way that was dragging him along like his shoe was tied to a runaway horse. He was about to raise his head and be on his way—the thought of licking the foamy suds off the splintery wood before him appealing to his lack of sensibilities—when there was a resounding *thud* on the rough boards in front of him.

His head snapped up, smile returning to his face.

"Rud, you sly old trickster! You had me believing all that nonsense!" he said as he grabbed the full mug of ale before him, praying this one hadn't been cleaned.

"Wasn't joking," the grumpy bartender said. "Lady at the end of the bar ordered it for you," he said with a thumb, before grumbling, "Gods know why..."

Elhurtan spun his head, running a hand through his sun-bleached hair as his grin pulled back, ear to ear. He took a sip of the delicious gift, staring over the wooden rim, swirling the frothy delicacy around with his tongue and wondering what the stunning beauty at the counter's end would taste like.

On second thought, perhaps ale was the gods' *second* greatest gift.

Part 2
MISGUIDED

Chapter Twelve

Desnia squirmed away, pressing her back to the paint-chipped wall.

Eyes like brown diamonds glimmered atop the Blue's smothering smile—a deceit as pedestrian and common as the beggars outside her window. Desnia knew better than to be consoled by such a rouse, no matter who it was from. It was to be intimidation, then, rather than torture, which would be the tool of these bastards' interrogation.

She could feel her heart *thudding* in her neck. It was doubtful that her captors knew of her revulsion to the stones' unconsented alterations and the privileged few who wore them. She'd thought, for a moment, Delvan to be different, but he'd turned out to be like the rest, just as her instincts had warned—a giving of trust that panged with fresh regret.

She wasn't sure what this newcomer was planning on doing to make her talk—she'd experienced pain her entire life, her threshold for it higher than most—and it made her mouth dryer than the air that hungrily stole away her perspiration to consider the possibilities. "A Blue?" she uttered in a whisper. *What kind of unknown abuse can she conjure with that gem?* she wondered. The question made her shiver.

Wait, really? asked Masini from his hidden location under her shirt, nearly making Desnia jump. *Interesting... There aren't many varieties of them that would be worthwhile to send for an interrogation. Try not to piss them off too much,* he said. As if she needed a reminder.

Was there a way out of this? Some way that she could twist it to her own advantage? Who knew if this woman intended on coming back to visit her again—she couldn't afford to waste an opportunity that might help her escape. Desnia scanned her up and down, looking for something that she could use. Aside from a belt and the buckles on her boots, the only metal immediately obvious was the sword at the woman's side. Desnia looked at it, her eyes glued to its white hilt longer than she'd intended, desperate imaginings running amok through her mind.

"I wouldn't recommend trying that," said the Blue with a smug smirk.

Desnia didn't respond, her brow furrowing. A blink of reflected light came from above the Blue's head as she turned it, and Desnia caught sight of something far more valuable to her than a sword: a silver hairpin, stabbed through the bun on the back of her head. *Finally,* she thought, *something that'll work on that damn lock.* The guards were too careful with their regular beatings to bring anything into the room—the bastards obviously experienced in their sadism. But a hairpin from someone more nonchalant? That was worth its weight in sapphires to her right now.

Not wanting the Blue to recognize the mixture of angst, relief, and anticipation she struggled to hide, she brought her eyes back to the sword. *These noble bastards always assume we're stupid and willing to try anything,* she thought with a sneer. It was best to play into their arrogant delusions—her pride was secondary to survival.

The Blue leaned forward, "Do you want to touch my sword?"

"No," spat out Desnia, a confused scowl smearing her face. She hadn't meant to say anything. Was her imprisonment beginning to wear at her more than she'd thought? *At least she didn't seem to notice me looking at the hairpin,* she reconciled.

"Excellent," said the Blue, leaning back. "Not a big fan of swords myself. They have their uses, and I've gotten quite good with them over the years, but they're usually attached to some asshole who thinks that everyone wants to ogle at theirs and can't hold their own in the ring for more than a few minutes. Wouldn't you agree?"

Desnia felt the hair on her neck raise on end, her mind distracted as though in a hazy cloud. "That's why I avoid them," she said, pulling her mouth shut as the last syllable left her lips, the creases of her confused scowl cutting deep canyons on her face.

"Do you now?" the Blue said with a wink, that gods-damned grin stuck to her face.

By the Greats, said Masini, *I think I'm in love. Des, I know I said to be careful, but*

I think you should 'unsheathe' me, as it were, so that I can get a look at this woman. To figure out what we're up against, obviously.

Desnia blinked and shook her head—as if it were enough to stop Masini's voice from poisoning it—now concerned about what was making her mouth work against her will. She clenched her jaw and steeled her mind. The most important thing now was biding her time, figuring out a way to steal that hairpin, and getting out of here before either the guards beat her to death, or someone decided it was time for her take a long walk to a short rope. *Assuming they'd be so kind as to make it quick.*

The Blue sighed as if disappointed there hadn't been a response. "*Fine,*" she drawled, "I suppose we can talk about something *boring.*" She leaned her head back on the chair, talking more to the ceiling than to Desnia. "Let's start with the reason you're here: did you start the fire at the clergy house?"

Desnia glared at the relaxed posture from below a darkened brow, wondering if it was some kind of feint to lure her into making a mistake, providing the Blue with a reason to slit her throat. As she sat there, her sweat soaking the wall through her linen-covered back, she felt a... force against her. A compulsion that made her want to vomit the words from her sealed lips. Her stomach turned as she began to gather an inkling as to which sect of Blue the woman before her belonged.

She managed to resist the clawing urge to speak, keeping her mouth tightly shut and letting out little more than a snort.

The Blue tilted her head forward, eyes narrowed—a telling expression, and one that often preceded spiteful scorn. *Like the rest of your kind,* Desnia thought with distaste, *not used to being denied what you want.* She could sense an annoyed curiosity from the Blue, as if it radiated from her. Desnia waited, wondering if her retaliation would be of a violent nature, or something more sadistic. *Maybe both...*

The vexation was gone in a blink, fast enough that most wouldn't have noticed it.

"You know," said the woman, her focus remaining on Desnia, "a lack of answer can be almost as telling as a spoken one."

"Fuck off," replied Desnia. *How's that?*

"Hmm." The corner of the Blue's mouth tugged upward, the smile devious and conniving. "Seems that I have been misled—and I promise you, that doesn't happen often. I was under the impression that this was going to be some stale back and forth that the general needed to send his report, then I could be on my way to more productive things. But you're so much more *interesting* than I'd originally thought, aren't you?"

There was a calm curiosity that filled the room, one which made Desnia's heart quicken. The last thing she needed was the attention of a perceptive Blue—she'd had her fill of their treachery. She flexed her jaw, clamping her teeth achingly together, eyes defiantly staring back at her interrogator's—a gaze that brought about it's own unwanted emotions.

"Oh," the olive-skinned temptress said in a half chuckle, "this is going to be so *fun!*"

Wow, said Masini, his voice lacking its normal dryness and seemingly energized, *she's good. Took all of a minute for her to catch on to you. If only she could hear me, I'd sing her a sonnet of our forbidden love. Me, a ring, winning her over with my irresistible charm and wit despite lack of appendages; her, a luscious and cunning beauty who stole away my silvery heart. Our duels of intellect would pleasure her through the day, my softly spoken sweetness gratifying her through the night. We could travel the world, and I could ride in her pocket—and by that, I mean the warm, moist depths of—*

"Would you shut up!" Desnia blared, her facing flushing, then rapidly turning snowy and cold as the woman across from her cocked an eyebrow. She unclenched her fists, looking away from the perplexed gaze of the Blue before her as her stomach launched into her throat.

What? I'm not allowed to fantasize? Masini asked, sounding legitimately offended. *It's pretty much all I've got going for me, you know. Not sure why you'd be so ups—oh! Oh ho ho! Do you?... By the Greats, you do! Wow, this girl was right, this is going to be so much fun. Aside from the, you know, impending trial and likely execution.*

Her hands balled back up into fists, shaking with rage.

"Afraid I can't do that," the Blue said with a shrug, "talking is kind of my *thing.*"

At least, Desnia thought, *she thought I was talking to her.* There was an irony that struck her at that notion, wondering what they'd bother doing with her. She was already locked away in the Asylum.

"Seems that my life is full of people who can't learn when to shut their mouths," said Desnia.

Wow, rude, said Masini.

"Really?" asked the Blue. "The guards don't seem like the talking type, and I didn't think you were allowed any other visitors."

The guards voice their opinions in other ways, she brooded. The other part of the statement piqued her curiosity. Had others tried to visit, but weren't permitted? *No, why would they? They've gotten everything they needed from me. There's Nerio, but he's safer hiding.* It's what she would have done, but it still wrenched her heart to think that she'd never see him again. *It's probably for the best—do what you need to to stay alive.*

"Maybe you should go chat with one of them, find out. I'm sure they'd want to talk to you a hell of a lot more than I do," Desnia said coldly.

"I think I'd rather hug a cactus," replied the Blue with a snort. "I'm pretty sure that one of them was checking out my ass earlier, left me more revolted than flattered. Anyway, let's get back to you. Tell me, where are you from, Desnia?" the Blue asked, a glean in her eye that was more intense than anything Desnia had seen from her before, her visage one of focus and concentration.

A sensation fell upon Desnia like a cresting wave against unsuspecting stone. Her eyes twitched, her head suddenly feeling as though it was being split by an axe. Muscles tensed to the point of threatening to strip from bone, the pulsing of her own blood through her veins an agony that beat like a torturous drum. She resisted the urge to huddle in a ball on her cot, trying to maintain a glare at her oppressor through watery eyes.

Through the cloud of pain that came at her like a hornet's nest, recollections of hearing about experiences like this one cycled through her mind. Those that were lucky enough to return to the streets after surviving such an encounter spoke of the unnatural compulsions to speak, babbling like children as they spilled the darkest secrets of their lives. This was the favored instruments of the Royal Inquisition, the ones capable of softly speaking questions which pierced one's mind like a siren's wail.

"Go... fuck... yourself..." she hissed out, struggling to think straight, leaning to the side, one arm outstretching to support herself.

The Blue's brief irritation at Desnia's curse subdued itself into intrigue, the probing glances a reprieve from the receding flaying of her mind that left her flinching from the brightness of the window's light. Each breath of the hot, sandy air stung her throat and lungs, and her shirt was now nearly completely soaked in clinging sweat.

The woman leaned forward, elbows on her knees and eyes little more than thin slits; an uncomfortable proximity—regardless of what Masini might think.

"Hmm," the Blue said after a moment. "Tell me, Desnia, what's your aversion to answering a few, simple questions? I just want to get to know you. I can be your *ally* here, but I need you to help me understand some things. You can trust me."

Trust, Desnia thought derisively. *These fuckers never think they have to earn anything.* She squeezed her eyes closed, shielding them away from the light as she prepared for the battery of the Blues power to once again plunge her into misery.

But nothing came.

She cracked an eye open, her entire being floating in a dizzying pool that seemed to fluoresce with residual pain, but the expected deluge that had drowned her before remained held at bay.

A deep, shaky breath did little to pacify the tremors, and Desnia thought on this woman's claims of "trust." Did the Blue think she was ignorant? An unknowing bystander to the workings of her and those of her ilk? It was more insulting than the infliction of the torture that left her with this power-induced hangover. *So much for intimidation,* she thought, wishing that it had been that simple—and painless.

"How many," Desnia croaked, "have you told that to before they were taken away with a black bag over their heads, huh? Do you know the number of people I've seen disappear from the streets, forced to give a false confession to save the hide of some spoiled shithead like you? I know what you do, I know what it is that no one bothers to ask when getting a report from you and the others with this fucking 'gift.' I know what the *truth* actually is."

There was a nearly imperceptible widening of the Blue's brown, glimmering eyes. The woman probably thought she'd revealed nothing, but it was something you learned to look out for on the streets, something that separated predator from prey. You learned to bury it, hide it away and shun its existence, or you died—or worse. Desnia knew it when she saw it, the hint of it filling the room in a way that only a select few such as herself could recognize.

Fear.

That's right, she thought, *sit there and squirm. If there's nothing else I'm able to do, it will be to ensure you know there are those of us who see through the likes of you.* She resisted looking to the hairpin again, wondering if she could use this turn of events to somehow bring the Blue closer to her. Could she antagonize her enough to bring her in for a strike? Desnia's bruised sides flinched at the idea, but what was one more beating if it provided a means to her escape?

"And what, exactly," asked the Blue, her anxiety well hidden behind a smile, "would that be?"

"That you *lie*," sneered Desnia, prodding for that exposed nerve. "Whether I say what you want or not, you're going to go report to your boss—some other highborn prick, I'm sure—and you're going to tell him what he wants to hear. Doesn't matter one bit what *I* say, no. You're going to speak, and he'll listen, never questioning *your* honesty, trusting that you're reporting what was said to you.

"All you Blues think yourselves so far above others, looking down from your mountain of shit and calling *us* filthy. And the crown bearers of that peak are the ones like *you*. Claiming truth in your titles when, in fact, you're the most dishonest among them, your mouths are like assholes that add to your own pile of self-esteem.

"So don't call me your 'friend,' and don't expect me to help you. My grave is deep enough as it is, and I don't intend to dig it any deeper. Go, tell the general and that other 'trusted' bastard whatever the hell you want, it's what you're going to do anyway."

Desnia could feel her headache getting worse, and looking at the Blue through the fog of increasingly bright light was becoming steadily more difficult. Determining if anything she'd said had set off the Blue was becoming strenuous. She knew that the smart thing to do would be to draw out the conversation, bide her time while she figured out which point of hers was the one that clawed under the woman's skin. Instead, her splitting head turned every miniscule filter and modicum of self-control off, a stream of resentment flowing forth towards her captor.

Never was great at keeping my mouth shut, she grimaced.

The Blue leaned back in the chair, the grin returning to her face. *Damn.* "Gods, I swear this is *not* what I was expecting today. You're much more than meets the eye, I can tell. But you're mistaken, Desnia. I *do* want to get to know you and hear about the things you've seen. More than you can imagine."

The breadth of my imagination is only matched by its depravity, mused Masini, *and the things I would do with this woman would be an enlightening that would make her gods blush. Feel free to use that line if you'd like, I was never one to not help a friend in need. And Des, believe me when I say: you* need *it.*

Desnia rubbed her temples, ignoring Masini—a skill that was being thoroughly tested at the moment. Why did she always attract the attention of those that wanted something from her? Asta, Mixton, even Masini had all sought to use her in their own way—the echoing of his voice in her skull making her question once more why she tolerated him. Now the sights of *another* Blue were set on her. *As if I haven't had enough of that in my life...*

The Blue reached down and pulled open the flap of a pouch at her side, producing from it a square block of pure white stone—muted inanite, tiny glitters of light refracting from it like snow. Desnia's attention was suddenly drawn to it, her throbbing head a background noise. It was everything she could do to not reach out and snatch the mineral from the woman's hand—its potency far greater than the paint she'd been forced to consume.

The Blue tossed the block into the air, catching and tucking it away back into the pouch. "Well," the woman said, "I think that's enough for today, don't you? Thank you for... being *you*, I guess. See you around."

Gods-damn it, Desnia thought. She was too encumbered with agony to force more words out. *I just have to hope,* pointedly avoiding the idea of praying, *that she comes back.* That was her luck, though. Everyone seemed to take unwanted interest in her, seeing a tool and not a person.

Fuck all of them, she thought.

The Blue stood, exiting the room and whistling for the guards. Desnia watched through blackening vision as the woman pulled the white sleeve back over her sapphire, giving Desnia a wink before the guards took the chair and slammed the door shut, the *clash* of iron and wood making her head spiral.

Desnia slid along the wall, vision getting lost in the encroaching darkness, and fell onto her cot. Unconsciousness consumed her—delivering her from one tormentor to another.

Chapter Thirteen

As requested, I have located and recovered Reedjin's journals.

Delvan sat motionless on the polished wood floor, his elbows atop bent knees as sweat seeped from his hair into the adobe at his back. Aside from a bed and desk, the once-occupied room was otherwise empty, its stirred dust hanging in the sun's window-born streak of resplendent yellow.

His heart felt as though it had been ripped from his chest, the hemorrhaging cavity as vacant as the room before him. Not but a few hours ago he'd said his goodbyes to Orne and Kolden, watching while they took the western road towards the mountain fortress. The reality of their absence hadn't fully set in until he'd watched them disappear beyond the horizon, their pack horses and the small supply train kicking up dust from the ancient road until they were eventually lost in the billowing plumes.

It was a suspended moment of relived torture, making the past few hours seem like days.

Since then, he'd sat here, unmoving from the unornamented floor. He rarely blinked as he gazed into an unseen distance, his mind burying itself and leaving him to sulk in vapid silence.

As night's shadow unexpectedly crept into the room, Delvan's legs slowly willed him to his numb and tingling feet. He walked down the stairs and out of the building in a slow stupor, the anchor of his abysmal sorrow hoisted only by the need to drown it.

Numbness alone was not a cure for his malady. No, only oblivion could remedy his woes, and even then, for only as long as the night lasted. His feet regained a semblance of feeling as they carried him down the brick-paved street, brightly painted walls dulled by grey ash. The blended tones of dirt and despair of those in the streets' gutters melded with his own.

Twilight had nearly washed away when he found himself standing before the alley's mouth. It was absent any mark or indication that something nefarious lay hidden in its shaded recess. But then, this type of establishment required no advertising. Its patrons lacked subtlety; as he stared down the hidden depths leading to an unmarked door, a group of boisterous soldiers emerged, reeking of ale. They caught sight of Delvan and gave casual salutes, returning to their spirited conversation as they walked away.

Orne and Kolden had frequently invited him here. He'd never joined them. A thought which only eroded his insides further.

As he stood there, people flowing past him like fish around a shark, an emotion overtook him, one that he couldn't explain and simply wasn't...*fair*.

Why do I feel guilty, *of all things?* he wondered. He'd been avoiding this for *him*, not anyone else. He'd wanted to prove to himself that there was no necessity to be here, that it had been a mere tool to deal with his grief, nothing more.

Why did the thought of stepping towards that door *hurt* so badly?

A voice lured his mind from its retracted depths, its breach making him notice a sensation that he'd been too incoherent to pay attention to but identified his gem-bearing addresser immediately.

"Are you just going to stand there or are you going to buy a girl a drink?" asked Ennui from his side. *No, that's not her real name,* he reminded himself.

"Are you following me?" he asked, his brow furrowing.

"Don't flatter yourself," she said. "This place has the best ale in the city."

Questions began to stampede through his mind, distracting him from why he'd come here and now focusing on the mysterious woman beside him.

"What're you doing here?" Delvan asked, his voice beginning to rise.

"Uh," she said, her lips tugging back and brow raising, "I just told you; they have the best—"

"*No,*" he interrupted, "I mean, what're you doing in *Brethefen*?"

Master Mornath's comments about her came to the forefront of his mind, the general's summons likely a convenient ruse. The question of which affiliates allowed her access to the guild's powerful inner sanctum became rekindled in a blink.

"Where's the fun in telling you that? You're going to have to work harder to get me to spill information, Sparky. A drink's a good start though. Where are the other—"

"I'm not in the mood for your games, Ennui," he interjected. "Or should I say, Knight Inquisitor Mithya."

Her only response was the small sliver of a smile.

"What are you in the mood for, then?" she asked, looking sly and leaning in.

He felt the gentle touch of her power, more delicate than any Truthsayer he'd met before. How she was this talented was just another mystery, but while the sect was powerful in their own right, their abilities were limited to the task of their namesake. He had been well trained in how to turn their questions against them.

"Answers," he replied, his gaze turning harder.

"Hmm," she said, putting her hands on her hips and leaning back, "clever. You already spoiled the fun in finding out my name, so what else is it that you're looking for?"

He didn't need to be evasive to answer this question. It was the beacon of his mind's storm.

"Desnia," he said.

Mithya's smile broadened. "Ah, I didn't realize that you two were a *thing*. She continues to be full of surprises."

"No," said Delvan, shaking his head with an annoyed grimace, "it's not like that. And what do you mean, 'surprises?'" *Has she managed to extract what I suspect already?* he wondered. *If she did then... What state did she leave Des in?*

"What I mean is that she's far more interesting than standing here empty handed. Come on, let's talk inside, this conversation is drier than my mouth," said Mithya.

Delvan could feel his face growing hot, anger bubbling inside of him ready to boil. The day had left him raw, and her evasions dug like sand against an exposed nerve. She took a long, confident stride towards the alley. Delvan couldn't allow her to leave, not until he knew that Desnia was safe, her mind unmolested. He grabbed Mithya's arm, stopping her mid-step. She looked down to his hand and back to him, and for the first time he saw a flash of anger cross her face, brief as it may have been. Her hand now rested on the pommel of her sword.

He let go, feeling shame roil with his anger. All he wanted to do was scream. This woman had managed to work her way under his skin like a flesh-eating insect, and the torment in his raw state was almost too much to handle.

"You need to..." he started, closing his eyes and taking a breath as he tried to think clearly. He needed to put this in a way that didn't focus more attention on Desnia yet kept her from harm's way. "Des is only going to fight you if you push for answers," he said. *A flood of your power could irreparably break her, if I'm right.* "Ask her your questions, but don't press. Tell her it will get her out of prison faster, make her trust you." *Just don't betray that trust,* he thought with a stab of guilt.

A Truthsayer's power was impossible to resist by the general masses. Power meeting power was a thin barrier of friction, even with a strong mind. With one that might be fractured...

"Hmm," she said, looking at him through eyes that were now thin slits. "A strange bit of advice, but maybe it has merit. Makes me wonder though, what aren't you telling me?"

"A lot of things," Delvan snapped. "And I swear, if I find out that you've harmed her in any way, treated her like a criminal, I will come after you. This city owes her its life, not imprisonment. I don't care what it takes, but—"

"Blood of my fathers," she cursed—the colloquialism unfamiliar to him—raising a hand and cutting him off. "I just want some questions answered, that's all."

"The general's, or yours?" asked Delvan.

She smiled again, crossing her arms and looking him up and down. "Asking questions is my job, Sparky. Although, you do have some good ones, maybe you should talk to someone about getting an inquisitor position."

Yes, Delvan thought, *I'll be asking questions. Ones I bet you'd rather not have answered.*

That, however, could wait. Desnia needed to be his first priority. He realized then that going down this alley did nothing but console his own pains—abandoning her to ones inflicted by the person before him. It was selfish, and too similar to mistakes he'd recently made with Knight Commander Ferrand.

He needed to be better. For her.

"What's it going to take for you to simply *ask* her questions?" asked Delvan, ready to commit to whatever it took to prevent her abuse of power upon Desnia. "Money? I can get it for you. Influence or a promotion? My father is Reagent of the Court," he said, avoiding statements that would reveal the rocky relationship between the two of them. *She'd know that was a lie in a second.* It was best to twist the words in his favor.

"Or," he continued, "let me speak to her while you sit in. She'll talk..." his mouth struggled to form the following words, the impressive subtlety of Mithya making his head ache and eyes water as he tried to say that Desnia would tell him what the general wanted to know.

Mithya's head listed to the side, a grin on her face. "You saved her life, and yet you know she'd still *lie* to you... Huh, maybe you're not as ignorant as you seem."

"What's that supposed to mean?!" he snapped.

"It's something you learn with this gift. Something that some people learn without it—and I'm betting our mutual acquaintance is one of them. It's the hidden truth of humanity."

"Enlighten me."

She let out a chuckle. "*Everybody* lies," Mithya said, her hands gesturing to her sides.

He glared at her, his teeth grinding together as his anger rose. "You especially."

She smiled, then winked at him. "Ain't that the truth. Now, you going to come join me? I might even buy *you* a drink."

With a turn and long strides, her boots *clicked* on the pavers as she walked away, weaving down the alley between those exiting it in a stupor. He watched as the sheen of her hair turned to darkened waves as she passed from the nearby streetlamp's light, her accentuated shape turning to shadow as the darkness of the alley engulfed her.

He knew Truthsayers to be notoriously tenebrous, smugly carrying themselves as though they were the merchants of others' secrets. That many did, in fact, hoard such knowledge was the reason their majority became inquisitors, and Delvan had always found their accompanying egos to fill the air with a toxic haze, regardless of their occasional usefulness.

And it would seem Mithya was as caustic as they came.

The thought of his former pursuit, which would have led him down the same path, was smothered. There was more he needed to do, more he owed to others than wallowing. His quarry followed that path, one whose challenges he intrinsically knew he'd succumb to. He couldn't face her there, with every advantage stacked against him. He would come at this from a different angle, one which could give him the upper hand.

Delvan turned on his heel, walking away from the alley and back towards the heart of the city. His steps were filled with vigor renewed, and his mind had once more become focused. He needed more than simple presumptions—a mistake he'd made with Ferrand. He was going to dig into Mithya's secrets, pull them apart and find the core of who she was. There was more to her, he was certain of it.

And once he had some answers of his own, he would use them to leverage Desnia's release.

Chapter
Fourteen

I was able to remove some of their protections, but the accessible contents were only half legible to my eyes.

Desnia winced, the volume of her own groaning enough to stab at her ringing ears.

Eyelids blinked away distorting grogginess. The clearing vision was followed by a residual throbbing in her temples, putting pressure against the backs of her eyes with each pulsing ache. Every creak of her cot's wooden legs cracked and resonated through her skull like nearby thunder, her stomach upside-down and filling her throat with acrid bile.

The room was refulgent with the rose-tinted gold of sunset, the day's inferno beginning to calm and become tepid. As the pain slowly faded like the receding sun, she looked around. Her dinner—a bowl of brown, tasteless mush—had been kicked over and spilled across the floor, a courtesy of her guards no doubt. Half a loaf of stale bread lay beside it—a chunk looking to have been bitten from it.

Is it the evening already? she bemoaned. She sat up slowly, a soreness pervading her entire being, making each use of her strained muscles careful and timid.

Oh, thank the Greats, you're awake, said Masini, sounding relieved. *You've been out for most of the day.*

"No shit. Feels like I just fell off of a building," she said quietly, hands pressed to her salty brow.

Well, if our eloquent enchantress is what I suspect, said Masini, *then you will find that resistance is often exhausting, if not untenable. The muted-in-in-in... ugh, the paint you're so rapaciously devouring is probably the main reason you didn't succumb to her wiles, as enticing as they may be.*

She took a careful, deep breath of the dry, dessert air that wafted through her barred window, eyes squeezing shut as the dulled agony continued drifting into the background. "I wish it did more to stop the gods-damned pain; hasn't been this bad before."

The hangovers of such visitations of power were familiar to her—there had been many an unpleasant morning after her mind's strings had been pulled by the puppeteer of her dreams. But this was something else entirely, even breathing felt exhaustive, her aches acuter than before.

Her interest in you is unfortunate—my own jealousy aside, contemplated Masini. *To your point with her earlier, she could just have told your imprisoners what they wanted to hear about starting the fire and be done with it. There's more that she's looking for here, I'd bet my left foot on it. Hmm, interesting, interesting...*

Desnia's eyes flicked to the door of her cell. Based on the state of her dinner, she knew who was on duty, and needed to keep her conversation with Masini as quiet as possible lest she unleash the man's temper, which snarled like a rabid hound collared by thin string.

"She must know what happened at the gate, right? De—" she cut herself off, not able to stand the vile taste of Delvan's name in her mouth. "They must have told her what happened there, or at least as much as that backstabbing bastard knew. She must want something else, something valuable, otherwise why decide to come back and talk to me more?"

Uh, I can think of a few reasons, he said. *Mostly they have to do with curves, and lips, and—*

Desnia grabbed at his chain—the consequences of the rapid motion be damned—and yanked him out from under her shirt. Listening to his absurd presumptions wore on her nerves when she wasn't exhausted, let alone in her current haggard state.

"I'm done with this." She looked for the clasp, feverishly trying to get the chain off. "You're going out the fucking window, at least then I won't have to listen to this bullshit."

I won't bring it up anymore! I swear! he said frantically as Desnia began tugging at the chain to break it from her neck.

"I don't have patience for this right now, Masini," she whispered maliciously, still holding the chain taught.

Fine! It's a wonder you're so uptight... he grumbled as she loosened her grip, the links and his ring falling atop her shirt. She glanced back to the door, tensely waiting to see if her ruckus had been noticed, or at least tolerated.

Back to your original point, he said after a thankfully quiet moment, *and what you said about the ga-ga-ga-fuck! The door. There are a few key things that Lord De-uh, I mean, that bad, bad Blue, doesn't know that a few psychotic and very upset, uh, people like me might want to. Specifically, the location of the person you were so kind as to reveal still lived—albeit in a less sexy, and almost as lustrous, body—and they think contributed heavily to foiling their plans.*

The realization struck her. *Of course, he blames Masini.* "Jerdine…" she whispered with a sneer, focusing once more on the problem at hand. The twisted bastard being behind this made too much sense. "You think she's his minion?" If the Blue was in the employment of the principle, then she was the last person that Desnia wanted to have unfettered access to her cell. *I need to get out here,* she thought with a new desperation.

A strong possibility—I wouldn't put it past him to also have Blues on his payroll, said Masini. *The lord general or even his superiors may also have some interest in the broader scheme of things, though I worry that your new, uh,* friend *has some ulterior motive—revenge on behalf of that limp-dicked pile of manure highest among them. Right after she figures out where I'm hidden.*

"Great," she sighed. Jerdine's wrath was a destruction that she'd been hoping to outrun; instead, she sat here like some sort of caged fowl waiting for slaughter. "Any ideas on how to deal with her?" she asked, hoping that Masini had something hidden up his proverbial sleeve.

Nothing you're going to like, he said. *But we don't have a lot of options.*

True enough, she thought, the knot in her stomach tightening further.

You think of any way out of here yet? he asked, voice tinged with hope.

"Maybe," she admitted. "But it involves the hairpin of my interrogator, which I need to somehow lift without her realizing."

There was a brief silence before Masini spoke. *You know, you're making it* really *hard for me not to make… suggestive arguments.* Desnia scowled and shook her head, trying to get Masini's voice and the image of the Blue out of her mind. It clung like a banner whipping in a storm, frustratingly refusing to be swept away.

"Just tell me what you're thinking," she said.

Oh, you definitely don't want to hear that… he said, his voice drifting off into what she pictured was his sty of an imagination.

"*Masini!*" she hissed.

Right, right, ehem. Resisting her ability is, obviously, a terrible idea. Agreed?

"No," defied Desnia. It was a basic law of the streets: keep your mouth shut, or someone will shut it for you.

Well then, maybe not *so obvious, but still,* he said. *You want to—and don't try to throw me out the window over this—get close to her, right? Otherwise, you can't steal this precious* hairpin, *of all things.*

"Makes a good pick," she said, wondering why she needed to justify her methods. The lock on her door was basic enough, but she needed something stronger than a wooden splinter to turn its mechanism. *And then figure out what to do about the guards,* she thought, fighting off a sense of resignation as she pictured getting past two armed men with nothing but a hairpin and Masini's ring.

I'll take your word for it. But, in case you haven't noticed, we're not on the streets, Des. We're in a small, cramped cell and have no way of sneaking up on this woman. So tell me, how *do you intend to get close to her, hmm? We're both aware of how... insubstantial your interpersonal skills are.*

Desnia crossed her arms, refusing to indulge Masini, yet struggling to think of alternatives. She could hope for the guards to make a mistake—assuming they didn't beat her to death first. Given their evident experience, she was doubting that either was likely. Assuming they kept their beatings non-fatal, there was only so much paint in the room she could consume before someone noticed and questioned her about it, or worse, took her somewhere absent the power-dulling flakes. With the dreams turning into fresh, hellish nightmares with increased frequency, she wondered how long it would be before she needed to become a more permanent resident of the Asylum. The thought sent an uncomfortable shiver across her skin.

"Let's hear it," she said with a loud sigh, her eyes widening at the sound of rustling armor outside her door.

Excellent! chirped Masini. *All you need to do is tell her everything.*

A growl began to arise from deep in her throat, her teeth grinding together as she prepared to scorn him for such an absurd suggestion.

Hear me out! he pleaded. *What do you need to do to get close to someone? And no, the answer is not break into their house and stand over them as they sleep. You have to earn their* trust.

That was a phrase that pulled Desnia lip with contempt. The only thing trust had done for her lately was land her in this cell.

Let her think that she's winning, continued Masini, *give her a reason to trust you and answer her questions—unless they're about me, of course. She doesn't care about the fire, we agree on that, so tell her about it. Ask a question of your own, you might learn more than you expect.*

"What then?" she whispered, hating every word of this idea.

Then we try to confirm our suspicions. That's *the information that's keeping you alive. Tell her the rest, but if we know what she wants, we can deduce who she's working for.*

Keep information about me and mine secret the best you can, since it'll give you more time to, uh, warm up to her. Eventually—I hope, though by the Greats, do you need work—you can cozy up to her and steal the means to our escape!

She shook her head. *Just talking to someone to get them to trust you?* she thought, rolling her eyes. Dressing and acting as though one belonged was one thing—subterfuge like that worked for short periods—but being here, at a complete disadvantage? It was lunacy, not to mention playing into her captor's hands. One slip up would be all it took to ruin the entire endeavor.

"There's no way chatting will be enough." The one thing that guaranteed an advantage was knowing what the person needed and bargaining with—or better yet, leveraging—it. *But how am I supposed to do that when the person asking can pry whatever they want from me, short of me paying a painful price,* she contemplated.

Ehem, coughed Masini. *And* how, *exactly, did you come to trust me?*

"Some days I don't," she grumbled. A common goal had brought the two of them together—finding Asta. The gate had just been a bump in the road, and his interminable dialog was merely another burden to bear as she sought her salvation. But, then again, she tolerated him more than most. In fact, now that she thought about it, she couldn't think of anyone that she'd spoken to this much over the course of more than a few weeks, let alone months... *Annoying fucker might have a point,* she thought.

And yet, aside from occasionally trying to defenestrate me, you treat me as a loyal confidant, Masini surmised.

Desnia groaned, resting her head against the wall. What other options did she have? As much as she hated to admit it, she had run out of ideas, and the Blue presented her best opportunity for escape. Although—and she'd *never* admit this to Masini—the thought of extended conversation with the woman twisted her stomach almost as much as resisting her abilities.

"Fine," she conceded. "I'll try your way, though I still think it's a stupid fucking idea."

I never have stupid ideas, defended Masini, *unless, of course, they involve alcohol or women.*

She let out a half-hearted snort. "Have you forgotten who—"

There was a pounding noise as fist met wood, her contemptuous tormenter now glaring at her with a scowl through the door's small portal. Her eyes went wide and heart raced as he opened the entry, a sadistic grin tugging at the man's hateful visage. "You're awake," he spat, "good. I was beginning to worry that my shift would end without being able to put you under myself. Fucking *Eka.*"

He raised his baton. Desnia pulled her arms tight to her side, hoping that he'd avoid hitting the exposed skin, but it did little good. Wood polished from use met bone and muscle with loud *whacks*, her body spasming from the sharp, repetitive pains and sending her from the cot to her knees on the floor.

From her huddled position she looked up, the man again raising the baton high in the air. Her mind had begun going numb during these beatings, but the survivor in her still fought, willing her to do anything in defense before her limbs gave out. With the little energy she could muster, she desperately tried to lurch her fist upward into the man's crotch.

The feeble—if defiant—act was for naught. Her arm was swatted away as though a pest, and the battering became more furious. All she could do was huddle tightly on the warm tiles of the floor, hoping for it to end as her mind burned with the hot white of agony and drowned out all other thought and functions. Time was lost, moments extending for what seemed like hours. Her mind screamed for it to end, drowning out any remaining instinct to fight back. The only concern now was surviving the next few, prolonged minutes.

After the beating finally ceased, Desnia remained on the floor, curled in a fetal position until well after the sun had crested down behind the mountains. Stars beyond the window and the dim light of torches from the hall were all that illuminated the room, the night's breeze still hot with summer's oppression. Evening had passed in what felt to be a shorter time than the span of her endured torture, her sense of time skewed by anguish.

Each flare of latent pain stoked her ever-increasing disdain for the guard, and she began to crave returning his displays of blame in kind as she writhed on the tiles. An eerily clear image of him bleeding from the neck while looming over her came to her mind and fed into her vengeful fantasy. It did nothing to sate it.

Desnia eventually unfurled, rotating and laying on her back while listening to the popping of joints and creaking of ligaments. Masini stayed respectfully quiet, as he usually did after these encounters. *I wish I could get him to do that with less effort,* she thought.

As time passed—she had no idea how much, the night blending together as the dark, dull face of the moon drove across the night sky—her body, and stomach, eventually settled. She gingerly turned her head, eyeing the food scattered over the floor like a drunkard's vomit. The gruel had long since dried up, leaving the half loaf of bread, which was surely hard as stone by now.

Desnia reached, ignoring the distal aches as well as she could, and grabbed the meager loaf. It tore apart with a loud *crackle*, stiffly fighting her fingers and teeth as she ate small, chewable morsels. For a brief moment, she was brought back to a terrace, high on a hill, overlooking an ocean sunset with a slice of grape pie before her. A serene recollection from what seemed like a lifetime ago.

Nothing more than pain and last week's bread now, she thought as the sharp edges of crust cut into her gums.

That moment of bliss all those months ago was a fever dream now. A memory that she almost wished to be erased from her mind, to send her back into ignorance of what a life could offer. *Maybe if Nerio and I had gone to another city. Del, for a moment... I guess the bastard did remind me how the world works.* Maybe he'd done her a favor, in a twisted way, humbling her back into the harsh realities of life.

As she tore off another chunk of bread her finger grazed something unexpected. It took her a moment to register what it had been, painfully tilting her head to look at the loaf in her hand—a piece of parchment protruding from within.

Her eyes went wide, flicking to the door to see if either of her guards were looking in on her. No one from outside could be seen, and she carefully pulled the parchment from its slot, which looked to be cut in with a long knife. She rolled to her side, keeping her back to the door, and with the utmost caution, unfolded it in the dim torchlight.

What's that? asked Masini, mirroring her own curiosity. She didn't respond, instead pulling apart the last crease and finding inked writing that she squinted to read in the dun room.

> *Desnia,*
>
> *I'm sorry it has taken so long to reach out, but you've been difficult to locate. Know that I am working through the proper channels to have the lord general release you from your unjustified imprisonment. I dare not do more, for I will not see you become a fugitive as I have. I'm confident that, with time, we can persuade the man to see he's made a terrible error in judging our characters. But it will take time. Hold fast and may the strength of Ursorner be with you.*
>
> *Nerio*

Her heart had fluttered with hope for a second while reading the note, before tumbling back into the pit of despair and disdain which her soul had recently become.

"Idiot," she cursed as she folded the letter.

He spent all that effort getting you a note, said a sardonic Masini, *and gave you nothing to get out of here with? What a guy.*

"He's naïve," she hissed. "For someone who's been exposed to some of the worst people imaginable... How can he *possibly* think this is going to work? Why is he still in the gods-damned city?!"

That boy's more full of hope than you are spite, and that's saying something, said Masini. *Sounds like it's not just Jerdine that might be looking for him either.*

Desnia shook her head. "Maybe Del tried to turn him over, too."

Well, on a positive note, someone out there is trying to get us out. Who knows, maybe he'll get lucky?

"You're failing at even *pretending* to sound confident about that," she said. While there was a tiny part of her that was happy to hear from Nerio, her instincts hated that he'd stayed. He was going to get himself captured, or worse. His complete lack of self-preservation was appalling.

"We'll still try what we discussed earlier," she said, dreading the prospect. "He's going to get nowhere with the lord general."

I agree, as much as I hate to admit it, said Masini. *Poor guy doesn't stand a chance out there; the streets are going to eat him alive. Literally, perhaps. Actually no, he's too scrawny, probably tastes stringy.*

Desnia crawled to her feet, shuffling to the window where the flickers of starlight were visible above the coronas of the streetlamps' light. Reaching between the bars, she tore up the note into the smallest pieces she dared, giving a few backwards glances to confirm she hadn't been heard. At the gust of a small breeze, she released the torn parchment, letting Nerio's inane hopes float away on the night's unforgiving current.

Help was a luxury, one which she'd rarely been able to afford.

The fact she'd ever had any felt like the greatest theft she'd ever committed.

Chapter Fifteen

I have sent them to your more knowledgeable self and am certain you will glean what I could not.

Nerio sat upon a crumbling stone block in the dull grey of sunrise, the dried blood on his hands and arms indistinguishable from his dark skin. Dirtied elbows dug into his knees as he rested his weight on them, his body feeling fatigued and ragged from the night spent in the triage tent. He could still hear the wounded wailing in the distance as lacerations were sealed or, in more horrific instances, limbs removed.

The injured had begun appearing the evening prior, hobbling in as quickly as they could, seeking refuge and healing. The other believers—whose numbers grew by the hour—were not prepared to care for the riot's numerous victims. He'd spent half the night directing the boiling of bandages, ensuring hands were clean, and feverishly attempting to direct the groups that had come to aid those in need.

Many had died. More still suffered.

There needs to be something more I, we, can do for them, he thought solemnly. He still wondered what had led to the attack against unarmed protestors. *Must they use such violence to hold their grip on power?*

Nerio squeezed his eyes closed, the agony's cacophony penetrating his soul. He wanted nothing more than to charge back into the tent and continue to help, but exhaustion had caused him to nearly faint a few minutes ago, and he'd been promptly sent out here to rest for a time by one of the other healers. It was the right decision, he knew, but every distant cry filled him with the guilt of abandonment.

Feet scuffed the ash-scarred stones close by. He looked up with red-stained eyes to see an old soldier before him, still wearing his uniform, proffering a small wooden cup of tea. It was a local captain, one who had been coming to Nerio's speaks for a time now and helping him out of tight situations more than once. His beard had more grey than black in it, and his hair was cut nearly to his scalp. His face was rugged and pocked, old scars creating trails across his face.

"Witness," said Captain Gernbard, "drink this, you look as though you could use it."

It didn't feel right to take the gift—tea, and other goods, was becoming difficult to come by after the fire—while others suffered. But the captain was a stubborn man, and Nerio knew that he wouldn't take no for an answer. After a moment, he nodded reluctantly and took the cup, sipping on the steaming liquid. It flushed him with its warmth, bringing a hint of vigor to his weary limbs.

"Thank you, Captain," said Nerio. "But, again, you do not need to call me that."

"Aye, I know that's what you think. Don't take my meanin' to be offensive, but you're wrong about that," he said in his gruff voice.

"I am not the one who should be worshipped," replied Nerio, taking another sip.

The old soldier shook his head. "Been doing this a long time, Witness. The way soldiers view their leader is important, the wants of that leader be damned. They need to look at you as something different, something above them, need to feel as though there's someone in this sand-blasted place that can give them a reason to help explain the grief.

"That's why they all come here," he continued, looking over at the triage tent with a distant stare. "Don't take that away from them."

Nerio stared into his tea for a moment, contemplating the captain's words. He could see the man's point—it hadn't been that long since he needed support like that himself.

"You're a wise man, Captain," said Nerio, "your point is a humbling one."

The man shrugged. "Soldiers don't get to my age without picking up a few things along the way. Those that don't are with the sands now."

Nerio nodded. He could see how his aversion to the newfound title was nothing more than selfish pride. He was glad for those in his life that were able to help him acknowledge such faults. The captain, those that came to worship, and those that had gotten him here. His mind wandered back to some of those influencers—more specifically, those currently absent from his life.

"Captain," Nerio said, his voice croaking from exhaustion, "have you looked further into what we discussed?" Asking for the captain's help had been difficult for him, he was always the one to help others. Requesting aid made him feel like a burden. But this was too important to let fall to the wayside.

The captain's lips became a thin line, his hand scratching at his beard. "Aye, and I still think it's folly."

The sun began to ignite the sky with orange flames as it struggled to crest the horizon, and in its newfound light Nerio could see the wrinkles of concern blending with the scars on the man's face.

"We must pursue every avenue," Nerio said, his voice quiet. "I will not break Desnia from her prison only to lead this life on the run alongside me. We must convince the Lord General to release her. Her acts of bravery alone should be enough to convince him of that."

"The lord general is a stern man," said Gernbard, his tone grim. "I've served under him a long time. He's fair, but not one to cross, and if he thinks that the Messiah has done wrong enough to imprison her, then I'd say there's little chance of getting her out through appeals and petitions. Even if they come from me."

The fires were an atrocity, one which Desnia had—ignorant of the devastation it would cause—started. Nerio had actively avoided discussing that event with the other believers. The miracle that had occurred and blessed her should not be overshadowed by unintended misdeeds. But if the lord general was aware of her wrongdoings...

It made Nerio's stomach drop to his feet.

"Then we must do something else," said Nerio. *But what could change the man's mind?*

"It would take an army to budge that man's orders," said the captain. "Unless you plan on marching one to his door, then I recommend that we free her and get the two of you to safety."

Perhaps not an army, but something else, Nerio thought in the background of his mind, an idea beginning to gestate. First, however, a more immediate concern needed to be addressed.

"And would you so readily help us, instead of your own commander, Captain?" Nerio asked. He trusted Gernbard, the man was insightful and full of advice that aided Nerio's navigation of these hard times, but he worried for a soul that had such conflicting loyalties.

He saw the captain's jaw clench tightly before he responded. "Like I said, been doing this a long time." He let out a sigh. "I know the lord general has good intentions, rebuilding this place is going to take a huge amount of time and effort. And it needs his guiding hand, no question. But it also needs hope.

"The reason that me and others flock here by the hundreds is because you give us that. It's good to hear that the gods are still looking out for us. Frankly, I don't think that the general needs the Messiah to rebuild the city and punishing her ain't going to do anything but push these people over the edge. The way I see it, getting her released will help both of you."

Nerio continued to be astounded by the man's sagacity. He felt as though a student, and not for the first time he wondered why the gods chose this duty for him. When there were men like Gernbard, why place the championing of this miracle upon his shoulders?

"I appreciate you being candid, Captain," Nerio said, wiping his hands on his robe, the white linen mottled with dried blood. "I have faith in you; I just fear that you will be put into a position that might test your own piety."

"Don't worry about me," the old soldier said with a cynical grin. "I made my peace with the gods long ago. Whatever happens now is their will."

"The gods cannot help everyone in their time of need," Nerio said, remembering back to his own begging for salvation from his tormentor. "But then again, we cannot know their plans. I don't know what they have in store for you, but I beg you to try and keep safe in the meantime. We've lost too many as it is."

"Mhm," the captain grunted. "So, you're saying that the gods ain't gonna help the Messiah, so we should go break her out?"

Nerio turned to see a sarcastic grin on the man's grizzled face, tugging the strands of his beard in tangled directions. Nerio shook his head, and if he hadn't been so tired, he might have laughed. "For now, I would like to try other options." He took another sip of tea, it and the rising temperature warmed him further, weighing his eyelids down under an overbearing weight.

"Fair enough," said the captain, "just know that we can't wait forever. Rosethorn is a lot of things, but I wouldn't say that patient is one of them."

He nodded, taking the last sip of his tea. As he tilted the cup back, he caught sight of a figure walking into the courtyard from over its rim. They were limping, carrying a small, bloodied body in their arms. He soon recognized it to be a woman, her face streaked with ash and scared by pain, the morning light failing to cast away the darkness she carried over her. He watched as she nearly tripped under the arch of the estate's former entry.

Nerio quickly put down the cup and bolted upright. His head became light, legs wobbling beneath him, and his arms waved in the air to balance himself. The captain's firm grip caught his spindly elbow, easing him back onto the makeshift seat.

"You stay there, Witness," the man said, his tone sounding like an order.

He pointed to one of the other soldiers—a surprising number of which had become regulars to his speaks, like the captain—and barked for him to go help the woman.

"I didn't think that any more were coming in," said Nerio sadly.

"Aye, not many, but they're still trickling in. I'm gonna send some of the boys out to make sure that their tracks get covered, last thing we need is a blood trail leading the unenlightened here. Might have 'em give some false reports as well, keep them chasing their tails." The man's tone was dark, and Nerio's heart felt stabbed as he imagined some of the soldiers standing their ground against their brothers-in-arms to defend him. He knew that whatever potential heartbreak he felt was a grain of sand compared to the captain's dune.

"Have you heard more about what happened?" Nerio asked, watching the woman get assisted into triage.

The captain's eyes also followed the woman and her child being carried into the tent as he nodded. "We went and asked around the Merchants' Guild, checked with some of the soldiers who were there. No one can say for sure if Brother Meneham was the one who incited it or not. He was there speaking beforehand, but then the mob was broken up and gathered again elsewhere before it marched on the place. Once some of these people are well enough, we'll start talking to them and see what we can learn."

Nerio's heart sank, his eyes too spent to fountain more tears. *If these people were hurt because of my message, the one delivered by Meneham, then how am I better than our oppressors?* He would need to pray that sending others out to spread the word of Desnia's resurrection was the right decision. He knew that he couldn't do this on his own, but the maimed and dead that now filled the courtyard here struck an unexpected fear into him.

"How many have made it here?" he asked hesitantly.

"Nearly sixty, at last count. Eight died of their wounds, and some were healthy enough to keep in rooms under the watch of others. We're running out of space, though. Twenty rooms that were in the stone section of the building still stand, and we got the rest in tents throughout the grounds, but more people arrive by the day. Keeping them all fed and watered—even on single-meal rations—is becoming extremely difficult.

"Not to add to your woes, but I just received word that the lord general is going to be imposing a stricter curfew and looking for more patrols to take to the streets. They're gonna be stationed near high-risk locations. Seems the incident at the guild set him off."

Their housing crisis was something he was all too aware of. The logistics of keeping a surplus of homeless housed and fed had never occurred to him. His only goal had been to do the gods' bidding, and now he found himself being asked to make decisions that affected the lives of hundreds. *A number growing every day.*

"What if we found other estates, like this one, and started housing people in multiple locations?" asked Nerio. "I could travel between them, giving speaks through the day, and at night stay somewhere that I don't put these people in danger."

If the lord general were to stumble upon a large group of refugees in the fire-scorched section of the city, there was little he could do aside from dispersing them. He'd have no proof that they were Nerio's followers. If Nerio was present though... He shuddered to think of what might happen. *But then I'm leaving everyone who needs me behind,* he thought at the sound of another cry from the tent.

"Aye," the captain agreed, "it's not a bad idea. Doesn't solve all our issues, but it's a good start. I'll look for someplace safe for you to hide. This portion of the city's rife with the remnants of lords' estates and manors, I'm sure we can find some stone ones that are at least partially sound."

Nerio nodded, feeling more pangs of sorrow at abandoning the devout. *It's for the best,* he tried to tell himself, failing to alter his despondent mood.

He admired the captain for his strength of will, being able to confidently stand by his ideals, even if in a convoluted way. Nerio's conviction was firm, his need to spread the will and word of the gods more profound than ever before. He knew the people needed this.

Despite that, he still wished for some of that strength.

His thoughts drifted back to Desnia, the person with the strongest will he'd ever known. A woman who could stand by her decisions and never seem to waver from them. A confidence that he'd never experienced. *If she were in my place, she'd face these obstacles. She'd find a way to make everything work.*

He needed to continue trusting in those around him, the captain first and foremost. His experience on the battlefield meant he was familiar with the necessities of caring for large groups of people.

"What else do you need, Captain?" asked Nerio.

The man scratched at his beard again. "Steady supply of water; got some boys looking for bathhouses nearby that might have burned down but have a working pump. Food. Specifically, rations that will keep and can be made in mass quantities. Bandages, bed rolls, clothing... The list goes on, Witness."

Nerio cringed at the list. He would be of little assistance in acquiring most of those items. It made him feel not only responsible, but useless.

"Is there anything that I can do for you?" he asked.

"Unless you can find a way to either get us a legion's worth of supplies—or a way to pay for them—then I'm afraid there's not a whole lot."

The captain's comment brought him back to the person he'd yet to contact—and their generous offer to pay his way out of the city. *And they have proximity to the general. Closer than most.*

"Captain," said Nerio, "do you think that you could get a message to someone in the army? I may have a way to help."

The captain gazed at him through squinted eyes. "Aye, but there's no telling what they might do if they're unenlightened. Whoever delivers the message could be imprisoned and lead them back here. Who are you looking to send a message to?"

Nerio looked down at his bloodstained palms, the morning sun revealing skin that was painted red, now flaking away. The needs of the many outweighed the risk to himself, and reaching out was a danger that he was willing to put himself in if it meant a measure of peace for the masses. While he did not expect the harm the captain was concerned about, he understood there was a risk all the same.

"There is someone I trust, a friend that I believe would be willing to help."

"Who's that?" asked the captain.

"Lord Delvan ce Saffstar."

Chapter Sixteen

Additionally, accompanying this message is a full, transcribed ac-counting of the events at the gate, several parts of which I believe you will find most interesting.

Everything about this vile town repulsed him.

A camp, more like, Jerdine thought. *Shanties everywhere, no proper inn or housing to speak of. And the filth...* It wasn't the cold that made him shiver as he stared down his nose at a beggar on the street, their face caked in grime and hair matted flat, the tangled carpet hosting a mess of flying insects.

He tugged his horse's reins to halt before the shack of a Royal Mail outpost, the fetid scent of pigeon droppings assaulting his already offended olfactory. The purr of their incessant cooing droned through the air. Heads of the few faces in town turned to stare at the newcomers, their visages wrinkling into disgust or horror upon seeing his scabbed, healing skin, puss seeping from the cracks of his scowl.

Dismissing the indignance of the peasantry, he awkwardly dismounted his horse, wincing and sucking gushes of air through his teeth as the twisting of skin burned like the fire that had caused it. Pain crawled along the cracks beneath his robes like lightning through the sky. Every jostle of his saddle, twist of his body, or flinch of his face sundered the scabs anew, leaving him in constant agony. The task was made doubly excruciating and complicated as he gingerly avoided excessive use of the hand previously stabbed by the man watching him struggle.

"You move like a cripple, old man," said Valander haughtily from his horse.

"Yes, well—" replied Jerdine as his boot landed in the road's slop, splat-tering the brown, icy mixture over his robes. He sneered, letting out a hiss. "Perhaps if we'd waited a few more days, as I'd requested, my Lord, I would be more fit for travel." *You apathetic sadist.*

Valander's impudence, it would seem, was only matched by his impatience. His ridiculous plan would take months—the parts that he had shared—but yet he seemed determined to arrive within the coming weeks. So, they pressed on, his compatriot ushering him with contemptuous threats all the while.

"You were fit enough to go searching for more alcohol," said Valander, "so therefore you must be fit enough to ride. You've been managing, albeit slowly and with a great many annoying complaints."

Jerdine shot a glare at the man, his black armor disguised as leathers, runic tattoos hidden beneath gloves and an illusion of unblemished skin upon his face. The cold stare that was returned hid the maleficence that he knew lurked behind it. He turned his eyes away, flexing his riven hand with a grimace. "Maybe, my Lord, you should see about finding us accommodations while I conduct my dealings here."

Valander's gaze did not waver, remaining silent atop his steady horse.

Fine, he thought. *But your nepotistic entitlement will not get you far in this realm, where one must scavenge. You strut and make demands, but your blatant misuse of our precious supply will eventually dwindle it to nothing, and you will have to answer for your failures. For they will be that: yours. Do not expect to snare me in such a trap.*

He turned, stepping through a puff of his own misty breath. How did these accursed people stand living north enough that summer's peak left the ground half frozen? Surely the furs which consisted of this, and the surrounding towns', livelihoods were not valuable enough to offset the winter's perpetuity? Jerdine shook his head as he climbed the flimsy planks of the building's stairs—his grunted protests louder than the boards' with each crooked step.

Inside of the stifled coop was worse than he had expected. A hearth laid cold, filled with naught but ashes that glimmered with fading flecks of red. The vermin—stacked to the ceiling in cages—fluttered as he limped through, his presence a disturbance to their strange senses. A bearded man—the other breed of vermin—wearing a Royal Mail uniform looked up from the stick he'd been whittling, an appalled expression rippling across his face. He attempted to mask it with a false cough. *Speak one word of my disfigurement, mortal, and you shall become its remedy.*

"Good day," the man said. He looked to the side, unable to maintain eye contact.

"What's so fucking good about it?" Jerdine snapped.

The man's lips went white as they pressed together and he scratched the nape of his neck. "Can I help you with something, stranger?" he asked.

"I'm expecting messages, why the fuck else would I be here?" Jerdine asked. *Asinine livestock.* He provided the false name the scrolls would be filed under. Assuming the man was capable of reading—and that Valander had mailed his instructions from their last dismal accommodations to forward his mail to the next pathetic town.

The attendant nodded after shaking off his dumbfounded expression, turning to the wall behind him. He seemed thankful to avoid Jerdine's mangled visage. "Right," he said, pulling open a small drawer, "looks like we've got a few here for you, sir. Do you have the code for them?"

Jerdine recited the four digits embossed in the wax seals. *Hopefully he can count.*

"Alright then," he said with a gulp, avoiding eye contact, "here you are." He dumped the half a dozen miniature scrolls into Jerdine's waiting palm.

He shut his hand and glanced around—letting out a snarl of pain as he did so—searching for a room in which to digest the messages in private. However, the only space available was a tiny writing desk coated in the dung of the flying rats.

"Is there nowhere else for me to pen my responses?" he demanded to the station's keeper.

"Uh," dumbly gaped the man. It was the only expression he knew, it would seem. "That's always worked before. Honestly, sir, I write most of the letters that go out. Most folk around here don't know how to read or write."

Of course not. This backwoods village is so far removed from civilization it might as well be a different epoch. Jerdine scowled. He couldn't decide what would be more excruciating, remaining in this foul sty to read his missives, or finding a more suitable location somewhere else in the town. *Assuming such a place exists.*

Cursing in whispers, he pulled out the chair from the desk, turning it so his back was to the attendant. With delicate care—his face twisting with a reddened, malformed grimace—he eased himself down into the seat. After a few labored breaths, he unfurled the first scroll with a glance over his shoulder. The attendant had gone back to whittling, a blissful ignorance on his face.

Imbecile.

Jerdine began reading the first of the messages, brow furrowing as he ingested the words. *No, this cannot be correct.* He read the incongruent syllables again. The letter began shaking as his hand formed a tremor, the words' impossible assembly coalescing in his mind.

Seized? SEIZED?! How dare they! His body began to tremble, an all-consuming fury burning within him. *Those* fucking *merchants! I will see their guild destroyed! Their coffers empty! They will pay! Them and that fucking general!*

The anger blinded him, but through the constricting, numbing chains of his betrayal, a question arose. His stomach turned, and his face lost its flush. He broke the seals of the remaining scrolls in a hurried panic, searching for the one from Elhurtan—the man who had been tasked with delivering his payment and securing the most precious of cargo.

One by one, the wax broke, dry chips falling to the floor.

More assets claimed by the crown and Court. Along with notice of his excommunication.

More chips fell to the floor.

Updates from friends on the southern continent.

A mound of wax began forming.

The locations of that wretched group who'd humiliated him at the gate.

Flakes of colored seals littered the wood at his feet, masking the ground.

Updates from Brethefen, and his Nerio's unfurling of that wretched religion. He would come back to that later.

He turned to grab another scroll, frantic to tear it open, but no more of the unbroken seals remained, the desk covered only with the twists of unbound parchment.

There was nothing from his intermediary.

No, no, NO! he thought, nausea bubbling in his throat. He *needed* this, if for no other reason than to gain favor with Valander—and provide himself with relief. *If he couldn't withdraw payment... Damn it!* The majority of his holdings in Brethefen had been in the guild's vault, and the report claimed that even the banks were being pressured into forfeiting his assets.

It took every fiber of self-control he had to not release a blood curdling scream. Tremors pulsated through his body like shivers of pain.

He ignored the detestable condition of the desk and began writing a flurry of letters and inquiries, the man behind the counter whittling in an annoying rhythm all the while.

He needed to ensure the merchandise was held in Elhurtan's absence—the man had his vices, after all, and while it was possible he'd forgone his duties in the throes of a bender, he would still not have neglected to message Jerdine as to the delay. The man was a drunk, but reliant, nevertheless. Jerdine gritted his teeth, wishing there had been someone else to send that hadn't been executed, ostracized, or imprisoned. The general, it would seem, had been keeping a closer eye on him these past years than he'd realized. That man was a nuisance.

He'd have to hire others in Elhurtan's stead. There was a possibility that Elhurtan was curled up in an alley somewhere, covered in his own vomit, soon to be sober enough to travel. But Brethefen was a chaotic mess, the incompetence of the general shining as his martial law had—by all accounts—the reverse of its intended effect.

There were still a few he could trust or at least trust in their sins' wants. Hate, lust, and greed; his three most reliable allies in these trying times. The spoils of centuries were no longer at his disposal, but he had enough caches to hire suitable candidates. The money was irrelevant compared to the riches he sought, regardless. He would send another letter to Elhurtan, to be safe, but he would also set others into motion, though finding any willing to take the risk would be an endeavor unto itself.

As for the others, the ones that had left him mutilated and disfigured, killed The Hunter, and stolen his moment of triumph, well, the needs of the detestable were easily sated when one had the means. There was nothing he wouldn't give to drain the life from them himself, but given his situation, knowledge of their most prolonged, excruciating demise would need to suffice. There were a few agents that came to mind, as well as some that would make it... personal.

He looked again to the scroll regarding his former disciple's progress in the city. It broke the only smile Jerdine managed that day. The boy was proving to be more than Jerdine had thought possible. *And with no instruction from me.*

He was determined to allow this achievement to be Nerio's, and his alone. He wondered if the boy saw it yet, the cauldron of violence and rebellion he was stirring. There were even some among his followers that showed promise in their own way. Fruit to be plucked once fully ripened, for it was too early yet, but they had his eye.

Satisfied with the dozen scrolls he'd written, he sealed them with wax that struggled to melt above the candle that emanated more warmth than the ashy hearth. Curses streamed from under his breath as the nearby metronome of knife through wood drove him to madness with its disjointed beat.

With no small amount of agony, he stood and placed the scrolls onto the counter before the attendant. "I need these sent."

The man nodded, his eyes fixed on his carving. "Yep, will do, sir." He did not stand.

"Immediately!" barked Jerdine.

The man raised a bushy eyebrow, his incessant cutting of tinder finally ceasing. He set the wood and blade aside, examining the scrolls. "Some of these are going pretty far off. I got a few carriers that can take 'em, but we've got some other notes that are going to take precedent—been waiting a week or so already. I'll get them out as soon as—"

Jerdine's eyes darkened. Arraying his fingers at his side, hidden from view, a fractal of purple light coalesced around them. The thin, wispy lines snapped into place with a glow and the man before him became quiet, his face blank as his mind emptied in preparation of new thoughts and wants. *His* thoughts and wants.

"You," Jerdine grated, glaring through trembling eyes, "have no deliveries more essential than these." The man nodded, still gaping as he stared at the scrolls. "They are to be sent with as much haste as you can muster." Sweat began dripping down Jerdine's brow, his knees shaking as his muscles threatened to give way. "Then," he snarled, "you will take that accursed knife, and *shove* it into your eye." The man nodded blankly.

He released the casting, catching himself on the counter as he nearly collapsed. The healing spell was draining his reserves, and casting anything—let alone a spell powerful enough to drain him at full strength—brought blackness to the edges of his vision, his heart threatening to burst.

In that moment, he did not care for anything aside from his own satisfaction. A way to redeem something from this miserable day. This would easily delay his own healing by weeks, but it was gratifying all the same.

He would not allow indignity against his person, no matter the state of his appearance. Watching while catching his breath, he leaned against the counter as the mail attendant attached the scrolls to the legs of several pigeons, releasing them through a window in a flourish of feathers.

Contented, and with his meager strength returning, Jerdine exited the shack as the last few carriers flapped their wings with notes tied to their legs. The air outside stung with a chill, deep into his raspy lungs. *Better than the scent of that damned coop.*

His horse was tied alongside Valander's, but the ksatsimtri was nowhere to be found.

Jerdine glanced around, the sweat upon his balding head becoming icy in the evening breeze. *Where has that man gone off to now?* He leaned against a post. *He best have found somewhere to stay for the night, I can barely stand. I could use some respite. Speaking of which...*

He approached his horse, taking the steps from the walkway cautiously, legs shaking and sweat streaming. The flaring pain reminded him, as it was wont to do, of his torment's creator.

Fuck, he thought with the creak of the first stair. *That sniveling,* with the second's groan. *Whore-mongering,* with the final's bend. *Masini—*

As his foot fell into the slop of the street, it plunged through the soupy mixture of cattle and horse defecation to the layer of ice beneath and slipped out from under him. His arms flailed as he fell backwards, the pain of the motion forgotten in the wide-eyed moment. The stairs rushed to meet him.

The treads jousted into his shoulders, back, and hind, forcing the air from his lungs in a bout of agony that left him gasping. He struggled to breathe, managing little more than shallow wheezes, while the immense anguish spread through him. With squeezed, tearing eyes, he laid there, desperate for the pain to subside.

"Are you alright, mister?" came a diminutive voice beside him.

Jerdine cracked a watery eye and found a young boy standing over him, perhaps no older than ten.

His heart skipped a beat.

"B-Be a good lad," he gasped, "and get the bottle of whiskey out from the saddle bag of that chestnut there. Yes. Yes, that one. Thank you, boy." The fair-skinned child handed him his bottle, and he took a long swig, desperate for relief. He let out a long sigh as he removed it from his lips, feeling its comforting warmth abate the inferno ever so slightly.

He looked at the boy who still stood at his side and proffered the whiskey. "Here, have a sip."

The boy clasped his hands behind his back. "Father says I'm not supposed to."

"Bah," said Jerdine, "what he doesn't know won't hurt him. Here."

After a moment the boy hesitantly took the bottle and took a sip of the amber liquor. He cringed. "It burns!"

Well, it is *shit whiskey.* "Yes, but you come to love it. Help me, would you?" He extended his arm, and the boy grabbed the wrist of the hand Valander had stabbed, helping him sit upright. Flinching as his body trembled with pain, he took another long draft, then looked back at the boy. A vigor surged through him, the exhaustion of the spell he had cast inside seeming to wither away.

Holding his hand from the boy's view, he twisted his fingers, threads of purple light sparkling in the air as they gravitated toward one another, snapping into the beginnings of a pattern.

"Tell me," Jerdine said, the boy's eyes beginning to dull as he became enraptured, "what's your name?"

"Reitler," the boy said.

"Such a... handsome name, my boy." In the light of the setting sun, some of the child's features made him reminisce. The rise of the cheek bones, cut of the brow, width of the lips. *Yes. Much like him. Much like my Nerio.*

A scream came from inside the coop behind him, curling the corner of Jerdine's lips, joy helping to diffuse the exhaustion within him. The boy's head went to turn towards the cry, his eyes and motions dull, but Jerdine turned the boy's head back towards him with a touch.

"Focus now. Don't worry about that. Tell me, is there somewhere quiet we can—"

"What are you doing?" cut in Valander's icy voice from his side.

Jerdine's head torturously snapped to the right, the fractal around his fingers vanishing with a wave. "Where were you?" he retorted.

"Supplies," Valander said, unslinging a sack from his shoulders, his hostile gaze fixed upon Jerdine.

"Did you find accommodations for us?" The ksatsimtri held his dark glare, silent. "...my Lord."

His companion's eyes finally shifted to Reitler. "Leave us." The glaze of his eyes faded, and a shake of his head reintroduced him to the reality he now found himself in.

The boy's eyes went wide. "Papa!" he yelled, turning and running into the coop.

Damn it, thought Jerdine. "Well," he snapped at Valander, standing like an onyx edifice beside him, "are you going to help me up or just watch me suffer?"

"You haven't answered my question."

"Nor you mine," said Jerdine, painfully rolling on his side and forcing himself up with his good hand.

"Mount your horse. We're leaving."

Jerdine glared at him incredulously. "Leaving?! We've only just arrived!"

"And clearly I cannot trust you to not bring unwanted attention to us," he replied coldly, the sound of a crying boy now suffusing the air from inside the coop. "We can travel a few more leagues before dusk. Let's go."

"But—"

"That's an *order.*"

Jerdine sneered, a growl rumbling in his throat, but he kept his tongue still. *Idiot child, rushing us as though on campaign. Have you ever even fought in a true war? Seen those around you fall? Or have you been handed everything your entire life? Titles do not bestow experience, boy.*

It took several attempts to pull himself into the saddle, his companion watching stoically from his own mount. The wretched beast kept shifting and pulling away from him, and more than once he stumbled into the street and caught himself on a nearby railing—the stairs at their side mocking him with their yellow, worn treads.

Humiliated, he eventually tumbled himself into the saddle, and their horses trotted them from the town's tiny limits as a few people gathered in the mail station, tending to the wounded attendant. It brought Jerdine little satisfaction now, knowing that there were ampler opportunities which he had been denied. He remained silent for a time, bitter resentment tainting his already malignant mood.

"What do you have to report?" asked Valander as the last vestiges of dusk's light were dragged down to the horizon.

Jerdine debated not responding, but the ache in his hand reminded him to think better of it. "There is a settlement, perhaps a week's ride from here,"—*or sooner with the way you charge forward*—"with a bank that I should be able to withdraw a sizable sum from. At least enough for us to travel with some form of comfort."

"You spent over an hour in there, and that's all you have? Or are you indeed as slow as you are lazy?"

"I had personal business to attend to!" *You arrogant fool.* "You are not privy to my every act. I had several letters to write."

"Tell me what you were doing."

Jerdine's eyes suddenly bulged, veins popping from his neck and temples as the sensation of hot iron spearing his mind cleaved his head in two. Twisting his head with a great deal of strain, he saw a fractal illuminated around Valander's hand, his now-revealed tattoos glowing in a pattern as specific lines outshone others.

"You *dare*?!" he sputtered, spit flying from his lips. "You'd-You'd dissect my mind for your petty—"

"The truth, before I lose my patience. What were you doing? With whom were you communicating?"

His chest was tight, every muscle taut with hellish pain as he struggled against the truth spell. He wanted to resist, for no other reason than to spite the ego of his companion. But he could feel the tendrils of power prodding within his brain, wrapping around the truth and forcefully tugging it to the surface.

Such a spell was intended for the feeble masses, compelling them as easily as a scythe through grass. To use it on someone as potently filled with vidut as him was akin to bludgeoning a tree with a war hammer—resistant, but a hard swing could take a chunk out. And the young mage seemed to have inherited more than some of his father's brawn.

"Assassins!" he yielded. "I was hiring assassins!"

"Interesting. For whom?" the tattooed warrior asked with a twist of his hand. The fingers pulled apart his thoughts, revealing what had laid hidden.

"For those vile children who destroyed the gate! And-and..." his teeth clenched, but the words still hissed behind them. "And for others that do concern you!"

"Does it concern our mission?"

"No! Not yet. It was-was to gain..." he hunched forward in pain. "It's something to gain her favor! A plan in motion. Now *stop!*"

"Hmm," said Valander with a sidelong glance. With a wave he dismissed the spell. The hot blade of power was extracted from his skull and Jerdine wheezed out a long breath, pulling in the cold air as his muscles loosened. The immediate agony abated, but the lingering fractures created a painful soreness in his skull. "I trust," said Valander from his side, "that you will inform me of this scheme of your own volition?"

Why, so that you may claim credit? No, I think not. "It has run into some issues, my Lord. Most of my funds in Brethefen have been... confiscated. Besides, that which I am seeking may not exist, many others have falsely made such claims before. Once I am able to confirm their claims true, I will share what I know. I do not wish to create false hope before then."

"The High Chair is not the only one who despises disappointment," Valander said. *I'm sure you have little tolerance for anything aside from your whims. Much like your mother—in the worst ways.* "Safeguarding this plot is acceptable—for now. Update me after each message. Also, you're to rescind the contract on the First Born and the other I fought."

"What?!" asked Jerdine, taken aback. "But why? They destroyed the gate! Drained it of vidut by all accounts! They must be punished! ...Sire."

"I would fight them again," said Valander calmly. "I had not expected to find such... proficient foes in this realm. One was not a child of the twelve yet fought with the skill of one of my vanguard. I was impressed."

"You give them too much credence—"

"And you not enough, as we've discussed. You have a history of such underestimations, or have you forgotten what left you abandoned here in the first place?"

A scowl cut deeply into his face, but he remained silent. He cared little for the wants of his companion. *I cannot deny his request, however. But he has said nothing of that bitch who manipulated my Nerio. She will suffer the same violation she imposed upon me, and she will beg for her death before it is over. And if that is unsuccessful...* He felt at the round chunk of jade tucked away in his pocket.

Well, then a messier, more gruesome ending may be needed. And if some of her cohorts become collateral damage by happenstance, then I shall not forsake the day. He grinned.

And with their deaths, a small amount of balance will return to this cursed realm.

CHAPTER SEVENTEEN

The remnants of Reedjin's hold linger in his absence, but the city's morale fades with his dissipating grip.

Delvan leaned with crossed arms against the building's corner, the setting sun ducking below the awning's cover and pressing its vestigial heat against his back. His finger tapped against his arm, and he shifted his weight to ease the stiffness in his muscles as he waited with eager impatience.

The day's earlier efforts had produced scant results. Spent mostly among the fetid company of cooing pigeons, the morning and afternoon hours had been engorged with writing letter after letter, the acrid scent of droppings burning his nostrils all the while. Unfortunately, his inquiries would take days to arrive at their destinations—when he'd get a response was another matter entirely.

All that effort and half of the letters will, likely, be lost on some bureaucrat's desk...

Whether the inevitable "misplacing" of his inquiries was due to the indolence of those he reached out to, or because it better served their own goals, was a coin toss. Such acts were prone to occurring when the requestee did not outrank you, and Delvan's lack of anointment to full knighthood put him into an all-too-avoidable position. He thought back to the general's comments about his possible ascendance.

He couldn't help but wonder *why* he wanted it. Because of expectation? Honor? Years of being told it was his duty?

Regardless of his other flaws, Hilbrun's disdain about their life's paths being decided and chosen for them were valid, and they impregnated his mind with a thought that still gestated within all these months later: who did he *want* to be?

His lips turned down as he let out a long breath through his nose, pondering the question and reminding himself why he was here, lying in wait. He tentatively eyed a patrol of soldiers as they walked by. Discretion in his endeavor was vital, but the general's stricter curfews and regulations since the incident at the Merchants' Guild meant Delvan's uniform was one of the few things affording him an exclusive freedom.

Recognition—and his superior's discovery of his avoidance of ordered duties—was a necessary risk. One that he hoped to mitigate by keeping a sufficient distance from his quarry.

The soldiers shot looks at him, some wide-eyed and fearful, others holding the uncomfortably reverent stares that he'd been catching increased glimpses of. Each passing toll of the bells seemed to bring additional numbers and confidence to the gazes, their bearing steadier and expressions awed. It felt like they'd transformed from sidelong looks into soul-piercing, unbroken stares in mere days.

I must be imagining things, he thought. *Maybe it's just that song Kolden and Orne were talking about.* Thinking about them made his stomach turn, but he steeled himself. He needed to focus on the issue he was able to solve, not the distance that seemed an impassable canyon between him and the brothers.

The soldiers gave salutes, some adding stiff nods as they passed. Delvan wanted to shrink within himself, hide away to keep his position hidden from those occupying the building he observed in the distance.

He gave a nod back, briefly watching as they continued down the street before turning his attention back to the distant entry. *Where is he?* he wondered, frustrated.

The letters, requests, and petitions that he'd sent were his fallback in case this didn't work. *Not that I can afford to wait that long.* They asked the question that shadowed him like an indomitable foe, decimating the battlefield of his thoughts.

Who was Lady Mithya?

Delvan doubted she was solely here acting as a knight of the Court. The woman's mysterious nature was masked by the glamor she readily exuded, her attractive physique distracting everyone as she flirted her way around even benign questions. *Gods know it captivated me, at first,* he admitted. But now, unbeknownst to her—or so Delvan hoped—she posed a threat to someone he cared for, someone he owed his life to. *Someone I inadvertently put in prison...*

Mithya's affiliation with the guild piqued his interest. While it was a common enough partnership for nobility, Mornath's cautionary words had led him to believe there was a great deal more to her than she would let others believe. He would need to discover something she was hiding, something he could leverage to free Desnia, or at least remove her from the danger of Mithya's power.

If Mithya does *figure out Desnia's secret, then she—and the general—are just going to become more curious,* he thought nervously.

He empathized with the general's desire to know more of the High Realm mages—their foreign powers warranted curiosity and caution alike—and he wished that he could provide the answers the man sought. *Unfortunately, he correctly assumes they lie with Desnia,* thought Delvan with a cringe. *Gods, I wish they'd let me just speak with her, rather than requiring the forced confession of a Truthsayer.* This stank of his father's influence, further twisting the knife in his gut.

A sudden breeze whipped the street's fine sand against his face, his eyes squinting against the assault. The smell of dust and ash still clung to the air, a pervading scent which replaced the once odorous market that now stood nearly barren a few streets away. Another belated victim of the inflated costs incurred by the fire's savagery.

Finally, an hour after the bells had tolled, the man Delvan awaited emerged from the imposing tower in the distance. An enforced reduction of speaks left the normally crowded streets scantly populated, making Delvan's task of following someone from the lord general's headquarters simple. The man began walking towards Delvan, his head low and hands in pockets, before turning down a nearby street and disappearing.

Delvan stood straight and began walking at a brisk pace towards the same corner. He rounded it and caught sight of the man walking a few dozen paces ahead, one of the few silhouettes in twilight's approaching shadow. Delvan took long, forceful strides as he approached the man from behind, trying to close the distance, the loud *clomps* of his boots never garnering the man's oblivious attention.

"Wellos, right?" said Delvan, loud enough to tug at the man's impervious focus as he came up to his side.

The lord general's scribe nearly jumped out of his uniform—it was blatantly apparent that his experience in the army never amounted to more than sitting at a desk.

The scribe turned to face Delvan, his brow digging deeply into his nose, offence blending tumultuously with his annoyance. "Lord Delvan," he replied, color returning to his face. "I've told you before, if you wish to make another appointment with the general, you're going to have to submit a formal—"

"No, no," said Delvan. "I just saw you leaving and realized that *you* might be able to help me with something."

He stared narrowly at Delvan. "And what would that be?" he drawled after a moment.

Delvan had spent his time at the street corner considering what he would say next. His previous experiences with Wellos gave him the impression that direct requests would be denied, perhaps out of spite. The man seemed perpetually annoyed, having turned Delvan away at every opportunity. *Though I do suppose I did send him a* lot *of petitions...* But there *was* something that the man—and most who met Lady Mithya, Delvan suspected—could relate too, and he hoped that requesting it in a more informal setting would bring a change to the man's attitude. He also couldn't afford the general overhearing his inquiries and asking why he wasn't searching for Nerio.

"Well," Delvan said, running his hand through his hair, "I'm a bit embarrassed to ask..."

The lieutenant tilted his head and rolled his eyes. "My Lord, it's been a long day, and I really don't have time for—"

"Listen, Lieutenant, have you by chance met, uh, Lady Mithya?"

Wellos's eyes perked with interest. "Why do you ask?"

"When I met her the other day, it was just... I don't know, it was like we had a connection. I can't explain it. Problem is, I don't know where to find her, or even what her house name is. I assume she checked in with you before seeing the general, right? You *must* have gotten her address, maybe her house name?"

Wellos shook his head, eyes turning to avoid Delvan, his face embittered. He began muttering under his breath, not attempting to hide his words. "Always thinking you can get whatever you want, every one of you..." His hardened gaze returned to Delvan. "Maybe she has interests elsewhere?"

Of that, Delvan thought, *I'm certain. But where is this animosity coming from?* There was something about the way the lieutenant's words bit, like a wolf guarding its kill. *He almost seems... jealous.* He had a sudden realization. *Oh, you fool.*

The lieutenant didn't honestly believe that he stood a chance with a woman like Mithya, did he? He wasn't a lord, and more than that, she was a Blue. *He* has *to know better. Unless... Oh, she flirted with you, didn't she? I wonder if the woman knows how many hearts she breaks?*

"Well, I can't know unless I ask, right?" Delvan posited. "Come on, Wellos, help me out here. At least give me a name. And who knows, maybe she's got some friends that would be interested in an officer? Especially one so close to the general. You help me out, and I can try to return the favor."

Wellos's face became a scowl, and Delvan noticed his face flushing despite his dark skin. "Of course, because I'm only good enough for your scraps, right?" he snapped.

This isn't going well, he thought. "Look, Wellos," he said, forcing out a lighthearted chuckle. He tried to phrase his next words delicately, "I know she comes off as kind of flirty, but you have to realize that there can't be something between a Blue and... you, right? I mean, nobles are very strict about bloodlines, believe me, and—"

"Clearly you don't know how to take a hint," Wellos said, his words harsh and volatile. "She's *not* interested in you, Lord Delvan. Drop it."

By the gods, is he always this petty? wondered Delvan, trying to hide his frustration. "I'm not sure why you're so confident about that, Lieutenant, but if it's all the same I'd like to ask her myself."

"I know because we've *already* begun courting. So no, I'm not going to give you her house name or any other information for that matter. But who knows, maybe she has some friends I can send your way."

Delvan shook his head, jaw hanging open. *He's lying, surely,* Delvan thought, his brain confounded. "I think you might have misunderstood her flirting with court—"

"Say whatever you want to appease your ego," spat Wellos, "but when I'm sharing a meal with her tomorrow night I will revel in its injury. Now, if you don't mind, *my Lord*, I'm going home."

He turned and stormed away, leaving Delvan frozen in place. There had to be some mistake. She'd misled him, said something to get what she wanted... but why? *She couldn't* actually *want to... With him? No,* Delvan contended in his mind. He shook his head, trying to rid it of his stupor. Wellos had made it ten paces before he managed to close his mouth.

He was about to be left empty handed. Again.

With each of the lieutenant's steps, Delvan saw his chances of discovering Mithya's secrets dwindling. This had been his only contingency—he couldn't even find out where she was staying in the city. Waiting for a response to his carriers—assuming he got any—required time he couldn't afford. Without this, he had nothing, no idea where to look next. His heart quickened, and a stream of sweat born of desperation beaded down his temple.

"Don't make me give the request as an order, Wellos!" he blurted as the man began shrinking into the distance. He *needed* this. He didn't know how often Mithya visited Desnia, or what damage might have already been done.

Wellos abruptly stopped and spun to face Delvan, the air between them tense and parted by the lieutenant's visage of scorn. "You might be a *lord*," Wellos barked, "but you're still a *cadet*, and as a lieutenant, *I* outrank *you*. Take your jealous threats somewhere else!"

He spun and stomped his way into the distance, leaving Delvan standing in the middle of the road, flabbergasted. Another patrol of soldiers marched by him, hesitantly saluting as they glanced between Delvan and the now-distant Wellos. Delvan pulled his jaw back closed, lackadaisically saluting back to the men.

So much for subtlety, he thought with a grimace.

His teeth began to grind as he watched Wellos blend and vanish into the obfuscating awnings and darkening shadows. He chided himself for his choice of words, though he still struggled to see how he'd made such egregious errors in judging Mithya's whims and Wellos's... charm. *Something's wrong here. There's no possible way she's interested in* him.

He kicked at the ground, scuffing the pavers with his boot and spraying up a small cloud of dust and pebbles. He'd truly believed this would work. To find the situation this... *confusing* deflected his mind astray. *Damn, Wellos,* he thought, *how could you be so blind? She's using him, but to what end?*

He looked around before collecting himself, trying to pull his thoughts away from whatever foreign power was clearly at work here.

The walk to his quarters would be an arduous and lengthy one—exasperated by his soured mood. Bewilderment and frustration filled the space between his steps, but in the short moments of clarity, he realized that there was one more place he could try to find information on Lady Mithya.

It was going to be tedious, boring, and take no small amount of effort, but it was better than waiting for responses that might not come. But by the gods, he was going to hate it.

Don't say I never do anything for you, Des.

CHAPTER
EIGHTEEN

It simmers in turmoil, and I hope to witness its demise.

I need you to tell me ways to deal with my interrogator before her next visit," whispered Desnia.

It had been a blessed few days since her first meeting with the brown-eyed Blue. Every minute of which Desnia's head had needed to finally clear and return to a semblance of normalcy. *Or as normal as it ever is,* she thought grimly.

Sleep had become a visitation to a fog-covered land, ravaged with images of death and pain. It was not Asta that she saw—the god strangely holding her tongue—but they had her... aura about them. *The hangovers feel the same, that's for gods-damned sure,* she sneered, remembering all the times Asta had spoken to her in her dreams.

Well, said Masini, *not to brag, but I am somewhat of an expert in this area. Once you get in close, you will need to take your time—warm her up, so to speak. A woman like her will require a delicate, but confident touch, and I happen to have a few methods that will arch her back more than a eunuch's frown when you ask him, 'How's it hang—*

"For fuck's sake, Masini!" she hissed, her face flushing. "I meant about her *power!* I'm going to throw you into the fucking chamber pot if say shit like that again."

She shook her head. Waiting for the Blue to return had been a double-edged sword. Time to recuperate was a necessary relief, but her anxiety had been building with each toll of the city's bells as she contemplated her captor's motives and what she was going to have to endure. *I wonder,* she thought, *if this is part of her method, making me sit here and overthink everything.*

She loathed the idea of what she'd have to do to get close to the Blue, feeling strangely nervous about the entire endeavor. And Masini seemed to always know exactly how to twist the knife in her gut.

Don't say I never tried to help you out, grumbled Masini. *But fine, I will try to describe what I can. Her 'gift' as the Blues are wont to call it, makes you want to, almost irresistibly, have an explosive, truth-ridden word-gasm—*

"Masini..." she growled through grinding teeth.

Shh, it's lesson time, he chided. Desnia rolled her eyes but remained otherwise silent. *The trick is not to resist, as you so painfully learned, but to answer in a way that is true, but dodges their actual question. Say, for instance, she asks what your favorite color is, and it's, oh, I don't know, blue. Instead of flatly saying as much, you'd say, 'You are, my sweet, untasted indulgence of succulent—*

"I get it," she said, shaking her head. "You're worse than a damn street dog."

It's part of my magnetizing charm, he beamed.

Masini's crass enamoring aside, the information *was* helpful. *If,* she considered, *I can find ways around the questions without making her suspicious, it might buy me time.* The half-shod plan relied heavily on possibilities that could easily go awry, worsening her pensiveness. Success came from careful planning, knowing your mark's weaknesses, and having contingencies—none of which she was afforded from a prison cell. Everything rested on what she could think of in the moment—her few hidden advantages aside.

She looked down at her cot. Hidden behind it, the wall of otherwise white-covered paint had been nearly scraped bare, her consumption of the muted-inanite colored paint growing with each day in preparation of the Blue's next conversation with her. *Going to have a hard time hiding that, soon,* she thought. She reconsidered the snowy white floor tiles, and whether she could find a way to somehow scratch the edges off—

Her mind was pried from its spiraling as a raving scream tore the quiet air asunder. Loud grunts followed, a struggle occurring down the hall. Desnia raised an eyebrow as she crept to the door, trying to catch a narrow glimpse of what was happening through the tiny viewing portal.

"Damned crazies," she heard one of the guards—not the sadistic asshole, fortunately—mutter.

"Not sure why they can't keep 'em with the others," the second of her sentinels griped. "Was nice and fuckin' quiet up here for a while."

"Place is fillin' up fast," the first guard replied, "heard they're gonna start sending more of 'em back up here, what with keepin' all the recent arrests downstairs. They got four to a room, I hear."

"Dunno why people keep resistin' Rosethorn's orders. Dumb as bricks if you ask me."

You're one to talk, she thought. A door slammed in the distance, and the wild screams began to calm. She shuddered to think about the person's madness, and how a similarly fevered insanity was digging its claws deeper into her with what felt like every passing dream.

She walked back to her cot, looking out the window above it and to the dusty streets beyond, yellowed weeds forcing their way desperately through gaps in the pavers as they struggled to survive. Among them, hidden in the shadows of alleys, was an unsettling sight. One that grew in number each day.

The hunger of deep-set, ghostly eyes.

They stared up at her window as though she were a morsel which could sate them, a craving in them that reminded her of the iguan addicts from the streets of Calentine. *Fucking creepy,* she thought with a shiver.

They were dispersed by the guards a few times a day, some being arrested and probably thrown into one of the cells downstairs that her guards had mentioned. Yet they seemed to flock back to here, and in greater numbers with each return.

The *creak* and *clang* of another door in the distance caught Desnia's attention, pulling her eyes from the dark outlines of figures in the alleys outside. A voice called through the hallway, clear and confident—making Desnia's heart skip a beat.

"Gentlemen," she heard the crystalline voice of the inquisitor call out, "please bring a chair and then see yourselves off. Hurry now, I hate to be kept waiting."

Desnia quickly tucked Masini under her shirt—much to his whining complaint—and faced the door, crossing her arms. The heavy wooden slab swung open, a chair being rushed in by an eager-eyed guard and placed on the floor directly before Desnia. Following behind him was the click of high boots that went over the styled, clinging pants, a loose, silken shirt of azure blue doing naught to hide the curves beneath.

The guard looked at the soft visage that covered what Desnia knew to be a granite resolve, being graced with a smile that caused his face to flush as he excitedly left the room. As Desnia looked her visitor up and down she felt her heart begin to race—before it fell into a pit with the rest of her insides.

She'd looked upon the smiling face, distracted, before eventually shifting her gaze to the woman's brown, shining hair. It cascaded to her shoulders, unrestrained—her hairpin devastatingly absent.

A weight of defeat crushed Desnia from within, her shoulders slumping with resignation as days of careful planning crumbled into dust.

"Desnia!" the Blue said excitedly, taking a seat before her. "Please, sit. This is going to get awkward if you just stand there and loom the whole time."

The Blue pulled the white bag off the end of her necklace's chain, the heavy sapphire matching the color of her shirt, the light dancing and casting rainbowed glimmers over the walls. Desnia became drenched in its power, a chill running down her spine as it enveloped her completely. From down the hall she heard a scream, and her and the Blue's face flinched in unison as pitiful pathos filled the room.

Her interrogator recovered herself, turning her full lips into a broad smile as Desnia slowly sat on her cot. "I'm sorry to have kept you waiting," she started, "but it seemed like our last meeting took... a lot out of you. How are you feeling?"

Desnia ground her teeth, her mouth clamped shut as she fought the restrained outreach of power.

Des, chided Masini, *answer the question. Remember, we* want *to talk to her.*

Desnia took a deep breath. *Doesn't matter much,* she thought, *if she doesn't have what I need.* Masini, however, was right—which she'd never admit—and this still presented as her best chance to learn more of who was coming after her, as well as securing a means of escape. *Assuming I can get her to come back after this, and that she wears her damn hairpin...*

"I'm better," she said, scowling. The answer was like releasing a tense muscle, relief flooding her as the power got what it wanted.

"Great!" said the Blue cheerily. "I felt like we got off on the wrong foot last time," she said, leaning forward. "My name is Lady Mithya, I'm here to ask you a few simple questions. I take it you prefer Des over Desnia?"

Desnia's brow furrowed. "How'd you know that?"

"Your overprotective friend called you by that name. Was on the verge of threatening me, if you can believe it."

Friend? asked Masini. *Ha!*

Through narrowed eyes, Desnia thought on the words. *Friend? Did she meet Nerio? Oh, no...* Her stomach flipped as she began to worry that the priest had been captured. *Probably turned himself in or some stupid fucking nonsense.*

"What did you do to him?" Desnia asked, raising her voice.

"Oh, you two *were* a thing? Huh, I must admit, I'm a little disappointed," she said, leaning back, her face turning down. Desnia cocked her head to the side as a strange emotion seemed to fill the air. *Is that... jealousy?* "I mean, he's handsome, I'll give you that. But he seems so... serious, like the world's resting on his shoulders or something. What did you see in him? Was it the money?"

Money? she thought, a realization striking her. "Oh," she said, her voice turning sour, "you mean the asshole."

Mithya sucked a rush of air through her teeth. "Oof, have a rough falling out, did we?"

Desnia sneered. "We were never a 'thing,' so stop spreading rumors. And the fucker put me in here, so no, we're not 'friends.'" *They're nothing more than a burden anyway.*

"Hmm," said Mithya, raising an eyebrow. "Maybe someone should tell *him* that. The way he was talking, I think he'd be willing to face a pit of vipers for you."

"Well, he did talk to *you*, didn't he?" Desnia quipped. She heard an annoyed groan from Masini.

Mithya's response was a broadened grin. "True enough, I have been known to bite."

Desnia heard a moan come from Masini, making her squirm in her seat. She sat quietly, averting her gaze, her instincts screaming at her to keep quiet, despite the plan that she and Masini had devised.

The Blue eventually let out a sigh, clearly hoping for a retort other than extended silence. "Alright, be that way... Now, I wouldn't normally do this, but since you seem so averse to answering my questions, I have an offer for you." *You mean you couldn't get what you wanted,* she thought, *so you need to try something different.* "Answer my questions today, and I will have something brought to you as a... let's call it a reward. What do you want? A good meal? I bet the food here isn't exactly what you can find in a local tavern. Or, speaking of which, maybe something harder to drink than the water they serve?"

"How about a key to the fucking door," snapped Desnia.

Now, Des, be nice, said Masini.

She rolled her eyes at his condescending tone, and the Blue let out a light chuckle. "I probably should have seen that answer coming," she replied. "How about I have a hot meal sent up?"

Despite the saliva wetting her mouth at the thought, Desnia remained defiant. "Going to give me something good as a last meal?" She could almost feel Masini's chagrin.

"Oh please," said the Blue with a wave of her hand. "You think this is the last time I plan to come see you? Answer my questions, and I promise to make it worth your while."

Desnia drew her knees to her crossed arms, the aches of the bruises below her clothing a mild annoyance compared to her detestation of the scenario she found herself in. *She's promising to come back, for whatever that's worth,* she thought. She needed that hairpin. Eventually, after her own consideration and Masini's prodding, she gave Mithya a curt nod.

"Excellent," she said with an ambitious smile. "Let's start with something easy: did you start the fire at the Grand Clergy House?"

Desnia felt the tendrils of power raise the hair on her arms, seeping into her and buoying the words on a tide of persuasion to her mouth. She thought back to Masini's instructions, answering honestly to question, but dancing around the blunt truth.

"All I did was serve a small amount of retribution to Jerdine. Man's a perverted fuck who deserves worse," Desnia said derisively.

The Blue narrowed her eyes at Desnia, tapping her finger as she thought in tense silence. "A dozen disciples confirmed they saw someone they described an awful lot like you fleeing the tower, Des. The tall creep confirmed that you started it, even if the other two you were with refused to say anything, so there's no need to beat around the question.

"That being said, when I talked to the disciples, too many described what the principle had been... capable of." Mithya became silent, her tone having turned morose. "Frankly, I wish you had done more to the bastard. Burning down half the city was an... unfortunate side effect."

"No shit," muttered Desnia. Her eyes bored through the floor to her side, an unease at the destruction she'd caused swelling within her, though it was shadowed by her hatred for the man. If she had known what the outcome would've been, would she have done anything differently? *Yes,* she thought, *I'd have made sure he was in there when I lit the wick.*

"Tell me about him," said Mithya.

Desnia glanced back at the Blue. *Cutting right to the point, are we?* she wondered. *Looking to see what I know about your employer? Maybe how much I've told the others?* "He had decent taste in booze," she said with a shrug. *How's that for an honest answer?*

"I'm more interested in what your not-friend, Lord Delvan, told the general," Mithya replied coolly. "Something about being a 'High Mage' from a different realm? Sounds interesting, if you can believe it."

Yet, Desnia noticed, *you don't feel the least bit skeptical.* "He put on a hell of a lightshow, if that's what you're asking. Maybe you should ask him about it."

"If anyone could find him, then perhaps I would."

"If you want to know more about the bastard," Desnia said, "perhaps you should try reviewing some of the journals I... collected. Makes for some light reading. Lord Dipshit took them to the general, last I knew." *And when you grab the pages, I get a small dose of revenge for the torture you put me through a few days past.*

"Mhm, would if I could," said the Blue, "but they've been stolen."

Desnia's stomach lurched into her throat.

Well, said Masini, *that can't be good. Bastard had who-knows-how-many secrets in there. Assuming he's the one who stole them back, I wonder what it was that he didn't want the general to know.*

Maybe, thought Desnia with a glare to the woman before her, *the person who stole them wasn't Jerdine himself, but his agent.* "Somehow, I bet you'll find a way."

A slyness crept into Mithya's smile. "I am resourceful like that," she said. "But, for now, I have you. Delvan explained to the general that you seemed to know a great deal about the group that he was involved with. These 'Magridi.' What can you tell me about them?"

Desnia's brow furrowed as an unexpected emotion reached out from the Blue. She wondered at it, confused as to why someone in the principle's employ would feel such a toxic emotion about the man and his affiliates. It was so intense it felt as though it poisoned the air.

Loathing.

"I know," said Desnia, watching the Blue's reaction through slit eyes, "that you hate them."

Wait, what? asked a confused Masini.

There was a flash of surprise on Mithya's face, so miniscule that it would have been imperceptible if Desnia hadn't been looking for it. She suppressed a grin from tugging at the corner of her mouth. *Good to know that I* can *catch you off guard.*

She had to admit Mithya was talented. She swept away any expressions and buried her emotions, remaining cool and calm in her chair, listing to the side as she casually lounged in it. "I don't know anything about them, aside from what was given to me in a report. That's why I'm here."

"*Now* who's the one lying?" asked Desnia.

Mithya only grinned, remaining still. "Where did you pick up such acute observation skills, Des?" she retorted.

"Where I grew up," Desnia said bitterly, "if you couldn't read someone, you ended up as their next victim."

"And where was that?"

"Don't pretend you don't know," grumbled Desnia, slouching further. "I'm sure Lord Dipshit told you all about the Valley. Fucking Uppers, always thinking themselves better than the rest..."

She began to regret agreeing to this ridiculous plan of Masini's. Talking about this did nothing but revive heartache and buried pain. She didn't miss Calentine per se, nothing as sentimental or pedestrian as that. Her escape from its underground's grip had been anything but what she'd expected—a night rife with betrayal, death, and grief. Events that were now being repaid in kind. *And now she wants the details of it, I'm sure,* she thought. *Probably wants another knot to add to the end of my rope, confirm that was all me.*

"You're from Calentine then?" asked Mithya. "I knew you weren't a local, but that's a hell of a journey. What brought you out here?"

"Misplaced trust..." Desnia said quietly.

"Hmm," said the Blue quizzically, "I bet that's an interesting story."

Desnia snorted. "That's a word for it."

Ahem, she heard Masini say, *remember the plan, Des. You'll never get her to warm up to you if you keep giving her the cold shoulder.* She stifled a sigh, resignation anchoring her back into the conversation.

"When you were in Calentine," said Mithya, "did you know Knight Commander Ferrand ce Lione?"

"No," Desnia said, thankful to be able to answer a question without doing a mental dance.

"The impression the others gave in their report was that you and the commander were part of the same group. Something called the 'Sraddhana.'"

"Is that what they were called?" asked Desnia coyly. Masini had never been able to speak the name aloud. "I just thought they were a bunch of rude, self-absorbed assholes."

Now you're just trying to hurt my feelings, said Masini.

There was a mixture of annoyance and anger that came along with the Blue's narrowed gaze. Desnia smiled inside, hoping that she was finally getting under Mithya's skin.

"Alright then," continued Mithya. "What about the body that was in the bath house? The one that the others said was called 'The Hunter.'"

Desnia scowled. "He was a twisted fuck, if that's what you're asking."

Ahem, coughed Masini.

Desnia closed her eyes and sighed. With a slow, reserved cadence, she continued. "He was a High Realm mage, like Jerdine. He liked to hunt down his own kind as a challenge. That's all I know."

The lack of surprise that Desnia felt from the Blue was enough to pique her own. There was animosity, more of the fiery loathing fueling it. *I suppose she would know about him, working for Jerdine,* she considered. *Perhaps she had a distaste for the man.* Scant little of this conversation had gone the way she'd expected thus far.

"Do you think this 'Hunter' could have been a Blue?"

Desnia dug her brow into her nose, looking into the inquisitor's eyes. "No,

I know a fucking Blue when I see one. He didn't have a sapphire, he used... something else."

"Are you sure—"

"Are you *deaf?!*" she asked. "Not. A. Blue."

After a moment Mithya gave a nod. Desnia shook her head and looked to her side, frustrated that even with someone supposedly able to discern absolute truth she had to repeat herself to dispel misplaced doubt.

"Are there any other members of your group, these 'Sraddhana,' still around? Any that I could talk to?" Mithya asked. There was a strange... nervousness that filled the air.

"I'm *not* a 'member.' I just happened to... fall in with the wrong people. And to answer your question, no, there's no one *you* can talk to. Besides, you wouldn't want to even if you could."

Masini gasped. *Does your impudence know no bounds? To think that I offer such sage advice, only to be tossed in the proverbial gutter.*

Keep it up, thought Desnia, *and I might throw you in the* actual *gutter...*

She waited with bated breath to see if Mithya would push the issue of Masini further. If finding out more about him was Mithya's end goal, as she'd originally suspected, then she doubted that the Blue wouldn't resort to extending the full brunt of her abilities. Desnia braced, waiting for the onslaught.

"Hmm," said a narrow-eyed Mithya, the creases at their edges giving her a weary appearance. She reached into the pouch hanging beside her sword, looking in and raising an eyebrow. Desnia tried to elevate her head and see inside, but the flap was quickly thrown shut. "Looks like that's all we have time for today," said the Blue with a tired smile.

She called for the guards, hovering at the door as she made her way out behind them. She turned back, looking at Desnia with glisten eyes. "Thanks for making this... interesting, Des. Look forward to the next time," she said with a wink.

Desnia threw back a contemptuous, sardonic grin. "Can't wait," she said.

"Oh," said Mithya as the door slammed shut, "I'll let Delvan know you said, 'Hi.'" With that, she walked from view, her boot's *clicking* fading in the distance.

Desnia sneered, sulking as the sound eventually vanished.

That could have gone worse, Masini said. *You still need work, though. Unlike myself—who knows that you show affection by angrily spiting those closest to you—Lady Mithya will need just a* little *more coaxing.*

"Something feels... off," whispered Desnia, ignoring Masini's jabs. "She felt so... angry about Jerdine and the Magridi."

Felt? asked Masini. *How would you-Oh! Did her sapph—*

"Doesn't matter," hissed Desnia. "Just... trust me."

Well, said Masini, *just because she doesn't like them doesn't mean she can't work for them.*

"True enough," she conceded. "I did help *you* out, after all."

Aw, you do care about me, said Masini.

She groaned, rolling her eyes. He wasn't worth arguing with, she knew—not that it often stopped her. She instead focused on the conversation, and its possible implications. She told herself that this Blue was nothing but a danger to her, that she'd sell her out as soon as she had what she wanted. There was a mystery to the woman, an intrigue that was beginning to deviate from what Desnia and Masini had originally suspected, and she doubted that it was to her benefit.

What does she really *want?* Desnia wondered.

Asking the question, Desnia was left pondering what *she* wanted. Escape was the most obvious, and perhaps that's what was making her feel this way. But there was something else, an anxiousness that was different from even the most daring of crimes she'd committed.

She wrapped her arms around her chest, trying to squeeze the fluttering of her stomach from her throat.

Reading others helped her survive, but fear of discovering hidden truths kept a blind eye on the person's secrets that she dared not reveal. The ones that could hurt her the most.

Her own.

Chapter Nineteen

I have also confirmed our suspicions and discovered Reedjin was contacted regarding the cache's purchase. Plans had already been set in motion to procure the entire sum.

The freshly risen sun drained the morning air of moisture like an army at an oasis. Delvan stared up at the building's outline against the crisp blue sky, carved effigies tucked into alcoves dotting its façade, ornate stained glass filling the space between up to the vaulted peak with magnificent splendor. A fascinating shell to contrast the banal contents.

Aside from the night of the fire, Delvan couldn't remember the last time he'd willingly set foot in a library. The curriculum of his youth required regular attendance to the one in Calentine, accompanied by the many tutors his father hired, but he'd never *enjoyed* it. By the time he'd graduated from the academy, he guessed he'd spent more time in taverns than he ever did with books.

And now everything rests on what I can dig up here, he thought. He could almost hear his tutors laughing at the irony.

He took a disgruntled breath and walked up the wide stone steps leading to the imposing wooden doors which required a strong heft to open despite the greased hinges. The smell of leather, parchment, and the too-common accompanying dust sprang forth at him like the memories that the scents invigorated. His knuckles began to ache at the recollection of Master Tunner rapping them.

A spectrum of light painted the building's imposing interior through the colored glass. It filled the main hall and towering shelves on the floor above—looking down from a balcony to the arranged tables below—with beams of concentrated hues, making thick streaks through the dusty air.

Delvan took in the sight, awed—yet desperate to leave.

Before him stood a wide, heavy desk. An old, crooked priest sat behind it, squinting down at a text which crinkled dryly with the turning of its yellowed pages. He walked up to him, standing at the edge of the antique, dusty workstation, waiting for acknowledgement.

None came.

Delvan tilted his head, trying to get a better view of the man who was certainly older than most of the tomes housed in the grand building. His eyes were squinted, his lips moving slightly as he read the page before him.

"Hello?" said Delvan. The man continued reading.

Is he ignoring me?

"Hello!" Delvan repeated louder.

The geriatric practically jumped from his chair, his hand pressing against his chest. He looked up to Delvan, squinting again before putting on spectacles that were beside the book he'd been previously enthralled by.

"You nearly scared the blood from my veins, my Lord," he said, catching his breath.

"Sorry," Delvan said, "wasn't my intention."

"No, no, it's quite alright. Happens more than I care to admit. King and His grace upon you."

"And you."

The elderly man took a shaky breath. "Is there something I can help you with?"

"Maybe," Delvan said pessimistically. "I'm looking for records on noble or elite houses, specifically ones that have Blues currently in the family."

"Mhm," the elderly priest nodded, wiping his brow with his heavily ringed sleeve. "We have many such records, yes. Which particular duchy are you looking to find records for? Looking for some insight into your own ancestry, are you? The library is the most complete in the western half of the empire. What, uh, did you say your name was?"

"Delvan ce Saffstar," he replied.

"Ce, you say? Hmm. Well, we house a great deal of information here, my Lord, but you might have better luck writing back to the capital, their records on such matters will be more complete than—"

"No," Delvan cut in. "That's not what I need. I want the records for *all* Blues, in *all* duchies."

The old priest stared at him blankly for a moment, assessing him with a slacked jaw. Delvan shifted uncomfortably.

"My Lord," he said, "I think, perhaps, you do not realize the *scale* of your inquiry."

Delvan shook his head. *It can't be that bad, can it?* "What do you mean? There are a lot of houses, I know, but surely you must have a few tomes with their lineages, or ones that focus on living members?"

The priest scoffed. "A few? Mhm, yes that's one way to describe it." He removed his spectacles, cleaning them with his robe and carefully adorning them before readdressing Delvan. "My Lord, there are likely over a *hundred* tomes meeting that criteria in this library alone. Not to mention additional details kept in the private estates. Surely a Blue from Calentine of all places knows this, your tutors must have spent months reviewing the annals of influential houses, no?"

They certainly tried... "I spent more time pursuing... other means of getting to know my peers," Delvan said.

"Ah," the librarian said with an understanding nod. "Yes, yes, swinging a sword and chasing dresses, as youth is wont to do. You know, if a few more men your age spent half that time studying, you'd outpace your peers and leave your names in the marks of history. I've seen youth who can excel with such studious natures..." he trailed off, his focus distant. "Anyway," he said with a wave, "back to your request.

"If you can narrow down what it is that you're looking for, then perhaps we could reduce the quantity of tomes you require. What is it exactly that you wish to research?"

Delvan's lips tugged back before letting out a sigh. "I have a first name, but I don't know their house. I was hoping to look through the records and see if I could find them."

The librarian cocked a gangly eyebrow. "My Lord, there are dozens of duchies in the empire, many have multiple cities that contain affluent enough members of high society to afford sapphires. Many birth-names are in common circulation, as I'm sure you're aware. Perhaps we could start with the duchy here? Are they from the region?"

Delvan parted his lips, but after a moment of silence, closed them again. *I don't even know where she's from...*

"Pull the records for this region and the surrounding duchies," he said, his tone resigned. *This is going to take* forever. Maybe he was better off waiting for responses to his letters. His short stint in the city left him with few contacts, and his efforts to buy information has so far led to dead ends.

"Hmm, as you wish, my Lord," said the man, standing with loud creaks and pops from his joints. "It may take some time, you're welcome to go sit and wait. I'm going to have to requisition the help of some Hands to assist the disciples that have to pull these from the shelves. Best that you take one of the longer tables."

Delvan groaned, reminding himself that he was here for Desnia as he rubbed his forehead.

"Been a long time," said the librarian as he grabbed his cane and began shuffling, "since we've had Blues in here. The Lord General has lived here decades, but this hall is yet to be graced by his presence. Although I do suppose the man himself is a part of history."

Can't say I blame the man, thought Delvan, looking around absently at the towering rows of bound parchment and vellum. *If I were the general, this is probably the last place I'd be spending—*

Delvan's head snapped straight, alert as his mind caught up to what the librarian had said.

"Wait," he said, taking two long strides towards the creaking man, "did you say *Blues,* as in more than one of us?"

"Mhm, well of course," he said. "Lady Mithya was here not two days ago, asking to look at some histories. Those Tennish women... pardon my language, my Lord, but they can make even a man my age stand a little straighter."

"Tenn... Tennish?" Delvan said with a gaping mouth. "She's from Tennefen?"

"Did you not know this?" asked the librarian. "I assumed you already knew of her; you Blues tend to congregate once you're within a few hundred feet of one another. I'm surprised you haven't met her, my Lord."

Oh, we've met. He couldn't believe that he'd learned more in a few minutes than an entire wasted day. His breath began to quicken, anticipation building like a pressure inside his chest.

"Do you know her house?" Delvan asked, anxiously waiting as the man slowly turned himself to face him, like the hands of a clock dragging the last few minutes of the afternoon hour before tolls.

Delvan began to worry about the ancient librarian succumbing to his age before the man finally faced him, looking up from his bent posture. "Yes, she gave it when we were chatting the other day. Mithya te Rytta, I believe it was. She was rather interested in some exciting histories, yes."

Delvan let out a sigh of relief, his anxiety melting away. *Thank the gods,* he thought, *I'm not going to have to go through* hundreds *of books to discover her identity.*

"I'd like to change my request," Delvan said excitedly. "Can you please give me the records for house te Rytta only? And..." Delvan put his hand to his chin for a thoughtful moment, "and can you give me the histories Lady Mithya was reading?"

A sly grin creased the heavily wrinkled face of the librarian. "Ah, I see. The vitality of youth..." he shook his head, still smiling. "The women of one's life can move mountains more than even the magic of your sapphire, can't they? Well, if it gets one reading, who am I to argue? Take a seat, my young Lord, and I will have someone pull those records for you, post-haste."

Delvan thanked him and nodded before walking to an empty table, illuminated in the vibrant orange glow of Amenesol's portrayal in a nearby pane. The librarian's words rang with a truth that he suspected was lost on the elderly man.

Maybe he does *understand my plight,* Delvan thought with a shrug. His tutors had always gone on about history being cyclical, and the man appeared old enough to have lived through a few repetitious eons.

As he sat there in the dusty air, he begrudgingly conceded that maybe—though he'd still contest the point—he should have spent more time studying.

Looks like you're finally getting your way, Master Tunner, he thought, rubbing his knuckles. At least now he had a place to start.

The soft rustles of turning pages and the ever-constant scratching of quills were the only sounds in the main hall—until Delvan let out a loud, exasperated sigh. The sun had sidled to another window, casting green-tinted light upon him as he contemplated his decision to come here, and the major flaw he now saw in his plan.

He had *severely* underestimated the volume of documents that it took to chronicle one's family lineage.

Three books, their spines nearly as thick as Delvan's palm, sat unopened on the table at his left, another weighty tome open before him. Within their enormous heft was the te Rytta bloodline—the family was prolific, even by nobility's standards. Based on what little he'd managed to divulge from the scribed pages thus far, they were likely the largest and most complex house in the western half of the empire.

So much for this being easier with her name... It was obvious now that the old librarian had been right, searching for a house with a first name alone would have been a vain effort. *Not that this is much better.*

He sighed a breath that dragged dust over his tongue as he glanced to his right, where the equally dense tomes which Lady Mithya had requested during her visit mounded. Their topic, fortunately, was something that Delvan was at least somewhat familiar with.

Gods know why she was looking into that, though—

The scuff of slippers on polished stone broke Delvan's concentration. He looked towards the sound's source: the reappearance of the head librarian's bent frame. "Is everything to your satisfaction, my Lord?" he asked in a sharp, but creaking voice.

'Satisfaction' isn't the word that comes to mind. "I have what I need, I think," replied Delvan, giving a weary eye to the pages open before him.

"Mhm, is there something that I or one of the disciples could help you with?"

"I don't know, maybe?" he replied, tossing up his hands. "This house's lineage is the most convoluted thing I've ever seen. There must be a hundred cousins alone that all bear the name, not to mention the direct descendants of just the *legitimate* wives of a few patriarchs... I feel like I'm more in the dark than when I started."

The librarian nodded. "Mhm, yes the te Rytta line is rather infamous in these parts for its complexity. The arguments between sects of the family are rather ancient, each believing it is entitled to this or that. They practically run the entire city and port of Tennefen. I recall one of the disciples, decades ago now it must have been, attempted to create a comprehensive accounting of their family history, to settle the disputes, as it were."

Sounds like torture. "How'd that go?" Delvan asked, wondering if what was piled before him were the results of such tedious labor.

"Hmm? Oh, he was murdered," the Librarian stated.

Delvan's eyes went wide. "*What*? What happened?"

"He claimed that two matriarchs from four generations prior—both bearing the same first name, mind you—had been confused by the respective descendants, and that one's inheritance should have been the port, and the other's the grain mills. Neither one appreciated such prospects, and when he presented his findings before the city council, a mob of te Rytta's from both sides stabbed him to death. Some fifty-seven times, if I recall correctly."

Delvan blinked his dry, reddened eyes, gaping at the old man. "And what did the city council do about this?" he asked, astonished.

"Gods, nothing. They were all te Rytta's themselves, mhm." He nodded his head again, lips pursed, as though that answer covered the breadth of a full explanation.

Delvan shook his head, mouth still gaping. *They don't even know who their own ancestors are, so what can I hope to discover in these gods-damned books?* he thought, disheartened.

"I was hoping to learn more about Lady Mithya in here," he said with a wave of his hand. "You make it sound futile."

"Oh, there very well might be some information to glean, though I understand that roughly fifty percent of te Rytta's possess sapphires. But I would warrant caution with your assumptions, as the family is a prideful one. Wouldn't want you ending up on the wrong side of a blade, now would we?" the crooked man said with a lighthearted laugh.

Delvan pulled half his face into a disingenuous smile, his eyes still wide.

The fact that there was little to learn which could provide him the leverage he sought began to settle in. If he made claims about Mithya, there would be nowhere for him to contest such statements, and if he were presented with the opportunity, the chances of him accidentally slighting some obscure sect of the family became another risk.

Delvan pinched the bridge of his nose, his eyes pressing tightly closed as he thought about his predicament. "Do you know why she was reviewing these?" Delvan asked, gesturing to the stack of books to his right.

"Ah, the last Trethish war," the man said with a knowing nod. "I can't say for certain, my Lord, though I do know that several members of the te Rytta family, Blues included, fought in it."

"On which side?" Delvan asked.

"Pardon?"

"Were they among the traitors that defected to the Trethish side, or among the King's army?"

"I'm not entirely certain, my Lord," the man said with a shake of his white-haired head. "I suppose it was possible that they fought on both. As you will find in those tomes, the records of exactly who and how many defected was either intentionally poorly recorded or expunged from the records at the King's command."

"Mhm," Delvan grunted. He'd been taught roughly the same. The number of sapphires which now resided in Trethefen was a secret closely guarded by the King and Court alike. It was entirely possible that even his father wasn't aware of the exact number, given the shadow of shame the event cast on the throne.

What was she looking for in there? Hidden clues as to her family's involvement? Delvan struggled to consider what her exact motives could be.

"If you're that interested, my Lord, perhaps you could speak with the Lord General. He's quite the authority on the subject," the librarian said.

"Rosethorn fought in the war?"

"Mhm, indeed. He was probably about your age at the time, though it's always hard to know with you Blues. I spoke with him briefly about it once, trying to document a few major battles that occurred. I would not be born for another fifteen years after the war ended, you see, and my father had been a veteran, so I was quite curious."

The general's older than I thought. Even by Blue standards he was incredibly fit for his age, assuming the librarian was correct.

Delvan couldn't say that he was surprised, the general was obviously a combat veteran, and from all accounts an excellent tactician. *One doesn't collect the memorabilia hanging on his walls without a few lifetime's worth of experience.* He recalled several of the items hanging within the general's quarters, his mind wandering to those that he hadn't recognized.

"Are you familiar with the strange dagger he has on the mantle in his office?" Delvan asked.

"I've seen it before, yes," the librarian said, leaning with both hands on his cane. "Taken from an enemy captain in battle, if memory serves."

Delvan scratched his head. "Is that the whole story?" he asked incredulously. "It's just that... it's the *centerpiece* of his collection from what I can tell, and given the man's evident combat experience, I find it strange that a captain's accessory is the trophy he prizes most."

The librarian's lips pulled back into a knowing grin, but his eyes remained somber. "You would be right at that, my young Lord, but it's far more significant than you give it credit for, in this case. Though your ignorance is rather excusable."

"What's that supposed to mean?"

"Given the lack of records, it's not surprise you don't know. The owner of that weapon," the elderly man said, "was a *Blue*."

Delvan blinked, his stomach turning. "One of the traitors?"

"Mhm, yes," he said with a slow nod. "I will let the lord general discuss it further if he wishes, for it's not my place. But suffice to say, it was a defining battle for the man, yes. Lady Mithya asked about the battle as well, after looking through some of the records."

I wonder what her interest was? he thought. *Distant relation, perhaps? Or was it something more?* Delvan leaned back in the chair, his shoulders slumping, knowing he wouldn't get an answer to his question.

Rosethorn's mantlepiece, now at least, made a little more sense to him. The death of a Blue was always difficult to contend with, his previous desire to turn against Ferrand had taken every fiber of will to fight against the instincts derived from their bond in violet blood. The man's death—even after the berating, belittling, and degradation he'd experienced from the knight commander—still hung remorsefully over his head. To actually follow through and hurt another Blue... it chilled him, despite the desert's summer heat.

"What's written on it?" Delvan asked, his voice low and solemn.

"Hmm?" the librarian said, leaning closer.

"The blade," he said, recollecting the strange patterns on it, "it looked to have writing on it."

"Ah, yes. It's been an age since I've laid eyes on it myself, but I imagine it's the aphorism which was the core of the Trethish uprising. Do you not know it?"

"Uhh," drawled Delvan, trying to pull at memories as thin as the crinkled parchment before him.

The elderly man shook his head with a sigh. "It went, 'For the blood of my ancestors.' Derived from some pagan nonsense or another."

Delvan's head tilted to the side, trying to recall the phrase. It seemed familiar, but he couldn't quite place it. *I really should have spent more time paying attention,* he griped. *Maybe I'll ask the lord general about it next time I see him.* He considered the idea for a moment, then thought better of it.

"Also," the elderly man continued, "there is a soldier waiting for you outside, he was rather intent on speaking with you."

His gut turned into a pit, and he immediately wondered if Wellos had wormed something into the general's ear. "Did he say what he wanted?"

"Not specifically, no. But he was rather insistent. He tried to claim access via martial law, but I pointedly reminded him that we are one of the few exemptions under the lord general's explicit orders. He can wait outside, take all the time you need," he said with a wink.

"No," Delvan said, leaning on the table. "I don't think there is much more for me to learn here anyway. You've been a great help, thank you." The thought of facing Wellos or the general right now was a nauseating one, but if he put it off it could have severe repercussions, and he couldn't allow anything to get in the way of trying to help Desnia.

"Best of luck in your... endeavors, my young Lord," the librarian said with a smile before turning and shuffling back towards his desk.

"Thanks." *I'm going to need it,* he thought as he stood to leave.

Knowledge had proven disappointingly insufficient in providing a leash he could tie to Mithya to rein her back from Desnia. He had more than when he started but felt more lost than ever; what he'd thought to be a spring in the desert was no more than a cruel mirage leading him down a path of illusion.

Another day wasted, with what to show for it? He needed to figure out what to do next and waiting passively for responses that he was growing certain would yield nothing wasn't an option.

A lack of prospects caused his heart to begin racing, a cold sweat beading on his skin as familiar pangs shot through his jaw and arm. He was at a loss, and it began to make him simmer in panic as he strode through the library's hall.

He squinted as he stepped though the behemoth wooden doors and back into the blazing sun, his eyes struggling to readjust to the glare. He shielded them as he tried to look around, searching in the canvas of sun-bleached glows for the soldier the librarian had mentioned. A motion to his side and the familiar rattle of a sword and scabbard brought his attention to someone nearby.

A captain, his head shaved and beard peppered, approached. As Delvan's vision cleared, he saw brushed ash on the fringes of his uniform and a worn scabbard with polished hilt at his side.

"Lord Delvan, I presume?" the captain said with a salute.

Delvan nodded, waiting with bated breath to hear what the general—or his petty scribe—had in store for him now.

"Do you mind if we speak somewhere more private?" the captain asked, jerking his head towards a nearby alley.

He raised an eyebrow, his nervousness changing to curiosity, and followed the man down the steps and to the shaded side-street.

"My Lord," the captain said, taking a cautious look up and down the street, "I've been sent to make a request of you."

Waiting, Delvan remained silent, his heart pounding harder once more. "Well?" he eventually asked, the captain unbearably quiet.

The gruff man let out a sigh. "A great deal of trust has been placed in you, my Lord, and I suppose that I am just going to have to do the same... I should warn you now that my request is in direct conflict with your orders, Sire."

Confusion tweaked Delvan's face. "Explain."

"I'm here on behalf of the Witness," the captain said. "He wishes to speak with you."

He narrowed his eyes. "The who?"

The captain seemed genuinely surprised. "*The* Witness, Sire. As in Brother Nerio."

Delvan pulled his head back in surprise, relief releasing the tension in his shoulders. *Nerio? Doesn't he know half the army is looking for him?* "Why?" he quickly asked. "Does he want to turn himself in?" The thought knotted his muscles tightly back together. The general was extremely displeased with the priest's actions—one of main reasons that Delvan had *not* been actively seeking him out. *And how the hell does this captain seem to know him? By this strange title of all things.*

"No, my Lord," the captain said. "He's asking for your aid."

I don't have time for this. "Look," he said, running his hand through his hair, "I don't know why you haven't arrested him, let alone why you're helping him, but Nerio isn't my biggest concern right now. I like the guy well enough, but if he knows what's good for him, he'll lie low for a while. These damn speaks that he's doing have the general furious at him, as I'm sure you're aware. Tell him I can't help him right now, I need to help Des first. He'll understand."

"Sire," the captain said firmly as Delvan turned to leave, "people's lives are at stake here. Please, it won't take but an hour or two of your time."

Delvan groaned as he tilted his head toward the sky. *Of course there are,* he thought. *It's better than sulking while I think of what to do next, I suppose.* He tossed his arms to the side, "Fine, lead the way then."

"Thank you, my Lord," the captain said with a nod. "You won't regret this." He turned and began walking towards the razed district, Delvan trudging behind him.

I somehow doubt that.

CHAPTER TWENTY

*With him absconding from the city his plans were easily foiled. The
unwitting assistance from parties unaware of our true intentions
was involved, I hate to say, by no design of my own. I attempted to
manipulate their future meddling to my advantage, but I fear I only
raised further suspicions.*

Tightly packed gravel crunched beneath the iron shoes of horses. The
caravan's carts groaned as their wheels traversed the worn, mountain
passage.

The pervasive, pale stone of the White Mountains deceived the eyes. From
a distance, one could believe that the snow-capped summits tumbled their
chilled, icy breath down over the huge, sheer faces of the surrounding slopes.
Yet the air was little more than brisk, and water flowed freely down through
crevasses and nooks in the weathered stone.

Kolden looked to his left, where a mere few yards from his horse the trail
plunged from a precipice, a slope of scree leading down to the valley below
at an impossibly steep angle. To his right, Orne sat rigid on his horse, his
knuckles white as he gripped the reins and steered the beast to the opposite
edge of the road, the soaring backdrop of rock which rose to obstruct the
horizon comfortably within his reach.

Eyebrow cocking at the sight, he scrutinized his brother's odd posture.
What's gotten into him? he wondered. He twisted his head back to his left, then
spun it again to Orne. A realization dawned upon him, and he burst into an
uncontrollable, spine-bending laughter, drawing gazes and turning heads of
the other caravan members and horses alike.

"What's so funny?" Orne asked with a scowl.

His laughter echoed from the valley's trickling river to the surrounding
spires of stone. He tried to take a breath and explain, but he was soon gasping

and wheezing between fits, his horse wavering and tucking its ears back while he listed from one side of the saddle to the other. "You're," he managed to rasp out, "afraid of heights! The mighty Orne, terrified. Of a *hill*!" His back arched with another uproarious outburst, his watering eyes streaming tears down his face.

Orne's lips tugged further down as he glowered at his brother. "Fuck you," he spat, trying to look menacing. Kolden knew him well enough to recognize the fear in his eyes, a confirmation that made him once again lose his breath and grab his aching sides.

"Oh," said Kolden, gasping for air, "oh this is great. I'm going to have to send Del a carrier when we get to the fort. He's going to love this."

"Don't you dare!" cursed Orne, his pale face now tinged with red. "And it's not just a fucking 'hill,' dumbass. It must be three-hundred feet down to the basin. I didn't realize the mountains here were so... tall."

"How's it feel to be so tiny?" Kolden asked, wiping his eyes.

"I don't know, you're the expert. Asshole," Orne retorted, his jaw muscles flexing tightly.

Kolden rolled his eyes. "It's perfect safe, you giant baby. This road is cut right from the rock. Tell him, Phrenwa," he said, calling to the merchant riding a few yards ahead of them.

The leader of their accompanying traders turned his head, long curled hair bobbing around brown skin that contrasted the salt-colored surroundings. "This road has seen over a thousand winters, Lord Orne, and carried many armies. Our caravan is nothing to this one."

"See," said Kolden with a wave of his hands. "Nothing to worry about."

"I wouldn't say that, my Lord," replied Phrenwa in his heavy accent. "Stones have been known to tumble from the slopes above, killing men and animal alike. I lost a horse on this very path last month."

"That would've been nice to know!" shouted Orne, who was now craning his head to stare up the slope to his right. He shifted his horse slightly to the left, eyes darting to both the road's edges with thin-lipped concern.

Kolden watched as his brother slumped in the saddle, his visage a storm of concern and scorn. He considered mocking him once more, but he found his own eyes drifting up the slope that seemed to pierce the sky in the unfathomable distance. "Well," he said, a shaky nervousness catching his voice, "at least we're out of the desert."

"Wouldn't say this is much better," grumbled Orne. Kolden was hesitant to reply.

He'd thought the heat was oppressive in Brethefen, but the brutality of the late summer sun was unmatched out in the open dunes. The brazen rays burned skin like boiling oil and cooked his muscles to the bone. More than one member of the supply train had slid from a saddle, succumbing to the omnipresent heat. The scarce oases had determined the groups meandering route, carefully rationed water barely lasting between each.

Kolden had stared at the spikes of rock from the mounds of fine, scorching sand and exposed rock, a longing pulling at him like a leash. The pinnacles pierced the earth and tore into the sky like the fangs of a bear through flesh, outcroppings and crags jutting out at wild, pointed angles. The longer his mind beheld the sight, the more he craved their shade's respite like a starved man salivating before a bakery.

The foreboding peaks had become increasingly gargantuan with the setting of every sun. The relief of finally reaching their bases had been palpable, their shadows a reprieve that escaped words. Now that he was here, however, he wondered if maybe Orne was right.

Not that I could ever admit that to him. Bastard would never let it go.

"How much farther?" Orne called out, the tension in his voice cutting like a sword.

"We arrive before nightfall," Phrenwa replied.

"About time," Orne muttered under his breath.

"Agreed," said Kolden, "two weeks in the damned desert's left sand in every fucking crease and hole. Pretty sure the skin on my ass has rubbed off," he said, adjusting the fabric of his uniform. "And I'd thought the journey from Drunt had been bad."

Orne's face turned sour. "Still can't believe after everything I did, she managed to get us sent back into the middle of fucking nowhere."

"You're surprised, really?" Kolden asked. "Only thing that shocked me was how long it took. Almost managed to get comfortable. Almost. And what do you mean, 'Everything I did?' I was there too, remember?"

"Yeah, locked up in a cage while Del and I did all the fighting. I remember."

"Oh, fuck off." His brother's mood was foul, and like a plague he felt the need to infect those around him with his pestilence. *He knows damn well what happened, he's just lashing out 'cause it makes him feel better. Or so he thinks. Idiot.* Kolden just shook his head with a sneer—it was easier to not play into the petulant games.

The next few hours passed with little more than the sound of ungreased wheels and the occasional chatter of the other members of their party. The sun's glare off the grainy stone was akin to a blanket of snow reflecting the midday winter's sun. Kolden was forced to squint as his eyes watered from the bright sheen, taking care to watch the road's edge and steer his horse clear.

They eventually came upon a section of road that swelled into a clearing, the charring of cookfires and animal refuse on the stone field evidence of the area's use as a waypoint. A stream of icy water flowed from the escarpment adjacent and continued around the encampment's ragged edge.

With practiced form, the caravan came to a halt. The merchants began refilling waterskins and preparing their midday meal with a routine that was little more than rote motions.

Hardly a word spoken among them, as usual, Kolden thought.

Several members of their company were as conversational as an ox, communicating with little more than grunts and nods for the length of the trip. Kolden had tried speaking to several but found them either lacking understanding or avoiding him with an obstinacy that would rival Orne's. Whether they were hiding something, nervous, or paid to remain quiet, he couldn't say, and after a week of trying, he'd given up on discovering whatever secrets they were safeguarding.

And then there was that itching feeling that he recognized them from somewhere...

"Hey, Phrenwa," Kolden asked. The man was one of the few willing to have regular, semi-intelligent conversations with him. "How often do you all come up here?"

The middle-aged man shrugged his shoulders while he poured water for his horse. "Once every month or so. We bring supplies from Brethefen, then circle back. This one is our primary trade route. It might not make us wealthy, but it's steady work."

A merchant who doesn't want to get rich, never thought I'd see the day, thought Kolden. *Doesn't explain all the silks you and the others wear, though.* "Huh, that's... interesting." He decided it was best not to press the issue until there was a greater distance between him and a fatal cliff edge. "Anything we should know about this place they're sending us to?"

The man shrugged again, this time his shoulders drawing up unevenly as his face twisted with a squirm. "It is," he said, hesitating to choose words, "less than it once was."

"What's that supposed to mean?" Kolden asked. He saw his brother turn his head to listen from nearby.

"There are legends about it and its kin. Black Bastions, they were called in your tongue. But the inanite has turned gray, as has the vein it sits atop. Some say..." the man drifted off, shaking his head after a moment. "I mean no offense with this one, my Lord, but what crime did you commit to be assigned to this place?"

Kolden's head jerked back. "Crime? We didn't commit any crime." *Aside from being born to an overprotective matriarch.* "What the hell makes you think that?"

"I'm sorry," Phrenwa continued, Orne now listening intently from a few feet away. "Most of the soldiers here, they are ones that do not have, how do you say, the best of reputations. I always understood this station to be one of punishment and assumed... Forgive my ignorance, my Lord."

Both Orne and Kolden's visages turned dour, the fetid words wrinkling their eyes and noses. His brother let out a loud huff and trudged off to oil his weapons for the second time that day while Kolden stood in disbelief. *Oh, we're being punished,* he thought, *we disobeyed her orders, and in her own ignorance, mother has seen it fit to throw us in with the dredges of the army in a vain attempt to keep us 'safe.' Wonderful.*

"Thanks for the insight," he grumbled before walking to his brother and sitting on the gravel-dusted stone beside him. Orne's whetstone slid along the edge of a darksteel blade. A saddlebag of weapons—including his precious halberd—rested on the ground before him. The gritty sound was smooth and unwavering, until it flared with a snap of the wrist as Orne swept it from the tip of the broadsword. The time between strokes was filled with the sound of Orne's grinding teeth.

"This is bullshit," his brother spat. "Sending us to a station full of fucking degenerates. She's gone too far this time."

"Mhm. At least you're getting a command—"

"Of criminals!" His brother's face turned crimson, spit landing in his beard with each over-punctuated word. "Rosethorn better follow through and get us out of here after a few months or I swear, I'll march back to Brethefen by myself. Fuck whatever father says."

Kolden's response was an extended silence. He wanted to remain optimistic, to not allow Orne's usual over-reaction to dampen his spirits. *But he's got a point. The Court themselves confirmed father's order to send us here.* "Well," he finally said, "Del's father is on the Court, maybe he can—"

"Gods, do you ever listen to *anyone?*" Orne asked derisively. "Del's relationship with his father is worse than our own. For all we know his father could make us stay here *longer* if Del sends him a letter, for no other reason than to spite him."

He rolled his eyes and let out a long sigh. "Do you have any suggestions?"

"I don't know!" Orne shouted, tossing the sword and stone into the pile of weapons before him then throwing up his hands. "I need time to fucking think about it, alright?"

Yes, give orders and get everyone else to figure it out, sounds about right, he thought bitterly. He clamped his mouth closed, however, knowing full well that his brother's fury would continue to build for as long as they remained on the topic, regardless of what he said.

"I think you brought enough for the whole fortress," Kolden said with a nod to the pile of weapons, changing the subject. "What are there, another four bags over the pack horse with the rest of your arsenal?"

"Three," Orne grunted. "And what was I supposed to do, leave them? Also, what are you complaining about? You're the one who made most of them."

"I'm not—" Kolden pressed his lips together, fighting back the argumentative words that would shake Orne's rage loose like an avalanche. "Whatever. And you can do what you want with them. I just like making the things."

Orne shook his head, his temper finally being cooled by his perplexity. "You're fucking weird, you know that?"

"We're from the same stock, idiot. You think that being a hulking giant is *normal?*"

"You're just mad because I got all the brawn."

"And you're just mad because I got all the brains."

"Oh, fuck you—"

A sharp cry from the camp's rim snapped both their heads to attention. Curses in a foreign tongue pealed from their normally mute companions as the band of merchants clamored.

The scatter of rubble from the looming slope to their side drew Kolden's gaze upward, and his eyes bulged as he caught sight of the commotion's cause.

A boulder the size of his horse's torso had dislodged from the mountainside and now pressed against a leaning cart. *Great,* he thought, *now we're going to be delayed* and *have to blow out our backs moving that gods-damned—*

Kolden stopped his movement towards the commotion as the three men trying to shove the boulder away were joined by Phrenwa. Much to his surprise, the stone's tonnage shifted and fell harmlessly to the side with a resounding *thump,* leaving the cart twisted, but functional.

"Good," said Orne, "now we can get to lunch."

Kolden stared curiously at the merchants. *That was... impressive,* he thought. He wasn't sure if Orne would've been able to help to the extent their caravan's leader had. *Must have been on a weird angle,* he considered as he also secretly wondering where the food was.

The sun had descended behind the peaks ahead of them an hour ago. As it slowly fell to the distant, barricaded horizon, the sky became awash with the color of burning coals, casting a red glow that gently suffused the valley around them as it reflected off the soft white stone. They had been plunged like iron into the cool fires of the gods' forge, and Kolden wondered what weapon the lord of death planned to create, prompting him to search the surroundings for owls.

"The valley's called the Bloody Scar," said Phrenwa beside him, noticing as Kolden craned his neck to the left, staring over the road's edge to the distant gulch floor.

As if this place wasn't eerie enough. "Seems fitting," Kolden replied.

"It's seen countless battles, that narrow strip. This one was once some of the most contested land on the continent."

"And now?" Kolden asked. He saw his brother shift his attention to the conversation.

A tiny smile crept onto the merchant's face. "Now? Little more than a stream that claims the title earned by its raging past."

"What's that supposed to mean?" Orne asked.

"The passage was blocked, my Lord," said Phrenwa over his shoulder, "a hundred winters ago. The Trethish dammed it west of here, creating a lake where the road once stood."

"That seems fucking stupid," Orne grunted.

Phrenwa shrugged. "Perhaps, but the next nearest mountain pass is three-hundred miles to the north. They ended the war without further blood-shed."

Orne grunted but didn't speak further.

"If the pass is closed," Kolden said, his brow knitted tightly in thought, "then why is the general worried about enemies sneaking past? Why even have it manned at all?"

The merchant let out a soft chuckle. "Good questions. Ones you can ask the keep's occupiers yourself. We're here," he said jutting his chin forward as they crested over a knoll.

A fortress thrust out and up from the mountain's slope, colossal and rugged upon its perch. The member of the infamous Black Bastions domineered the craggy landscape, its sharp corners like blades, the spires along its walls angular and steeper than the narrowest peak. The stones constructing its outer walls were to Kolden as he was to a pebble, their incredible mass supporting the towering fortifications rimmed with parapets and outcroppings sized for siege weaponry of the grandest scale.

A stepped wall extended from its exterior down into the distant valley, where a fortified bridge guarded the babbling creek that had replaced the once-mighty river. Kolden suspected that even from there, the imposing fortress would strike terror into those who once dared assault the pass.

The ballistas, stone-throwers, and other machinery that once line the walls must have reaped death upon any force bold enough to clash against the walls below. Devastation would have rained in sharpened arrows and a hail of stone, shattering even the most hardened of armies. *No wonder the Trethish decided to block the pass, they must have gotten slaughtered down there.*

As they approached, Kolden noticed the ground beneath their feet—as well as the area surrounding the bastion—turn from the milky white of muted inanite into the fading black of the castle's walls. The monstrous keep stood in the center of a great patch of inanite, now slowly muting with time, standing out like an eye blackened against the white skin of the range it guarded.

Kolden doubted it affected its efficacy.

As they reached the gate of rusted, woven iron, voices called out from the interior courtyard, and the great mass of metal began crawling upward with the squeals of unoiled gears and the clatter of corroded chains. It locked into place, and Kolden spurred his horse as he passed below it, keeping a cautious eye on the hanging, barbed blockade.

The courtyard was unkempt. Weeds clung to crevasses in the stonework, refuse piled high in the corners, and the scatterings of gravel covered the once-perfect flagstones. A dozen or so soldiers were gathered, awaiting their arrival, and began to unload the caravan's wares as the carts came to a halt and the merchants started unhitching their steeds.

Kolden hopped down from his mount and handed the reins to a nearby sta-blemaster before joining his brother's side. The pair stood amidst the churning labor of the keep's guards, eyes grazing the landscape as they searched for a commanding officer. A few soldiers parted before them, and between the wares-laden men sauntered a man with a frayed captain's patch stitched to his shoulder.

He tried to suppress his incredulity as their new commander stopped a few feet from them. The captain's uniform was spotted with stains, the fabric stretching to fit the man's bulbous girth. His chin rolled down to the base of his neck under a thin, wiry beard of grey which twisted in whatever direction it pleased. Bags hung low and dark beneath drooping eyes that discriminately scanned them from head to toe.

"So," the captain said, his rancid breath choking Kolden, "you two must be the ones Rosethorn wrote to us about."

"Yes, sir. I'm Kolden, he's Orne."

"Great, didn't ask. I'm Captain Mathin. We had a couple rooms made up for yer lordships. Hope you wasn't expecting anything fancy though. Lieutenant Villera will get you your assignments, he manages the day-to-day orders and all that." The captain's low-lidded gaze drifted to two soldiers nearby, unloading a barrel that dropped heavily onto the ground. "Hey!" he snapped. "Watch what the fuck yer doing!"

The soldiers both looked up with wide eyes. "Yes, boss. Sorry 'bout that," one of them said.

The captain shook his head and turned to leave without so much as a dismissal.

"Sir!" said Orne. "We were given orders before we left."

The captain twisted his rotund body back towards them. "I never saw no orders. Villera's my second in command, you'd be wise to just do as he—"

"Sir," Orne cut in. Kolden rubbed his brow, trying to cover his rolling eyes. His brother tended to agitate commanding officers, and it seemed like he was attempting to set a record for the shortest time to receive disciplinary action. "The orders are from the general himself," his brother said, pulling a writ from his pouch and shoving it towards the captain. "And as lieutenants, we don't take orders from peers. Only the general or you, sir. Assuming they don't override Rosethorn's, that is."

The captain took the writ from Orne's extended hand as quickly as his enormous form would allow, opening it with aggressive jerks and crinkles. A tall, pudgy man that Kolden assumed to be Villera—based on the lieutenant's patch on his shoulder—walked up to the captain, looking at the writ from over his shoulder.

The captain looked up from the document and handed it back to his lieutenant, his eyes held onto Orne. "Command of yer own squads? Great, the boys are gonna love that. Not sure what in the name of the gods the general thinks we need more squad leaders here for, not but a hundred of us here. But Villera will pull some of the lads for you, won't you lieutenant?"

"Aye, sir," Villera said with a cynical grin.

"Sir," stated Orne, "we—"

"Listen to Villera," the captain rasped, "that's my order." Orne shut his mouth and glowered at the lieutenant's baggy eyes. "And you," he said, turning to Kolden. "Says here you're a smith and yer to take over the keep's forge."

"Doesn't look like he's big enough to lift a hammer," said Villera with derision.

"Maybe," Kolden retorted, "if you got me one the size of your brain, I'd be able to swing it easier."

The lieutenant's face twisted in confusion for a moment before his brow slanted as he became irate. "Listen here, you little shit, I—"

He stepped forward, hand on the hilt of his sword, but cut off as Orne took a step towards him, half drawing his own side sword from its scabbard. The two glared at each other, Orne's visage fixed with anger and confidence, while Villera's flickered with doubt, despite his blistering rage.

"That's enough, boys," the captain croaked. Orne held fast, waiting until Villera took a reluctant step back before he slid his darksteel blade back into its sheath. The captain spared the two a short glance before turning back to Kolden. "We need hinges for the doors. Tools are in short supply as well; hammers, chisels, and the like. Think you can manage that?"

As well as you can manage a meat pie, you fucking lard, he thought with a sneer. "Probably. Any of your smiths members of the guild?"

"Only have the one right now. He *was* an apprentice, but he, let us say, didn't get a chance to finish. Mostly just fails at making shoes for the horses. Forge is across the courtyard, I'm sure someone as smart as yerself can find it."

Great, a washout, Kolden thought, ignoring the jab. *At least I don't have to worry about someone reporting me for making darksteel.* There was always the risk of the guild discovering someone outside of their senior members knowing the secrets of creating the rare metal. But, given the isolation he now found himself in, he guessed his hidden skill wasn't at great risk. *Though I would rather be working with cadentite, not that I'm going to find any now that I'm in this shithole.* He was going to need to make attempts to remedy that.

He felt his gut wrench in disappointment. Cadentite was new, misunderstood, and, in his mind, the key to whatever mystical powers the High Realm mages possessed. The image of his dagger glowing with the soul of that boy still plagued his mind with questions. *Not to mention that sword...*

"Right," said Captain Mathin, "now that we got that out of the way, I'll be retiring. The boys can get you shown to your rooms. Might be some scraps from supper in the mess, but don't expect much." He turned towards the two men still struggling with the barrel. "I expect that brought up double time, you hear?" They gave a succession of nods before the man waddled away through the courtyard and into a door in the distance.

The sky's red ambiance faded as the sun made way for the moon, and the courtyard was plunged into shadow. Guards began lighting torches and braziers, throwing flickering light across grey stone.

Lieutenant Villera's sly grin returned when he said, "You boys are gonna help the others carry this up to the mess, ya hear?"

"Go fuck yourself," Orne replied. The soldiers around them froze in place, the area becoming quiet as Orne stared the man down. "If you think we're taking orders from you, then you're sorely fucking mistaken. Now, be a good little lap dog and tell my new squads that I want them in this courtyard tomorrow an hour after the first bell. I've heard this keep has been lax in its duties of late."

The lieutenant sneered, hand once more falling to the hilt of his sword. "*You* don't give the orders here, you underst—"

"Listen, dumbass," interjected Kolden, "clearly you don't have this through your thick skull, but if you keep giving us shit, you'll have not one, but two generals demoting and court martialing you as fast as a pigeon can fly. And you'll probably get assigned to a place that makes this one seem like luxury. So, if you're done with the dick-measuring, maybe show us to our rooms and give it a rest."

The man flared his teeth, his face flush as he glared at them from under a low brow. He spat on the ground at their feet. "Find it your-fucking-selves." With his curse he turned and trotted towards the door the captain had vanished through, leaving them alone with the quiet group of caravanners and soldiers—only now resuming their labor, avoiding eye contact with the brothers all the while.

"That went well," said Kolden.

"We've had worse," replied Orne.

"Not by much."

"Fuck 'em. I don't intend to be here long."

Kolden sighed. *We never do.*

Chapter
Twenty-One

Despite this unwanted attention, and with our regular information brokers fleeing south, I have managed to procure sources of the highest caste, as well as those that kneel in their shadow.

The surroundings quickly turned from clean, polished cityscapes to charred, ash-stained ruins, the eerie silence of the city's black scar enveloping Delvan in its disquiet. The scorched, black marks upon stone, brick, and timber filled the air with more than just their drab, dark tones; a grimness hung amongst them, a weight of souls that bore heavily down upon those in its midst. They had been claimed by the impartial, ravaging fire, and their ghastly cries felt like familiar nails being dug into Delvan's chest by a too-tight grip.

"How much farther?" Delvan choked, his eyes flitting across the mural of destruction.

"Another half mile or so, sir. Shouldn't take long," the captain said over his shoulder from a few paces ahead of Delvan.

The sooner I get out of here, the better, he thought. It had not taken him long to regret following his enigmatic guide. Why they were trekking this deeply into the metropolis' wounded heart was one of the many questions that Delvan had—his curiosity one of the main reasons he hadn't turned back from this hellscape conjured from his darkest nightmares.

"Hey," Delvan called out, "what you said before, calling Nerio the 'Witness,' what did you mean by that?"

The captain glanced back but continued his march. "It's the title that the people have assigned to him, my Lord. I'm surprised you haven't heard."

"What surprises me, *Captain*, is that Lord General Rosethorn has a standing order to arrest Nerio on sight. Yet you clearly have been communicating with him for some time and have disobeyed that order. Why?"

The burly man stopped and spun to face Delvan, his hand on the hilt of his sword—whether out of habit or intention, he couldn't say. The man glared at him with tight lips, as if trying to judge his soul. "Is that what you intend? Why you've agreed to come?" asked the captain. "To arrest the Witness?"

From its place at his hip, Delvan turned his palm toward the man before him, his other on the pommel of his own sword. The deadened air seemed to suspend their quiet suspicions of one another, the silence extensive and taut with mistrust. *What* am *I going to do?* he wondered. *I have orders, but does Nerio deserve the general's punishment? Probably no more than Des does, less even...*

"No," Delvan finally said. "I'm not going to arrest him. He... he helped when the odds were against us, and if not for him we'd never have been able to stop the invasion. I owe him this much."

They both visibly relaxed, postures loosening as they finished studying each other, coming to a quiet agreement. The captain turned and once again began his rigorous pace, stepping over the charred detritus that littered the once orderly street.

Delvan followed, still burning with questions. "I'm still confused, Captain," he said genuinely, "you know why I'm here, but I can't understand why you'd risk everything to protect Nerio. Who is he to you?"

The man was silent for a time, until he eventually turned his head and spoke a single word over his shoulder, "Light."

His face wrinkled. "What's that supposed to mean?"

"This is a dark time, my Lord," the captain said, facing forward, "many of us have lost everything, feeling adrift. He's a beacon and his story of what happened to you and the others reminds us that the gods still care, and guide us to their light. You should stay for one of his speaks."

"I'm quite familiar with what happened that night," Delvan muttered, flashes of Ferrand and Desnia's lifeless bodies scrolling through his mind. "I don't need to hear one of his retellings."

"It's not about that, my Lord," commented the captain. "It's about those who attend and letting them see the gods' conduit themselves. They could use that right now."

Delvan halted mid-stride. "What did you just call me?" he asked, recognizing the term. *The whispers outside of the guild... What has Nerio been saying?*

The captain stopped and half-turned towards Delvan. "The gods' conduit, my Lord. Surely you must know. They did act through you, after all."

They what? Delvan was baffled, failing to comprehend what the man was talking about. "Enlighten me."

The captain's expression mimicked his own. "Is this a test, Sire?"

"No, I just... I'm curious what Nerio is saying, exactly."

The man's expression remained incredulous, but he responded, "Through you the Messiah was resurrected, a blessing sent by the gods as thanks for delivering the city and their domain from the foreign invaders."

Delvan's eyes squeezed shut, a sharp breath pulling through his nose as his fists clenched. *Gods-damn it, Nerio. What have you been telling these people?* The priest was obviously ignorant to Delvan's newfound abilities and was now spreading the misinformation as if scripture. *I admittedly know little more than he does,* he griped. "That's—" he started, clamping his mouth closed. Correcting the captain would get him nowhere, he would need to go to the source. "Lead on," he finally said with a wave.

The captain nodded and fell back into a hurried pace, but this time Delvan was on his heels. He and Nerio had much to discuss.

The camp was bleak and nearly destitute, reminding Delvan of the slums in the Lower Valley. Haphazardly erected tents lined the edges of the courtyard, and through the nearby passages of the once-magnificent estate he could see the huddled forms of gaunt bodies, their clothing bending sharply over boney frames and draping the floor beneath them. The coughs and moans which floated uneasily through the air brought back memories of the caravan attack's aftermath not long ago, the wounded and dying cursing those around them with the songs of their pain.

Delvan's nose wrinkled at the smell of blackened flesh, pressing his hand to his sleeve as he continued to trail behind his guide. "Why does it smell like a battlefield, Captain?"

"Many of the wounded from the clash at the guild came here, my Lord," the man replied solemnly. "We did what we could, but resources are difficult to come by. Most medical supplies have been allocated for the army due to martial law and rising prices."

He winced, remembering all too clearly the onslaught of unarmed civilians falling upon rows of pikes like martyrs into a predator's fangs, futilely attempting to choke it to death. *I hope they haven't brought me here to heal these people...* Without cadentite it would be impossible, and were they able to provide it, he wasn't certain he could control the gift—making the turning in his stomach even more turbulent.

He refrained from asking additional questions as he felt sunken eyes fall upon him. Any not distracted by the burden of daily chores and duties caught sight of him and hooked their gaze into his heart. He managed to pull the attention of some of the wounded's caretakers as well, their eyes glistening with pitiful hope and awe, locked upon him with mystified expressions. Delvan wanted to squirm, to sprint through the courtyard and escape the oppressive attention.

He increased his pace, thankful to the captain for doing the same. As they made their way through the courtyard, the captain motioned to one of the nearby soldiers—the number of which alarmed him—and the passage they walked through was quickly blocked, preventing the small mass of people that had been hesitantly trailing them from following suit. He glanced over his shoulder, seeing the whites of eyes hidden deeply in skeletal faces bobbing over the guard's shoulders in an exhausted effort to catch another glimpse.

They wove through a maze of halls, the ceiling open to the sky and the wooden roof's remains brushed from the floor. Eventually they entered a small room, cramped by two motionless figures laying on the ground, the scrawny frame of a young, short-haired priest kneeling above one, dabbing their face with a wet cloth.

"Witness," the captain said, "I have our visitor."

Nerio turned his head, his eyes going wide and a smile coming to his face. "Lord Delvan!" he said. "It's a pleasure to see you again, thank you for coming. Captain Gernbard, would you mind if I spoke to Lord Delvan privately?"

Gernbard gave a stiff nod, then a short, but cautious glance at Delvan before turning and leaving. He suspected the soldier wouldn't travel far.

"Forgive my rudeness," Nerio said, still kneeling, "but these men have both succumb to fever, and require constant attention. I'm also afraid that we have run out of tea, though I could ask Gernbard to have someone fetch some water for you."

"I appreciate the hospitality, but I'm fine, thank you," said Delvan. Nerio's lack of etiquette was the least of his concerns. "What is this place?" he asked.

"We offer sanctuary. Treat those who cannot find aid elsewhere. House who we can, though what we can offer right now is little more than pieces of patched, salvaged canvas. And it serves as a place to spread the gods' will."

"Yeah, about that last part," Delvan said, the stain of those starved eyes saturating him still. "Do you mind telling me why Captain Gernbard—not to mention random people in the street—called me 'the Conduit?' And what's with him calling you 'the Witness?'"

Nerio turned his face to him, an earnest expression upon it. "Because that's what you are. The gods channeled their power through you, and Strigifious's owl returned Desnia to us as a result. As to my title..." His voice drifted off, a resigned expression on his face. "It is the one that has been chosen for me, willed by the people despite my... reluctance."

Delvan rubbed his temples, taking a deep breath as he processed the ridiculousness of what he was hearing. "Nerio, that's not... What I did wasn't an act of the gods, alright? I may not have a deep understanding of it, but I know that much. I didn't know it then, but cadentite unlocks, I don't know, *something* between me and my sapphire. It allows me to heal, I guess..." He let out an exasperated sigh, cursing his own ignorance. *Gods, I wish I could talk to Des more about this, she was the only person who seemed to know anything.*

Nerio continued treating the two men on the floor, unfazed by Delvan's words. "Was it not Almedia who delivered the sapphires?" Nerio stated. "After Amenesol gave part of his heart to the King, Almedia delivered pieces of the sky down to those worthy of its bearing, thus creating the King's loyal legion: his knights, his Blues."

I didn't come here to listen to scripture. "Nerio," Delvan said, his voice becoming harsh as his annoyance stirred, "you saw the same thing as me that night. One of those mages used at least four *different* gifts, which should be *impossible*. Not to mention the powers I've never seen and can't explain.

"Blues get *one* gift. One. Or... well, maybe two, I guess..." he stumbled over his own words, the questions that had hung over him like a cloud these past days muddling everything he thought he knew.

"It sounds to me," Nerio said in his level tone, "that the gods chose to reveal this hidden power to you at a time that served their will."

"That's just coincidence," he said. His faith was on rocky ground, his steps unsteady as he tried to walk a path of understanding. "I've rarely seen cadentite, let alone been around *that* much of it."

Nerio shook his head. "Where you see coincidence, Lord Delvan, I see the posturing of gods. We were a group brought together with a purpose, for without any one of us, Jer... the principle would have succeeded."

On that, you and Des would agree. He wondered if she'd ever shared her plans to seek this "imprisoned god" with the young devotee. *Given everything he's done here, I'm disinclined to think so. Can't imagine he'd take it well.*

"Whatever your reasoning, it needs to stop, Nerio," Delvan said, his hand cutting through the air. "I heard the captain call Des 'the Messiah!' Do you not remember what she said about worshipping her? Based on the time I've spent with her, she's going to be furious! You know her better than me, how do you think she's going to react to the piety coming her way?"

Nerio froze, his gaze distant, eyes growing incrementally wider. He shook his head and went back to treating the men before him. "She... won't be pleased, I know. But I hope that she will come to understand that this is bigger than her wants. These people need to know that the gods have—"

"Yes, 'willed it,' as you've said," interrupted Delvan, burying his forehead in his hand.

"Perhaps we could get her opinion on it," said Nerio hesitantly, "were you able to secure her release."

Delvan narrowed his eyes, wondering if the words had been accusatory or a plea. Nerio was diverting his eyes, a pup scared of its master's scolding, waiting for punishment. Delvan slumped his shoulders. "I've tried, Nerio. The general is convinced that she holds the secrets to the groups Ferrand and Jerdine were part of, and unfortunately, he's right. He wants to know everything she does, and to have her read Jerdine's journals on top of it. Not that that's going to happen any time soon..."

"What do you mean?"

"The journals have vanished. Stolen from the barracks, somehow," Delvan said, exasperated. He looked to Nerio, brow furrowing, "You wouldn't happen to know anything about that, would you?"

The priest shook his head before his gaze became distant again. "I have no desire to touch anything that once belonged to that... man." There was more disdain in the words than he'd ever heard from the timid priest, fueling a curiosity he decided to smother. *Best to let it lie.*

"However," continued Nerio, putting his hands on his legs and hanging his head low, "If they'd be willing to release Desnia in exchange, I... I could turn myself in. Tell them what little she told—"

"Stop," Delvan cut in. "He's not going to release her, Nerio. Not in exchange anyway. He would have you in a room with that gods-damned Truthsayer making sure your answers align." *And likely forcing Des to endure even more of Mithya's gift.* "It would just make for more problems, trust me."

"A Truthsayer?" asked Nerio. "I didn't realize there were any in the city."

"There weren't," he grumbled. "This one came at Rosethorn's summons. And there's something about her. I've been trying to find out more but so far it's been mostly wasted time."

"You do not trust her," said Nerio. "Strange for Blues, is it not?"

Not nearly as much as I once believed... "The Court's become involved, which means my father. *Him* I don't trust. And because of that they won't let me just talk to Des and get the answers they want. I'm worried about—" Delvan stopped himself. He didn't think that his suspicions, correct or not, should be shared, lest Nerio have more to preach about. He let out another sigh as he leaned against the blackened stone door frame. "I don't even know where they're keeping her."

"The Asylum," Nerio stated.

Delvan's head snapped straight as he looked to Nerio, eyes wide with shock. "You know where she is?! How?"

"Some of the attendees of my speaks," said Nerio, toiling away with helping the febrile men, "are Hands—or are related to them—and are assigned work there."

Delvan's mind spun. Not knowing Desnia's location had kept the possibility of extreme measures from his mind, unable to act upon them. Now that he knew, the options weighed more heavily than he would've expected. He wasn't willing to go that far, was he? "Have you... done anything about that?" he asked, his voice tense with anticipation.

Nerio nodded. "We have gotten her a note, stating that we are trying to petition for her release."

"So, you're *not* trying to break her out?" Delvan felt a stab of disappointment.

"I would not see her become a fugitive. This life is... challenging."

He blinked, his jaw going slack. *I thought he knew Des?* "You do realize she's been a fugitive since she fled Calentine? I think she'd manage."

"I do, Lord Delvan, but I still see it as a last resort."

He shook his head. Nerio couldn't possibly be this naïve, could he? "Please don't tell me this is why you brought me here? The general has already told me he has no intention of releasing Des soon; despite the slew of petitions I sent his way." *And any more are probably going to be 'lost' by Wellos...*

"It was not, though I admit I hoped that you'd be able to help. No, I..." Nerio strained to force the words out, his body tense. "I need to ask you a different favor."

After a extended moment of silence, Delvan said, "Being?"

Nerio stopped what he was doing, putting his hands back onto his legs. "I'm sure you saw the people outside. They come here—come to me—because I give them words that heal their souls, fulfilling the duty laid before me. Words, however, do not fill stomachs. Nor do they protect from the sun's heat or the rains that come at summer's end. I want, *need*, to provide for these people, otherwise they're just going to be starving *here*, instead of on the streets."

"Philanthropy," Delvan replied flatly.

The priest nodded, giving Delvan cautious, shamed glances from the corner of his eyes. It seemed to take everything he had to request aid from others.

Delvan pulled in a deep breath, exhaling it slowly. He didn't have an issue helping Nerio, though he wasn't sure if what he could provide would be enough to support the mass of people gathered in the compound. "My father gives me an allowance every month, after my expenses it's more than I can spend anyway. I might also be able to go to a bank and withdraw next month's in advance. I don't know if it will be enough to feed half the people here, but would, say, four-hundred suns help?"

Nerio coughed, and for a second Delvan thought he was choking. "My Lord, that... that is most generous." Nerio looked to him, tears welling in his eyes. "We can go several weeks, at least, with such funds. Thank you and may the gods bless you yet again."

Weeks? How meagerly are they eating? "Well," said Delvan, a thought brewing in his mind, "I do have conditions."

"Of-Of course," Nerio said, worry creeping into his tired eyes, "I will do whatever I can."

"First, stop calling me 'the Conduit,'" Delvan said. "I prefer 'Del.' People who know me don't need to refer to me by my title, so you can stop with that too. Second, I want to meet with the Hands that are working in the Asylum."

Nerio's relief was visible as the diminutive muscles on his frame relaxed. "I am not sure what I can do about the designation, my Lo-um, Del. I have made several requests to those that come here to stop calling me 'Witness' to no avail." *Great, so I'm stuck with the sidelong glances and whispers...* "And arranging a meeting should be simple enough but, dare I ask, why? What are your intentions?"

"Rosethorn isn't the only one looking for answers," he said. "For right now, I just want to check and make sure Des is alright and see if she can help me figure out a few things."

"I... I do not wish to do anything that would put Desnia in danger," Nerio said quietly. "Please tell me that you do not intend to put her or the Hands in a situation that could bring them harm."

"She's in danger sitting in that cell, Nerio." Delvan watched as the young priest seemed to crumble, his body pulling itself inward. Trying to ease the man's concern, he added, "But I'm not intending to do anything drastic." The words felt disingenuous.

Nerio slowly nodded his head, despite the pain in his eyes. "I understand. Please, give her my best, and let her know I'm doing what I can."

"If she's guarded as well as I suspect, then I don't know how much I'm going to be able to say about you. As it is I have to think of a way to make sure Rosethorn doesn't find out."

"I will speak with the Hands, and perhaps we can think of something that will give you time alone with her."

"I'll give it some thought as well, thanks," Delvan said.

The priest wiped his hands on his robe, looking pensive. "Would you like to stay for my evening speak?" Nerio asked after a pause.

"I think I'm good," Delvan said. Nerio seemed crushed by the decision, but despite his guilt at injuring the priest's pride, he'd had enough of the strange, reverent attention that had followed him the past few days.

As he left there was an irritation itching at the back of his mind. Part of him had wished that Nerio planned to break Desnia out. It left him feeling guilty, knowing that the desire was born of wanting to keep his own hands clean, a way to obtain what he wanted without hindering his potential future.

The only thing that didn't leave him feeling ill with selfishness was leaving Nerio to his work and not turning him in. He wasn't sure he could live with himself if he were responsible for two people he knew being imprisoned on account of his involvement—negligent or otherwise. He didn't crave knighthood badly enough to permanently mar his conscience to obtain it.

Still, it was leaving him with fewer and fewer options. He wondered what he would even say to Desnia, and if she would forgive him if he secured her release. He doubted it.

But it would not deter him from trying.

Chapter Twenty-Two

These new relationships have proven indispensable, allowing me to identify and eliminate other couriers Reedjin might have utilized. I worry that there are some I may have missed, or who have already been dispatched. It is a certainty that he has machinations beyond what I have unraveled.

A cracked, wooden bowl sat empty on the scuffed, tiled floor, save for the smeared remnants of the dark brown curry that had once filled it. It had been delivered, its contents still on his breath, by Desnia's least favorite guard, leaving her with nothing but whatever dredges his spoon couldn't scrape clean—not to mention a few additional bruises.

She winced as she sat upright from her cot, her muscles aching no matter the position she found herself in. A pang of hunger emerged from under her rainbowed abdomen, her eyes staring at the empty bowl while saliva drenched her mouth. *So much for that hot meal,* she thought with no small amount of disdain.

On the plus side, said Masini, clearly having a similar train of thought, *at least Lady Mithya* tried *to follow through on her promise.*

"Was probably poisoned anyway," she whispered. *Or so I hope.* The death of her tormentor would provide an intimation of happiness, perhaps enough to take the edge off her impending walk to the gallows.

Yes, said Masini, *keeping up that kind of outlook will definitely get you out of here with expedience. You need her to trust you, and if you don't at least* appear to trust *her, then this is never—*

"I get it!" she hissed under her breath. She shook her head, the frustration of the entire situation far more agonizing than her physical injuries. "She sent the food to try and win me over," she said, eyes keenly on the door, "sorry if I'm not thrilled about a bribe meant to make me confess to who-knows-how-many crimes."

Yes, starving yourself will definitely spite her, well done, said Masini dryly. *Assuming the meal is actually delivered to you next time, maybe* consider *eating it.*

Desnia grumbled under her breath. She'd seen these juvenile tactics before and remembered well how she and too many others learned one of life's great lessons the hard way: nothing was *ever* given for free. Her stomach, however, argued its disagreement with a loud growl, twisting her face with hunger. The daily consumption of paint was doing little to sate it, and stale bread had begun leaving her with ribs that were becoming more visible by the day.

On a more exciting note, he said, *do you think this means Lady Mithya—the jewel of my life, queen of my dreams, voice of my heart—will be here today?*

There was a cry from down the hall—they'd been frequent since some of the Seers had been relocated back to this floor—and Desnia swore that she heard utterances of "dreams" and "heart" in the mad ramblings. *I hope those poor bastards don't have to listen to Masini too,* she thought with a cringe.

"Probably," she said with a shrug. She tried to temper her hopes that the inquisitor would arrive with her hairpin in place. Its absence during the last meeting a few days past had been a catastrophic setback, leaving her at the mercy of the guards and their malice. *And one day closer to whatever the general has planned for me.*

Wonderful! chirped Masini. *I mean... wonderful for* you, *obviously. If you put aside her tendency to crack your mind like a mongoose eating an egg, I think she could be really good for you—*

"Can we focus on the fucking problem at hand?" asked Desnia, exasperated.

Which one?

"Getting out of here, what else would I be talking about?"

So many things. Like, was our contested love sent here to kill you? To find out where my lustrous self currently resides? Or perhaps we could address your loneliness-induced anger issues.

"I'm *angry*," she said through barred teeth, "because I'm stuck in a *cell* with *you!*"

Mhm, I think not. I've seen you outside of prison. Still angry. Also, occasionally violent.

"I'm not having this conversation right now," she snapped as loud as she dared, her fists balled up to her side. She took a deep breath, calming her simmering blood. There was another cry from down the hall, eerie and cackling. She cringed at it, then a plan formed in her mind. "The hairpin, Masini, I think

I have an idea as to how to get it."

I'm listening.

"I think some of the other Seers might be able to hear you," she said. "If you can do something to get them to create a distraction—enough to get Mithya to turn her head—I can use that opportunity to grab her hairpin. Although it might require me doing something to make sure she doesn't notice it's missing..."

Tantalizing... Alright, what are you thinking? Spare no details.

"I don't know," she said with a shrug, "punching her, probably. Don't do anything unless I tell you though, not even sure if she'll be wearing it again."

Masini was quiet for a moment, then spoke. *That's far less... invigorating than what I'd had in mind. But fine, I will do my best to rally the troops, as it were.*

"Just try not to make them any *more* insane," said Desnia.

Rude.

She ignored him as she sat in the hot room, beads of slick sweat crawling down her back. As the radiant sunlight drifted across the floor, filling the room with an iridescent glow from the snowy tiles, she thought back to her last meeting with Mithya. Some of the questions she'd expected—her inquisitor's motives plainly ulterior—but the way she'd reacted...

Maybe, she thought as midday crept toward evening, *she's here on someone else's behalf? Someone who also despises Jerdine. Or maybe Masini is right, and she's just upset to be working for him?* It was difficult to say, but her gut was telling her it was more than just revenge on the principle's behalf. Nothing about such scenarios superseded the need to approach the conversation with caution, but perhaps it warranted more than her previously terse responses.

Or, she thought, *I'm just saying that because part of me* wants *it to be true...* She shook the thought from her mind, burying it in the deepest, blackest, most quarantined part of her soul, forever hidden from the light of her conscious mind.

A door opened and shut in the distance, and Mithya's now-familiar voice rang through the halls. Desnia tucked away Masini and watched from her cot—too sore to move otherwise—as a chair was rushed in by a guard, with the Blue following close behind.

Desnia scanned from the boot that first entered the door up to the legs that followed, to a shirt of light, flowing green, upon which her hair... draped down over, free and unpinned.

Her stomach twisted into a knot, curses flying through her mind at the lack of her means to freedom. *It's like she's fucking taunting me! What do I need to do to catch a gods-damned break?!*

"Don't look so happy to see me, Des," said Mithya mockingly. Desnia did her best to wipe away the scowl that had unintentionally marred her face, feeling the redness slowly fade as she pulled her attention from the stabbing chagrin.

Off to a good start, I see, snarked Masini.

Mithya glanced to the bowl on the floor as she removed her sapphire's covering, the residents down the hall becoming boisterous. A waggish grin tugged at the Blue's visage as she looked from the bowl to Desnia. *What's she look so gods-damned happy about?*

"Did you enjoy the meal?" Mithya asked as she sat down.

Desnia resisted answering, glancing to the door as it was being pulled closed. *Someone certainly did,* she thought as her abuser glared through the narrowing gap, his insinuation clear as he pulled the door closed and began walking away: if she revealed his sins, there would be hell to pay far greater than anything Mithya could concoct for her.

A headache began to form as she tried to twist an answer that would appease the Blue and keep herself out of harm's way. "It's practically licked clean, isn't it?" she finally said. There was a small release of tension, but the power's grip had not completely relaxed. She felt herself straining, her sweat turning to runnels as they beaded on her forehead and beneath her clothes.

"I guess it is," said Mithya. Desnia let out a silent exhale as the Blue's gift laxed, a quiet satisfaction in her interrogator's eyes. "How are you today?"

"I'm still locked in a fucking cell," quipped Desnia, "so needless to say I could be better."

"Fair point," said Mithya, thankfully lacking a condescending smile. "I spoke with the general. While he's pleased with your... cooperation, he's still looking for some additional details."

The general, she thought, *or you?* "Like what?"

"Ugh," she sighed, "boring specifics, but questions I have to ask, nonetheless. To start: can you identify any additional members of the Sraddhana or Magridi?"

Back to Masini, then, she thought, trying to figure out how to disguise her answer. "Who're still breathing?" she asked carefully. "Only that sick fuck principle."

The disappointment emanating from Mithya was nearly palpable, despite her face holding its coy mask tightly. "But you knew one, correct? The mage that taught you how to read Old Trethish? At least that's what the others described as your reasoning behind being able to decipher a long-dead language."

Those gods-damned journals, she recalled. Reading them with Masini's aid in front of everyone had been born of urgent necessity, and the excuse was as good as any at the time. "Those idiots don't know what they're talking about." *At least about one part,* she thought, desperate to twist the truth. "I have no idea how to read Old Trethish."

There was a flash of genuine surprise that widened Mithya's eyes. "But you *did* know one of these High Realm mages, did you not?" Her anxious anticipation suffused the room, causing Desnia to cock a curious eyebrow. *Why are you so determined to find out?* Her earlier second-guessing about the Blue's mysterious motives once again became lost in a turgid haze.

"I did, yeah." *And I still do.*

"Tell me about him," Mithya asked, eyes glistening excitedly.

"I can tell you he's a pig," said Desnia with a shrug. "But he was never able to tell me much, and I've never met him in person." *Technically.*

Desnia's eyes began to water as surges of power were pressed against her, her mouth wanting to vomit a stream of information. She clenched her jaw until the sound of grinding teeth echoed in her skull as it threatened to rive, refusing to elaborate further. If the Blue *did* work for Jerdine, this is what he wanted, and it was her only leverage. Possibly the only thing keeping her alive.

Aside from being mildly insulted, Masini chimed, *I'm impressed. I knew you could be clever. Though I'm mostly perturbed by the fact that 'pig' was the best you could come up with. Surely you must have more eloquent insults to throw about after basking in my brilliance for so long.*

She ignored him as Mithya leaned forward and narrowed her inquisitive eyes, watching Desnia's every muscle twitch, searching for what she could only assume was a tell. Eventually she leaned back, and the weight of the Blue's power was removed like a wagon unhitched from its beasts of burden. She blinked away the water in her eyes, trying to keep her expression stoic.

"Hmm," said Mithya with another grin. "You're just full of surprises, aren't you? I'm going to have another conversation with Lord Delvan and ask how he could be so 'mistaken.' Want me to pass anything along?"

"You could kick him in the crotch for me," she spat.

Mithya chuckled—her amusement far more enthusiastic than was warranted. Desnia then noticed that the Blue's brow had begun to glisten with sweat. *Trying harder than you're showing, are you?* But there was a strange... affection that seemed conjoined to Mithya's strain. It left Desnia even more confused.

Nicely done, Des, said Masini, *you're doing much better than last time. I'm so *proud.*

"Well," said the Blue, "can't find answers that aren't there, can we?" The warmth that had filled the room shifted to dismay, swamping the air. "Moving on then. What do you know about the chamber below the city, where you and the others found Jerdine?"

Mithya probably knew most of her story, based on what Desnia had told Delvan and the others, and this seemed as good a place as any to attempt following Masini's instructions. *Here goes nothing,* she thought.

It felt as if every word were hooked into her throat, torn painfully as she went into detail and fought her instincts to remain silent. "It's... it *was* a gate. To another realm. It had been dismantled, but Jerdine spent gods-know-how-many lifetimes rebuilding it. He wanted to bring an army here, and nearly succeeded... One of the bastards still managed to get through—then decided to stab me in the chest."

"So I heard," replied Mithya. Her tone and expression were more serious than Desnia had expected. Most people's reaction was laden with disbelief, and Desnia thought maybe the Blue was thinking something else entirely. *Is that... pity?*

"Don't look at me like that," she snapped.

"Like what?" Mithya asked sincerely.

"Like I'm... Like I'm deranged, or something," said Desnia with a scowl.

"I don't think you're crazy, Des," Mithya said in a tone that seemed to sound genuinely caring.

That makes one of us, she thought. The words—which told Desnia just how talented of an actor the Blue was—hung in the air, dangling like valuables in a shopkeeper's window, asking to be taken. But she kept her hands tightly to her side, arms crossed as she waited for Mithya to steer the conversation.

The Blue tapped her boot after a pause, then continued. "So, what was it like?"

"What was what like?" said Desnia, her face painted with consternation.

"Dying, obviously."

Desnia pulled her head back in surprise before turning it to the side, the agony experienced that night lingering in her chest. "Fucking hurt," she grumbled. The vision that she'd had during the span that her heart had stopped beating was crisp as the night it had happened—the promises of a god not easily forgotten.

Desnia wiped the sweat from her brow before asking a question of her own. "Why do you care?"

"Because who doesn't want to know what comes after? Why else?" the Blue said with a dramatic roll of her eyes.

"No..." Desnia said quietly, eying Mithya and gauging her captor's anticipation. She was far more eager for something than she was letting on, and the aloof tendencies were no more than a mask for it. "You want something. I don't know what, but you're hoping that I have information, information that you're *desperate* for." *She couldn't possibly know about... No, that can't be it, can it?*

Mithya cocked her head to the side, a corner of her lips pulling up to her rich brown eyes. "That talent you have for reading people, it's amazing. Almost like it's a... gift." Desnia's stomach lurched into her throat, her heart beating like mad. "Tell me, what else do you see when you look at me?"

Desnia's jaw defiantly fought to keep itself clenched as power curled around her like vines, their thorns digging into her skin and poisoning her blood. "I think," she reluctantly began, "that you're here for no one but yourself. I think you wink and smile and flaunt because you've always held power over people, and it gives you some sick fucking rush to find other ways of making them squirm.

"I think that you sit there, leaning back, pretending not to care when you're actually on the verge of an anxious breakdown. You could have said whatever you wanted about me and been done with this, yet you keep *coming back.*

"Which is how I know—not think—but fucking *know* that you're not here because of the fire or the general's stupid fucking questions. So why don't *you* try being honest for once and tell me what the fuck you *actually* want. Otherwise stop wasting both our time and leave me to what we both know is coming."

Mithya was motionless for a period that seemed to stretch beyond the horizon. Desnia couldn't bring herself to look the woman in the face, her eyes instead spearing the floor with her anger.

That had *been going well,* grumbled Masini.

All the effort these past few meetings, and she'd jeopardized everything because of her gods-damned temper.

Again.

The Blue stood, looking down at Desnia. "You want me to leave? Alright," she said with a shrug. Desnia's throat and gullet became so tight she had to fight the urge to vomit. "But I'm the only hope you have right now. I had thought that we could help each other, Des, but I'll find another way to get what I want. One way or another. If you want to sit here and rot instead, fine by me."

Desnia could feel the slightest hint of sadness beneath the avalanche of frustration coming from the Blue. She hoped that it was a bluff, that Mithya wasn't about to abandon her like everyone else.

Her instincts knew better than to hope.

She sat silently, her only response the flexing of her tight jaw muscles. To Mithya's credit, there was less hesitation than Desnia would've expected, and before long the Blue spun on her heels and took two long strides towards the door.

All her plans, her hopes for escape, were *clicking* away in tall boots. Nerio wasn't going to come to her rescue, nor, she knew, could she count on anyone else—a wound that still dripped with fresh blood. This was her only chance; she couldn't let it walk away.

"Wait!" she said.

Still glaring at the floor to her side, Desnia heard the footfalls cease, and the rustling of silk as the Blue turned to look at her. Desnia forced out her words, each one fouled by the taste of chagrin. "Don't... Don't leave."

The sound of the Blue's smile was clear in her voice. "Are you saying that because you're willing to help me? Or because you just enjoy my company?"

Desnia's mouth moved before she had time to think about the question, her resolve wearing thin as the continuous waves of power crested over her. "Both."

Ha! Masini cried victoriously. *I knew it!*

Her eyes went wide as she realized what her tongue had unconsciously blurted out, and her body quickly shrank in on itself. She curled herself tightly, forehead digging into her knees as her back pressed tightly against the wall. Sitting in the cot left her feeling exposed, her fatigued armor having finally cracked. Part of her wanted to crawl under the cot and wait for her executioner to arrive. *Anything to escape this feeling...*

A plethora of emotions emulsified the air, and Desnia didn't have to look at Mithya to know a satisfied grin now plastered the Blue's face. She heard the chair's legs *scratch* against the floor as Mithya sat back down.

"I'm going to tell you a secret, Des," said Mithya. "You're *right.* Partially, anyway. The fire is the least of my concerns—the general's too, I would think, considering most of the city would rather see him hanging right now instead of you. Part of why I come here is because I do have questions. Questions whose answers could change the very world we live in, effects that you've seen in person. But do you know the other reason I'm here?"

Desnia kept her eyes averted, clamping her mouth shut lest it stupidly betray her once more.

"I'm here," said Mithya in a low tone, "because I find you *fascinating.* You're a mystery. And let me tell you, there are a scarce few who I can make such claims about. Spending time here is *far* more interesting than everything else I'm doing in this city."

So, what, she thought, *you're going to figure me out and then toss me to the wayside when I become boring?* She wanted to scream the accusation but no longer trusted herself. She tried to rein in her emotions, remember the end goal of these meetings, but the extended conversation was a strenuous battle which had left her exhausted. Distress sank through her at the idea of being left in the cell, like a solved, discarded puzzle.

Once again, a thought came to her mind, a repetitious realization that she couldn't help but speak aloud, her mouth yet again turning against her. "I'm only interesting to the people who want something from me. Been that way my whole life. You're no different."

Desnia could feel the Blue's confident regard burst as her words punctured it like a dagger of disillusionment. She thought that her lashing of truth would bring her a sense of satisfaction, a revelry of returning a blow. Instead, she, too, was left feeling embittered and dejected.

There was a long silence, and the air was thick with emotion, stifling Desnia's every breath far more than the torrid summer heat. Seconds seemed like minutes, minutes like hours. Neither one spoke, the removal of veils communicating more than words could manage.

She felt a tightness in her aching stomach, and the silence was finally broken by a loud growl from her starved gut that echoed through the room.

From the corner of her eye, Desnia saw Mithya glance from her to the empty bowl on the ground, her brow knitting tightly together. "Still hungry after all that?"

Desnia kept quiet, the aches on her torso and legs a persistent reminder of the consequences should she reveal anything.

The Blue leaned forward, eyes narrow. "You *did* eat—"

"Stop!" Desnia hissed, finally turning her glare to Mithya. Her words were filled with anger, spite, and fear as she punctuated them under her breath. "Don't you *dare* ask me that. Because if you do, you're condemning me. You might as well slit my throat now and save me the trouble."

"Tell me wh—"

"*NO!*" she nearly screamed, glancing to the door with wide eyes. "Unless you plan to be at my door night and day, there isn't anything you can do. If you tried it would only make it worse. I'll answer your other questions, but I need you to *leave this alone.*"

The abuse was wearing on her. She could feel it chipping away at her defenses as day after day the baton left its mark. It kept sleep at bay, and what little she managed to get was filled with another form of torture. The Blue's involvement would only make matters worse.

Mithya pursed her lips, obviously reluctant to take orders. They locked eyes, fear and resentment twisting Desnia's face. The Blue eventually nodded, and she let out a breath she hadn't realized she was holding in.

Mithya leaned back in her chair, resuming her leisurely posture. "I'll be sure to deliver it myself next time, then."

"Thanks," she grumbled as the word burned her tongue like bile.

"I'm going to hold you to that, by the way," said Mithya.

"To what?"

The Blue grinned. "Answering my other questions."

Desnia's stomach twisted in a knot. "Fine," she quietly conceded. *At least it gets her back here... Gods I hope she wears the damned hair pin.* She wasn't sure how much more of this she could take. It felt like her skin was being removed, revealing secrets she kept from everyone—herself included. *Everything's simpler when I can just... ignore these feelings.* She cursed Delvan once again for putting her in this gods-forsaken cell and the mind-bending torture and abuse that came with it.

Mithya opened the bag that hung alongside her sword, the leather sack hanging heavily. The Blue raised an eyebrow before shutting it and giving Desnia a smile. "I think that's all I have time for today, unfortunately." The Blue stood and walked to the door, turning her head back before she crossed the threshold back into the free world. "Looking forward to next time," she said.

The door closed behind her, leaving Desnia with nothing but the tumultuous emotions her absence brought with it, fresh questions, and the regret of being born with a mouth capable of leaving her shamefully exposed.

Chapter Twenty-Three

Hopefully I have bought my brother time to complete his task in the mountains, although I am suspicious of the quantities claimed to be stored there. The claims must be false. A fraction of the supposed hoard would be worth a king's treasury.

The wagon creaked as is jostled over the broken cobles in front of Nerio, the horses giving a shake of their heads as they came to a halt. The drivers of the supply laden wagon looked disheveled, their scars and creased scowls portraying a life crueler than that of simply delivering goods to those in need.

He dispelled his unease about them and stepped forward to begin helping the soldiers that had surrounded the cart and were making efforts to unload its burden. His attempt was stopped as Captain Gernbard rested a hand on his shoulder, pulling him back. "We've got this, Witness," the captain said. "Besides, we have to leave soon for the other camp for your afternoon speak."

Nerio slumped his shoulders. More often his duties were pulling him away from aiding those that needed it—a conflict of necessity that battled within him daily. He looked again to the men delivering the sacks and totes of much needed supplies for the camp, their tones full of anger and bile as they spoke to the contents of their haul, a few words that he thought he recognized as Trethish slipping in. Their presence left him disquieted, and his hands fidgeted nervously with his robe.

"Don't worry about them," said the captain. "Smugglers are a means to an end, and as long as you pay them you can generally trust them. Had a few campaigns where we used them extensively for resupplies—hard to find food for an army when you're in enemy territory. Besides, it's a hell of a lot cheaper than buying this stuff second hand from merchants in the city; with the damned guild masters gone, prices have gotten out of control."

"I just want to make sure these people are safe, Captain," Nerio said.

"I know. But I trusted you with Lord Delvan—who, true to your and his word, came through for us—and now I need you to trust me."

Nerio thought for a moment, then nodded his head. It was difficult to put his fear to the side, but the captain's words held a veritable truth, and once again he was reminded of his greater duty. "Must they draw weapons, though?" he asked, nodding to the ring of soldiers guarding the wagon, keeping gawking bystanders at a distance.

"One thing you learn in battle," said Gernbard, a remorseful pang in his voice, "nothing ever goes as planned. I don't think they're needed, but I like having a contingency all the same."

"Surely we must be able to trust our own people?"

"I *want* to, but I think it's best if we err on the side of caution—especially with everything that's been happening."

He felt his heart sink at the reminder of recent reports from throughout the city. "Have we heard anything further?" he asked solemnly, afraid of what the answer might be. "Are the speaks that are turning riotous... Are they preaching my words?"

Gernbard frowned, then slowly nodded. "From what we can tell, yes. The people are on edge, Witness. Their patience is wearing thin, and they're lashing out. You can't blame yourself for that."

And blame who in my stead? he wondered, knowing the captain would argue otherwise should he speak the dark thought aloud. *The gods? The priests? The people? No. This violence is my responsibility.* "I know the people are angry," he said, "but I refuse to accept that the gods' plan involves such additional pain. The people have suffered enough, and I fear this will only make things worse. Perhaps emphasizing the need for pacifism in my speaks from now on will help suppress these outbursts."

He saw Gernbard raise an eyebrow and glance at him from the corner of his eye, but the grizzled soldier remained otherwise silent.

Nerio was not ignorant to the animosity that people held against the reign of the army and the taxes it imposed. Even within the camps, there was strife between the soldiers and peasantry. With food enough to now prevent starving, those who were not injured or sick were becoming restless, tension filling the air of the speaks—whose attendance rose with each passing bell toll. Yesterday Nerio had stood before a gathering of nearly a thousand souls—all listening with an intensity which was becoming frighteningly overbearing.

He shook away the concerns as he reminded himself that this was the will of the gods, and he was simply the messenger.

Ready for the welcomed distraction of his next engagement, he began speaking to the captain, "Perhaps we should start walking to—"

"Brother Nerio!" called out a young voice from behind him.

Nerio turned, seeing a young disciple—no older than twelve—working his way through the crowd gathered around the smugglers' caravan. The boy's white robes were dusted with ash at the fringes, and he wore the blue sash of Almedia—causing old memories to form a pit in Nerio's stomach. Gernbard did not move from his side, but he could feel the captain's cautious eye upon the boy.

"Yes, Brother?" asked Nerio as the disciple approached.

"Brother, I, uh, come..." the young boy glanced around, a nervous expression on his face as his eyes flitted from guards to commoners. "Actually, is there somewhere we could speak that's less... crowded?"

Nerio felt his stomach turn into a knot. He tried to silence the fear in his mind, attempting to dispel the notion which his thoughts jumped to. *He's gone. Gone far away from here. This boy is here for something else,* he consoled himself.

He nodded and turned, leading the young disciple down a nearby hall, Gernbard in tow. The rooms were full of the sick and injured, but a nearby exit led them to the outside edge of the building. A few guards could be seen in the distance in either direction, standing as lookouts at the building's corners.

"What is it that you wished to discuss?" Nerio asked the disciple, the tremor in his voice betraying his apprehension.

"I come bearing a message," said the boy, his head hanging low and eyes darting to the sides.

"From whom?" Nerio asked. There was no hiding the pitch of his voice, the cold sweat on his face, nor the shake of his hands.

"Principle Jerdine."

Nerio went numb. His heart slammed against his chest, pulsing in his neck. *No,* he thought, *it can't be. He's gone, out of my life. I watched him vanish.*

Captain Gernbard immediately dropped his hand to his sword's hilt, the *scratch* of steel against wood filling the air as the blade dragged along its scabbard.

Nerio's eyes went wide as he raised a hand. "No!" he cried as the captain nearly finished drawing the blade. "I-I would hear the message. Besides," he said, looking to the shamed eyes of the boy before him, "it is not of his own volition that our messenger is here. We cannot blame him for what he has no say over..."

The child hung his head, staring at the ground. Nerio knew that feeling, that powerlessness. He empathized with the boy and wished he could do more than simply listen to whatever words he had to say. The disciple stared at the ground as he spoke, reluctant to look at Nerio in the eyes. "He wanted to say... He said that he's proud of you."

The words pierced Nerio's heart like frozen steel, chilling his bones. The boy continued, each syllable full of regret, "He said that the work you're doing here, bringing these people together, is more than he could have asked of you. He's... excited to see where it leads, and wants you to know that you..." The boy pressed his lips together as he swallowed loudly. "That you hold a place in his heart, and he will continue to watch and admire what you're becoming."

Nerio wanted to vomit, to purge himself of the feelings coursing through him. His shaking hand dragged along his face, his dark skin whitening a shade. He saw a sneer pull at the captain's visage as he stared contemptuously at the disciple, releasing a string of words that were full of disdain. "I never thought I'd consider hurting a child but coming here on behalf of the man who tried to bring ruin upon us, tortured the Witness, and brought the death of the Messiah is crime of the highest degree."

"He did not have a choice in the matter, Captain," Nerio said quietly, his mouth struggling to find his voice. "And I would venture that he might welcome your punishment. It would be a relief from the one he now suffers."

The disciple's head sank lower, his body shrinking.

The captain grumbled, then waved his hand to the side. "Fine. Leave then, and don't find your way back here, understood?"

The boy gave a quick nod before shuffling quickly away, refusing eye contact with either of them.

Nerio stood there, motionless, the words replaying in his mind.

...Proud? he thought, bewildered. *No, this is the work of the gods, not him. Why... Why would he be* proud? Nerio fidgeted again with his robe, wondering how anything he was doing could be to the benefit of the principle. He felt the foundation of his convictions crack, his duty now in question. *On the run, unseen by anyone in weeks, and the man has yet again influenced me.*

Gernbard watched the disciple scurry away before he turned to Nerio, whose eyes were gazing into the unseen distance. "We should get going, Witness. Don't let him get under your skin."

Nerio nodded, eyes still affixed to that distant, unseen point. As he walked, his head spun. *This is what I am* meant *to do, my duty. But, if it's playing into Jerdine's hand, could it be maligned? Have I misjudged my own purpose?*

He shook his head, tightening his jaw.

No. No, this is the truth, and it is a power greater than Jerdine. It will overcome the actions against it, just as we overcame his actions against us. This is the path I must walk.

Isn't it?

CHAPTER
TWENTY-FOUR

My more immediate concern is that I have not heard from my brother in some time, a deviation from convention completely out of character.

O rne stood with crossed arms in the courtyard's center, tapping his foot firmly on the marred flagstones. The morning sun was two hours into the sky, its glare only just piercing the valley. His breath steamed the mountain air, creating an ever-growing haze with each exhalation.

Not *one* of his new squad members had reported to his roll call, leaving him irate. There could be only a single explanation.

Gods-damned Villera, Orne seethed, *he better not have told them to come later, or worse, not at all.*

There would be retribution for this petty injustice. The longer he stood in the fog of his lungs' breath, the more he came to detest the man.

His stomach grumbled. The pickings from the previous night had been meager, and he'd been able to find little more than hardtack when searching the pantry stores this morning. The keep's cook hadn't arrived until Orne's storming exit, and he'd been in no mood to ask where they kept items that were actually edible. *Fat-ass captain or Villera probably ate it all.*

The *thump* of boots on stone turned his head towards a staircase against a far wall. Walking down it was a woman in a shambled uniform, her hair a short, cropped mess of brown, her eyes as muddled as her motions were groggy.

About time, he thought. "Hey!"

The woman turned her head with a start and, upon noticing Orne glaring in her direction, looked around to see if there was someone else present.

"Yes, you," Orne boomed. "You're late."

She scratched her head. "Late, sir? For what?"

Gods-damn it. I knew it. "Roll call," he said, his breath still fuming.

"Uh, I didn't know nothin' about no roll call. I was just on my way to the mess—"

"You *are* in one of my squads, aren't you?" He wondered if she'd been here by happenstance, rather than attendance. The possibility that the lieutenant hadn't informed his squads of their new command rooted in his mind, sending tendrils of anger through his veins.

"Um, I think so?" she said, a dumb expression on her face. Despite her indecorum, Orne let out a small sigh of relief.

"What's your name and rank, soldier?"

She languidly snapped her heels together and saluted, the motion awkward on the stone steps. "Helona. Infantryman, Second Western Army, sir."

"Did Lieutenant Villera tell you about your new attachment, Helona?"

"Yeah, he mentioned something about that last night," Helona replied, relaxing. "Though I told him it doesn't matter to me much who I—"

"Did he tell you," Orne asked, "what time to be here?"

"No, sir. He only said me and some of the others would be reporting to someone new is all."

Orne's fists trembled as his nails clawed into his palms. It was all he could do to force out his words, each grating like steel over stone. "Do you know who else was transferred?"

She shrugged. "I reckon. If not I can find out easily enough. Just gotta ask the right—"

"Go get them," he growled.

"Uh, yes, sir. Just going to get my morning meal first and then—"

"*Now!*" he bellowed.

Helona jumped, her baggy eyes going wide as she saluted and huffed her way up the stairs.

Villera was a pebble against an avalanche, and nothing short of the act of a god would save him from being crushed and swept away. His obliteration—his humiliation—was set in stone. He just didn't realize it yet.

It had taken another hour, but Orne's two new squads now stood at attention in the courtyard before him in two evenly spaced blocks. He'd had to drag the last two away from their meal, and several had still been asleep when the soldier he'd tasked with their retrieval had found them.

He made little effort to hide his disdain as he addressed the soldiers. "My name is Lieutenant Orne, and I am your new commanding officer," he barked, his voice echoing through the courtyard. "Starting immediately, you're each to report here, every morning, an hour after dawn for training exercises." Disconcerted mutterings and groans buzzed through the forty soldiers, their whispers harsh.

Orne ignored them.

"We're going to start each morning with a two-mile march, full gear, at double pace. Then, combat training and sparring. Afternoons will be drills and—"

"Oh, fuck this," said one of the squad members, looking to those around him, his gaunt, hollow eyes seeking affirmation. Orne recalled his name from roll call, Steddus.

"We don't have to listen to this!" Steddus said, gesturing towards Orne. "No one cares enough about this rat's nest to treat us like we're still in the army, why bother acting like it? Y'all can stand here and take this, but I'm done." The man turned to leave, the resolve of the others around him wavering as they shifted and relaxed from their attention.

Orne's teeth ground together like millstones. How *dare* any soldier of the King's army be this insubordinate? He planned to make something of this haphazard, lackadaisical group, and he wasn't about to let this first act of defiance go unpunished.

An example would be needed.

"Steddus!" roared Orne, causing a few members of the squad to start. The outspoken rebel turned an angry glare towards him. *Not afraid, huh? We'll see how tough you really are.* "Are you defying a direct order?!"

Hesitation shivered through the man's posture. The repercussion for such disobedience was simple, if ghastly—a way of removing the rotting flesh to save the host. The soldier well knew it, based on the look in his eyes.

Execution.

Punishment was at the discretion of commanding officers, and while many could be lenient, Orne wasn't about to fall into the trap of showing weakness on his first day as this group's superior.

"What makes you think," Steddus asked slowly, his voice slow to regain its recent confidence, "that we want to take orders from some *noble.* You didn't earn this station and we've been disciplined enough by being sent here. The military stopped caring about us a long time ago, so why should we bother caring about it?"

Gods-damn it, thought Orne with a sneer. He'd hoped his status as a lord had remained with the captain. *Instead, the bastard undermines me. Again.* "I am your squad leader per the orders of Lord General Rosethorn, regardless of my title. Furthermore, this fortress is critical to the protection of the empire—"

The soldier laughed, prompting a chuckle from the rest of the group surrounding Orne. "*Critical?* Are you mad? There's nothing here!" the man said between fits of laughter.

Orne's heart pounded with enough power to make his neck throb. Animosity churned and roiled inside of him, turning his face a deep ruby. He refused to stand here and be mocked by his own soldiers.

He stomped over to the nearby weapon's rack, pulling forth two wooden training swords. He walked through the array of watching soldiers and threw one at the feet of his would-be challenger. Silence fell, the surrounding walls forgetting the echoes of even the passing breeze. Steddus looked down at the wooden blade, his face curious, and then back to the storming Orne before him.

"You want to leave?" Orne asked, spittle flying from his lips. "Then pick it up. If you manage to land a blow on me then I'll release you from my command. But when you're not able to—and I know that your lazy, inbred ass can't—know that you're going to wish that you'd never been stupid enough to pick it up in the first place."

The soldier seemed bold enough to consider the offer, looking at the faux blade on the ground and then back to the Orne, his face only a shade lighter than the mountainsides.

To the man's credit—or his stupidity—he reached down and picked up the practice sword, spinning the handle in his hands before gripping it far too tightly. The soldiers around them backed away, breaking their formation and forming a circle around the pair as they murmured and like judgmental spectators.

Orne swung his foot behind him, standing tall with the wooden hilt loose in his hands, held before him and pointed at his feet. His opponent lowered himself, lightly bobbing as he glared with a malicious intent.

Orne was the first to mark the start of the duel. "Swords un—"

The soldier suddenly lunged, not waiting for Orne to finish, let alone provide the traditional response of acceptance. Orne had patience for a great many things when dueling. The drawing of blood, the mishaps caused by the environment, even a loss. But this man had been sent here—he imagined, as his type were all scoundrels—for an offense truly unforgivable.

Being a cheat.

With a step to his side and an arcing swipe of his sword, Orne batted away the miscreant's sword with a loud *clack*. Steddus's horrid lunge had been a complete committal, leaving him within arm's length of Orne—and utterly exposed. A second *clap* echoed off the surrounding stones as Orne slapped the cheat's face with an open hand, spinning him around and dropping him to a knee. Normally, Orne wasn't one to embarrass someone so thoroughly.

But this bastard had it coming.

"Do you yield?" asked Orne as the man spit blood onto the flagstone.

The soldier snarled as he twisted his head to look at him, the side of his face a red welt in the perfect silhouette of Orne's hand. He pulled himself to his feet, hunched as he gingerly prodded at the side of his visage, wincing and once again glaring at Orne. With the wooden handle gripped like death, he raised his sword, his knees bending as he prepared to strike.

Fine, I'll happily kick your ass all day.

Steddus decided to try something new and swung with all his might in a wide arc from his side, aiming the wild attack directly at Orne's head. In a quick motion, Orne stepped into the attack, his sword sweeping up and meeting the soldier's hand in a loud *crack*, blocking the weak attempt. Pain contorted his foe's face, but the true satisfaction came as Orne dug his fist deeply into the man's gut, just below the ribs.

Eyes bulged as their air rushed from his lungs in a wheeze. The soldier dropped to the ground, gasping, the practice sword clattering to the stone beside him.

All around him was silent.

Orne stared down at the scum triumphantly. Picking up his opponent's practice sword, he looked around at the paled onlookers, standing in their circle around him. "Form up!" he ordered.

Everyone rushed into place, standing at quiet attention, eyes forward and ignoring their writhing squad member.

He walked through the ranks, locking eyes with the rest of his two new squads, the defiance drained from their eyes. "Alright, training begins now!" he called out. "I want two-hundred pushups from everyone. Once you're done, stand at attention and wait for the others to finish. Then we begin drills."

There were grumblings as the soldiers shared glances at one another, shifting uncomfortably.

"Now!" he shouted.

There were a few hushed murmurs, but the soldiers slowly got on their hands and began their pathetic excuses for push-ups—slow and shaky after only a dozen or so. *We'll fix that soon enough.*

He looked up, noticing Kolden standing in the doorway of the forge, looking at him with a cocked eyebrow and an expression that said: *Really?*

Orne returned one, stating: *What?*

Kolden's response was simple: *You're an idiot.*

A low growl shook his throat, and he left his squads to continue their weak exercises and stomped towards his brother, who rolled his eyes with that gods-damned, egotistical grin he always wore.

"What's your problem?" he snarled, rage building anew in his chest.

"Beating the hell out of them the first day? Really?"

"He was disobeying orders!" Orne replied, pointing a finger at his brother, who remained unperturbed, the only flinch of his eyes coming from the contact of Orne's flying saliva. Kolden just stared at him, moving Orne's growing temper to the side and forcing him to consider his actions. "Whatever," Orne said with a curt wave. He refused to acknowledge his brother being correct, regardless of the circumstances. "What matters is it got the little shits in line."

His brother sighed and shook his head. "Right. Because who cares if they all resent you?"

"What matters is they obey orders." *What does he know about leading, anyway? He only obeys half the orders given to him, hypocritical asshole.*

"*Sure,*" said Kolden.

Orne just shook his head, refusing to play his brother's games. He knew when he was being manipulated.

They stood and watched the soldiers struggle for a while, many lying flat on their faces, heaving the warming air with puffs of dust from the courtyard's flagstones. *It's going to take them all morning at this rate,* he begrudged. He looked down at Kolden, still standing and watching at his side. "What are you doing, anyway? Don't you have a forge to run or something?"

His brother shrugged. "The chimneys are clogged. I'm just waiting for someone to get here with the sweeps. Place hasn't been maintained in probably a hundred years." His head suddenly cocked to the side, that annoying, contemplative look on his face.

"No," said Orne, before his brother had a chance to speak.

"You don't even know what I was going to say!"

"You want me to do something for you. My answer is no," he said with crossed arms.

"Fine," replied Kolden, "but don't come to me when you need a weapon or repairs."

His uniform tightened around flexing muscles as he held himself back from strangling Kolden. "What do you want?" he asked through barred teeth.

"The forge is a mess," he said. "It's going to take me a week to clean it, at least. *But...*" he said, turning to meet Orne's glare.

"There's *no way* it's going to take you a week to clean one measly forge," he said derisively. "Stop whining and deal with it yourself."

"It's not *one* forge. It's *ten*," Kolden said, glaring at him. "The place is immense. Has to be bigger than the barracks at Drunt. I can only imagine what it was like when it was fully staffed. Regardless, there's garbage and dust and rusted tools and scraps everywhere, the faster I can get it cleaned up and working, the faster you get a smith who's competent."

Orne stood there and thought for a moment, nostrils flaring as he debated his brother's request. *Blackmail, more like.* "Fine!" he eventually conceded. "I'll have my squad help you clean your stupid fucking forge."

"See? That wasn't so hard."

"Do you want my help or not?!"

"Alright, alright. Gods, lighten up."

"You're the one instigating! You're still pissed you don't have any of your precious glowing rock, aren't you?"

His brother's face curdled, a nerve being struck. Now it was Orne's turn to grin.

"Fuck off," Kolden snapped. "You know as well as I do how important cadentite is, so don't give me that. Besides, I spent the morning sending carriers to anyone and everyone that might have connections to the smugglers that were in Brethefen. Hopefully I hear back from one of them sooner or later, 'cause I sure as hell am not going to spend my time here making more *chisels.*"

"A bunch of letters aren't going to get you anywhere, Kolden."

"I don't know about that," his brother replied, his grin returning, "Del is pretty resourceful. I'm sure the one I sent him will get me somewhere."

"You sent one to Del?" Orne asked, his flush face cooling as the blood drained from it. "You didn't... I swear if you told him about what happened on the pass I'm going to—"

"What?" asked Kolden. "Beat me up with a wooden sword?"

Orne shook his head with a tightened jaw, his indignance at his brother's gibes leaving him simmering in his own tumultuous anger. He looked back to his squad, none of the soldiers yet standing as they struggled to complete their assigned regiment. Once they were finished—and only then—he would send them into the forge to assist Kolden with his tasks. *He can wait a while longer,* he decided.

They stood there watching the sun begin to pool in the courtyard as it poured over the wall behind them, raising sweat and soaking the backs of his command's uniforms. Amid the grunting and rustle of soldiers, something to his left caught his eye.

Atop a wall, leaning on a parapet near one of the tower entries, was Lieutenant Villera. He was watching the soldiers in the yard with a grimace beneath sagging eyes of malice. He caught Orne's gaze, holding it for a second before spitting to the side and walking into the nearby tower.

Orne's lip tugged in contempt. *That's right, go back into the hole you crawled out of.* There was a good chance the man was running to the captain like a child to its mother's teat to make some false, derogatory claim. It mattered little. He would show the captain—even if he had to drill it into the man's thick skull himself—that he was far superior to that miserable lieutenant, regardless of whatever venom the man spewed.

I will *show Rosethorn that I can get these sloths in shape. I will show that I'm worthy of the promotion out of father's shadow and trust Rosethorn's given me.*

And I'll be damned if that bastard gets in my way.

<h1 style="text-align:center">CHAPTER
TWENTY-FIVE</h1>

I worry that communications have been somehow sabotaged.

Each hot breath brought with it a restrictive, stabbing pain in Desnia's side.

She'd heard the rib crack during her most recent beating after the guard's overzealous partner joined in the now-ritualistic sadism. Her tormentor had the experience to display a certain level of restraint—you couldn't perform interrogations if the inmate wasn't breathing. His partner, unfortunately for her, had been young and maleficently eager.

After a stab of grueling agony, she squinted her watery eyes and gazed out the window, desperate for anything to take her mind off... everything.

Stuck in a cell, she thought as the weight of her circumstance began to suffocate her like the snapped rib, *plans going to shit, always in pain, and mentally degrading by the day...*

Her dreams had become more frequent, disregarding the barrier of her ever-increasing paint consumption, and too often they were filled with blood and death by her own hand. Sleeping or awake, there seemed to be no reprieve from one form of torment or another—and the promised salvation hidden in the mountains outside her window might as well be on the other side of the kingdom. She began to long for the misery's end, anything to escape the near constant suffering she found herself drowning in. *If only I were so lucky...*

You, uh, alight there, Des? Masini asked hesitantly.

A melancholy silence filled the room, Desnia avoiding the answer for her own sake as much as Masini's. Eventually she broke it with an admittance that cleaved her heart as much as it did the quiet. "I don't think we're getting out of here, Masini."

That's just the torture talking, he said. *Happens to the best of us. I remember this one time, I was tied up on a bed for weeks, teased endlessly by this domineering mistress. Halfway through I was ready to have a go at a rabid racoon if she'd let me, and by the end of it she had me crawling around on the floor barking like a dog, having forgotten why I was even there. Anyway, my point is: stay strong, you've got this. Also, don't trust a woman who's into ropes and weird foreplay.*

Desnia sat quietly, a storm of emotions raw and turbulent within her, threatening to sink her in their wake. She felt her bottom lip begin to tremble as a tear trickled down her cheek. She rested her head against the wall at her back, closing her eyes and taking a shaky breath. "It's like I can feel Asta, hovering and watching me. Every day her angst grows, mine worsens, both of us trapped in cells we can't escape."

Well, that's not true, for either of you, said Masini.

Desnia shook her head. "She told me as much herself, going as far as to bribe me to help her. People who have options don't do that. And let's face it, there's no one coming here to help *me*. I'm beginning to wonder if seeing Mithya's hairpin wasn't just a figment of my imagination. It was never realistic anyway, let's be honest."

Did you ever consider that maybe there's a reason why I, along with a demigod, specifically sought you out? asked Masini. *If there's one attribute that defines your capabilities, it's your resourcefulness. You're the best at what you do for a reason, Des, and I'm here to remind you, in incessant perpetuity, of that fact. Also, I need someone to talk to, and the other Seers are a little difficult to have conversations with.*

Wiping the tear from her face, she took another deep, shaky breath. "Gods forbid you don't have someone to annoy," she said with an amused snort. His words—as much as she hated to admit it—did help lift her spirits, but only enough to prevent her from drowning.

The only deviancy worse than my own would be its absence from this world. And, although I realize my banter may be misconstrued to make you believe otherwise, I am rather fond of you, Des. I have the utmost faith that you'll get us out of here.

Desnia sat quietly, feeling more tears catch in her eyes, refusing to open her mouth lest it release the foreign well of emotions behind it.

Also, Masini continued after a moment, *do you, uh, mind elaborating what you meant by 'bribe?'*

She shrugged. "Asta mentioned something about 'power beyond imagination,' and 'glory.' People like to promise shit they can't deliver when they're desperate." *I'd offer someone the King's Jewel to get me out of here right now...*

There was a pause before Masini replied. *And you thought that one of the most powerful beings in the re-re-re-fucking-damn-it, in this world was making empty promises? I'm not trying to call you thickheaded, Des, but by the Greats, are you thickheaded?*

"In my experience," she said bitterly, "the most powerful people are the ones who you should trust the *least*. Besides, the only promise I cared about was the one she made about making sure I didn't, you know, go crazy."

You, drawled Masini, *might be the most jaded person I've ever met, and I'm older than some* continents. *Were you planning on, uh, sharing this at some point? Did she happen to say anything about yours truly?*

"What? Are you saying I'm wrong?" she chided. After a moment, another trembling exhale, and silence from Masini, she continued. "She didn't mention you, aside from saying to listen to you—clearly unaware of how difficult *that* is. And I *was* planning on telling the asshole about it at the meeting where he promptly had me arrested. So, tell me again how I should trust those in power."

Hmm, said Masini, sounding disappointed. *Does this, uh, mean you don't intend to seek Asta out still?* There was a nervous edge to his voice, a concern that she could almost feel.

"She's still the best chance I have to keep myself sane... Even if it's as realistic as the hot meal I was supposed to get." Her stomach panged at the reminder of food, her meals failing to arrive with increased frequency.

Ah, excellent, said Masini with no small amount of relief. *I know you have your own motivations, but there's still an enormous risk of, you know, invasion and torture and such.*

She let out a long sigh, flaring the pain in her side. *Might be an improvement from this,* she thought bitterly.

There had been situations aplenty in her life that she'd needed to struggle through, fighting with sheer determination and force of will to merely survive. But this was something different. Every day dragged her further down into a dark abyss, the will to fight being beaten out of her, eroded with every new bruise. She knew it happened to everyone in these circumstances, but being aware of it only seemed to weigh her down more. If it hadn't been for Masini's companionship, she suspected she would have succumbed to the despair days ago.

Time was measured by the stabs in her side as her lungs struggled to overcome the pain and draw full breaths. As the sun neared its mountain cradle, Desnia heard a familiar voice in the distance, and soon a chair was rushed into the room—prompting her to tuck Masini away. She had a hard time looking at Mithya as she strode through the door, giving her no more than a cursory glance before staring off into the distance beyond her window once more, listening to the guards' footsteps fade down the hall.

Gods, she thought, *I don't have the energy for this today...*

A scent wafted through the room, one that twisted Desnia's stomach and made her mouth water. She looked back to the Blue—standing there in a black shirt and customary boots over clinging trousers—holding a steaming bowl of curry and smiling at her.

Desnia's wide eyes were unable to pull themselves away from the meal, her mind forgoing conscious thought and craving nothing more than to steal the food and devour it with fervor.

"I thought I'd deliver this myself, this time," said Mithya with a discrete glance at the door. She walked over and handed the steaming sustenance to Desnia, who stared at it in disbelief before glancing back up at the Blue. She could feel her eyes welling—despite her resistance—as she looked up to the supple smile. Her heart quickened and then, at a glint of light, nearly burst from her chest.

Holding a twist of hair, protruding just above Mithya's head, was her polished, silver hairpin, its long, dagger-like shape stabbing through a bundle of hair.

Desnia nearly forgot about her food, her body feeling light as an anxious euphoria fluttered within her. She forced her gaze away, her eyes skimming along the curvaceous Blue before her as they made their way back to focusing on the meal.

A part of her told her not to trust the handout, that it was some kind of trick. But her thin, weakening figure and bony limbs argued overbearingly against it, and she was forced to succumb to her body's needs. "Thanks," she eventually said before using the wooden spoon to take a massive bite of the dark brown curry.

Flavors exploded in her mouth—not that she took much time to taste it, swallowing the stewed mixture half chewed. The curry was so filled with spices that its texture resembled sand, but it was more food than Desnia had eaten in days, and she attacked it voraciously. She consumed it in such a ravenous fashion that she hardly managed to breathe, ignoring the pain in her side.

"The innkeeper that makes that is a little heavy-handed when it comes to seasoning," said Mithya as she sat across from Desnia, "but I didn't think you'd mind."

She shook her head as she scraped the bowl and shoved another morsel into her mouth. Her stomach began cramping, and she was forced to slow down as the bottom of the wooden bowl began to appear.

Mithya reached into a pouch at her side and drew a flask. Desnia eyed it as the cork was pulled before being extended to her.

"What is it?" asked Desnia warily.

"Whiskey," replied Mithya, raising it closer to her.

Woman after my own heart, said Masini. *As though I needed another reason to lust over this musing paramour.*

Desnia hesitated, staring at it as her instincts fought against accepting the offer. Mithya lolled her head and rolled her eyes, taking a sip from the flask before extending it back to Desnia. "If I wanted to poison you, it'd be in the curry. Here."

Desnia's eyes went round as coins as she looked down at her food. Her hunger had gotten the better of her, overriding the cautious instincts that normally protected her. *Was that the plan?* she thought, panicked. *To starve me for days and then bring the means of my demise?* She looked back up at Mithya, who sighed while still holding the extended flask.

"The food isn't poisoned either, Des. Want me to eat some of that too?"

Now, Des, she heard Masini say, *remember what we talked about?*

She slowly reached out and took the flask, giving it a hesitant smell. *Masini's probably right. Why kill me when she still has questions?* she thought. She took a swig, swallowing a large gulp of the burning liquid, the warmth flushing her body and easing her turmoil. *Fuck it,* she thought as she took another long draft, relief flooding through her like water from a broken dam.

She handed it back to Mithya, who took another sip and then put on one of her coy smiles. "So," said the Blue, "where were we?"

Desnia took another bite of the chalky curry, replying while she chewed. "You were about to get to the real reason you were here." The whiskey had loosened her tongue, it would seem. *Worth it,* she decided.

"You mean aside from our mutually enjoyed company?" Mithya asked. Desnia stopped chewing, her body freezing in place.

Ooh, said Masini cheekily, *well done, Des, well done. I'm happy for you. And turned on. I didn't think my silvery body could get any harder.*

There was adoration dancing through the air, whether it was her own, Mithya's, or Masini's was impossible to say. "Yeah," she said, looking at her bowl, "aside from... that."

"Alright then," said Mithya with a wink, leaning farther back, "let's help each other out then, Des. You answer my questions to the best of your knowledge, and I will go to the general and work to secure your release in exchange."

Desnia resisted letting out a snort. *That's never going to happen.* Even *if* Mithya went back and argued for her freedom, the general wasn't about to release the person responsible for burning down half the city. "Fine," she replied. *As long as it gives me time to snag that hairpin, I'll answer your questions, damning as they may be.*

The Blue's grin broadened. "Perfect. Let's start with something easy: do you know where Jerdine is?"

"No," said Desnia, looking up from her food and straight into Mithya's eyes. "Why? Worried I'm going to go after your boss? I'm stuck in a cell, remember?"

Masini groaned, and the Blue's face turned more serious than Desnia had ever seen it, a scowl pulling down at her lips and scorn emanating from her like light from a candle. "I don't work for Jerdine, Des."

She held her gaze, searching for any sign that Mithya was lying. A stern visage chiseled of vile hatred stared back at her, and Desnia could find no signs of deceit. It was impossible to be certain, but she sensed that the Blue was being honest.

"Say I believe you," said Desnia, "why are you so interested in where to find him?"

"For the same reason you were," she said with a shrug. "To protect our realm."

Did she say re-re-re-fuck! cursed Masini. *Where'd she learn that term?*

"Did Del tell you about that?" asked Desnia through slit eyes. *Did he get that detailed in the snitching he did to the general? Or does she know it another way?*

"Sure," said Mithya with a wave of her hand. She took another swig of whiskey and handed it back to Desnia. "But we're here to learn about you, Des, not me." *Speak for yourself,* she thought before taking a long pull of liquor. "You mentioned before that there was a High Realm mage you knew but never gave his name. What was it?"

She felt her head begin to ache, the whiskey rapidly taking its toll on her starved body. "Um," she said with a slow blink, handing the flask back, "I don't, uh... I don't know his real name."

"What one did he give, then?" Mithya pressed.

"Um," she said, the light seeming brighter, "Masini."

Uh, Des, Masini said, *excuse me for asking, but what the fuck are you doing?*

She shook her head, her throat tight as she looked up at Mithya's smug smile. "Well, isn't that interesting," said the Blue. "I'd heard he was dead."

By the Greats, Des, Masini said nervously, *what'd you say that for? Alright, at least this means she probably doesn't work for Jerdine, since you decided to also tell him about me. I swear, no one can keep a secret anymore.*

Desnia was less concerned about her slip of the tongue, and more curious as to what had caused it. *Am I that drunk already? Has being trapped in here destroyed my entire tolerance?*

"A little weird," Desnia retorted, "someone like you being misinformed like that."

"I'd thought so too, until I met you."

Lucky me, she thought, rubbing her temples.

Mithya took another sip of whiskey before continuing. "Was the gate the reason you came to Brethefen? Were you meeting Masini here?"

"Yes and no. I was on the run," Desnia said. "I was made an offer, and closing the gate was my part of the deal."

"An offer made by whom?" Mithya asked, leaning closer.

Desnia cursed her loosened tongue and struggled to salvage her failed misdirects. "Ast-Ast-A stubborn bitch," she stammered, "someone I only met once in person—in a way which I have no desire to repeat."

Mithya leaned back in the chair, seeming disappointed. Desnia didn't dare divulge what had brought her to the city—more questions meant more time in this cell, and she hoped to the gods that Delvan didn't stupidly mention what she'd told him regarding the trapped deity. She turned to put the empty bowl on her cot, the motion spiking a sharp pain through her side. She winced, hissing as she gingerly pressed her hand to her ribs.

The Blue dug her brow deeply into her nose, her concern genuine enough to knot Desnia's stomach. "What's—"

"Don't!" spat Desnia. "Just... don't. I told you before, if you ask me, you're condemning me more than I already am."

Mithya leaned forward, as close as she'd ever come to Desnia. She outstretched her arm, bringing it close to Desnia's side, her face less than a foot from her own. Desnia resisted glancing at the hairpin above the worried visage. *If there was ever a moment...*

Another opportunity to steal her prize might never again present itself. On impulse, she moved to strike and distract with her left hand, her right motioning to grab the pin. Misdirection was the key to any good lift—distract the person with a bump of the shoulder while you snagged their purse, hiding the lesser sensation from the greater. Only, in this instance, she was going to need to suffice with a slap instead of a bump.

Her body, however, refused her. She managed to twist little more than an inch before her rib screamed out in agony at the sudden motion, stopping her cold and causing her to suffocate a scream behind gritted teeth.

To Mithya, it would have seemed little more than a flinching aversion to being touched. To Desnia, it was a mockery to her skill, her torturer finding ways to bring her pain even when he was out of the room. The failure did more than curse her with derision, it crippled the little will she had left, leaving her feeling further broken and defeated.

"Let me see," said Mithya, not having flinched from Desnia's laughable efforts.

Desnia shook her head, her eyes red and leaking as she squeezed them shut.

"Des," she said firmly.

Desnia didn't see the point in resisting anymore. The one thing she'd needed was within her grasp, and her best attempt had left her half keeled over in pain. A part of her began to wonder if having this over sooner rather than later might be for the best. *Better than ending up like the others down the hall...*

Finally, Desnia gave a short nod, her face still pained and moved her hand from her side. Mithya grabbed the side of her shirt and gently lifted up a corner below her rib. Her touch was the softest thing Desnia had known in what felt like a lifetime, and she felt her face relax, her breathing turning steadier.

Mithya's expression, however, turned to stone. As the white top lifted, it revealed skin that was no longer its original pale white. Instead, a mixture of blues, blacks, greens, and yellows covered it like a drunkard's, ulcer-stained vomit. Mithya revealed no more than a hand-span of skin before looking at Desnia, her eyes glowering. "Who?" she asked, the Blue's power resting on her shoulder like a comforting hand.

Desnia hung her head. "The guards," she whispered, fear spiking her heart like ice.

Mithya stood, the chair kicking backwards behind her, hand on the pommel of her sword. She turned to leave, and Desnia reached out with a hand as quickly as she dared and grabbed her arm, trying to ignore the searing pain in her side. "Don't. You'll only make it worse," she pleaded.

The Blue looked down at her, eyes of ire locking with her tear-filled plea. There was a retribution burning in that glare, which assuaged the agony of Desnia's mind and flesh. There was a moment that Desnia thought the Blue would leave despite her silent begging, but she slowly sat back down after a tense hesitation.

"You weren't to be harmed," said Mithya sternly, her normally lax and flippant nature vanishing. "Those were orders directly from the general."

Desnia let out a short, dry laugh. "I bet you think I'm being fed meat every day too, maybe a side of wine with it." She shook her head with a sneer. "Gods-damned highborns," she half whispered. "You have no idea what it's like, fighting just to survive, having everyone look down on you every day like you're no better than mutts begging for scraps. You, the general, Delvan, you can all tell yourself whatever you want to keep your conscience clear at night, but it doesn't matter who you put at that door, because I'm nothing more to them than a stray dog to kick."

Guilt suddenly saturated the room, Mithya's mask uncharacteristically fracturing to reveal the emotions beneath.

"*Don't* look at me like that," Desnia snapped. She didn't want pity. Pity was for the weak, for the broken, for those who couldn't survive. *Those like... like... me.* Resentment erupted within her, burning inside like an acid that she wanted to spew at anyone she could to purge it from her body.

"I promise, Des, I'm going to help—"

"Help? *Help?!* The only person you're trying to help is *yourself*." The press of Mithya's gift surrounded her, carrying her as if on a tidal current. "We both know the general is *never* going to let me out of here. Del probably thought he was fucking *helping* when he told him about me starting the fire, the stupid fuck. And you're doing nothing more than taking advantage, you—"

She grunted as she pressed her hands to her temples, her head suddenly split by an invisible axe, blurring her vision. She thought she heard cries from down the hall, then a louder, familiar voice shouting furiously in the room with them. *Del? He's here?* She cracked her eyes open to see only Mithya, sitting and staring at her with sorrow in her eyes.

"I'm only trying to protect the people I care about, Des," said the Blue.

"Then why," she groaned through barred teeth, "do you feel so fucking *guilty* about it, huh?"

"I don't—"

"Oh, fucking stop!" Desnia said "Gods, you're practically fucking oozing regret, it's like I'm swimming in it."

She wiped her runny nose and glanced at her hand. Her face turned white as the walls, her heart thrumming impossibly fast as she looked down at the gut-wrenching sight.

Blood. Her blood, running from her nose. Desnia stared at it for a second, realizing that Mithya was doing the same. Looking at the streak, and more vitally, its color.

Crimson, tinged with blue—emulsifying into an unnatural violet.

Mithya went uncharacteristically silent, her full lips parting ever so slightly. Desnia looked at her through searing, blurred vision as the light played tricks on them, casting shadows from the Blue and herself onto the walls, taking the alien shapes of the emotions that filled the room like a gallery of demons.

She saw Mithya's eyes unwittingly flick from her blood-stained hand to the bowl at her side. Desnia glanced at it, then back to the Blue, her heart sinking to the floor. She felt the omnipresent warmth of Mithya's power retract, hidden in shame.

"What did you do?" Desnia asked, her mouth dry and throat ragged.

"I, uh—"

"*WHAT* did you do?!" Desnia screeched.

"I... needed answers," the Blue said, her confidence fleeing.

"You... You put something in the food," Desnia realized with horror.

Mithya swallowed loudly before giving a subtle nod. "...Inanite."

Oh, fuck, said Masini.

Desnia nearly choked. Adrenaline rushed through her veins. Her head pounded until it trembled, the other pains in her body now little more than a second thought. She smacked the bowl away with an angry shriek before scrambling from her cot to a corner of the room, putting herself as far from Mithya as possible. She slid down to the floor while digging her hands through her hair and into her scalp, eyes wide as the shadow's voices became louder. *No,* she thought frantically, *no, no, no, no, NO!*

"What have you done?!" she asked, the terror in her voice cold and shrill as she looked up to Mithya, now standing a few feet away, returning an expression of confused anguish.

Desnia stared at her, shaking, eyes wide with fear as the betrayal set its claws in and tore at her. She'd been a gods-damned fool, tricked by the one thing she'd always denied herself: desire, buried deep. The same which so many fell victim to, herself now included.

And the price was now set to be paid.

Chapter Twenty-Six

Unfortunately, I do not have time to investigate these concerns, as I may have discovered something which surpasses all else. A woman, who is more than she appears.

Kolden's head jerked upright, his eyes snapping open as the chair loudly creaked in complaint to the jarring motion.

Hand pressed against his jumping chest, he took deep, ragged breaths as he steadied himself. He glanced around the dark forge, the coals beside him long extinguished, searching for an explanation for the frantic chaos stampeding through his mind. Only the dim light of the courtyard's dying braziers flickered through the tall windows of the forge, and all around him was a stilled, dusty silence.

He wiped sweat from his brow, the cool air chilling his skin and sweat-soaked back with a shiver. *A dream,* he thought, leaning forward and resting his elbows on his knees. *When was the last time a dream woke me up like that? Drunt?*

Its details sieved from his recollections like sand between his fingers, and within moments he was left with little more than a blank void where his slumbering wanderings had recently drifted. He squeezed his eyes closed, trying to remember, but was left with little more than grogginess he was forced to blink away.

Standing slowly and stretching his aching joints—reminding him with stiff pangs of discomfort the hazards of sleeping awkwardly in chairs—he felt his way through the inky darkness. It was made easier by the recent cleaning, the members of Orne's squad making short work of the disaster that the once-glorious foundry had been. By the time they'd left, they were covered in more soot than the equipment they'd cleaned.

Probably could have done without Orne shouting at them all the while, he thought, recalling his brother's particular leadership style.

Kolden twisted his neck with a grimace, trying to get the crook out of his muscles. He had not intended to fall asleep, only to watch the coals and confirm the efficacy of the newly swept ventilation. Instead, he'd fallen back into old habits.

What's the point? he thought with a sigh. *Anything aside from figuring out how to protect ourselves is moot. There's a threat out there, and all we have are questions. What happens when they inevitably come for us—*

A sound from beyond the windowpanes to his left broke his thoughts. He stopped and squinted, looking through the streaks on the freshly washed glass into the courtyard beyond, wondering who else could be awake at this hour. *Wall guards, maybe?* He didn't realize the captain bothered to man the battlements of this forsaken fortress.

A heavily accented voice fell upon his ears, muffled by the stone and glass. The rhythm of the speech was familiar; he recognized it as one of the members of their caravan. *I know I've heard that accent before, but where?* he wondered with a scrunched brow. It had bothered him the entire journey here. The answer was not unlike his dream, slipping from grasping fingers as he struggled to recall his other encounters. His eyes went wide with realization.

The smugglers! He had only heard them speak for that brief moment when Orne had barged into his meeting in Brethefen, but it was the same tongue, he was certain.

An identical accent did not necessarily identify the traders they traveled with as smugglers, merely that they called the same land home. But a meeting in the blackest hours of the night as it weened the coming sunrise was circumstance enough to give him pause.

Two shadows shifted in the murky darkness across the courtyard. Hooded and cloaked, Kolden's view was obfuscated, their words little more than unintelligible pitches and tones.

A desire grew within him, an interest sparking and seeding the need for him to know what this discussion pertained to. An itch he couldn't scratch.

After a few more hushed whispers, the two figures turned and walked along the courtyard's edge before passing beneath an arch to an unknown part of the keep.

He scampered to the door, taking great care to open it slowly and stop short of the ringing squeak that it was prone to. He closed it as quickly as he dared before stalking between the light of the braziers, half-stepping on the balls of his feet. He threw glances to the surrounding walls and windows, seeing no lights beyond the few torches that were lit around the gate.

All was silent. All was still.

The courtyard was immense, meant to house a legion of soldiers preparing for march, and Kolden cringed with every scrape of gravel on stone beneath his toes. No other sounds befell his ears, however, as he anxiously made his way across the wide flagstones. As he reached the arch the two figures had walked into, he pressed his back against the masonry, letting out his held breath.

He couldn't explain what had driven him to such precautions. After all, he was a lieutenant and had every right to ask questions of anyone meeting in such a clandestine way. But there had been this... feeling, a sort of premonition since arriving at this archaic place, that told him to trust in nothing.

He thought it was best to heed such instincts.

Crouching low, he turned the corner and crept along the wall of the passageway, his own outline becoming one with the smoky black. Every step warranted vigilance, lest he accidentally strike some unseen object and create a ruckus that would alert his quarry. After a few dozen paces, he heard voices coming from ahead, and he soon found himself adjacent to a cracked doorway, the speakers' words carried down the echoing stone halls of what lay beyond.

"...told you what this one is we wish to purchase," said the first voice in the heavy accent. He tilted his head, bringing his ear closer.

The next voice he recognized as Villera's. "You can buy what I say you can buy. Besides, I never said I had anything to sell aside from—"

"I will give you fifty percent over your current offer. And stop pretending that you don't have any. We've bought enough product to know what process you're using. It could never be so potent otherwise." *That's Phrenwa,* he recognized. *What is he trying to buy at this hour?*

There was a silent pause. Kolden craned his head closer to the door's gap. After thirty heartbeats that pounded like a drums through his ears, Villera responded. "Even *if* I had what you're asking for, how do you know I haven't sold it all?"

"I promise, Lieutenant, the people I am here for are not ones you wish to dismiss. Name your price, and it will be granted. If protection or asylum from your client are what you seek, then perhaps we could discuss this one as well. But I do not intend to leave empty handed." Kolden had never heard the man's tone sound anything other than pleasant and friendly, but the words he spoke now were punctuated and deep, carrying the weight of a threat, speaking implications even Villera should be capable of picking up on.

"Sorry, Phrenwa," said Villera unapologetically. *Guess he didn't get the hint.*

"The money and the buyer's man are already on their way here to collect. And he ain't the type to renegotiate."

"Ah, but it's late, is it not?" asked Phrenwa coyly.

"How do you know that?!" The lieutenant's tone was beginning to brim with the petty spite Kolden had met upon their arrival. "I swear, if you have something to do with that—"

"I do not. If you do not believe me, ask those we traveled with. We did not see or attack any on our journey here."

"You think I'd believe the word of a couple spies from the city?! I trust them less than I do you!"

Spies? Seriously? How paranoid is he?

"Regardless," said Phrenwa calmly, "My sources say the man you were conducting business with is suddenly much less wealthy. To the benefit of the crown, no less."

"What're you talking about?" Villera grated.

"His money and assets were taken the day before we left Brethefen. Surely he made you aware of his sudden... poverty?"

Kolden's eyes lit up as he nearly gasped. *The principal?!* Jerdine *is Villera's buyer? What could he possibly have that that bastard would want?*

"Bah!" the lieutenant snapped, the dismissal echoing across the stones in the corridor around Kolden. "You're making this up! You don't know who our buyer is, and even if you did, who says you didn't sabotage their convoy on your way here, huh? What's your plan, beat them here and try to steal it out from under our noses?"

"Write to Brethefen, you will find that what I say is true—"

"No! Don't forget that I saw everything that was on your carriages. Unless you've got some Blue that can pull a cart's worth of gold out of his ass, you don't have the means to outbid our buyer."

"We have ways of delivering payment, I promise you."

"Promise? As if that's worth anything from someone like you. You're as daft as those two you brought with you from the city."

There was a pause before Phrenwa responded in a level, chilling manner. "Like me?"

"Yes! Like *you*. Don't think I don't recognize that accent. You're pretty good at hiding it, I'll give you that, but your boys have let a few slips of the tongue out since they've been here. Wasn't much, but then it doesn't need to be for people here to recognize. So, if you think I'm going to go with you for 'protection,' let alone trust that you'll actually pay me, you can think again."

"I see," replied Phrenwa quietly.

"Yeah, you'd better. Here," Villera said with the *thud* of something being tossed to the ground, "your next order."

"It looks smaller than the last one."

"Aye. More expensive too. Two hundred suns for the lot."

Kolden heard the jostle of a coin purse. "I hope that you reconsider—"

"Keep hoping. I want you and yours gone come morning."

"We will make it so. And you should know, this man you are dealing with, his lack of funds will not deter him from acquiring what he wants. It would be better, and safer, for you to sell this one to me."

Villera let out a grunt. "Goodbye, Phrenwa."

Kolden heard the shuffle of boots, his heart nearly going into his throat. He spun, scurrying away as fast as his feet could quietly carry him. The sound of a door creaking reverberated down the passageway behind him, ushering him with haste.

Ducking around the end of the arched tunnel, he frantically searched for a hiding place. He ran, ignoring the sound of scattering pebbles flung from his shoes, and skidded behind a pile of decrepit crates, desperately trying to slow his breathing. He pulled his shirt over his mouth, attempting to hide both the fog of his breath and the noise as he pressed against the splitting wood.

The cloaked figures of Phrenwa and Villera strode from the black depths of the tunnel as though torn from shadow itself, parting ways and walking in different directions without a word of discourse.

He peeked above the crate into the dim courtyard, watching as the lieutenant climbed the stairs. He and the merchant appeared unaware of Kolden's current or former presence, and he eyed the merchant as he seemed to glide with an unnatural grace towards the stables, a large sack in his hand.

What the hell is going on here? he wondered. Who was it that they'd traveled through the desert with? The man he'd listened to speak tonight was one whose flat tone implied capabilities of a depraved, dispassionate nature. *And we shared meals with them,* he thought, his gut wrenching.

Then there was Villera. What was he selling that could pique the interests of a High Realm mage? *And he said that he had a man on the way... Oh, no.*

If he or Orne were recognized, the former principal was likely to come for them himself.

He spun and rushed into the tower that led to his and his brother's sleeping quarters, racing up the stairs two at a time.

They'd been moved to keep them from danger. Yet it had found them all the same.

And the coals are stoked into fire. Gods-damn it.

CHAPTER
TWENTY-SEVEN

I believe she may be able to guide us to our salvation, and has a companion you may be acquainted with. I shall spare no details...

Mockingbird

The evening sun settled behind the western mountains, filling the sky with swirling hues of blood and water and blanketing Delvan in unease. He stood at a street corner as the city sank into shadow, staring down to its end where the stark white walls of the Asylum were just visible, standing apart from the brightly painted buildings that otherwise surrounded it.

He fiddled with his sapphire, a feral anticipation scratching under his skin as he thought about what waited for him inside the distant edifice—and what crossing its threshold risked for his future.

He played his reunion with Desnia through his mind. What would he say? The apology he owed, for one. More than anything he wanted to promise her release, to protect her from more danger. But could he do that, not knowing if it was possible?

Hopefully she's happier to see me than Mithya, he thought. *She's in a more dire situation than she might realize, surely, she understands what Mithya's gift used on her could—*

The *scuff* of sandals on brick caught Delvan's nerve-racked attention. He turned to see a middle-aged woman wearing a white robe, the customary white rings of the Holy Hands stitched around the garment's cuffs.

"Conduit," said the woman with a reverent bow of her grey-specked head, her skin beginning to show the wrinkles of time that the desert sun bestowed.

Not with the title again, he thought with an annoyed grimace. Each utterance of it was increasingly reverent, and made him increasingly uncomfortable. "My Lord or Delvan will suffice," he replied tersely. "I'm assuming Nerio has told you what I need help with?"

She nodded, glancing down the street. "Getting inside will be simple enough, given your rank, but..." she said, shifting nervously, "you're going to draw a considerable amount of attention."

I usually do, especially recently. "I can deal with the guards' questions; they normally don't push questioning a Blue."

"Um," said the woman, "I did not mean from the guards, Con-um, my Lord."

Delvan raised an eyebrow. "Who then?"

"The Asylum's residents, of course."

"What do you mean?"

"Do you not know what the Asylum is?" she asked curiously.

He shrugged. "I know they've turned it into a makeshift prison. It was a little hard to find, but I can't say I know what it was used for prior. Why?"

"Some would argue that the Asylum was a prison long before the recent fires," she said with a solemn shake of her head. "It houses your kin, the ones who the Court seems eager to hide from view."

Kin? The Court? "What're you talking about?"

"Seers, my Lord," she said, giving him a look of confused dismay. "Did you not know where they were sent?"

Delvan's head jerked back, turning wide-eyed and looking from the building to the Hand at his side. "Blues?" he asked, his gut turning over.

She nodded. "Mhm. The Witness used to work here, you know. Given their temperament, there were few who were willing to come and help. The other Hands speak of this place as though it's cursed."

His initial shock turned to a somber remorse. That other Blues were cast out to the other side of the empire for nothing more than being different was a sentiment that he felt to his core, and he fought back a geyser of emotion that tried to force its way from his chest.

"I will need to cover my sapphire then," he said, remembering back to his last experience with a Seer back in Calentine. The ravings induced by once more being in the presence of their long-removed jewel took hours to recover from.

"Mhm," she agreed with a nod. "That would be a kindness."

"Thank you," he said, "for watching over them all this time."

The Hand shuffled her feet, turning her head to the side. "I... I must be honest, my Lord, as I feel it would be a sin to do otherwise. I didn't want this assignment, originally." Her voice was crestfallen, her head low. "I... resented it. These people are troubled, and it takes a strong heart to return here, day after day. But I see now, the gods wanted me here, so I could aid you in protecting the Messiah. May they forgive my doubts. May *you* forgive my doubts."

He stifled a sigh at the reverence. "It's... fine. Just get me inside for now. Do you know where Desnia is? How many guards she has?"

The woman's posture straightened, as if a few simple words from him had been enough to renew her faith. *Gods-damn it, Nerio.* "She's on the second floor," the Hand said, "most of the first is now only used as a prison. The guards there won't think twice about you, I suspect, but up with the Seers and the Messiah might be another matter. She has two guards at her door at all times, and they only allow the Truthsayer and those of us fortunate enough to bring her food to come to the door."

Damn, he thought, *I was hoping that wasn't the case.* He felt at his pocket, the parchment within it crinkling. On it was a writ that he'd forged—poorly, in his estimations, but hopefully well enough—from the general stating to provide him access. If he managed to fool the guards, there was still the inevitable outcome of word reaching the general about his visitation. He cringed at the thought. "Let's hope an opportunity presents itself," he said, more to ease his own nervousness than anything else. "Lead the way."

"Of course. Follow me, my Lord. We will approach the entrance that the guards keep clear."

Delvan furrowed his brow. "Keep clear of what?"

"The worshippers, of course."

He looked from her to the building. In the shadows of the surrounding structures, he noticed dark outlines shifting and kneeling in seething, undulating masses. *By the gods,* he thought, seeing more and more the longer he looked, *there must be hundreds of them.*

Going through such a crowd, given his "Conduit" status, could be disastrous. *We don't need another incident like what happened at the guild,* he thought, his hair raising at the memory of the uncomfortable stares and gawking protestors.

Nodding, he let the Hand guide him through a maze of narrow alleys and cluttered streets. During the interminable trek, he began to think again about his priorities, his convictions, and the thoughts hidden beneath the surface he dared not reach in and reveal. All the while an urgency propelled him forward, a foreboding sense that he was somehow running out of time.

The room's shadows circled around Desnia, mocking and berating her as their dark outlines blurred across the contrasting walls.

She crumbled to her knees in the room's corner before hunching forward in pain, her arms and forehead pressing against the hard tiles. Her lungs battled tense muscles and stabbing pains at her side with shallow breaths. The pain was subdued by the greater agony that throbbed throughout her body, emanating from the hammering in her skull. Cold sweat seeped from her pores, shivers running along her skin.

Despite the pain, there was a noise in the background that was impossible to ignore. Although no one but Mithya was present, she thought she once again heard the shouting of an argument between the Blue and someone else, their voice ringing with familiarity. *Is that Del?* she wondered again between the haze of pain and phycological anguish.

Mithya had nearly leapt from her chair upon seeing the blood trickling from Desnia's nose, her visage plastered with shock at what the off colored letting exposed. The Blue quietly stammered, "You're... You're a—"

"No!" growled Desnia, pulling her head up from the floor, glaring at her captor through soaked locks of hair. "I'm *nothing* like you, so don't you *dare* fucking say it."

"I would never have... Why didn't you say something?!"

"Fuck you!" Desnia spat as she rolled to her side, causing a flash of pain from her rib, doing little to diffuse the other acute aches. The hot pressure of Mithya's abilities had abandoned her psyche—it seemed she'd begun restraining herself at long last. But it mattered little at this point, the damage was done, exemplified by the voices which now jeered and clapped, the cacophony sounding like a misaligned rhythm of clashing steel as they danced over the walls.

Mithya fell to a knee, her voice apologetic and sullied by remorse. "Des, I-Wait, what is *that?*"

Through pressed, narrowed eyes that blurred and struggled to focus, Desnia saw Mithya's hand come for her throat. She tried to bat it away, feeble as her weakened muscles may be. The effort was as meek as her arms were frail, however, and Mithya easily pushed her paltry defense to the side as she grabbed at something. Desnia felt a tug, and then, with abject horror, saw the Blue lifting the chain bearing Masini's ring to her eyes.

Oh, fuck, she heard Masini say, *Des, you look terrible. Listen, you need to focus, and... By the fucking Greats, she is* gorgeous, *no wonder you let down your guard. Sorry, focus, right. Whatever you're seeing or hearing, you can control it, just take a deep breath and choose one thing to focus on, don't try to take it all in, you can't.*

Desnia reached out an arm from the floor, desperate, tears streaming down her cheeks as Mithya held the ring to her face, inspecting it closely. In the end, she was as helpless to wrestle Masini back from Mithya as she was to escape—the distance as insurmountable as reaching the horizon's edge beyond the sea.

"This is..." said Mithya, narrowing her eyes, "this is a *contract* spell. An incredibly powerful one. *Where* did you get this?"

Wait, said a confounded Masini, *how does she know that? Blues shouldn't know that... Not even Truthsayers should know that. Unless... Ohh, Des, I, um, don't like this.*

"Give..." Desnia sputtered, spit flying from tight lips, "give him back."

"*Him?*" Mithya said with a furrowed brow. The Blue glanced from the polished, patterned ring to Desnia, her eyes going wide with realization. "Blood of my fathers, you're good. If this is what I think..." Admiration blended with regret in her words, an angry remorse following behind. "But damn it, Des! If you'd just fucking told me, I would never have... I didn't want to hurt you!"

"Gods forbid," Desnia groaned spitefully, "you don't get what you want."

Her head pulsed behind her eyes as if a brick had suddenly collided with it, the voices shrieking like sirens. They cried of death, ruin, and failures like an uproarious stadium. Desnia held her hands to her ears, shutting her eyes from the blurring figures that began translucently filling the room, moving in streaks of blue and black. She thought she heard Mithya bursting into the hall, calling for medicine, but she couldn't be sure it was truly her, or one of her many figments.

Desnia let out a guttural scream, trying to drown out the stridency surrounding her. The racket continued, and she thought back to Masini's words, attempting to find one voice in the mesh of thousands she could focus on, trying to save her mind from further, irreparable shredding.

There was one. Distant and deep, it overshadowed the others. She clung to it, letting it float her above the sea of sounds. Her tremors ceased, the waves of pain steadying. She opened her eyes, seeing Mithya kneeling above her, surrounded no longer by shadows, but the light that cast them. Its warmth soothed her chills, its presence quelled the uproar, and its unspoken control was absolute.

Despite Desnia knowing it could do with her what it willed in that moment, the presence made a request. She held an inherent understanding of the harm acquiescence would entail, but within that same comprehension was the knowledge that her own future, along with that of everything she knew, was at stake. With great sufferance she released her mind from her physical being, and when her mouth opened, her voice no longer her own.

But that of a god's.

Delvan's finger tapped the pommel of his sword as a cold sweat beaded his brow. He was relieved that his guide had been correct—the guards had given him nothing but a few glances as they passed through the halls of groaning inmates—but an angst still burned in his veins. And this place did little to calm his nerves.

They'd walked past rooms with as many as a half dozen prisoners crammed inside. The putrid odor of blood and defecation insufficiently masked by the hay strewn over the floor, and Delvan was constantly attempting to suppress a gag as they walked the filthy corridors.

Inversely, the second floor was comparatively pristine, the air fresh and floors still shining with a worn polish. The walls were covered with flaking paint, and the fixtures were aged and rusted, true, but he felt as though he'd entered a palace after the journey through the nightmare below.

He fidgeted with his sapphire again—now wrapped in a cloth dyed white with muted inanite—as they walked through the maze of halls. Masking the power that emanated from his gem would keep it from affecting the Seers populating these halls, but such suppression did not discriminate.

He too would not be able to tap into its power, suffocating his gift.

Without it, he'd be able to light a candle at most, and his gift's absence left him feeling exposed and hollow, as though a piece of him had been carved from his chest. He reminded himself of the havoc it would create, and the turmoil he would expose those around him to should he remove the protective covering.

Still, the gem twisted between his fingers all the same.

There were fewer guards present on the second floor, the long white halls lined with barred, unmanned doors that stood out from the surrounding walls like headstones in a field. Through the small viewing portals, Delvan could see the residents—the Seers—staring with hollow eyes back at him, a lack of understanding and cognizance behind some, others agonized by the awareness of what he was and his representation of the life they once had.

A surge of pity crested over him, and he wished for nothing more than to be able to restore these lost souls to their former status, to free them of their madness.

"Do their houses know they're here?" Delvan asked as they strode down the hall.

"Sadly, my Lord, yes," the Hand in front of him replied somberly. "Worse yet, they are often disowned, leaving the care—and cost associated with it—on the church to bear."

Delvan scowled. *Of course they do. Can't risk blemishing the family name now, can we? And it saves a few suns? Typical.*

After a maze of twists and turns, the Hand slowed to a stop in the middle of a hallway, turning to face him.

"Wait here, my Lord," she said. Delvan's brow dug down, his impatience urging him to move quickly. "The Messiah's room is around that next bend, down the hall," she continued. "Let me go, I can make it seem like I'm doing rounds and will come back and let you know what I find."

Delvan ground his teeth, his first instinct to go sprinting down the passageway. *But if there's a chance I don't have to use this fake writ, then it might be worth waiting a few minutes,* he decided. It would be foolish not to attempt to avoid inciting the general's persecution.

He gave a nod and then watched as the woman grabbed a jug from a shelf nearby and walked around the distant corner, the sound of her sandals *clapping* against the tiles fading with each step.

It only took a few stagnant seconds for him to begin pacing in the hall, eyes low as his mind raced. *Even if I'm able to avoid using the writ, there's still a risk of discovery by the general. What am I going to tell him? What if I do have to use it?* he wondered as he considered the litany of crimes the forgery entailed.

A voice to his side made him nearly jump from his skin, his hand instinctively raising, palm facing the source. "The boy with wings has flown back to see me once more, has he?" said a woman whose face was pressed against the iron rods of her door's window. Her grey hair was a chaotic, tangled mess, twisting and curling as to defy the pull of the ground. Her teeth were yellowed, and the wrinkles on her face were deep-set crevasses that sank into her skin as she adorned a crooked, manic smile.

Delvan lowered his hand and cocked his head to the side, trying to place the woman he faintly recognized. He blinked and his eyes went wide as the realization struck him. "Rockin' Mari?"

The Seer he'd met in Calentine all those months ago broadened her smile. "Aw, you remember. Faster with your hands too, well done, well done."

"What can I say," Delvan said hesitantly, lowering his arm, "nearly getting stabbed by you last time made me a little more cautious."

"Not personal, not personal. Did you come all the way here to visit?"

He shook his head. "No, sorry. I'm here for someone else."

"Right, not the companion from last time, though. That's certain. Tried to warn you about him, I did. You didn't listen."

Delvan's heart raced, his face cross as memories of Hilbrun's death deluged into his mind, the claws of a shadowed hand dragging against his chest. "What do you mean? What warning?" He thought frantically back to their last encounter, the woman doing little more than spouting rambling nonsense.

"Doesn't matter, that future's now in the past. Not that you listen. I listen, listen all the time to the voices. A great many souls. They say you're the First to be reborn. A threat you might not seem to her now, but you will. You will."

He closed his eyes and took a deep breath. *What am I doing?* he wondered. *Trying to understand these ravings is going to just lead me in circles.* He was assuming that she was talking about Hilbrun, but for all he knew he was just twisting her words into what his own subconscious wanted to hear.

"Whatever you say," Delvan said skeptically after a moment. He shook his head. He pitied those cursed with this insanity, no Blue was deserving of spending their adolescence dreaming of a future as a knight to only be locked away and taken from their sapphire. But he had little desire to listen and be reminded of the most painful mistakes of his past—wounds that were healing, but still raw. He moved to walk farther down the hall, looking to separate himself from the crazed Seer and the tragedies she caused his memory to induce.

"Listen!" said Mari before he'd taken two steps. "Do you hear him? The mage harks now, speaking to us. To her."

He stopped in his tracks, turning and taking a step closer to the door. "Mage?" he asked, tense. "What mage? Jerdine? The warrior mage? Are they here?" He felt the prickle of needles down his left arm, his throat going tight at the thought. He'd barely managed a draw at their last encounter, and that had been with Orne fighting at his side. Against even one of them he questioned whether his skill would be enough.

"No. No, *listen,*" she said, relief lifting a weight from his shoulders. "The other one, the one who talks like a bovine's asshole."

Delvan shook his head. "The... what? There's a different mage? Here?" *Who is she talking about?*

"Here, not here. A piece of him, trapped here with the girl. He talks, keeps us up at night. Annoying anus, that one."

"None of that makes any sense," said Delvan tossing up his hands. "Can't you just speak plainly?" he asked, exasperated.

"Listen, not much time left, I can feel him coming. His presence..." the woman winced and let out a cry of pain, looking back at Delvan. "Find your brothers, they begin the path. Truth and deceit are joined sides of a coin, and they will pay your toll. And most importantly, accept your fears, or they will consume you—"

Mari's eyes suddenly rolled back as her body shook, her head pulling away from the bars. Delvan stepped forward, reaching for the door's handle, but Mari went suddenly still. Her head was leaned back, mouth open, with eyes displaying nothing but an eerie white. Her mouth moved, but the voice from it was not her own, nor that of anything natural.

A deep resonance came forth, an exultation of power and force that rattle the doors hinges. Delvan felt it reverberate through him, a bass that beat against him like a war drum, the chords of some unknown stringed instrument singing its song of divinity with each booming syllable.

"YOU HAVE ENDANGERED EVERYTHING, CHILD."

Delvan took a step back, mouth agape and hands trembling. The words enveloped him with the grip of a giant, assailing him from every direction and shaking his very core. It was the predator in the grass, the hidden poison of existence, the knowledge of one's final fate.

It was terror incarnate.

His eyes went wide as his head whipped from side to side, finding entranced Seers in each of the rooms, all chanting in unison. The air felt different, turbid, as though it were laden with emotions that clawed at him like the hands of thousands of tortured souls. It filled him with dread, the pain of his worst days boiling within him and the bubbles bursting to foul the air with suffering and loss.

He felt his breath become shallow, his jaw aching and arm and leg going numb. The shadowy phantom he thought he'd dismissed cried with glee as it sank its fangs into his heart. He struggled to breathe, his vision spinning as his heart threatened to explode. But a thought burst through the chaos, dispelling the gloom like the sun's morning light searing away the night's darkness. He fixed his vision down the hall, wiping the sweat from his face as a single, all-consuming charge took precedent in his mind, pealing as loudly as the voice echoing through the halls.

Desnia.

He knew, without question, that she was in danger. She was within arm's reach, a distance that was thick with the barrier of grief and apprehension that muddled the air. It took all he had to not drop to his knees and curl up on the floor as distress crashed over him, but he had no choice. He wouldn't let Desnia fall.

With gritted teeth, he sprinted away down the hall, refusing to allow another's demise while he still drew breath, the voice haunting him with every step.

The words poured from Desnia like fiery ash from a mountain. She rode as a passenger, watching with horror as her mouth moved, bellowing the words of another in a tone that shook the walls around her. She was granted penitent knowledge of her body's inhabitant, bringing her a rueful understanding of the damage that was occurring as a result of such an allowance.

She tearlessly wept, fearing for what her life would look like after this damning event. But she allowed it, for the awareness that rained upon her was vast, its expanse incomprehensible to her diminutive mind. Possibilities filled her surroundings like stars—emotions blinking them in and out of existence—one guiding her course like a beacon of salvation. Set in the dark sky by this moment, it was clear that this was her path to take, though she couldn't understand why.

The assurance did nothing to repair the harm she was enduring. The future, in that moment, seemed irrelevant, and she began to regret this silent agreement.

Her life was beyond her control, and that realization cut at her like the blades of a thousand daggers. No display, no feeling, no matter how convincing, could distract from the helplessness she now felt.

Through eyes not her own, she saw Mithya's face twisted by shock and horror. The Blue knelt before her, her face close enough to Desnia's that she could feel her breath upon her skin—or skin that was once hers.

"YOUR ENDEAVOR JEAPORDIZES MY DISCOVERY. CEASE THIS INQUIRY AT ONCE, OR YOU SHALL BRING RUIN UPON ALL," the voice projected from her throat in its unerring tone.

Mithya became deeply disturbed, shaking her head. The woman's regret seeped from her like fog down a hillside, and Desnia could do little but observe, muscles frozen in place and belonging to another.

"I didn't know," muttered Mithya. Her face was apologetic and pallid, her eyes begging in fear. "I swear, I didn't know."

"I KNOW YOUR HEART." The words were tempered, placating. Whether it was meant for the Blue or Desnia was unclear, but it did little to mend Desnia's fracturing soul. "THE PATH YOU SEEK IS BEFORE YOU, FULFILLMENT

AWAITS YOUR ACTIONS."

Mithya gasped, her hand covering her mouth. After the briefest of pauses, she dropped her hand away, questions flying from her. "What do you need me to do? Where are—"

There was a release, and Desnia felt her body's mobility return to her as she slid back into it like it were a robe being adorned. It felt leaden, her muscles unable to support its immense weight as she collapsed the short distance to the floor. The light that once engulfed the room dissipated, the warmth it provided fleeing and leaving Desnia with the bones, sinew, and skin that now felt as though a shell.

Mithya cut off, her face's excitement diminishing as she realized the presence had abandoned them. It then took on a quiet reverence, leaning in closer to Desnia's huddled form as a pain in her head grew beyond anything she'd ever known.

Her vision blurred with fringes of black as aches and pains blossomed within her, and she was barely able to make out Mithya as the Blue leaned in close. Wiping a lock of hair from Desnia's face as she slowly writhed on the floor, Mithya whispered to her, "I've been looking for you for a *long* time, Des, I think—"

She was cut off as the door burst open with a head-splitting *crash*, fogging her vision further. Through the haze, Desnia could see Delvan over Mithya's shoulder. *Is it Del, isn't it? Or is my mind playing tricks with my eyes once more?*

Delvan—or her mind's projection of him—stood there, face emblazoned with rage. Delvan's hand grasped Mithya's shoulder and turned her to face him, and through the spinning, pulsing waves of black, Desnia saw before her—not a foot from her face—the glint of a polished, metal spike.

Mithya's hairpin.

She felt her breathing quicken, causing the gales of pain to violently storm. What little movement she could manage happened by instinct, her mind in a fog so thick she couldn't discern up from down. The muscle memory of thousands of lifts, the picking of hundreds of pockets, and swiping of more valuables than she could fathom, took control.

As Mithya went to stand to confront Delvan—whose shouting sounded muffled, the words indistinguishable and garbled—Desnia's fingers pinched the hairpin's end, letting it slide free as Mithya pulled away, the hair casually unfurling as it was released and unnoticed in her confrontation with Delvan.

The precious jewelry slipped masterfully into Desnia's hand, fingers tucking it from view in a single motion. She slipped it into her pocket, the distal sensation feeling as though it were still a foreigner, hiding the metal sliver away. She felt the briefest exultation, but even that elation was soon lost as everything became opaque.

She watched Delvan and Mithya as though staring at them through frosted glass as they screamed at each other, and she couldn't help but think she'd seen this happen already. The sensation was fleeting. She felt her body and mind quickly give out, muscles no longer capable of basic functions and her eyelids closing like weighted curtains to quiet her thrashing mind.

The world went black, and she dreamt of a cave that echoed with the rattling of chains.

END PART 2

Interlude

T he Messiah and Her grace upon you!" called out Brother Meneham over the crowd.

The words, as they always did, calmed the gathering's cacophony, drawing a cloud of silence over the people packing the sunny street before him. He scanned their faces. Some he recognized; others were merely mirrored, gaunt visages, a hunger gleaning in their eyes.

They were starved, he knew—bodies and souls panging alike, deprived of the Witness's teachings. Lacking the knowledge of the gods' hands in their lives, in their collective circumstance, left one emptier than any stomach.

Like their predecessors, he would nourish and nurture them through enlightenment.

"Our benediction," he said, "begins with this recognition of the gods' recent favor, for she is blessed, and through that blessing provided us with salvation."

Meneham peered down from his perch atop an overturned crate, questing for the light of faith to glimmer in the gazes fixed upon him. It smoldered there, lost, untenable in the face of their daily oppression. He would rekindle their piety; remind them of the blaze it once was.

He spun for them the tale that had once enamored him so. That day, he had stood among a gathering like this, listening to the Witness recite this new chapter of scripture. How he envied those around him, wishing that he could once again feel the ecstasy of that epiphany. The realization that the gods had not condemned the city and its people, but freed them, had profoundly changed his life.

And oh, how free they were.

After countless recitations of the gate's contest that fateful night, many would come to find the act rote. But not Meneham. He leaned into the words, exuberance saturating the highs, and hushed whispers carrying the lows to attentive ears. Faces began to shine with the light of discovery, and they radiated upon him, bolstering his feverous display.

He finished his retelling, the crowd's awe lifting his spirit into the air, levitating him amidst their unspoken appreciation. The time had come to provide them with a purpose, in the way he had been deigned with direction.

"I share this with you," he continued, "because you must understand, as I have come to, that the gods have made an announcement. A divine edict. It is simply this: the regime of old is contested. By granting the gift of returned life to another, they have shown that the time for change is *now*."

There were nods among members of the crowd, their awe transforming into interest. Into *impetus*.

"Let not ancient laws hold us to the dirt beneath their heel. Let not those who would deny the actions of the gods control your lives. And let not the greed of the wealthy subjugate those who struggle to simply feed their family!"

His words were the binder that joined the throng into a single entity as fists raised and voices jarred the air. Meneham raised his head high, approving of their newfound faith.

"The merchants whose carts overflow with *your* coin not one street over do not *care* about you. They do not *care* about the will of the gods. They are their own deities. Worse, they are *godless*," he said, leaning forward and shaking a hand in the air.

A jeer from the crowd cut through the turmoil. "This is the gods' city, not theirs!" A chorus of cheers rang in agreement.

Meneham righted himself, standing straight and resuming in a calm, even tone, the riled crowd once again quieting themselves to listen. "The gods are with you. You know this now. This city is no longer the King's, nor the guild's, nor the army's! It is the Messiah's! It is of those you worship! It is *yours*! And it is your responsibility, your *duty,* to sow the seeds of renewed deliverance and reap for yourselves what has been given to you!"

The mob roared.

"Go!" Meneham shouted over the discordance. "Reclaim your city! Reclaim your home! And carry with you the assent of the gods!"

With a final rallying cry the group moved as one amorphous entity, marching down the street to the merchant stalls lining the road adjacent.

He allowed himself the smallest of smiles, praising the gods for their intervention in his life, for directing him to the Witness and, through their grace, becoming a voice on their behalf. He would speak the truth of their intent; of the decision they had made.

The King was a lone deity no longer. Another walked this plane.

He would not patiently wait for the gods to act. The words of the Witness himself stated it was in the people's hands to carry out their will. This was not a place to be contested over by those who sullied the youth or claimed invalid birthright. It was the people's. It was his. And he would see it reclaimed.

Meneham stepped down from his makeshift pedestal and sauntered down the street, the riotous din fading in the distance behind him. This day was not over.

His dissemination had only begun.

Part 3
Heartbreak

Chapter Twenty-Eight

Delvan stormed out of the Asylum, tearing the cloth off his sapphire as he closed the distance between him and Mithya.

Desnia had gone unconscious after her fit, and Delvan had been frustratingly unable to extract an explanation from the Truthsayer. The argument which ensued after he'd found Mithya over Desnia's convulsing body was fraught with screams and beratement before transitioning to tense silence as the healers arrived. He had forgone continuing their discourse to hurriedly clean the blood from under Desnia's nose—the less others knew in that regard, the better. Mithya, strangely, had forbidden the healer from removing any of Desnia's clothing to search for wounds.

Their disquiet had stifled the air with tense animosity. They couldn't risk the priest and guards becoming privy to too much information, and Mithya, though upset, seemed satisfied to be excused from his questioning for a time.

The healer eventually concluded there was nothing more for either of them to do aside from wait, prompting their dismissal. Mithya managed a head start as Delvan had hesitated to leave Desnia, forcing him to hasten his pace to speak with the enigmatic Blue beyond the range of undesired ears. She propelled herself with a determination and fervor nearly matching Delvan's own, and he jogged to close the last few feet as they turned down a street lit by a single, dim lamp and the sparkle of stars above.

"Wait!" he shouted as he grabbed Mithya's arm and spun her to face him.

"You're not going anywhere until you explain what happened back there!"

Mithya pulled her arm free, her face sterner than he'd ever seen it. "How should I know?" she asked.

Delvan was confident her normally disinterested ignorance was feigned, another distraction from her true wants. But her tone and expression provoked an urge to believe her words—her eyes looked bewildered, her body shaken, her mind racing. Most would have believed that she was as confused as they were.

Delvan, however, did not.

"Don't *lie* to me!" he exclaimed. "How hard did you press her, huh? I *told you* not to push your gift, to just ask her questions! Why didn't you *listen*?!" Air poured from his nostrils in torrents as his chest heaved, an hour's worth of pent-up anger finally breaking free.

Mithya stared at him with scrupulous eyes, her brow slowly slanting as a conclusion was drawn. "You *knew*!"

Delvan clenched his jaw, taking a moment before answering. "Don't try to pin this on me! This is *your* fault!" he accused with a pointed finger. "I swear, if her mind's gone, I will—"

"Maybe," she said, raising her voice, "if you had mentioned she was a *Blue*, I wouldn't have pushed!"

"She's *not* a Blue." Delvan's voice wavered, struggling to hold his conviction.

"You're a terrible liar," Mithya said in a low tone, shaking her head. "Are you just going to pretend you didn't wipe the blood off her face? The *violet* blood."

Delvan's stomach turned. Before today, he had seen Desnia's blood in daylight once before—the morning after she had been stabbed at the gate. The stains produced by her pierced heart *had* been violet—but the shade was off, too red to be that of a pure-blooded Blue. He had wanted to ask, to confirm his suspicions, but sitting on those steps, with the smoke of the night hanging in the air, he had just been glad for her survival and decided not to press the issue. Opportunities to ask had been cut short by her incarceration.

"What about you?" Delvan retorted. "Are you going to pretend you were there solely because of the general's orders? What selfish desire drove you to hurt her?!"

Mithya gave a short, sardonic laugh, roving her eyes to the sky. "I don't know where you're getting these wild theories from."

"Don't give me that! I'm sure you could have reported to Rosethorn days ago and been done here. *Something* brought you back. *Something* made you force Des into that fit!"

"Maybe I just enjoyed her company. Don't tell me you're jealous. Is that what this is all about—"

"Fine!" he barked, his balled hands shaking at his side. "If you won't answer me then I'll go and report you to Rosethorn myself."

Mithya put her hands on her hips, her eyes narrowing as a confident grin pulled at her face. "No."

Delvan's throat tightened. "What do you mean, 'No?'"

"You're not going to go tattle or whatever nonsense to Rosethorn."

Her attitude held as his frown deepened, shifting his weight uncomfortably. "Of course I am, why wouldn't I?"

"Because, then you'd have to explain what you were doing here. Last I checked, you weren't on the approved list of visitors. In fact, you were specifically listed as not being allowed in. So, tell me, what *were* you doing here?"

Her contented smile was pinned and unmoving, a satisfaction gleaming in her eye at having turned the conversation around. Delvan kept his mouth tightly shut, frantically thinking of an excuse to pull him from the collapsing mine he'd dug himself into.

Standing there, quiet, eyes locked with Mithya, he slowly felt the faint touch of her power raise hairs on his skin, tickling the inside of his skull like an infestation of pests. His muscles tightened as he resisted, his gaze becoming a glower. *After what just happened, how* dare *she use her gift on me?*

A low growl, guttural and deep, came from his throat as he felt the rage boiling over, the indignation of such actions burning hotter than any fire. He threw his clenched fists with a cry, hands opening and releasing an explosion of fire to his sides that scorched and cracked the clay pavers. The flash illuminated the entire street, torching the dried weeds, their flickering glow fading like Mithya's smug grin.

Breathing heavily, sweat dripping into his vision, he glared at the wide eyed Blue. "Use your gift on me again," he said, panting, "and I swear on all of the gods that I will make it the last time."

After a moment—the fire's heat vacating and leaving the warm desert night in its wake—she squinted and asked, "Are you in love with her or something? You seem pretty defensive about the whole issue, and it could make things pretty awkward."

"No! I..." Delvan's teeth clenched together tightly enough that his jaw ached. How could she keep making light of what had happened? "You," he asked, beginning to tremble, "don't even *care* about what you just did to Desnia, do you?"

Mithya had the gall to roll her eyes. "Look, before you consider doing something stupid, you should know something," she said, almost nonchalant. It seemed that the effects of whatever had happened in the Asylum had begun to wear off, and she was back to her old self. Regrettably.

"Rosethorn isn't going to care that Des is hurt," she said. "He only cares that he gets answers. Also, I am *supposed* to be here, so, if he does reprimand someone, it's going to be you for disobeying a direct order. Not a good look on your part, I must say.

"And believe it or not," she said, her tone becoming slightly more serious, "yes, I do care about Des. More than you know."

"Could've fooled me," he grated.

"For the hundredth time," she said, exasperated, "I didn't mean to hurt her. I *had* to push her because she wasn't just good at avoiding questions, she legitimately resisted them. Which, I shouldn't have to tell *you*, isn't something even Blues can do all that well."

"But you didn't just push. You forced your gift on her so hard that *something* took possession of a dozen Seers and told you to stop."

He regretted the words the moment they left his lips.

"*Something*?" Mithya asked, her eyes scrutinizing him. He held his lips tightly together. "What else aren't you telling me? Did Des tell you something?"

Delvan waited, itching for her to use her gift and give him an outlet to focus his ire.

Disappointingly, nothing came.

"What she told me isn't important," he lied. "And why is it you don't seem the least bit disturbed about what happened in there?"

She shrugged. "Reasons. Also, considering you thought not mentioning to me that Des was a Blue wasn't important, I would say that your judgement isn't exactly worthy of credence."

"Even if I did know any of Des's secrets, what makes you think I would tell them to you?" he said with a sneer.

"Well," she said with a prolonged, feigned innocence, "I could just, you know, make you."

"Try it," he growled, "and I will make your boots your own personal pyre."

She gave a flippant wave of her hand. "No, you won't, Sparky." He felt the rage building inside of him again. "But fine, I know everything I need to anyway." Without hesitation, she spun and began walking away, leaving him in the shimmering heat of his own anger.

Delvan's stomach turned as her words settled, the implications chilling his temper with icy veins. *She can't know. Unless... Did Desnia tell her? Does she know that Des was planning on seeking and freeing a* god? He hoped not. Before this evening, he would've said it was because such nonsense could result in her becoming a permanent resident at the Asylum. Now... now he wondered what amount of truth was behind the claims.

Furthermore, if Mithya did know, why hadn't she told the general? *Or has she?*

"Wait!" he shouted.

Mithya stopped, turning back and giving him a triumphant grin. He felt some of the ice melt.

"Have you..." he grimaced, hating that he was backing himself into a corner. "Have you reported any of your discussions to the general?"

She shrugged. "We've spoken, yeah." Delvan felt the blood drain from his face. Her smile broadened. "But only about the fires and the principle. What were you so worried about me saying?"

"I wasn't-uhm, I wasn't worried," he stammered.

"Is that why your face went whiter than the mountains?"

Delvan opened his mouth, but his tongue refused to bend. There was no argument to be made, no excuse for his question that wouldn't entrench him further. Eventually he shut it, his words chained to anchors of possible outcomes—each threatening to drown him.

"How about this," she said as she stepped back towards him, "you tell me what I want to know and I won't tell Rosethorn about, well, everything."

How had this conversation so completely turned against *him*? "You *wouldn't*," he said with a quiet desperation. She might be right about Rosethorn being indifferent to Desnia's condition, but there was always the chance that he'd be irate about his primary source of information on the principle and his group becoming incognizant by her hand. Unless she misconstrued and twisted that, too.

"You sure?" she asked with narrow eyes. "Like, really sure? Who knows, I might have some slip of the tongue and whoops, the general knows that Des is a Blue. I bet he will have a lot more questions after that."

Delvan's instincts told him that she was bluffing. She was manipulating him, using his fears against him.

He glared at her with a sneer, thinking about turning to leave, walking away and ignoring her—hopefully—empty threats. Maybe he could get Desnia out of the Asylum before Mithya was able to visit her again. Or maybe she would undermine him at every turn—starting with giving what Delvan suspected would be a lengthy report to the general. Someone who lied with the ease of breathing could want for naught but their own gain, Desnia's pain could be little more than a means to an end for her.

Even with leverage in hand, he still had no idea what Mithya wanted. And there was the possibility that, in this last effort, she'd gotten all the answers that she needed from Desnia.

Delvan didn't know what condition Desnia would be in after she woke up—assuming she did at all—and he couldn't risk Mithya giving up her secrets, lest she be forced to endure more torturous visits.

Gods, I'm really starting to hate this woman. "What is it," he asked through barred teeth, "that you want to know?"

She gave him that gods-damned grin again. "I knew you'd come around," she said jovially. "Tell me, does the name 'Masini' mean anything to you?"

"If I answer your questions, do you swear that you're going to keep it from Rosethorn?"

"Sure."

"That's not an answer!"

"Well," she replied casually, "it's the best one you're going to get. So come on, out with it. Masini. Does the name mean anything to you?"

He hated this situation. He hated that he'd dug himself into it. Most of all, he hated not knowing what would come of it.

But what choice did he have?

"It sounds familiar," he said, "but I can't say I know who it is."

She scrutinized him with lips pursed. "Hmm, I'll take your word for it since you're so... touchy. Alright then, tell me, why aren't *you* bothered by what just happened in there?"

Delvan's face became cold. "What do you mean?" he asked.

"Mhm, don't play coy," she said with a knowing smile. "You said that I didn't seem bothered by all the Seers who suddenly, as you put it, were 'possessed by something.' Only, you're the one who came running into Des's room, almost like you *knew* that she was in trouble. Give me every detail, and don't hold back or I'll know. Your innocence has a certain charm, but it means you can't lie to save your life."

"What does that say about you, then?" he snapped.

"That I'm better at getting what I want? Now, answer the question please."

Delvan could feel his heart beginning to race, the thought of exposing Desnia's request to him bringing back the phantom hand that pierced his chest with its claws, spreading pain through his body and black venom through his blood. He would have to give her something, but he couldn't expose the heart of the matter. He wouldn't. Besides, he needed to keep a slipping grip on some semblance of leverage in this conversation. *Not that I've managed to retain any so far...*

"She... asked me to join her," he said hesitantly. "After the night at the gate, she asked if I would accompany her to seek someone out."

"This *someone* have a name?" Mithya asked, leaning in with an eager glimmer in her eye.

"Not that she mentioned, no."

Mithya wilted, ever so slightly, before bringing herself back to her normal repose. "Still doesn't explain how you knew Des was in trouble."

"Call it a gut feeling," he said, putting all his spite into the chomped words. It was a half-truth, which was more than he expected from Mithya, and he hoped his disdain was enough to cover the other half.

Her lips tugged down, gaze narrowing. "Well, that's disappointing." Delvan let out an internal breath of relief. "What were you doing here, anyway?"

"I was here," he grated, holding onto the frustration that had worked to mask his nerves, "to speak with Des."

"Why?"

"Because you aren't the only one with questions," he replied honestly, and tersely. Mithya knew these details of the night at the gate, and it allowed him to answer truthfully.

"...About?" she said after a pause.

"More information about how I healed her, for starters," he said.

"Ah, yes, cadentite makes us do some *weird* stuff," she said, as though it were common knowledge. "Too bad you muted our largest supply."

Delvan blinked, his jaw dropping in shock. "H-How do you know that? Did Des tell you that?" She'd revealed the source of his healing gift with knowledge bestowed by a High Realm mage. He'd only admitted in his report that he suspected cadentite was what allowed him to heal, omitting Desnia's statements. But Mithya's words were so... certain.

"I know a great many things," she said with a wink. "But a girl can't share all of her secrets in one go, now, can she? Need to keep the intrigue alive."

"I'd really prefer you didn't and tell me what you know. I..." he pinched the bridge of his nose, taking a deep breath. "I *need* to know."

"Another time, maybe. I might want to have another one of these conversations, after all."

"I'd rather—"

"So," she interrupted, "you came all this way, and the *only* thing you were going to talk to Des about was yourself?"

"Well, no... I mean, when you put it like that it sounds... This is important!" he said, frustrated. *She doesn't even have the whole story, and she's judging me after everything she's put Des through?* Mocking him about an honest answer was simply impudent.

She leaned back, eyeing him up and down. "You really don't understand women, do you?"

"What the hell is that supposed to mean?! I understand women just fine."

"You took the risk of coming here, and you weren't even planning to apologize? You do realize she's a bit upset about the whole being locked up thing, don't you? Kind of blames you, as I'm sure you're aware."

"Of *course* I was going to apologize," he said. Why would she suggest otherwise?

"And you think that she'd forgive you, just like that?" she asked.

"Well... no. But I had... I mean I was going to... Never mind," he dismissed with a wave.

"Oh, I see," Mithya said with her sly grin.

"See what?"

"You were going to make it up to her somehow, weren't you?"

Delvan's gut lurched. "I don't know what you're talking about."

"Uh huh," she said, smile curling. "You know, having had some time to get to know her, I can tell Des isn't the type to forgive easily. Sort of holds a grudge." *Thanks for the reminder.* "I assume you know this, so what could you offer that you think would warrant her forgiveness? You must have had *something*."

"I was going to start with 'sorry,'" he said, his mouth dry. The answer, disappointingly, did little to sate her curiosity.

"What was it? What did you think could buy her forgiveness? And don't tell me it was your charm, as good of a laugh as that would be."

He felt pain begin to throb in his jaw, familiar pins crawling down his left arm as terror froze him in place. The twisting vortex of insatiable malice consumed his thoughts, taking the reins of his consciousness. His brain refused to provide an answer that would satisfy the Blue before him.

He had been betrayed by his own mind. A cold, wicked realization.

Was this how Desnia felt about him?

In the whirlwind that was his stagnant posture, he missed the creeping sensation that wormed through. The tendril of power moved with the delicate touch of a lover, and cut with the exactness of a surgeon, reaching in and finding what it wanted before he realized.

By then, it was too late.

"I'm going to break her out," Delvan blurted.

His eyes became orbs, dry and wide as his hand smacked against his mouth.

Mithya's smile tugged all the way to her eyes.

The answer, he realized in astonishment, was an honest one. It had been there, driving him forward under the guise of a belief that any other means to Desnia's release was possible. His requests and letters were never going to go anywhere. The general would have more questions than answers, and the city wasn't going to settle in time for Desnia to escape her affliction. Not after that outburst. There was no alternative.

And he found, most surprisingly of all, that he was comfortable with that. He *did* want to choose his own life, and that meant selecting the people that resided within it. A title did little to replace the connection he felt in his veins. This was a secret he'd kept from himself, one that he would have needed to face eventually.

Until Mithya ripped off the veil.

It did not excuse her invasion into his mind.

The tremor that washed over him took the pain of fear and focused it into rage. He'd warned her. Told her to restrain herself.

And she'd done it anyway.

His hand rose before him, fingers shaking as he thrust his palm towards the Blue. His chest heaved as he glared, the indignity of her actions pushing him over the edge he teetered upon. A part of him screamed in protest of hurting another Blue, a bonded brethren. He suffocated it, preparing himself to immolate Mithya where she stood to protect Desnia and his secret.

She had the audacity to smile back at him.

"What did I tell you?!" he said.

She seemed unfazed. Death stared her in the face, and she didn't carry a single worry on her shoulders. "You're not going to do anything," she said confidently.

"And what," he rasped, "makes you think that?"

"Because," she said, "we want the same thing. I'm going to help you break her out."

Delvan blinked, his arm slowly lowering to his side. Surely, he hadn't heard that correctly. "You... what?"

"You heard me. Now come on, we finally have something exciting to talk about."

She spun on her heels, walking away into the star-ceilinged street. Delvan scratched his head, the anger having vanished, completely replaced with a profound confusion. Was this what she had wanted all this time? But why? A compelling curiosity drove him to begin walking after Mithya, and he decided in those hesitant steps that one thing was a certainty.

He absolutely did not understand women.

CHAPTER
TWENTY-NINE

This woman's release is now your primary goal, at the cost of all others. I am still uncertain how the seal will be bypassed, but Asta would not have gone to such lengths if they did not foresee a solution.

O rne!" Kolden said in a hoarse whisper, rapping on his brother's door in the dimly lit corridor.

He held the rusty lantern to the side as he pressed his ear to the worn wood, the latch to his brother's quarters locked tightly. Snoring reverberated off the stone walls like a line of drums. *I'm surprised he doesn't rattle this thing off its hinges...*

Knuckles tapping against the thick wooden planks more firmly, he rasped as loudly as he dared. "Orne! Open the door, gods-damn it, it's me!"

The rumbling of his brother's nose-trumpet ended in a snort, and all went eerily quiet. He pressed his ear harder, listening, waiting, trying to hear the slightest—

The door flung open and Kolden tumbled into the room, waving his arms and nearly dropping the lantern as he struggled for balance. He caught himself and, after standing straight, turned an ire-filled eye to his brother, standing in his undergarments by the door, sword in hand.

"What were you going to do," said Kolden in an angry hush, "stab me?!"

"The thought's crossed my mind a time or two," replied Orne groggily. "What do you want? What fucking hour is it?" His brother did *not* like to be awoken ahead of schedule.

Sometimes I wonder if he's actually a bear, or a person. "Listen, I saw something. It's bad—"

"Someone get murdered again?"

"What? No, that's not—"

"Then someone's about to be."

Kolden rolled his eyes as he shut the door. "Gods-damn it... Would you just *listen* for a second?!" Orne crossed his arms—the dim, flickering light amplifying his darkened mood. *Grumpy bastard.* "Look, I was coming out of the forge just now, and I saw Villera meeting with Phrenwa out in the courtyard—"

"What were they doing there?" Orne asked, brow furrowed.

"Fuck... I'm getting there! Just, shut up." Orne's brooding worsened. "They went into this room and Phrenwa bought something off Villera, *but* he was trying to buy something else. Like, *really* trying. Only Villera refused. The next thing Phrenwa says is that he knows who Villera's buyer is for whatever he wouldn't sell him. Guess who the fuck Villera is selling this mystery item to?"

"Did you drink like eight cups of tea or something?"

Kolden smacked his hand to his forehead. "Jerdine, Orne! Like, the fucking *principal.* And he's got a man *on the way* here. Right now!"

Orne stood straighter, his face hardening. "Why didn't you start with that?" he asked. "Fuck. Did he say when he was supposed to be here?"

"He said he was late. *Probably* because he has nothing to pay Villera with after *we* helped take all his money from the guild."

"Mhm," Orne grunted. "He's probably pissed about that."

"You *think*?" asked Kolden.

"Wait," said Orne, the gears attempting to turn in his head. "You said it was his *man,* right? Not the actual principal?"

"That's what they said, yeah."

"Oh, then what do we have to worry about?"

Kolden's jaw dropped. "Right. Nothing to worry about. Except maybe an early funeral."

"How would this man know what we look like? No one is expecting to find us out here in the middle of fucking nowhere, Kolden. He could just arrive, buy whatever this 'mystery' thing is, and leave none-the-wiser. Stop worrying."

His fists balled and shook, the lantern quivering. "What if the person he's sending is the man he pulled through the gate, huh? You think *he* wouldn't recognize us?!"

"Oh," replied Orne, the three cogs of his brother's mind finally spinning at capacity.

"Yes, 'oh.' Besides, you think him not having money is going to prevent him from getting what he wants? Phrenwa implied that this wasn't something he was going to let go. What if it's something related to the High Realm? What if he's coming to collect it *himself*?"

"What the hell could be out in this fucking pit that he'd want?"

"I don't know," Kolden admitted. "This was a critical defensive position at one point, maybe it was left here during the last Trethish war? Whatever it is, it's important. That I know."

His brother crossed his arms, scowling. "We need to tell the captain," he said firmly.

"Tell him *what,* exactly? All the things that we were ordered to *not* tell anyone? All we're going to be able to say is, 'Hey, Captain Sloth, there's a really scary priest on the way, and we should prepare. Not that there's anything we can do if he shows up.'"

"Well, we need to tell *someone!*"

Kolden rubbed his forehead in thought. "I'll send a carrier to Rosethorn and Del, they at the very least need to know something nefarious is going on here. Maybe we can get some help—if it shows up in time. In the meantime, we need to figure out what the hell is going on in this castle."

"Mhm, agreed," said Orne as he began taking his armor off the nearby stand.

"What are you doing?"

"I'm going to beat the answers out of Villera, obviously," he replied with a shake of his head.

Kolden groaned. "Stop. Look, I want to give the guy a beating as much as you do—"

"I doubt that," said Orne with a glare.

"But, if we do that before hearing from the general, and the captain finds out, he could have us arrested. Hell, he could have us *hanged.* And I like my neck at its current length, thank you very much."

"But if we can prove—"

"Prove what?! That Villera sold something to a *merchant?* No, Orne, we need to be smart about this, at least until the general gets orders to the captain or we can find *actual* proof."

His brother hesitated, his hands resting on his armor's pauldrons. Kolden could hear his teeth mashing together, digging the ends into his brain no doubt. "If we're not going to force him," Orne grated, "then how the fuck are we going to figure out what he's hiding."

"We could try using our *eyes* instead of our *fists,* for starters. Let's see what we can find around here, maybe we'll figure out whatever it is that's so valuable it would attract Jerdine's attention. Just... try to not let too many people see you doing it."

"What are you going to be doing then?"

"Sitting on my ass," he said with a wave of his hands. His brother's glare intensified, some angry comment sure to bubble to the surface soon. "I'm going to be doing the same thing. What did you think? And I'm going to talk to Phrenwa, hopefully he hasn't left yet."

"You won't let me speak to the lieutenant, but you can go talk to Phrenwa?" said Orne.

"You have no intention of actually *talking* to the man. And yes, though the guy makes me nervous."

Sneaking around the castle didn't bother him. Between his rank and title, there was little most would do to stop him. But the way Phrenwa had spoken to the lieutenant tonight sent chills along his skin, and his stomach churned at the thought of broaching the man's secretive dealings.

"The little, cheery merchant is what bothers you, out of all this?" Orne asked incredulously.

"You didn't hear the way he spoke tonight. I don't know, but I think he's more dangerous than you think."

"Great," said Orne, "is there anywhere we can go where people *aren't* trying to kill us?"

"Good question."

Orne took a few long steps to the window, undoing the latch and pulling back the frosted panes to glance outside. A sliver of gray light striped his face before he returned to his armor to continue adorning the darksteel and leather plates.

"What're you doing?" asked Kolden.

"Sun's rising. Time to see what my new squads are made of."

"We have other priorities, Orne, haven't you been listening?"

His brother shook his head with a scowl. "Yes, Kolden, I've been fucking listening. You might want to know what Villera is selling, but I'm not going to waste time searching for something when I don't even know what it is."

Kolden's face tightened in frustration, his words starting as a growl. "Orne, this is *important*—"

"You know what else is important?" cut in Orne. "Knowing whether or not the people that might have to fight alongside us are capable of actually *fighting*. I intend to find out."

"You don't even know if you can trust them!"

Orne's face twisted. "Some of them might be an issue, but Villera can't have corrupted the *entire* keep. Besides, I'm not going to just sit on my hands and do nothing while we wait for the general or Del to get back to us."

"Fine!" exclaimed Kolden, tossing up his hands. "It's not going to matter if Jerdine comes but go do drills or whatever. I'm going to do something useful and see if I can find Phrenwa before he leaves."

With Orne's only response being a dismissive grunt, he pulled open the door and stormed out. *Idiot. Why is his only response to a bad situation to fight his way out of it?*

As he made his way down the spiraling stairs of the tower, the light of his dying lantern was joined by the dull hue of morning as it bled through the black of night. The castle remained quiet, the stones offering no voice to counter the concerns rampant in his mind.

This is ridiculous, he thought. *If I didn't know better, I'd say someone is* intentionally *putting us in these situations. What fates have aligned to bring us face to face with ancient powers a* second *time?*

As he entered the courtyard—the braziers now cold and black—he dismissed the thoughts with a shake of his head. He needed to focus on how to broach his overheard conversation with someone who had completely hidden what Kolden was certain was a malicious nature. His heart began to race as he approached the carriage house where the caravan members had been sleeping, its windows dark and stalls quiet.

I just need to let them know I'm on their side. Right. I can do that, just need to say, 'Hey, I also happen to know how dangerous that ancient magical fucker is, mind explaining how you—

The double doors of the large building's entrance had swung open effortlessly and without a sound. Maneuvering the hulking door had not been what distracted his thoughts, however. Eyes flitting in disbelief to the sight around him, Kolden's stomach sank, leaving him frozen in place at the entrance as his lantern finally dwindled and, with a flicker, extinguished.

Phrenwa and his company were already gone.

Chapter Thirty

We must act with haste. Reedjin's failure at the gate will have infuriated him but will not deter another attempt. I doubt the plots you've sabotaged were his only efforts.

The latest tally is up to seventeen, Witness," Captain Gernbard said.

Nerio's heart sank. Seventeen people. Could he live with this death toll, spurned by his message? He wiped his eyes as he watched more injured enter the triage tent at their newest sanctuary. The makeshift cots and bedding—mostly blankets spread on the stone floor—were filled with the dozens wounded during the most recent insurrection. The mending of spilled blood had become a theme of his daily life, leaving his heart fractured further with each painful cry.

"Are we certain that Brother Meneham was the one responsible for this?" Nerio asked, praying that it wasn't true.

The captain grunted. "Mhm, unfortunately. Some of the soldiers sent to break up the riot were among the enlightened, and they questioned a few of the participants. After speaking to them, there's no question in my mind."

The tent's shroud of darkness suddenly felt as though it was pressing down on him, suffocating him in a heat borne by despair. His sleeve wiped tears mixed with sweat as a sickness filled his stomach with heinous urgency. He ran out of the tent, past the dense congregation of guards around it, and vomited into an ash-filled corner of the courtyard.

Hands held to trembling knees, he heard footsteps behind him. Gernbard came to his side, offering him a scrap of cloth to wipe his face after the forceful heaves. Dots of white filled the vision that wasn't blinded by the blazing sun, his eyes struggling to adjust from the dim lamps and braziers inside their pauper's hospital.

"How... How can he twist my message like this?" Nerio asked, appreciative-ly taking the cloth. "My words are meant to be a light of hope, not a torch of destruction."

"I'll see that a stop is put to it."

Nerio shook his head, concerned about Gernbard's gruff tone. "Please, do not bring him harm. We must be better than that," he said, the bile still burning his mouth.

"I know you don't want to hear this, but I don't think that is a wise decision, Witness."

"There has been so much death," Nerio said quietly. "I could not face myself were I the cause of anymore. Please, find him and bring him back to me, perhaps I can speak with him."

Gernbard scowled. "Yes, sir. I already have people looking for him, but he's been moving around constantly. It shouldn't be taking this long..." The captain's voice trailed off, his gaze becoming distant. "The soldiers, as much as I trust them... well, let's just say the city's citizens aren't the only ones that are struggling."

"You worry that they are helping Brother Meneham stay hidden?"

The captain remained quiet, a response that disturbed Nerio more than words could have. He had come to rely upon the captain's confidence to strengthen his own. Seeing it falter caused his sense of hope to whither.

"Do you not have faith in your own men?" asked Nerio, wiping away a deluge of saliva as the nausea struck again.

"Let's just say I have some... concerns, sir."

He closed his eyes, focusing on suppressing the urges and twitching mus-cles of his gut. The captain's worries bolstered his own, the man's wisdom seldom wrong.

The churning in his stomach eventually subsided, allowing Nerio to stand straight and take a deep, cautious breath. He needed to do something about this shift in his followers' ideology. It would seem preaching at his speaks would only get him so far—he'd been vehemently suing for non-violence in each of late—and it was yet to take root.

Or, he thought, sickened further, *willfully ignored.*

He looked at the numerous guards standing around the tent, hands on swords, eyes intense as they watched any who walked or hobbled past. There were at least a dozen standing there as though protecting the King himself.

"Are so many necessary?" asked Nerio with a nod of his head. "Those who come here are not of a violent nature."

The captain's lips pulled back, turning them thin. "I think it's better if they stay, Witness."

Nerio turned and looked at him. The response was terser than his normal pragmatic responses, and it was clear that he was holding back. *I cannot have those closest to me remain a mystery. Not after everything that has happened.* "Speak your mind, Captain. I wish to hear your thoughts. Please. There are so few others who are willing to do so with me anymore."

The captain rolled his shoulders, considering. "I know you have a tremendous trust in the people, Witness, but I've seen the depravity of people pushed into corners. Sieges are wicked and vile. They turn the best of people into thieves and killers, and morals do nothing but get you killed. Caution would be best in this case. I ask that you trust me on that."

"But, Captain, we are not under siege."

"Not by some outside force, no, but this isn't all that different. The people are starving, poor, unable to find or afford what they need to simply live. It keeps them trapped here, and the poorer they get, the more entrenched they become. There might not be an army at the walls, but no one here is leaving."

Nerio wanted to reject the concept. His followers were benevolent, having seen the cruelest side of life's indiscrimination. He did not expect them to rise and riot.

"I worry about the contradiction," Nerio said. "I preach, pray, beg, for peace and pacifism, yet we station a dozen guards around a tent of wounded."

Gernbard's face darkened. He spoke hesitantly, as though maneuvering through a thorn thicket. "Except that the wounded include several of the merchants the people attacked, Witness. I would rather be cautious than allow for a mob to form and complete what some might see as unfinished."

It had been a point of contention with the guards and residents of the camp alike, he knew. But Nerio wasn't about to turn away those in need, and though their supplies were meager, there was nowhere else for these poor souls to turn to.

"I cannot leave people to die, Captain. If I did, I would be no better than our oppressors," he said mournfully. *Or others...*

Nerio felt the turn of his stomach once more at the thought. He'd been shaken these past few days, the foundation of his faith undermined by the few simple words of a young boy.

Jerdine was *proud* of him.

His message had been built upon the tenant of spreading that a new messiah had been given to the world. There was no twist to his words, no subtle meanings or violent undertones. Only the soothing reprieve from the hardships of recent tragedies.

Yet, the most scornful, selfish, and malicious person he'd ever known had sent a message to pronounce his awe of Nerio's accomplishments. The proclamation was caustic, eroding the pillar of his faith and leaving him to crumble. Was this Jerdine's intention? Did he wish to return the faith to as it had been during his tenure? Or was there something that Nerio wasn't seeing?

Have I created something irrevocable? Have I given Jerdine something that he wanted?

He let out a bile filled burp, the back of his tongue burning once more.

"I know the situation isn't ideal," Gernbard said, glimpsing Nerio's paling face. "But it will keep the peace."

Unless I am destroying that peace, he thought solemnly. "I understand, Captain. I just wish there was a better way." *And a clearer one.*

Gernbard's response was little more than a grunt, a grain among the sands of bemoaning produced by the sick and injured nearby.

They stood there for a time, silent, Nerio wondering why Jerdine had forced the boy to deliver his message. *Perhaps it means he is out of the city,* Nerio thought with a small flicker of hope. *Otherwise, he may have delivered the words himself.* The flame was extinguished, the knowledge that Jerdine could control his life if he chose settling in.

Again, he felt his sweat turn icy.

Pleads for help burst into the courtyard as a pair entered, their backs hunched under the weight of the limp body they carried between them. A few people ran to help, but Nerio could recognize from even this distance that an owl had already stolen away the person between them. Nonetheless, he took a step forward to assist.

"We should be going," said the captain, putting a hand on his shoulder, "there's a supply delivery coming to the western camp in about an hour."

Yet another one of Nerio's growing concerns. "Captain," he said hesitantly, watching as a healer rushed over. Keens of the lost soul's friends followed shortly after. "I worry about these smugglers that we're using."

The captain let out a disgruntled snort. "You and me both, Witness. But we don't have many options, and they're well paid. Should be enough to keep them civil."

"It's not just that," Nerio said. Over the past several shipments he'd noticed something about the often-quiet deliverers. They occasionally let slip a few curses, or turns of phrase, that Nerio would recognize—but not from where he would have expected. "What do you know about them?"

"What do you mean?"

"Do you know where they're from? This group specifically?" he asked.

"No idea," Gernbard responded with a shrug. "But they come through—most of the time—which is better than I can say about most of their kind. Accents are a little odd though, nothing that I've heard before."

"Therein lies the crux of my concern, Captain," replied Nerio, his voice laced with worry. "I often hear them speaking Trethish." Nerio hoped he was wrong. He'd told himself time and time again this past week that he was mistaken. The doubt had prevented him from mentioning it earlier, but the more he thought about it, the more it ate away at him.

The captain raised an eyebrow, turning slowly to face Nerio, looking down at him inquisitively. "A third of the city still speaks Trethish, Witness. You're not implying what I think you might be?"

Nerio shifted, his arms wrapping around his sides. "It's a different dialect than what's spoken here," he pointed out. "One that is more closely related to the roots of Old Trethish."

The captain chewed on the information for a minute. "Are you sure?"

"I... can't say," he admitted. "I speak the local dialect well enough, but it could be that they're Tennish, or from one of the northern duchies. Perhaps it was nothing, forget that I mentioned it."

The captain remained silent for a time, a look of consternation setting into his visage. "I'll ask around," he said. "I hope you're wrong—Trethish in the city, at a time like this, could be disastrous. If they are though... I might have to go to the general with this."

Nerio's throat went tight. He worried for the captain. The man's dual allegiances would have torn at most men, but the captain remained resolute, separating the two in his mind like he'd cleaved them with his own sword. By all appearances, anyway. How he was able to request the duty of searching for Nerio in the Scar to avert suspicion and not be racked with guilt over his deceit was difficult to comprehend. He saw the captain as a friend, one of the few that he had, and the idea of the man feeling turmoil over Nerio's words broke his heart.

"I could be wrong," Nerio pointed out. "A Trethish spy has not been caught within the city in decades, after all."

"None that have been made public, at any rate," grumbled Gernbard. "All the more reason to watch over the next delivery. If you're ready, we should get going."

Nerio nodded. His feet shuffled as they walked, sandals scraping on the marred stones and bricks of the broken streets. *There must be something that I can do,* he thought, still carrying the moans of the triage tent with him.

Peace was needed, a tranquility founded in faith that he could disperse to the people.

Despite his teachings of late, the violence only seemed to be increasing—more than he thought even Brother Meneham could be responsible for. Combined with the enigmatic words of Jerdine, Nerio began to feel a deep fear rise within him. The shift in mentality among his followers was disturbing, and against everything he'd ever stood for. Peace was needed, and he would need to disseminate it not just in the gatherings at the growing camps, but to all of his followers.

He had little idea as to how to accomplish such a feat.

It was another concern to add to the list. The litany grew as quickly as his followers, and it was increasingly difficult to temper their ire. Each day under the extended rule of martial law further eroded the people's resolve, and Nerio could see in their eyes a desperation that was a thirst, a hunger. For what, he could not say, but he knew that it was not founded in the pacifism that he preached.

It had begun to chill him to his core.

An alcove to his side drew his attention. Tucked inside of it was a masterfully carved effigy of Amenesol, the sun's golden crown upon his head. The paint which had once brought it to life was now flaking ash, the stone cracked and crumbling, stained black by the fires. The massive lintel above had split and half-toppled, leaving what was left of the alcove shadowed from the light of the god's own visage high in the sky.

Nerio stopped and stared at it, the simple remnant of a time not far past striking him. Was this what his faith and those that followed him could become? He had thought the blessing of the gods to be enough, that there was nothing which could cause him to falter. *Or have they put their own faith in me for their deliverance? Is this the ship's final thrash in the storm? Or am I able to right the course?*

Something new was needed. Words that could not only show the people the path of righteousness but refresh his own soul in its cleansing light. He bore the death of what must now be hundreds upon his shoulders, a weight that made his knees buckle as he walked. What he needed was something grand, something that could bring the people together, something that could earn the gods' attention.

And their forgiveness.

Chapter
Thirty-One

My greatest concern lies with the one who crossed through and dueled with the First Born and his compatriot.

The rhythm of wheezing and clattering armor followed Orne like a leashed dog pulling against its master. Several soldiers—coughing as if plague-stricken—began falling behind as the dust of the narrow road kicked up and covered their armor and sweat streaked skin in a layer of white. It was all Orne could do to keep them in a group, let alone in step.

There was, however, one benefit to their hacking fits—they couldn't complain, which had been their incessant wont since he woke them at dawn.

Nothing like a good march to shut up a group of dissenters, he thought.

He fell back a dozen paces and lifted a hunched soldier by her armor's collar, standing her straight as green bile dribbled down her face, eyes glazed and head bobbing. Two more of his squads' members needed to be righted before he jogged back to the column's front, his darksteel armor quietly jostling thanks to the leather padding between plates and halberd loose in his hands.

"Keep the double time up!" he shouted. "Or expect another march this afternoon!"

For the first time in the past hour, a sound besides the pants of exhaustion filled the stony valley as the group rasped out a collective, pathetic moan.

The first few miles of their forced march had left him irritated to no end, rife with the grumbling protests of the early morning exercise. He'd taken them out the main gate and along the road he and Kolden had traveled with the merchants. Six miles out, six miles back.

Of course, the first half had been *downhill.*

The return journey was a steady hike up a constant incline, and it had dragged the objections from his squads with each of their labored breaths.

Can't believe they're this exhausted, and we still have two miles to go, he thought with a shake of his head. He heard more vomit spill across stone. *Gods-damn it.*

After Kolden's visit that morning, he'd been determined to know what state the men were in. They were, after all, the only defense against that fat priest bastard—or worse, the warrior in black. Delvan had said his swordsmanship hadn't been a power. *But he's wrong. Has to be. Hell, the idiot didn't even know he could heal until a few weeks ago, who's to say there isn't something those mage fuckers can do to be better with a sword?*

No one could fight him and Delvan at the same time like that. No one. And the creepy fucker in the bathhouse only used a *dagger* while fighting Orne and *two* Blues. It was incomprehensible. Much of that night had been.

To say his men's first test had been lackluster would be akin to calling a recruit a general. A twelve-mile forced march was *the* standard for soldiers of the Royal Army. This wasn't just unacceptable, it was embarrassing.

He was beginning to think he'd have better odds fighting on his own.

These idiots aren't going to stand a chance, he thought, looking over his shoulder at the gaping mouths sucking in the thin, mountain air as if it were their last breath. *Then again, well trained soldiers don't stand much of one either.* A recollection of Knight Commander Ferrand's corpse laying on the ground in a pool of violet blood vividly formed in his mind. The man had been more than competent—thanks mostly to cheating, but that was beside the point—with a sword.

His sword. Which he hadn't been able to reclaim after the commander's death. Instead, it and the man's sapphire were sent to his extended family back in Calentine. As if any of them knew how to handle a weapon like that. *Fucking waste.*

Regardless, if this group of soldiers were to fight against even a singular mage, they'd be slaughtered like fowl. He itched for redemption, wanting to prove that he could stand against one of the magic-wielding bastards in a fair fight. He also knew that was never going to happen and wondered if a tactical retreat might be best.

The sharp, angular points of the keep eventually appeared in the distance, dark grey lances puncturing the blue sky above. "Oh, thank the gods," rasped one of the men behind him, his voice dry and gravely. Orne hoped that Kolden had managed to search through whatever he needed to, though he still thought it was lunacy to go looking for something when you didn't know what you were even looking *for.*

He's probably going to bitch and moan more than my squads when I get back. When Kolden saw a way of doing something, it became the *only* way. Orne hadn't felt like arguing that morning, but he doubted his idiot brother knew the reasoning behind this forced march.

Aside from testing their abysmal fitness, it had allowed him to search the road for anyone traveling along it. Six miles wasn't a long ride for someone on horseback, but the layout of the valley gave him a vantage from their midpoint for what he guessed to be ten miles further out.

He'd seen nothing, not even the merchants who had quickly vanished this morning—he assumed the downhill journey and empty carts had made for fast travel. Furthermore, it served one additional function which he imagined helped Kolden out immensely.

Not that he realizes it...

They crossed the main gates and marched into the courtyard, his soldiers struggling behind him. A few dropped to the gray flagstones, others began stripping the packs of gear and soaked armor, their putrid stink filling the air.

He looked around, trying to see if he could glimpse Kolden anywhere. When he didn't catch sight of the little ferret, his gut synched slightly. He hoped he was in the forge, or really anywhere that the soldiers weren't going to be prone to wander.

"One hour water break!" Orne shouted. He'd only planned for a quarter hour, but he didn't think most of the stragglers would have even caught up by then. "Then back here and in formation. Dismissed!"

As predicted, no one moved. A few more laid down, coughing up wads of phlegm.

He was surprised to see Helona there, the woman he'd sent to collect everyone this morning. She must have been on his heels. He eyed her up and down, impressed. Too bad the rest of them were a disgrace.

With a disapproving scowl he left and walked to the forge. He let out a small breath of relief at the telltale sound of hammer to steel, the ringing crisp and vibrant as he opened the door and entered the brightly illuminated space.

Dust hung in the windows' light like snow drifting lazily in early winter, and of the ridiculous *ten* forge pits in the enormous space, one was alight with an orange glow. Kolden stood beside it, hammering away at a thin, wiry piece of steel, twisting it at odd angles.

Orne took a moment to glance around and ensure they were alone before speaking. "How'd it go?" he asked.

Kolden looked up from the anvil, his face smeared with its usual soot. "Well," he said, also looking around as though Orne hadn't checked, "aside from finding the captain has a stash of absolutely *delicious* smoked pork, I didn't find shit."

Orne's eyebrow raised high. "You say smoked pork?"

His brother rolled his eyes, a slight smirk on his face. Obviously, he knew Orne wanted some but always found pleasure in these petty manipulations. *I swear, if he didn't get me any...*

Kolden walked to a nearby cabinet and produced a wrapped bundle, maybe twice the size of Orne's fist, and tossed it to him. He peeled back the cloth to reveal a chunk of meat dusted with seasoning, and using the short knife from his belt, cut away a slice.

If his jaw hadn't been so busy chewing, it would have dropped to the floor. "Holy fuck," he said, eyes wide, "this is best smoked pork I've ever had."

"I know," Kolden said in that condescending tone. Orne decided to let it slide. This meat was fucking *delicious*. "It had to cost him a small fortune to buy *and* deliver. Gods know what else he has hidden away here. Whatever he's selling, it pays damn well."

"You search the whole castle, then?" asked Orne with a full mouth.

"In a *morning*? No." Orne gave him a quiet glare. "But I also couldn't get into half the rooms in the place."

"Why not?" he asked.

Kolden stared at him dumbly for a second before answering. "Because the doors were *locked*. Why do you think?"

"Well, no shit," snapped Orne. "But can't you, I don't know, figure out a way around them or something?" For all his boasting about his capabilities, his brother did love to complain about problems he couldn't immediately solve.

Kolden held up the thin spindle of steel, its glow beginning to fade. "That's what this is for," he replied, as though it were obvious.

"And?..." he said, since it absolutely wasn't.

His brother rolled his eyes. "It's a lock pick. Or, well," he said, his confidence cooling like the metal in his hands, "it's *supposed* to be, anyway."

"What do you mean, 'supposed to?'"

"I know *how* the locks work; I used to help put them together back in Drunt. But I've never actually, you know, picked one before. I'm pretty sure this will work, though."

"Seems like a lot of wasted time for being 'pretty sure,' Kolden."

His brother glared at him before turning and tossing the steel back in the forge in a spray of sparks. "I'm not the one," he started, turning back to Orne with his face hotter than the coals, "that found out impending doom was approaching and decided the best way to deal with it was by going on a stupid *march*!"

Orne sneered, annoyed enough that he stopped chewing. He had known this was coming, and yet it still infuriated him more than the whines of his own squads. "That march showed me there was no one approaching on the road for at least the day. Not to mention emptying the castle so that *you* could snoop without getting caught!"

Kolden's jaw snapped closed with a dull *click*. If anything, his face became more frustrated as he struggled to think of a retort. "Whatever," he finally said. *Little weasel can never admit when he's wrong.* "I'm going to wait until it's dark and search some more. Everyone in this castle sleeps like the dead."

"I still don't understand how knowing what Jerdine wants to buy is going to help us. Who cares? We should tell the captain—not everything, obviously, stop looking at me like that—and set up patrols and night watches in case he or that other fucker shows up in person."

"Once I hear back from the general, then fine." Kolden said, folding his arms. "It's a short flight from here, I expect to get a pigeon back by tomorrow morning, maybe even tonight."

"And what happens if they show up before then?" asked Orne pointedly.

"I don't know," said Kolden, tossing up his hands. "Maybe we'll get lucky, and he just kills Villera, takes what he wants, and leaves, we get to sleep through the whole ordeal, and he never even learns we're here. Or..."

Orne had already concluded his brother was still working out on his 'stupid march.'

"Or," said Orne, "he decides he can't risk anyone here knowing something and talking, so he kills the entire lot of us."

Kolden's lips tightened and turned steeply down. "Fuck," he finally said. "We'd be better off just hiding in the mountains for a while. Find some cave and wait the whole thing out. Can't say I'd lose much sleep over the whole affair."

Orne had come to the same verdict but, on principle, refused to utter an agreement with his brother. "We'd be hunted for deserting and hanged, Kolden. Not going to work."

"Still worth a thought..." he grumbled. "If I find whatever it is they want, though, I'm taking and hiding it."

Orne's brow dug into his nose. "What? Why?"

"For leverage," his brother stated. "If they do show up, I'd rather have something to bargain with."

Orne grunted. He didn't think it would matter in the end, but it was better than nothing. Their situation, to put it bluntly, was fucked. If they were lucky—which they'd been in a drought of recently—the principle's man would never show, they'd spend whatever time they needed to here and then head back to the city. Although, if things went as well as a sword breaking in a duel, they'd be facing a very affronted, very powerful, mage.

Orne looked back out to the fodder that was still catching their breath, the last of the soldiers crawling through the gate. He hated that they had to wait for a response from the general. They needed to be proactive about the whole situation, waiting to react would be too late, their throats likely slit in their sleep.

Fuck what the captain says, he thought, *I'm going to set up a watch for tonight.* A few shifts of guards on the walls and some lanterns weren't unreasonable acquisitions—not that he'd do anything differently if it were. Hopefully by the time the captain found out, or that prick Villera, they'd have orders from the general, and the authority backing them.

Maybe it would be enough.

Or maybe it would just announce their death's arrival.

Chapter Thirty-Two

I have little doubt that he is of the ksatsimtri. Likely a leader among them.

Desnia awoke to something worse than pain yet lacked the faculties to describe it.

Every pore of skin felt raw, her joints stiff and creaking as they resisted her feeble struggles. Her head throbbed with indescribable agony, each bead of sweat applying the pressure of a boulder upon her skull. She let out a whimper as she attempted to roll over, her back cold as the sweaty garment clung to it and peeled from the tiled floor. Her eyes remained tightly squeezed together, the thought of opening them a dizzying anathema.

Slow, shallow breaths were all she could manage for a time, every heave of her chest twisting muscles that protested with violent spikes of torment. With time, and bending joints that groaned louder than her, she brought hands to her dripping temples, caressing them with a feathery touch—if feathers were made of lead.

She laid there, waiting for the pain to diffuse as time passed, cursing it as it crawled along, slowing to make her live in this tortured aftermath in perpetuity. Its silence rang deafeningly in her ears and swirled in colors behind her eyelids, sickening her in its saturation.

Eventually, she managed—with the grace of a drunken sailor—to lift her head and prop herself up on her elbows. She slowly released the tension pinching her eyes closed, opening them in a distorted haze.

Despite the room being dark, and little more than starlight sprinkling in through the window, she was blinded, the faintest flicker appearing brighter than the sun. She flinched as she tried to blink away the feeling of daggers stabbing through her eyes and into her brain, inching her head from side to side to take stock of her surroundings.

Gods-fucking-damn it, she thought as she realized she was still in her cell at the Asylum. She wasn't sure why she expected any different but for some reason she'd envisioned finding the mud-red of brick around her, the warmth of wood beneath her feet. *This hangover is playing tricks on my mind,* she thought groggily.

A dull glimmer of a dying lantern peeked through the portal in her door, a dozing quiet emanating from the hallway beyond. With stifled grunts and twinges of seized muscles, Desnia sat up, hands gingerly rubbing her neck.

Everything seemed like a dream. Plucking the imaginings from reality as she drew upon her recollections of what transpired was a mysterious blur of the intangible, seemingly impossible to separate.

Had Delvan been there? She was fairly certain he had but seemed to recall his voice multiple times. Mithya had come at her, *hard.* That was difficult to forget. Her food had been spiked. Not assuming as much had been idiocy on her part, the conniving of her captors should never have been underestimated. The betrayal bled like its dagger was still between her ribs.

And then something else, something distant and—

Desnia's throat went tight. Memories flooded back to her. The realization of an overly tenacious Blue. The brink it had pushed her to.

And the god that had pushed back.

She had been a passenger in her own mind, watching as Mithya discovered the force backing Desnia's quest. But, after the initial shock, she remembered the Blue being... reverent? *As if this shit wasn't strange enough as it was.*

"How long have I been out?" she whispered. She glanced around the room, wondering what else she might have forgotten.

There was an extended silence. Not so much as a, *'Hmm,'* or dry, sarcastic retort echoed in her head.

"Masini?" she whispered, pressing her hand against her chest.

Her eyes went wide, engorged with panic. Her hand patted frantically around her neck, feeling for the absent chain and ring. She sharply spun her head, the adrenaline forcing her past the winces of pain as she swept her hands across the floor searching for him.

She found nothing but dust and tears as a memory dangled in her mind, one of Mithya holding up Masini's chain before her, staring at it in awe. Desnia wanted it to be a nightmare, a concoction of her own fears and years of loneliness. But as her hands dragged over more empty floor—her head vacant of vulgar quips—she came to the crippling realization that he'd been taken, probably now traveling in the pocket of her interrogator.

She crumbled to the floor, forehead pressed against the white tiles as her balled fist slammed down upon them. Her body shook, eyes gushing and nose flowing as the gravity of her situation fully settled in.

She was alone. Again.

The months since fleeing Calentine had been mountainous progressions of events, from some of the quietest moments of her life, to by far the most dangerous and deadly. Through it all, she'd had the consistent companionship of Masini—prude, crass, and disgusting as he may have been.

She'd taken him for granted, an accepted part of her life. Time and time again she'd told herself that it was temporary, a means to an end. After all, she'd discarded him once and attempted it repeatedly since. But now, in a moment of exposure and vulnerability that filled her with terror, when she needed his voice the most, he was nowhere to be found. And it carved away at her insides like she was a quarry to be harvested.

The world, the cruel bitch that she was, had cursed her. She'd fought against it her whole life, yet never won, only delayed. She turned to roll onto her back, eyes red and lips shaking as she—

Something jabbed into her thigh as it pressed to stone, causing her to swear under her breath as she flinched. She tilted her head up as she flopped onto her back, reaching a hand into the offending pocket. Her heart nearly stopped as fingers touched the cool metal, a long, blade-like pin of polished steel smooth beneath her fingers.

With a quick glance to the darkened door, she pulled the glinting metal from her pocket, hand shaking as she gaped at the hairpin resting upon her palm. The memory was fuzzy, and despite holding the needle-pointed finery before her, she was still half convinced she'd dreamt stealing it. It was here, it had happened, and the key to her freedom was now in her grasp.

Holding her breath as her face wrinkled and teeth snarled, she sat herself up. A few slow, shallow breaths later, she leaned forward and pulled herself to her knees, then her feet, hunched like the moon itself rested upon her shoulders. A corpse would have been easier to bend into shape, her lower back quivering as it pulled her fully upright.

More deep breaths. More shaky exhales.

Finally standing, the pains dulling their sharp edges into blunted aches, she crept to the door. Remaining in the comfort of shadow, she peered through the portal, and her gut twisted into a tight knot.

Lids fluttering near closed, sitting on a stool beyond her door, was her abusive guard.

Her rib flared as though pierced by a spear, a reminder of his most recent flogging. She could hear the light breathing of another guard on the other side of the door but didn't dare sneak a glimpse. She held the pin and its sharpened point tightly in her hands, gritting her teeth together as she tried to overcome the growing, excruciating pain as her rib recalled its former frailty.

It's now or never, she thought, preparing herself. There was no plan, no contingency. Only one option stood before her.

Run.

She couldn't wait here with an opportunity like this in hand. There was no one to rely on for her release, as she'd painfully realized. Nerio's naïveté left him ignorantly believing he could change her circumstance through discourse. Delvan couldn't be trusted after getting her thrown in here. And the look in Mithya's eyes... she wanted something from Desnia. She knew that glint all too well. *Bitch already took Masini,* she thought with a contemptuous sneer. She'd be back, of that Desnia was certain.

Her escape *had* to be tonight. The only person that could get her out of this situation was herself. *Just like old, miserable times.*

With great effort she knelt, slipping the tip of the silvery point into the keyhole of her door. The mechanism was antiquated, she just needed to put the point in, rotate a half a turn, and the latch would release. Now that she had something which could overcome the bolt's heavy weight, it would be quick work. But also, *loud.*

The weight would fall into a place with a ringing click—she'd heard it enough times when they opened her door. *Not like I have any other choice.*

Slowly and with great care, she began to turn the pin, the latch smoothly moving out of place. An eighth of a turn, then a quarter, and soon she had crested nearly the entire half circle, the bolt ready to slide and drop into place.

Desnia held her breath, bracing herself to move her ragged body as fast as it could be willed. Adrenaline flooded her veins, narrowing her vision and making her heart race. The latch was almost there, any second and—

A picture flashed in her mind. Then another. A guard drawing a sword, bursting through the door and beating her to blackness. Then her running through the halls, walls echoing with... snoring?

She froze. *What the hell was that?* she wondered. Was it paranoia eating away at her? She'd been in tight spots before but never had her imagination produced something so... vivid. Uncertainty kept her there, still as stone, her gut telling her to wait to turn the pin.

A sound made her nearly jump from her skin. The telltale snort of a snore, a brief pause, then again. Instinct flicked her wrist. The bolt fell into place with its audible *click* as the corridor beyond reverberated with the gargled snoring of one of the guards. She cringed, waiting in place, tendons screaming for her to straighten.

There was a rustle that nearly made her heart burst, then silence disturbed only by the soft breathing of a sleeping guard.

They hadn't noticed. Or were they toying with her, hoping for an excuse to execute her for escaping?

Again, it didn't matter. Death's owl had been circling her for weeks now, waiting to sink its claws in and reclaim what had been stolen from it. *The feathery bastard will have to wait a little longer*, she decided. Well, hoped, really.

The door let out a muffled groan as it turned on its hinges, Desnia pulling it open with all the care she could manage. Time dragged as she creaked it ajar, inch by inch, the miniscule feat taking what felt like hours. Eventually she had it slivered open enough for her to slip through, a fissure of dim lantern light streaking upon her face.

With trembling hands—the hairpin held tightly in one, point sticking out opposite her thumb—she released the air from her lungs, pulled in her stomach, and turned as she slithered through the opening. Her eyes were pinned to the sleeping sadist, her vengeful tormentor, as she finally pulled herself through the gap with little more than a rustle of her white linens.

His eyes remained closed, mouth slightly open as spittle dripped down from its corner. Her lungs refused to pull in air, straining and burning as she stood beside him, waiting for the prick to open his eyes or suddenly lunge. Another snort of air pulled through his nose, and he remained blissfully unaware of her presence.

It was almost enough to relieve the tension, a small drag of air working its way into her desperate lungs. She turned away from him, towards the shorter end of the hallway where she assumed a door stood between her and the stairs to her freedom. Two dozen paces and—

Desnia stopped, her face turning ghostly pale and gut lurching to her throat.

The other guard, sitting upon another stool, was now face to face with her. His eyes were half open, the lids drooping lazily down—at least until they started to blink away his oncoming slumber.

His eyes grew almost as wide as Desnia's. "What the—"

She didn't let him finish the thought, lifting and slamming the pin's protruding end at his face. He screamed, blood squirting from his eye as the makeshift weapon plunged until she felt a scrape of bone. She ripped the point free, his wails sharp and cutting as he fell to the floor, writhing, gripping his face and cursing as crimson splattered the crisp floor and walls.

She spun, the pain in her side flaring, to see her torturer shaking off the disorientation of being roused by his partner's cries of agony. His eyes locked with hers. A red glare of hate beamed from them in a blinding fury. He tried to jump forward, but Desnia was already plunging the spike in her hand down, piercing it deeply into his upper thigh.

Which was a shame, as she'd been aiming for his crotch.

He buckled and fell back against the wall, his wail coarse and haggard. "You Eka *bitch*!" he spat. He reached for her, but another quick stab sank the needle into his arm, another angry scream echoing in the hall. The pain of the sudden motion nearly caused Desnia to vomit, her body fighting every motion with crippling pain. With a final, agonizing movement, she slashed the point across his face. The deep slice poured blood into his eyes, his arm reaching blindly as a hand attempted to wipe his face clean.

Desnia hobbled away, her tight muscles threatening to snap and shear from bone as she tried to sprint to freedom. His cursing faded behind her, bouncing down the halls as she turned a corner, trailing drops of blood from the dripping pin in her hand.

Desnia wiped the blade against her leg, desperate to not lead them directly to her. The halls were a maze of twists and turns that led to nowhere, and she found herself down dead-end passages, branching corridors, and barred windows. Her mind was a frantic tumult of chaos, racing to try and remember her way through the building as she frustratingly led herself in circles while constantly looking over her shoulder.

She was gasping for air, her heart throbbing in her neck and dizziness making her darkened surroundings swirl in a turbid haze. Her shoulder slammed into a corner, arm scraping against the plaster walls as she teetered in her mad dash. She grabbed a door jamb to stop herself from collapsing completely, blinking as she drank massive gulps of air, perspiration flooding from every pore.

She leaned against the wooden door, so alike to her own, trying to concentrate. Every hall looked the same, strange corners and unnatural angles making the place a mess of indistinguishable cells. *It's almost like they were trying to make people here insane.*

Voices, angry and accompanied by the ring of steel, resonated in a dull, muffled tone from a distant corridor. She looked over her shoulder yet again, the faintest flicker of lantern light glowing at the distant hallway's end. A rat trapped in a sewer, that's all she was. Drowning in shit and unable to escape, the sickening dread of dying in this gods-forsaken place nagged as—

"Oh good, it's you," came a voice that spun her with a start, her joints protesting painfully to the sudden movements.

An aged, wrinkled face was pressed to the bars of the door's portal, eyes—wide with madness—peering from behind grey, twisted locks of equally deranged hair. The woman smiled, her yellowed teeth visible even in the faint light.

"Be a dear," she said, "and let Mari out of this cell, would you?"

Desnia managed to close her gaping jaw, looking back to the light which was beginning to brighten at the corridor's opposite end. She glanced back to the eager eyes and then to the pin in her hand.

Did she have time? They didn't deserve to be in here; she empathized with them on that front. Each second lost was another chance for her to be captured. Her instincts told her to leave, to flee with as much haste as possible and, most importantly, survive.

But after weeks held in this white-washed prison, the thought of letting others rot here felt like a punch to her gut.

Glancing back down the hall and gritting her teeth, she pushed the pin into the lock and began turning it, the voices growing louder in the distance. The bolt slid with ease, taking nothing more than a turn of her wrist. But, as she almost had it opened, an image flashed in her mind. She pressed her hand to her head, eyes pinching shut as her vision filled with blood, blood that soaked her with guilt. Resting above it was this woman's visage, her demented grin upon her face.

Desnia peeled her eyes open, horror upon them as she looked at the weathered Seer before her. "You..." she struggled with what to say. "I can't..."

"Ah," said the Seer knowingly. "You've seen. Yes, yes, one possibility. Live as long as I have, favored child, and you learn not to let those control the day. Throw them in the shitter with everything else. Better that way. Better."

Desnia gawked. "But... you're going to *die*," she said, wishing she could ignore the words or how she knew them. She shook her head and knew, despite her desperate desire to release this trapped soul, that she couldn't. "I'm sorry," she said, sadness fountaining from her trembling voice, "I can't. You're safer in there."

"Can't and won't are two very different things," replied the Seer. "Lives, ours, tied together. Release me and live. There are many ways out of here, and ol' Mari knows which one brings you to where you need to be. We, all of us, want the same thing, same thing. You must succeed. Now, stop being a coward and open the shitting door."

Desnia frowned, taken aback by the nonchalant attitude of the Seer. A yell, clear and close, punctured the darkness. She snapped her head towards the light that now glowed brightly, cutting a sharp shadow around the corner of the passageway's end.

"Fine," said Desnia tersely, "if you have a death wish, then what should I care?" With a flick of the wrist the bolt clicked, and Desnia pushed the door open.

"Many thanks, many thanks. Oop," she woman said, peeking around the corner, "time to run." And with speed that defied her hunched, ancient stature, she turned and ran down the hall in a flurry of grey and white. Desnia staggered back, watching in disbelief at the spryness before another shout caught her attention. Her pursuers were closing in like hounds on her scent and barking wildly.

She turned, chasing the old woman's trail in a crippled hobble, struggling to keep up.

Hearing became difficult as her heart hammered in her ears. The glow of torches and diffused lanterns seemed to loom around every corner, yet the Seer kept twisting them down different halls, sometimes stopping halfway down one and turning around, muttering nonsensically to herself.

The longer they tried to escape, the more voices Desnia could hear from all sides. The guards must have called for reinforcements. They seemed to come from everywhere, an omnipresent babble which swarmed the air. Her mouth had long since gone dry, her eyes refusing to blink as she tried to cautiously peek around each corner, her companion barging ahead all the while, as though danger didn't surround them.

"Where are we going?!" rasped Desnia in a whisper, checking over her shoulder once more.

The Seer continued mumbling, head down as she stopped in the middle of a hall, looking about and up as though there were no ceiling. *This is madness,* thought Desnia. *I'm going to get captured if I keep following her around, she's just leading us in circles!*

Not that Desnia had been doing much better on her own, the labyrinth of halls having been laid out by someone more insane than the occupants.

"Ah! This way," the Seer said, nodding to herself. "Yes, yes, right up ahead, left, past a hall, and then the stairs! Yes, just had to try a few dozen ways to get my bearings, yes, yes."

Desnia shook her head and blew out a puff of air. She didn't trust the woman's sense of direction, but at this point, she was willing to try anything. She could hear the stomping of boots, the clamor of armor and the shouts of those searching for her. As they rounded the first corner, Desnia sucked in a painful breath through barred teeth, eyes pinching closed as pictures flashed in her mind. An empty hall, then the same, but three soldiers in it, faces lit by torches. Then back to the dark shadows as they vanished. Blood sprayed, red and violet, covering her, then vanishing and leaving her clean.

She shook her disoriented head, stumbling forward into something in front of her. Her eyes fluttered as her vision cleared, having realized that she'd walked straight into the back of the motionless Seer before her. *What the fuck?*

Over the hunched shoulder of the wild-haired woman Desnia saw a familiar hallway, and standing in it, their mouths open in disbelief, were three soldiers. "Oh fuck," she hissed under her breath.

They brushed off their own initial shock. "That's her!" one of them said.

"Aye," said another, "matches the description. And ma'am, I don't know who you are, but you're going to need to come with us."

The Seer let out a low cackle. Desnia felt her knees go weak, legs shaking as they prepared to sprint. She glanced behind her, ready to flee, when she heard the shouts of another group coming from the direction they'd approached. Her heart sank as she spun her head from side to side, trying to decide which direction gave her the best chance for escape.

Her gut told her it was neither.

"Now, now, lads," said Mari, "you wouldn't risk endangering your new Messiah, would you?"

Desnia's face turned confounded, a reflection of the soldiers before them.

"Her?" said one, pointing at Desnia with an incredulous finger. "She don't look like much."

Desnia's brow dug into her nose as her eyes flitted between Mari and the guards. *What the fuck is this mad woman talking about?*

"Tell them your name, child," said the Seer.

"We *don't* have time for—" started Desnia.

The Seer cranked her head around, that crazed grin carved on her face. "Humor me."

Desnia sneered, the distant footsteps growing closer. Her heart was on the verge of bursting from her chest, and she was trying to see a way out of this but coming up dishearteningly short. *Whatever she's thinking, it had better work.* "Desnia," she hissed out. "My name is Desnia."

Shock and doubt intermingled on the soldiers' faces. "She can't be the same Desnia, can she?"

Same as who? she wondered. *How do these idiots know my fucking name?*

"Her hair is blonde, like the stories," said another.

"Not a lot o' fair skinned, gold haired women around these parts."

"But what's she doing in here then?"

Desnia's teeth ground together. The *thumps* of several pairs of boots drew closer by the second. "For fuck's sake. I don't know *why* any of this is fucking important," she said, shooting a glare to the Seer beside her, still wondering where this plan was leading, "but my name is Desnia, I'm from Calentine, and I was locked in here after the general arrested me for saving this gods-damned city. Does that answer your fucking questions?!"

The trio gaped at her for a second, slowly turning their heads towards each other as their eyes widened. Desnia tightened her grip on the hairpin, preparing to leap forward and throw a wild stab that would hopefully slow one. If she were lucky, she might escape in the chaos.

Not that luck and her were on speaking terms at the moment.

One of the guards suddenly dropped to his knees, prostrating before her, the other two quickly following.

"The Messiah!" one said reverently.

"Forgive us!" said another.

Desnia's jaw dropped, grip loosening on her makeshift weapon. *What. The. Fuck?*

"Yes, yes," said the Seer, unimpressed and ushering them with waves of her hands. "Now, get up and protect your Messiah, help her flee."

"Of course," they said as they stood, still staring at Desnia with wonder. "Go, down this way, turn at the second hall on the left and you'll be at the stairs." They walked past her and Mari—the youngest being tugged by his shirt, gawking—and around the corner, calling out to and confronting the oncoming patrol.

"What... what just happened?" Desnia whispered. She half expected some cynical retort from Masini, her heart crestfallen when all she heard was Mari's crackled reply.

"Your friends, hmm, looking to join you once more, I think. The priest worships the wrong deities out of his own ignorance. Time's almost up. Now, come, this is the only way. Crowd outside would tear you apart in adoration, mhm," said Mari before scuttling off down the hall, the sounds of the soldiers' marching paused around the nearby bend. She could hear their muffled voices in the distance.

Mari's response left Desnia with more questions than answers. *Can't this woman just speak plainly?* She empathized with her, to an extent. They were both, as much as she hated to admit it, suffering from the same affliction. But nothing about what Mari just said explained why three men just *bowed* before her and called her "the Messiah."

With a last look behind her, Desnia shook her head and hastily attempted to close the distance between her and the invigorated Seer.

They approached the first intersecting hall, a frame of darkness surrounding a canvas of black. Desnia opened her mouth to ask more questions, desperate for answers, when Mari stopped and turned to face her, a gangly smile twisting her face. "See you in the sea of stars, girl. I'll tell Asta good things for helping out ol' Mari."

Desnia came to a halt, eyes narrowed by the words and wondering why they'd stopped. For a cryptic message of all things. *This woman,* she thought with a minute shake of her head.

"What're you—" Desnia started to say, until a wave of hatred washed over her. Her head pounded against the odium, making her stagger back a step.

A shape emerged from the darkened corridor to her left, a painting brought to life with the strokes of a demon's brush, for the person who hobbled forth could only be the creation of such malevolent deviancy. Her sadistic abuser flashed a glint of steel across Mari's throat, violet blood pouring like a waterfall, soaking her white robes from below her twisted grin.

Desnia watched, frozen in horror, as the Seer's body collapsed to the floor, tinged blood slowly creeping outward.

She looked up at the guard before her, a rag tied around his bleeding leg and forehead. He looked pale, drenched in sweat and barring his teeth as he held one hand above his wounded thigh, a dagger in the other with blood dripping along it from his arm. His eyes, however, were reddened with hate, a fuel that burned hot as the desert sun in his glare.

"Killing an inmate's a capital offense," he wheezed. "Now that you've done that, I'm free to use whatever force needed to bring you to justice, you Eka cunt." A sick, contemptuous grin tugged at his lip, his expression becoming hungry. A look she was, unfortunately, familiar with.

Her grip on the hairpin tightened, a growl emanating from deep in her chest. "You fucking *bastard*!" She lunged forward, raising the sharpened pin high. She should have fled. Even in her fractured state, she could outrun a man with a limp. But something drove her forward. Guilt. Loss. Grief over someone—for reasons that she couldn't explain—who she felt a deep kinship to, now lying dead on the floor.

Her fury blinded her. The bastard needed to pay.

The murderous fuck was faster than she expected, however, and he reached up with the hand gripping his wound and caught her arm. Her free hand grabbed her wrist, tugging down with her meager body weight to force the needle into his neck.

It hardly budged.

The guard wrapped his fist tightly around the dagger and punched her in the chest, avoiding use of the blade. An explosion of pain from her rib deflated her lungs in a long wheeze, and she was thrown backwards, ramming into the wall as another burst of pain left her gasping, her head whipping back and skull smacking against the plaster. She heard the hairpin clatter on the tiles.

She slid to the floor. The world was spinning, a dark figure looming above it. Her limbs refused to work, the pain more excruciating than any she'd ever felt.

The dark figure shadowed her entire vision. She heard a hiss, vile as poison, "Jerdine sends his regards."

The world was suddenly drowned in a blind panic. There was nothing but the racing of her heart, the rapid heaves of her chest, the blackness of her vision. The phantom pain of a blade delving into her chest flared like hot iron, her panic worsening as she thought through the scenarios the vindictive principle could have in store for her, how he would want to see her in endless pain for spoiling his machinations.

Kicks assaulted her legs, crushing flesh against bone and causing her to scream, the excruciating pain turning them limp and useless. She felt his body press against hers as he knelt, spitting virulent words all the while. The breaking of her body had overwhelmed her, deadening the words' meaning, but a terror grew as she began to comprehend, a hidden recess of her mind still listening. She felt his clammy hands pull at her clothing, his disgusting skin against hers. Her legs didn't work to kick. She flailed, trying to force him away, but agony pulsed through her, every motion a beating's worth of torment.

Her vision began to clear. Her clothing was torn away from her body. The guard kneeling before her, struggling to undo his trousers, the wound she'd given him wrapped tightly around the top of his leg and obstructing his efforts.

Her throat went tight, breathing becoming impossible as she frantically reached around for something, anything. Her fingers groped wildly, searching, begging, pleading—

Metal. Her fingers fell upon a sharp pointed end of it.

The hairpin lay there beside her. She gripped it tightly. With all the will she could muster, she sat up, her abdomen a ball of furious, resistive pain. With a scream, she plunged the needle point into the guard's neck in a flash of silvery revenge.

His eyes bulged. His hand came up to grip her wrist, but she yanked it free as blood dripped from his lips with a cough. She drove into his neck again.

And again.

And again.

Her arm was a flurry of motion, blood splattering over the walls and spraying across her face as she shrieked a wild cry. He fell back with a gurgle, body landing limply on the floor.

She sat there for a moment, watching as his twitching corpse stilled, hand gripping the pin so tightly it dug and cut into her palm. The fucker was dead. After endless beatings and threats, he'd gotten what he deserved.

But not before the senseless murder of someone who'd dared to help her. Again. An owl had been circling her this night, and when unable to claim its prize, found another. A punishment. A paltry atonement. All because of her own defiance.

She'd imagined killing him. It was one of the few things that got her through these days. But, unlike those fantasies, she felt no victory, no triumph. Only... empty.

And *angry.*

Desnia crawled backward, pulling her clothes back on, feeling tears streaming in torrents down her face. Everything felt like a blur, the world around her spinning. Her whole body ached, as though her very skin were poison. Her head screamed and made her vision swirl.

She needed to run. She needed to escape. They wouldn't take her, not again.

Not alive.

She forced herself to her feet, taking two wobbly steps forward, legs burning and swollen, fighting and failing to support her. Her head became light, her stomach fluttered, and vision tunneled. She stumbled against the wall, trying to fight the encroaching oil darkening her sight's edges. She pushed herself off, attempting to walk. Her knees refused, buckling beneath her.

Shadow enveloped her. All went black.

And she collapsed to the floor.

Chapter
Thirty-Three

While I am perturbed by your descriptions of what I assume to be a powerful vi-blade, you glazed over what I find most alarming. His armor.

Kolden twisted the barb of metal, the scraping and rattling of iron a din in the otherwise silent passage.

He knelt in a pooling absence of light, the door only a few inches from his face almost imperceptible. Farther down the lengthy passage, the light of braziers in the open courtyard winked and shimmered in the night's cool gusts. The scent of must wafted around him, the damp penetrating and dripping from stones as the mountain's runoff soaked through them. The arched masonry echoed with each jostle of his makeshift lockpick, leaving him constantly checking to his left and right for anyone approaching.

Would be just my luck, he thought, wiggling the tool's end, *that one of the people Orne put on night duty would find me trying to break in here.*

The unyielding mass of wood and strapped iron was the same he'd seen Villera and Phrenwa enter the night before, and he'd decided this was as good a place as any to start his late-night search.

Assuming he could get in.

His lockpick had almost immediately gotten stuck, though he couldn't fathom why. *This* should *work,* he thought while his teeth gritted together, forearms straining as he tried to unwedge it. He worked it harder, pulling and pushing, torquing left and right. The mechanism *should* be simple, yet it fought him like a bear protecting its cub. He tried wrenching it more vigorously, arms—muscled from years of blacksmithing—burning from the exertion.

Stupid fucking... gods-damned... piece of—

There was a loud *ping,* Kolden grunting as his wrist twisted rapidly away from the door. Righting himself, he looked down at this hand, the shiny glint of fresh iron staring at him from the end of the tool's half still clutched in his grasp. He stared at it, dumbfounded for the briefest moment as he glanced at the other half still firmly lodged in the door's lock.

His fists balled up as he started swinging them violently from side to side, screaming silently, lips quietly forming every curse he could conjure—and a few expletives that he concocted in the moment—as his face became hot. He pulled back a fist to punch the wooden obstacle, holding it there, resisting only to prevent the noise that would accompany it.

Settling instead for resting his burning head against the cool, moist stones, he pounded the butt-end of his balled-up hand against them with muffled *thuds*. Panting heaves slowly turned to steady, deep breaths as he leaned against the wall, trying to think of what to do next.

An all-powerful mage with a grudge had a henchman, or was himself, on the way here, right now, and Kolden couldn't even get a gods-damned door open to figure out *why*. Admittedly, he wasn't sure why it mattered. There was the faintest hope that he could use whatever it was to bargain with, but this was someone who was accustomed to putting people—Kolden among them—in cages to be harvested. He could only imagine what the man's idea of torture might entail.

But a driving curiosity propelled him forward, an itch that he couldn't explain nor sate. He *had* to do this. There wasn't a choice, or sliver of doubt, in his mind.

I'm going to have to go to the fucking forge, he thought, trying to work out how to remove the lodged bit of metal, *and get pliers.* He glanced back at the hefty barricade. *Maybe an ax, might be easier than all this sneaking around, noise be damned.*

Turning away from his victorious opponent, Kolden began shuffling back towards the light at the tunnel's end. His shoulders slumped as he tossed the bit of twisted steel in a nearby crate. He moved into the courtyard, high walls reaching up into the star-filled sky, the parapets cutting sharp outlines against the pinpricks of light. He glanced up at them, wondering if any of the post guards would see him, despite mostly sticking to the shadows.

Probably all sleeping, he thought. The ax was becoming a more promising idea by the second—

There was a loud *crash* in the courtyard a few dozen paces away. He started, turning to see the crushed and splattered remains of someone wearing a Royal Army uniform on the ground a few feet from the wall. He took a few steps forward into the light of a nearby brazier, eyes going wide, lump in the back of his throat, then craned his head upward.

Along the top of the wall, another outline was blotted against the night sky. The silhouette seemed to be staring back at him, and he half expected to see two red stars appear within the mask of the darkness. That was no soldier of the King upon that wall. The guard's tumble wasn't an accident to be investigated. Kolden felt, deep in his gut, what this was.

They had come.

And just gotten a very long look at Kolden's ghostly face.

Adrenaline flooded his veins. His feet skidded out from under him as he burst into a sprint, heading for the bell tower across the enormous courtyard. The familiar, distant *twang* of a bowstring snapped from atop the wall, followed by an arrow that skittered across the stones by his frantic feet.

He didn't slow as he approached the tower's door, an arrow whistling past him as another wave of cold air shifted it off course. He prayed for the laziness of the castle's soldiers as he leapt, hoping they hadn't locked the tower's entrance as he turned his shoulder and focused all his weight and momentum into smashing against it.

With a crash like thunder, the door's latch snapped and flung open as he barged into it. The stone floor met him in a rush, sending a secondary pain through his arm and side as they skidded across it.

He let out a long, low groan as he rolled onto his front, hissing in the air that had been punched from his lungs. Clutching his arm, he forced himself to his knees, staggering to his feet. For all he knew, a purple-light-spitting bastard was right behind him. He had to move. Had to alert the keep. Else he and everyone in it were doomed. And he was *not* going to be put back into one of those gods-damned cages.

He stumbled forward, neck too sore to check behind him. He wasn't sure he'd check if he could.

The bell's rope dangled a few paces ahead, hanging in the dark room from a small hole in the ceiling. It was thick as his wrist, frayed, bleached, and worn, looking as if it hadn't been used in decades.

With several twists, Kolden wrapped his working arm around it, high above his head. Gripping firmly, he lifted himself upward, feet barely grazing the stone floor beneath. He tugged, squirming his weight to budge the ancient alarm.

It refused him.

He was too light to move the tons of bronze dangling the hundred feet above. The pin had probably seized, so he couldn't be blamed entirely, but still, he couldn't help but hear Orne mocking him in the back of his mind.

"Fucking thing," he cursed, unraveling his arm and grabbing the end of the coil laying on the ground. He hurried through the opening between the bell room and one adjacent, sitting himself on the floor and squarely planting his feet against the stone wall near the entry's edge, body facing towards the bell's drooping cord.

He pulled the rope taught as he could, the line lifting from the floor and bending where it rubbed over the chute in the ceiling. He tucked the thick, rough hemp beneath his half-limp arm, the weight trying to pull him forward, and wrapped his free arm thrice around it.

With a great groan of stress, he pulled at the rope, feeling it beginning to give way as it creaked over the chute's edge, sagging in the air under its own weight. He released the tension, letting the cord pull him forward, almost dragging him to his feet. He rocked back, heaving with all his strength as his ass landed down on the stone once more.

"Gods-damn it," he said through grinding teeth as he repeated the motion, frayed hairs of rope hanging in the air. With one more strenuous rip, he landed back down, the rope in his grasp coming back to his face. Above, far in the distance, a great bell pealed through the air.

He let go of the cord, hearing it ring out again as it swung high above him, alerting the castle to the coming attack. *For whatever that's worth,* he thought grimly.

Struggling back to his feet, holding his throbbing shoulder, Kolden looked around for another exit. He didn't dare go back through the courtyard, the whistle of arrows as fresh in his ears as the chimes above.

There was another door at the back of the room. He stiffly ran to it, jiggling the handle, the door holding fast. He wrenched it harder, desperate, his heart beating like war drums in his ears. He turned and slammed his good shoulder into it, the wood and metal rattling loudly in the dimly lit room as it rebuffed him. It felt like hours were passing as he began kicking at the door, the seconds tilling up dread within him. Minutes must have passed, each one more and more panicked as he tried frantically to get out.

The room's faint light dimmed further, and Kolden felt a sickening horror in his stomach. He turned, looking towards the doorway he'd charged through moments before.

Black against the glow of flames beyond was the outline of a figure, ebony robes wrapped tightly around his body and face. The glean of steel reflected from the long, curved sword in his hand. A blade for slashing. One he had little defense against.

He felt like he was choking as he pulled the long dagger from his side, holding it in his functioning left hand.

"I don't suppose," said Kolden shakily, "that we could come to some sort of, I don't know, arrangement?" There was no response, only a quiet, eyeless stare. "No? No. Right. Maybe if you, uh, tell me what you want, I could help you find it?"

The only response was a strong, steady stride forward. Whatever was choking him crawled higher in his throat. He was never going to win in a fair fight in his current state against whoever this was, their sword held loose and comfortable in their hands. Hell, he probably couldn't win if he were in the peak of health. He needed to find a way out, to run—

There was a muffled *smack*, the prowling figure stopping in his tracks. The would-be attacker looked down, hand coming to his chest, before dropping his sword with a clatter and collapsing to the floor. It was then that Kolden saw the length of spear shaft protruding from the man, the leaf-point blade having penetrated his upper back and thrust out from his chest.

An even more domineering shadow darkened the door, Orne's massive figure impossible to mistake.

"Did you have that in hand, too?" his brother asked.

Kolden rolled his eyes. "Obviously," he said, trying to hide the tremor in his voice, "took you long enough though."

"Should've rang the bell sooner, then."

"I... well... it was..." Kolden stammered. "You know what, never fucking mind. Someone killed one of the wall guards you had posted, tossed him into the courtyard. Might have been this asshole, but I'm not sure."

"Doubt it," said Orne, jerking the spear free. Kolden doubted he'd taken his halberd if he was fighting in hallways. "Dealt with another one in the halls on the way down here. Fucker fought like a demon," Orne said, scratching at a mark on his darksteel armor.

"Did you sleep in that?" Kolden asked, wondering how his brother had managed to adorn the full suit so quickly.

"Don't fucking judge me," snapped Orne. "If I hadn't, then you'd be dead right now."

He had a point. "Any of them throwing around purple light and draining souls?"

"Not that I've seen. Doesn't mean there isn't a mage here somewhere." Orne pointed to the dead man's sword. "Take it and let's get going."

Kolden bent over with a wince and grabbed the sword. He was pretty flexible with which hand dominated—using tools in both for years had given him a certain level of ambidexterity—but he wasn't confident about wielding a sword against anyone Orne deemed a "demon." He was a much greater admirer of projectiles. They did most of the work, all one really needed to do was point and shoot.

Orne cautiously checked around the door's frame into the courtyard, the clashing of steel beginning to sound in the distance. Without so much as a nod, he turned and strode out. Kolden's cheeks puffed in a blow of air before he followed a few steps behind.

More dead soldiers littered the courtyard, Kolden assuming they were the remaining posts along the wall. Screams bounced off the stone, horrors unseen from throughout the castle as soldiers were woken to the gore of battle. *Massacre might be a better word.*

They'd been taught about night raids like this. Assuming even a small force of attackers, given their lax security and the poor training of the soldiers stationed here, all that was needed was a dose of chaos and the castle could easily be taken, even with Kolden having rung the alarm. *Hopefully we can overpower them, assuming—*

As though on cue, a flaming arrow flew from an obstructed walkway, landing at main gate's base—which Kolden assumed to be covered in oil, as it burst into a blinding light. Flames wove and vined up the steel barrier, turning their primary exit into a gate to hell.

Other blazes sparked throughout the castle, burning away the night's veil and illuminating the keep. Kolden's eyes darted, the flames igniting at the entrances to different levels. He saw shadows move along the wall, maybe a dozen, though it was impossible to be sure. They all waited, armed and poised, near the flames, watching the smokey tendrils intently.

They're boxing everyone inside, he realized. What were they planning? To smoke everyone out? Burn the entire castle? *Or are they trying to buy time?...*

"Orne!" he hissed as they hurried along the courtyard's outer walls, the shadows few and far between. "Orne!"

"What?!" his brother growled over his shoulder.

"I think I know where they're going!" He pointed to the archway he'd been in earlier. "Where I saw Phrenwa and Villera last night!"

Orne glanced at the tunnel a few dozen paces away and nodded back to Kolden. There was no guise of black for them to creep through, no hidden recess from the flames' light, licking at the crevasses of their entire path. "Try not to get shot," said Orne as he sprang forward with an agility that defied his mass.

Asshole, thought Kolden as he took one last look around, eyes grazing the walkways and towers above, before lunging forward with as much speed as he could muster.

For the second time that night, he ran across the dark flagstones, arrows ricocheting off the stone around him, one glancing off the back piece of Orne's armor. All he could hear was the gushing breaths leaving his metallic-tasting mouth, his legs burning like they'd been set alight in the fires. He felt a tug at his ear, ignoring it as his feet pounded against the stone.

They burst through the tunnel's entrance, arrows *clicking* across the ground behind them. Five or ten paces in kept them out of the archers' lines-of-sight, and Kolden hunched over as he tried to catch his breath. *Gods, I really don't want to do that again—*

A noise from ahead.

Fewer than twenty paces away, standing before the door Kolden had been struggling with earlier, were three men draped in black, lit by the torch in one of their hands. One was swinging an ax, cleaving at the door Kolden had incidentally locked shut with his failed lockpicking attempt.

Bastards beat me to it, he couldn't help but think.

The third man, his face also covered except for a thin slit at the eyes, stood behind the other two. Head back, posture straight, he was imposing without towering over those around him. He stood there, silently watching as the door was being broken down.

At least, he *was*, until he and the others turned in unison to face Orne and Kolden.

"Ah, *fuck,*" he muttered as the two with the ax and torch immediately ran at them.

Orne wasted no time, raising the spear above his head and hurtling it down the wide corridor. The man with the ax turned his shoulder, the long blade missing him by a hair, but the man with the torch—busy drawing his sword—had not been as nimble, and the spear lodged itself deep in his gut, dropping him to the ground in a cry of pain.

Kolden ran up beside Orne as he drew his side sword, the dead man's saber held before him. The man with the ax came in swinging, his movements not the wild or careless motions he'd been expecting. The weapon swung in wide, graceful sweeps, the momentum carried into the next strike to make it a blurring wall of steel. Orne was side-stepping and deflecting the blows while Kolden took a step back.

He and Orne kept trying to reach for an attack, but as a foot went forward, the curved head of the chopping instrument was there, ready to cleft. It was a whirlwind, a level of mastery and skill that took Kolden by surprise, one that he rarely saw from anyone besides Delvan or his brother.

Who he was—though he'd never admit it—thanking the gods was at his side right now.

They were back-stepping, avoiding the flurry of arcing swings as often as blocking them. Kolden knocked one incoming blow to the side as hard as his single arm could manage, twisting the assailer's body slightly. Orne stepped in to take advantage, stabbing forward. The man contorted, bending impossibly backwards and to his side, as though a serpent, the tip of Orne's blade nicking his shoulder, drawing a spray of blood.

Who the fuck are these people? Kolden wondered, shifting on his aching legs, looking for a time to strike. He was still expecting, at any moment, for a flash of purple, or for fire to burst from their attacker's hands, or for them to become suddenly frozen and immobile. For all he knew he could be turned into a fucking chicken in a blink.

They couldn't afford to waste any more time. He went to lunge in, raising his sword to slash as the man finished a flourish.

There was movement to his side, a faint glint of steel from the quiet shadows. He cursed, dropping himself low and keeping the sword raised, held tightly in his hand. Another sword struck his, hammering a numbing vibration down his arm, pushing his blade back to where his face had been a moment ago.

Kolden felt his sword being pulled, wrangling his wrist as it tried to move away from him. He looked up, seeing his assailer's blade biting deeply into his, the weapon a shimmering black—something he knew well.

Darksteel.

He was lucky his sword hadn't snapped in half. His dagger was made of the same unbreakable metal, as was Orne's sword, but the one he'd claimed off his last attacker was of more common steel. It would be like wood against a chisel.

The man yanked at his sword, firmly lodged into Kolden's, trying to reclaim it. Attempting to grip with both hands—one numb, the other almost immobile—Kolden fought against him, twisting the blade and pulling at it to either pry it from his attacker's hands, or to delay him long enough for Orne to help.

His brother was still prodding and slicing at the ax-wielder, their fight a dance compared to Kolden's drunken brawl. He doubted this person, who he assumed was the break-in's leader, was any less capable than the others Orne or he had encountered. Better, in all likelihood.

Therefore, he could *not* allow him to get this blade free.

Pulling on his own hilt, he tried to drag the attacker towards him, kicking at his leg to throw him off balance. The man swept his foot with ease, dodging, causing Kolden to be the one struggling for footing. He leaned on the interlocked blades for support, but the torque and pressure were too much, because he heard a gut-turning *ting* as the opposing force vanished, his sword finally snapping.

Kolden stumbled backward, back slamming against stone. His eyes refocused as a slash of the darksteel sword came down towards him. Sparks sprayed as steel hit stone, Kolden ducking away, grimacing as he rolled over his shoulder and back to his feet.

All that remained of his saber was half an arm's length of steel. It wasn't going to be useful against darksteel, so he whipped it at sword-bearer. The man easily deflected it to the side. *Gods-damn it.* He drew his darksteel dagger, cold sweat dripping down his face. His vision tunneled as the man stepped forward, raising his sword, and—

Spinning, to find Orne, leg raised and driving downward. Before the man could react, Orne's metal-clad boot drove into his knee, twisting it sideways with a *crunch* that made Kolden flinch. He collapsed to the ground, grunting in pain, Orne's foot stepping on the wrist holding his sword.

Kolden stepped over, pulling the darksteel blade from his assailer's hand as his brother touched the tip of his blade to the man's throat.

"That priest fucker send you?" asked Orne. Kolden listened, still catching his breath, seeing the man with the ax on the ground in a pool of his own blood nearby.

There was no response, only a glare. The eyes, in the dim light... He thought for a second that he recognized them.

"Is he here?" asked Orne, obstinately refusing silence as an answer.

Quiet.

"Enough of this," grumbled Kolden, reaching down and unfurling the black wrapping on the man's head.

Kolden's jaw nearly fell to the floor. His brother let out a surprised, "Huh," as they stared at the person before them.

Even in the light of the fallen torch, flickering shadows across the walls, Phrenwa was unmistakable. His eyes were red, pained by the agony he assuredly felt in his knee, yet alert. And nothing whatsoever like the kind, cheery merchant they had come to know on their journey here.

"Son of a bitch..." said Kolden. "You came to steal whatever Villera wouldn't sell you before it went to Jerdine's man, didn't you?"

Orne turned narrow eyes to Kolden, then back to the merchant. He swore he could hear flint trying to spark a thought in his brother's head.

"You know nothing of this one I seek," he said in his thick accent.

"You'd be surprised," quipped Orne.

"What is it?" asked Kolden, leaning down close. "What the hell is here that a gods-damned mage could want so badly?"

Now it was Phrenwa who looked shocked. "This word, how do you know it?" he said angrily.

"Let's just say that we've had some experiences recently that we'd sooner forget," replied Kolden.

"Cheating bastards," said Orne.

"What happened in Brethefen, this was you?" Phrenwa asked skeptically.

He and Orne shared a looked, their statement clear: *Worst kept secret in the gods-damned empire.*

"Tell me," Kolden practically pleaded. "I *need* to know. What's he coming here for?" His drive had risen beyond simple curiosity, the need burning at him with an all-consuming flame.

"He won't stop hunting you," said Phrenwa with a hiss as he grabbed his knee. "Any of you, for what you've done. If I had known... perhaps this one could have been different. We're on the same side, you cannot trust the people here—"

"What's this?" echoed a rhetorical voice down the long, arched passage. Kolden stopped breathing for a second, iron bars flashing in his mind, a blade of brimming power forcefully sheathed in an unwilling heart.

Turning slowly, he saw the outlined shadow of a group of soldiers at the courtyard end of the tunnel. They took a few heavy steps forward, the dying light of the dropped torch illuminating Lieutenant Villera's visage.

Kolden exhaled, for once thankful to see the walking excrement. The sphincter atop pulled its shit-pumping lips into a grin.

"Prisoner," replied Orne tersely.

Villera looked from Orne to the battered door, then to Phrenwa, eyes narrowing. "Knew I couldn't trust you. And you two," he said looking back to Kolden and Orne, "you just been hiding in here the whole time, while we're fighting, forcing the intruders out?"

Says the man without a speck of blood or ash on him. "I'm the one who rang the alarm, asshole."

"What?" said Villera with a poor feint. "Steddus, you was the one that pulled the alarm, wasn't ya?"

"That's right, sir," said the soldier beside him, cheeks so hollow he appeared emaciated, eyes a reddish haze. Kolden thought he recognized him as a member of Orne's squads, which explain his brother's grinding teeth.

"What're you telling lies for, yer lordship?" asked Villera.

Kolden was glaring at him from beneath a darkened brow, venomous hate pumping through his veins. Before he could say anything, Orne stepped forward. "Try selling that story, and I'll hang you from the ramparts myself you fucking waste of air."

"Tsk," Villera said, smug and gloating, "I've got five witnesses right here that say it was Steddus who pulled that there bell rope. And threatening a fellow officer? That's a serious offense, even for a lord."

Orne snarled, contempt flooding his voice. "It's not a threat. It's a *promise*."

Villera flashed a hint of fear, opening his mouth to spew more verbal diarrhea, when another voice called down the tunnel. Pulling his glowering eyes from the lieutenant, Kolden shifted his attention to the newcomer.

Wobbling as he shifted his bulging girth from foot to foot, Captain Mathin approached, two soldiers at his side, both far more alert appearing than the ones with Villera.

"What's happened?" he rasped. "Give me a status, Villera."

"The keep is secure," the lieutenant replied. "And me and these five managed to capture a prisoner." He pointed to Phrenwa.

"Fuck you!" said Orne, grabbing Villera by his collar, the man's eyes going wide. "Kolden and I captured the prisoner, sir. What this man says is nothing but lies."

"All I see is one officer assaulting another," said the captain, needing a wheezing breath between every other word. "Let him go, soldier, and I won't toss ya in a cell for the next few days."

The smug grin returned to the anus's face, Orne's hands shaking almost as much as Kolden's.

"Now, Lieutenant!" the captain commanded.

His brother sneered, veins threatening to burst from his skull. With no small amount of force, he shoved the lieutenant away, careening him into the wall. The captain looked as though he wanted to reprimand further, but then probably realized that much speaking would cause him to break a sweat.

"Boys, take the prisoner to a cell," said the captain.

Kolden looked to Phrenwa, his many questions unanswered, his cravings unsatiated. "Sir, we should question him, find out if there's another attack planned or—"

"My orders are my orders," the ruddy-nosed man replied as several of Villera's men were taking Phrenwa away.

Kolden's tongue twisted itself into knots as his jaw hung open. He locked eyes with Phrenwa for a second as he was dragged into the distance, seeing in them the panacea to this craving. There had been something he was about to tell them, and in his gut he knew it was vital, somehow, to his and Orne's survival.

Orne's face was carved with anger as foul and heinous as Kolden had ever seen it. The captain seemed to ignore him as he was leaving, saying first, "Good work on ringing the alarm, Steddus. Probably saved the lives of half the castle. We'll have to get you something special."

The man's leaden eyes lit up, following behind the captain like a puppy chasing a fresh bone. "Really, sir? Thank you, I was just doing my job, sir." Kolden's stomach dropped to the floor.

They all exited the passage, leaving Orne and Kolden standing there, their anger building like a pressure around them, the betrayal choking them like a noose.

"I'm going to kill him," said Orne, voice hard as any steel.

"I'll join you," Kolden said. And while his fury had turned his focus to the captain and Villera, something else nagged his mind. *Phrenwa knew. He knew Jerdine was a mage. How?*

As they stood there in motionless silence, the torch sputtered, blinking slowly as it dimmed lower and lower, until the flames extinguished. The darkness enveloped them, sounds of soldiers in the nearby courtyard little more than the wind's breeze to their ears. And in that darkness, another question came to Kolden's mind. One that he swore would be answered.

What else does Phrenwa know?

CHAPTER
THIRTY-FOUR

I believe it is crafted of hide. Only one creature in—or out—of the realms possesses scales which any ksatsimtri would deem worthy of adorning. To my knowledge the feat of slaying one hasn't been accomplished in millennia. And not from lack of attempts.

What a fucking waste.

Efforts without end, all culminating in utter failure. How difficult was it to travel to the mountains and make a simple exchange? Did he need to hold their hand through every endeavor? He was becoming increasingly certain that every native of this abominable realm was incapable of wiping their own ass.

Had we not laid their foundations, civilization might have withered and died here altogether.

Jerdine grumbled further as he sat down on a log, tossing the burlap bag on the ground beside him. He rummaged through it, pulling out the first item he had acquired in this wretched town, setting the glass jar on the soggy ground strewn with wet, composting leaves between his feet.

For weeks now, he'd been attempting to find some contingency to his reliance on Elhurtan, to no avail. At each of these towns they passed through—their single street paved in saturated manure—he went to the mail coups expecting positive missives yet found little besides disappointment.

Elhurtan had ceased responding, probably taking Jerdine's money and running to the nearest brothel. *The flippant insect will regret having been born when I am done castrating him,* thought Jerdine as he pulled out the clippings of a wolf's mane from the bag and sprinkling it into the jar. He couldn't believe the huntsman he'd bought it from had charged twenty moons. Regret from not killing the extortionist hung with him still.

Or perhaps it was residual wrath at mass incompetence.

Despite his lack of success, tenacity had won the day. Elhurtan might still possess the wisdom and self-preservation to attempt completing his contract, but in the event he did not, Jerdine had managed to at last contact two men of ill repute—the valuable quality precisely what he sought—willing to assist him.

He knew little of them, but their recommender regarded them highly. And, considering the rest of the dregs of Brethefen were either run out of town, drowning in cheap booze, or unreachable, it left him with little alternative.

They best be more reliable than the last one, he thought, inspecting a small vial from his pack. *How that bitch managed to gain the upper hand...* He'd met the woman, she was no larger than his Nerio, her resistance should have been easily overcome.

Pathetic.

Jerdine poured the vial's contents into the jar, careful not to allow the venom to touch his skin. He flicked the side, ensuring each drop of the expensive fluid dripped into the vessel. Finding the substance had taken extensive—and frustratingly discrete—searching, and he doubted he would come across such quantities again, short of draining a serpent's fangs himself.

The trees groaned and creaked in a breeze, rustling their leaves beneath a sunless sky as he turned his head, checking to ensure Valander had not followed him. The ksatsimtri was like a hound—aware of Jerdine's every move, rarely leaving his side. The child was currently reporting to the High Chair, affording Jerdine this brief window in which to further ensure his own plans' success. The first time to himself in nearly two weeks. Of course, it could be over without a moment's notice, depending on the communication's duration.

He had no time to waste.

Shoving his hand into the depths of the bag, his fingers clutched the next necessary ingredient. He removed and inspected the polished fang—a bear's, probably, which wasn't quite correct, but it would have to suffice—and with an approving grunt, dropped it with a *clank* into the jar.

The one piece of information gleaned from his messages which had drawn his lips to his eyes was the sheer momentum of his Nerio's movement. He had even acquired some rather zealous followers, by all accounts. The cataclysm of *that* he would watch most intently. If he were fortunate, that conniving woman and tainted First Born would become casualties in the inevitable crescendo.

And if not, then that is what this is for, he thought as he poured enough clear alcohol into the jar to cover the other ingredients.

The mixture needed to be as close to the desired result as possible. As there were no khimaira native to this realm, he'd substituted with the closest he could find.

He held a scabbed hand over the jar, aligning his fingers as thin lines of purple coalesced around them, snapping into fractals along a plane parallel to the ground. *Now, to picture khimaira vomit...* It had been several thousand years since he'd laid eyes on one of the atrocious creatures, but their disgusting methods were difficult to forget.

The liquid mixture below his hand began to bubble, noxious steam rising and burning his hovering palm. He winced, holding his breath with a cringed scowl as the toxic fumes ate away at his skin, inflicting a burning pain that amplified the one still throbbing through the rest of his body. It was not an agony one simply grew accustomed to. *A few... more... seconds...*

He ripped his hand away, the other gripping his wrist, avoiding touching the newly bubbled flesh. Gritting his teeth, he released a loud grunt as he kicked a pile of leaves, his toe jamming hard into hidden rocks.

"Fuck!" he screamed. He was far enough from the town's limits that he didn't worry about attracting attention, but his companion's... This was a mere fraction of what he could inflict. He gritted his teeth, pressing his lips into a white line as his face turned a deep shade of crimson.

Time was of the essence, he needed to continue, quickly. He focused what little vidut he still possessed to healing his hand—the transmutation leaving him in need of recharging, *again*—and while he attempted to ignore the scalding pain, he dug through his pocket and pulled out the round, jade stone which he'd kept hidden these past weeks.

How Valander had not noticed its absence was perplexing. Perhaps he had not looked into his trove; why risk exposure and possible discovery, after all? *How much competence can one who wears faux custodian scales truly have?* Or, *had* he noticed, and decided to stay silent? Was he hoping that Jerdine would do exactly this and use it as an excuse to extricate him from his life?

It's what I would do.

Jerdine dismissed it. Even if he were aware, Sylvain would never allow it. Not while he remained useful. The boy would just have to deal with one of his trinkets being taken away. Still, it was best to ensure that if he *didn't* know, it remained that way.

Sitting back on the log, Jerdine lowered the rock—its cloudy, crystalline depths refracting the dots of light from above—to the rim of the jar, its contents now a putrid, churning green, the air above it shimmering with caustic vapors. With a *splunk* he dropped the stone into the acid, ripping his hand away to avoid any splatter. With as much haste as his disfigured body could manage, he stood and took several steps back.

The potent acid began to bubble, the surface fizzling and popping toxic sprays through the top of the jar, the leaves surrounding it shriveling and dissolving with a touch of the liquid. The glass began to rack, tilting side to side as something tapped against it with a *chink*. The virulent mixture began to swirl like a tempest in miniature, rocking its vessel until finally it tipped beyond its limits, and teetered down to the ground.

Acid spilled and contaminated the soil with a corrosive hiss, sending smoke and hot toxins into the air. Jerdine knelt, bringing his face as close as he dared to the fumes, and felt his lips and eyes crease as he gazed upon what lay squirming amid the lime-tinted solution.

A creature, no larger than his palm, began to blink its reptilian eyes, taking in its new world. Its small, bat-like wings unfurled and took their first stretch as its scaled tail unraveled. Its body and head were as a wolf's pup may be, with a short snout and thin fur that would eventually grow to a lush mane.

The newborn khimaira turned its head, searching, until it found Jerdine's waiting smile. *That the giants ever considered you pests... Well, they never were known for being intelligent.* His chest filled with glee as he locked eyes with the creature, the energy of his soul's vidut imprinting upon the freshly hatched animal, bonding it to him permanently. *How fortunate that you were not driven entirely to extinction by those absent-minded barbarians before we conquered your realm.*

It stared, unblinking, locked in a trance of its own instincts, until it eventually turned its head and broke eye contact. The ritual was complete.

The khimiara took a little hop forward and let out an extended squeak in its first attempt at a roar, revealing a mouthful of pointed fangs. Jerdine would have laughed had he not once heard the earth-shaking rumble of a grown adult—which one of these creatures could reach in a matter of weeks.

Provided they were fed well enough.

The kit took another step forward, begging with voracious eyes and annoying squeals. *At least I must only deal with you the once.* What he would do after the animal completed his task, he wasn't certain. Despite their ravenous and deadly reputation, their bonds were notoriously... persistent. Jerdine shuddered, grabbing his pack and removing the final and bulkiest item within.

He dropped the goat's leg on the ground, the khimaira's barbed teeth digging in before the limb had a chance to settle. The sound of tearing flesh filled the humid air as the creature gorged and quickly devoured meat and bone alike. It would be capable of feeding itself within hours, growing at an unprecedented rate. Before he went to rejoin Valander, he would provide it instructions as only he would now be able and send it to aid those who would deliver what he sought—that bitch's head, and the mountain's bounty he so desperately required. Perhaps the tainted one would fall in the pursuit; after all, the minds of beasts could only be influenced so much.

After that, well, it would be useful to keep, but if it proved too great a nuisance, their pelts made exquisite cloaks.

They will not be able to hide now. My only regret is that I will not be there to witness the terror upon their faces.

They said vengeance was an indulgence, but then, what was life without its pleasures?

Chapter
Thirty-Five

If you ever cross his path, run.

The room's few windows cast garish panes of sunlight against the bare adobe walls. Its only furnishings were a round table and accompanying antique chairs where Delvan had sat until his backside was sore. Then he paced over the groaning wood until his feet similarly ached. Now he stood near one of the deep-set windows, eyes straining to adjust as he looked out into the bustling street, filled with soldiers and citizens alike, tapping his foot.

He felt unsteady, like his mind was a lode of shale, slipping from under his feet whenever he climbed near the semblance of an answer to his many questions.

The voice from the Asylum haunted him, making sleep elusive. The image of Desnia convulsing on the floor was an accompanying vision whether he was asleep or awake. Guilt tore at him. For not being there in time. For inadvertently getting her incarcerated to begin with.

Each time he felt he understood the world, he slipped again on its ever-changing complexities, never able to shore his footing.

Beyond the tea shop's empty patio a floor below, Delvan watched as people went about their days. Some pretended to be willfully ignorant of the omnipresent soldiers, whilst many wore dark expressions, and cast glances that were darker still. Few had the money to afford bare necessities—many businesses, such as this tea shop, were slowly dying as the spirit left the eyes of their customers.

He hoped the donation to Nerio was working to restore some of what was lost. His family had never been known to be overly philanthropic; he himself had spent most of his money in taverns or in pursuit of well-fitted dresses. But knowing that he'd given some level of reprieve to even a few made him feel strangely proud. He would give more if he could, but he suspected it would take what little remained to aid Desnia.

There was a *creak* of a hinge from room's entrance. *About time,* he thought, turning to see Mithya enter. In their discussions the night before her face had taken on a hint of seriousness, evinced by fewer of her flirtatious gibes and less forceful smiles. Now, however, the few pleasantries were completely absent, her face stern.

"You were supposed to be here hours ago," snipped Delvan.

She dropped herself into a chair, shaking her head. "We have a problem," she said, her tone making Delvan suddenly feel ill.

"What do you mean?" he choked.

Mithya ran her fingers through her flowing hair, rubbing them against her scalp as she ground her teeth. "Something happened at the prison last night. A guard and a Seer are dead."

"You don't mean..." His mouth went dry.

"No," Mithya said, shaking her head. Delvan felt his muscles unfurl. "Good news is, Des *did* wake up—like I told you she would." The corner of his mouth tugged down, but she ignored his contempt. "The bad news is that she tried breaking out last night. Got pretty far by the sounds of it.

"I just came from the general's office, trying to see if I could learn more. He wasn't willing to discuss much, but I have an informant that gave me those few details. The only other information I've gathered is that she was moved to a different location. Rosethorn's *furious*. Mostly about the dead Seer—which he blames Des for, by the way. Ironic, that he should care so much about a dead Blue..."

"What do you mean they moved her?" he asked. "Where to?" Breaking her out of the Asylum would be difficult enough. If they didn't know where she was, they'd be digging blind.

"*That's* the problem," she said with a sigh. "I have no idea."

Delvan leaned his hands against one of the chairs. "What about this 'informant' you have? Do they know?" *It's probably Wellos,* he thought, thinking back to the jaded scribe. He was fairly certain that if the lieutenant knew Mithya and Delvan were having clandestine meetings, he wouldn't take the news well. There was a glimmer of elation in his chest, a triumph in being right. *I did try to warn him that he was being used...*

"No, this is being withheld from even them. They would've told me if they did."

Willingly, too. No need to use your gift on someone so infatuated.

Lips pressing into a line, he stared at her. He wanted this to be her fault, to focus blame *somewhere*. But, for once, he struggled with a justification—making him all that much more incensed. *Gods-damn it, Des. A few more days and we could've gotten you out.*

"Maybe," he said, "the general will have you interrogate her again. Perhaps this time you could *refrain* from using your gift?" The words held a sharp edge, his anger still raw.

"Wow, why didn't I think of that?" she said, tossing up her hands. "Oh, wait, I *did*. Do you seriously think that wasn't the first thing that I asked? What do you take me for?"

"I have no idea."

Mithya leaned her chair back on two legs, staring at the ceiling and continuing to rub her temples. "The general wouldn't even consider it. And it's not like I can use my gift on him, he'd throw me in a cell next to Des—"

"So, you *are* capable of restraint," he said, his expression flat but voice snide.

She ignored his gibe and continued. "He said if I didn't have anything new after speaking to her that many times, then there was nothing else worth learning. Men." She shook her head.

"I'm assuming you didn't tell him anything about the other day?"

"You know, speaking of men and assumptions, I thought you had half a brain. You're *really* making me second guess that."

Delvan's lips shut as his chin pushed them upwards. He wanted to retort but also had no desire for this to spiral into an argument. Disregarding the comment, he decided to focus on the issue at hand.

The information was problematic, of course, but something about it sat uneasily with Delvan. "So, wait," he said, his face scrunching, "if the general doesn't think that there is anything more to learn from Des, and he holds her responsible for the death of a Seer..." His eyes went wide.

Mithya snapped her head upright, dropping the chair back onto all four legs. She stared at him with eyes that were equally peeled back.

Neither one wanted to say the words aloud. Desnia had been sentenced to a fate, one of condemnation. One that left them with little time to fashion a rescue.

He's going to execute her, he realized with abject horror.

Despite the fiery tension between the two of them, the fear that gripped them both was as shared as the air they breathed. He expected the Truthsayer's reasons for concern to be more self-serving than his, but it was obvious that neither wanted harm to come to her.

He wondered for a second whether he could appeal to the general. It had taken days just to get a meeting with the man, despite Delvan's house and title. He suspected that, given the general's ire, he was going to be unlikely to acquiesce to his appeal.

Whatever they were going to do, they would need to do it soon.

It was Mithya who began to pace now, standing from her chair and voicing thoughts aloud as her eyes bored into the floor's planks. "I've already reached out to all of my contacts in this damned city," she said, "and none of them know where Des is. *Maybe* they will find out before... Anyway, I don't want to only rely on that. There has to be something else we can do."

He held his chin in his hand, heart beginning to gallop as ideas stampeded through his mind. *We need someone who has access to eyes and ears throughout the city. Someone we can trust to stay quiet. Someone—*

"I know how to find her," Delvan said, eyes coming alight.

Mithya stopped pacing and spun to face him. "How?"

"Not a how, a *who*," he replied, feeling the slightest flicker of Mithya's subtle power. *You're not getting it from me that easily.* It still impressed—and infuriated—him how precise she could be. "First, I want you to tell me what you're planning once we get her out."

Crossing her arms, she stared at him for a moment, her boot *tap-tap-tap-ping* against the worn floorboards. She'd refused his inquiries the night prior, remaining mysterious and vague during their, albeit brief, discussion. Delvan finally had leverage, and he intended to get the most out of it.

"What does it matter?" she asked. "I intend to keep her safe. Isn't that what you ultimately care about?"

"No," Delvan said. "I'm not risking all of this just for you to try and take her to get what you want. What is it that you want, anyway?"

"You're really going to delay Des's rescue to play these games?"

"I'll get her out without you, if need be," he said with a shrug. He already didn't like that he'd been roped into working alongside the enigmatic Blue, and while he suspected she could be of substantial assistance, he held no reservations against doing this on his own. *She won't turn me in, this is what she wants, too.* It was a conclusion he'd drawn while waiting here this morning, one that freed a burden from his shoulders.

"Hmm," she said. "I'll admit, I didn't think you had it in you. I like it." She gave him a wink. "Fine. Once we get her out, I'm going to get her out of the city. Quietly."

"How?"

"That involves a few friends of mine, people who are used to moving things unnoticed."

He gave her a blank stare. "Smugglers. Your plan is to use *smugglers* to get Des out of the city?"

"Oh, don't look so appalled," she said with a dismissive wave. "They know all the least guarded routes for a hundred miles in every direction. She'll be in good hands."

"They're common criminals! And the routes are only unguarded because they bribe the patrols, which means that gangs of bandits travel them instead! There were a dozen raids and robberies last week alone!"

Many of the newly arrived soldiers we being stationed along the roads to combat the increasing marauding, but the men were still spread thin, the great lengths of trade roads into Brethefen too numerous to protect entirely. Half a legion had arrived from Tennefen this past week and they were barely managing the riots and tax collections. Desnia could possibly be *safer* in a prison cell.

"I trust these men with my life," said Mithya. "Besides, I'll be traveling with them, if it makes you feel any better."

"It doesn't," he said flatly.

Mithya rolled her eyes as she sat back down in a chair, dropping her feet on the scuffed table.

Am I helping Des escape only to snare her in another's trap? he fretted. He hadn't decided what he was going to do once Desnia was free, his priority until now being her release. Was there a way to aid in her escape without being discovered? Could he free her *and* cling to a shred of his old life?

Did he want to?

A part of him still wanted the title he'd been groomed for since conception. But his heart—despite the dangers of the unknown—wanted to follow a different path. It had just taken his expulsion of wanting to break Desnia out to realize it.

Beyond that, Desnia's request was a cloud on his thoughts' horizon. It hovered there, obstructing the beyond in a grey veil, making all else seem irrelevant. He'd almost dismissed it, wondering if it was merely a hallucination or after effect of her death somehow playing tricks on her mind. But after the display at the Asylum, he could disregard it no longer.

He wasn't sure who he was meant to be, a strange and unsettling sensation for someone whose life had always possessed directive. One thing was certain, however, he wouldn't leave Desnia's fate to anyone else again. He would help her in pursuing this... *god.*

"I'm coming with you," he said.

Her lip tugged back, head shaking. "No. Not happening."

"It wasn't a request," he said sternly.

"Why? I thought you wanted her free? We can do that and, more importantly, make sure she *stays* that way."

"A few reasons. Making sure you don't break her mind again, for starters," he said with a glare.

She rolled her head. "We've been over this; I'm not going to use my gift on her again. Believe it or not, I think she can help me with something. Something *important*. Having you along with us is just going to make things more difficult."

"So you plan to use her?"

"By my ancestors, you're incorrigible," she said with a sigh. "No, she and I want the *same thing*. I help her, she helps me. Everybody wins."

Delvan stood there, lips pursed, choosing his words carefully. "And what is it, *again*, that you want?"

The obvious answer was the name she'd mentioned the night before, Masini. He thought he recalled him being the High Realm mage Desnia said she knew—why Mithya would be interested in him was escaping Delvan. She knew more about the voice than she'd let on, that was clear to him. She'd spent a good deal of time trying to drag it from his lips the night before, the disappointment of not getting it giving him a small amount of gratification. Maybe it was his turn to spin the conversation, see what he could learn.

She gave him a wide, tooth-filled smile. "You wouldn't believe me if I told you."

"Right, I mean, it's not as though you plan to go searching for an imprisoned god or something," he said, hoping for a reaction he could gauge. He disliked revealing so much of what he knew, but he needed to know Mithya's intentions.

Mithya, to her credit, was *exceptionally* difficult to read. But Delvan watched, seeing her breath catch just slightly, her eyes flash the hint of a surprise, and her smile turn down for the briefest of moments. The reaction was gone in a blink. She plastered on one of her smiles and gave a hearty laugh. "That's one hell of an imagination you've got there. Makes mine seem banal by comparison."

Delvan stared, his visage returning a half-hearted smile, a knowledge in the depths of his eyes. *She knows. And she wants Des to lead her there.*

The answer to Mithya's mysterious wants left him with more questions than he'd started with. It was more than he had before, however, and it cemented his decision to accompany her further.

"Are you just going to sit there and gawk?" Mithya asked, breaking the uncomfortable silence. "Or are you going to finally tell me who can point us towards Des?"

"Yes," he said, feeling that faint brush of power and glaring at Mithya. "But only once you agree to take me with you when you leave."

She let out an exaggerated sigh as her head lolled back, hanging behind the chair. "*Fine*," she drawled.

Delvan had little to no faith in her promise, but he knew it was the most he was going to get out of her. *I'm going to have to watch her. Closely.* He was confident she would abandon him and take Desnia with her at the first chance, but the truth was that he had no idea how to get Desnia out of where she was being imprisoned, let alone how to get her safely away from the city once he did. Besides, he couldn't risk Mithya getting there before him if he tried it on his own. Keeping her within arm's reach was the best option.

"Alright," he said. "Follow me."

"Where are we going?" she asked, feet plopping onto the floor and springing to her feet.

Delvan pulled open the door to the stairs, the street a dusty oven beyond. He hoped that he was right. If there was someone that had or could find information on Desnia's location—not to mention the motivation—it was the person he sought.

"We're going to talk to a priest."

Chapter
Thirty-Six

Your brother's silence is unnerving, but not unheard of. You must trust that he is capable of completing his task and focus on your own.

The room stank like a tavern. Stale ale pungently diffused the space, potent enough to stick to Orne's tongue. His boots had gripped the floor in places, satin stains dully reflecting where polished wood has once shone. Two large casks rested on their sides on a table behind the red-eyed Captain Mathin, the man's ruddy cheeks and cherry nose hinting that he wasn't wont to share his indulgences.

Orne sneered.

Since arriving in this barren castle, he'd scoured the stone halls and carved cellars—the unlocked ones, anyway—for ale or liquor of any kind. The cook had attempted to scold him for digging through the pantry, but the pudgy man had been quickly shut down when Orne pulled rank. Nonetheless, he'd concluded that this gods-damned place was as bereft of drink as this captain was sense.

"What do you mean, we can't talk to the prisoner?!" expelled Kolden from beside him.

The captain stared at them from behind half lidded eyes, his exhaustion from being woken in the raid last night apparent as he slouched low in the chair behind his desk. *Not sure why he's so tired,* thought Orne, *he slept till midday.*

"You best start callin' me 'sir,' boy," said the languid captain, "else yer gonna end up in a cell right next to him."

"At least I'd be able to talk to him, *sir,*" quipped Kolden.

"What I do with my prisoner is *my* business, Lieutenant. I know you lords are used to gettin' yer way, but my answer is no. You don't have anythin' to talk to him about anyway."

"He tried to kill me!" his brother exclaimed, tossing up the arm that wasn't in a sling. "Sir," he added.

"So you keep sayin'," Mathin said gruffly.

Orne's sneer twisted into deep scorn, affixing to his face like a hilt to blade. Villera stealing credit for his and Kolden's deeds had left his own eyes bloodshot, his rampant ire keeping him awake in the hours after the attack. The crash from dissipating adrenaline had begun to droop his eyes in the time before this afternoon meeting, but the snide comments from the captain rekindled his fury, pulling his eyes wide once more.

"This is bullshit, sir," he growled. "We attacked and apprehended that prisoner. General Rosethorn is going to want to know—"

"The lord general will get his report in due time," the captain interrupted. "Until then not a word goes to him about any of this, understand?"

Selfish and *incompetent, great. How the fuck did he become a captain?*

Kolden's voice was becoming fevered and pitched, verging on raving. "You're going to *wait*? We lost twenty-three men last night, and you don't want to send for reinforcements?! It'll take them *weeks* to arrive as it is! What if we're attacked again—"

"That's enough!" the captain's voice gurgled. "If yer so concerned, then take a post on the walls. Not like I have much use for a smith that can't hold a hammer." Kolden opened his mouth to speak. "Quiet, Lieutenant, that's an order."

His brother's face became a gradient of red, his body trembling. *Like a vicious little otter.* If he wasn't so irate, he'd have laughed.

"Sir," Orne said, "we should be doing patrols, full marches down the roads and anywhere the attackers could hide—the valley, mountain passes, the like. They might be nearby, waiting for an opportunity to come rescue their leader."

"You mean the man y'all spent weeks travelin' with?" the captain asked, leaning forward. "For all I know, you two were involved in this somehow. Now ya ask to pull resources away from our dwindled guard? No, not happinin'."

Orne and Kolden locked eyes, their contained indignity on the verge of erupting.

The proficiency and skill of the attackers spoke to a level of training and competency that this sow of a captain could only dream of achieving. They would come again, Orne was sure of it. The question was whether they would return before or after the priest or his man did.

Neither scenario boded well for them.

"Sir," Orne grated, "if we could talk to the prisoner, we could learn where the rest of his gang might be. If we're not on the offensive, then—"

"That's enough." The captain was, frustratingly, as immovable by simple logic as he was from his creaking chair. "I only brought you two here to make one thing clear. I don't care what orders you might have, or what fancy titles you hold. You haven't been here all of two days, and nearly two dozen of my soldiers have had their blood spilt by cowards in the night.

"Between yer gods-damned attitude since arriving, and the reports that you were hiding during the attack"—*I'm going to kill that lying fuck Villera, I swear*—"I think it's past time to deal with yer insubordination. I'm demoting both of ya to sergeant."

Orne's jaw went slack, then clamped close, his fist digging nails into his palm, his sword hand instinctively resting on his weapon's hilt. Kolden shook his own flabbergasted face before exclaiming, "You can't do that!"

"I *can*, and I am. Another word from you two and—"

"No, you fucking can't," Orne thundered. "We're here with direct orders from our commanding officer: Lord General Rosethorn. Not you. Not the slimy, dim fucker of a lieutenant you have here as a lap dog, but the commanding officer of the entire Western Army. Unless you have a writ from him then, frankly, sir, you can go *fuck* yourself."

Orne hadn't paid the closest attention in the classes they'd been forced to take in the academy, as his brother often smugly pointed out. What he *had* listened to he didn't retain well, but one thing he knew as well as any historian, better than his brother even, was military hierarchy.

He'd finally earned a promotion, and he would fight the gods themselves before he let this drunken slob take it from him.

The captain's already veiny, ruby face bled a shade deeper. He pointed at the door, spit flying as he shouted at the pair. "Get outta my office, the both of ya! If I hear one more thing about you two causin' problems then I'll have ya hung above the main gate, ya hear! Go!"

Neither Orne nor Kolden bothered saluting as they turned and left the dim, damp quarters. Orne slammed the door, hoping it was hard enough to break the lock and trap the bastard in there. Which, on second thought, would've been a shame, as he had the only hoard of ale in this gods-forsaken place.

"What a fucking idiot!" his brother shouted, echo ringing down the halls. "He's involved with whatever Villera is doing, he has to be. It's the only reason he would defend the prick."

"Obviously," retorted Orne.

"We *have* to speak with Phrenwa. Gods, I wish we'd had more time last night. He was about to tell us something, I know it."

"The captain probably has the man surrounded by guards. Fucker might not be able to demote us, but he can give orders to keep us away from a prisoner easily enough." It twisted in him like a knife in the back but, for the same reason Orne and Kolden remained Lieutenants, the guards could ignore their orders.

"Well what do you fucking suggest then?"

"Don't get fucking snippy with me, Kolden." His brother being unable to hold a hammer would be akin to Orne losing his sword hand. He'd recover, eventually. The interim, Orne suspected, would be miserable—for both of them. *I can only imagine the whining...*

"Whatever. Well, the first thing I'm doing is going to the carrier station, then I'm going to see how much security the captain has around Phrenwa. Who knows, maybe I can sneak in."

Didn't work out well for you last time. "Have you heard anything back from the general or Del yet?" Orne asked.

"No. I should have though. Hopefully there's something up there now. Either way, I'm writing to the general again, the captain's orders be damned."

The delay was worrisome. Even if the general was busy, Del wasn't one to procrastinate. If he wasn't responding then he was either in trouble, or something had gone terribly awry. *I hope he didn't do anything stupid.*

"How are you going to write with a bum arm?" Orne asked.

"My left is still legible. Barely."

He questioned that, but his brother did have a knack for weird talents. "Let me know what you find when I get back," he said.

"Why? Where are you going?"

His brother wasn't the only one capable of ignore asinine orders. Orne refused to sit here and wait like a rabbit in a snare. "Out."

"Hmm," Kolden grunted, looking at him sidelong. "Well, I don't suppose the captain can get much *more* pissed off. Not sure if your squads are going to be a help or a hindrance though."

Don't I know it. "We won't be attacked in the day, there are too few of 'em. Now's the only chance we've got."

"Mhm, get to sleep with my crossbow drawn and a knife under my pillow. Is it just me, or does it feel like the gods themselves are putting us into these situations?"

"If they are, they better have a good fucking reason."

The hallway came to an end at a spiraling stairwell. His brother began climbing, the pigeons' roost a few floors above. "Maybe," Kolden said, before stepping from view, "try taking a few alive, if you can. I don't know what, but something strange is going on here, more than what we've seen. I can... I don't know, feel it."

"Don't you start with that cryptic shit," Orne replied.

Kolden rolled his eyes. "Gods, I don't know why I bother sometimes. Try not to die."

"Try not to break another arm," he said, turning and stepping down the stairs. He could hear his brother mumbling in the distance. Likely something he thought would be witty and offensive, though probably neither.

His footfalls echoed down the tower as he took the worn stone steps. With each armored *clank* he festered on the injustice of what had happened. Accusations. Belittling. Robbed of credit. Dishonored by those devoid of it.

By the time he reached the base of the tower, he could feel the blood in his veins, flowing like burning oil.

The courtyard, filled with gloom and the stench of death, only darkened his mood. Bodies covered with makeshift palls lined a wall. The flagstones were a bloody patchwork of grey and black; the life spilled across them dry and flaking in the afternoon sun. The attacker's bodies wouldn't be afforded a proper burial, Orne assumed. Instead, they'd be tossed and left for the scavengers, the vultures denying the owls their prize. Splitting up the soul or some nonsense. The details of scripture didn't keep him alive on the battlefield. The gods, maybe, but the exact words made little difference, so he had never bothered to listen too intently.

Which is why, upon finding a few members of his squad praying over the fallen, he approached and interrupted. "Helona," he said to the short haired infantryman. She turned, her eyes baggy and red. "Go grab some of the squad, we're heading out." He didn't have time to wait for them to finish their grieving, lest the captain try to stop him.

"Are we going after the bastards, sir?"

"Mhm. Now, go find who you can, and quickly. We leave in ten minutes."

She saluted, and then ran off, a spring in her step that he'd yet to see from a single soldier since his arrival. He appreciated someone with drive, and she was one of the few with promise. *The circumstances are shit, but maybe...*

He refocused.

The captain and his pet lieutenant could sit here and wait all they wanted. Orne would show them what it was to take action, what it truly meant to be a soldier of the King's army. And when the general bestowed the accolades that he deserved, he would revel in the indolent bastards' chagrin.

First, he had to find where the enemy was hiding, undoubtedly waiting to strike once more.

Let's see how they like it when the fight comes to them.

Chapter
Thirty-Seven

To settle your mind and ensure his success, I will send others to investigate the troublesome silence, although they will take several weeks to arrive.

The demons danced.

A revelry. Faces, twisted and fanged, laughed, cried, and keened. Celebration in all its innate forms rose tall above Desnia's huddled figure, circling her in the dark, their shadows casting night upon the sky. Their skins dripped liquid essence, rippling like water over their misshapen forms.

Gold glistened over the folds of the obese, coins dripping into the shallow midnight pool in which she crouched, diamond eyes sparkling above a glutenous smile.

Blood covered the grotesque, mace and armor crafted from the bones of its conquests, smiling behind tusks of black and mouth of razors.

A face, kind, gentle, soft—yet *wrong*. A crescent pulled to its ears, black teeth barred, laughing a cloud of pestilence. Behind its back, a hidden hand clutched a dagger. Waiting gleefully, it wanted her to flee—presenting an opportunity to drive the steel into her back.

More. More of the monsters joined the spinning debauchery, begging for their chance, pleading for her to succumb.

The circle became tighter, the revolving horrors teasing her, tantalizing with their promises and remedies. They were almost touching her, their sins raining into the choppy water splashing at their feet, Desnia at their center.

She was shaking, mind screaming to flee but body frozen in abject terror, hoping to not be seen, to endure this no longer. It would never come, she well knew, survival did not come to the still. To the stagnant.

To the prey.

Instincts of old began to leak through the cracks of her dammed emotions. Legs tensing and eyes flitting, she searched for an escape, for freedom from this torment. Then she saw it. The blackened sky which hung like an eerie sheet of pure, distilled darkness tore. A sliver of light—faint but stark against the celestial ceiling—speared forward from a distant horizon, its origin blocked by the domineering figures surrounding her.

Their dour expressions pulled away from her, their frolic coming to a halt as their visages went blank, staring up at the needle of light piercing into their haunt.

Desnia's body moved before she was able to will it, her subconscious forcing her onwards, her terror-stricken mind struggling to keep up. Distal and foreign feet—which she recognized after a time as her own—splashed through the icy water as she sprinted between two of the living nightmares and beyond their ring of lustful misery.

She ran towards the growing speck of light, inviting her in like the warmth of the rising sun. Her ankles dragged through what became an endless sea, stretching with glass stillness in all directions. Looking over her shoulder she no longer saw the coven of fiends. Worry filled her, a paranoia that warned of their eyes swarming around her, ever watching, ever waiting. One and all would consume her, she was certain, if she allowed it.

The faint glow had grown into a blinding ray, and the uncanny black retreated as Desnia was torn from its grasp and into the embrace of the light. She shielded her eyes, blinking against the brilliant radiance.

Her eyes reopened to a world once again dark. A pervasive sound had taken the light's place, a static drone.

Rain.

It began to wet her skin, moisten her hair, steadily pattering the land around her. Her head spun, flinging droplets of water from soaking locks. The grains of the desert sands dug abrasively between her toes. Water cut runnels through the dunes, the storm above releasing its body in torrents upon the arid plains.

A glimmer in the distance came alight. Desnia's breath caught. Heart racing, she trudged through the clutches of the wet sand, panic pulling her forward. The flicker she worked towards, this point of grief and loss, began to grow. Like a sun emerging from the waves of sand, it domed outward, reaching into the sky, surging to meet her.

She didn't slow. Water sprayed from her lips as she let forth a silent cry, the roar of fire drowning her pain. Hands grasped her arms, holding her back. The salt of her tears diluted the rain, a mere drizzle to her deluge. Voices to her side whispered, asking if it was time. If now was the right moment to strike.

The ball of fire was fast approaching, pressing its untamed heat against her face. She glanced to her left and right, the men holding her unfamiliar, yet her stomach sank. One looked down at her, his face inviting and kind. He smiled and Desnia felt, for a moment, reassured. But then the smile pulled farther back, past his eyes, clawing towards his ears. Teeth of black revealed themselves, and the demon drew a knife from behind his back.

Desnia screamed, head spinning to see the other captor at her side. Tusks drenched in violet blood, a helm formed of skulls, eyes black as death's heart. She cried louder, pulling and twisting with all her strength, body immovable against their grip. Blade, and mace of bone, were raised, her name echoing in their malice.

The fire wrapped around them, a hot breath against frozen fear. Desnia squeezed her eyes closed, bracing, trying to fight the onslaught.

And then it was gone.

She cracked an eye—a thin, cautious blade of sight. Another environment greeted her, one of stone and iron and indignity. Someone stood before her. A surge of anger washed over her. She was done running. Done trying to flee from the phantoms that pursued her.

She charged the man before her, ready to fight, prepared to claw the life from him.

He smiled, a band of golden luster glinting from the curved grin. Desnia tried skidding to a halt, her eyes wide as the ones before her refracted and sparkled—jewels that assessed her, valued her, seeking profit. She knew them well, for she'd been trapped by their bearers before.

The figure lifted a leg, thrusting it forward into Desnia's chest. Air gushed from her lungs as she was thrown onto her back, her bones and body a flare of agony. Grasping at her chest, trying to draw air, she looked up, the golden smile and jeweled eyes staring down at her.

Her eyes squeezed closed, the pain spreading through her body a radiating ache that crested over her like waves emanating out from her chest. Each ripple was torture, the heart of her pain a white fire. Color pulsed behind scrunched eyelids; greens, yellows, and reds flashing like bruises.

A slow, unsteady breath left her lips, the air hot and stale. Her arm left her aching ribs and reached out, sliding across hewn timber. She tried to roll, to adjust herself, but a sharp pain in her side left her immobile, a hiss of air sucking through her teeth.

It was with great care that she opened her eyes, the muscles easing back ever so slowly. The dim light of a torch was harsh against her vision as it crept into the room from a slit at the base of a nearby door. She let out a groan, turning her head away, allowing her eyes to adjust to the dark room.

Walls of brick surrounded her, the rough wood beneath her back pricking her with splinters. She tried to sit up, but the pain in her side returned with ferocity, her arms hurrying to press gingerly against the broken rib. Eventually she rolled onto her side, twisting her body to its knees with careful, testing motions. Her legs felt like little more than dead weights. It was as though every muscle in her body was connected to her rib, pulling or displacing it with each of the measured, sluggish movements.

She knelt there for a time, focusing on breathing, trying to ignore the pain in her body and head. The air was dry, drawing the moisture from her mouth and nose. There was no window in the room that she could see, nothing adorning it aside from a pot in the corner.

The wood felt tactile and solid beneath her knees, the air was warm and heavy on her skin. It felt real. But then, so had the glee of the demons which had just given her chase.

Desnia closed her eyes tightly, holding them shut, hoping, begging, for this to be a figment, an illusion of her mind.

She opened them, the same dark room around her, its brick walls solid and unchanged. A sigh left her lips, a sharp intake of air cutting it short as her side throbbed. Her eyes began to adjust. Turning her back to the sliver of light from the door's base, Desnia took stock of her surroundings.

The room was small, less than twice her height in width and length. The brick rose from floor to ceiling, nothing allowing her to see if it was night or day beyond their confines. She guessed it was night based on the ambient temperature, but she was so disoriented that it was difficult to discern.

Lifting her arm to rub her forehead, she saw stains covering her hand and sleeve. Dark splotches and splatters climbed above her elbows, inked into the white shirt. She looked down at her body, her front equally covered in the dry, dark coloring.

She grimaced, memories coming back to her. The rush of an escape. The smile of a woman's mad death throes. And blood. A man's. Her tormentor's. Spilling everywhere, dripping a crimson reminder of his permanence on her soul as it soaked into her clothes and skin.

She suddenly wanted to rip the clothing from her body, to burn it on a pyre fueled with rage and revenge. There should have been a sense of justice, a satisfaction at rendered revenge. Instead, she felt disgusted, a hollow pit carved from her.

Rather than the void being filled, a flood poured from her eyes, stealing from what little she had left to give.

Her mind had become a portentous theater; of what, she didn't know—if it meant anything at all. The ones like... her, well, there was nothing but chaos in their words, words which they clung to, each heavy with importance, yet surmounting to nothing. Desnia, however, did not see them as such. There was no credence to give, no message to deliver. She refused to be like *them*. This wouldn't control her, not while she had the ability to recognize real from dream.

However long that lasted.

Fuck this curse, she thought, clenching her teeth.

"And where were *you*?" she croaked, looking beyond the ceiling above. She didn't know if Asta could hear her, but it didn't stop her. "You ask me to help, yet can't give any in return? I thought you were a *god*? Or maybe you're just a coward, like everyone else."

She longed to hear Masini's voice. He'd been an anchor, her tether to reality these past few months. Before, whilst living in the streets of Calentine, her own grit had carved her way forward. But her vision had been short-sighted. She'd focused on the tomorrow, hiding the condemnation borne to her and burying it in temporary remedies of white, powdered stone. Why worry about the coming years, months, even days, if tomorrow held the perpetual question of life and death?

Delaying the inevitable had allowed her to cope, and while she wouldn't describe her life as *living*, she'd survived. *To what end?* she wondered. She felt as though all those years of struggle had been for naught. A moot effort, leading her straight to what she feared most.

What might be worse than even her mind breaking, a punishment that she could not have prepared herself for, was the loneliness that surrounded her now. It moved the walls away, pulling them into the unreachable distance, leaving her on an island of misery. To have found companionship in not only one but multiple people had been unexpected. She'd retracted from it out of fear, fear for a moment such as this. But they'd forced it upon her, and it had, for a time, shone a light into her life.

A light now extinguished.

To have found and lost, to her, seemed far crueler a punishment than to have been left in the bliss of ignorance.

A rattle of metal pulled her aching head to the side, slowly twisting her body as the door behind her opened. Desnia needed to squint against the licks of the torch's light, the man holding it a uniformed guard. Her stomach jumped into her throat as she wondered if he was here to kill her, revenge for the comrade's blood that covered her.

She should have tried to run or at least defend herself. But she hadn't the energy to pull herself to her feet, her legs like stone. The pain was too immense, her exhaustion too absolute to resist.

At this point, she simply hoped that they would make it quick.

Desnia tried to turn herself to face the man, still on her knees. She'd spent most of her young and adult life trying to prevent someone from stabbing her in the back, and she wasn't going to allow it now. There was still that much dignity flowing through her veins.

The man stepped up to her and bent forward. She couldn't stop herself from flinching, waiting for another heavy-handed beating. A swift death was more than she could hope for, it was childish to think otherwise. No matter her justification in killing the abusive fuck that had tormented her all this time, her new guards would never see her as a victim. In their eyes, she would always be the murderer who had killed their friend.

She began to shake. The thought of torture too much to bear.

The guard rested a wooden bowl on the floor before her.

What is this? she thought, angry and taken aback. *They're going to let me eat before they beat me to death? Is it poisoned, again?* She didn't know what to think, staring at the bowl of grains, lip trembling. Distrust and hunger warred within her.

After a moment steeped in her own fear, she pulled her eyes upward. The brown eyes of her dark-skinned guard were young, full of the life that had long left her own, gleaning with what she could only describe as hope. This was not the visage of a torturer. Not unless he was somehow more twisted than the last bastard.

"Eat," he whispered. She stared at him, refusing to look away, expecting that if she did, she'd miss seeing her own death coming. "It's not poisoned, look." He pinched a couple grains between his fingers and ate them.

"Wh-What do you want?" she uttered, so quiet she could hardly hear herself.

"There are a few of us here—the ones loyal to your cause. We want to help."

"Why?" she asked, wondering what cause he was talking about. "What's in it for you?"

He appeared offended by that. *As if you're the one who should be offended in this scenario...*

"What do you mean? We seek to aid you, in the name of the gods."

She hadn't the faintest idea what he was talking about, but delusions were better than beatings, she supposed. "If you want to help me, then get me the fuck out of here."

He pressed his finger to his lips, shushing her. "Too many of the other guards are unenlightened, we can't risk anything. But there are whispers; they say that the Witness himself has a plan to free you from this place. He will make a plea that not even the general can ignore, not with the gods at his side."

"The who?" she asked.

"I can't stay to explain," he said looking over his shoulder at the sound of feet coming down the hall. "It was an honor to meet you, Messiah. Grace upon you."

With that final, mysterious comment, he reverently bowed his head before exiting the room. When the door closed it was a din to her ringing ears, making her start. The room was once more plunged into darkness, her eyes slow to adjust.

What... What just happened? Hadn't those other guards called her "Messiah?" Who was this "Witness?" A hundred more questions swam in her mind's muddy river, leaving her blind to anything that wasn't an inch before her.

She resisted hoping, objecting to her wants on the contrary. Part of her was still convinced this was some form of trick, some plan of her captors to seek their revenge. Her stomach cramped in protest. When had she last eaten? How long had she been in this cell? Hours? Days? She had no idea.

Reaching down, she picked up the bowl, giving it a sniff. Her mouth salivated, gut twisting into painful knots.

She looked to the ceiling once more, her voice hoarse and cracking. "I hope you're not expecting a fucking 'thank you.'"

With a final sigh, she pinched some grains in her fingers, brought them to her dry, papery lips, and delicately chewed, wondering what tomorrow would bring.

Chapter Thirty-Eight

What he seeks is too valuable to ignore, and given Reedjin's interest, our prerogative shall be to secure it before he does.

Scree tumbled down the mountainside beneath Orne's feet, the winding path scarcely wider than the length of his boot. The slope was nauseatingly steep to his left, disappearing at a cliff's edge. To his right, the incline rose ever upward, supporting the sky in the distance. Jutting boulders and bones of rock emerged from beneath the mountain's gravely skin around them. It was a barren waste, absent of verdant life.

Behind him hiked seventeen members of his two squads. Thirteen had been lost in the attack and, of the remaining, this group was all he could quickly assemble to search for the night raiders. He'd marched them down the access road for less than half an hour before finding this hidden trail leading up into the slopes. If he hadn't been searching for it he could have passed by it a dozen more times, ignorant of its camouflaged existence. Which made him wonder how the enemy had known of it.

The perilous trek had one benefit—it kept them inaccessible to horses. Although he wasn't sure what the caravan had done with theirs or the carts. He'd kept expecting to hear the thunder of hooves—the captain, sending someone to reprimand Orne and order him to return. He doubted anyone would follow them here, let alone find the trail.

Of course, that did not free him from opposition.

"Sir, we shouldn't be up here!" came Steddus's petrified whine from further back in the column.

Orne had debated throwing him from the trail a multitude of times. When Helona had dragged the man into the courtyard in their rush to leave, he'd immediately rejected the idea of taking him. Then he realized that if he didn't, the little worm would run immediately to Villera or the captain. They wouldn't have made it ten minutes into their pursuit before being chased down.

"The road is a few hundred feet down that way," said Orne over his shoulder, pointing down the slope to his side. "Do us all a favor and take the short way."

There was no response.

This was the raiders route, he was certain. The path was recently traveled, doubling them back towards the keep—which he expected would be coming into sight in a short while. With any luck, their attackers would be camped nearby.

Or so he kept telling himself. *Damn trail never seems to end,* he thought with a grimace.

He hated that he'd left his halberd back at the castle, but he kept picturing someone getting leverage on it and throwing him off balance. The idea of rolling off the side of a cliff had *not* been appealing.

As Orne pulled his vision away from his feet and towards another bend in the distance, a stone slipped from under his boot, sending his leg kicking to the side and onto the slope's edge. A splash of loose stone rippling downward with a clatter as he caught himself on a nearby outcropping, fingers digging into the stone. *Fucking place is a death trap,* he thought with a long breath, trying to slow his frantic heart and to not look at the vanishing ledge to his side.

His legs had been like leaves in the wind for most of the climb, though he did his best not to show it in front of the squad, especially Helona. *She's the only one worth a damn, as far as quality soldiers go.* There was also something about the cut of her jaw, the blue of her eyes, her overall... shape. He shook his head, focusing again on the trail, and marched onward, the *crunch* of stone resonating from the line behind him as they moved with their breath collectively held.

The sun had lowered itself behind the range's peaks, filling the sky and valley with reddish hues, taking on an otherworldly ambiance. Orne was torn between wanting to rush forward and taking cautious steps. Climbing this trail in the pitch of night would up the keep's death toll to an even forty, he imagined. But the people who'd attacked them had to have camped *somewhere*, and after hours of hiking, he was confident they would come across it. *Let's just hope it's before the damned sun goes down.*

He increased his pace the little he dared, the chill of the night's breeze upon his clammy skin. Attempting to pull his focus away from the treacherous plummet a few feet away, he tried to dwell on other thoughts.

There was Kolden, who he hoped wasn't doing anything *too* stupid while he was gone. His brother had a tendency to overreach, and without Orne there to keep him grounded, he worried that he'd become overzealous and get caught. The captain and Villera were looking for excuses to punish them both, they didn't need it to be made easy.

The fact they hadn't heard from Delvan yet gnawed at Orne. It could have taken Delvan some time to respond, or the pigeon could have struggled flying through the desert, but it should have returned by now. He wasn't sure what was happening in Brethefen, but his gut told him it wasn't anything good.

He wondered how Helona was doing. His leadership was obviously superior to Villera or the captain, and she must have been impressed by the way he—

His foot slipped again. Barely maintaining his balance, he shook his head. *Focus on the fucking path, you idiot,* he told himself. He fixed his eyes squarely on the trail, intently focused on each step.

Eventually—much to Orne's relief—they rounded a bend and the trail opened, traveling along a shelf of rock roughly six paces wide and eighty paces long. He planted his feet firmly on the solid outcropping, the tension in his shoulders and back finally unbinding. He walked to the other end of the shelf, keeping away from the edge, and looked out.

The distance beyond gave way to a flatter slope, crags rising high in the distance. The trail branched, heading off through the rolling scree towards the mountain's summit, the other direction switchbacking downward.

Directly to the keep below.

Thank the gods. From this distance, the monstrous fortification appeared small but remained imposing—impassable to any but the idiotic few who would brave these slopes. The descending trail must have led to some part of the castle he'd been unable to explore, likely to an old escape tunnel from its more active days.

With the sun rapidly setting, he wasn't going to be able to explore much farther. They were going to have to wait until morning, camping here without torches or fires marking their location in dull moonlight. Footsteps approached from behind him, Helona carefully stepping to his side. He stood a little straighter.

"We heading back down there, sir?" she asked.

"No," Orne said, shaking his head. He turned to look at the line of exhausted soldiers, boots planted squarely on rock. He tried to keep his voice low, the rocky slopes easily carrying sounds for miles. "This is where they waited," he announced. "Up here, until the time was right. We'll take shifts, watching for anyone coming up our rear or from the trail leading further into the moun—"

"Wait, do you really expect us to camp up here? All *night*?" asked a rebellious Steddus. His aggrieved voice was loud enough that Orne heard it reflect from across the valley. "The captain said he had... something special for me! You can't keep me—"

With heavy strides along the stone shelf, Orne made directly for Steddus. Grabbing him by the collar and pulling his sickly face close enough that his breath threatened to make Orne gag, he hissed, "You listen, and listen closely. Speak louder than a whisper again, and I will throw you from this mountainside myself. And I'll do it with a fucking *smile*, you bastard. It's bad enough you took credit for Kolden's alarm last night, but if you reveal our position to the enemy because you're fucking *annoyed*, then I'll make sure they can hear you scream all the way down. Understand?"

Steddus nodded, swallowing loudly and looking pale. Orne was disappointed. He'd been looking forward to throwing the fucker off a cliff.

"Now," Orne said, shoving the vermin to the side, "we have a few packs of supplies, so eat while you can. *No fires*. I want two guards at the rear, two at the front, and two with eyes on the keep. Hopefully the bastards try again tonight, and when they do, they'll either pass right by us, or we'll be able to cut off their escape and flank them. Change shifts at the moon's crest."

There was a susurration from the group as they hesitantly pulled off packs, speaking low amongst themselves rather than rummaging for supplies. *What are they waiting for?* he wondered.

"Uh, sir?" came Helona's voice behind him. He turned to see her with her shoulders hunched, biting her lip and rubbing her hands. "Are we *really* not going back to the castle tonight? I mean, it's not like we can see anything up here once it's dark and all."

Not you too, he thought. He had higher expectations for the infantryman. When he'd said they were taking the fight to the attackers, she'd seemed one of the most eager. "Why is that such a gods-damned problem?" he asked, his voice clipped.

"Well, uh, it's just that when we headed out of the castle, most of us didn't take anything we would, you know, *need*, for, uh, making a camp. Maybe a few of us could go down there and get some things, you know—"

"Do you want to avenge your friends or not?" he grated.

"Well, course I do, but—"

"But what?" Orne interrupted. "What's so difficult about sleeping on the ground for one fucking night?"

"It's just... sir, most of us didn't sleep after, and we might not be doing so good if we stay out here all night." Her eyes flicked from Orne to the distant fortress, a craving in them, a desire that he couldn't explain. "We don't have the... items that we need, sir."

He couldn't believe the excuses he was hearing. They had enough food for a night; even if they hadn't, skipping one meal wouldn't be the end of them. As far as he'd been able to discern thus far, there wasn't a single *actual* soldier stationed in the entire Black Bastion. "We have enough. Anyone that leaves will be court-martialed for abandoning their post, understood?"

She gave him a nervous glance, her mouth opening as if to argue. But she shut it, giving a short nod in response.

"Good. I want you to be on first watch, and I need you to do me a favor." Orne didn't intend to sleep much tonight. He doubted that any of the squad would be adept at catching motion in the darkness. Still, he needed rest, even if it was only for an hour or two, and he didn't like the idea of not being alert in the current company.

"Sir?"

"I need you to keep an eye on Steddus. Make sure he doesn't try something."

She looked from him to the disgruntled infantryman a dozen paces away. "What did you mean earlier, sir? When you said he took credit for Lieutenant Kolden's alarm? Wasn't it Steddus who rang it?"

Orne's teeth pummeled together, refusing to separate as he spoke. "No, it fucking wasn't. Kolden rang the bell, then that bastard Villera and Steddus took the credit."

"Always did think Steddus was a slimy shit." He could see her sneer—a small vindication. At least someone had their head on straight. "If I had known, I wouldn't have grabbed him to come, sir, he was just in the mess and easy enough to—"

"It's fine." He snapped the words out, though he hadn't intended to. *If he gives me a reason to kick him from a ledge, it'll have been worth it.*

"For the record, sir, I never did believe what they said about you hiding during the attack."

"Don't know why anyone would," he retorted. "A lot more people would've died if I had. Fuckers. Some thanks I get." He shook his head. "Take your post and keep your eyes sharp. If I'm asleep then wake me before you switch shifts."

She nodded with a bob of her cropped hair, moving to the end of the stone shelf. Orne watched her walk away longer than he intended.

At least there's one *soldier in this gods-damned post that might be redeemable.* The general's orders seemed more impossible by the day. These soldiers were assailed in the middle of the night, comrades dying by the dozens, and the best among them were more interested in getting back to their beds than they were in revenge. Their blood should have been boiling, their fury righteous and unquenchable. It was as though an illness plagued them.

He wouldn't settle for apathy. If he did, death would find them all. It felt like it had been circling him for weeks now as it was, round eyes waiting for him to drop his guard, directing enemies into his path. Well, if the raiders decided to attack again tonight, he'd be ready for them. If they didn't, then he'd tell the captain to fuck off and keep searching.

He rolled his shoulders, trying to shake the concerns. He had to focus, not just for the enemies beyond, but the ones within. Vigilance was his greatest ally in times like this.

Settling down onto the stone, he took some dried meat from a pack nearby. He tore at it with his teeth, eyes sharp and ears tuned as night drew over them like a god's shadow. Orne shifted uneasily, glancing around as he felt the hair rise on the back of his neck.

He had the odd, itching sensation that someone, somewhere, was watching him.

Chapter
Thirty-Nine

Do not allow yourself to deviate because of grievances, for they are trifling compared to the oncoming storm.

Y ou still haven't answered my question," said Mithya.

Delvan ignored her, stepping over a pile of charred rubble in the street. A dreary grey imbued all but the sky itself here in the Scar—the locals' apt name for the fire-ravaged wedge of city—but even the blue ceiling felt less vibrant when framed by blackened skeletons of once colorful landscapes. Ash clung to the breeze, softly mixing with the scratching desert sand. The most disturbing thing, to Delvan, was the utter quiet of it all.

He felt the slight tug of Mithya's power as she spoke, agitated. "Why do you think your priest friend is going to be able to help us find Des?"

"Not so fun, being in the dark. Is it?" replied Delvan without glancing back, the itch in his mind unrelieved.

He heard a huff from a few steps behind him like an exasperated laugh. "Are you always this petty?"

Only when reciprocating. "Nerio has... Let's just call it a large network in the city. If anyone has the resources to find her, it'll be him."

"Sounds like his preaching has spread faster than I would've thought. Now I definitely want to meet him."

"I'm surprised you haven't. Figured the general would've sent you after him too."

A Truthsayer could've found Nerio in a morning without using more than a small block of inanite. With half the city seemingly giving small bows to Delvan these days, he wondered if Mithya realized all she needed to do was ask any random person on the street to lead her directly to the priest. *Better that she thinks she needs me. I wouldn't be surprised if she was still looking for ways to do this on her own.* Perhaps the idea of Nerio being able to help her hadn't occurred. *Or maybe I'm not the only one trying to keep the competition close...*

"He did. I tried," she said casually. He stopped and turned back to look at her, incredulous. "What?" she asked.

"What do you mean, 'tried?'"

She shrugged. "Maybe 'tried' is a stretch. With the amount of people flocking to him, I just thought the city would be more... *interesting* with him still running around in it." She put on a small and mischievous smile.

"Are you *trying* to sow chaos?"

"Sow? No, no. *Reap?* Well, that's an entirely different story. Besides, I thought you'd be happy, he's *your* friend, after all."

"Don't act like any of this was for me," he said. He couldn't tell whether she was saying all of this to get under his skin, or if there was any truth to it. "And I don't know if *friend* is the word I would use. But we both care about Des, so I know he'll help."

"Well, then it was a good thing I didn't go looking for him too hard. See? You should be thanking me."

Delvan's mouth opened wide, then hung there, silent, while his tongue twisted itself into a knot. *I cannot believe this woman!* He turned around and stormed down the street, avoiding detritus while attempting to outrun Mithya's arrogance. He swore he could *hear* her smiling behind him.

Retracing his steps from the last time he'd been led to Nerio, Delvan wove them through the streets of ruin, taking moments at intersections to scratch his head, attempting to remember the exact path. Burnt to cinders, the buildings throughout the Scar all appeared similar, almost indistinguishable.

After nearly thirty minutes of walking, Mithya broke the tolerable silence. "Are we going to tour the *entire* Scar or are we actually going somewhere?"

Delvan quickened his pace, his feet trying to outrun the question. There was another turn up ahead. "They're around here somewhere," he said. "Besides, people make their way here every day, we should—"

Rounding the bend revealed a posting of guards before a once grandiose entrance. Now it was a crumbled arch with pillars that stood half as tall as a man, their remnants cleared, and area swept.

Finally, he thought, relieved. He walked towards the guards, who, upon first seeing his uniform, visibly tensed. Then, as he drew closer, dropped to one knee as their eyes filled with recognition, bowing their heads. *Not this again.*

"Well," said Mithya, "that's... unexpected."

"Just... *don't.*" He hurried by them.

And strode into a temple of the devout.

The sick and hungry were waiting in a line near the large tent on the courtyard's edge. Others sat on the ground, gathered in prayer. All while a great many moved and labored as they attended to daily duties. More had gathered here since his last visit. Many, *many* more.

How his trifling donation was feeding a group this large, he couldn't fathom. A grimness hung in the air, but not the haunting exhaustion he'd experienced on his previous visit. Instead, faces were irritable, tired—and Delvan couldn't say that he blamed them. They'd lost everything, and whatever little remained was being taken by taxes and the army. He understood that it was meant to benefit the people, but while the rebuilding happened, the desperate and hungry were left with nothing to lose. The only thing that could not be taken from them were the words of hope that Nerio preached, and it became their world.

A world he was, unfortunately, a part of. The courtyard quickly became devoid of motion or sound upon his entrance, the entire populous turning to stare at him.

"Fans of yours?" Mithya leaned over and whispered. Delvan ignored her.

"I'm looking for Nerio," he said, barely needing to raise his voice for it to carry through the silence.

Murmurs, hushes, and whispers were cast behind covered mouths. Knees were bent and steps were taken, forward and back, as the group tried to decide how to react in their nervousness, his presence akin to an idol come to life—or so it felt.

This is ridiculous, he thought, waiting impatiently for a response, their eyes like a stone's weight. *Nerio has to stop this.* The reverence had gone from uncomfortable to oppressing, weighing on him like a boulder.

"Alright!" came a loud shout over the group, catching them by surprise. "We have work to do, food to cook! Let's give the Lord some space."

The crowd slowly began to clear. As they parted Delvan saw through the throng, finding Captain Gernbard standing tall and watching everyone with the commanding eyes of an officer, Nerio at his side. People parted as the pair approached the two Blues, distractedly performing their duties as they continued flicking their gazes towards Delvan.

Nerio was beaming with a smile as they approached. "Lo-uhm, Delvan! It is a pleasure to see you again. I had actually hoped to speak with you regarding some troubling things I've heard this morning. And I apologize for not knowing your name, Lady?..."

Mithya gave a close-lipped smile.

"That would be Lady Mithya, Witness," said Captain Gernbard before Delvan had a chance to respond.

She raised a curious eyebrow. "I don't believe we've met, Captain."

"Your reputation precedes you, my Lady." Delvan saw the slightest twitch of Mithya's brow.

"Ah, yes. I've heard of you. It is a pleasure," said Nerio with a small bow. "Tell me, what brings you here?"

Delvan turned his head, every direction filled with keen ears and pious eyes. "Is there somewhere... private where we can speak?" He caught Gernbard's gaze shifting just as cautiously through the crowd.

"Yes. Yes, of course," said Nerio, oblivious to the people surrounding him. "Follow me."

He led them back through the front gate to a building across the street—another once-estate that was in far worse condition than the one that housed Nerio's camp. Its halls and the courtyard they eventually came to were quiet, and Delvan was thankful for the reprieve from the burden of voracious eyes.

"You're fortunate," said Nerio as they gathered, "we were just about to be on our way to another camp when you arrived."

"You have more?" Delvan asked, astonished.

Nerio, a small amount of pride in his voice, said, "Half a dozen or so total. Thanks, in large part, to you." The comment raised a curious look from Mithya. "More and more people are coming here, seeking refuge from the streets. So many were displaced by the fire that even the alleys are becoming crowded in the untarnished portions of the city. We do what we can for them."

"I'm a rather avid admirer of the riots your followers are inciting," said Mithya. Delvan glared at her, once again unable to tell whether she was being sarcastic or genuine.

He wanted to strangle her all the same.

Nerio's face flushed, his head turning in shame. Delvan caught the flicker of a sneer from the captain to his side. "Some of our more zealous followers have misconstrued what it is that I wish to teach," said Nerio. "I plan on guiding them back into the gods' path, away from these violent outbursts."

"And in what capacity," stated the captain in a flat tone, "do you come here today?" Delvan noticed his hand resting on the hilt of his blade, the strap already undone. Despite her nonchalant attitude, he knew that Mithya realized the same.

"I have no interest in stopping you, Captain, if that's what you're asking," said Mithya. It was the first honest sounding answer Delvan had heard from her that day.

"We need your help," said Delvan. Nerio's eyes lit up, the captain relaxing slightly.

"Of course!" the young priest said excitedly. "After everything you've done, it's the least I can do."

Delvan glanced at Mithya, a curl to her lips as she added Nerio's words to the leverage she held against him. "We need you to tell us where Des is," he said.

Nerio's face fell, the excitement vanishing. The captain shifted slightly, appearing uncomfortable. "As it so happens," Nerio said hesitantly, "that is the matter I had wished to discuss with you. Is it true, the stories I have heard? Did she speak the words of a god?"

"I wasn't in the room," said Delvan, glancing at Mithya. He should have known this question would come, and he could see where his answer would lead. If a hint of divine intervention fell upon the priest's ears, he would add it to his doctrine, and the idea of Nerio's following gaining additional momentum wasn't just disconcerting—it terrified him. "What I know is—"

"I was there," interrupted Mithya. "And it was a god's voice—of that I'm certain. Loud and exalted, he possessed—"

Delvan grabbed and pulled Mithya's arm, whispering harshly into her ear as he dragged her away. "What are you *doing*?!"

"Making things more interesting," she replied with another impish smile, before jerking her arm free from his grasp. *Is this woman insane?!* he seethed. He saw Nerio with his head bowed, praying, and the captain making a small motion and raising his hand. Delvan groaned.

He and Mithya stepped back towards the two, a fury still roaring in Delvan's chest. "Look, Nerio," he said, trying to temper the priest's benediction, "I don't know what happened, and presumptions will get us nowhere." He shot another glare at the smugly contented Truthsayer. "But Des is *not* safe. That episode yesterday nearly killed her; from what we've heard she's *just* regained consciousness."

"The gods are protecting her," said Nerio, looking to the sky. "She won't succumb to the owl's talons, I assure you."

"You didn't see her, Nerio!" Delvan said, trying to control his anger. He closed his eyes, taking a breath before continuing. "We cannot rely on the 'gods' to save her. We need to do something. We need to get her *out*."

"Is that why you're here?" asked Nerio. "To ask for my aid in her freedom?"

"Waiting around for her execution," said Mithya, "seemed, well, kind of boring."

"They've moved her. We need to know where," said Delvan. "You have the eyes and ears of half the city, if anyone is going to know where she went, it's you."

Nerio's face turned down, his lips pressing tightly together. He shifted on his feet, his eyes having difficulty meeting Delvan's own. "I'm sorry, Lord Delvan. I cannot say."

"Why?" asked Mithya. Delvan felt the telltale trickle of power emerging from her, a spark, faint but warm.

"Because I have a plan to ensure her release," said Nerio. *He probably would've told us that anyway,* Delvan thought, looking at Mithya. "One that does not resort to violence. I am going to make an appeal that even the general cannot ignore. He will see that it is the will of not only the gods, but of the people, that she be released. Her freedom will not come with pursuit, as I have told you before."

"While I appreciate your flare for the dramatic," mocked Mithya, "who says we're going to resort to violence?"

"I know you're well intended, Lord Delvan," said Nerio hesitantly, "but you're a knight, a soldier, and I cannot risk more violence as a result of my actions."

"Well, personally, I don't plan to rely on the general's integrity to come through for Des," said Mithya with a hint of a sneer. "Where is she?"

Delvan wanted to scold her for pushing her power outward once more, although he was growing increasingly certain that she was incapable of doing otherwise. As much as he hated it, however, he agreed with Mithya. Someone had to be willing to take the measures to ensure Desnia's release.

"An old building," said Nerio, "a few blocks from the Devapuram. It was a former housing block but has been commandeered for food and supply storage by the army." The priest's eyes went wide, his hands running over his short-cropped hair. "I-I-I didn't mean..."

Gernbard looked both furious and... relieved? Delvan narrowed his eyes. *Maybe I'm misreading him?* "Nerio, listen," he placated, "we've tried every avenue to get her out legally, it's just not working. I hope whatever plea you make works, it will save us a lot of trouble, but one way or another, Des is going to be free."

"You don't want this life, Delvan," said Nerio, his head hung low. "If you do as you intend, you will step from a precipice from which you cannot return. Why would you do that?"

Delvan's heart sank. He'd told himself the same words before, that there would be consequences. And he thought he'd accepted that. Hearing the words aloud though... It hit him differently. "For the same reason you give speaks multiple times a day, Nerio."

There was a protracted, weighted silence. Nerio could not pull his eyes from the floor. The captain was stoic and silent behind him. Delvan's mouth was muzzled with guilt.

And then Mithya spoke. "Are you all always this glum?" Delvan slowly turned his head, staring at her flatly, resisting the urge to gag her. She had the audacity to roll her eyes. "It'll be *fine*. You'll see."

"I... should be going," said Nerio. He looked at Delvan, his eyes wet and downtrodden. "I don't expect you to have the King's grace in this endeavor, and I know how you feel about the words of those that listen to me. So I will merely wish you to be safe, and may the gods watch over you." He gave a short bow of his head to Mithya. "My lady." He then strode between them, his sandals dragging long lines through the ash on the floor.

Delvan watched him leave, turning to Mithya with a glare of disappointment in his eyes. "Why do you always have to be like... you?" he asked.

"Because it's what makes me charmingly irresistible," she said with a wink.

"Ehem," came Captain Gernbard's voice from their side. Delvan had almost forgotten the man was there. "My Lord, I wish to have a word."

"Yes?" asked Delvan. Gernbard eyed Mithya, gaze laden with concern. "Give us a minute," he said to her.

She looked at Delvan with low eyes. She would probably try to pull the answers out of him later, but he couldn't deny there was a certain level of satisfaction in knowing something that she didn't. She rolled her eyes after a second and left. Delvan waited until he felt the warmth of her gem dim to a small ember, knowing that she was far enough away not to overhear.

"Sorry, my Lord," said the captain. "I know I shouldn't be saying so, but I don't much trust that witch."

Have to appreciate a soldier's candor. "Neither do I, Captain, but we can't always be picky with our allies."

"Mhm, true enough," he replied with a knowing grunt. "I wanted to express my gratitude, sir. I had my doubts when we first met, I'll admit. Been on a few campaigns and met a few knights, can't much say I thought highly of most of 'em." Delvan tried to hide a grimace, thinking of too many Blues he could say the same about. "But, you came through, and I can tell that you care about the Witness."

"What is all this about, Captain?"

The man clenched his jaw, looking at the door for a moment before speaking. "I... have some concerns. About the Witness's plan."

"To free Desnia? I tried to use every political favor I could think of, and the general wouldn't budge. His orders are coming from the Court." *And my father's even more stubborn than he is.*

"He intends well," said Gernbard with a sigh, "but it's the riots that worry me."

"I've seen them firsthand, I can't disagree with you." The carnage at the guild was still enough to send a shiver over his skin. "But what does that have to do with Nerio's plan?"

"He's intending to give a speak, sir, before anyone and everyone who will listen. He's asked those true to his cause to come—a sign of the peoples' will. He thinks that the display will convince the general to release the Messiah."

"What?" asked Delvan. *If he thinks a speak is going to convince the general, then it won't be here in the Scar. It will need to be somewhere he can see it, where he'll feel pressured.* "Where?"

The captain shook his head, his face reserved. "The Devapuram itself, sir."

"All he's going to do is *anger* Rosethorn! Has he lost his mind?!"

"That's why I wanted to discuss this with you. I've served under the general, I know how he is. We've been out of his way until now, an annoyance to him, yes, but not a direct obstacle. But this..." the captain grimaced. "He'll bring a legion down on us, and these people are on edge, as you're well aware."

Delvan's fingers pulled at his hair. "We have to talk to him, stop him from—"

"I've tried, sir. You won't be able to. And if you do anything excessive, you'll have a revolt in the camp. He's the only thing holding together half the city, so if you think the riots are bad now..."

Delvan began pacing. He wanted desperately to tell the captain he was wrong, that they could talk sense into the priest. But he remembered the stares, the reverence shown to *him*, let alone the devotion to Nerio. He couldn't help Desnia if he was torn apart by an angry mob. "How many people, do you think, are going to be at this speak?" He braced himself, petrified of the answer.

"Honestly, sir, I can't say. We have more people here every day, the worship's growing at a rate that surprises even me."

"Guess," said Delvan.

The captain was quiet for a moment. "Ten thousand, at least. Maybe more."

Delvan felt his face grow cold. "That's twice the count of the legion patrolling the streets. If they turn violent..."

"My thoughts exactly, sir."

"We have to do *something*," Delvan stated. "Why tell me all of this if you don't want me to talk Nerio out of it?"

"We will protect the Witness, sir. I have men, loyal to the cause, and I expect the crowd's anger will be directed outward, rather than in."

"What's to stop them from seeing your soldiers as more oppressors? I watched a mob throw themselves at *pikes,* Captain, I think you overestimate their minds in the moments of chaos."

The captain's lips turned down as he nodded. "I expect you're right, my Lord. We'll be wearing no uniforms, only covered armor. It's the best we can do."

"I don't know about that," said Delvan. He couldn't think of anything to do differently, not that wouldn't end in violence. With time, perhaps, he could concoct a solution, but he still had Desnia to worry about. "You never answered my question. What are you asking of me?"

"Get the Messiah out of the city, sir. I pray that the gods keep this peaceful, that everything goes as the Witness hopes, but if things go wrong... The crowd is going to want two things: revenge, and their Messiah. You said yourself, you can't trust a mob. Especially not a starved, broken one."

Delvan rolled his head back, staring at the blue sky framed in crumbling stone. *Save Desnia, at the cost of what? The entire city?* Nerio's plan was idealistic, but mostly foolish. *But with everything he's done already, could he keep the masses calm? Could his plan work?* Was he really beginning to believe in the priest? There was a certain aura about him, his conviction true and endearing enough that it made one want to believe everything he said, to conform to his ideals.

As much as he wished he could, Delvan couldn't rely on such hopes. "I'll get her out, Captain, I promise."

The grizzled man gave a short nod, relief again loosening his shoulders. "There are some soldiers stationed where she's being held, ones that are enlightened. I will have them meet with you and provide whatever they can."

"Thank you," said Delvan.

"No, thank you, sir. And, in the words of the Witness, may the gods watch over you."

Delvan nodded and watched as the captain left. He stood there for a moment, quietly hoping that Gernbard and Nerio's words had been heard and, if he was lucky, would be answered.

Chapter Forty

In the meantime, I will review the journals, as they should be arriving within the week. Though I suspect I will be sorting through a great deal of egotistical drivel.

This place was beginning to remind him of Drunt.

Kolden wiped his head of the cold drops that had fallen from the arched passage's ceiling, cursing the leaking stone. Drunt at least had a tavern. People also weren't actively trying to kill him; not most of the time, anyway. The captain there had been an ass, but Mathin was a step above even that cranky bastard. He had a better forge here, but blacksmithing with only one arm was nigh impossible. He supposed they both had old, crumbling castles, but this one was still—despite its decrepit state—a far superior fortress.

In fact, the only thing that the two had in common was how absolutely fucking miserable they were.

Which made them basically the same.

He tried to roll the shoulder that hung in the sling, wincing as the tender muscle burned like a fire. The bones weren't broken, he suspected, but it would be weeks before he had mobility back. *Sure could use some of Delvan's healing touch right about now,* he thought with a hiss.

After the captain and Villera had nearly given themselves aneurisms screaming in the courtyard after Orne's departure, Kolden had thought it best to keep his head down and out of sight for a while. The carrier coup had been distressingly absent of messages from Delvan or the general. Not hearing from one of them was one matter, but both? Kolden couldn't help but wonder if something had happened in the city, or if their messages were being intercepted somehow. Which raised the question of *who* might be interfering with their correspondence?

Kolden had sent a few more this morning. Some to the barracks, others to the general's scribe, another to a few people that he suspected would be able to find Delvan in a hurry. He tried to put the missives out of his mind. His distraction was, yet again, sneaking around the castle at night. *Hopefully with a little less bloodshed this time...*

Based on the placement of guards, a little common sense, and the complete lack of creativity on Villera's part, he'd determined that Phrenwa was being held in the keep's old prison wing.

Likely intended to house prisoners of war and hostages, it branched from the main building, was two stories tall, and contained scores of cells. Kolden had quickly gone poking through it the other day when looking for hidden stashes of Villera's, but it hadn't seen foot traffic in years.

Except for the guards that now stood at each of the entrances. *The idiots aren't even trying to be subtle,* he thought.

What he needed was a key—and a good distraction, but one thing at a time—to break in. The guards, he assumed, would have one, but he couldn't just walk up and take it from them. Despite the temptation, he decided against forging another lockpick. Not only would it have been annoyingly difficult without help, but the results of his last attempt had left a sour taste in his mouth.

He'd hoped to find another entrance to the prison wing, or an old guard post he'd missed the day prior with a hidden stash of keys, forgotten to time, but they'd been locked or cleaned out. *The* one *time those idiots do something competent, and it has to be something that gets in my way.*

Instead, he was forced to creep down the one hall connecting to the jail, a surplus of torches along its length making it unfeasible to travel unseen. He held tight to the wall, the dewing moisture clinging to his clothes and skin while the snapping flames of torches grabbed at his face with grazing warmth.

The entire castle was alight with braziers, the few lanterns they had oil for, torches, and a large fire built on the courtyard's flagstones. Kolden could only shake his head. There wouldn't be fuel to maintain this level of illumination for more than a few nights; all the enemy had to do was wait for them to run out and then attack when it was dark as inanite in the keep. If they were in fact the merchants that had traveled with Phrenwa, then they would be well aware that another supply train wasn't coming for several weeks, minimum.

Kolden had to get in to see Phrenwa before then, find a way to prevent his men from attacking again, and hopefully gather information on who the man was that the principle was sending—assuming it wasn't the bastard himself.

But first, he had to get *into* the place. The cold, wetted stone sent a shiver down his spine as he slunk closer to the single bend in the long, narrow passage. He needed to think of a way to get past the guards at its end—a convincing story, maybe? He could try to pull rank, but the captain or lieutenant had probably specifically stated to keep him and Orne out. Maybe he could bribe them? He had several darksteel blades, worth considerably more than even the decent sum of golden suns currently in his purse. That and... and...

And what was that *smell*?

Pungent, sticky, burning at his nostrils, the scent clung to the inside of his nose like tar. It was herbal, like an incense burned at an altar. He swore that he recognized it from—

His eyes popped as it struck him. *Iguan.*

Given how much time he'd spent in those damned iguan dens in Brethefen, he was shocked he hadn't recognized it sooner. What was it doing out here? Finding it in the midst of a large city wasn't surprising, but on this desolate slab of rocky mountain? It hadn't occurred to him that it would be procurable.

Once he recognized the scent, he saw the telltale wisps of hazy smoke hovering in the air, twisting in the heat of the torches. His eyes squinted in a curious expression, watching it churn in the air. He slid farther along the wall to where the stones turned at a crisply cut corner and peered around.

The two guards were there, as expected, on either side of the door. Both were perched on stools, their backs pressed to the wall and heads lolled to the side. They were slumped and enervated, heads listing from one side to the other, a thick cloud of smoke hovering around them.

They're high as a treetop! thought Kolden.

He'd seen the effects of iguan use firsthand, the many dens offering little discretion for their patrons, who didn't care if they were in a pig's troth or silk sheets as long as they could get their fix. It was nasty, vile, and most importantly, extremely convenient. *Maybe there is a bit of luck in the air tonight. That and hallucinogens...*

They wouldn't be able to differentiate between him and their visions. Hopefully. He'd been called everything from demon to god when going through the dens, at least by those conscious enough to recognize him as being within their proximity. He *should* be able to walk straight up to both of these idiots and take the keys to do as he pleased. Probably. Maybe.

He could feel his heart beating against his chest, despite knowing that he wasn't *technically* doing anything wrong. It was the captain and Villera that he worried about. If they were hiding something that warranted an attack by masked assailers in the night, who knew what lengths they'd be willing to go to protect it.

With a shake of his unslung hand and a deep breath, Kolden pulled away from the wall and strode down the hallway, trying to keep his head high and walk steady. The guards' eyelids were sagged low, eyes twitching and roving underneath. Kolden's nose cringed and flared as he came within a few steps of them both, the haze thickest around their limp figures, a nearby torch casting long shadows down their faces.

Neither so much as shifted as Kolden came to a halt between them, the locked door within the reach of his good arm. He spun his head, looking between the two, and then shrugged before searching for a key.

A ring—several iron keys hanging from the patinaed metal—hung from a loop at one guard's waist. Not wanting to challenge the shred of luck he'd been given, Kolden gingerly pinched the ring between his finger and thumb, lifting it as smoothly as he could from the guard's waistband.

A twitch from the man's body rolled the half-limp head to face Kolden's own. Breath held, he slowly raised his eyes—and met the guard's.

Oh, shit.

The locked gaze held for a moment that felt suspended in time—Kolden too petrified to move, the guard's foggy eyes too slow to process what was happening.

"Wha-What are you?" the guard asked, his words slurred.

"Uhh," said Kolden, his mouth choosing a terrible time to stop working. "I'm a, uh, demon!" he said, trying to sound menacing, but mostly sounding ridiculous.

The man's eyes narrowed. "You don't look like no demon," he said, tongue like molasses.

"That's because, uh, I'm a *shapeshifter*. Yeah. That's it."

The guard's eyes went wide, his head pulling back. "You *are*? Please, I don't want trouble."

"Well, just let me be on my way, and we won't have a problem."

"I'm not, uh, supposed to, for some reason. I think..."

Kolden wanted to smack the man but refrained. "Look, let me go and I won't, uh, eat you."

"Eat me?!"

"Yes, but I'll only do that if you don't let me through. Or if you tell anyone you saw me. Or if you don't tell me where the prisoner is."

"That's... a lot of things to tell you..." *I'd be surprised if you could tell me your own name right now.* "But I don't want no trouble." *Yes, you said that.* "I... I think there's someone on the second floor inside."

"Perfect," said Kolden, lifting the keys from the inebriated man's belt. He didn't seem to notice. "Now, forget you saw me. Or... else."

"No! Please!" The man's voice was shaky as he pulled himself away from Kolden, fumbling off the stool and landing in the hall's corner. Kolden rolled his eyes.

He took the keys, testing a couple before the latch made a satisfying *click* and the door loosened in its jamb. *If only I could've done that last night,* he thought with a sigh. He walked through, leaving one guard quivering on the floor and the other half asleep and heedless of his actions.

Locking the door behind him, he began making his way through the prison wing, searching for stairs to the second floor. They weren't hard to find.

Following the guided path, he glanced around at the nearby cells. He didn't much like the idea of being in another prison. This one might have a notable deficiency of purple-glowing cadentite—not to mention psychopaths—but it *felt* like a cage all the same. Still, the idea of swiftly approaching death was a hell of a motivator.

He trudged forward, climbing the stairs on the balls of his feet, trying to remain quiet in case there were more guards posted. When he reached their summit, he slowly peered around the wall towards the long hall's single light source—the distance beyond and to the opposite end black, bottomless wells.

Sitting in the flickering light on another stool was a guard, motionless and relaxed. Kolden sniffed the air, thinking that he smelled iguan once more. Given that its scent was lodged into his olfactory after the last passageway, it was difficult to tell if the woman was just asleep or amid opiate-induced hallucinations.

Looking around, he grabbed a small pebble from a tread's crumbling edge, then tossed it at the guard's feet. Or, at least, he *aimed* at her feet, but his uncooperative left arm decided to shift his throw—right onto the woman's face.

Kolden cringed and sucked in a hiss of air as the pebble bounced from her cheek, landing with a soft putter on the floor. There was no flinch from her face, no shift of her body, just the remaining stillness and gaping jaw. *Probably out of it,* he thought. *But maybe sleeping?* Whatever her condition, he needed to get over there and speak to the man in the cell she was supposed to be guarding.

Taking the risk, he turned the corner, steps cautious as he approached, his eyes stuck to the guard. The smell of iguan intensified, and he soon saw smoldering ash on the floor. He kept light on his feet—he had no idea if he could talk his way out of another confrontation. If he couldn't, then one twist of her head, one flutter of her eyes and he might have to turn and run for—

"You need not worry about her," came a calm voice from nearby. One which made Kolden almost jump from his skin.

His head spun, twisting his body and aching shoulder. Wincing in pain and calming his thumping heart—which mostly involved cursing like a horse-kicked farrier—he looked to his left, the cell opposite the transcended woman housing a single, slumped figure, sitting on the floor, leaning against the greying stone behind the iron bars.

"Phrenwa," said Kolden. "Nice of you to not try and kill me this time."

The merchant's face remained stoic, a quiet indifference on it. "Lord Kolden. Had I realized earlier that our goals were aligned, then confrontation could've been avoided, I think," he said in his thick accent.

"Aligned?" asked Kolden. "I don't even know who you *are*."

"Someone who wishes to prevent the man you know as 'Jerdine' and his Magridi from accomplishing their goals. I believe you have already succeeded once in this one?"

Kolden glanced over his shoulder at the motionless guard behind him. "I... might know something about that. But I *need* to know, what is his man coming here for? What is Villera selling that he wants?"

"You fear this man, no?"

"What kind of question..." Kolden rubbed his forehead. "Have you had the pleasure of meeting the fucker? Seen what he can do?"

"Mhm," he said with a nod of his head. "I am familiar with the High Realm's magic."

"Then you can understand why I'm asking about who's coming. I need answers, not more questions. Gods, if he's sending the other one... None of us are going to stand a chance."

"Other?" Phrenwa asked, his face puzzled. "I was informed that The Hunter was dead. There are few other mages on this side of the mountains that could've arrived in such a short time."

"That twisted bastard *is* dead. Roasted like a pig on a spit." Kolden still wished he could've heard the bastard scream, but the headless body of blackened skin and flesh had brought about a certain level of satisfaction. He could still see that demented smile, the glee of murder the creature had reveled in. A chill bit him, one not of the cold.

It seemed that Phrenwa was willing to share and knew a great deal more than anyone he'd encountered. Kolden didn't know what better possibility might present itself to learn more about their possible pursuers. Orders would need to be... ignored, for a short period. "I meant the one in black armor. The one that managed to come through the gate before we closed it. And what do you mean, 'other' mages?"

The deadly merchant's stony eyes finally cracked, the whites growing large in contrast to his deeply tanned skin. "Some managed to get through?"

"Just the one, thankfully. Fought unlike anyone I've ever seen, though. Gave the sense that he was far more dangerous than Jerdine, or even that sick fuck pet he had."

Phrenwa drew a deep breath, his lips turning steeply down. With tremendous effort, he pulled himself to his feet, leaning against the wall and wincing as he held his knee and hobbled closer to Kolden, who took a short step backward. "Then things are more dire than we'd thought," Phrenwa said, his face nearly pressed to the bars. "You must get me out of here, back to my people. A warning must be sent."

"*Why*?" asked Kolden. "You've answered none of my questions while leaving me somehow *more* in the dark. Give me a reason I would even *consider* helping you."

"Because you are here, and because you know there are greater dangers to this world than the tiny goals of petty men."

Kolden stared at him, lips pressed tightly together. *Gods-damn it,* he thought, hating that he was considering the proposal. He glanced over his shoulder again, the guard still a sagging mass of armor.

"She smoked enough iguan to be like that until morning, by my guess," said Phrenwa.

"Her and the other guards," mumbled Kolden.

"Most of the castle uses the drug. Habitually. It's how they're kept in line," said Phrenwa.

"Kept in line? What is that supposed to mean?"

Phrenwa shook his head. "First, get me out of here, and then I will explain this one."

Kolden's hands balled into fists. "I swear, if you don't give me one gods-damned answer soon, then I'll leave you here to rot."

"We do not have time for this! There are still many who abstain, the ones with real power in the castle. More than we expected. We will have to get past them with my mangled knee."

Crossing his arms, Kolden stood there, waiting.

"You know what is at stake!" hissed Phrenwa. The man gritted his teeth, appearing deep in thought. "Fine! I do not know who it is that Jerdine is sending. A courier or another mage, either is possible. I have been coming here for months now to try and purchase or steal this one before he had the opportunity or became aware of its presence."

"Is that what you bought from him last night?"

"No. I purchased iguan, a large supply of it. We heard of its potency and traced its source to this castle."

Kolden blinked, his mind whirling as he began to think through the implications of what Phrenwa said. *He was hardly interested in the iguan,* he recalled. *If he was following the drug, then something related to it must have—Ohh. Oh, shit.*

The word escaped his lips in a low, air-draining breath. "Cadentite."

Phrenwa gave him a slow nod. "Yes, you see it now, no? We cannot allow the keepers of this castle to hold it, nor for it to change hands with Jerdine. They require it to use their magic, and if they gather enough, they *will* try again to take this realm."

Bile burned the back of his throat as he listened to Phrenwa's words. The man was right. Nothing else mattered. If the principle managed to acquire however much was stored here, then who knew what kind of damage he could reap.

A flood of questions came to Kolden's mind. What was the stone's source? How much did they have? Did Phrenwa know more? He didn't have time for any of those right now, however. He needed to get that cadentite before anyone else did, for their survival.

And also because he *really* wanted it.

He spun, taking the rattling keys off the unconscious guard.

Hidden stashes of cadentite and secretive groups looking to take it for their own gain? Yeah, this seems familiar, and if it goes the same way, then things are about to get much, much worse.

He'd been right. This place was *exactly* like Drunt.

Chapter
Forty-One

Onto the final matter at hand. I know of this "Masini," although I believed him to be dead.

Wind twisted and spun the street's sand into funnels of whipping grit. It had picked up earlier that morning, the dawn bringing growing gusts in its wake. Life on Brethefen's roads had come to a standstill, the homeless having dispersed to better sheltered areas, soldiers stretching the time between patrols, and the already quiet bustle of businesses taking another downturn.

Delvan put the strange silence out of his mind as he walked, guarding his face with his arm as a blast of sand rushed over him.

He and Mithya were set to meet with guards from Desnia's prison in a few hours. With any luck they would be out of the city before midnight. The idea should have pleased him, his mind set on the decision. Instead, he felt his throat tighten while claws dug into his heart. Change was inevitable, and while he knew what he had now wasn't a life of his own choosing, setting out and creating a new one was a plethora of possibilities that overwhelmed, freezing his mind like a glacier.

There wasn't much time. Not to do the few things that he wished, the few things that truly mattered. Not knowing what to expect, he'd gone to the bank, forging a letter and seal from his father and withdrawing an assortment of gems worth the better part of a thousand suns. They'd realize what he'd done eventually, but that would take weeks. The kingdom was vast, his father's reach extending well beyond its borders. Delvan would, as much as he detested the idea, have to trust that Mithya's smugglers could provide undetected escort. What he did after that was a matter to be concerned about later.

His second errand brought him before the entrance of the Royal Mail Service. Stone steps led to a facade of chiseled cornices, smooth blocks, and pillar-supported dormers. A Calentinian style that was stark against the bright, adobe landscape. He hurried inside, the floor-to-ceiling polished rock continuing within and providing relief from the desert's abrasive breath. Delvan brushed himself off, then strode through the main chamber and approached an attendant, his boots echoing off the reflective stone. The man's desk sat before a wall of slots and stacked paper, his nose buried deep in a ledger. Delvan could hear the cooing of pigeons from behind a door at the desk's end, humming constantly.

The attendant looked up from his scrawling. "King and His grace upon you, my Lord," said the balding, portly man Delvan recognized from his frequent visits.

"And you," replied Delvan. "Has anything arrived for me today?"

"Yes, in fact," said the attendant with a nod. Delvan perked up, watching intently as the man spun on his stool and ran a finger along the column of boxes. "Ah," he said, pulling out a small scroll. "This arrived just a few minutes ago, my Lord."

Delvan anxiously took the scroll, looking at it to find a signet he didn't recognize. His shoulders slumped. "Was there nothing from the Traskors?" he asked.

"Sorry, my Lord, nothing that I've seen."

They should have been there days ago, he thought, wondering if his messages had made it.

There was probably nothing to fret over, they were both capable of handling themselves. Perhaps they were settling in still. *Or maybe something has gone terribly wrong...*

He tried to shake the concern, his own assurances falling flat, a worry festering in his heart. He had to trust that they were safe, after all there wasn't much out in the barren slopes of the White Mountains aside from, as he understood it, the White Mountains.

I'll write them again before I leave, tell them... well I guess I don't know what to tell them, he thought as he broke the seal on the small scroll. Would he see the brothers again? And if he did, would it be as friend or foe? He liked to think their loyalty lied with him, but the shackles of family obligation were difficult to break. The realization of what kind of situation he was putting both Orne and Kolden in became suddenly apparent in his mind, and a sense of dread filled him. *What am I—*

Delvan froze. The words on the scroll before him completely engulfing his focus as they registered.

From the hand of Matriarch Payuess te Rytta

Lord Delvan ce Saffstar, I have received your inquiry regarding the woman pronouncing herself as "Mithya te Rytta," and admit I was most perturbed. Whomever this callous imposter is, I can assure you, she is not a member of our house. After the untimely death of my eldest, infant daughter (of the same name), none in the family have taken it. A rare, unified respect this woman patently ignores. As this was close to sixty years past, I doubt even a Blue would remain as youthful as the woman you've describe. Given this, I have reached out to Brethefen's governing families but would be indebted by your assistance in her arrest and prosecution. I wish her brought to Tennefen, so I may see her face to face, and issue her sentencing personally.

King and His grace upon you.

Hands frozen, face cold, Delvan read the words again.

Part of him glowed with victory. Mithya, Ennui, whatever her given name was, was not the person she'd led him and everyone in this city to believe. She'd teased, smiled, and manipulated her way to the highest levels of nobility and power, and he now held proof that she could not be who she claimed.

Yet, with this damning evidence, she could—*would*—be imprisoned, tried, and condemned. Taken away to Tennefen in all likelihood.

Right when he needed her.

No, he thought, eyes scrolling over the words again. *No, no, no, no!* If the general received the same letter as he did, then he'd have Mithya in chains before lunch, Blue or not. He needed to warn her, help her into hiding before anyone else came searching, or else his and Desnia's escape route would vanish with her.

Regardless of her conning her way into prestige, he doubted he and Desnia would be able to traverse the desert without Mithya's help.

He shoved the parchment scroll in his pocket before sprinting out of the building, the attendant's farewell as indiscernible as the pigeon's cooing in the room behind him. The doors were grabbed by the wind and flung open, ripping their handle from his hands. He struggled to shut them, giving up after a few fruitless pulls.

Shielding his eyes against the sun and grit, he ran through the streets, making his way back towards where he and Mithya were set to meet with Desnia's prison guards, hoping she was there. As he neared, the warmth of the Truthsayer's sapphire glowed against his senses, directing him away from the meeting spot and to a nearby building. He followed the energy's source, entering the open storefront of a rug vendor.

Weaving through the leaning stacks of rolled fabrics, he ignored the smiling merchant calling out to him with the deals he could provide and walked towards a closed door in the back. He forced it open; the muffled voice he heard through it becoming instantly distinct and emphatic.

"—need that key, Mithya! Please, take another look for it. If anyone finds out—" All went quiet as Delvan burst into the room, finding Mithya cross-armed before Wellos, the young lieutenant's face a shade darker than normal. He turned his head and glared at Delvan, brow digging down as he peered over the cluttered crafting stations.

"I told you, darling, I couldn't find it," said Mithya innocently, ignoring Delvan's entrance. "But, for you, I'll take another look around my place."

Wellos didn't seem to hear her, his burning gaze fixed on Delvan. "What is *he* doing here?"

"No idea," replied Mithya with a casual shrug, somehow maintaining a believable naivety. "You need something?" she asked.

Delvan glanced between the two of them; one a face of vehemence, the other a dispassionate feint. "I need to talk to you. Alone," he said to Mithya, before looking at Wellos.

The lieutenant's fists balled up. "What is it you need to say?" he asked, his voice rising. "Can't you see we were in the middle of a conversation? I don't care if you're a lord, you don't have the right to just barge in here and make demands—"

Mithya reached out and put her hand on the lieutenant's arm. "Hey," she placated, giving him a smile that made even Delvan's knees weaken, "it's fine. I'll see you tonight, where we talked about, yeah? I'll check my place right after Delvan and I talk. I'm sure he's here on *official* business, right?" she asked, giving him a look.

Yes, but not the officials you *want to be hearing from,* he thought. "That's right."

"What?" asked Wellos, incredulous. "No, I would've known. Hell, I would've been the one to scribe the order—"

"You can't scribe it if you're not there," said Delvan, becoming impatient. "Now, it's urgent that I speak to Lady Mithya." *Or whatever her name is.* "Immediately."

Wellos glanced from Delvan's scowling face to Mithya's entrancing smile, caught between vehemence and lust. "Fine!" he eventually burst out. "But I'm going to find out what that order is," he said, pointing to Delvan, who had to resist rolling his eyes. "And, my Lady, I will see you tonight?" he asked. Delvan could see disappointment in his eyes—the flicker of betrayal, the hint of doubt, the telltale signs that he was beginning to see the coming of his and Mithya's end. *The denial is all over his face,* Delvan thought, feeling pity for the man. *It took him long enough to see it, but a woman like her can be blinding. Given her identity is a farce, I've done you a favor. Not that you'll ever realize it.*

"Of course. I cannot wait," she said, running a hand along his cheek. He forced a smile before turning and walking out, glowering at Delvan once his eyes left Mithya's, holding it until he slammed the workshop door behind him.

The smile immediately vanished from Mithya's visage, her lips pulling down to her jaw. "Seriously? You couldn't wait five damn minutes?"

"Can you not play with your food before you eat it?"

"Why? Jealous?" she asked, a hint of a smile returning.

"Hardly," he choked, resisting the touch of Mithya's gift while his voice pitched up an octave. Her smile broadened. Ignoring her gloating, he reached into his pocket and drew out the scroll, walking over to Mithya and handing it to her. "We have a serious problem."

Her eyes narrowed as she took the parchment and began reading. With each flick of her eyes her brow delved deeper, her smile diminishing and jaw beginning to gape.

When she finally finished, her eyes raised to meet his own, a fury in them, her head following slowly behind. A fire burned behind the brown wells, one that grew from a flare to an inferno. "You absolute *idiot*! What did you *do*?!" she shrieked, shoving his shoulder and forcing him to take a step back. Breathing heavy, the note clutched in her grasp, she began pacing in the crowded space.

"Maybe if you'd actually answered *any* of my questions, I wouldn't have needed to reach out and ask about you!" he responded. How was this his fault? She was the one who faked her identity.

"Years of effort, work, all gone," she said, staring at the floor in front of her stomping feet. "And why? Because... because I didn't answer your questions? No. What was it, really? Were you looking for blackmail? Angry that I didn't fuck you? What was it, huh?!" she said, glaring at him again with eyes like sharpened steel.

"No!" he exclaimed. "I was worried about Des!"

She sneered, looking away as she continued to pace. "Gah!" she burst, the scream ferocious enough to make the building's bones quiver. "Why do men always have to be so fucking *stupid*?!" Delvan wanted to make the point that impersonating a noble was a risk she had willingly accepted but decided against it—he still needed her, and making the argument worse wouldn't accomplish anything.

He glanced cautiously at the door. "If you keep screaming, the owner of this place is going to hear."

Mithya shook her head, her anger steeping with his words. "I don't care, because at least I know I can trust him to keep his *mouth shut*." Delvan's jaw instinctively snapped closed, lips pressing together. While he could see what his actions had wrought, he still didn't see himself as being in the wrong.

There was a litany of other questions they didn't have time for. Everything about their plans had broken like a timber set. Nonetheless, he couldn't help himself, the foremost question on his mind running past his lips. "Who are you, really?"

Mithya gave him a sidelong glance. "I'm still the person who wants to get Des to safety."

"That's not an answer," replied Delvan, crossing his arms.

"It's the best one you're going to get. Now be quiet and let me think."

Delvan shook his head. "No. Not good enough. If we're doing this, I need to know I can trust you. It was hard before, but now? Give me a reason to not walk out of here."

"Because the only thing that's changed is my name. And if you try this on your own you won't make it two days outside of the city, assuming you make it out at all."

As much as he hated to admit it, she was right. *I'm going to have to look over my shoulder and keep an eye open while sleeping the entire journey.* He swallowed hard before asking his next question. "And what about your sapphire? You clearly grew up with it, but if it's stolen—"

"Don't you *dare*," she said, turning and pointing a shaking finger. "This gem is *mine*, by right, as it was my grandfather's before me. You might not know much about me, but that, I assure you, is an unequivocal fact."

"Fine," Delvan conceded, raising his hands. "But everything that we're about to do just became a *lot* more difficult. Like you said, getting out of the city and staying hidden was already going to be challenging, but now? It's going to be impossible!" Delvan threw his hands to the side and leaned back against a nearby workbench. It wouldn't be long now before search parties were organized to find Mithya. He let out a sigh and rubbed his forehead. *It's like we've been defeated before even beginning,* he thought solemnly. Questions still ate at him, but with their plan in shambles, his burning curiosity was becoming secondary to his dismay.

Mithya stopped pacing, running fingers through her hair and massaging her scalp. She took a sharp breath. "What we're doing, where we're going, and who we're looking for," she said, glancing from the corner of her eye, "is more important than me, you, anything. Do you understand that?"

"My first priority is Des," he replied. "I owe her that much. The rest... Well, I don't see how much of a choice I have once we're on the run. It's important to her, and if it gives us a chance against the High Realm mages, then I'm willing to help."

"It's our *only* chance," said Mithya. She closed her eyes, jaw flexing. She was quiet for a long moment before speaking. "I'm not from... here," she admitted.

"Obviously."

"No, I mean—" she rubbed her temples, eyes squeezing tightly. "I mean that I'm not from this *empire*."

Delvan's head tilted. "Wait, you don't mean—"

"Do I have to spell it out for you?!" She lowered her voice. "I'm *Trethish*."

His jaw dropped, eyes going wide. "You... You're a *spy*!"

She scoffed and rolled her eyes. "Oh, get over yourself. Kingdoms have been spying on one another since their inception, it's hardly anything to be surprised about."

An imposter from an enemy kingdom? Delvan hadn't thought that he could become more uneasy about this endeavor, but now he felt the racing of his heart, the cold sweats and pricks of pain in his arms and chest. "Has everything you've said been a lie? What's even your real name?"

"Mithya is as good as any other," she said dismissively. "Or maybe not, based on this fucking note."

"What possessed you to choose a name no one took any longer?" he asked, genuinely curious. "You call me an idiot but that seems like a massive oversight, wouldn't you say?"

"It's not like we're all knowing," she said with a derisive shake of her head. "Last we knew it was the most common te Rytta name. It didn't seem like much of a risk when I chose it before coming here."

"And why *did* you come here?"

"Certainly not to spy on the King's men or this dying city," Mithya replied before taking a deep breath. "I came here because of *you*."

Delvan stared at her for a moment, thinking. "The gate."

"Not bad. A few hundred more deductions like that and I might start re-considering your monumental stupidity."

That's a bit hypocritical. "Why?" While there was an overflowing abundance of unknowns he wanted to vocalize into existence, the single word was all he could force out.

"Even if I was willing to explain, we don't have the time. What's important is getting Des out, and fast. All while trying to avoid the soldiers that are going to be looking for me, thanks to *you*."

Delvan opened his mouth to retort, then thought better of it and snapped it closed. A few days ago, he would have been the first to assist in Mithya's capture and trial. Now, the truth and situation had become a murky river of right and wrong, needs versus wants. The one thing keeping him afloat, the single surety, was helping Desnia. The morals or origins of whomever helped him seemed trivial now, regardless of his own biases.

Planning the escape and getting the people in place had seemed daunting before, but now a legion's worth of soldiers would be looking for Mithya. Waiting wasn't an option. They would need to act fast and would be lucky to be afforded the luxury of hours prior to the search going into full swing. *There's maybe one thing that will work in our favor.*

"We might not have to worry about too many soldiers, actually," he said, standing straight.

Mithya stopped her pacing, staring at him for a prolonged moment. "Well?"

"This evening, Nerio is going to give a speak from the steps of the Devapuram," he said, recalling the details of his conversation with Captain Gernbard. "It's going to draw thousands, maybe more."

She raised an eyebrow. "That many people, plus one of the general's most elusive fugitives? Aside from me now, I suppose," she added with contempt. "Huh, you might be right, Rosethorn is going to bring his legion's fist down on them like a hammer. And with all the people on edge? Oh, I *like* that little priest."

Delvan stared at her, jaw agape. "How can you say that? Nothing good is going to come of this."

"That depends on your perspective. Also, as you've implied, it will give us a perfect opportunity to help Des. Sounds like everyone wins to me."

"We have very different definitions of winning."

"Maybe that's why you never get to experience it."

"What... I, well... Tha—" His mouth fumbled, tying his tongue and leaving him looking the fool.

"Don't worry, you'll have *some* success, so long as you stick by me and don't do anything else stupid," she mocked. "Alright, I'm going to go talk to my friends about moving up our timeline. I'll meet you at Des's prison."

"By 'friends,' I'm assuming you mean the smugglers? Still not sure why you trust them." He didn't care how much they were paying, anyone whose silence could be bought was at risk of being outbid.

Mithya turned and gave him a flat stare.

"No..." he drawled. "They're Trethish too?"

"Most of the smugglers around here are," she replied casually. "What better way to know the best ways to hide in foreign lands? But I told you, I trust them with my life. Stop worrying."

Attempting to look past the implications of how deep Trethefen was imbedded into the local society, Delvan asked, "Are you going to be able to get to them without being noticed?"

"The only thing I'm worried about is you somehow making things worse. Were you thinking you'd like to send another letter? Maybe ask permission to break Des out? Tell Rosethorn about—"

"I get it," he interjected. *Gods, this woman can be insufferable.* "I'll talk to the guards and meet you where we discussed before the first bell."

Mithya walked up to him and slapped her note of condemnation against his chest. "Pack light." She brushed past him and out through the door, leaving him standing in the quiet workshop, wondering how everything had turned against him so quickly.

His every action had shattered his goals with consequence—noble, selfish, or otherwise. Following his heart had led him astray time and time again, to the point where he wondered at his own ethics. Somehow, despite that, he *knew* this is what he needed to do. Without an inkling of doubt. Although, in hindsight, he could say that about every decision leading to this moment and place.

Was he truly so misguided? Or was this where he was meant to be?

Chapter
Forty-Two

To trap a soul in such a way requires talent and skill surpassing my own, along with boldness which borders on stupidity.

A hand pressed to his armored shoulder.

Orne jolted awake, his body moving before his eyes had opened. The foreign wrist was suddenly clamped firmly in his grasp, a dagger drawn from his belt in one swift motion. Eyes opened to nothing but the polluted dark. A flash of black steel brought his blade to the throat of the person hovering over him.

"Woah! Lieutenant, it's me!" came Helona's panicked voice.

Her disc-like eyes came into focus as the adrenaline cleared his groggy vision. He twisted his head to the left and right. Everything seemed normal, most of the squad was sleeping, a few guards sitting restlessly at either end of the rock shelf. He released his grip, slowly sitting straight from the ledge his back had been resting against.

Helona took a step back, breathing heavily. "Gonna be more careful the next time I wake *you*, sir."

Orne grunted. The edge from the attack the previous night had yet to dull. That, combined with Steddus's tendency to be a conniving miscreant, meant sleep had been light, and vigilance high. "How long was I out?" he asked.

"'Bout an hour, sir," said Helona, her voice still shaky. Orne could just make out her figure in the darkness, the muted grey light of the black moon glowing at its apex in the sky. Even in this gloom his imagination filled in the shadows.

The rule preventing officers from fraternizing with their direct reports seemed fucking stupid, in his opinion. It's not as though he was going to make whatever piss-poor mistakes the people who the rule was created for had. And, assuming they lived long enough, and their luck didn't flip like a coin, he would be heading back to Brethefen in a few months.

Clearly the rule wasn't meant for someone in his position. Therefore, there was no reason not to ignore it.

Trying to put the thoughts aside for the moment, he stood up, assessing his surroundings. Something seemed off. "Did anyone see anything?" he asked, inspecting the lumps of curled up soldiers.

"We didn't see nothin'," she said, hesitation in her voice. "But, well, I woke you because..." She trailed off, and Orne's concern worsened.

Sixteen, he counted. *Wait, that can't be right.* He counted again. Moving away from Helona, he crept along the rock shelf, inspecting each of the soldiers and their gear, Helona a few steps behind him.

He stopped, turning to face the infantryman and hissing, "Where the *fuck* is Steddus?"

Helona's shadow wilted. "Uh, that's the thing, sir. Why I woke you," she chattered nervously.

"What happened?" he asked, punctuating each syllable.

"Once you were asleep, he started pitching a fit. Complaining 'bout not being given notice, not having... what he needs. Cursing you out like a storm in whispers to all the others. Said he wasn't gonna put up with it anymore, and headed back to the castle to—"

"That fucking prick!" Orne hissed, struggling to keep his voice down. *I should've thrown him off the cliff when I had the chance.* "How long ago was this?"

"Uh, a few minutes, maybe?" Helona responded.

"Gods-damn it." He debated chasing down the insolent deserter, but the thought of scrambling down the pitched hillside in the dead of night made his heart beat fast enough to throb in his neck. If he were lucky, the idiot would trip on his way down, doing them all the service of breaking his neck. *Or,* he thought, *he's going to run into a bunch of enemy combatants and alert them to our position.*

Gods, he couldn't stand it when people didn't obey his orders.

Their only advantage right now was the security of their position's footing. It was defendable enough that if Steddus did draw the enemy to him, they could hold off a force larger than their own. As much as he hated letting Steddus get away with anything, the better tactical decision was to remain here until either they or the keep was attacked, or daylight broke.

He walked to the guards at either end of the rock shelf—all seeming shifty and on edge—reminding them to remain vigilant. With a wave he motioned for Helona to sit, then squatted down on a boulder nearby.

Despite his scowling frustration, he tried to put on a smile but then remembered that she probably couldn't see his face, and returned to scowling. "So, uh, what got you stationed out here?" he asked her. *That was a stupid question,* he thought, immediately trying to think of a remedy.

Helona fidgeted, her voice distracted. "What? Oh, well I kind of... I guess you could say I was sick, sir."

"Sick? What's that supposed to mean?"

"I'd... rather not talk about it," she replied.

Orne shook his head, the silence becoming loud between them. This was *not* going the way that he wanted. He shifted uncomfortably and opened his mouth to speak, this time planning to *avoid* saying something idiotic.

Helona couldn't see it, but in the black of night, Orne did his best to force a smile and start over.

Gods, Kolden loathed this place.

It didn't help that, even with a splinted leg, Phrenwa's arm was digging into his injured shoulder, burning like glowing steel as he helped him limp along. *Stupid fucking castle and its gods-damned thousand stairs,* he cursed as they reached the top of another stairwell. The keep's enormity meant that they could avoid others in the maze of passages, but at the rate they were moving, it would take until morning to get out of the place.

Kolden wiped sweat off his brow and adjusted his crossbow's sling.

"How do you intend to use that?" asked Phrenwa in a tone Kolden didn't much appreciate.

"Easy. I'm going to have you load it," he quipped. His lack of mobility was a hindrance, but he refused to leave the fortress unarmed, so he'd left Phrenwa in a dark hall and ran to his quarters to grab the weapon. *Maybe a crank and gear of some kind,* he pondered, considering ways to improve its design. *With the right ratios, it could be easy enough to arm one-handed—*

"Turn down this way," said Phrenwa as they came to a branching hallway.

"Are you going to tell me where we're going soon?" he asked, his voice clipped. He'd been following the merchant's—or was it assassin? Smuggler, maybe?—directions since they'd left the prison wing, the man guiding them around every corridor and bend as if he'd been raised there.

"Down this passage, there is a room that has the means to our escape."

"Because that's not vague at all," mumbled Kolden. The man had been both confident and adamant about being able to guide them to safety, yet all they'd seemed to do was get lost deep into the bowels of the immense keep. *He got in here somehow,* Kolden thought. All the entrances he knew were guarded and therefore left him with little choice but to listen to his enigmatic guide.

Hunched under the taller man's weight, Kolden grudgingly turned them down the corridor. Almost dark enough to warrant feeling his way through, he stepped by the faint light of fires glowing through vacant windows as they hobbled along.

His impulsive plan hadn't considered the well-lit walls and exits. Nor had he given thought to his or Phrenwa's injuries. In fact, he'd done what he constantly scolded his brother for, and just acted without thinking of the consequence. *How does Orne do this?* he wondered, checking over his shoulder again.

"This one," said Phrenwa as they reached the last door.

"Please tell me we're almost there," said Kolden as he turned the loose handle and pushed against creaking hinges.

"Almost," replied Phrenwa, blessedly removing his arm from Kolden's shoulder and hopping along the room's wall, one hand against it for support.

The room was filled with dust. It was spacious enough to be an officer's quarters and based on the size of the built-in bookcase at the end, it likely had been. That time had long passed, with anything not bolted to the floor removed, the walls left with little more than bits of iron for lamps, and the floor's once lustrous polish faded and weathered.

Kolden popped his head through the door to check down the hall once more before closing it as quietly as possible.

Which was to say as loudly as a wailing goat.

He flinched at the protesting, unoiled hinges until the latch eventually clicked. *Gods, I hope nobody heard that.* "Well?" he hissed as Phrenwa was doing something at one of the shelves.

"Now," said Phrenwa as a dull *click* came from the bookcase, "we leave." He pushed the bookcase open, revealing a dark passage behind it leading to... more stairs.

Gods-damnit. At least these ones go down. "How could you *possibly* know this was here?" he asked.

"My forebearers knew this bastion better than almost any still alive. Once I knew we were coming to this one to search for the cadentite, I learned as many of its secrets as I could. Now, come."

There was a lamp and what looked to be a bag of supplies on the landing beyond. All lacking the thick layer of dust and cobwebs apparent in the rest of the gloomy passage.

"Where did this come from?" Kolden asked.

"We left a few items at each of these entrances on previous visits, in the event they were needed," said Phrenwa. *Each?* thought Kolden, his gut turning. "Now hurry and light the lamp."

"How about you stop giving orders to the guy helping you escape?"

"There's no time to argue, and I cannot bend with my leg. Hurry!"

Kolden groaned and rolled his eyes but bent down and found what he needed in the bag to light the lamp. As it ignited, Phrenwa quickly shut the bookcase, and Kolden wrapped the man's arm around his neck again in a flare of agony.

There were a dozen questions on his mind. Despite his gritted teeth, he asked the foremost among them as they began their descent. "Where does this lead?"

"It will take us beyond the walls and to the mountainside," replied Phrenwa, face writhing in pain as he gingerly avoided use of his leg.

"How many escape tunnels are there like this one?"

"Caves, not tunnels. And half a dozen, perhaps, though some are too well hidden for us to find."

"Caves?" asked Kolden, thinking back to the door he'd spectacularly failed to open. "Is that where you think they're storing the cadentite? Where the door you were trying to open led?"

Phrenwa nodded as he sucked in a gush of air, each step leaving his face tortured and twisted. "That is my belief. There is but one that is unconnected to the larger network, used to store the bastion's food in ancient days. You and your brother—along with the unfortunate luck of the lock being jammed—prevented us from discovering if we were correct."

Kolden grimaced. *Perhaps it's best not to mention* why *it was jammed.* "Sorry about that."

"We were both victims of our own ignorance," replied Phrenwa. "Once we reach my camp, we will reconsider our approach. Hopefully before it's too late."

"And what do you intend to do with it, once you have it?" he asked.

"Why?"

"Because," said a straining Kolden as they reached the last step and entered a narrow, ancient cave, "I want some."

Phrenwa gave him an incredulous look. "This one is of no use to you. Why do you wish for this?"

"Why do you?" he retorted.

The assassin was quiet for a moment, hobbling along as their shoulders grazed rough protrusions of greying stone. "It is one of my people's most valued possessions. I cannot speak more to the matter, but, for your assistance, I am willing to give you some."

Willing or not, there wasn't a man nor god that was going to get between Kolden's curiosity and that glowing stone. Phrenwa agreeing made it easier, at least. Although he was still unsure how much he could trust the man, given the little he knew about him.

"And who, exactly, are *your* people?" Kolden asked, trying to ignore the water dripping onto his face from the spiked ceiling.

"Perhaps, in time, I will explain." *Right, because you've been so forthcoming.* "But, for now, we should focus on our escape, and the mage's interests, no?"

"Fine," said Kolden, too tired to argue, the stabbing pain in his shoulder becoming increasingly difficult to overcome.

The cave was a twisting, uneven path shaped by stone formed into an annoying, obstacle-ridden passage. It would've been difficult to traverse if Kolden had been alone—with Phrenwa limping alongside him, it was downright impassable.

After what felt like hours, they reached a small hatch, the wood cracked and faded with age. Kolden extinguished the lamp and pushed it open, seeing the stars and dimly lit sky beyond.

With no small amount of effort—along with Kolden's whispered curses—he pulled Phrenwa through the portal, closing it behind him. Once closed, the gravel-dusted door vanished, blending perfectly with the stone surroundings. Despite knowing exactly where it was, Kolden found it to be completely imperceptible. *I wonder how many of these are tucked away throughout these battle-torn mountains?*

The thought was brief, as Phrenwa silently pointed in the direction they were to travel.

Directly up a winding trail on the mountainside.

Gods-fucking-damnit, thought Kolden with a long sigh. In the back of his mind there had been a hope that he could return to the keep before morning, no one being the wiser as to his absence. He was certain that the captain and Villera would blame him, regardless, but at least if he were in his quarters he could easily deny it.

This, however, was going to take hours to climb. *Maybe, if I get him hidden up there, somewhere, and if I run back to this door fast enough, I can be back in my quarters before anyone's the wiser.*

That was too many "ifs" for his liking. But what choice did he have?

With as much haste as he could muster, he and Phrenwa began trudging up the mountain's path, the switchbacks leading them slowly higher and higher. His eyes burned with exhaustion, sweat drenched his clothes, and knees threatened to buckle under the dense weight of his gimped companion.

Kolden wasn't sure how long they climbed—though he was absolutely sure how long it *felt*—and his concern about getting back to the keep before dawn began to make him increasingly anxious.

As the slope began to finally level out, they approached an outcropping of boulders. *This will have to do,* Kolden thought. He could leave Phrenwa here, run back to the castle, and come back out here the next night to take him the rest of the way. The pack they carried should have enough supplies to—

Phrenwa suddenly raised a hand for them to stop, holding a finger to his mouth. Kolden froze, wondering what warranted the immediate halt.

Voices. Kolden could hear them, speaking well above hushed whispers, either ignoring or neglecting prudence. Phrenwa's face looked grave, and made Kolden believe that whoever was on the other side of the tall stones must have been from the castle, or worse, agents of Jerdine.

Kolden heard a voice he recognized: Steddus. He and Phrenwa took a few daring steps closer, trying to step and hobble between large stones to avoid the *crunch* of stones underfoot.

"—boss said to draw him away, convince the squad that he had an accident," he heard Steddus say. "If not, we give out extra rations to all of them, whatever it takes to keep 'em quiet. Understand?"

Kolden heard grunts in response, perhaps from two or three others, his heart dropping into his gut.

"Good, let's go give the big bastard what he deserves," Steddus said.

Kolden heard the telltale sounds of steel sliding from scabbards, weapons being checked, and the adjusting of chainmail. Feet soon crunched into the distance, and the shadows of murder along with them.

Fuck! Kolden screamed in his mind, his throat tightening to the point of making it difficult to breathe. He unstrapped his crossbow and handed it to Phrenwa. "Load this!" he hissed.

"Why?" Phrenwa asked. "We should leave them and continue, my camp is not—"

"Load it, *now*! Or I'll throw you off this mountain myself!"

The assassin hesitantly took the weapon. "This is a mistake, we should avoid conflict until—"

"They're going after *Orne*, you bastard! And 'we' aren't going anywhere, not with your leg. Now, hurry!"

The man used his good leg to hold down the crossbow's front and pulled back the string before handing it back to Kolden. He threw a bolt in it, turning to leave and follow the men in the distance.

"Your brother can handle himself, no?"

Kolden looked back. "Your men would've said the same about you, I'm guessing."

The only response was a short, silent nod. Kolden turned and began hiking, free of Phrenwa's burden, a nervous fear itching at the back of his mind, telling him he had to warn his brother, and that something was about to go terribly wrong.

Chapter Forty-Three

He poses no threat to you. A soul without a living host is a figment of its whole self and likely renders him incapable of casting. Most mages would never consider such a thing.

Ol' Breig hadn't known what he was missing, 'fore the drink came flowing into Brethefen.

Used to be that he would have to sneak into the Devapuram, findin' the best of the offerings and making away with 'em. He'd always been good at sneakin', was like no one could see him. They'd walk right on past his little home on the street, eyes never even looking at him or all his stuff. Which was good, because he had a lot of really great stuff. He didn't even need to try, and no one noticed.

Except those annoyin' Holy Hands.

If they saw him at the big temple, they'd always try and recruit him, spoutin' nonsense about, "You don't need to be homeless," and, "We can feed you." Ha! Like he wanted to *work* to eat. Or that he was "homeless." Fools. Why bother workin' if he could just take some of the food that folks left lying around? He didn't much expect the gods to mind just a little goin' missin' to feed Ol' Breig.

Then those damned fires blew through and ruined everythin'. Now he had to hide all his valuables from the *other* people on the street. Didn't they know he was here first? Who did they think they were, livin' all around him like the street wasn't his?

But Ol' Breig knew a thing or two they didn't. Oh, yes, he had his second home by the Devapuram, hidden away from those pesky soldiers. One could never have too many homes, in his opinion—which was basically fact. Better to keep his things spread out, in case some of the new dwellers got the idea of barging in. 'Sides, all those rich people had a bunch of houses, and Ol' Breig was the richest of all, so why shouldn't he have a bunch too?

He checked in his crate—another treasure nabbed from the Devapuram—and checked again that everything was there. The head of an old walking stick, carved like an owl. A piece of blue silk, a bit stained but soft as a cloud, big, like a headscarf or fancy napkin the rick folk liked. The page of a book he couldn't read, but words, words were worth money, he knew. Which is why it was one of his most prized bounties.

Tucking it back into its hole, he nodded. It was a good hidin' place.

He grabbed his bottle and took a long draft of the liquor. It burned, which he didn't like, but then it made him feel good, which he liked plenty. It reminded him of the feelin' of findin' new stuff, so he took another swig. He coughed a bit, his house spinnin' around him.

Good stuff, this liquor.

He put the bottle down and then crossed his house in three swerving steps. He lifted the wooden roof—the bottom of an old box, a find he was rather proud of—and looked out onto the street. No one noticed him, probably because he was down in an old stairwell, eyes barely above the street's pavers. A group of soldiers walked by—lots of those around these parts—lookin' like they were in a hurry. Ol' Breig watched as they marched quick-like towards the great big pillars of the temple. Probably goin' to listen to that priest talk, like everyone else.

Everyone but Ol' Breig, that was. Couldn't give anyone the chance to steal his treasures. No, better to sit here, or go huntin' for new ones while the whole city was distracted. If they cared about their stuff, they shouldn't leave it lying around. Fools.

The street slowed its spinning, people comin' into focus. That told Ol' Breig it was time for another drink.

He went to close the roof back up, but a sparkle caught his eye. He squinted, wondering what could make the sun twinkle like a star in the middle of the day. Ol' Breig didn't have too many things *that* shiny. He should try to get some.

Then he saw that it was one of those sapphires, hanging round the neck of some Blue. The boy didn't look like much, but he knew better than to mess with those mystics. Bad luck those stones were. He wanted nothin' to do with 'em after one of them Seers told Ol' Breig he'd die by drownin' in his home.

In the desert? Ha!

He kept a cautious eye on the boy as he went past, not even noticing sly Ol' Breig. Couldn't be too careful around those types, especially the old, tall one. *That* man scared him somethin' fierce. Although he *had* cleared out all the other dwellers from Ol' Breig's street, so maybe he wasn't too bad. Best that he stay hidden, just in case.

That bottle was callin' to him. Time to maybe—

Another soldier. Gods, they were everywhere now. Ol' Breig recognized him, that scribe or something that worked for the tall scary one. He looked angry, like someone had stolen his stuff and he was lookin' to take it back. Ol' Breig understood that feelin'. Though why he was glarin' at the Blue boy was beyond him. He didn't want to know, it was better that way.

He squinted as another cursed gust of wind blew sand in his eyes. Stupid sand. At least it wasn't water, Ol' Breig wasn't a fan of that wet nonsense. Lookin' up at the sky, he saw a bunch of clouds rollin' in, dark and angry. Storm was comin' by the looks of it. He quietly closed the roof of his house—it would keep him dry, he was sure of it—sat down, and took another long swig from the bottle.

Good stuff, that.

Chapter Forty-Four

It would be prudent to attempt removal of the contract spells you mentioned, but likely futile. Despite your skill, the mastery of a pinnacle mage is difficult to overcome. I'm impressed you were able to remove any from Reedjin's journals. Although the man has a habit of reclining into sloth.

The gathering was a seething mass unlike any Nerio had witnessed. He could barely move among the throng of the street, strangers' shoulders pressed tightly against his own, their breath hot against him. From under his hood, he could see the packed terraces above, and at the road's end the massive steps of the Devapuram were covered in mounds of people, amassing like sand upon a dune.

Thousands—tens of thousands, possibly—had gathered around the dome's pillars, brimming with reverence and disquiet, whispering among themselves. Soldiers could be seen along the crowd's fringes, overwhelmed and confounded, their faces conflicted and eager, cold and desperate. They were people, not unlike those that surrounded him now. Citizens of a ravaged home. Some yearned for justice, while others were devoted to duty.

Nerio saw the energy of the crowd. Felt it. The people were angry, rightfully so, but there was another emotion buried beneath the veil, one that brought them together to this grand place of worship and unified them in their time of need.

Hope.

The great emulsifier. The bond of a despaired community. The gods, on this day, had brought them here, to listen to words that reignited it, reminding them they were watching, their hands reaching down and affecting their lives in ways unseen.

And the words the crowd sought were *his*.

He tasted bile. His stomach had been in his throat all afternoon. The breeze to his back sent chills into his marrow, the oncoming clouds turning it to ice upon his skin. He'd never spoken before a group so large. This was no speak in the Scar, to what he had ignorantly considered a massive congregation. Even the principles' speaks on King's Day didn't compare to those who had gathered.

Fear must be overcome, whether by him or the people. The gods had chosen him for this path, and along the way it had become twisted into the violent outbursts that now plagued the city. The people were no longer following the guidance of the gods, the doctrine he passionately preached. He would channel their rage into the benevolence he knew it could be, shepherding them back into the gods' graces and away from the perversion of his words.

Nerio wiped his palms on his robe. "I think it's time."

Captain Gernbard stood uneasily at his side, his sword's scabbard unclasped and hand resting on the hilt, his eyes surveying the crowd. "I don't like this, Witness."

"I have nothing to fear from these people, as I've told you, Captain."

Gernbard grunted. "Too many things can go wrong in a crowd, and then there's that storm that's rolling in."

Nerio shared the man's concern. Rain in the desert was a dangerous thing, but he could not remain idle any longer, not while people were being hurt on account of his words. "I will endeavor to keep it short."

"Mhm, that would be best. I've got enlightened soldiers at the general's tower today, they should keep him from getting news of the crowd. But, at some point, the man is going to look out a window and see us, and he has a wrath to rival the gods' own."

He took a deep breath, his voice shaky. "Then lead the way, Captain."

With a curt nod from the aging soldier, the dozen plainly dressed soldiers surrounding them began to march forward, parting the crowd as Nerio followed in their wake. Hushed whispers spread behind him, and his heart began racing, thundering in his chest.

This is the gods' will, he reminded himself. *I am their servant, my words of their design. Their light shines down upon me and the people who heed their diligence and involvement in our lives, for that is the anathema to this city's pain.*

As they approached the polished stone steps of the Devapuram, white treads wider than the height of a man, the people began to part ahead of them, easing their passage. Nerio found he could not force himself to walk any faster, however, his feet feeling heavy as the stone they fell upon.

The final step was a podium of burden, the weight bearing down on him forcing the air from his lungs and blood from his face. His knees shook. From this vantage the pillars of the temple appeared to sit on a foundation of his followers, a field of wheat waiting to reap his words. He turned to look down upon the streets which converged at the holy temple, each swimming with the city's occupants.

He removed his hood and an unnatural quiet fell upon the crowd, the wind coming to a sudden still. The eyes of a forlorn city turned their gaze upon him, and with their attention he felt their anguish, connecting to it in a way that crippled him with empathy.

Mouth dry, he glanced to the sky, the sun touching the crest of a cloud's peaking wave. The blanket of black rolled in from the east, a wall of water greying the distance beyond the city's walls. Almedia had her own plans for today, it would seem, and despite the odious, oncoming torrent, Nerio took a deep breath.

The sun slipped behind a cloud, and as the first drop of rain touched his skin, he began to speak.

Chapter Forty-Five

Communicating with him will be impossible without an Eighth Born or a mage, and despite your first instincts, I would suggest against sending him to me.

Delvan felt the first drop of rain touch his skin as he stared at the clouds roiling the sky. Flashes of light could be seen behind the cage of grey, trying to escape its confines with roars of thunder and pent-up rage. It brought an early night to the city, the sun trapped behind its thick veil, spreading from the horizon like a plague.

He'd heard of these summer storms, and if the stories carried any amount of truth, a deluge would soon be upon them. If they moved quickly enough, it could work in their favor, or it would turn their escape into havoc as it brought destructive floods and gales.

Quickening his pace, he continued down the desolate street, making his way towards Desnia's prison. With most of the city collected a few blocks away at the towering Devapuram, he was left thankfully unobstructed, letting him make up time lost to the last of his errands. He shifted the strap of the sack over his shoulder, wondering if there was anything he'd forgotten, remiss over what he'd left behind.

The sound of trailing footsteps turned his head over his shoulder once more, but the street was empty. He shook his head. *Ears are playing tricks on me,* he thought. This was the third time he'd mistaken the echo of his own boots for that of another. His nerves were frayed, the near-constant thought of this breakout making his heart pulse needles through him with every rapid beat.

He finally reached the alley's mouth, Desnia's prison visible a few buildings down. He could feel his sapphire pressing against his chest beneath his armor—wrapped in cloth dyed white with muted inanite, masking him from

Rosethorn's senses.

He would need to endure the loss of his gift for a short time while they endeavored to stay hidden and flee the city.

Mithya was there—likely only waiting because the guards were expecting him, specifically—dressed in her normal attire and sapphire hidden under her shirt, similarly wrapped. A thin cloak draped her shoulders, similar to the one Delvan was wearing over his armor. She greeted him with arms crossed and eyes stormier than the sky. "Took you long enough," she snipped. "What were you doing, sending *more* letters?"

Delvan gave her a flat stare. Had she followed him? Or was she merely making a derisive comment? "Yes, actually," he snarked as she let out a sigh and rolled her head, "but not for the reasons you think."

"What did you do?" she groaned. There was an absence of her gift, her inability to dredge the truth from him was likely driving her mad. Delvan resisted the curl of a gratified lip.

"Don't worry, it doesn't affect you."

"You can't *possibly* be that naïve, can you? Everything you do affects me. Affects *us*. Maybe someone recognizes you, remembers who you sent a letter to, they find the recipient... Do you see where this is going yet?"

Delvan ground his teeth. "I was sending a letter to Orne and Kolden, al-right?" he said, exasperated. "They should've arrived days ago and I haven't heard anything from them yet. I was just... concerned." Not knowing when, or if, he would be able to speak to the brothers again left him feeling as though he had an open chest wound and was by far one of the most difficult parts of what they were about to attempt. He'd needed to send them *something*.

A worry crept onto Mithya's normally facetious visage. "Is that strange? For them not to write?"

"They said they would," replied Delvan. "At least one of them should've responded by now." Mithya shifted, her feet shuffling in place. "Why?" he asked hesitantly, afraid of what was making her uneasy.

She paused for a moment before speaking, her words dragging as if each was being forcefully pulled from her throat. "The people they're traveling with..." She sighed. "Let's just say that I know them, and I also haven't heard anything yet."

"Wait," Delvan said, confused, "they left with a merchant caravan, how do you—" A realization dawned on him. "They're smugglers, from your... homeland, aren't they?" Mithya gave a terse nod as the pressure of fury began to build in his chest. "Were you planning on mentioning this to me?!"

"Would you keep your damn voice down?" Mithya hissed. "They wouldn't hurt your friends, they wanted—"

"Right, because what would a group of foreign spies have against a few Royal Soldiers?"

"—something from the fortress they're going to," finished Mithya, ignoring his comment.

Delvan stood there, silent and glaring.

"What?" Mithya asked.

"You know what."

The Truthsayer rolled her eyes. "They were trying to buy cadentite, alright? There's a good chance there's a reserve at the castle and we wanted to get it before anyone else."

Delvan's jaw dropped. "By someone else, you mean Jerdine, don't you? Of course you do." She looked away, avoiding his indignant eyes. "*Why* didn't you tell me this?! I could've at least warned Kolden and Orne! I can't believe you. Every time I think I'm starting to understand you, you just... gah!" He couldn't form the words, his shaking hands digging through his hair as he tried to temper his ire.

"I'm not going to stand here and justify my actions to you," she retorted. "Besides, there was nothing to worry about, the man Jerdine was sending isn't going to make it—"

"Nothing to worry about?!" he cried, his voice carrying down the empty street. "You don't know what he's capable—"

"His courier is dead!" she interjected. "I got his name from someone at the guild the day you were there and found him before he left. And I know, better than you, what he's capable of. I bought my people—and your friends—time, so stop scolding me and acting like a petulant child."

Delvan took a minute to breathe, processing Mithya's words. "Do you really think," he said slowly, his voice low, "that Jerdine will stop because one of his couriers is dead? What if he decides to go himself? Have you considered that in your grand wisdom?"

Mithya's lips pressed into a thin line. "We don't have time for this," she said. *No, of course not. Gods forbid you admit your mistakes.* "We need to get Des out and then flee the city. We can figure out how our messages are being intercepted later. Bastards probably paid off someone at a mail station."

A sprinkle of rain began *plopping* against his armor's darksteel plates, drying in a sizzle of steam. "Fine," he finally replied, conceding that she was probably correct. "But we're *not* done with this conversation." Every word from her flared an inferno of hate and mistrust. The only person who'd ever managed to drive emotions like this to the surface was Ferrand. She might be worthy of replacing the man as Delvan's personal Monarch of Scorn.

She had the nerve to once again roll her eyes. "Whatever you say, Sparky. Leave your bag here," she said, pulling back a lumpy cloth in the alley, revealing a few more sacks of supplies. "I have people coming to grab all of this who will meet us beyond the walls."

Still leering, Delvan tossed his few possessions beside the others before Mithya covered them. They began walking down the street, the sound of clapping thunder at their backs, the flashes of light illuminating the dim, abandoned roadway. The lack of pedestrians gave the city an eerie feeling, and a dark sense of dread conjured urgency in Delvan's steps.

Putting his disdain to the side for a moment, his thoughts returned to another unanswered question that refused to stay quiet. Knowing that Mithya and her counterparts were aware of the High Realm mages gave him a sliver of hope, the words of Master Mornath echoing in his mind. The guild was not as cohesive as it might seem—people vying for their own goals, secretly seeking opportunities to gain an advantage. Was there a chance that some members didn't align with Jerdine, but instead with someone, or someplace, else? "Was finding Jerdine's courier the only reason you were at the guild?" he asked.

"This really isn't the time," she replied as they neared the makeshift prison's entrance.

"It's as good as any other we've had recently." He tried to subdue the harshness of his voice, choking out his words. "I *need* to know... please." *Tell me my friend wasn't the monster he seemed.*

Mithya gave him a sidelong glance, sighing after looking at his face. "No. It wasn't."

His stomach tightened as he waited for an explanation that never came. "Well?" he asked. "Why were you there?"

"We... exchange information with the guild. In return we get the funding we need for operations here."

"What kind of information?" he pressed as they reached the door. An ember sparked in his chest, fueled by the bellows of hope.

Mithya grabbed the worn, bronze handle, waiting to open it. "I can't tell you that. No, keep your mouth shut this once. Answering that would betray... everything. Maybe, in time, but for right now that is a secret I have to keep. Now, stop pouting and let's go."

Before Delvan had a chance to reply, she pulled the door open and strutted into the stout, three-story building. Was she incapable of having a conversation where she didn't tease or taunt?

He watched as she strode with the confidence that drew eyes upon her, wanting to pull her back into the street and force answers from her. But she was right. Desnia needed to be his sole focus. There would be time in abundance to ask his questions once they were out of the city. All the worries about Kolden and Orne, his inquisition about Hilbrun and the guild, they would need to wait. As much as it pained him to do so.

Jaw flexing tightly, he strode through the door after the Trethish spy, the wind whipping a spray of water against his back and slamming the door behind him.

Inside were two guards, dimly lit by the single lantern hanging from the wall. There was a tense silence, Delvan unable to discern the pair's expressions from beneath shadowed eyes. This was where they were to meet the guards loyal to Nerio, but what if there had been an unexpected shift change? Or they'd been pulled to deal with the crowds amassing a few blocks away? Neither he nor Mithya were permitted to be here, and their entire plan could quickly end before it had a chance to begin.

"Messiah and Her grace upon you," said one of them. Delvan felt some of the tension leave his muscles.

"Captain Gernbard told us you'd be coming," said the other guard, her voice proud.

"Did he tell you why we were here?" asked Delvan.

The first guard nodded, his expression resolute. "We're prepared to help you, whatever it takes, sir."

"Some of the others," said the other guard, "they weren't too keen on going against the Witness's wishes. But we've served under ol' Rosethorn, you see, and we agree with the captain. This here is the only thing that makes sense."

"Where is she?" asked Mithya.

"Second floor," the second guard replied. "In one of the old storage rooms."

"Are any of these other guards going to be a problem?" Mithya asked.

"No, my Lady. Those who stayed behind when some captain called for reinforcements are all enlightened. Couldn't talk no sense into some of the ones that decided to go hear the Witness, but they're as bullheaded as the general. Although, uh, you should know..." He shared a glance with his partner, who continued for him.

"The Messiah, she ain't in a good way," she said.

"What do you mean?" asked Delvan, his face pallid.

He and Mithya leaned forward, waiting, hoping that something hadn't happened. That Desnia was safe. Delvan wasn't sure he could forgive himself if he lost someone else.

"It's best if you come see for yourself, sir."

The walls screamed while the shadows gawked. Their wails ricocheted inside of Desnia's skull as she sat huddled on the ground, knees pressed to her chest.

The dark, quiet room was a maleficence that permeated her soul. The Asylum had been a torture to endure—physically and mentally—but this... *cage* was a special type of cruelty. There was almost no light, the void around her shifting into confounding, blurred shapes. Voices whispered from the distance and cried from over her shoulder as the midnight phantoms haunted her every waking moment and then seeped into her sleep.

Determining whether she was lucid or dreaming was a confusing fog of faces and words spoken in hushed promises. She'd heard of the prisoner's madness before, tales spoken by drunken attention mongers in shady taverns, but she'd always passed them off as the ravings of idiots. How could sitting in a dark room for a few days be enough to break one's mind? Weak-willed fools, she used to think of them.

Now she knew that the only fool had been her.

How long had she been here? A part of her conscience, the shred that remained sane and rational, guessed it to be a day or two, assuming they fed her at normal intervals. But the raving, scared, and panicked ramblings of her fractured mind decried it to be an eternity, an endless, hopeless torment of darkness and fear. It paralyzed her, had her hearing what wasn't there—not that her mind wasn't wont to do that on its own already—and shaking while she curled herself up, cowering in the room's center in a feeble attempt to avoid the voices' pining.

Even now, as the aches and pains crippled and shackled her to the floor, she thought that she heard familiar voices, one among them whose loss had been the most devastating.

Desnia pinched her eyes closed, attempting to expel the sounds of demons, their padded footsteps drawing nearer. Chatter, endless and droning, surrounded her, lying and deceiving her with its wiles. She needed to resist, to focus on the real and ignore this temptation of familiarity that was baiting her to the abyss.

A light burst into existence before her, the creaking sound accompanying it harsh and shrill. It stung her eyes from behind closed lids, her head turning away from the fresh pain. The sounds became tumultuous and overwhelming. She wanted to resist, to block her ears and kick and run and flee. But it was all so... loud.

"Des!" came a troubled voice. There were others, layers of panic over calm, soothing words. A cacophony that drove spikes through her ears. A hand rested on her shoulder, firm and steady, yet foreign.

The brief meeting she'd had with her guard—a figment or real, she was unsure—had given her a sliver of hope. One that left her both craving for her dreams to become realities, and for her reality to stay a nightmare of distant slumber. Hope, however, was a cruel bitch of a lover. It elated, invigorated, and drove one forward, but to lose it, to have it quashed... She knew no worse torture—something she'd become an expert on of late.

In the end, the temptation, the possibilities, became too great to ignore. She cracked an eye, the light blinding her in its brilliance, shying from it as the owner of the hand before her came into a hazy focus.

Armor, black and glittering with filigree procured only by the pretentious affluence of nobility, with blue leather that glowed with an unseen radiance. Locks of dangling brown hair. Either her imagination had concocted a new way to infuriate her, or the person before her was real.

"If it isn't the asshole," she said, her voice hoarse.

Delvan's face sagged, his eyes looking to the floor. "I... deserve that."

"You deserve worse. I'd tell you to go fuck yourself, but you'd probably enjoy it," she sneered. She thought she heard a laugh, another among the shadow's jesters.

Delvan sighed, then shook his head. "Look, I'm sorry. I know that doesn't make up for it, but we're here to get you out. Can you walk?"

Desnia narrowed her eyes, struggling to see beyond the light and hand held before her face. "Who's 'we?'"

"That'd be me," came a soft and supple voice. Desnia felt her heart melt, muscles somehow going weaker. She looked up, still shielding her eyes, to see the lithe figure of Mithya standing there, her face forcing a smile, her soul, however, was an outpouring of regret and angst. Desnia gazed at her lissome figure. She would not be so easily fooled, not again. More accustomed to the betrayal of her own wants, Desnia tried to envision what lay hidden beyond the façade of beauty, remembering who had brought this living hell down on her.

"You selfish bitch," Desnia spat.

Mithya recoiled, and Desnia felt pain bleeding from Blue. It wasn't enough. She wasn't sure it ever would be, despite her own words digging a dagger into her chest.

"Des, I know you're upset," Delvan said, "I'm not happy about this arrangement either. But we can't afford to idle too long, so you're going to have to wait and curse us out when we're beyond the city. Can you walk?"

"Does it fucking look like it?" she asked. *Gods-damned Uppers, always so stupid. Can I walk? Can you shut your mouth and use your eyes? And-and... And why does he have blue shadows coming out of his back?* She looked at Mithya, her shirt wet and running with violet blood, dripping onto the floor. *No...* she thought, hidden desires boiling into bubbles of guilt. *Nononono!*

Something was wrong, terribly wrong. What was missing, like a key from a lock? She couldn't quite pin down what it was, but it made the voices in her head scream, telling her this was a lie, an illusion manifested in her throes of madness. Desperate to believe her freedom was before her, she tried to rationalize with herself, say that it was fine, that it was the voices lying, not her eyes. Why wouldn't they be—

Desnia's eyes went wide, her voice trembling. "You d-d-don't have them."

"Don't have what?" Delvan asked.

How had she not noticed? There was no chill down her spine, no presence of power polluting the air. *They don't have their sapphires,* she realized. *They're not real, none of this is...*

Desnia pulled herself away, refusing the touch of an imposter's hand. The motion sent pain cutting through her, stars filling her vision, and air wheezing from her lungs. In a series of frantic, groaning hobbles, she dragged herself to the back of the room, raspy screams shaking the walls between ragged gasps. "Get away from me!"

"Des," said the one that wore Delvan's face, "we're here to help you. Just come with us—"

"You're not real!" she shouted. "This is in my head," she said to herself. "In my head, it's all in my head."

The seductress that masked itself as the traitorous Truthsayer pulled a bladder from her bag, unstoppering it and proffering it to Desnia. "Des, drink this. It's us, I swear. Please."

"I won't let you poison me again," hissed Desnia. "Even if you aren't... No, no poison, you manipulative bitch."

Delvan's illusion appeared perturbed by this—it would seem her mind was delving deep into this altered reality. "What does she mean, poison *again*?" he asked, glaring at his fictional counterpart.

"We have to get her to drink it," said Mithya, not deigning the demon masquerading as Delvan a glance. "Des," she said softly, leaning forward. Gods, it was like the wraith truly cared about her, the devious actor putting kindness into its voice and caring in the air. "I'm sorry, but this is for your own good." *What?* "Guards!"

Two more demons, confused and hesitant—clearly the more dimwitted ones, the best were reserved for her, apparently—entered the room. "Hold her," said the false Mithya. Desnia's heart fell to the floor.

"What are you *doing*?!" asked Delvan's phantom. They were at odds. Good. Maybe she could use that as an escape—

"We don't have time for this, and she clearly isn't in control of her faculties. If she doesn't drink, then we're getting nowhere," said pretend Mithya. "Hold her, now!"

The guards hesitated. Desnia couldn't allow them to trap her, to poison her again. What would remain of her if they did? Was there anything left of her to take as it was?

With all the strength she could muster, she tried to lurch forward and sprint away. But a riving pain tore through her legs, and she landed with a lung-draining *thud* on the floor.

Hands held her as she tried to struggle. They turned her over, despite her agonizing thrashing, and pinned her to the floor. Something pressed to her lips and a chalky fluid poured into her mouth. She tried to spit it out, her screaming blending with the clamor of others in the room. Her head was held straight, nose pinched as the fluid filled her mouth and involuntarily flowed down her throat. Face soaking and hair drenched, she coughed a spray of liquid, terror filling her as she thought about how much of the devil's venom she'd swallowed.

There was nothing left of her energy to thrash, her adrenaline drained, and flesh exhausted from the events of the past days and weeks. Her resistance became weaker, and as she lay on the floor, the voices around her calmed, and the shadows began to recede. The overwhelming flood of emotions that constantly berated and crashed against her fell away like the tide, and for the first time since coming to this hell of a dungeon, she felt her own senses regain control.

Desnia blinked away the haze, her body stilling. The light that had blinded her earlier was a lantern, now resting on the floor to her side, and the only omnipresent sound was that of rain pelting against the exterior wall. The once-firm grip on her arms released, the two guards backing away with faces covered in pain, fear, and regret, as if they'd committed some mortal sin. She tilted her head up, finding Delvan and Mithya standing on either side of the door, anxious.

Meaning they were, in fact, quite real.

Gods-damn it, she thought. "The two people I wanted to see most..." she said, wiping her face with her sleeve. "I think I preferred you as demons."

"Are you alright?" Delvan asked. As if caring now would make up for the past.

"No, dumbass, I'm not alright. No thanks to *you* and this..." Gods, she couldn't even think of which curse to use in describing her feeling towards Mithya, her anger masking hidden feelings below. "Liar."

"What did you give her?" Delvan asked Mithya, his face pained.

"Medicine, from the Asylum. It quits the voices that the Se—"

"Shut your *gods-damned* mouth," Desnia snapped.

"Look, Des," Delvan said, kneeling in front of her. She used her arm to slowly right herself to be seated on the floor, dragging herself slightly away from him. "We don't have a lot of time. We're here to get you out of the city, and we need to go, *now*."

So, that was *real,* she thought, slightly relieved. "Have either of you spoken to Nerio? Do you know if he's alright..." Her words faded as Delvan and Mithya shared a look. Her gut knotted. "He's done something stupid, hasn't he?" Did she dare ask the question that scared her most? Had anything befallen the one person who *hadn't* betrayed her? "Is he... alive?" she asked slowly.

"Yes," replied Delvan, much to her relief. "But you're right about him doing something stupid..."

"You shouldn't speak of the Witness in such a way," said one of the guards.

Desnia's brow furrowed. "Is he talking about Nerio? Why are people calling him that?"

"Don't worry about it," said Mithya. "You two, go scout our route and make sure it's clear." The guards begrudgingly took their leave. Desnia tried bringing herself to her shaking feet, her legs swollen, bruised anchors. Delvan tried to help. She swatted his hand before landing hard on the floor with a groan.

After a grimacing moment, Desnia said, "Tell me what's happened to Nerio."

Mithya shuffled uneasily, her eyes flitting to the door. Delvan sighed and said, "He's giving a speak at the Devapuram. In front of *thousands*, maybe more. An appeal to get *you* released."

"Which is going to backfire spectacularly," said Mithya, "and why we need to get out of this building."

That absolute idiot. "They're going to listen to *him*? Why?"

"Long story," said Delvan.

Desnia gritted her teeth, unable to believe that she was going to suggest something this asinine. "We need to go get him. If he doesn't get himself killed then he's going to end up in a cell like this, or worse."

"No," said Mithya firmly with a slash of her hand through the air. "Absolutely not. We're behind as it is and with the storm—"

"You have no *fucking* right to tell me what we can or cannot do," cursed Desnia. "You poisoned me, stole my... ring, and broke me. At least this asshole," she said, pointing to Delvan, "apologized. All you've done is give orders. You want me to come with you? Then go. Get. Nerio."

Mithya's jaw hung open, contorting as it struggled, her emotions tempestuous as the contents of a shaken cask of ale. Grief, embarrassment, regret, deprecation, were only a few of what Desnia felt circulating around Mithya.

Delvan, meanwhile, had ire wrinkled so deeply into his face that it resembled that of an ancient, weathered stone, deep-set eyes driving spears into his Blue companion. "You *what?!*" *Don't think you're off the hook for this, bastard.* "You *were* responsible for what happened!"

"I didn't... That's not... If I had known..." Mithya stammered, her confidence vanishing in a rare moment of vulnerability. The Truthsayer took a deep breath, collecting herself, a mask once again pulled over her soul. "I'm sorry," she said. She dropped the bag on her shoulders before Desnia's feet. "There's a change of clothing in there, hurry and get dressed. I'll go and see what I can do about Nerio. There's something that I've been wanting to take care of that I'll handle while I'm gone." *Of course, it's still about what you want.*

The Blue turned to Delvan, pulling a black, linen bundle from her pocket. "Take this," she said, handing it to him, "use it to help Des when you get far enough from this building."

"What is it?" he asked, moving to open it.

Mithya quickly pressed her hand to it, stopping him. "Cadentite," she said, "only a pebble, but all I have. Don't open it until you're farther from the general's tower."

Delvan's eyes went wide. "You've had this the whole time?"

"What? It's not like you needed it. Besides, I needed to try and lift the contract spells from this." Mithya pulled another black bundle from her pocket, opening and pulling a long silver chain from it, making Desnia's heart jump into her throat as—

FINALLY! came Masini's voice. Desnia found herself smiling despite the pain. *By the Greats, you people never treat your elders with—Des! Thought I heard your voice. Oh, it's good to see... Wow, you look* terrible.

And the smile vanished from her face. *Gods,* she thought, *I wish I could kick him between the legs.*

I mean, continued Masini, *I thought I looked bad after this one time this mistress in Tennefen drugged me and—after blaming me for something I clearly would never do—tried to cut off my—*

"Would you shut up already?" said Desnia, snatching the chain and ring from Mithya.

Don't pretend as though you didn't yearn for my soothing, sensual, salacious voice, said Masini. *You missed me, I can tell. You haven't sworn or threatened to throw me into the sea yet, clear signs of your unfettered gratitude for having me back in your life.*

"I'll be sure to throw you out of a window, for old time's sake," she replied.

"What?" said a confused Delvan.

"Not you, though it's tempting," replied Desnia.

"I wasn't stealing him," said Mithya. "I wanted to see if I could lift the contract spells binding him. But whoever cast them had skill that far surpasses my own."

The tantalizing beauty doesn't give herself enough credit, said Masini. *She's clearly been trained by a ma-ma-ma-fucking damn it. Someone like me. Unless, of course, it's a weird coincidence that she knows about the, uh, things she mentioned and happens to have a full back tattoo of a fra-fra-fra-gah, a pretty pattern.*

"What are you talking about?" asked Desnia, cringing from her many aches.

"What's he saying?" asked Mithya.

Delvan, his mouth agape and head tilted, dashed his eyes between the two of them. "*What* are you two talking about?"

Wait, Desnia thought, *how would he know about a back tattoo?* "Did you, by chance, leave his ring outside of that bag somewhere? Your quarters, maybe?"

"...Why?" asked Mithya.

Oh-ho-ho, did she ever! said Masini. *Shall I describe it in extreme, curvaceous detail? By the Greats, it's been lifetimes since I've met a woman endowed with such sublime beau—*

"No reason," Desnia said, interrupting what she was certain would be an hour-long monologue.

Don't act like you don't want to know, retorted Masini. *Anyway, I hadn't considered tattoos on Blues before, it's rather ingenious. It would certainly explain her, uh, talents. You should find out more about it, there's no way she knew about that on her own.*

Desnia rubbed her throbbing head and refocused, still bitter despite the gesture of returning the kidnapped Masini, regardless of the intentions. "This," she said to Mithya, pointing to Masini's ring hanging around her neck once more, "does not make up for what you did." She felt the words wound the Blue, but the torture she'd endured these few days left a deep, dark stain of resentment. "And there are things that we are going to need to discuss. Later."

Masini's words hadn't been lost on her. If Mithya was trained by a mage and possessing knowledge of Asta and Desnia's quest to find her, there were questions that carried a grave concern upon their shoulders. But they would have to wait until they were out of the city, the urgency of their situation fully settling on her.

"Go, follow the route we talked about," said Mithya to Delvan. "I'll meet you by the edge of the city."

Delvan ran a tensed hand through his hair. "This is ludicrous," he said. "We don't have time for this, and Nerio is surrounded by loyal soldiers. He'll be fine!"

"Like I said, I have something I need to do anyway. Who knows when or if I'll be coming back to this city to get it. If I'm not there in time, I have two of my people waiting beyond the wall with horses and supplies. I'll catch up eventually."

Delvan tossed up his hands. "Fine. But don't expect me to wait long."

Mithya rolled her eyes. "See you soon," she said to Desnia, giving her a wink before turning and striding from the room.

My non-corporeal flagstaff is fully raised right now, said Masini. *Don't worry, my envy over her adoration of you won't come between us. Though if you don't let me watch I may hold a grudge.*

Ignoring him and grabbing the bag on the floor, Desnia withdrew the clothing. Something heavy fell from it. She reached down and picked up a sheathed dagger, the one that Delvan had given her on the steps of the Devapuram. The darksteel blade was loose in its sheath, the top inch exposed and glinting in the lantern's light. Dizzying images flashed before her eyes; the dagger, covered in blue blood, Delvan on patterned stone before her, chest carved open and motionless.

She blinked, looking to Delvan with terror in her eyes and gipping the leather blade cover tightly in her hand—which he mistook for something else.

"Yes, I'm an asshole, I know," he said, exasperated. "You can stab me once we're safely out of here, if it's all the same to you."

Desnia snapped her mouth shut, teeth pummeling together. She grabbed the bladder of medicine and took another draft, trying to expel the images. The ghastly visions slithered away, the grief and self-loathing lingering for a few moments longer. *A nightmare, nothing more,* she consoled herself.

She wouldn't allow it to be anything else.

CHAPTER
FORTY-SIX

He was one of the pinnacles ordered to remain and be their charge's sentinel. His, as I recall, was Asta.

People of Brethefen!" Nerio shouted, hoping his voice would carry to the distant reaches of the endless sprawl. "My neighbors. My friends. My family."

The stark white of thousands of eyes were fixed upon him, shining against the oncoming darkness of the storm above. They were a great field of seeds waiting to blossom, and by his hand he aspired to guide their growth away from the harmful intent which many had come to reap of late. For if he did not, disaster and sin would poison what he knew to be benevolent hearts.

There was a greater purpose for them, a calling he needed to shepherd them towards. He could not allow for his benedictions to be contorted or misconstrued any longer.

"Our city has befallen difficult times of late," he said, drops of water beginning to lightly drizzle onto his face and robe. "The gods, in their designs for the protection of this city, have left us trodden upon hardships. Babes go hungry beneath roofless homes. We beg for meals, for water, for the basic necessities of life."

There was a murmur from the crowd, their energy shifting from hope to despondence.

"Their wisdom, I realize, is difficult to comprehend, for it is above us all," Nerio continued. "There cannot be salvation without cost, a blessing without reprimand, success without failure. This is the toll we pay and is the eternal formula that creates the beauty of our divinely blessed life.

"The ashes that now stain us are a reminder of the gods' protection of our city, and the ascension of one amongst their midst. We mustn't forget that our sacrifices allowed others to still walk this plane alongside us."

The tone of the mass changed once more, regret filling it, gazes downcast and grey. The sky darkened further, the clouds blanketing the sky and pressing their chilled breath harder against Nerio's back, carrying his words across the crowd.

"I want you to look to the person to your left, and then to your right," called out Nerio. "Know that your grief is shared, your loss felt, and it is righteous, but because of it those that now surround you were sheltered from a demise too horrible to speak of. For if it were not for the gods' hands interfering, *all* would've fallen, and even the owls would've wept for the tragedy this world would have witnessed."

Nerio could see their pain, its corona blending into the jet clouds of the storm above. He understood their plight and knew it was this burden which drove them to lash out, to find an outlet to direct their anguish. This was not something to be condemned, as the city's martial law would lead one to believe. It needed to be *healed*. Only then would the grandeur of this magnificent city begin to reform.

"I believe that we have once more been ignorant to the gods' plans, as our mortal minds are wont to do." Nerio stared out at the rapt throng, his voice filled with the torment of the souls that surrounded him. It shaped his words, molded them into the ones that already hung in the thoughts of those around him, though they had yet to hear or understand them.

"Look at what they have accomplished this day!" Nerio continued, his hands spreading outward. "The people of this city, brought together and unified in singular purpose. To see their Messiah freed!"

The crowd lifted their heads and spirits, and then broke out with an echoing cheer, fists rising towards a thunderous sky.

This was the moment, the pivot upon which he would sway the masses and bring them to heel, to remind them of the power of their voice, and disregard the temptation of violence.

Nerio held out his arms, calling for silence. The throng and storm alike tempered themselves to a low, grumbling quiet. "Let our voices be heard, for the decree of a city, its people, its *gods*, cannot be ignored!"

From the center of the crowd, a chant slowly began, growing steadily, reaching outward until it engulfed the tongues of the thousands gathered. "Free the Messiah! Free the Messiah! Free the Messiah!"

Nerio allowed himself a moment of pride, hearing the calls of the people demanding Desnia's freedom. It was not bloodshed, nor perceived retribution which would bring about Desnia's release. Such acts were not what the gods willed, they would not wish to see their worshippers destroyed by their own maliciousness. A protest, peaceful yet vehement, would be a call the city's oppressors would be unable to ignore, the chant loud enough to shake the heavens above, where Nerio was certain the gods were smiling upon them.

Looking to his right, Nerio saw Captain Gernbard shifting uneasily, his hand resting on his sword, eyes darting. He appreciated the captain's caution, it was a soldier's habit and one that served them well, but there was nothing to fear from—

"Carry your voices to their doorstep!" came a shouted voice over the crowd. Nerio looked to his left—where the voice originated—as the crowd's voice began to dim, the wind lashing out with whips of rain. "Their tyranny cannot resist the will of the people. The will of the gods!"

Nerio, horror filling his eyes and heart as he heard the words, saw the shift of the people's attitudes as they began to listen, to *agree*. He finally found the speaker, near the bottom of the wide temple steps. The man had stepped upon a makeshift dais, raising him two heads above the crowd, their attention now completely focused on the young priest.

Brother Meneham.

Nerio, voice stolen in the shock of the moment, heard an angry growl from Gernbard. The captain nodded to a few of the nearby soldiers, sending them pushing their way through the crowd in a struggled, futile effort to reach the other priest and silence him. Nerio's mouth went dry, his body frozen as the man responsible for the surge of violence in the city enthralled the crowd.

There was an alteration to the mood of the masses. Nerio could see the glowing halo of their energy morphing, their pain once again being channeled into the wrath which had been born of their despair. It threatened to break his heart, eating at him from the inside out. He needed to stop this, before it was too late.

"No!" Nerio shouted, trying to draw attention back to him. Eyes, dark and riled as the sky above, turned and gazed upon him. "We have seen enough death! More than one should know in a lifetime! We must bring the peace that is needed in times like—"

"Peace wrought from the removal of the oppressors!" interrupted Mene- ham. Nerio began to choke, his worst fears unfolding before him. "You cannot have peace without freedom! Do you feel free?!"

A susurration spread through the gathering. A few jeers broke through the static—angry, embittered, and tainted with contempt. The crowd quickly followed, becoming a din. Nerio felt as though he were about to vomit, color vanishing from his face. His voice shaking, he cried out over the crowd as they began to quiet. "We must seek freedom from—"

"From those who would shackle us to debt! Those who would claim this city—*our* city—as their own! As the Witness has said, we are the gods' chosen. The survivors! The true believers!" cried Meneham. *Gods, what is he doing?* thought a horrified Nerio. *Why must he hate so ferociously?*

An uproar erupted, deafening and drowning out Nerio's pleading calls. Claps of thunder became its chorus, torrents of rain its applause. Nerio begged—his voice no longer heard—for the people to calm. Tears began streaming down his face as he saw the hate burning like coals in their eyes, the unadulterated resentment for those leveeing taxes and repressing them possessed one and all like an amorphous entity of loathing.

Nerio's voice cracked and strained as it was drowned by the flood of outrage. His screaming pleads for mercy were lost among the single-minded mob. Soldiers surrounded him as the mass of people began to undulate and seethe, a pot of emotion nearing its boiling point. Gernbard was shouting, pushing people away and trying to grab Nerio's arm.

Nerio pulled away. He could save the crowd, stop this madness. He had to. Stepping back to the stairs' lip, he frantically waved his hands, trying to draw the attention back to him. But heads were turning away, facing the newfound screams and shrill cries in the distance.

The edges of the crowd rippled as though a stone had been dropped, and from the epicenter Nerio saw an array of shields, spears leaning forward, being driven into the crowd. Blood sprayed, metal rang, and the stench of death began filling the wind-swept air, only faintly dulled by the rain that was now soaking his robe and cascading down the steps before him.

Behind the unyielding wall of soldiers, Nerio could see a lone, tall figure, sword of black metal in hand, barking orders that carried out over even the roar of the masses. General Rosethorn had heard their calls, it would appear, and decidedly refused them.

Gernbard's hand gripped his arm again. "We have to go, *now*!" he shouted into Nerio's ear.

"No!" he shouted. "I can't! I won't leave them like this to rip each other—"

"There's nothing you can do!" the old soldier shouted back at him. "If we stay here, we die!"

Nerio looked back to the crowd. A curtain of soldiers, the ones among the gathered crowd, had formed a line of opposition to the shield-wall that the general was relentlessly driving forward, slaughtering people by the dozens, possibly hundreds.

Bystanders were caught in the middle, swiveling their heads from left to right as they became caught between the two opposing sides. Nerio almost fell to his knees as he watched them clash in a clamor of steel, crushing anyone between them. The screams clawed wounds into his mind. A legion of soldiers brought to bear arms against their own now fought relentlessly for their beliefs. Beliefs that Nerio had instilled.

No, he thought, *I did not mean for this. Gods, what have I done? How can* this *be part of your design?*

He refused to believe that the gods who had protected him, chosen Lord Delvan, and resurrected Desnia would be responsible for the blood-stained waters that now ran through the streets like rivers. This was not the salvation of a city, but its utter destruction.

"Why?" he whispered.

The pull of the captain's grip was too much for his thin arms to resist, but as he began to be dragged backward into the churning throng, his eyes scanned, taking in the sight, viewing the desolation he had brought upon his home. With the last glimpse of the wider riot before him, he caught sight of Bother Meneham, locking eyes with the rebellious priest.

He gave Nerio a smile—not condescending but, instead, reverent. Thankful. Meneham then clasped his hands together and bowed his head as the narrow gap of people closed before Nerio and vanished behind the clashing frenzy.

As Nerio was being hauled away, fending off the reaching hands and indiscriminate shoving, the sight of a gracious Meneham haunted him. And he realized, unequivocally, the responsibility for what was happening, what was to come, fell upon but one person, who it would crush with guilt for the rest of their days.

Himself.

Chapter
Forty-Seven

I did not know him personally, but he was infamous for numerous reasons, the only one of importance being his involvement in the cataclysm.

Desnia hobbled along as fast as she could, her arm slung around Delvan's neck as he carried the brunt of her bruised and battered weight. Her rib stabbed at her with each lumbering step, her discolored legs straining and burning as if their veins were filled with molten metal. She cursed that sadistic bastard for leaving her like this, wishing she could've made his death linger, sting the way her body did now, agonizingly reminding him that each throb of pain brought him closer to his demise.

Instead, she was left dissatisfied, her vengeance unquenched and poisoning her thoughts. The only thing her recently reclaimed clarity of mind bestowed was the revelation that the monsters of this world were far more terrifying than the ones of her visions.

Those faces in the clouds are going to need to try harder, she thought, looking up and mimicking their scowls.

Rain barraged in a deluge that drenched them both, hair clinging to their faces, leather squishing, linen melding to the skin it touched. Her new clothes were a variety meant for the desert, not a summer storm, and fared terribly in this weather—sagging, chafing, and miserably adhering everywhere they shouldn't.

The distance in all directions was shrouded in grey as the showering water fell in waves and folds, carried on the gusts of the black storm above. Lightning flashed and lit their way, the sun blotted out entirely.

The rain was a roar, submerging their feet in water that rose above their toes as it ran through the street like a channel, heading from the city's central peak at the Devapuram to its outskirts. They flowed with it, the water becoming increasingly deep as they trudged on.

Over it all, Desnia heard the howl of another beast. An army of voices called out as one, their cry beating back the storm in combative anger. She struggled to look over her shoulder, back to the dome's outline in the distance, faintly visible through the onslaught of cascading water. A sickness rose in her throat. What was happening back there?

"In here!" Delvan shouted, his voice raising just above the storm.

Desnia let him lead her through a storefront, absent of light, the door un-locked. Even by the dull illumination of grey shadows, she could see the place had been ransacked, its wares thrown and smashed upon the blood-stained floor. "What happened here?"

"The whole street," Delvan said, straining as he helped Desnia onto a stool, "was attacked by a mob. The merchants who survived fled the city." He shut the door, delving them into a colorless blend of hues that barely lit either of their faces.

Mhm, said Masini. *I heard about this during my euphoric stint nestled against the skin of our mutual love. The people here are not fans of price gouging. Who could have guessed?*

"What the hell's happened to this city?" Desnia murmured.

"Nerio," Delvan said, struggling to dig into a wet pocket, "*may* have started a new religious sect by preaching about what happened at the gate, and me healing you. They, uh, basically worship you now, and—"

"*What*?!" she said, flinching at the tensing of muscles.

"I'd tell you it's not as bad as it sounds, but honestly, it's probably worse," he said with a cringe. He managed to finally rip the small black pouch Mithya had given him from his pocket. "His intentions were innocent enough, but it's started to take a mind of its own."

With shaking fists and a clenched jaw, she grated, "I'm going to kill him." How *dare* he? She hadn't wanted attention, in fact, she'd specifically told Ne-rio to stop his ridiculous groveling and come to his senses. Now it seemed the idiotic sheep of the masses had found another shepherd to flock to, believing his naive notions that what had happened to her was the divine intervention of their gods. She hated the fact that *a* god had a hand in her life—if Asta was indeed such a thing—and couldn't fathom why anyone would *intentionally* welcome such mediation into their lives. When she next saw Nerio, they were going to have a *long* conversation, or a very, very short argument.

Devan dropped the pebble of cadentite into his hands, flushing a com-forting warmth through Desnia's chest. It cast iridescent hues that gently shifted and swirled around them, throwing crisp black shadows onto the walls. Despite the calm, welcomed sensation it sent into her, it did nothing to cool her ire.

"Not if Rosethorn beats you to it," said Delvan as he pulled a chain out from under his armor.

Desnia's eyes flicked to the white pouch hanging at the silver chain's end, her stomach turning as Delvan went to pull it off. Her hand snapped out and grabbed his wrist, terror overpowering the pain the rapid motion caused.

Delvan looked at her, his eyes sympathetic. "I have to, Des. I can't carry you through the desert. And we need to move faster if we're going to beat the flooding."

"Hold on." She pulled the bladder from their bag and took a swig of the chalky "medicine." *At least it's not paint*, she thought.

"Does that... help?"

"Better than nothing," she replied, pulling wet hair from her face. "It's best if you grind it up into powder and snort it, but this works well enough."

Delvan tried to hide his flabbergasted expression. Poorly. "You really do that?"

"You hear voices in *your* head and tell me what you wouldn't do to shut them up," she said. She looked down at the cadentite sitting in his palm. *It's worth relieving the pain,* she told herself. "Do you even know what you're doing with that?"

It took a moment for Delvan to respond, his jaw hanging open as he searched for an answer. "I... think so?"

"Well, that's fucking reassuring."

Oh, it's not that difficult, said Masini. There was a long pause, as though no explanation was needed.

"Mind explaining?" The one time she needed him to talk...

"What?"

"Not you," she said with a shake of her head.

"Uh," said Delvan hesitantly. "Didn't you just say that the medicine... helped?" He was having a difficult time meeting her eyes, an awkward tension radiating from him.

"It gets rid of the ones that aren't real." *Mostly.* "But unfortunately, it just makes this one a little quieter."

Rude, said Masini. *I see the joy of our reunited companionship was as short-lived as your patience.*

"...Whose voice do you... hear?"

"Don't look at me like that," she said adjusting herself in her seat in a failed attempt to relieve the aches. She sighed, having hoped to keep Masini's presence secret, but there wasn't much of a choice on her part. Not if she wanted Delvan to be successful and heal her.

Hating that she was going to have to trust in someone who had a *long* way to go towards earning it, she grabbed at the chain around her neck. "*This* is Masini, or his, I don't know, soul, I guess. My *normally* incessantly talkative... companion, who also happens to be a High Realm mage. And he just said that, for you, healing should be 'easy.'"

Actually, I said 'not difficult.'

"Oh, stop with the fucking semantics," she said.

Delvan stared at her, his jaw gaping. He was quiet for what felt like minutes, causing her to shift with uncomfortable angst. Finally, after an eternity of the Blue being dumbstruck, she said, "Would you stop fucking gawking and get on with it already?"

"Sorry," he said in a burst of shame. "Does, uh, *he* say what I need to do?" he asked, still sounding incredulous.

"I don't know, does he?" she asked, waiting for Masini to speak up.

He doesn't appreciate your attitude, replied Masini. *And I didn't bother to explain because I shouldn't* have to.

"What's that supposed to mean?"

Ugh, Masini sighed. *Blues, and the... ones they descend from, have the fortune of being able to ca-ca-ca-blah! to do what they do, intuitively. None of you even need to try, or make the, uh, special patterns or motions. It's infuriating! I spend centuries learning the minutia of, uh, transformation—admittedly to create some stellar aphrodisiacs—and one of you just waves a hand and poof! Stone into steel. I still don't know how she managed to create entities with such concentrated—*

"Masini!" Desnia barked. "We don't have time for bitter ramblings. What does Del need to do?"

Bit hypocritical of you, but I'll give you another pass on account of all the torture, he said.

"How kind," she replied, deadpan, Delvan doing his best not to stare.

I know. It's one of my greatest attributes, now that I no longer have a physical member. As I was saying, he continued, before she had a chance to retort, *while it comes so unfairly naturally to you, there are ways to enhance or concentrate abilities. Focus them, if you will, so that you don't just send the power out wildly.*

"Get to the point, Masini."

"Does it always take this long to get an answer from... him?" Delvan asked, looking worriedly at the door.

"Unfortunately..."

By the Greats, do your manners need work. We don't have any *of what we need for*

Lord Delvan to reach his true potential, so, for now, have him press his fingertips in a circle—evenly spaced, this is important, and three inches in diameter—to wherever your pain is the greatest. Have him press the ca-ca-ca-fucking glowing rock! to the side opposite. Then, all he needs to do is picture it in his mind, and that will mostly work.

"Mostly?!"

It's a pebble *that our lady friend already used a portion of the vi-vi-vi-guh, energy from,* he replied. *So yes, mostly.*

Desnia sighed and rubbed her brow before repeating the instructions to Delvan. She had him put his fingers over her rib, hissing in pain as he pressed his fingertips to her side. Masini gave a few corrections, and Desnia helped him shift his positioning until the mage was satisfied.

With not just her ribs, but her entire body covered in severe bruising, she hoped whatever Delvan did would saturate into her legs—assuming it worked at all. The instinct to pull away from his touch made her squirm, despising the idea of anyone being this close, to leaving herself this vulnerable. He was gentle, but her skin crawled all the same.

"Ready?" he asked.

"Are you?"

Delvan shrugged, his face devoid of confidence. He removed his sapphire's covering, the glistening azure gem pressing its heat against her like a hearth's fire, her hair standing on end. A pressure built in her mind, as if the voices were beating at the thin membrane of the medicine's potency, trying to break back in. Shadows blackened, the grey light from the window dancing in the rain. With a slow exhale she did her best to loosen her body's taut sinew, the voices held at bay.

For now.

"And I'm supposed to just, *picture* it?" he asked, holding the small, shimmering stone to the other side of her ribcage, the purple light casting undulating shadows on his face.

"Not great instructions, I know," she said uncomfortably.

It's not my fault you're terrible students, Masini said dryly. *Tell him to focus, as though he's expelling fire, but to draw his power from the, uh, opposite energy. Opposite isn't the right word, but you understand what I mean. Anyway, he will draw it from one hand to the other, passing through you. Should work quickly—which I'm definitely not insanely envious of, as it takes us weeks or months to do the same level of repair. Oh, and just be careful not to concentrate too hard on fire, otherwise he's apt to turn you into a torch.*

Desnia groaned, then repeated the instructions—for whatever the vague directions were worth.

Delvan stared at her for a moment, then gave a half shrug and focused back on his hands. Desnia waited, her arms held awkwardly to the side, nervously hoping that what appeared from between the Blue's hands didn't incinerate her.

The only sounds were that of the wind pelting rain against the building, the expensive glass of the room's wide, grey window doing its best to resist the storm's might. Desnia sat there, abashed, the hands of someone she could hardly proclaim to trust touching her, waiting in pain. Time was counted by the pulses of her heartbeat delivering a ticking agony from skin to marrow, all while the gem hanging from the neck before her taunted and toyed in the faint light.

"We don't have all night," she said tersely.

"I'm trying!" Delvan said, appearing to focus harder. "It's not like I'm experienced with—"

A green hue began to diffuse the air, rising in whisps from her skin and falling like drifting fog from Delvan's clawed hand against her broken rib. His eyes went wide, as if he were in disbelief of his own capabilities.

A surge of warmth flooded her, her heart racing as a euphoria seeped into muscle, bone, and tendon. The sensation was akin to the buzz of alcohol rushing through her veins, but while this was intoxicating in its own, unique way, it did not give her a heady, floating feeling. Instead, it invigorated, sutured not only her body, but her body's will.

The purple illumination quickly went dun, exchanged for the thin tendrils of verdant green. They faded shortly after the cadentite turned a deep black, evaporating and taking their ecstasy with them. Delvan exhaled and thankfully removed his hands from her sides, looking inquisitively into Desnia's eyes.

She slowly lowered her arms, a fatigue still burning in them, but the acuteness of the pain's barbs had subsided. As slowly as she could manage, she pulled in a deep breath, waiting for what her mind assumed would be the inevitable jab of agony from her side.

Which, blessedly, never came.

Air whistled slowly from her lips in relief. She forced herself to stand, her legs wobbling for a moment. Delvan quickly stepping forward to grab her, but she held a palm forward, stopping him. Gaining her bearings, she stood upright and stretched. The muscles were sore, but it was manageable. A step forward proved her legs capable of transporting her on their own, and with a few paces through the littered space she regained her stride.

See? asked Masini. *I told you it was simple. You're welcome, as always.*

"Did it work?" asked Delvan, now holding a bead of inanite, the energy fully drained from the cadentite.

"Well enough," she said, grateful for the lack of pain. Or, rather, its mitigation. The weight bearing down on her mind, however, continued to press like a building upon a foundation. "Can you cover that?" she asked, pointing to Delvan's sapphire. "I barely have space in my head for my emotions, let alone yours."

He looked down at his chest. "Oh! Yeah, sorry," he said, putting the white pouch back over it.

Desnia felt her shoulders slump and neck loosen as her unseen demons receded. "That won't have brought us unwanted attention, would it?"

Delvan shook his head. "I stopped sensing the general a few blocks ago, that's why I brought us in here. Besides, I think he has other priorities right now."

And, chimed in Masini, *I doubt Jerdine is still in the city. With the, uh, door rendered useless, there isn't a reason for him to stay. Although I do worry about where he and his newfound confederate went off to.*

"Hopefully in the opposite direction of wherever we're going," mumbled Desnia. Grabbing their bag and walking to the door, she turned to Delvan as she clutched the handle. "Don't think this has earned you forgiveness," she said bitterly.

Her pathos crumbled the Blue's figure, his head hanging low as he rubbed his brow and hid his eyes from view. "I... I know. For what it's worth, I never intended any of this."

"Maybe think before you act, next time."

Oof, cringed Masini. *Des, you're harsher than a scrotum-scrubbing cactus. Look at the guy. The least you can do is thank him for getting you out.*

"He's the reason I was thrown in there in the first place!" she hissed off to her side.

Oh, yes, because your decision-making skills are impeccable. I seem to recall someone setting half a city on fire. Who was that again?

Desnia's lips drew into a thin line, her foot tapping against the blood-stained floor. Too much had occurred, the wounds still fresh and only partially healed, for her to simply look past Delvan's actions. Masini was twisting events entirely out of context to fit his argument. What Delvan had done was a betrayal, and she wasn't yet prepared to offer forgiveness for such a deplorable act.

"Let's go," she said, her body rigid and voice terse. She pulled at the door, a gale wrenching it from her hand and slamming it into the wall with a clatter. Wind threw rain at them like shards of glass as they trekked once more into the riverine streets. A tumult could be heard rising in the distance behind them, and the wind carried waves of anguish, fear, anger, and hate that no amount of medicine could block from her senses. A tide of blood was rushing towards them—attracting a full parliament of owls in its wake—coming to engulf them in its fury.

Something floating in the street's current caught her eye. She bent down and grabbed the square of blue fabric, which appeared to be finely laced silk, and quickly rung the water from it. Her hair had become too long for her liking, and she used the cloth to tie back the unruly mess.

Despite the storm's resistance, they covered the ground to the city's edge in less time than it had taken to travel the short distance from her prison to the abandoned store. Her legs burned, but a quick check had shown the bruising was almost entirely gone. There had been times when she'd been forced to do more in worse condition. It wouldn't be easy, but it wouldn't be the struggle it would have been prior to Delvan's healing.

The water was above their ankles now, logging her boots and leaving her feet swimming. Shielding her squinted eyes from the onslaught of rain, Desnia watched as Delvan approached the door of a building that stood adjacent to the squat, city wall. She climbed the steps behind him that rose a few treads above the water, looking over her shoulder as Delvan jostled the handle.

Shadows shifted and swirled in the darkness, hiding in the street behind them. They approached from the Devapuram in the distance, masked by the wall of spraying rain. Were they tricks of the eye by the boiling clouds above with its curtains of rain and flashes of lightning? Nefarious haunts trailing at a distance, waiting for her to slide back into her delusional state?

She shook her head, ignoring their presence and walking through the well-lit door as Delvan managed to get it open.

The interior was dry, albeit bare. A single lantern hung from the wall of the windowless room and with the exception of the door they'd walked through, the only other exits were a long hall leading towards the side of the building facing the city wall, and a set of stairs that rose to the second floor.

Desnia grabbed her hair and tried wringing it out, a pool forming beneath their garments as they splattered dripping water onto the adobe floor. "What now?"

Delvan nodded at the hallway. "Down there is a false, wooden wall that leads to a tunnel under the city wall. Takes us about a hundred yards out behind a small outcropping. A few of Mithya's people are waiting there for us with horses and supplies."

Assuming they're not drowning, she thought. She began pacing in the small room while Delvan went down the corridor, presumably to check on their exit. Freedom was a few feet away, yet she lingered. Not for Mithya, though with her people—whatever that meant—waiting for them, it was unlikely they'd get far without her. Instead, she hoped for Nerio—the idiot clearly couldn't survive on his own, and—

There was a rap at the door.

Desnia touched her fingers lightly to the hilt of the dagger at her side. She couldn't say why she'd kept the double-edged blade. It was a reminder of the worst of her dreams, ones filled with the death rattles of those close to her, images that plagued her waking moments. And yet she'd tied it around her waist all the same, an... *urge* compelling her to keep it close.

Loosing the sheath, Desnia crept towards the door, careful to keep her shadow away from the narrow gap at its base. She stepped to the door's side. As she pressed her hand to the crude lock and drew the darksteel blade from her hip, she felt another rap on the boards.

"It's me!" came Mithya's familiar voice.

Desnia's gut jumped. Thrusting the dagger back into its leather covering, she threw the bolt and pried the door open, the wind pulling against her all the while. Mithya slipped in, and Desnia—after seeing nothing but horizontal rain and flashes of lightning outside—let the door slam back into its place, a deep concern growing within her.

The Blue was soaked, her normally pristine clothing stuck to her bronzed skin. A strange, embellished dagger now hung from her hip, opposite the short sword she typically carried. Desnia looked at her, breath held, and asked, "Where's Nerio?!"

Mithya threw her soaking hair back, the regret emanating from her making Desnia fear for the worst. "I'm sorry. I tried to get to him, but the crowd... they've turned into a mindless mob. Soldiers fighting each other, people being slaughtered by the hundreds... it's chaos out there. I tried Des, I swear, but I couldn't get within a hundred feet of the Devapuram."

"Could you at least see him? Tell me he's not..." She couldn't say the words, the thought painful just to fathom. An anger welled within her, sudden and fed by her own clawing resentments and disappointments. "You didn't even try, did you?! I swear, if you left him there to die..." She felt her face flush as her fingers found the hilt at her side, her eyes low and darkened by shadow.

Mithya shook and hung her head before looking back up at Desnia, her expression as serious as she'd ever seen it. "You can read me better than anyone I've ever met," the Truthsayer said, "do you think I'm lying to you?"

Desnia was trembling with each sharp breath, her fury decrying the words as false, begging to be unleashed. But there was no deceit in Mithya's statement, and Desnia was forced to choke down her anger, the beast thrashing in her chest. "I... I can't just leave him."

"That mob wasn't far behind me," said Mithya. "They're calling for *you.* If we go anywhere near them, they'll tear us apart. I'm sorry, we'll just have to trust that his guards got him to safety."

"Or he's..." *already dead.* Tears began to cloud her vision.

Des, said Masini solemnly, *she has a point. This is our only chance at getting out of here, we can't afford to waste time.*

No. She refused to believe it. He was alive, she knew it in her heart, and he would need help. "I'm going after him." She took a step towards the door.

Mithya stepped in her way. "I'm sorry, Des," she said with pain that was masked from her voice but filled the air. "But I can't let you. Nothing is more important than you getting to safety, nothing. You're our best chance. Maybe our only chance to find—"

"We have a problem," Delvan interrupted as he came rushing from down the hall.

"Perfect timing, as always, Sparky."

He gave Mithya a glare but continued. "The tunnel's flooded, there's no way we're getting through—" He cut off, his mouth gaping as his eyes fixed on the long dagger at Mithya's side. Pointing to it, he shakily asked, "Is that... Where did you get that?"

Mithya crossed her arms. "Seems to me like you might already know the answer."

Desnia's head snapped back and forth between them, perplexed. "Someone mind telling me what the hell you're talking about?"

"You *stole* from the *general?!*" Delvan proclaimed.

Ooh, said Masini, *this is getting juicy.*

"I *stole* nothing! This blade is *mine* by right!" Mithya screamed. Desnia had never seen the Blue lose control in such a way, her emotions an assault as vengeful as the storm outside. Mithya took a deep breath, composing herself. Her words, however, still bit with sharpened fangs. "It was my grandfather's, and the only thief is that bastard Rosethorn who cut him down in cold blood."

"You found time to get a *dagger,* but not Nerio?!" Desnia asked.

"It's not like that! I *barely* made it to the general's tower, I couldn't go any farther, and it was the only opportunity I would have. The place was swarming with violent rioters and soldiers, and if I had gotten closer to that damned temple I would've been cut down."

Desnia ground her teeth, but again, she failed to detect a lie from the Blue—as much as her pent-up rage would've liked her to.

"*That's* why you got close to Wellos!" Delvan exclaimed. "You stole his key to the general's office so you could steal that blade."

"It's not like it was hard," Mithya drawled. "After all, the man *is* kind of a sap."

They began volleying curses back and forth, Delvan going on about some ancient war, Mithya talking over him and making his words indistinguishable as she corrected his every assumption. Desnia dug her fingers into her scalp, trying to block the present voices that berated her senses with almost as much vitriol as the imagined ones. It reached a point where she could no longer take it, her own emotions being rallied by those of the argumentative Blues.

"Stop!" Desnia shouted. The idea of Nerio being lost in a bloodthirsty mob tore her apart, the uncertainty surrounding his survival or demise consuming her. She desperately wanted to go searching for him, to seek him out and protect him from himself. But an unseen, consoling hand rested on her shoulder, calming her erratic nerves. Mithya was right, they would never find Nerio in the thousands rampaging through the streets, they'd be lucky if they were still able to make it out of here themselves.

Assuming she and Delvan didn't tear each other apart first.

There were other, more immediate concerns they still needed to address. "If the tunnel is blocked," Desnia asked, "how are we going to get out of the city?"

"If this one's flooded, the others probably are too," said Mithya, her eyes still throwing knives at Delvan.

"Others?" asked Desnia. "How do you know about so many?"

There was a tense silence, Delvan audibly grinding his teeth while Mithya glanced between him and Desnia with arms crossed.

"Do you want to tell her?" asked Delvan.

"Tell me what?"

Delvan didn't give Mithya a chance to speak. "Mithya here—or whatever her *real* name is—is a spy. From Trethefen."

Oh, Masini said, *she's good. By the Greats, I never even suspected!*

Desnia did her best to blink away the surprise. A spy? Trethefen had always seemed a far-off place, more than even Brethefen. A place where old women said demons lived; somewhere she'd overheard fat, drunken men regaling heroic war stories from their great-grandparents to other fat, drunken men. Somewhere she thought of as more an idea than an actual place.

Is that how she seems to know about all I've kept hidden? Desnia wondered.

Mithya merely gave her a wry smile and slight shrug. Delvan appeared perturbed enough to spout off another round of rhetoric. Mithya's origins, however, were far less critical than their current situation, off-putting and question-raising as they might be.

"Enlightening," Desnia said, "but something to deal with later." Delvan grumbled but didn't argue. "What other ways are there out of the city?"

Mithya thought for a moment. "Aside from the west gate? None nearby that aren't probably underwater. And I don't know about you, but the irony of drowning in the desert *really* doesn't appeal to me."

"Then the west gate it is," said Desnia.

Delvan rubbed his worry-stricken face. "If anyone sees us—"

"We have to take that risk," Mithya agreed. "The guards are all hopefully dealing with the riots."

There wasn't time to stand around and argue, as Delvan appeared wont to do. Desnia was the first to grab her gear, leading the other two into doing the same. The three of them forced the door open, battling their way back into the storm's gales.

The going was slow, the water now flowing halfway to Desnia's knees. Wind swayed her side to side, the street dark as dusk with the sun continuing to hide behind the storm's wrath. The gate was less than a quarter mile away, the break in the wall normally visible above the roofline but obscured by the inundation of rain. The alleys to their left and right were blacker than the abyss. Desnia tried to avoid looking into that darkness, worried it might reach out and pull her into its sickly embrace.

She should know better, the rational part of her brain tried to say. But the fear, even buried and blocked by the effects of muted inanite, was unforgettable. She tried to hold her resolve, keeping her eyes fixed straight ahead. But a pair of alleys to their either side pulled at her attention in a way she couldn't ignore, though it was difficult to explain why. She just knew they hid something... terrible.

"Wait!" She had to shout to be heard. Delvan looked over his shoulder, but Mithya, walking in the lead, hadn't heard Desnia's call.

She was about to cry out again as shapes burst from the dark portals to their either side, dragging the shadows behind them like cloaks. Desnia's couldn't decide if the assailers were real or manifested from her addled mind. Instincts, honed over a life of running, spun her around to flee.

Delvan shouted and Mithya spun in surprise. They were real.

She found her path blocked, two more black figures charging from behind her, spears pointed downward. Desnia turned around, desperate for a way out, and saw Delvan facing two more spear bearers. He ripped the shroud from his sapphire as Mithya drew her short sword, blocking another soldier's sword strike with swift grace as her darksteel blade cut arcs and ribbons through the water-filled air. The sword flowed like a leaf twisting effortlessly in the wind, streaming in a black streak through the air with the precision and skill of a master. A nimble dodge and adroit upward cut felled her attacker, the slash sending blood spraying from his neck.

Delvan raised his hands to his either side, the air before his palms beginning to shimmer and glow. Steam hissed and spat from them as the spearmen began tightening the circle around them, cutting off their escape.

The flowing water's indiscriminate, dragging grasp hindering Mithya's footwork, delaying her spin to face her next attacker. He grabbed her from behind, and in a single, swift motion pressed a knife to her throat, shouting, "Stop! Don't do anything!" The spearmen halted, their glinting spear heads reflecting the flashes of lightning a few feet from Desnia's every side.

The young soldier's eyes pierced into Delvan with malice, and what Desnia could sense to be deep, burning jealousy. The light flickering at Delvan's hands dimmed, returning a cautious glare of his own at Mithya's captor. "Drop your sword!" the young man demanded. Mithya reluctantly released her grip, her short, straight sword falling into the running water with a *splunk.*

Desnia slowly stepped to Delvan's side, avoiding the floating corpse Mithya had left, eying the two spearmen behind them and glancing to the two flanking Mithya. They were trapped.

Her heart began pounding against her chest. She couldn't be captured. Never again would she be put into one of those cells.

She would die first.

"Wellos!" Delvan screamed to the man holding Mithya hostage. "What're you doing?!"

Ohh, this is not good, Masini said. *Des, do something!*

"I'm thinking," she said under her breath.

Wellos's jealousy was only matched by the anguish gushing from him, tears pouring from red eyes in floods as ferocious as the ones rushing over her feet. "I knew you were trying to take her away from me!" the man's voice cracked. "I knew it!"

Mithya tried speaking, keeping her voice calm and barely audible over the storm. "Wellos, my love, this isn't what it looks—"

"Shut up!" The blade pressed tighter to her throat, and Desnia saw a trickle of violet blood blending with the runnels of rain. Her heart beat impossibly faster—finding herself overly concerned for the Blue's well-being. "I'm done listening to you! When the general learns what I've done... I *love* you! How could you betray me?! Betray *us*?!"

He does not seem, uh, stable, said a concerned Masini.

"Listen to me!" Delvan shouted, looking at the surrounding soldiers. "I am a knight of the Sapphiric Court! I order you to stand down and arrest this man!"

"Don't even try it!" Wellos exclaimed. "You're not a knight! You're a traitor! I saw you break *her* out of prison, and I made them well aware of your crimes. You'll all hang!"

A blurred vision came to Desnia's mind, muddled and more of a feeling than the clarity she'd had of late, the medicine still flowing through her. It was grief, and blood, and... fire.

"You need to do something, Del," she said as loudly as she dared.

"Let her go, Wellos," Delvan attempted to placate. "If it's me you want, then take me and let them go—"

"NO!" Wellos screamed. "You always thought you were so much better than me! That you could steal her from me just because of your title! This is all *your fault*!"

Maybe don't let Lord Delvan speak anymore, said Masini. *Just a thought.*

Desnia had to try something, anything, before this man fully lost his mind. "Listen!" she said, the sound of a chanting roar rising above the storm. "There's a mob coming, right now! They're hunting for soldiers, like you. If we don't get out of here now, they'll kill us all!"

That's your argument? You and people, I swear...

Through the downpour, behind Mithya and Wellos, Desnia saw the flicker of torches and seething of shadows. She turned her head, where another amorphous mass, dotted with lights like malevolent fireflies, was approaching from behind. The sounds of wood smashing, jeering, and clay shattering rose to a clamor—the wave of people a destructive force working in tandem with the unstoppable, erosive power of hammering water.

Desnia's throat tightened, choking her breath. They would soon be crushed between the crowd's brutish rage, a fact that Wellos seemed to recognize in his own frightened eyes.

"Listen to her, Wellos," said Delvan. "It's the only way!"

The fear painted onto Wellos's face dissipated, a calm acceptance softening it. *Oh, no,* she thought.

"No, it's not," he said. Mithya's face snarled at the response, twisting and making the bleeding at her throat worsen. "No one can love you like I can," he said, his lower lip beginning to tremble. "I won't let them try."

He pulled the blade from Mithya's throat and raised it high. Desnia's heart sank into the water, eyes bulging as she tried to scream, to beg, to fight—*anything* to stop what was happening.

But there was nothing she could do, and before she or Delvan could react, Wellos plunged the knife into Mithya's stomach. The Blue's eyes went wide as Desnia, Masini, and Delvan cried out in shared horror. Wellos stared at them, outpouring tears, and shouted an order to the encircling soldiers.

"Kill them!"

Chapter Forty-Eight

If he was with this girl, then he is undoubtedly acting as her guide.
Reunite them at once.

Go! Run!" screamed Captain Gernbard, giving Nerio a shove in the back and pressing him forward.

Their accompanying guards had beaten a path through the hectic mass of flailing arms and panicked screams. Nerio had to dodge over-reaching hands as he slipped between their backs, bouncing off their hidden armor and jarring him from side to side as he snaked through.

They had opened a narrow gap to a yet-unfilled street, and as Nerio emerged after shoving his way past the last of the soldiers, he turned back to see the chaos rising behind him, the madness bringing forth the rain and the gods' fury.

The steps of the Devapuram were covered in a disarray of clashing forces—peasant against soldier, tools against blades. He could no longer see the stone treads through the press of bodies, the rain carrying their spilling blood down the massive stairs and over his feet, tinging his robe's edges red. Those that did not fight had begun to spread, chanting for their freedom, for their lives, for their rights.

And for the heads of their oppressors.

Doors were being broken down, looters filing in and raiding whatever precious valuables may be within. The few not afflicted by the havoc fled in terror—mother's guarding their children, husband's their wives, young their elders. Many were falling, trampled by the monster he'd created.

Nerio held himself, numbly watching as all he had worked for tore itself apart in a fit of widespread pandemonium. He had wanted peace, to assuage the people affected by the city's devastation and bring the gods' light back into their hearts.

The light which had now been smothered.

His certainty as to his divine selection for this role had been absolute, his convictions pure. But, as he watched the people's blood stain the white stone steps in a deep, gory red which no storm could hope to cleanse, he felt a tremor of uncertainty.

How could this be their plan? he wondered. *Unless it was I who misjudged. Was it me who went against their will? Is this punishment for my deviation?*

The gods could not be callous enough to allow for such destruction.

Could they?

Captain Gernbard broke through the gap and grabbed the awestruck Nerio by the arm. "We need to go! Follow me!"

Nerio was slow to respond, his eyes unable to turn away from the abominable sight as he was pulled, stumbling backwards. "I... I have to do something!"

"The only thing you can do right now is survive, Witness," said Gernbard, taking a cautious glance towards their rear. He continued moving them forward as he waved to a few of the soldiers working to hold the marauders at bay. A handful pulled back to join them, the rest holding the mob back with the makeshift barricade of an overturned horse cart and swords pointed towards the crudely armed rioters. "Come, we'll flee through the north gate."

Nerio gave in to the pull of the old soldier's firm grip, unable to stop looking over his shoulder at the mayhem, tears diluting the rain. The sky cracked and rent asunder as Almedia shouted forth her rage at the destruction below. *Yet she takes more lives in her fury. What have you and your ilk done? Is it possible that you've... erred?*

No. No, this was something else. It had to be. He could not accept otherwise.

The overwhelming emotions were too much to bear. His mind blanked, his body performing the rote motions necessary to keep up with the men who now led and surrounded him. Whatever they told him to do, he would obey. He was clearly incapable of leadership, the ruckus behind them a clear reminder of what he'd always, deep down, known himself to be.

A failure.

Gernbard towed them farther down the street, until they reached the double-wide doors of a stable. He and another soldier flung the doors open and ran inside while Nerio stood on the street, staring off into the unseeable distance, face slack and devoid of emotion. Three guards stood around him, weapons pointed outward, warning the few stragglers on the street to stay away.

A few moments later, the captain emerged from the stables with two reins in hand, the horses tied to each saddled and bearing sacks filled near bursting.

Nerio stared at them for a moment, his mind slow to process. "They're... They were already saddled."

"Aye," replied Gernbard solemnly. "I hope you accept my deepest apologies, but I was... concerned, with this plan of yours, Witness. I thought it would be wise to have a means of escape, just in case."

Nerio felt the cavern in his chest grow larger, his heart shriveling to nothing. Not even his closest followers had faith in him. Of course, it was a miracle they had believed in him in the first place.

All he could manage in response was a slow nod.

"I wish it had worked," Gernbard said. *Is that a tear? No, must be the rain. He would not weep for what he knew would fail.* "I really do, sir, and you almost managed it. We'll punish Meneham for this betrayal another day."

The captain helped Nerio into a saddle. The horse jittered as he settled down, the rolling thunder making it uneasy.

"We'll head north," said Gernbard as he prepared to pull himself into the other saddle. "There's a small town a few days ride away, I know some people there. We can lay low there until—"

There was a commanding shout, one that reverberated off the soaking walls and shocked them all into silence. "I order you to stop!"

Through the veil of rain and spraying mist, Nerio saw a wall of black, its parapet the helms of soldiers, its towers the shafts of spears. Feet marched forward in a uniform beat, splashing through the floodwaters. At their lead was the lean, imposing frame of a greying commander, his stature firm and rigid. His crisp uniform was stained in blood, and upon a raise of his fist, the shielded block at his back came to a unanimous halt.

Nerio knew, instinctively, this to be Lord General Rosethorn.

Nerio saw Gernbard's shoulders slump. Their eyes met, the captain's looking as defeated as Nerio felt. Gernbard flicked his gaze to the road leading north, empty aside from the wall of water dropping from the sky, and then stepped closer to Nerio's horse, who wouldn't stop twisting around in circles as it trembled with each rumble from the black sky.

"I'm sorry, sir," Captain Gerbard replied, "but I can't do that."

"We've served together a long time, Captain," the stern-faced general replied, "but do not think that my patience is limitless! That *boy* is responsible for the carnage tearing through my city, and I will see him answer for it!"

A small trickle of fear dripped into Nerio's chest, but the numbness quickly snuffed it out, keeping him hollow.

"He's not, sir. His words were twisted, his message abused—"

"His message?! Do you know the *truth* about his message? This criminal he calls 'Messiah' might indeed have committed the acts he claims, but do you know what is omitted from those tales he weaves?"

Gernbard remained silent. Nerio's stomach suddenly returned and constricted in a nauseating twist. *No, gods, please.*

"His 'Messiah' *started* the fires, Captain. The woman you've worshipped was the one who delivered this city's destruction. Now, and this is my final offer, hand him over, or I'll be forced to take him myself."

Nerio couldn't breathe. He'd gone cold, his horrified eyes staring at the captain while his horse continued to shift. The man who'd been his closest companion these past weeks, the foundation to Nerio's pillar of beliefs, would now see Nerio for what he was. What he, moments ago, had realized himself to be.

A fraud. Nothing more than a false voice of the gods.

The crippling of his soul was now utter and complete. He had known lows in his life, but this was a pit deeper and darker than any he could've imagined.

Gernbard stood silently for a moment, the rain beating on him as though a statue. He did not turn to look at Nerio, his face and gaze fixed forward.

Nerio would not allow anyone else to die this day because of him. The Lord General was right, he *deserved* this. He would present himself to Rosethorn, and surrender in exchange for the release of his friend. A friend he knew he'd forever lost.

Nerio began to dismount, but before he could pull his leg over the back of the saddle, Gernbard replied to Rosethorn. "Serving you has been an honor, Lord General, but I have found something more. A way to complete my life in ways service to you cannot. Forgive the disrespect but, frankly, sir, I don't believe a gods-damned word that you've said."

What?

The horse reared as it turned to another clap of thunder, facing Nerio and the mount north. His visage was one of shock, having been dumbfounded by the captain's words. *He doesn't know what he's done!*

"Captain!" Nerio shouted, his voice shaken. "Don't do this—"

Gernbard turned and looked at Nerio, his chin held high, face glowing with reverent surety as he cut Nerio off. "Messiah and Her grace upon you, Witness." He brought his hand down with a loud *slap* as it hit the rump of Nerio's horse. With a terrified neigh, the horse reared and then broke into a gallop as it carried him north towards the distant gate, nearly throwing Nerio from the saddle.

"No!" Nerio shouted, watching over his shoulder as Gernbard gave him a farewell nod, and then turned to face the outraged general and advancing wall of wood and steel.

Nerio tried frantically to pull on the reins, tugging the bit deeply into the horse's mouth, but a succession of thunder sent ear-splitting terror into the beast, and it refused to cease its flight.

He looked back over his shoulder, tears flowing in rivers, his throat choked and chest heaving. There were flashes of steel, the men who'd stood at his side falling to the points of spears. And in the flashing strobes of lightning, Nerio witnessed Captain Gernbard take his drawn sword and face the Lord General.

Who, with two inhumanly powerful strikes, cut his friend down.

Nerio tried to scream, but his constricted throat allowed for nothing but the sobs of grief. He went limp as the scared steed carried him onward to the gate, staring at the crumpled figure of the captain until it was engulfed by the storm.

Just like his faith.

Chapter
Forty-Nine

If Asta's prison was constructed as I suspect, his knowledge of the Astral Plane will be vital. Do whatever you must to secure their freedom. For without it, the realm shall fall.

Violet blood gushed from Mithya's punctured stomach, diffusing into her drenched, silk shirt as it ran in thick streaks over the blade and Wellos's hand. Time slowed to a crawl as Desnia met the Blue's shocked eyes—her own filling with anger, despair, and... regret. Though she had no reason to and had told herself there was no love lost between her and the Truthsayer, she felt a mirrored, excruciating stab in her soul, sharp as any blade.

The world came rushing back from her halted instant in the form of spears being thrust towards them, their points cutting ruthlessly through the falling drops of rain. She had to pull her eyes from Mithya, tracking the fast-approaching glints of steel, her heart attempting to burst from her chest.

"Get down!" screamed Delvan.

It was then Desnia noticed the heat rising from him, the water flowing around her warming as the current carried it from the bubbling pool surrounding Delvan's feet. The air around him shimmered, the rain landing on his armor spitting with a steaming *hiss*. As the spears' sharpened edges lunged forward, his hands extended to his either side, a righteous fury burning in his eyes.

Their would-be executioners' faces turned ghostly, and their attack fell fatally short.

An explosion of light, illuminating the encompassing buildings like the day's sun, burst from Delvan's palms. The twisting spirals of flame spouted outward, reaching beyond the length of the soldier's spears and consuming whatever lay in their voracious path. The blaze pressed its ferocious heat against Desnia's skin, and she felt the rain's damp evaporate in a searing flash.

She dropped into the water, attempting to submerge herself as Delvan twisted and flung his fury. The orange and white inferno roared with a cry of vengeance, and Desnia felt it pass over her exposed back as she forced as much of body as she could below the racing current.

As quickly as Delvan had ignited the outburst into existence, it faded back to the cool dark of the falling storm. Desnia pulled her head up from under the water with a gasp, her back steaming, to find the roaring onslaught replaced with the keens of death. The four spearmen were engulfed in flames, the immolation persisting despite the rain or the water they attempted to plunge into—falls from which they did not rise.

Delvan's vortex of incineration had avoided Mithya and Wellos, leaving the Truthsayer with a face of gritted agony, and the jealous lieutenant petrified. Desnia threw herself forward, trying to sprint the short distance between herself and the pair while Delvan, panting and hunched forward, began forming a glowing sphere above his upturned palm.

Before either of them was able to act, however, Wellos regained what little sense he had, his face returning to its dark shade of envy. With a piercing cry from Mithya, he jerked his blade free from her gut and raised it once more. Desnia was helpless. Delvan could do nothing without risking setting Mithya ablaze. Still, she had to try, urgency pressing her forward as—

In a spray of water, Mithya snapped her head back, her skull deftly shattering Wellos's nose with a *crunch*. The soldier cursed and stumbled, releasing his grip on the Truthsayer, who took a few hindered steps forward, clutching her abdomen, the profuse bleeding dripping through her fingers and blending with the rain.

Desnia leapt sluggishly forward as her feet dragged through the churning flow. She caught Mithya as she began to fall, letting out a grunt as the Blue's weight collapsed in her arms and nearly brought them both to the watery ground.

There was a loud cry of choking defiance, Wellos clutching his bloody nose and attempting to reach forward. "No! She's *mine!*"

"I wish you had listened to me, Wellos!" Delvan shouted. "I'll give you one—"

"Fuck you! I *won't* let you have her!" Wellos spat, blood sputtering from his lips. He raised the knife and careened forward, unyielding and determined.

He managed one step before combusting in a blinding ball of yellow, orange, and white.

The shrill screech he released was short, but the agony it etched in Desnia's mind would remain with her for the rest of her days. She could see his eyes, black against the white flames, staring at the crumpled Mithya. They were empty of hate, brimming instead with a deep longing. Not love—Desnia doubted he'd ever understood the meaning of the word—but an... infatuation. One he would take to his sodden grave.

Wellos collapsed into the water with a sizzle. Delvan slumped, shoulders rising and falling as he gulped massive breaths of air. They needed to get moving. Too much time had been lost already and, looking to Delvan, Desnia worried about how much more the Blue would be able to aid them.

Desnia tried to stand herself and Mithya straight, the Truthsayer's face flinching and rasping out, "Gah!"

"We have to go!" said Desnia, looking at either end of the street at the mob approaching like a rolling siege. A horde that claimed to be marching to propagate their cause in *her* name, without even knowing what she looked like. They would ravage her as they did everything else, the mindless fucks.

Mithya wailed as they took a few steps forward, doubling over in agony. Delvan grabbed her sword from the water, came to her side, and attempted to help but merely caused her to curse in further torment.

"Gods-damn it," said Delvan. "Listen, Mithya, I can cauterize the wound, but it's going to hurt like hell."

"Will that help?" asked Desnia desperately.

"It'll stop the external bleeding, but everything in her gut... Let's just hope she can heal fast enough to stop the internal hemorrhaging."

Hope is a strong word, in this case, said Masini worriedly.

There had to be a better way than torturing Mithya further. "Do you have any more cadentite?" asked Desnia.

Mithya shook her head, her face having lost its parlor and normal golden hue. "No, gave the last of it to you." Her voice sounded thin.

"Fuck," Desnia cursed.

"Do it, Sparky," Mithya hissed through barred teeth.

Delvan's lips turned into a narrow, white line. "Move your hand when I say, alright? Ready. Now!"

A spurt of blood sprang from Mithya's stomach as she removed her hand, Desnia feeling her weight press down forcefully onto her. Delvan quickly pulled the tear in her shirt wider before pressing his hand directly against skin. Blood flowed between his finger—Mithya's face turning sickly—until a glow of beaming light began to emanate through the viscous violet. Radiant lines grew bright between Delvan's fingers. The sound of bubbling and crackling turned Desnia's face green.

The scream from Mithya was enough to ripple the water.

It was all Desnia could do to hold the Blue upright, fighting against the curling of Mithya's stomach and the arching of her back. Fingers dug into Desnia's side as Mithya clutched her for support, straining as every muscle in her body tightened to the point of tearing.

Delvan pulled his hand away, revealing blackened, scorched skin beneath, raw and cracked like dried mud, dark red flesh filling the fissures from beneath and deepening with Mithya's every motion. Assuming they all lived through this ordeal, Mithya would bear a horrendous scar once fully healed.

The chants of the enraged riot drew nearer, their shouts turning to a single, continuous rumble. Looking through the rain-shrouded distance, Desnia searched for the west gate, but was unable to find the break in the city's wall. She had hoped they'd made more progress, but she suspected there was the better part of a quarter mile yet to travel—if not more.

"Come on, we need to move, before we're surrounded," said Desnia, trying to carry as much of Mithya's weight as she could, hobbling them forward through the canal that the street had become. For every step they took, the crowd drew four steps closer, packing every major causeway shoulder to shoulder. The darkened alleys to their sides hid possibilities—both of escape and capture—but were the only lanes where a visible threat didn't loom.

"This way!" Desnia said, turning them down an alley, weighing the risk of the unknown to be less severe than facing the crowd head on. Before they were fully engulfed by the alley's concealment, Delvan raised an arm and shot a stream of fire towards the throng, the licking flames falling short and simmering in the water. The mass slowed, but as the fire quickly dissipated into the torrent, they hesitantly moved forward, the lust for retribution still alight in their eyes.

The three of them began moving down the corridor. Desnia heard a *crash* from the alley's opposite end and quickly turned them down a branch between two buildings. The going was terrifyingly slow, and at their current pace Desnia began to have sickening doubts as to whether they could make it to the gate.

They passed another branching alley leading to the packed, torch-illuminated street. They just needed to slip past, discrete enough to avoid the notice—

"There!" came a shout from the crowd.

Fuck, she groaned internally. The Blues' cloaks had been forced to their backs, exposing armor and gem alike. *Might as well not be wearing them...*

Delvan raised a hand and another wide flare erupted forward, forcing the charging rioters back.

Desnia watched as Delvan hurled flames against the alley's walls, adhering to them with a dim, wavering flicker. The wind and rain fought for dominance over the blaze; one fueling, the other dousing.

"I can't keep this up much longer," said Delvan over the fire's roar and cracks of thunder. Desnia looked at him, her heart pounding in her ears. His face was frantic yet resigned as he glanced back at the throng and the few that were daring to cover themselves and run through the hot, licking tendrils. He opened one pouch of inanite, and then a second, to reveal blocks that were mostly white, their color drained by his conjurings.

Desnia wiped the ceaselessly running water from her eyes, glancing at Mithya's pale visage, her jaw tightly flexed as she too gazed out at the conflagration and what lay beyond. Mithya undid the similar pouch from her side and handed it to Delvan with a trembling arm. He took it with a nod and rummaged through its contents with fervor.

"Is it enough?" Desnia asked. Delvan looked at her, a grim expression turning his lips down beneath deeply set bags topped by reddened eyes. He shook his head.

Fuck, Desnia thought, *even if we had enough, he doesn't look like he's going to make it.*

Nonetheless, Delvan tied the bag around his waist and sent another fiery flurry down the alley, rekindling the dying barrier of searing heat. Beyond, she could clearly see the undeterred visages of the rabid throng.

"Come on!" Desnia called, trotting down the alley and away from their pursuers. Delvan was only going to be able to sustain their defenses for so long—until he quickly depleted his inanite, or his stamina. Their odds of success were crumbling beneath them by the second.

They traveled fewer than ten steps before Mithya keeled over in pain.

"Stop!" the Truthsayer pleaded.

"We can't stop," replied Desnia. "We have a long way—"

"Not with me you don't," cut off Mithya.

Desnia's heart sank, and she felt the color leave her own face. "Don't even fucking think about it!"

"We're not leaving you," said Delvan, his voice bitter, wavering, and guilt laden.

Mithya let out a weak chuckle, wincing halfway through. "You're never going to make it alive if I'm slowing you down, and you both know it," she said. "Don't look so cheery. I have no intention of dying because of *one* jealous lover, if you can even call him that."

Desnia should have felt satisfied, pleased, or any number of emotions upon hearing that the person who had been the catalyst of her mind's fracturing would stay here, wounded among an insatiable uprising. It infuriated her that these feelings lay dormant, and instead she was left with tears pouring from her eyes, her chest riven and heart removed.

What was wrong with her?

Mithya unbuckled the ornate, curved blade at her hip and pressed it against Desnia's chest. "Take this. When you reach my people outside the city, show it to them and say—" She let out a hiss of pain before taking a shallow breath. "Tell them 'for the blood of my ancestors.' Understand?"

Desnia didn't respond, her jaw flexed tightly shut, lips quivering. She was afraid that if she spoke, responded in some way, what was raging inside of her would somehow reveal itself.

"You'll die here!" cried Delvan.

"Thought that would make you happier, Sparky. And don't worry about me, I'll get myself out of this. Always do."

Desnia remained standing before her, frozen, any movement threatening to crack the dam. Even the approaching squall of shouts and curses quieted into the background. Every instinct was telling her to run and save herself, yet her muscles refused her. Left her paralyzed.

Uh, Des, said Masini, *you're not seriously considering this, are you?*

"No," she whispered.

"You have to," said Mithya, glancing down the dark alley. The beam of light from around the corner was shuddering, becoming little more than a candle's luminance. Delvan's blockade was dwindling.

Mithya locked eyes with Desnia. "You're the only hope we have of finding Asta. We don't have years or centuries to wait for another chance."

At what cost? Desnia wondered.

Desnia was still as a statue as Mithya straightened, one hand pressed to her wound, flinching as she pulled herself upright and took a step forward. Desnia's body was cold as stone, as if she was carved from it. Mithya reached a hand around the back of her head, fingers pressing against her hair. And, like a bust of marble, she was unflinching as Mithya leaned forward and pressed her lips to Desnia's.

Then, like a curse lifted, she melted on shaking knees.

There was nothing but the sound of pattering rain, her ears mute to the violence of thunder, the threats of lightning, and the tumult of those that would claim her their Messiah. The moment and its silent, warm peace, lasted longer than she could have dreamed, and shorter than her heart desired.

Mithya pulled away, a smile on her face, Desnia's a melted pane of wax.

There was a wince of pain in Mithya's eyes, but the smile persisted. "Go. I'll find you, I swear."

All Desnia could produce was a wilted sigh, her insides turned from chiseled stone to warm gelatin.

And then, of course, Masini ruined it. *By. The. Greats... That is going to forever live in my, uh, memories. Not sure I have a detailed enough image, though, maybe you should give it another go.*

"I absolutely do *not* understand women," grumbled Delvan from her side.

"No," Desnia faintly wheezed. "No, you... You don't get to do *that* and then just leave!"

"It's the story of my life," Mithya rasped with a wink as she doubled over in agony. "Now go, find Asta before you get any worse, before you no longer can."

Delvan—head twisting and turning as the rioters closed in—strode to a nearby door and attempted to wrestle it open. When it resisted, he kicked it, swinging it inward with a jarring clash. He came and put Mithya's arm over his shoulder while Desnia watched with shaking hands and welling eyes.

"See ya around," Mithya said with a forced smile as Delvan helped her limp away.

Wait, asked Masini worriedly, *Des, what are you doing? We can't leave her!*

"She's right," conceded Desnia, so quiet she could barely hear her own voice, "we'll never make it." *Not that I'm certain I want to anymore.* She was affixed to the ground, water impassively holding her in place as her desires warred. Despite knowing it would bring her demise, knowing that her chances of survival were likely null, she *wanted* to stay.

She was more broken than she'd thought.

Delvan carried Mithya into the building, and as she looked back at Desnia with her lip curled and eyes full of longing, he set her down, stepped out, and shut the door.

And Desnia began to sob.

There came the scraping sound of something being wedged against the door from inside, and Desnia wondered if it would be enough. Before she had a chance to ponder further, a chance to make a terrible, deadly decision, Delvan grabbed her wrist and towed her behind him as they left the alley behind.

Nothing she'd expected, yet everything she wanted, was being relinquished the moment she'd grasped it. Which, she realized in terrible irony, was her own tragic story.

Gods, did she hate her fucking life.

The water felt like lead around her feet, her mind in a frenzied haze as Delvan harried them between alleys, throwing occasional jets of ignited air to impede their would-be attackers. Eventually, as the instincts of a challenged upbringing took over, moving her without thought, she pulled her hand free and took the lead. Delvan, after all, was as adroit in winding through a city's maze of alleys, passages, and shortcuts as he was at understanding women, apparently.

Her mind did not contain thoughts, not as words or expressions. It filled with resentment, sadness, and a concoction of emotion whose presence was completely foreign. It was unfair. Everything felt dull and colorless. And she hated herself for allowing these rampant feelings to cripple her so.

Focus was needed now, although she found the distraction of fleeing for her life wanting in intensity enough to suffocate what she was experiencing.

They slipped between throngs, crossing streets in splashing sprints as gaps formed in the mayhem. They covered considerable ground, yet traveling in circles half the time meant it was taking an exhausting effort to reach the gate. Thirty minutes later—though her judgment of time was as skewed as everything else—the gate stood, tall and imposing, across the street from them.

With a press of wild insurrectionists before it.

Doors cracked and splintered as the horde attempted to steal weapons from the guard station. Soldiers worked to fight them back with ringing blows of steel, the crowd protecting themselves with tables and crates, forcing the resisting soldiers back with sheer numbers. The gate itself—a wide, thick collection of squared beams bound by steel—stood open, the empty road beyond fading into the rainy distance.

She and Delvan crouched behind a barrel, watching as the frenzy shifted, tore, and split like a sea's crashing waves. She glanced at Delvan, his face sagging, taking deep, long breaths. "Do you think you can spray enough fire to part a way for us?" she asked.

Delvan wearily hung his head, shaking it after a prolonged pause. "I'm out of inanite. I can feel some, in the ground below us, but I don't... I don't think I'll be able to do much with it. It's too deep."

Fuck, she thought.

"You go," Delvan said at her side. "You can blend better than I can. I'll... try to find another way around."

She glared at him, brow diving deep down towards her nose. "Shut the fuck up. I'm not leaving you behind." It was strange to say, considering the animosity she still held. But it was the truth, she couldn't—wouldn't—lose anyone else today.

Wouldn't be the first one you've left behind today, grumbled Masini bitterly.

"You know I didn't—" Desnia snapped her mouth closed, gritting her teeth as her body trembled with regret and rage. There was nothing she could say that wouldn't cause her to break down and collapse. Instead, she chose to ignore Masini and refocus on the few dozen yards that separated them from freedom.

Additional rebels were marching down the street to their either side, no more than a hundred feet in either direction. There was no room for subtlety. The well-honed skill of disappearing into a crowd was useless with a second person—especially one as recognizable as an armored Blue. She pulled Delvan's cloak back over his shoulders and grabbed Delvan's hand, legs tense. "When I tell you to, follow me as fast as you can."

"What? No, Des, we can't—"

Desnia saw their opportunity as a part in the shifting mass opened. She stood and began running, tugging hard on Delvan's hand and towing him forward before he could argue. They sprinted, splashing through the road and into the gap of looters.

With most of the people around them blinded by the infectious mania, they were able to follow the weaving path through the turbulent mass. They crossed half the gate's distance before Desnia had to avoid someone tumbling towards her, brushing her shoulder—and running straight into Delvan.

The reckless rioter grabbed his cloak for support, ripping it from Delvan's shoulders. Desnia heard a gut-wrenching cry from over her shoulder. "Blue!" Then, "A knight! Get them!"

Heads began turning, murderous shouts following closely behind. Their window began to narrow, and Desnia pushed her legs to their burning limits as she tried to force them forward. Shoving, ducking, and charging headlong began to become a losing battle, their pace slowing to a crawl.

A flare of heat battered her face, a spurt of flame spitting from Delvan's outstretched hand and surging over people's heads. It forced back some, but then quickly extinguished, sputtering like a well run dry, Delvan having no more left to give. She heard him pull his blade from the scabbard, streaks of black arcing through the air to her either side as Delvan brought the blade down upon the arms of those fearless enough to reach for them.

Blood sprayed as lightning streaked across the sky, shaking her to the core as it boomed. Their escape was now but a few feet away. Desnia drew the shorter of her two daggers from her side, pointing it at anyone who dared block their path, slashing at the ones stupid enough to test her mettle.

After leaving a trail of blood and appendages, they burst from the seething mass onto the road. Desnia was still pulling Delvan by his hand, not looking back as she broke into a full-on sprint, the water at their feet thinning as it spread into a delta beyond the gate's limits.

Their pursuers' calls and cries began to blend into the constant fall of rain—though far less expediently than she would've liked. A venturing glance over her shoulder left her feeling ill as she saw hundreds flowing out of the gate, chasing them with intent that was viciously clear through the haze.

They needed to find Mithya's people, flee from here with as much haste as could be mustered. Would they still be waiting by the flooded tunnel? Or would it have occurred to them to move to the only nearby exit still available? Desnia hoped that they had a shred of aptitude, but as she frantically scanned her surroundings, she struggled to see anything besides a muddled, blended horizon.

Delvan suddenly ripped his hand away, forcing her to slow and spin around. "What are you doing?!" she screamed, hardly hearing herself over the pounding of her heart in her ears.

He stepped a few paces off the road, standing atop an exposed crown of black rock. "Go!" he shouted, holding his hands with palms facing each other, a glowing mass forming between them as the stone beneath his feet began to blanch. "Find Mithya's people and get out of here! I'll buy you time!"

"You stubborn prick!" she shouted taking a few steps closer before staggering back as the heat radiating from Delvan became too much to bear. She was forced another step back, her skin burning, then another, shielding her eyes from the white ball of light growing like a newborn star between Delvan's shaking hands. She could see the strain on his face, the effort depleting him beyond his limits, his legs shaking and barely holding him upright. And in the distance the stampede of rioters slowed, uncertainty and fear gripping them as they were accosted by the warmth of Delvan's creation.

A jagged bolt of lightning plummeted from the sky and struck the rocky dunes in the distance, bringing the rolling landscape into clear view. Desnia's heart skipped a beat as she briefly saw—roughly a hundred yards from where they stood—two men among the muddy sands and low shrubs, attempting to rein in a group of horses.

They vanished back into the grey, stormy veil as the light faded, leaving their outlines burned into her sight. She looked from Delvan to where she'd seen them, the power burgeoning in his hands intensifying further. She was yet again left without choice. "Gods-damn you!" she screamed, though he didn't seem to hear.

The wet sand kicked up behind her as she sped away, running with all her strength towards the group she hoped were Mithya's awaiting people.

Des, said Masini, *are you really—*

"Fuck off!" she gasped between breaths. "I'm *not* leaving him," she shouted, leaving out the final word. "Too."

Delvan's hand-held inferno grew to such a potency that it lit her way. The sand was soft beneath her feet, denying her purchase to run faster. After a painstaking dash, she reached the collection of nervous horses and two shouting men. One held a bow with arrow nocked, the other gripped a sword's hilt. Both eyed her warily.

"We take none that flee—"

"Shut it!" Desnia barked, desperately trying to catch her breath. The first's bowstring began to tighten. "Listen, fuckers, Mithya sent me. I need your help—"

"Where is she?" the bowman asked.

"She... didn't make it." The words nearly made Desnia choke. "She gave me this," she continued as the men's eyes turned sour, grabbing the hilt of the dagger at her side and pulling it from the sheath. "Told me to say, 'by the blood of my ancestors.'"

The two men shared a look, concern in their eyes and hesitation in their posture.

"We don't have time for you to sit there and fucking think about it!" cried Desnia.

"We will discuss this later," said the same bowman after another pause from the pair. "For now, you speak true. We must hurry, before any follow—"

"No!" said Desnia with a curt hand gesture. "First we have to go get *him.*" She pointed back to the glowing sphere of light where she'd left Delvan, the clouds above now reflecting his beacon.

"We do not have time—"

There was a sudden, violent explosion of light. A plume of flames exploded forward from Delvan's location, a wide cone of death that reached taller than the west gate's crest and spread outward to engulf the wall in a blinding flash of searing death. The white of its core was decorated with tendrils of yellow and orange, dancing like leaves in the wind. The blast released a percussive wave that sent rain back towards the sky and outshone the brightest streak of lightning.

Desnia watched, wide-eyed, as a torrid wave of air rushed over her. The entire western gate became enveloped in a raging blaze, illuminating the area in a tinge of red even after the initial funnel of sorcerous fire faded away.

The men were rapt by the sudden inferno, and Desnia didn't bother to wait for their rediscovered attention before grabbing the reins from a near-by, unmounted horse and pulling herself into the saddle. She reached out and jerked the reins of another riderless steed from the hand of one of the dumbstruck assholes and dug in her heels, sending the skittish beast bolting forward towards the flames, the other following along as she yanked on its lead.

There was sudden shouting behind her, but she could hear little beyond the pounding of hooves, the wind whipping sharp thorns of rain into her face. She looked out to where Delvan had stood, the worst possibilities turning her gut into a tightened knot. The residual embers were still oppressive as she grew closer, the ground before the blaze's origin glowing a dull orange.

As she galloped onward, her eyes laid upon the crumpled figure of Delvan. He laid motionless on the ground, the field of sand before him now cooling, cracking glass, the stone beneath him a stark white. She pulled the horses to a halt, ignoring the heat bludgeoning her, and ran to his side.

His eyes were closed. Anything he'd been wearing that had not been dark-steel or dyed in the blue dust of sapphires was little more than singed car-bon. His sword was barely held in its charred, wooden scabbard, the belt it hung from frayed and cooked. Yet his skin and hair appeared normal, albeit dry—slowly becoming damp from the rain once more. Desnia reached down to shake him, hoping he was still alive, but her hand snapped back as it touched the scalding darksteel armor and burnt and blistered her fingers.

"Del!" she shouted as a herd of hooves thundered closer. She pressed her hand to his neck, his skin cool, and felt for a pulse. The breath she'd been holding was released as she felt the weak, thready beat of his heart. The rain splattered boiling droplets onto her as it fell and feverishly attempted to cool the armor, but despite the downpour, it remained impossibly hot.

Edges of her fingers burning as she failed to avoid touching the metal, she began to furiously undo the plates from him, pulling on the leather straps and releasing the buckles as she cringed with each new blister.

The voices of men reached her ears, and she turned to witness the arrival of her guides, their faces stricken with fear and shock. "Get down here and help me!" No one else was being left behind today, not while she was still alive to do something about it.

"My lady, we must—"

"*NOW!*"

They groaned and let out unintelligible complaints but dismounted and came to her aid. Before she could warn them, they, too, burned themselves on the slowly-cooling metal. One let out a string of curses in a language Desnia didn't understand, then ran to a horse and grabbed blankets—completely soaked through—and returned.

They draped the fabric over Delvan with a sizzle and hectically wrapped him. They continued shouting—orders or curses, it was difficult to tell—as they managed to lift Delvan from the ground and heave his limp body over the back of a horse. The layers of blankets kept the animal from being scorched, despite the fabric smoldering under his armor. They haphazardly tied him down, and Desnia hoped it would be enough to stop him from slipping off.

Desnia took a last look at the burning gate. The flames adhered defiantly to the stone and mud, the doors splintered and blazing. The fires did not spread beyond where Delvan had cast them, but they ate unceasingly away anywhere they'd succeeded in latching on to. Beyond the hellish portal she saw the boiling street, devoid of the people who moments ago had filled it. She shuddered to think what had happened to them in Delvan's effort to buy her time.

She wrangled herself into a saddle, one of the men taking the reins of the last unmounted horse—Mithya's mare—and spurred it into a gallop. Desnia and the other followed behind, riding through the storm and leaving the madness of the city behind them. Desnia accompanied the pair, not thinking of her coming obligations, nor the events that had led to this absconding. There was only room for one thought, one goal.

To get as far from Brethefen—and its memories—as possible.

Chapter Fifty

Stay safe and may your ancestors watch over you.

Svami

Orne smiled as Helona let out a small chuckle.

"You didn't really do that, did you?" she asked.

Orne couldn't help but quietly laugh, picturing the scene. "I did. Poor bastard had to walk all the way back to camp without any trousers after a fresh snow. Don't think he moved from the fire for two days after that."

Their words were whispered, quiet enough that even the soldiers on watch a dozen paces away couldn't hear them. His wants weren't about to overrule caution; their deadly enemy still roamed these slopes, after all.

"I think you take your wagers a little more seriously in Drunt than we do out here." Her voice was tired and edgy.

We take most things more seriously, based on what I've seen, he thought, but kept to himself, instead responding with a grunt.

There were a few hours left before sunrise, the waning glow of the moon their only light. It had taken no small amount of effort, but he'd finally managed to turn the conversation with Helona around. The thought of Steddus's recent desertion lingered, but every laugh and charmed response took a little more of the edge off.

He tried to think of a few more stories, avoiding the ones that were more well suited for a tavern or the dark humor of veterans. Although, Helona hadn't shied from any of the more.... visceral portions of his retellings—another trait on the growing list of reasons he enjoyed her company. Maybe this could be more than a basic connection of convenience.

The threat that still loomed in the mountains had not lost his attention, and his ears and eyes remained open. Yet again he found himself using the brief pause in conversation to assess what might prowl nearby.

Helona started talking, saying something about some post or another she'd been stationed at. Orne didn't hear most of it, his gaze having drifted and fixed upon something in the distance, further along the mountainside. With the way the moon had shifted in the sky, he thought he could now faintly see a glow, nearly imperceptible, in the distance.

Soft and diffused, the strange light dissipated just above the crest of a rolling hillside, perhaps five hundred paces away. Assuming it wasn't a trick of shadows and sleep deprivation.

Orne debated going to investigate, not wanting to abandon the conversation at hand. It was probably nothing.

Unless it wasn't.

Gods-damn it, he groaned as something itched at the back of his mind, driving him to scout the light's source. It was the responsible thing to do—which was tremendously annoying. *Maybe I should send someone. On second thought, most of them don't know their ass from their face.* He groaned again. Was it too much to ask to have soldiers under his command with a modicum of competency?

He stood up, Helona cutting off whatever she was saying. "Somethin' wrong?" she asked.

"Come with me." It was best to take some backup in case they ran into anyone unexpectedly. Might as well take someone he *wanted* to be around. The rest of these idiots were more apt to get him killed rather than helping.

He heard her shuffling feet scraping along the stone behind him. "We'll be back," he told the guards as he passed them. He prodded one in the shoulder, trying to pull them from their lethargy. "Don't leave until I return." The sentry gave a mumbled response and half-effort salute.

Careful of the slope to his side, he crept along a path that wound beyond the rock shelf they'd camped on. Down to his left, the path switchbacked into darkness akin to coal, the keep an ember in the distance. The rolling incline before him extended until it came to the escarpment of an adjacent mountain, and to his right the gentle climb rose to a scramble of boulders, dumped by the many avalanches of winter. The nestled valley was, fortunately, easy to traverse. Orne was able to take confident strides, knowing that what laid to his left was little more than a gentle descent, and not the cliff face they'd followed earlier that day.

The scree crunched beneath his boots, the sound falling strangely dead in the dry mountain air. They stopped occasionally to listen for anyone nearby, although their surroundings remained eerily absent of a whispering breeze or shifting stones, the mountain notch claiming the noise for itself. As they drew closer, the glow became brighter, giving a matte reflection off the abutting walls of rock. Cresting the knoll in a crouch, Orne's eyes glistened in the reflection of what lay before him, and he heard a slight gasp from Helona.

A field sprawled before them. Rolling crests rippled outward, the rocky surface covered in low, stemless plants, resembling a stocky cactus. They reached as far as Orne could see, covering acres of hillside. The most startling sight, however, was the ground beneath their thick, wide leaves.

It was glowing.

The purple hue shone from miniscule, powder-like specks on the ground, scattered like stars in the night sky. The subtle ambiance reflected its serene essence off Orne's grudging features and off Helona's dumbstruck face. *She clearly doesn't know what she's looking at.*

Orne enlightened her. "It's cadentite." *Which somebody has gone through the effort of grinding into dust and spreading through this field.* He recalled Kolden complaining—as he often did—about how grueling it was to pulverize the dense stone. Actually listening to his brother might have helped him in this instance, but he tended to drone and try to sound smarter than he was. *Probably didn't say anything important anyway.*

"Huh?" asked Helona. "Oh, right. Sorry, sir, I've just never seen so much in one place..."

"Not surprising. Shit's pretty rare." *Kolden would kill for what's laying on the ground here. Then, so would several others.*

"No, I meant the, uh, plant."

"Oh." Taking a long look around, he carefully approached one of the nearby crops, removing his helm and inspecting it closely. Not wanting to appear uninformed, he simply nodded. "There's a lot of it. Makes me wonder who's tending to it."

Helona came to his side, eyes flitting across the arrangement of plantings, unable to pull her gaze away from them. "Iguan's tough to grow. Or, so I hear," she rapidly added.

Iguan? Disdain curled his lip. *Those fuckers down in the keep must be growing it. I knew Villera was rotten, same with the captain probably. Gods, this field must be worth a king's ransom.* Orne's fist clenched into a ball as he thought of the soldiers that had died merely to keep the captain's supply of ale—which he didn't even share—flowing. He now hated Villera even more, which he hadn't thought possible. He was going to have to contact the general. The garrison had fallen further into the dredges than expected.

"What do you want to do, sir?" Helona asked from his side, her finger tapping her leg where it rested. Their discovery made him uneasy, too. The lack of guards was concerning—they were either sleeping, or the keepers of this field did not expect it to be found.

"Until morning, we do nothing," he replied. "Right now, our silhouettes would be visible from half a mile away if we started walking through this, assuming they're not already. We'll set up a watch to see if anyone comes, then we—"

The clatter of sliding rubble from behind them spun Orne around in a whirlwind. In a blink his sword was pulled from its scabbard, his stance wide and firm. Helona caught up a second later, drawing her rapier with a bewildered expression on her face.

Three men in full armor stood on the mounded ground from where he and Helona had descended. One held a spear, another a loaded, leveled crossbow, and the last held a sword—along with a despicable smile.

"Steddus," grumbled Orne, eyes scanning for anyone else that might be hidden in the distance. "I had hoped you'd done us all the favor of jumping off a cliff face."

"And give you the satisfaction?" Steddus replied surly, waving his sword. "No. The only one who's going to gloat today is me, right after I cut your gods-damned eyes out."

"You can fucking try. No Villera? No, of course not," he growled. "He seems like the type who would only fight if it was fixed. That's why he sent his bitch, because you're *expendable.*"

"Just like every other noble: a pretentious, overconfident asshole, expecting the world to bow to you."

"Just the pissants whose ass I kick," Orne replied, his off hand slowly drawing the short knife strapped to his waist behind his hip. "Don't even have the balls to fight me yourself again? Can't say I'm surprised you brought two others."

The crossbow was his priority, without his helm—which he was kicking himself for removing—he was too exposed. The one with the spear was second.

Steddus, he would save for last.

The man's face twisted slightly at the jab but remained haughty and shadowed in the pale light. "I shoulda known you couldn't count, you giant oaf."

What's he talking about? Orne thought frantically as he looked around for others. Were there bowmen hidden in the dark, arrows aimed at him?

"Helona, lass," said Steddus in a creepy way that he probably thought was smooth and enticing, "help us out here. This is where you belong, after all."

Orne snorted. How delusional could this ass-wipe be? "Your mother drop you on your head as a child? She's obviously not going anywhere," Orne retorted. He debated throwing the knife right then and there, but, despite the bravado, being outnumbered was never a good scenario. All it took was one lucky bastard to land a strike or sink an arrow and you could be done for. There was also the risk to Helona if he just started swinging.

"Fuck off, Steddus," said Helona, shifting her feet and fidgeting with her grip. "You should..." she gulped. "You should get out of here before you do something stupid. No need for anyone to get hurt today."

Orne grinned, but Steddus wasn't fazed by Helona's words of caution. "You haven't heard my offer yet. It's a good one. I don't think you'll be able to turn it down." Steddus pointed his sword to the field at Orne's back. "Help us with this arrogant prick, and the boss will let you take as much iguan from this field as you can carry. Assumin' of course that you don't tell no one about where you got it, or what happened to the lieutenant here."

What kind of pedestrian nonsense was this? "*That's* your argument? You really are a fucking rat, Steddus."

The vermin retained his confidence, but Orne could see the reluctance in the other two—weak knees, sweaty brows, dodgy eyes. Steddus might claim superiority, but clearly he was a poor judge of capabilities.

Silence hung in the deadened air, none daring to make the first move. Well, that was fine. Orne was plenty happy to be the initiator, as they tended to be the victors—though this scenario would put that to the test. He gripped the handle of his dagger between his finger and thumb, gauging the distance between him and the bowman, how much space the spearman could cover in a short burst, and—

There was a movement to his side, and he saw Helona shifting, turning to face him, rapier raised to his face.

There was a protracted silence, his brain obstinately refusing to process what was happening. He was frozen, his mind slow to remind him to blink, or breath through his hanging jaw. *She... can't be.* "What are you *doing*?!" he growled, slowly turning his head to face her.

"Sorry, sir," said Helona, angst painted on her face, covering a foundation of guilt and self-loathing. She swallowed hard, having a difficult time looking at him, her eyes still drifting to the plants at their feet. "I... I told you. I'm... sick. And it's the only thing that lets me feel something 'sides the pain."

Orne felt a rage building in him, staring down the length of the narrow blade and glaring at eyes that couldn't meet his own, their shame cowering to his fury. He felt his hands begin to shake, his vision tunneling, and teeth grinding together. How could she? Turned against him… because of a gods-damned *plant*?!

He hated that he'd cared about someone willing to turn on him.

He hated Steddus for succeeding.

He hated, most of all, being betrayed.

Craven bastards.

His vision went red as he spun and threw the blade pinched between his fingers, sending it whistling at the soldier holding the crossbow. It sank into his eye with a spurt of blood and force enough to violently whip the man's head back. Orne brought his armored bracer to the side of his face as the man's body spasmed, causing the latch on the bolt to release. The arrow darted out, wild and undirected, striking and skidding harmlessly off his chest plate.

There was a flash of steel to his side. Helona lunged at him, striking with her rapier's point at his unprotected neck. He tried to lean back and angle away from the stabbing thrust, but the knife throw had left him twisted. Awkwardly contorting his head backwards, it was all he could do to have the sharpened tine avoid his neck, but he couldn't dodge it altogether.

The heat of unrecognized pain burned hot from his cheek, and he felt the grinding of metal against his teeth. The needle-like tip of Helona's sword pierced through the side of his mouth, biting into his molars and slicing his tongue as she reached the limits of her arm's extension. Adrenaline and ire prevented him from experiencing what should have been excruciating agony as his mouth drowned in a rush of his boiling blood.

Helona's short reach brought her within the breadth of his own. He swung a backhanded fist, the darksteel gauntlet connecting to the woman's jaw with a peal. She flew to the side, ripping the rapier from his face and widening the wound, landing in an unmoving heap among her precious fucking plants.

Orne could feel the blood running down the side of his face and neck, trickling under his armor. The burning in his mouth was like scalding tea, but there was no pain—it had fled him, as his attackers should have done.

Steddus and the spearman finally regained their senses after seeing their two comrades fall within the span of a few heartbeats. To their credit, the terrified scoundrels had enough brains to attack in tandem. Steddus raised his sword high above his head, forcing it down in a wild, powerful swing aimed at Orne's unhelmed skull. In unison, he saw the spear being impelled towards his flank. A decision—obvious as it was—needed to be made.

And it was going to fucking hurt.

Orne brought his sword up in an arc to deflect Steddus's blow, redirecting the flailing blade past him. The momentum caused Steddus's strike to drive into the ground, leaving him hunched at Orne's side. Which would've been ideal for a riposte of his own, had the end of a leaf-tipped spear not been lanced into his side.

The mail between the front and rear plates of his cuirass prevented the point from piercing him too deeply, but a few of the links must have broken as a pain even his rage couldn't ignore ignited in the side of his abdomen. Orne let out a loud grunt, his teeth tightly fusing together.

Steddus was still attempting to regain his balance at Orne's side. The rodent was going to be a nuisance if Orne remained within the spear's extended reach. He did what he could think of in the moment.

And spit a spray of blood in the man's face.

Steddus stumbled back, eyes closed as his hands hysterically tried to wipe the coating of dripping red from them. In his clumsy stupor, he tripped on a bushel of iguan, falling backward and landing on his ass with the grace of a wounded boar.

Orne clutched the haft of the spear and pulled it from his side, ignoring the feeble resistance of its wielder. Once the oversized thorn was removed, he yanked on the shaft with all the strength he could muster, dragging the person holding it forward.

Why did these idiots never let go?

With a blur of inky steel, Orne slashed his blade across the neck of the wide-eyed traitor, sending him to the ground with a gurgle.

Orne turned to find Steddus recovered, standing there, blade held in trembling hands before him, like a child struggling with their parent's sword. He spat another mouthful of blood to the ground, picturing what he would do to the contemptuous fuck. A quick death wasn't enough. It needed to be more than that.

Slow.

Agonizing.

And devoid of mercy.

"Come on then," said Orne with a voice like gravel, blood flying from his lips like spittle.

Steddus's entire body was quivering now, eyes more white than black. The insolent bastard stared, unblinking, at Orne, his face pallid and knees beginning to buckle. Then he did what Orne should've expected.

He turned and ran.

No, you're not leaving here, thought Orne as he pulled another knife from his belt and flung it. The double-edged blade *thumped* into Steddus's back through the leather armor, dropping him to the gravelly earth. Orne strode over, breaths gushing from flared nostrils, chest heaving as his lungs fought to cool the furnace of his burning hate. He kicked Steddus, rolling him onto his back and digging the blade deeper. The man was gasping like a fish out of water, bloody bubbles at the corners of his mouth.

Orne wasn't one to watch combatants suffer.

Normally.

In this instance, he reveled in standing over the fallen, feeling disappointed that he couldn't make his anguish last longer. That he couldn't bring to bear the pain that he felt, deep in his soul. He had stolen from Orne an opportunity for something better. He'd revealed the nature of someone he had clearly misjudged, the bitch leading him on all this time, deceiving him. Then he'd used it as leverage, as a way to steal away her illusion of choice.

They would both pay, he'd see to that.

Orne raised his boot, seeing the fear in Steddus's eyes as the sole hovered over his face, his choking turning to convulsions. He flexed his leg, ready to stomp—

There was a snap. The familiar sound of a quarrel being released from the taut string of a crossbow spinning Orne's head around.

The first thing his eyes laid upon was Helona, standing there with a crossbow in hand, loaded and aimed directly at him. His eyes turned harder, reddening them as the embers of his rage burned into his already bloodthirsty vision.

Of course she was going to shoot him from behind, there wasn't an honorable bone in that witch's body.

She swayed slightly, a shocked expression draped over her face. The weapon fell from her hand and fired harmlessly into the ground, revealing a splotch of blood pooling around the fletching of a bolt protruding from her chest. She looked at him, sorrow in her eyes—as if begging for forgiveness, which she was unworthy of—as she collapsed to the ground, life escaping her with a final, languid breath.

Orne's breathing grew more rapid. Emotions warred within. But he wouldn't allow the pain to surface. No, only ardor would rise a victor in this battle, with weakness and doubt being dispassionately culled. She had gotten what she deserved—and come far too close to finishing him off in true, spineless fashion.

Which raised the question: Who had shot her?

Orne spun his head as a figure came scrambling forward from over the nearby knoll, the gravel crunching beneath his feet. Orne lowered his sword.

The short, mousey figure approaching could only be one person.

"Kolden!"

"Orne! I got here as fast as I—" His brother stopped in his tracks and gawked at his bloody visage. "Who tried to make your face look pretty? Fuck, they really—"

"She was *mine*!" Orne boomed, pointing to the fallen Helona.

Kolden looked from Orne to her, a dumb expression on his face. "She was about to *shoot* you, Orne. You could try fucking *thanking* me!"

Orne felt his throat tighten, dry and choking despite the blood pooling in his mouth. He struggled to form words expressing what Kolden had stolen from him. What this *night* had stolen from him. "You don't understand!" is all he was able to expel, along with a bloody mist from his twisted tongue.

Kolden's head drew back, his good arm tossing out to the side. "Right, next time I'll let them stick you from behind. My bad." Orne's sword began shivering, the grip creaking as he gripped it mindlessly. "Look, we need to get out of here," Kolden continued. "Villera and the captain are going to have the entire castle turned on us soon and—" Kolden's eyes turned to circles as he fixed on the field at Orne's back, only now realizing what was there. "Is that *cadentite*?!"

"I'm not running," Orne grated, ignoring his brother's fixation. "I'm going to go down there and kill Villera and the captain and whoever else is responsible for growing this shit." He pointed to the accursed plants at his side.

Kolden struggled to take his eyes off the field. He walked as he responded to Orne, leaning down and picking up some of the dust between his fingers. "We can't take them all on, Orne. Not by ourselves and..." Kolden managed to pull his eyes from the glowing sand, realizing he'd found lead that was covered in gold leaf. He flung a pinch of it back on the ground with a sneer. "Is that bad?" Kolden asked, pointing to Orne's side.

Orne pressed his hand to where the mail's links had snapped, pulling it away to reveal the dark stains of blood running down his fingers. "Looks like it."

"Gods-damn it," Kolden hissed. "Alright, we need to get out of here. Stop. Don't fucking say a word. Even with you charging in there like a bull with a dog biting its balls, we don't stand a chance. All this fucking iguan has the entire castle in the lieutenant's and captain's pockets—"

"I fucking know."

"—and they'll probably cut us down as soon as we get there. I have a plan though."

"If it doesn't involve Villera's and Mathis's heads on pikes, I don't want to hear it."

"It will. Eventually. But first, I need you to come with me."

"Why?" Orne had no interest in blindly following his brother's orders. He needed to be reminded of that. Frequently.

Kolden let out an exasperated sigh. "*Because*, I need your help."

"With?"

"For fuck's sake! Why are you being like this? I need help with Phrenwa, Orne. I, sort of, broke him out..."

"You *what*?!"

Kolden rolled his eyes. Idiot. "I don't need a lecture. He can help us, and I trust him a lot more than I do anyone from the gods-damned castle. So, are you going to help me, or are you going to keep acting like a fucking inquisitor?"

Orne frowned, his face cutting deep trenches into his skin, the stinging pain in his cheek and mouth beginning to surface. Kolden had a point—although he still thought breaking Phrenwa out was asinine—no one at the keep could be trusted, not if their brains were all addled by the same disease as Helona's. If Phrenwa's men were still holed up in these mountains, it could provide him the opportunity to eventually seek justice, though the burning oil in his veins craved vengeance now, while the heat of battle was fresh.

A dizzy feeling had him reconsidering the urgency, blood beginning to run down his leg.

"Fine." Orne would help his brother, but he refused to admit his plan's validity. The last thing he needed tonight was anyone else gloating.

They collected weapons and what little supplies the fallen soldiers had on them. Orne considered going back to his squad and grabbing what he could, but there was no way to know if Steddus had sent someone to convert them to his machinations. After collecting what he could, he walked over to Steddus.

The fucker had expired, mouth frothing with crimson bubbles. Orne pulled the knife from his back and then took one last look at the vile excuse for a soldier, wishing that he could have watched as the man suffered and been the one to inflict his last moment of agony. Instead, he lied here, taken quickly by Strigi's owl, denied the torture he deserved.

What a gods-damned shame.

END PART 3

INTERLUDE

Riding the storm's midnight winds upon a demon's wings, it arrived.

Smiyta had not, even in his most repellent nightmares, laid eyes upon such a creature. Beside him, the normally impassive Ksatri gripped his mace's handle firmer in his muscle-bound hand, feet shifting in the rain's puddles.

The creature had shaken the flat, wooden roof upon its landing. Sitting on its haunches, its strange, slitted eyes sat level with his own. Its motionless head had the features of a lion's, its mass broaching ursine immensity. Unnervingly, it simply stared at them, devoid of emotion, as its serpentine tail restlessly flicked from side to side.

"Do you think it's a demon?" Smiyta asked his partner.

"I think it's what we need," grumbled the brutish man.

"Yes, I suppose so." Smiyta's lips peeled back from ear to ear. "What do you think would happen if we told it to hunt during the day as well? We have a lot of ground to cover, after all."

Ksatri shrugged.

"Ever insightful, old friend. The instructions *were* rather specific in that regard, yet it seems such an odd demand." He narrowed his eyes as lightning flashed above, the crack of thunder rising above the calamity spreading through the streets in the rest of the city. "Do you think it would know what I was saying, were I to try? The eyes, they seem... intelligent. Or do you think it's more like a dog?"

"Found us."

"How you fit so much wisdom in so few words baffles me, Ksatri. Were you not so proficient with our trade, I would suggest you become a philosopher."

His partner grunted.

Through the deluge, Smiyta could see the glow of the west gate's remaining embers. It had taken until midnight for the priest's creature to greet them, and he suspected that their quarry had quite the head start. Although his gut told him it would matter little, given the ghastly creature before him. Day or night, the fair-haired maiden would elude them no longer.

"Well, no time to waste. Find us our little thief, and stay low enough that we can follow," said Smiyta to the beast. It looked at him, then blinked its vertical eyelids before spreading leathery wings wider than the house's roof. Knots of muscle tensed beneath its sodden coat as it crouched on its four legs, their tension suddenly released in a pounce that launched it skyward, wings beating against the gale, lifting it off into the night.

"Clever indeed," nodded Smiyta. "It has been a night to remember, wouldn't you agree?"

"The last, for some."

PART 4
GIFTS

Chapter
Fifty-One

My Lord,

It is with great regret that I must inform you of a failure most pro-found—my own. Brethefen has been lost, usurped by its own citizen-ry.

The head of Nerio's horse swayed in long drifting sweeps as it trotted over the runnels and slicked stones of the open desert. The rhythmic *clops* were a metronome, Nerio's body rocking side to side with the slow, languid beat. The last vestiges of the storm had finished drizzling down an hour past, and the cold night air had stung him with a chill through his soaked robes until he'd long ago gone numb.

It was a small penance when scaled against his debt, the lives lost weighing more than he could hope to atone for in this lifetime or the next. His convictions had been steadfast, the purpose of his life appearing obvious and guided by the hands of the gods themselves. Never could he have imagined the destruction which would be born of his words, nor could he have anticipated the way they would be twisted and defiled by the minds of those devoted to him.

Had he been unclear in his message? Was there a point at which his deliverance had deviated from his original intentions? There must have been signs, indications of what was to come which he'd been oblivious to all along—either ignoring or misinterpreting them in the ignorance of his faith's confidence.

As the stars relinquished the night sky to the morning grey, Nerio's head remained hung low. Moistened sand was an insipid scent compared to the carnage which had rooted into his olfactory. All his senses felt dull, the numbing of his skin seeping deep within.

It wasn't enough. The image of Captain Gernbard standing in defiance before the general had brushed its pigment upon the canvas of his mind, staining through the fabric and leaching into all other thoughts. It didn't matter where his eyes listed, for everywhere he looked he saw the captain falling, cut down for standing at Nerio's side.

For refusing the truth.

When Nerio had first started reciting the tale of what occurred under Brethefen's surface that fateful night, he'd omitted Desnia's involvement in the fire. He'd told himself it was to protect her, to ensure her image was as the gods would wish for it to be: pristine, pure, and divinely selected. Her failures and misdeeds should not have defined her. The people's focus needed to be on the *good* that had been accomplished. How was his message to be received in its full splendor if the cause of the listener's indescribable pain and suffering were the focal point, rather than their holy miracle? He'd been blind to his own arrogance, and countless more were now dead as a result.

Including his friend.

Was this all a test, a way for the gods to show him what Desnia had gone through, to know her pain? He hoped not, for if the mass cessation of life was the gods' means of merely making a point, he wasn't sure they deserved his faith. There was no redemption in this act of violence. What salvation could be pulled from the ashes of this abhorrence?

What, he wondered, *befell Desnia? Lord Delvan? Did they manage to escape the chaos?* He debated going back to the city to discover their fate, but if he were to find them among the deceased...

There was a limit to the shame he could bear, and what already resided within the hollow of his chest prevented him from turning around. In protecting him from further damnation, his own indignity only worsened his chagrin, spiraling him deeper into despair.

Regardless of whether celestial involvement played a hand in what had transpired, Nerio would accept the blame for the devastation. No longer would he degrade the memories of those who had been lost by claiming them to be part of the gods' schemes. This injustice resided with him, and him alone.

That epiphany presented him with a question, one which had left him staring mindlessly down at the swinging motions of his horse's mane through the night, the steed choosing their path while he contemplated. In the sleepless hours he'd come to no conclusion, unaware of how to proceed with the nagging question.

How was he to recompense their souls?

Every minute, hour, *day* that he lived beyond those who'd been snatched away by talons was a sin in its own right. His heart bled, his soul irreparably wounded. His eye's fountains had run dry hours ago, leaving him with a stinging ache as they tried and failed to drain what they did not possess. Perhaps he could find a keeper for his horse, then wander the desert until the vultures claimed him—he was undeserving of an owl. His ghost should have to continue to walk this plan in endless torment.

With a concerted effort he raised his head, finally deigning his surroundings with a glance.

They had been turned west at some point, the White Mountains rising high in the distance before him. Fleeing the city had been a blur. After rushing through the north gate, the ground around him had been smote by lightning, his horse rearing in a panic. It had turned and galloped in another direction, then another as more thunderous cracks rolled through the sky. Nerio had clung on, letting the beast take him where it willed like a tossing vessel through crashing waves.

The city was long behind him, no longer visible in the distance. Nerio did not know these lands the way traders and the like did, the oases known only to the maps staunchly held by the desert's most frequent visitors. Going back to Brethefen was not an option, yet he did not wish to allow his horse to falter beneath the unforgiving sun.

The north road led to several small towns. He could turn northeast, go to one like Gernbard had mentioned before... everything.

The thought made him wilt, his chest a vacuum, pulling all into the abyss. He pinched his scratchy eyes shut, taking slow deep breaths as he tried to avoid the agonizing numbness. There was little choice. He pulled on the reins, tilting the mount's head to the north. It lazily turned, billowing out an exhausted sputter. Traveling during the day posed a risk, he would need to—

What is that?

Nerio pulled on the tethers, his eyes catching sight of something in the distance. Settled low among a circular rock outcropping, he saw the flicker of light. He squinted, the sun's leading glow masking the smokeless fire.

But a fire it was. Someone had made camp nearby. Nerio looked to the north once more, gazing across the barren, shrubby landscape, considering the distance—which he could only guess to be dozens of miles—to the nearest town. He then looked back to the scantly perceptible light. The camp could be anyone; soldiers, traders, smugglers.

Bandits.

The northern route could mean death for his fatigued horse. If bandits were to attack him, at least they would keep the valuable animal alive. It certainly was worth more than he was.

His face stolid, he turned the horse back towards the encampment. If they were travelers willing to aid his weary animal, then it would be a much-needed blessing. If they deemed him prey to their ill-will, then that would suffice as well.

At least then he could begin his eternal roaming.

Chapter
Fifty-Two

After weeks of suppressing small, contained riots, the populace cul-minated in a single mass gathering at the behest of their leader, a young, elusive priest. The former disciple of the missing principle riled and instigated them into a frenzy which quickly took hold of the people.

Desnia sat atop a cold rock, shivering under the saturated wool blanket.

She and her new companions had ridden hard through the night to put as much distance between them and that gods-damned city as possible. Their horses had reached their brink in the dark, ephemeral hour before dawn—verging on going lame, foam likely to start clinging to their lips at any moment. They'd found this alcove, a notched scar in the desert rock large and low enough to file the horses into and keep their silhouettes out of sight.

The horses drank from a pool of standing rainwater in the corner a dozen paces away. The rocky walls glistened beneath pale green shrubs as the earliest of nature's risers began to shift from their slumber and skitter across the stones. Desnia contemplated sitting on the muddy, silt-covered ground, her stone chair hungrily devouring what little warmth remained within her. But she was too exhausted to bother, her body completely inflexible.

The night's frigid air had left her blistered fingers bitten and muscles frozen to the bone. Nighttime fire was too great a risk with the chance of pursuers being on their trail. Sitting there with her teeth painfully chattering together, she'd been prepared to say, "fuck it," and accept the danger, regardless of the others' opposition, but a glance to her side had her reconsidering.

Delvan lay there on a blanket with eyes closed as his mind floated through unconsciousness. His breathing was steady, but he'd yet to let out a grunt or word, even while they had been removing his armor and putting fresh—if damp—clothes on him. She'd also managed to hide a half-scorched purse full of gems that'd been on him without the others noticing.

Desnia brought her knees closer to her chest and pulled the blanket tighter. Looking at Delvan, she couldn't help but feel the urge to kick him. Not to wake him up, though that would make traveling considerably more convenient, but out of an annoyed spite.

She wanted to hate him. Ignorance was no excuse—Delvan was an idiot, but he wasn't stupid. He should have anticipated what would happen if he told the general about the street thief who had known about the doorway to another realm. She was the expendable one. Delvan and the other two were lords, no one was going to lock them away and torture *them* for information.

But then he had to come to her rescue. Him and... and...

She couldn't think about her, and squeezed her weary eyes closed.

It had been too little, too late. The damage was done, the voices in her head blended into her reality as if there was another world overlaid onto hers. The gritty medicine she forcefully swallowed was a reminder of just how decrepit her mind had become, tasting like the memory of paint's flavor in a cramped cell.

And what? She was just supposed to forgive him? Where was her retribution in that? Delvan hadn't just come to help her, he'd made a gods-damned spectacle of it. There was no deniability for him, not after that. Now the dumbass was another fugitive, like her. Of course, with the way nobility could mangle and rearrange a narrative, she would probably be blamed—again—and Delvan given another pass.

Why did he keep putting the effort in to redeem himself? *Why* couldn't he just let her be *angry* at him?!

On second thought, she considered with a sidelong glance, *maybe I should kick him. Might do us both some good...*

A *chip, chip, chip* sound drew her eyes like a magnet to the center of their boulder-strewn recess, watching as one of the men struck a piece of flint. Sparks scattered over the pile of sun-cooked dung until the flakes of dried tinder beneath it lit with a few *snaps* and *pops*. Desnia stood—sounds similar to the fire's crackle coming from her frozen joints—groaning from the exertion and took dragging steps towards the growing flames.

With daylight's breaking grey illuminating the eastern sky, they could finally light a fire without fear of discovery. It would be a few more hours before the sun began baking the desert with its torrid rays, and they would need warmth in the waxing morning hours. She shuffled closer, her feet touching the ring of stones around the pit and blanket steaming. The fetid smell of burning manure was almost as pungent as the Calentine sewers. It was difficult to breathe, the offensive odor sticking to her tongue and singing her nostrils with its acrid scent.

It was still preferrable to convulsing beneath a sopping blanket.

The night relived itself repeatedly in her mind, and each time she forced it back down, burying it alive and ignoring its keening. Other questions found ways to haunt her. What had happened to Nerio? The guilt of leaving him behind corroded like venom.

Her life had been turned upside down and filled with people that were willing to sacrifice for *her*. Worst yet, they asked for nothing in return.

How was she to cope with the loss of what she never wanted? And why did it *hurt*?

As she thawed before the fire, Desnia flicked her gaze towards her huddled guides, seeking a distraction. She knew almost nothing about the two men whispering argumentatively near the horses in hushed, undecipherable tones. She averted her gaze as one of them looked over.

The bowman who'd attempted to defy her the night before strode over as the heated conversation settled. "Myself and Freegrouse," he said in a thick accent, "believe it time for you to explain what happened to the one you call 'Mithya.'"

Desnia almost coughed, her throat tightly constricting. She wanted to ignore them, to stare blankly into the fire until these erratic, unfamiliar emotions dissipated. Instead, the two of them stood there, expecting an answer like a group of orphans waiting for a baker's stale scraps. "S-S-She stayed b-b-behind," Desnia chattered, the cold yet to abandon its grip. At least it covered the tremble in her voice.

"No," the man responded sternly. "She would not do this. Where we go now, nothing is more vital."

"H-H-Hard to run when you've been s-s-stabbed in the gut." Desnia endeavored to refrain from picturing the scene in her head, pressing her lips tightly together to stop them from quivering.

There were more whispers, a look of disbelief whitening the man's visage. "She... is unborn?"

"If y-y-you're asking..." Desnia struggled, her voice pitching as it caught in her throat. "I don't know. She was a-a-alive when we left her."

"She lies," said the other man, his voice low and eyes dark.

"Fuck you!" Desnia spat.

The man before her, the pair's apparent leader, raised a hand to his comrade. "She bears the blade and speaks our virtue. For her we will pray to the ancestors, but on our journey we must remain. Tell me," he said, looking at Desnia, "did she tell you what we seek?"

She nodded.

"And you, you be as she described? Are you to be compass and direct us?"

Do you really think that I intend to take you with me? she wondered. "I don't know you from a snake in the grass. What makes you think I'm just going to tell you?"

"I," said the man, pressing his hand to his chest and giving a modest bow, "am Bloodstone, and this is Freegrouse." He indicated to her fat mouthed critic, who was still pouting his disapproval. He could choke on that scowl for all she cared.

"Another 'spy?'" She could finally feel her neck begin to loosen, the heat driving away the chill.

"No, no. Nothing so devious. I am a smuggler, and Freegrouse is, how do you say, subservient?"

"What the hell is that supposed to mean?"

"The word you might use is not a good one. I believe it's 'slave?'"

"*What?*"

"He is from a different tribe. One that you would know as, uh, vassal? In our homeland, when one tribe conquers another, they become, um, indentured is the word? By our law, he must offer—"

"Forget I asked," cut in Desnia. She had no interest in listening to the affairs of foreign politics. Frankly, she had no interest in listening to *anything* Bloodstone had to say.

Bloodstone bit his lip, plainly choosing his words carefully. She recognized the look—it was what the broke wore when trying to barter. Revealing the depths of his desires would give her the advantage, and therefore he tried to act aloof. Little did he know his own attempted indifference exposed just how desperate he truly was. She would rob him blind without stealing if she ever got him in a game of pebbles.

"Madam," he said, feigning a smile, "please, Mithya spoke to us of you. We are seekers of the same spirit. We intend to find him ourselves, but your... guidance would point us in faster direction, so to speak."

Desnia mumbled under her breath. "It would help if *I* knew where we were going..." Everyone kept telling her that she could find Asta, yet no one had explained *how*. She felt as lost as the rest of them.

She waited for some snark comment from Masini, prodding him with opportunities she didn't think he could resist. He'd been silent since their flight from the city—which she imagined was some form of punishment. She hadn't thought him capable of being speechless for such an extended period. Letting out a sigh, she applied the little amount of knowledge Masini *had* shared with her to the conversation. "We head towards the mountains. I'll let you know more once we get there."

Freegrouse hissed a curse. Bloodstone managed to hold a smile but could not prevent his eye from twitching. "Then the mountains shall be our destination," he said, giving a short bow. "We camp here for the day, travel by night. Perhaps you should get some rest."

And not be able to keep an eye on you? she thought. *I think not.* She didn't like the wary looks they were giving Delvan. His sapphire alone was valuable enough to purchase a small duchy, and—assuming they were in fact from Trethefen—they could run beyond even the King's vengeful reach were they to steal it. No, it would be better to stay awake, at least until Delvan regained consciousness.

There would be rest nor reprieve in her sleep, anyway.

Desnia continued staring blankly into the reeking fire. The sun began cutting a ragged line of shade across the opposite wall of worn rock, drinking away the storm's residual moisture. Everything moved in a fog around Desnia, her eyes burning as she forced herself to stay awake, attempting to passively watch the Trethish guides finish setting up their camp. The sun had begun warming the back of her head when a shout made her start, hand instinctively grabbing the dagger's hilt.

Freegrouse had called, drawing his bow. Desnia watched through slit eyes as he and Bloodstone scrambled into hidden positions amongst the boulders. Without knowing why, she remained standing, unmoving from the fire.

The sounds of clopping hooves, slow and singular, bounced off the surrounding stone. The head of the steed appeared from behind a shaded stone, more exhausted than even theirs had been. Atop its back was a slumped figure, looking equally defeated and beaten by the night's tempestuous fury. Filthy white robes, adorned by a thin—

Desnia's mouth fell open, her heart racing as she realized who it was that she was seeing.

Nerio.

It was impossible. This... this was another dream. Were the effects of the silty swill wearing off, or worse, become ineffective?

No, it couldn't be, for the others saw him too, were reacting to his presence. Arming themselves...

Oh, shit. "Stop!" shouted Desnia. "Don't shoot! I know him!"

The two hidden party members looked at her, hesitant to lower their weapons as they questioned her with frowns. Nerio's head sprang upright, his eyes turning to round, white orbs against his dark skin as he locked them with her own.

"D-Desnia?" Nerio asked, as if he too were in a dream.

"You're alive!" she said, shedding the water-logged blanket and striding towards his mount, skeptical of what her mind was envisioning before her.

Nerio slipped down from the saddle, leaving the horse to drift towards the shrinking watering hole as he took heavy steps forward. They stopped a pace apart, staring in wonder at what turn of fate had brought them back together. She wanted to laugh, grateful for the one event of the past day that could bring her joy. Grateful that he had survived the riots. Riots caused by... by his invocation of her being allegedly chosen by his gods.

Her lips turned down and brow slanted steeply as a sudden burst of rage exploded within her. Nerio's face contorted into confusion as she reached out and forcefully shoved him.

"A '*Messiah*?!'" Desnia screamed as Nerio landed hard on the ground. "What part of 'don't worship me' did you not understand?"

Bloodstone and Freegrouse shared surprised glances before he spoke up. "Madam, we must be quiet—"

"Say another *word*," she interrupted vilely, "and I'll cut out your gods-damned tongue."

The men's expressions turned sourer, not that she cared. They remained silent.

Nerio dragged himself into a sitting position, staring abashed at the dirt between his feet. When he eventually spoke, his voice was soft and quiet. Desnia had to lean forward to hear whatever excuse he could concoct. "I'm sorry. I didn't think—"

"No, you *didn't*." Another apology, too late to make a difference. "You twisted what happened to fit into your neat fucking ideology without knowing the *truth*. I'm not entirely sure if I even know..." She gritted her teeth and sucked a breath through flared nostrils. "*What* did you expect would happen, huh? In what dream would this plan of yours end any other way?!"

Desnia could feel pressure in her face, her chest heaving with rage. It seemed that everyone wanted to use her. What about what *she* wanted? Did no one give a shit?

Nerio shook his head, and she saw that there were tears cutting lines down his face. Despondence and ire clashed within her, their throes a conflict for dominance.

"You're right," Nerio said solemnly. "This is all my fault. I know... I know there is nothing I can do to set it right." He stood, his movements sluggish, and looked at her with eyes spiderwebbed with crimson. "Please, keep my horse, and know that I will beg for forgiveness for the rest of my days. That you are alive is the one blessing of this day. One more than I deserve... But I understand that you do not wish to see me. Stay safe, Desnia."

He turned and began walking back from whence he came, head hung low while the Trethish men suspiciously watched. Desnia dug her fingers through her hair and into her scalp as she groaned behind gritted teeth. Part of her considered letting him leave to face punishment for what happened. There was an empty saddle among them because of his actions, and whether its rider lived or not was agonizingly unknown. Deep down, however, she couldn't watch him leave. Not again.

But she couldn't find the strength to ask him to stay.

She let out a scream as her nails dug into skin, then kicked a fist-sized rock nearby, sending it rolling. "Wait!" she called out. Nerio slowly turned, his eyes destitute of hope, his fate apparently accepted. There was a collective moan from the rest of the party. What was she to say? She looked to her side, seeing Delvan lying there in the shade and pointed to him. "He could use your help." She expected a quip from Masini, but none came. Which was fine, as she could deprecate herself well enough without his assistance.

Nerio turned his gaze to the motionless Blue, a look of surprise flashing onto his face, as if it was the first time he'd noticed him. "What happened?"

Desnia briefly recounted the... major points of the prior evening's events, omitting the parts that didn't pertain directly to Delvan. Nerio had walked over while she was talking, pulling Delvan's eyelids back and methodically checking him for injuries. By the time that she had finished describing what happened, Nerio was already digging through his small pack. "I know very little of Blues," he said, "but he appears to be suffering from some form of exhaustion. I have seen similar episodes in those that work the fields, though never for such an extended period..."

Nerio looked around, seeing the two men sitting there and watching them with mixed expressions. "Do any of you have yertwood root?" They sat there quietly, refusing to respond.

"Well?!" glowered Desnia.

Bloodstone spoke up. "We do not think it wise to add members to party, madam. Perhaps—"

"Perhaps you should keep your fucking opinions to yourself and *answer* him."

There was a quiet moment as Bloodstone flexed his jaw and pursed his lips.

He said something she didn't understand to Freegrouse, bickering for a time before the "slave" eventually hopped off his rock and began digging through a saddle bag. "We have some supplies, though I do not know this root you speak. I ask you be sparing, it is all we have."

Nerio took the bag with a quick glance at the disgruntled Freegrouse before digging through. "This will do," he said. "It's not what I would normally prescribe, but Lord Delvan might not react the same as you or I, so perhaps this will suffice."

Maybe not the same as you, anyway, Desnia thought. "How long will it take? For him to recover?"

Nerio shrugged, his shoulders slumping. "I cannot say. I'm—"

"Sorry. Yeah, I know." Desnia pinched the bridge of her nose, sighing as Nerio somehow wilted further. "Just, do what you can for him..."

"Of course," said Nerio, scurrying away and assembling a kettle and strainer that was set out nearby.

Desnia rolled her head back and let out an exasperated breath, kicking herself for her own temper. She went and sat back upon the rock where she'd been earlier, indifferent to its chill. Masini's tantrum must have been uniquely potent for him to not have said anything during the exchange, opportunities for gibes having abounded. Not that she needed to hear him to know what he would say. The worst part being that he was right, the annoying prick.

"Gods, am I bad at this..."

CHAPTER FIFTY-THREE

Attempts to quell the uprising were met with resistance from the commoners and, most disturbingly, our own troops. I have no insight or excuse for their insubordination.

The sun's blaring heat had long taken away Desnia's embedded chill. Sitting high overhead, it beat down on them with its oppressive rays, the shade of the small canopy above her doing little to prevent perspiration. She should have laid her head down to rest—gods knew she needed it—but she remained upright all the same, eyes on the sleeping figure ten paces away, the other Trethish member of their company on watch in the crevasse of two boulders nearby.

More than once her head had nodded forward, prompting a shake from her and a firm bite of the inside of her lip. The trick did little more than leave the taste of metal in her mouth, her eyelids weighted like a mountain rested upon them.

Nerio had dozed off some hours ago beside Delvan, who he had been steadily providing tea to. Desnia glanced over to the exposed sapphire resting on his chest, slowly rising and falling with each of Delvan's languid breaths. She had considered covering it but had been worried that it might prevent him from recovering somehow—though she admittedly had no idea if that was the case. The medicine was doing its job, and as long as she was in a dulled state she would tolerate the gem. Once Delvan awoke—which he *would*, because there was no way he was going to abandon her, too—she would ask him to cover it.

A rustle drew her rust-colored eyes to her side.

Nerio groaned as he sat himself upright, digging into his eyes with his knuckles before taking a swig of water—the air notorious for leaving your throat feeling as though you'd been drinking sand in your sleep. He looked at

Desnia, surprised in his groggy state to find her huddled there, knees at her chest, hand at the knife hidden beneath her linen clothing.

"Des? Have you slept?"

"Wasn't tired."

"Forgive me for saying, but your appearance would suggest otherwise," he sheepishly said as he began collecting his tea supplies.

She drew a long breath. "I just... don't like the idea of no one watching him," she said, nodding towards Delvan. The words came out more genuine than she'd wanted, despite the edge to her voice.

"Ah," said Nerio, surprisingly understanding. He looked at the dozing lump in the distance, keeping his concerned voice lowered. "I heard them speaking Trethish earlier. Desnia, I believe they may be *smugglers*."

Desnia snorted. "Wow, really? I had no idea..."

"Not surprising, as I'm sure you don't hear the language often in Calentine." *Oh, Nerio, how can you possibly be that innocent?* "We used smugglers to supply the camps—"

"You had camps?"

"Of course, how else was I to feed and shelter those in need?" Desnia raised a sluggish eyebrow, wondering why she was surprised. "As I was saying," he continued, mixing a concoction of herbs together, "I found that the smugglers often spoke Trethish, in a dialect that was more similar to Old Trethish than the modern version still often spoken in households in Brethefen."

"Is that right?" Desnia drawled, lacking the energy to converse more extensively.

"Indeed. I thought it odd, but, Desnia, I now worry..." He looked at her hesitantly, his voice dropping lower. "What if they're from *Trethefen?*"

If Desnia hadn't been so far beyond her body's limits, she would've laughed. "That's because they *are*, Nerio."

The priest's eyes went wide and his head spun from their companions to her. "*What?* Des, these people are dangerous!"

That managed to force out a half-breath chortle. "Less than the people hunting me in Brethefen?"

"Well..." Nerio's mouth hung open, short syllables staggering out of it as he struggled to counter her.

"I know where they're from, and what they want—" *Not that I intend to give it to them, not without...* her *here.* "—and I'm well aware of how dangerous they are."

"Is that why you haven't slept?"

"How astute..." Nerio blushed, hanging his head down. Desnia rolled her eyes, annoyed with herself for being too tired to prevent her mouth from spitting senseless gibes. "Sorry, I'm just... Sorry."

Nerio, in his typical fashion, was quick to forgive, nodding grimly as if the apology had been unnecessary. "Do you intend to stay with them?" he whispered, placing his prepared kettle on the remnant coals of the morning fire.

Desnia shook her head, whispering her own response. "We met with them because it was our only option. We were supposed to have someone else with us, someone that I would have stayed with, but without her I don't have any intention of trusting them." She looked over to Delvan. "I can't do much until he's awake though." *I can't leave another behind, regardless of how frustrating he is.*

"This 'other' you speak of," said Nerio, sitting back under the shade beside her while his tea percolated, "was it Lady Mithya?"

Desnia nearly choked at the name, a tear dripping from the corner of her eye. She quickly wiped it away, hoping Neiro hadn't noticed as she nodded. "How did you know that?"

His shoulders slumped. "I made a mistake, one which I must tell you how deeply sorry I—"

"You've mentioned you're sorry," Desnia cut in, "to the point that the words are losing meaning. Just... tell me what happened."

"Ah, yes. I'm sor—" He let out a slight cough as she glared at him. "She and Lord Delvan came to me, mere days ago, and told me of their intentions in helping you escape." Desnia stared at him, brow delving down, but remained silent. "I... refused them. I thought—well, I believed—that I could convince the Lord General to release you, with a show of the people's will. Everyone warned me against it. Lord Delvan. Captain Gernbard..." Tears now welled in his own eyes, and he had to wipe his sniveling nose with his sleeve. "I was a fool. I should've helped them with your release. Instead, Brethefen burns once more. Because of me."

We have that in common. Desnia should have probably offered words of solace, told him that it wasn't his fault or some nonsense. Knowledge, however, was a bitter taste, and that he could have aided in her release even when she was in the Asylum was a flavor that sat on her tongue, exaggerated with each mouthful of medicine she was forced to swallow. He could use the life lesson, as far as she was concerned, but given how devastated he already was, she didn't see a benefit to beating him down further. The best she could do was keep her mouth shut.

They sat there in silence for a while, long enough for Desnia's eyes to once again begin drooping. Nerio stared at the dirt until the whistle of his kettle distracted him from his aura of melancholy. He poured a cup of tea, cooling it with water from a bladder, and began administering it to Delvan. After a few cautious glances in her direction, he spoke once more. "If you wish to sleep, Des, I can stay on watch for a time. I do not see myself sleeping much more today, my dreams, they're..." *Haunted?* "Regardless, you need rest. And it would be nice to feel... useful."

Desnia wearily looked from him to the rest of the group. Sleep was a terrifying thought, though Nerio was right. She was apt to fall from her horse while riding if she didn't attempt to get some rest, and thus far the sediment-filled medication had been effectively quieting her additional... senses. Perhaps just a few hours while the others slept? Would there be risk in that?

"Alright," she said groggily. "But the moment any of them—or Delvan—stirs, you wake me immediately, understand?"

Nerio nodded eagerly. "Yes, of course. Thank you, Des."

She painfully rolled her eyes before giving the slumbering Bloodstone one last glance. She laid down in the shade beside Delvan, pulling her bundled bag under her head and rolling on her side.

Fear, she suspected, would keep her awake for a time, and if she did manage to rest, it wouldn't be for long.

Her enamored demons would ensure it.

Desolate solitude. A vast swath of emptiness, where time was irrelevant and the landscape remained an unchanged tomb of black.

And it was *quiet*.

It was a blessing, yet she still *heard*. Not voices, but she lacked the faculties to describe what else it could be. Emotions carved her surroundings, an image beyond the darkness that was like a statue beneath a sheet. Desnia could reach out, feel its texture beyond the veil, gain a sense of what lay there, shaped by hand and chisel.

But it fluctuated, shifting and ephemeral. At one moment it was recognizable, and then it would transform into an indecipherable, congealed glob of unknown thoughts and ideas.

She could see herself, as if watching like a bird hovering nearby, lit by an unseen light as if a beacon on the plane. The starless night that surrounded her, despite its appearance, wasn't static. It undulated, evanescent in its form, despite her eyes seeing naught but the fixed absence of light. Dynamic, yet comfortable. Solid, yet viscous. This place... left her feeling lost.

A sound pierced the silent abode. Distant and quiet at first, it approached like a coming avalanche, growing from a single echo to a colossal bellow. She recognized it.

Des.

Quiet, yet profound.

Des.

Bolstered and urgent.

Des!

Desperate and pleading.

Then another, familiar voice, turning the cascade into an unstoppable force.

WAKE, CHILD.

A frantic trepidation shifted the world around her, she could feel it, moving faster, the forms and molds beyond her shroud transforming in a racing flurry.

DES!

Desnia's eyes shot open, an anomalous assortment of sounds filling the dimly lit surroundings. *It's evening?* How long had she slept?

Des, wake the fuck up! came Masini's hysteric voice. What had convinced him to speak to her again?

She bolted upright, head spinning as she took in her surroundings, her heart beating in her throat. The sun had recently set, burying them in the mountains' shadows and leaving a lingering pink ripple in the sky.

The clash of steel to her left drew her gaze to where Bloodstone was deflecting the swings of a mace with his sword a dozen paces away. The spiked ball of steel moved in a blurred flurry, each arc bludgeoning the air with a *whoosh* as it was propelled by the tree trunks its wielder called arms. The enormous man moved with fluidity and grace as he swung the pointed mass of metal, forcing Bloodstone back and leaving him on the defensive, despite his sword's agility.

Desnia drew the darksteel dagger Delvan had given her and moved to aid Bloodstone's failing defense. She stopped and spun her head as the string of a bow snapped taut off to her right. Freegrouse knelt on a boulder, releasing an arrow that missed the nimble ogre, the man deftly keeping Bloodstone between himself and the ranged weapon's line of sight.

Out of the corner of her eye she saw Nerio huddled in front of Delvan's unstirring figure, keeping his unarmed self between the Blue and their attacker. *Idiot is* trying *to get himself killed,* she thought.

Oh, you're awake. Thank the Greats, said a panicked Masini.

"What, you're talking to me now—"

I don't feel like dying, so yes, a temporary armistice.

"Are there more?" she asked, searching their alcove's ridgeline for movement.

Well, that's why I started screaming like a baboon with its testicles in a vice, he said as Bloodstone deflected another blow from the whirling mace. His footing was becoming unsure as another arrow missed its mark. *We have a problem. Not a tiny, 'oh no, a parasite is about to swim up my urethrae' problem, but a massive, 'we're all about to die horrible—*

"Get to the fucking point—"

A roar broke the sky, the reverberations raising bumps across Desnia's skin and paling her face. It was a thunderous, predatory bellow which spoke to a creature that announced its arrival as a challenge for its prey to flee, knowing full well that it would dominate a chase. It drew her and Nerio's eyes skyward, her breath held and feet frozen in place.

That, said Masini, *is the problem.*

As she stood there waiting for the inevitable, a flash of movement caught her eye from behind a boulder at the rim of their sunken hollow. Sleuthing though the crevasses was a man of narrow frame and lanky proportions, slithering through the cracks and gaps soundlessly—directly behind Freegrouse.

Desnia tried to scream, to warn the bowman of the impending danger. As the air escaped her lips, she bolted forward, seeing a knife rise above the man's back. It was futile. Before her foot hit the sand in her third stride, the blade plunged into Freegrouse's back, forcing the breath from his lungs and sending him to the ground beneath an eerie, face-splitting smile.

Wait, Desnia thought, her eyes going wide as she stared at the man's widely curved lips. She spun, looking at the hulking warrior swirling his mace through the air until it finally connected with a bone-crunching *thump.* Bloodstone lifted off his feet before falling lifeless onto a nearby stone, blood and gore filling the cavity where his ribs had been. Desnia's heart began drumming in her ears. *I know these men... I recognize them from—*

Another roar made the stones and sand tremble.

Air kicked up sand beneath beating wings as the outline of a horrific beast emerged over the crest of their camp's outcroppings. The ground shook beneath Desnia's feet as claws the length of her hand dug into the sand, curling beneath the ropes of muscle that flexed beneath a coat of golden fur. She couldn't force her body to take a step back, her fear paralyzing her as the beast curled its lip with a malicious snarl, a rumbling growl emerging from behind rows of pointed fangs.

"By the gods..." Nerio whispered. Desnia wasn't certain what created such an appalling being, but it likely defied any of Nerio's "gods."

"As promised," said their smiling ambusher, casually hoping down from his perch, wiping his blade clean. "Most impressive, wouldn't you say, Ksatri?"

The man referred to as Ksatri twisted the mace's grip in his hands, turning from his inspection of Bloodstone's corpse. His face was expressionless except for the faintest furrowing of his brow. "Very," was his only response.

"You, my dear," said Freegrouse's murderer, pointing his blade to the trembling Desnia, her eyes locked with the green slits of death's amalgamation before her, "have been impressively difficult to locate."

"W-W-What is that?" Desnia forced from her dry mouth.

A khimaira, said Masini, sounding equally shaken. *I don't know how it got here, but Des, you need to distract it, then run. As fast and far as you can.*

"How?" she whimpered.

Uh, food. That's it, basically.

She could hear Nerio a few paces behind her, speechless. She held her gaze with the creature, her lids peeled fully back, wondering what would happen to him and Delvan if she ran. And what, exactly, qualified as food for this thing born of a demon's nightmare? Based on the way it stared at her, drool hanging from a sneering lip, she could imagine what it wanted...

Oh, gods, she thought. *No, no I won't...* "What do you want?" she asked.

"Oh, that's simple," said the mischievous smile's owner as he stepped over the flicking, scaled tail which was thicker than her leg. "We're here for *you.* Well, you and then some errands in the mountains, but you're by far the more... illusive of our tasks."

She swallowed hard, her throat choking. There was nowhere to run, and even if she did, how far could she make it before this fucking thing found her again? What did she have left to bargain with?

"If it's me you want..." she said shakily, "leave them out of this." She pointed to the crouching Nerio and subdued Delvan.

"Mhm," said the man, pondering beside the creature's folded wing, his partner stepping over and standing on the animal's other flank. "They weren't part of our contract, but our... *interesting* companion here has a surprisingly large appetite. I think it deserves payment as much as we do, wouldn't you agree Ksatri?"

The man slightly shifted his bulky shoulder.

"Ah, well, that's that, then," said the man with a further curl of his over-sized mouth. "We were asked to make this as slow and painful as possible, but the creature's patience has so far been, um, *wanting*. I don't think Jerdine is going to mind *too* much, though. Hopefully he doesn't request a small discount as an apology."

Of course it was that fat bastard, Masini said, echoing her own thoughts. *Des, I'm sorry. For everything.*

"This is what it takes to get an apology from you?!" she quietly shrilled, her mouth somehow moving despite the panic.

The man's smile dimmed, his face puzzled. "I take my client's requests rather seriously, you should know. But, if torturous pain is *really* what you want, we could abide—"

There was a blur of movement from her side. The creature's head dipped lower and folds of its brow deepening as Nerio was suddenly standing between her and the beast's white, shining fangs, its hot, fetid breath moving the fabric of his robe.

Desnia's head drew back as she gasped. "Nerio! What the *fuck* are you doing?!"

"I won't let you take her!" he shouted to the creature, his voice wavering and hands visibly shaking. "Des, run!"

Uh, Des, said Masini, *I like the kid and all, but I'd take his advice and, uh, run for your fucking life.*

She couldn't. She *wouldn't.*

Not again.

"Nerio, no!" she grabbed his robe, pulling on it, but he dug his feet in, standing fast between her and the deadly maw. She felt tears well in her eyes, her lip trembling as all their lives shined like dying candles in those cold, reptilian eyes.

The smiler let out a chuckle, and a singular eyebrow rose on his companion's face. The khimaira took a step forward, bringing its nose mere inches from Nerio's chest, his robes trembling as if a breeze were passing through it. Desnia was helpless, fear compounding itself as she failed to think of an escape.

Desnia felt the humid air of the sniffs that the creature pulled and released through its black, feline nose, smelling Nerio with gushes of air through its nostrils. Petrified, she could only watch as it brought its massive head from his chest to his feet, then back to his face.

The sniffing stopped. The khimaira pulled its maned head back, dropping its lips and tilting its head to the side. *It looks... confused?* thought Desnia.

The malice suddenly vanished from its eyes as it took two light steps forward and nuzzled its head against Nerio's chest, a purr emanating from its chest. He looked back at Desnia, his face impossibly pallid and sweaty. "W-W-What is happening?"

"How the fuck should I know?" she asked, her jaw agape.

Masini gasped. *Oh-ho-ho! By the Greats, oh I never thought I could be ecstatic about Jerdine's abhorrent urges.*

The smile was vanquished from their attacker's visage entirely, his companion stepping back, looking concerned. "So much for being clever. We don't have time for you to play with your damned food. End them and let's be on our way!"

The beast ignored them, rubbing its face against Nerio and nearly lifting him from the ground. It was all the priest could do to remain standing upright, his hands extended to his side, unsure of what to do.

There was no glee on their ambusher's face as he sneered. "Fine! I'll do it myself." The lanky man took two steps forward, blade in hand, and pushed Nerio to the side as he reached for Desnia. The khimaira twisted its head towards him and snarled, hissing and revealing a mouthful of needle-sharp fangs. The killer took a step back, his own face turning a light shade of white. "Yo-You're supposed to listen to *us*, you stupid abomination!"

The creature lowered its head, muscles constricting into defined bunches as it readied to pounce.

"Something's different. We should go," said his companion, who had been slowly taking steps back.

With eyes transfixed by the salivating, pearly-white points, the other tested a lean forward, his prodding met with another snarl and revealed claws. He backed up further and nodded, his face turning into a plunging scowl. "I will discover what you've done," he said, eyeing her and Nerio, "and return." He took several paces backward, never turning away from the predatory gaze.

Desnia opened her mouth to threaten them, to reinforce the idea, somehow, that they should stay away from them. But she too was distracted by the mass of winged muscle, and before she could say anything, Nerio took a step forward, pointing to their assailer. "No. You will stay away from us, understand? I never want to see you again." His voice was shaky, but he somehow stood his ground. Desnia couldn't help but be impressed—despite how fucking stupid he'd been.

Oh, not the best choice of, uh, intent, said a chuckling Masini. How was this funny?

In less than a heartbeat, the beast sprang forward, snapping the man in two between its jaws, his life evaporating before he could manage a scream. Behind the khimaira, the imposing warrior spent no time dallying and spun in an instant to sprint in the other direction. A gleam of light reflected off the black scales of a tail that was as long as the beast's body, the end wrapping around the man's ankle and dragging him to the ground.

He flailed, kicked, and grunted wildly as he tried to pull his foot free. He raised his mace to strike, but before the heavy weapon reached the peak of his swing, the tail flung him effortlessly through the air, slamming him with a sickening *crunch* into the side of a tall stone. The twisted remains of his body landed motionless on the ground.

The khimaira twisted its bulk between the two corpses, as if confirming the kill were somehow necessary. Satisfied, it relaxed and stood tall and proud on its four paws, spinning with terrifying speed to face her and Nerio. Lowering its head, it rubbed its face against him with enough force that Desnia had to catch him from falling. It turned and hopped in a manner that was almost playful to the first body, shredding into it and soaking its snout in blood, chewing through leather and bone alike.

Nerio slowly righted himself from Desnia's arms, his jaw hanging low as he gazed in horror at the surrounding carnage. "What... I don't... Why?"

I am so glad you and him are friends, said a cheery Masini. *Oh, you have no idea how pissed Jerdine is going to be about this. Where did he even* get *a khimaira?*

"What. The. *Fuck,* just happened?" Desnia asked.

Do you remember how the young priest was able to enter the passage leading to the, uh, door?

"Because it recognized him as..."

Jerdine, correct. The twisted bastard's 'influence'—a word which diminishes his vile desecration of the boy, but makes my point—altered Nerio's, uh, energy to nearly match his own. It thinks the boy is Jerdine! Ha!

"That explains basically nothing," said Desnia, standing alongside Nerio with similar revulsion as the sounds of cracking bones filled the air.

Khimaira bond to the first person they see when they're born, normally their mothers. My people have been known to use them as, let's call them companions, in battle and during conquests.

"You keep these as *pets?*"

Well, some do. They're incredibly expensive, and equally rare. The one bastard that managed to come through the door—*that is so annoying to have to keep saying—must have brought it. But if it's bonded to Jerdine... Hmm, strange.*

"Des," said Nerio, his knees wobbling uncontrollably, "who are you talking to?"

"My ring," she replied. He turned and looked at her, confounded and still utterly terrified. "It's a long story. But, apparently, this *thing* thinks its bonded to *you*."

"*Me?*"

"Yep. So maybe be a little more careful about who you say you don't want around anymore, yeah? Also, have I mentioned that I'm sorry about this morning?"

That's what it takes to get an apology out of you*?* snarked Masini.

"Really? *Now?*" she asked. There was no response. *Stubborn prick*, she grumbled.

Nerio had not spoken for a moment, his shoulders slumped and hands at his quaking side. "These men... They're dead because of *me?*"

Desnia stared at him, the coming night darkening her flabbergasted expression. "Nerio, they're dead because they were assholes that were going to *kill us*. You can't *honestly* feel guilty about that?"

His mouth hung open as he watched the khimaira's gruesome, effortless mutilation of its meal as it laid flat on its belly and used its curved claws to hold the body in place, grinding the skull between its teeth. A feeble sound escaped his mouth, the beginnings of a word—

"What the *fuck* is that!" came a shout from behind them. Desnia, Nerio, and the khimaira spun in unison, finding a wide-eyed Delvan sitting up, his palm extended forward. The khimaira slunk forward a step, pulling back bloody lips and digging claws deeply into the shrub-covered soil.

Nerio dashed between it and Delvan, raising his hands. "Wait! Friend! He's a friend!"

The beast narrowed its strange eyes and then relaxed with a dismissive shrug before turning and dropping itself back before its dinner.

Desnia turned and looked at the ghostly, sweat-slicked Delvan, her stomach in her throat. "*Now* you wake up?"

Chapter Fifty-Four

We fought through the night, but in the end, we were forced to retreat. Of the two legions' loyal soldiers I now have but fifteen hundred accompanying me.

*F*inally, whiskey that doesn't taste like horse's piss, thought Jerdine as he sipped on the passable excuse for honey-stained euphoria.

The recent weeks had melded into a month and then dragged vexingly beyond. Fortunately, each day had brought them further from the northern, desolate tract of pleasure's antithesis into a clime far more hospitable to his preferences. How any of those inbred fleas could live in such a place was beyond him.

Unfortunately, he'd spent the entire time jumping at each of Valander's whims, mostly explaining in painstaking detail the history of this wretched realm—a surprising amount of which the pampered progeny was already familiar with. Not that he told Jerdine what he did or did not know. *He's testing me. The gall... Who does he think reported these events?*

Now, approaching civilization once more, he and Valander had found their way to an inn with a tavern that catered to a plethora of indulgences. There was a constant buzz of chatter that filled the stone-walled space, a mighty hearth in the wide room's center glowing with a thick bed of coals, the scent of meats roasting above it wafting through the air. He would almost dare call it comfortable, were it not for the company.

"The arrangements for our meeting are proceeding?" asked Valander. His disguise today was of high nobility, silks and colorful garments presenting him as a man of stature and wealth.

"Indeed," he replied, smacking his lips and savoring the sip on his tongue. *Yes, I have labored while you delegated in sloth.* "Although, I cannot guarantee we will be able to meet directly with—"

"If you are unable to procure my audience, then I will do it myself."

Jerdine's lip twitched. *Go ahead, barge in with your haughty demands and face the consequences, you naïve child. At least then I would not have to coddle your almighty ego.* He took another drink, choosing not to retort the lambasting.

If the ksatsimtri ran in headlong, he would see them *both* executed. A handful of those tainted knights might be manageable, but neither he nor Valander were immune to their abilities, or the bite of enough blades.

There was a balance he maintained with this indentured servitude, offering guidance needed to keep the oblivious scion from harm, all while appearing obedient with his every demand in an effort to retain value. The edge he stood on, however, was becoming more precipitous by the day.

"I have other news that may be of interest," Jerdine said.

Valander glanced at him, silent and waiting. *Every word to be judged. I tire of this. If it were not for your mother's wrath, and my desire to see home once more, I would slit your throat in your sleep.* But she would learn of his betrayal, eventually. Considering the consequences sent a shudder through him.

"The city of Brethefen has fallen to internal strife," he continued. *Thanks to my Nerio. The boy seems to have run off, however.* "The peasants have overthrown the nobility, if you can believe it. The small portion of the army that remained faithful to the crown has retreated, and now one of the jewels of the kingdom has slipped from its fingers. Guarded by a sizable force of deserters, no less."

"Gloating is a distasteful attribute. That it fell after the removal of your influence was an inevitability."

Jerdine scoffed, the pleasant buzz helping him ignore the derisive gibes. "Obviously. I *built* that damned city you know, laying out the streets without the imbeciles ever noticing what they walked upon. They were in the palm—"

"Fascinating. Is there a point to all of this?"

"My *point*," he replied snidely, his voice growing harsh as his inhibitions softened, "is that our goals cannot be flatly stated, nor can we admit who we are or from where we hail. We must provide—"

"Your assumptions that I am unaware of these facts are not only condescending but trying my patience."

Of course, because you've been so forthcoming. "I was simply stating, my Lord, that we could use this uprising to our advantage. Brethefen is a foothold defense against some of this kingdom's longest held enemies. Were we to reclaim it, a debt would be owed to us."

There was a silence between them, the ungreased spit nearby letting out high-pitched squeals as it rotated. It and the babble of the crowd fell to the background of his focus.

Valander didn't look at him, his gaze drifting elsewhere. "No."

Jerdine swallowed his angry retort, his eyes darkening beneath a deepening brow. "And what, my Lord, makes you so casually dismiss something that could earn us much needed favor?"

"For the same reason I do not intend to rebuild the gate. Time."

A tremor ran through his flexing muscles—his body's resistance to the impulses that now flooded him. Did the fool truly plan to only act on his own schemes? Did he not think that having an alternative would be wise? *Impetuous ambition will serve neither of us. No one knows this realm better than I, and he continues to ignore my ideas!*

"Listen," Jerdine hissed, leaning forward in the polished chair, "no one wants to be free of this miserable place more than me, but we *cannot* barge in and make demands. We need leverage, people on our side that could provide the Fifths' assistance without the blessings of—"

"The High Chair is out of patience. We need expedience—a trait you seem devoid of."

Jerdine's jaw ached as it tightly constricted his teeth, preventing them from separating while speaking. "Do you care to enlighten me of your plan, my Lord?"

"In time. For now, know that the egg you stole was not the only tool that I brought with me."

Jerdine nearly spat out his drink. When had Valander realized it was missing? *It was only a matter of time,* he thought, his hand shaking slightly. His reasons for taking it had been justified, deserved even. But could he convince his companion of that? *Likely not. Perhaps I can convince him it was not me, before he decides on further punishment.* A flex of his sore hand was all the reminder he needed of his companion's patience, remembering the blade being driven excruciatingly through it. "Egg? Do not dare to blame me for your mishaps, sir, I will not sit here and bear the brunt of-of-of..."

His throat began to choke, a searing pain riving his head in two. His tongue ceased exercising his will and instead moved to that of another's. Lies fell to his mind's wayside. The truth bubbled to the surface, itching insatiably to be expelled from his lips. Somewhere, unseen beneath the table, Valander's fingers were arranged with thin lines of vidut encompassing them, forcing him to surrender to this compulsion.

"Attempt to lie again and I will begin removing fingers. I have been aware of its absence for some time. Your petty lust for vengeance has now cost me dearly, and regardless of the High Chair's instructions, I will carve you in two should you tell me you took it for parochial ends."

"No." His mouth formed the words, empty of choice. "This was important, I swear—"

"Where have you sent the khimaira?"

"Searching..." Jerdine's lips were snarled, spittle flying from them as his face turned red. "Searching for the girl who destroyed the gate, and... and..."

"Settling grievances? You've lost sight of the High Realm's values, old man."

"Cadentite!" he forced out. The spell fell away, the pain vanishing from his brain. Gaps where Valander's proverbial fingers had dug in slowly formed back into shape, leaving a dull throb in their wake.

"There's a stockpile," he said between gasps, fingers white as they clutched the table's edge, "in the mountains. I've been trying to send people to retrieve it, bring it to us, but I've run into... complications. It was too valuable to let slip through my—I mean, um, *our*—fingers. I needed assurances. The khimaira was the best I could think of."

Valander stared at him with thinly slit eyes, quiet for a moment. Even the sound of crackling flame and surrounding chatter seemed to dim.

Surely, he does not believe me lying now? Even he cannot deny the value of that much vidut, not here, in this desolate place.

"How much cadentite?" asked Valander, still pensive.

Jerdine shrugged. "They've made large claims; how true they were is difficult to say. But, if their accounts were accurate, then nearly three hundred pounds worth."

There was the slightest jump of Valander's brow. "Such quantities should not exist in this realm."

"They *don't*. Which is why I assumed the man was trying to swindle me. But still... I did not gather enough for the gate's reconstruction by only pursuing sureties. I did it by chasing every lead, across every continent, regardless of the expense. Most were merely a farce, I expect this to be the same. Nonetheless, I couldn't leave it to chance."

His companion's finger tapped slowly on the table. "What if it *was* accurate?"

"Bah," said Jerdine with a wave and another long draft of whiskey to cool his burning skull. He sneered at the empty glass before raising it and catching the attention of a waiter. "This is why I didn't want to discuss it with you until I knew for certain." *Among other reasons.*

Valander's face was growing steadily more concerted. "Then your caution has been a grave error."

"Error? If there is nothing there, the khimaira will return—you know how *attached* they become. Aside from the expenditure of *my* coin, I don't see what we've lost."

"Potentially everything."

Jerdine's face twisted into an exaggerated, dismissive scrunch. "That's a bunch of dramatic—"

"It is little wonder you failed so cataclysmically during our last incursion into this realm." The ksatsimtri's face had become dark, the points of his mouth turning downward. "There is only one question you must ask, yet you are blinded by arrogance."

Jerdine growled while the veins on the side of his head bulged. *He believes me arrogant? Perhaps he should look in a mirror.* "And what, my Lord, is the question I am so oblivious to? I, who has spent an eternity here in this forsaken place?"

"Where would one," the man replied as though he were speaking to an infant, "if they were inclined and ignorant, find such a wealth?"

"I just told you, there's nowhere—" Jerdine's stomach sank, the burn of whiskey bubbling up his throat as it threatened to rear from his stomach.

"No," he said, shaking his head. "No, it's not possible. It would take hundreds of mages to undo any of their *seals*, let alone bindings. I was *there* when you were naught but a babe. So do not think to lecture me on things you obviously don't understand."

"You are so set in your own delusions that they become your failings."

"My—" Jerdine cut off as the waiter arrived and began pouring him another whiskey. Jerdine took a second to admire the tall, teenage boy. He tucked the thought away, pulling a sun from his purse and handing it to the wide-eyed lad. Before he could satisfy his other wants, he needed to first deal with what were clearly mad ravings.

"My *failings*?" he said as the waiter walked away. "Those seals were *perfect*. The problem with youth is you believe everything must be new and different, changing what *works* for no reason than your own hubris. Had you the experience, you'd understand that the beauty in those simple, elegant designs is how utterly *unbreakable* they are.

"To shatter one—which is what would be necessary to provide as much cadentite as you suggest—would require there to be an existing imperfection. A flaw to exploit. In fact, it would have had to been put there *intentionally*, by one of our... our..."

He became still. *That spiteful, drunken fool wouldn't have sacrificed everything for... For what? Her?* A wave of nausea overcame him, his mouth wet with nervous salivation. *No. No, the risk was too great, even for him. For all of us. But if there were anyone willing to act on an eternal grudge...*

"I see you are not completely devoid of faculties," remarked Valander.

"*Masini*," said Jerdine, the word burning like acid.

"The traitor. Yes, that makes the most sense. It would seem his betrayal began long before his more recent actions against the High Chair."

Jerdine pounded a fist down on the table. "That sniveling worm! I said, time and time again, trusting him was a mistake."

"Why was he selected to remain? He should've been a part of the closing ceremonies with the others."

"Because," hissed Jerdine, "his astral aspect was the only one strong enough to watch over his charge."

Valander raised an eyebrow. "A *talented* fool, then."

"Far more fool than talent, I assure you." Substantially more whiskey was going to be needed, and soon. He glanced around the bustling room, wondering where that serving boy had gone to.

"Tell me more about him. Where did he acquire such skill?"

"He was hand selected to be a student of your aunt's, the cunt. No doubt an early sign of her failing judgement. Once the calamity was said and done, he was the only one of her protégés left alive and refused to teach her secrets to any of us."

"And yet he was permitted to be a guardian? The lack of foresight from the Council prior to the High Chair's ascension is truly appalling."

Do not pretend your mother would've done differently, Jerdine thought. *I know the reason behind her interest in this realm, and given her ambitions, there would be flaws in* all *of the seals. It would be best if she let it lie, for I will not face them again.* "It was a time of desperation and necessity. He made some bullshit claim that he wanted to 'right her wrongs.' I never believed him, but the Council did—probably because none of them were willing to take our places, the cowards."

"Regardless of their incompetence," Valander said, watching Jerdine drink more amber solace with those damned judgmental eyes, "the possibility remains that a seal is broken. I hope I need not explain the prudence in sending the khimaira and your agents to investigate. *Immediately*."

The empty glass slammed down on the table. Jerdine pulled another sun from his pouch and raised it high.

"Do you intend to spend all of our coin on drinks?"

Only enough to tolerate you. No, actually, even I do not have funds that extensive. "*My* money is paying for our room and board, along with your meals, and horses—not to mention bribes for the meetings you've requested. There's plenty more available, under different aliases. Where do you think this sagging purse came from?"

The waiter hurried over with another drink. Jerdine handed the eager lad the golden coin and said, "I'll be needing two rooms, baths drawn, and clean linens. And stick around, I'll like to utilize more of your services later. Oh, and leave the bottle."

The boy nodded and placed the sloshing glass container on the table before rushing off, clutching the stamped coin tightly.

"The khimaira," Jerdine said, pouring an excessively full glass, "should have led the men I hired to that cretin woman by now. I suspect they're already halfway to the mountains." *Which I would feel more assured about were they to* write *me.* He held his face firm, fighting the nervousness he felt slithering under his skin.

"This woman, she is the one that I dispatched at the gate?"

"Yes," he replied cautiously. *He couldn't possibly want to claim her for himself, too?* "Why?"

"She is Astral aspected."

Jerdine coughed, sending some of the burning liquid into his nostrils. "What? You're mistaken, you must be." The glare he received was enough to make him sink in his chair.

"I am certain," Valander said, resting his hand on his sword's pommel, glancing at it. "I was surprised by it myself."

"She seemed... competent. Her mind was not at all addled," said Jerdine in disbelief. "But I'm sure you're right, of course," he quickly added.

"You'd said she was aligned with the traitor?"

"Based on what she said before your arrival, yes. Though at the time I couldn't fathom *why*. If her aspect is why he sought her, then perhaps the gate was not his primary goal. Perhaps..." His face turned cold as he looked up and met Valander's eyes—displeased and smug. He'd come to this conclusion minutes ago and had led Jerdine on a trail of humiliation. *Indignant little shit.*

"He is elevating his defiance against us and risking their release. Have you received confirmation that the girl is dead?"

Jerdine brought the shaking glass to his dry lips. He dared not lie, but feared accountability if the girl—and Masini, if he could find him—were to survive. This was no longer a quest for retribution, but his own survival. "No," he admitted. "But the last I'd heard, they were on her trail. She will be no match for the khimaira, no matter who assists her."

"Assuming you fail, which—"

"How *dare* you?!" snarled Jerdine, leaning forward. "I did not spend monotonous centuries rebuilding the gate and hunting our own kind to have you insult me with—"

"A gate you could not protect when it was most vital. And if you do not wish to be insulted, then begin succeeding. We must assume this girl and the traitor will reach the entrance before you or me; and as you neglected to inform me of this information until now, we are too far to port ourselves back without utilizing our entire supply of vidut."

And no doubt you will be eager to direct Sylvain's fury at me. "I can salvage this! Even if they were to somehow reach the chamber, they could not possibly—"

"The impossible has become reality far too frequently around you. We plan for the worst, which means that we need a handful of the Fifth's children in far less time than your plotting would allow."

Jerdine wiped beading sweat from his brow. The air suddenly felt thick and heavy, the pungent smell of roasting meat choking him. There had to be an alternative, otherwise destruction could rain upon them all. "My *plotting* has kept this realm in check during my entire tenure. Give me time and I will think of a solution."

Valander blissfully kept his mouth closed, his face stoic and unreadable. *Lacking ideas of your own, are you?* he thought, taking another drink. *Your unguided aspirations will send us headlong into a wall.* He well knew that haste in this matter was sagacious, but not all problems could be solved with the edge of a blade or the brunt of a hammer. He threw back the last of his glass's contents, trying to consider solutions to their predicament one at a time.

"I will send word directly to the ones claiming possession of the cadentite," he said, thinking aloud. "I will increase my offer to something irrefutable, as well as put a bounty on the heads of any others who may come to claim it."

"If only you had considered that earlier, we might not be in this position."

Yes, because you have proffered so many ideas of your own, he thought with fists balling up tightly. "I *had*, but who knows if they did not seek other buyers regardless. As I'm sure you've learned, these plebians are unpredictable."

"And if they should succeed regardless?"

"I don't know! We raise an army of our own?" he said, tossing up his hands and letting out a demented, drunken laugh. "Convince the knights of this realm to make a stand with us against a being of unfathomable strength? We could return to Brethefen, I could reclaim my power over it and use the forces there. Why not see my city fall a third time?"

"It is in the tainted one's blood to refuse the spillage of their own kin's."

Jerdine glared at the man across the table from him. "I am *sick* of being patronized by someone who has not so much as present the *glimmer* of a plan. Do not pretend that you do not fear—or are incapable of—failure. I have known your mother since long before your bastard birth and I'm well aware of her wrath—"

Valander's hand shot out and gripped the air between them in a fist, then yanked back towards him. An invisible rope, tied to his chest, ripped at him, violently tugging him forward. There was no resisting the Reach, not when used unsuspectingly, and before Jerdine could react, the unseen tether flung him towards the table and planted his face onto its surface hard enough that there was a *crack* from the wooden boards—or perhaps his skull, based on the bloom of agony. Several patrons throughout the establishment turned concerned and curious eyes towards them.

"You've let the drink allow you to forget your place, old man." The cool calm of Valander's voice was gone, and now fraught with contempt. "If the next words from your tongue are anything besides details pertaining to our situation, I will cut it out, understood?"

Jerdine nodded, his body fixed in place and face pressed to the table. The possession of his body was released as if the rope he was tied to had gone suddenly slack. He slowly lifted himself, groaning as his face and head throbbed. Before sitting fully upright, he leaned to the side and spit a wad of blood onto the floor, the white of a tooth visible in the purple pool. His chest heaved as he tried to contain his fury, hot breath rushing through his mouth as blood dripped from his clogged and broken nose.

The urge to scold, to retaliate, was almost overwhelming. But, as his eyes flicked to the sword that Valander's hand rested upon, fingers loose and waiting, he decided against it. *Your time will come, one of these days, and you will regret dismissing my patience.* "In my humble opinion, my Lord," he said cautiously, "our approach should be more... indirect. Given that we were attacked by several of the tainted knights, I am under the assumption that knowledge of us exists within the realm's upper echelon. If we announce who we are, they may attempt to detain or execute us."

"So, you are capable of making a valid observation."

He felt his eye twitch and cleaned the taste of blood and annoyance from his mouth with a drink directly from the bottle before him. Better to say nothing at all.

"There is merit to some of what you said," Valander stated, his fingers tapping the tabletop once more. He stood, causing Jerdine to flinch back slightly—a reaction that he saw curled the lip of the ksatsimtri's face. "I'm going to retire and will think further on this. It may be wise for you to do the same." He gave the bottle a last glance before walking away and up the stone stairs on the room's opposite end.

Jerdine grumbled under his breath, watching as the man's militaristic stride carried him from the room. Once he was gone from sight, he took another long draft from the bottle, ignoring the metallic flavor that now blended with it as he tried to numb the pain in his face and douse the fire of contempt. He needed a distraction from this fresh hell his life had become, an escape from the reality of his companion's zealous pursuit of their demise.

The world around him was crumbling—a world which he had held intact and maintained a status quo for thousands of years. All undone within a matter of weeks.

Another drink. More fuel to his ire.

Masini, the girl, that cursed, tainted First Born, Valander. They will pay, each of them. And I will have what I deserve, what I am owed.

Now, where had that server boy run off to?

Chapter Fifty-Five

I estimate over four thousand remain in the city and, if they're smart, will begin training all the men they can muster.

Is that thing going to follow us everywhere?" asked Delvan as they slowed their horses.

Desnia looked to the sky, the khimaira's winged outline dark against the grey of morning's earliest emergence. "It basically thinks Nerio is its mother," she replied, trying to steady her uneasy mare. "So, I think we're stuck with it."

"I still don't understand how that is possible," said Nerio, also looking upward.

"A few months ago, I would've said the same about riding alongside a priest and a Blue," she retorted.

Delvan shook his head, pulling the map they'd found amongst Bloodstone's possessions from his saddle bag and aligning it with the stars' vestigial light. Desnia kept a wary eye skyward, feeling a sense of malaise little different from their pack of horses. Despite the exhaustion from being ridden hard through the night—switching to the three riderless mounts at midnight and letting the others run unburdened to cover more ground—the animals were still skittish anytime the strange beast drew near.

"There should be an oasis half a mile from here," said Delvan, pointing southwest.

"I hope so," said Desnia, licking her cracking lips, "since we passed right by the last one."

"The horses do appear to be at their limits," said Nerio, petting the swaying neck of his mare.

"We need to put as much space between us and Brethefen as possible," said Delvan, the air of nobility repugnantly fouling his voice.

Desnia turned her head away, scolding herself. *Stop that, he's made sacrifices, too. Not that he'll let me forget it...* She ground her teeth together. "Let's go then. I'm starving."

They spurred their horses into a canter, following Delvan's lead. The desert had not taken long to return to its dry, natural state after the deluge, and Desnia had spent more time than she would've liked chewing on the grit of sand clouding the horses' trail.

After a few minutes, Delvan brought the train to a halt. A small depression in the rocky, sandy plain sat before them, a tiny pool surrounded by reeds sitting in the center. Desnia dismounted her horse, thankful to stretch her sore legs, blowing hot breath into bundled fists.

They set up camp, tying down the horses as they reared and neighed upon the landing of the khimaira nearby. Nerio had cautiously approached the excited creature, prancing around like it were a pup, and voiced a request for it to lay down and rest.

Which, to everyone's surprise, it did—albeit with a whine in protest.

The three of them sat before a fire as the first rays of sunlight itched to break over the horizon. She was fairly certain their meal of dried jerky was rat—the rodent's flavor more familiar than she cared to admit.

Nerio was the first to speak—probably because he detested the stringy meat as much as Desnia did. "I do not mean to sound ungrateful or rude," he said hesitantly, "but do we have a plan? A place to go? The desert's limits far exceed our own, and it would seem I now have a... *creature* to care for."

"Khimaira," Desnia corrected.

Nerio furrowed his brow and looked over his shoulder at the beast, both its pairs of eyelids nearly closed in slumber. "I'm still confused as to how you know that."

Desnia and Delvan shared a glance. He knew. Her deepest secret had been laid bare to him and... the Truthsayer. How she wished she could go back and change what had happened, done something differently and kept everyone unaware of this curse she carried. It left her exposed, vulnerable in ways that made her writhe in her own skin.

It was easier to pretend that it wasn't there, inside of her head. Life had seemed simpler, but she couldn't say whether it had been better.

She took a swig of the chalky medicine, keeping the voices at bay, reminding her why she had to undertake this journey.

The fear that gripped her was as tangible as the fanged monster nearby. It sat and ate away at her, slowly dissolving her psyche until it would one day send her over the cliff's edge, just like it did with all the other afflicted.

There was no choice. She *had* to get to the mountains and find Asta, even if her chances of salvation were slim. With her mind deteriorating, and her search looking to be a haphazard one, there was a doubt seeded within her, one which wondered if she could do this on her own.

Do I have a plan? she thought. *Yes, but you're going to ask questions... Fuck, do I hate this.*

"Do you know," Desnia started, regretfully chewing each syllable as she struggled to spit them out, "what a 'canary' is?" She looked directly at Delvan. Maybe he would understand. Then she wouldn't have to explain it; wouldn't have to relive it. But if he *was* aware... It could mean he was guilty of sins she could never forgive.

Delvan shook his head, appearing genuine—a relief, and a disappointment.

Nerio swung his head, looking at them both. "Are you speaking of the bird?"

Desnia scoffed. "No. No, I'm not." She took a deep breath, staring into the fire, unsure if she could look either of them in the eyes. "The mines in Calentine, well, they're supposed to be run under the bastard King's strict laws. And since neither of you has had the pleasure of entering one, let me tell you, the shift foremen and overseers can be tyrannical about enforcing them."

"What do you mean?" asked Delvan. She almost wished he would ask to get to the point, to skip everything she was about to explain. Relieve her of this pain.

"You're searched at the end of every shift, stripped practically naked after spending a day in hot, thick air so dark you're basically blind. Humiliated if they think you might have tucked even a speck of sapphire somewhere they can't see... If they're real pricks they'll make you shit in a shallow latrine for a few days and check to make sure you haven't swallowed one. They turn you against each other, offering a fifty-sun reward if you rat on someone who tries to steal one of those blue fucking rocks."

She took another draft of the medicine, hating every word that escaped her lips. They tasted sour, each stinging like vinegar.

"I had always pictured the mines... differently," said Delvan.

"Oh, I'm still getting to the best parts," she said. *Gods, I would kill for a fucking drink.* "Aside from people being falsely accused for money and force-fed laxatives, the foremen had quotas they were required to meet. The more sapphires they brought sun-side, the bigger their day's purse."

"What?" asked Delvan. "That sounds... exploitable?"

"Pretty sure that's the idea." The chalky liquid did nothing to wet her barren mouth, her hands revealing the slightest tremor. "Unfortunately for them, most of the sapphires are found in thin, long veins, surrounded by inanite, which can be a bitch to mine through without shattering the gems. Frustrates the hell out of 'em, sitting in the depths of a narrow crack they can see but can't reach."

It was obvious from his expression that Delvan was wondering where this was coming from, why she decided to delve into the odd subject. Nerio was equally confused, but he was too polite to speak up. *Please, give me a reason to stop talking. Interrupt, be rude, do* something.

There was nothing from either of them, the bastards.

"Doesn't matter that plenty of fucking sapphires come out of there, enough to build the King's wealth and army." Desnia tightly balled her fist. "No, they always need more. There's so many of the gods-damned things in the Upper Tier... That was my first lesson in the poison that runs in men's blood. Greedy fucks, the lot of 'em."

Still staring at the fire, she could see Nerio shifting and Delvan scratching at the back of his neck. "Not you two, idiots. Just... in general."

"I had not realized the conditions the mines presented," said Nerio. "Though I suppose that I shouldn't be surprised, given how the King covets the jewels."

Delvan was staring at his own gem, quietly contemplating with a sunken face.

"Mhm, well, like I said," she continued, "there's a lot of the things sitting where no one can reach. Almost no one, anyway. Do you two know what else Calentine has an endless supply of?"

Delvan shrugged. Whether he was ignorant or afraid to answer was tough to discern. Nerio was the only one to break the silence, "Many things, I suppose, but I doubt I could guess what you're about to tell us."

"Orphans." It made her skin shudder and raise the hair on end. "There's practically an endless supply of them, running through the streets, wanting nothing but survive, to find a dry place to sleep, if they're lucky. Tough to do that when you're barely over three and got no parents, let me tell you."

Delvan looked up and stared at her, his face crestfallen. "*Three?*"

Swallowing hard, she wiped her eyes on her sleeve, trying to hold her scowl tightly, lest it break and let spill years of pain. "Tiny hands, when you're that young," she said. "Can reach into all the cracks the adults can't. Could even earn yourself a meal or two, if your fingers are nimble enough."

"They aren't... they can't... that's too young!" said Delvan, his brow burying into his nose. "They risk over exposure! They risk them gaining..." His eyes went wide, a sadness in them.

Nerio was once again caught between a hidden conversation he didn't understand. "What? What do they gain?"

"The foremen," Desnia continued, "pay the guards to look the other way, with an unspoken agreement between them. After a few years, they kick the children back to the streets and get new ones, that way they don't risk them developing *gifts*." A sneer pulled at her lip. "I still don't know how you can call it that."

"Exposure," Delvan said to Nerio, "to a sapphire changes you, alters who you are and grants you one of our gifts. It needs to be near constant, though, from before birth through puberty. Otherwise, it doesn't take hold, or so I've heard."

"So, these children," said Nerio, "if they worked the mines longer than they were supposed to, they could become Blues?"

Delvan shrugged. "Without a sapphire you wouldn't be able to do much, but, yes, I suppose so. Although I suspect their power would be far weaker than someone who carried it from birth." Delvan's face became contemplative. "But the King would never allow it. Only those approved and ordained by Him are permitted to raise a Blue. He'd do... *terrible* things if He knew that children were working the mines."

Desnia pointed a finger at Delvan, lips thin, still staring at the flames. "Exactly why their little rule exists. Too long in the mines, and everyone gets to spend a few weeks in hell with a special inquisitor. Or months, if you're really unlucky."

They'd all heard the stories; a few had even seen the mangled bodies, dumped in the sewers as a last, sadistic gesture. The one time she'd seen such a corpse, the flesh was little more than ribbons and was hardly recognizable as human. The image still made her gag.

"But every now and then," she said, "someone comes along who's too talented to let go, who is able to get the largest gem out of the slimmest gaps." She looked down at her own hand, flexing it open and closed. "They can't just send you back to the streets, not when you're their means to endless ale and whores. So, they cut your hair, muddy your face, pay the guards double, just to keep you going into the mines. For years and years, until you begin to forget any other life aside from the sweat and dust and dark."

There was a silence that filled the air, burdening their shoulders with its weight. She had never told anyone about this, she realized. Part of her still wished she hadn't, fearing judgement, or blame, for what she'd done. Those fuckers had kept her in their debt, using her for years, and yet what had she done to resist? Before she had known it, it was too late, and the damage was done.

"How long?" Delvan quietly asked.

"Until I was eleven," she whispered. "I had my first nightmare around then. Tried to ignore them at first, but they kept getting worse. I was afraid to sleep; went four days without it, once. I finally broke and told the miners that I worked with. One of the old-timers taught me the trick with muted inanite. Worked great, for a time. Then my foreman found out." Her words trailed off, her stare becoming distant.

"What happened?" asked Nerio. How was he always so concerned?

"There are special inquisitors whose sole job is to find canaries—those of us who've overstayed our welcome in the mines. The King might not be aware of what happens in those tunnels to hell, but the Court sure-as-shit is. Can't be having any non-sanctioned Blues running around—His whole society might fall apart. Asshole."

"I swear, Des, I had no idea," said Delvan, his eyes aching.

"Yeah, well," she said, wiping her face with her hand, "someone does. They came for me while I was eating dinner with my foreman and the other miners. The fucker tried to hold me for them to take, like I meant nothing to him. I stabbed him with my fork and ran for my life, barely managing to escape. Started stealing to eat—then found out I was good at that, too, for all the good it did me."

"I'm so sorry, Des," said Nerio, tears streaking down his own eyes. There was pain there that wasn't solely for her, but she understood that better than most.

"Well, anyway," she continued, "you asked where we're going? Why? I'm heading to the mountains, where there's someone that has a cure for this curse."

"What do you mean, a *cure*?" asked Delvan, his eyes narrowing.

"And who could possess such a thing?" asked Nerio.

Desnia rubbed her face, this conversation and answering their questioning was draining her entirely. "You, of all people, Nerio, should know the answer to that."

"How could I—" His head pulled back as his eyes darted side to side. "The *Seers*?" he asked. "Does that mean that you..."

She nodded.

Now it was Delvan who was confused. "What're you talking about?"

"The Seers in the Asylum," Nerio said, "they would say things; in their sleep, in strange trances, recalling things they'd heard in dreams—"

"And?" asked Delvan. Desnia could almost hear the pieces clicking together in his mind.

"And the things they said *repeated*," said Nerio. "People who had never met, had no way of communicating, would recite the words, verbatim, to these strange, prophetic ideas or predictions. To most it sounded like gibberish or hysterical nonsense, but there was a pattern, I'd heard it.

"I had always suspected that they were, in fact, hearing a voice, a singular one which spoke to them and tried to communicate to us with them as a vessel. The voice of... of..."

Desnia looked at him for the first time since beginning her chronicling, seeing a terror in his eyes. He knew the answer, he just couldn't bring himself to say it.

"A god," she said flatly.

Nerio's stare went straight through her and into the distance. He had gone mute, his face blank and body still. This was going to be more of a struggle for him than she'd expected. It had been hard for her and she didn't even *believe* in gods, but to be told ones different from your own might exist? Ideas like that started wars.

"Des," said Delvan, leaning forward, "I know you have high expectations, but you should know, there's no... *reversal* for this, for what *we* are. I'm sorry this happened to you, but I can't in good conscience let you take this route without telling you that there's a good chance there's *nothing* this 'god' can do."

"It's... all I have," she said, her voice pitching higher. "You've seen what the others were like, in that place—the mad rants, the visions, the blank stares." She let out a shaky breath. "If there's a *chance* that I can do something about it, I have to take it. I can't become like them, Del, I *can't*. I already have to drink this swill night and day to keep from hearing things, from seeing whatever it is the others can't escape from."

He nodded. "I had already decided to come with you, regardless." Desnia coughed to cover the crack in her emotional dam. She couldn't speak for fear of what might accompany the words' release. "I can't exactly go back to my old life, not after everything the past few days," continued Delvan. "And there are other dangers out there, ones that are a threat to everything I've ever known. Maybe this god of yours will be able to help, because after what happened at the gate, I think we're going to need it."

The young, not-quite-a-knight is right about that, came Masini's voice, making her jump with a start.

"Gods-fucking-damn it, Masini," she growled with nails digging into her palms. "*Now* you join the conversation?"

My entrances are always perfectly timed and comedically strategic.

"I didn't find it funny..."

But I did. Oh, your face! A delight, truly.

Delvan looked at her, eyes narrow but more... understanding than they had been previously. "Your mage friend?"

"'Friend' is a strong word, considering the asshole wasn't talking to me after we left..." Desnia swallowed dryly. "*Brethefen* behind."

I have decided, said Masini, *to forgive you for your abandoning of our mutual love. She was a treasure, a star among the clouds, an island in the endless sea, an oasis—*

"Fuck off!" Desnia practically screamed.

Right, obviously my loquaciousness being subdued all this time has left me with an itch that must be scratched, like an insect bite on your scrotum. But I digress. Lady Mithya made her choice—which you could have, in my most humble of opinions, argued against slightly more fervently—and committed the most noble of sacrifices. Is that dew on my lustrous, silvery skin? I'm not crying, I swear, he said with a snivel.

"Are all of your apologies going to be backhanded?"

In perpetuity.

Desnia groaned.

Delvan was looking at her with a cocked eyebrow. Nerio had partially pulled himself from his trance and was staring at her, looking from her to the medicine at her side.

"Des," he said lightly, "do you, perhaps, require more muted inanite? I could assist—"

"Don't." Desnia pointed a firm finger at him. "Don't do that. I'm *not* a patient for you to treat. And while I wish this voice was imagined, he's annoyingly real." She held up Masini's ring. "*This* is Masini, a High Realm mage. What's left of him anyway. I can hear him because... of what I am." Saying that left a taste like bile in her mouth. "And he's the one who's been guiding me, all while incessantly talking my ear off."

You're welcome. Also, I think your people skills might be improving, well done! Although, after the past few days, the bar has been set admittedly low, even by your atrocious standards.

Desnia rolled her eyes.

Nerio was staring at the ring, an incredulous fright in his eyes. "A mage... like Jerdine?"

Desnia sighed and dropped the ring to hang from its chain. "In that they're from the same place, yes. I'd say he's less despicable, but that bar's pretty low, even by his standards."

Ha! That was actually well done, I'm proud, Des. I must be rubbing off on—

"Shut it, Masini, before I feed you to the khimaira."

"What's he saying?" asked Delvan.

"Nothing worth repeating."

"Well, how about some insight as to where we're going?" Delvan asked.

Ah yes, my chance to shine like I'd been freshly polished—which I could do with a little more of, by the way, said Masini. Desnia didn't bother responding. *You're on the right path, keep going straight into the mountains. We're going to be looking for a cave along the old pass. There's a road there that follows it, if we take that, it should get us to the right area.*

"Should?" she bemoaned.

I've told you, my memory from back then is sort of a drunken haze. It was a... dark time.

Delvan remained quiet, staring at her patiently. Nerio's semi-skeptical expression was doing nothing to ease her disquiet.

"He says to follow the road along the pass, we're just going to have to look around for a random cave, I guess."

Delvan flashed a surprised expression and seemed to let out a held breath as he leaned slightly back. "That's... actually better than I was hoping to hear."

"Why?" she asked.

"Because, I..." He scratched the back of his neck again and sighed. "I wasn't sure how to broach the subject, and I was afraid to ask because of, well, everything."

"Spit it out," said Desnia.

"I haven't heard from Kolden or Orne since they left. With that *thing*," he said, pointing to the khimaira, "and the assassins showing up, I'm worried that something might have gone after them too."

There had been a nag at the back of Desnia's mind regarding the brothers, but she hadn't had the time to give it much attention. "Where are the troll and ogre?"

"They were sent to a fortress, in the same pass. One of the Black Bastions. A sort of punishment for disobeying their father's orders. I've been sending pigeons for weeks but haven't received a single response."

Huh. Well, that seems a little too coincidental, said Masini.

As much as she hated to do so, Desnia agreed with him. "Given how much Asta has... *manipulated*, I strongly doubt anything about them going there was accidental. Fuck, do I hate being a gods-damned puppet."

Nerio spoke up, his voice shaken and shoulders slumped. "This *god* of yours," he said, struggled to produce the word, "they would alter your life?

Change events for their own gain?"

Desnia snorted. "I don't know the extent of her influence, but yes, Nerio, she absolutely would. I know you have some idealistic image of how perfect and righteous your gods are, but I can tell you from experience, they're far more human than you'd expect in that regard."

There was a long silence.

"I have reached a similar understanding," Nerio replied, hanging his head down low. "I have been left to wonder at what lays beneath the husk of what I've worshipped my entire life, and if it's as fallible as I am, then perhaps my life has been... a waste." He wiped his eyes, his breathing shaky.

Desnia felt his pain—reminding her to take another sip of the medicine—and knew that his revelation was tearing him apart inside, a reflection of her own cracking soul. She reached out and put a hand on his shoulder, and his eyes released their floodgates as he softly sobbed.

Well, aren't you lot a motley crew, chirped Masini.

"Not now," she grated from behind clenched teeth.

What? Any eyeless, ancient fool could make that observation. Also, I believe that you are correct. Asta does not have the same type of 'influence' as some, but she's more than capable of nudging people into certain directions. If the brothers are in this bastion, I'd bet my left testicle that's where we need to be.

Great, thought Desnia, *just who I wanted to see.* The short one she would tolerate, mostly because he'd asked Delvan to give her the shorter blade at her side—despite what she'd seen of it in her dreams. The little shit had a way of getting under her skin nonetheless, and she wondered how long it would take before she wanted to stab him with it. The big fucker was, in her opinion, little more than an obstinate asshole. But they were important to Delvan, and she was back to owing him. Or did he owe her still? It was difficult to keep track.

"So," said Delvan, "we head into the mountains, then?"

Desnia nodded.

"And you're sure about this?" he asked. "Do you think this god will follow through?"

"She made a lot of promises," said Desnia. "Though in my experience, they tend to..." *Be empty.* "All I can say I hope this is different. If you don't want to come, then I'll understand." She said the words but had no heart in them. She'd been alone her entire life, and while she'd managed all that time, there was a nervous uncertainty that made her believe without them at her side, she would fail.

Nerio was silent, his tears wetting the arid soil beneath him. After a moment he said, "Wherever I venture, death's talons seem to follow. I fear that if I go with you, I will carry our demise upon my shoulders. Perhaps it would be best if you left me here."

"Without you, none of this would've been possible," Desnia said. "Brethefen would've been destroyed, and we'd *all* be dead." He looked at her with bloodshot eyes. "Please," she whispered.

He hung his head low again but nodded. If anything were to happen to them, he'd blame himself, she knew. What she was asking was selfish, but at the same time, he couldn't be left alone to his own devices. She'd seen this look of defeat in him before and remembered well what he'd attempted to do.

She wasn't going to lose anyone else.

"You already know my answer," said Delvan, taking a cringing bite of the dried rodent meat. *Should I tell him what that is?* she wondered before thinking better of it.

The first rays of sun broke through the sky and began drawing downward along the mountains' slopes, igniting the sky in a resplendent splash of color. Warmth pressed against her skin as the desert manifested its first trace of heat, and a few small mice could be seen scurrying towards the basin of water nearby.

I'm still debating, you know, whether I want to come, said Masini. *In case you were interested.*

"I wasn't," she replied.

I figured, but my opinions must be known by any and all blessed enough to hear them. She rolled her eyes. *Oh, also, since the priest seems to be becoming attached to the voracious vanquisher of vile, uh, give me a sec, I'll think of something. Eh, vile... damn, 'V's are hard. Anyway, I probably should have mentioned a little thing about khimairas during the day—*

The sun broke over the horizon, and Desnia felt the first ray press against the back of her head. There was a strange crunching sound nearby, causing all three of them to turn their heads. There was a gasp from Nerio as he stood up and took a few cautious steps forward.

The khimaira, curled into a ball and dozing peacefully as if it weren't death's deliverance incarnate, had transformed into a solid carving of light green stone.

Desnia's jaw dropped as she stood and took a few steps beside Nerio, finding the detail of the effigy to be minute, and to a degree that shouldn't be possible by even a master craftsman. Individual strands of hair were visible, the scales of its tail polished and shining.

"Is it... dead?" asked a horrified Nerio, his shoulders slumping low.

If only they were that easy to kill, said Masini. *No, it's fine. Once it's out of the sun it'll return to it's vindictive, vicious self. Ha! Knew I would get it eventually.*

"Gods-damn it, Masini," she grumbled. "That would've been nice to know beforehand." Nerio looked as though he was on the verge of crying once more. "It's fine," Desnia said to him, "it'll turn back to normal once the sun is gone."

Nerio and Delvan both looked as though they were expecting more of an explanation than that, but she was too exhausted to give it. She went to her makeshift tent, which was more of a canopy than anything else, and laid down, jealous of the khimaira's deep, undisturbed sleep.

Desnia woke, blissfully unaware of what her nightmare had been about, but still feeling the lingering terror. Her heart was pounding, the desert's heat unable to steal all of the sweat from her soaking back.

The sun hovered directly above, glaring and watchful as it spread its torrid heat, leaving her throat raw and withered. Something else hung in the arid shimmers, something that made her want to curl into a ball and weep—an emotion that crushed her soul's will.

Remorse.

It clung like humidity, soaking into her skin with its turgid pestilence. Its crippling symptoms—regret, grief, guilt—were enough to draw droplets from her eyes' corners. She fumbled with a reaching arm for the waterskin of medicine, grabbing the sloshing bladder and gulping a mouthful of the gritty tea, letting out a sigh as the overbearing sensation evaporated from her psyche.

Desnia sat up straight, rubbing her forehead and shading her stinging eyes. It did not take more than a moment of searching to find the source of the radiating self-loathing, sitting in the shade of his pitched canvas covering.

She groaned, debating going back to sleep. *It wouldn't be much of an improvement*, she eventually decided.

With a heavy sigh, she stood and walked to where Delvan sat, facing the watering hole at the center of camp, the khimaira's daytime sepulcher beyond. He turned his head slightly, watching her approach from the corner of his eye, saying nothing as she took a seat beside him.

"What's got you so gods-damned glum?" she asked, resting her arms on her knees.

I swear, said Masini, *you have the emotional intellect of a shark...*

She ignored him, waiting as a silent void filled the space between her and

Delvan. After a while he hung his head, looking down at his hands. "I keep seeing them," he said quietly, "the faces of all those people charging us from the city's gate. Running headlong into the fire." He gripped his hands into fists and shook his head. "Sorry, I hadn't meant to dump this on you. I know there's a lot on your mind."

Desnia's lips pursed into thin lines. "They would've killed you—killed *us*. You realize that, right?"

"That's what I keep telling myself. Hasn't helped me sleep."

"If you can figure out how to solve insomnia, let me know," she scoffed. The glazed stare didn't waver. There had to be something she could say to change his attitude. "Sometimes you just have to deal with it and move on."

Mhm, that'll be sure to improve his mood, said Masini.

Delvan's brow dug down, and she distressingly realized that Masini may have been right. "You're telling me you've just moved on from Mithya, then?"

Her throat choked and water blurred her vision. An anger bubbled in her chest, masking the pain with its scalding heat. "You know what, I don't need this shit. Sit here and sulk by your-gods-damned-self."

She moved to stand, but Delvan lightly grabbed her arm. "Wait! I'm sorry, this is just... hard. I shouldn't have snapped at you."

Leaving would've been the easiest thing. Then she could ignore the turmoil within her heart. She wiped a streak from her sandy cheek and sat back down—why, she couldn't say.

"No," she squeaked out. "I haven't moved on. I try not to think about it, but it's always hanging there like a fucking cloud. I don't even know why, after everything she did to me."

"Can't say that I'm going to be able to answer *that*. Her and I argued constantly, and it was still hard to leave her behind."

"Maybe we're both piss-poor judges of character."

"Mhm, well I am the idiot who decided to break you out of jail, after all."

"That *was* pretty fucking stupid," she replied, earning a chuckle from the downturned Blue. "Although, so was getting me thrown in there in the first place."

"Yeah," he replied with a slow shake of his head. "Not one of my better moments."

It was quiet then. The two sat in that comfortable silence, listening to the movement of the desert's lungs as it drew air over them, the creatures that called it home cautiously scurrying towards the watering hole. She would almost dare to call it peaceful, had she a point of reference.

"What are you going to do after this?" Delvan asked.

"What do you mean?"

"Say we're successful, we find this 'god' and you get what you want. What then?"

Desnia's eyebrows flicked up as she shrugged. "No idea, honestly. Haven't thought much past getting this fixed," she said, tapping her head.

"I can't go back," Delvan said somberly. "Not after all this. Leaves me wondering."

"Spent my life on the run. It's as familiar as breathing at this point."

"Guess we'll figure it out when we get there."

Desnia looked at him, his eyes still fixed on the distance. After everything she'd gone through, could she consider a life after finding Asta that included others? People who *knew* her, yet stayed regardless?

Betrayal, in her experience, was company's dark shadow. Yet, it begged the question: was there a light which cast that darkness?

"Yeah," she eventually replied, "I guess we will."

Chapter
Fifty-Six

Kolden tried lifting his elbow as slowly as he could, crawling upward inch after inch past the burning in his shoulder. *There, further than yesterday, maybe it'll actually go—*

"Ah! Fuck!" he blurted as a stabbing pain exploded deep in the joint's tissue. His arm fell back to his side, swinging in its sling. He kicked the ground in front of him, sending a spray of stones into the fire.

"Hmff," grunted Orne from where his ass was planted on a boulder nearby. Even with his face wrapped in bandages and his jaw basically tied shut, Kolden could still perfectly understand what his brother was saying.

"It'll get better," he said defiantly. "Just needs time."

His brother looked at him, his eyes saying: *Seriously? You're dumber than you look.*

"Oh, fuck off, pretty boy. I think whatever herbs Phrenwa mashed up and put on your face are making you delusional."

Orne shrugged, running his whetstone along the edge of his sword.

"Really? You're going with the 'ladies love scars' idea? You'll be paying double at the brothels, you'll see."

Orne shot a glare at him. "Af leaf I can gef laif."

"Yeah, you seemed to be doing really well for yourself with Helona."

The sword's leather grip began to creak as Orne strangled it, his face turning flush and eyes attacking Kolden like lunging lances. For a second, Kolden worried that the giant oaf would fling the weapon at him, despite knowing it would tear all the stitching in his side. Instead, Orne huffed—with some muffled curses that were reserved for soldiers and sailors alone—and began digging his stone into the blade harder, a *ring* filling the air each time it slipped past the point.

Kolden shook his head and eyed the camp around them. Two dozen men—who he recognized as the traders from their caravan—sat around them in the mountain crevasse. Fires within the tall, sheer walls were hidden from outside view by the weaving entrance, the red blanket of sunset filling the scar-like opening above. Twenty paces of width and a length stretching a hundred yards back provided plenty of room to keep their new companions well beyond arm's length.

There were a few who did not give them a wide berth, and Kolden wasn't surprised when he heard the awkward gait of a foot followed by a crutch.

"Any updates?" Kolden asked as Phrenwa carefully lowered himself onto a stone near the fire.

"They burned through most of their firewood last night," replied Phrenwa, rubbing his splinted knee, "but the scouts saw them bringing furniture out into the courtyard this morning. The oil lamps still burn brightly."

"Great..." he grumbled.

"Gofs-damn if!" cursed Orne, grunting something after Kolden couldn't discern.

"Patience," said Phrenwa. "We are outnumbered and they are expecting us. Even with the hidden entries the risk is too great while they keep the fortress so well lit."

"Not sure if you've noticed, but patience is *not* one of my brother's virtues."

Orne's face turned a deeper shade of red, the repetitive grind of stone on steel ceasing as the man's muscles tightened and bulged beneath his armor. He moved to stand, pointing the sword at Phrenwa and doing his best to shout muffled threats—until he dropped back onto the stone seat, clutching his side with a long groan.

"It would seem this one could do us all some good," said Phrenwa, watching Orne's labored breathing. "Do not worry, we will all have what we wish, soon enough."

"Nof eferyfing," grumbled Orne.

Kolden glanced at his brother. *Gods, she really got to him,* he thought. Part of him felt for Orne; after all, no one deserved to have their trust betrayed like that. But he also knew that his brother would seek vengeance, and no amount of spilled blood would satisfy him—even if it were his own.

"Well, in the meantime," Kolden said, "how about we make our way down to that iguan field?"

Phrenwa gave him a quizzical look. "I would suggest against use of the drug, you've seen its hold over people firsthand."

"Eh wanfs hif fuffing roghs," mumbled Orne.

"Exactly. I don't care about the damn *plant*. I want the cadentite they spread all over the ground."

"Ah," said Phrenwa, seeming relieved. "We searched, hoping for much the same. Unfortunately, it was little more than sprinkled dust. We tried collecting it, but we spotted many soldiers from the castle approaching."

"Probably coming to harvest and keep it out of our reach," Kolden said, his mood turning sour.

"Mhm, we assumed the same. Which is why this one is now a field of ash."

Kolden blinked, looking away from the fire's entrancing dance to the crippled man beside him. "You burned it *all*? Oh, the captain and lieutenant are going to be *pissed*."

Orne grunted, the trace of a smile gracing his lips. Kolden couldn't help but swell with his own feeling of satisfaction, despite the lack of usable cadentite.

"It is the reaction we hoped for, yes," replied Phrenwa. "We assumed they would chase us, send parties searching that we could ambush."

"The cowards have holed themselves up instead, haven't they?"

Phrenwa slowly nodded. "Unfortunately, yes. So, we must continue to wait. The element of surprise is no longer on our side—darkness is our only advantage now. Do not fret, you will have plenty of usable cadentite once we take the castle. A repayment, for my freedom."

After being the one who got you locked up... Hopefully the assassin wasn't having the same thought. Kolden didn't need another supposed ally to turn on him.

Orne was still grumbling, obviously upset that they weren't attacking sooner. It was probably for the best, regardless. Supplies wouldn't arrive for weeks, and his brother was looking rather pale from the blood loss.

He thought it odd, his brother's craving to attack soldiers of their own. Given that they valued their precious plant over even a shred of morality, let alone the crown, he couldn't care less, but Orne had always been a loyalist. For his ire to overrule his camaraderie this soundly, the betrayal he felt must have run to his core.

Of course, the entire castle probably itching to kill them both was no small motivator.

A commotion from the entrance to their stone-walled hideaway turned all three of their heads. Scree flew from under the moccasins of an assassin adorned in white as he came sprinting in, shouting for Phrenwa's attention in whatever language it was the group spoke. Nearly sliding to a halt beside him, the man began speaking rapidly between gasps of breath.

Phrenwa listened intently as the man rattled on, Kolden and Orne flitting their eyes between the pair, unaware of the conversation's content. Phrenwa's head pulled back, his face twisting in confusion as he glanced at the brothers. The scout finished his report, standing there with a billowing chest. Phrenwa leaned forward, chin in hand, silently staring into the fire.

"Whaf?" asked Orne.

"Yeah," agreed Kolden, "what's happened?"

"Something... unexpected," replied Phrenwa. "I am trying to decide what to make of it."

"Care to elaborate?" pushed Kolden.

"Riders approach along the mountain road."

Kolden's stomach cinched, and he felt some of the feeling in his face fade away. "Oh, fuck. Did that fat prick Jerdine finally send someone here to collect?"

"How mamy?" asked Orne.

"Three riders," said Phrenwa, "and, based on the sapphire around his neck, one appears to be a knight, which is a serious problem."

Kolden's face turned incredulous. *A knight? Working for Jerdine?* Something seemed wrong. There was an itch of possibility at the back of his mind, one that, regardless of its likelihood, begged a question. "Describe them," he said. Both he and his brother leaned forward.

Phrenwa said something to the man beside him. There was a back and forth in their foreign tongue, the master assassin nodding before eventually translating for the pair. "Two men, one of which is the knight. The other wears the robes of a priest, an acolyte of the mage's, no doubt. The last is a woman with golden hair, wearing the clothes of a man."

He and Orne's eyes locked together in shared understanding.

Delvan.

Their eyes grew wider as another realization dawned upon them. *He has Desnia with him... Oh, gods, he actually did it, that crazy idiot. And he has the priest, too? If they're on the road heading this way, then that means they're traveling to...*

Kolden bolted to his feet, looking at Phrenwa. "How far from the keep are they?" Orne slowly dragged himself up beside him, sliding his sword into its scabbard.

There was a short discussion between the assassins, Phrenwa turning back to answer them with a curious expression. "They should be arriving at the keep within the hour. Why? Do you know who the mage has sent?"

"They're not Jerdine's people," he said, speaking rapidly. "It's Delvan! We need to get to them, cut them off before they reach the castle!"

"Does that mean the woman is—"

"Yes! Now fucking take us to them before they walk into that sack of shit's hands!"

Phrenwa barked a command to the scout beside him before saying to them, "Go, he will lead you to this one. And hurry—even in the best of health you might not reach them in time, and night is fast approaching."

Kolden grabbed his crossbow and pointed for the scout to lead the way. Orne trailed behind him, hand pressed to his side as the trio moved with cautious haste from the hideaway to the unsheltered mountainside, following a narrow and precipitous trail. Orne's grunts from behind him indicated an anger derived of nervousness, but this wasn't the time for him to prod his brother's phobias. Their near-reckless pace sent gravel tumbling, the sounds sure to draw attention if the captain had been smart enough to send scouts this far into the hills.

The man wasn't that competent, but even if he were, their pace wouldn't have slowed. There was only one thing on his mind as they clamored and scrambled along the path, a thought driving him impetuously forward.

What the fuck are you doing, Del?

Chapter
Fifty-Seven

Lord General,

I do not know what has emboldened the rebellious nature of Brethe-fen's people, but it is clear they are owed the heavy hand of order.

The road, cut directly from the white rock, seemed to climb endlessly upward. The slight slope, stretched over the uncounted miles they'd traveled, had slowly brought the three higher into the thinning, cooler mountain air.

Delvan was grateful they had begun traveling during the day, now that they were beyond the limits of the open desert. It meant he only needed to look over his shoulder, and not to the sky as well. Having the khimaira catch up and rest near their camp for half the night was nerve-racking enough—causing him to wake to every minuscule sound—but having it overhead all day left him feeling exposed in too many directions.

Desnia had said they "shouldn't" need to worry, but it hadn't stopped her from seeming equally nervous around the grisly creature. Their three remaining horses clopped steadily along the path, burdened with the weight of gear and packs from the ones which had been eaten during the night by the voracious predator. It had continued to grow at an alarming pace—Delvan now had to tilt his head upward to look into its eyes while it sat on its haunches—although it seemed to have finally stalled with a body size that could rival the largest bear's.

A few more nights on the path, and we'll be walking, he thought with a grimace. *And what would it eat then?*

"Any idea how much farther this place is?" asked Desnia from her adjacent horse.

"None," he replied. "Your mage friend doesn't know?"

She scoffed. "Unless he's talking about some barmaid's tits from a hundred years ago, he's basically useless." Delvan raised an eyebrow, looking at her. She looked like she was about to say more before her face puckered like she'd eaten something rotten. "Gross, stop. No, just stop talking! Gods..."

"He seems... different than what I was expecting," Delvan said, trying to infer what had been said.

"Age doesn't grant maturity, apparently."

"Lord Delvan," said Nerio from behind, "to answer your earlier question, I believe the bastion should be nearby, based on my recollection of some maps we held in the library."

"At least there's that," Delvan said as a breeze tumbled down the white slope to their side, blowing his hair in his face. He struggled to part it to the sides, the unmanageable locks obscuring his vision.

"Do you think anyone out here has heard about what happened in Brethefen?" Nerio asked, his voice dripping with solemn anxiety.

"Hopefully not," replied Delvan. "I've been sending pigeons here for weeks and haven't gotten a response. I've never heard of them losing their way, but this place is nothing if not remote."

"I'm not relying on luck or lost fucking pigeons," retorted Desnia. "We should assume they know."

"If that's the case, we're doomed already," said Nerio.

The logic in Desnia's argument was sound, if not a little derisive. Something else could have happened to his letters, not that he was certain what. That he had received nothing from the brothers was disconcerting as well. Nonetheless, there could have been circumstances that prevented their communication.

But if he was wrong, they'd be walking into a potential ambush.

Desnia's head rocked side to side, her face pensive. "Well," she said, dragging the word, "we *could* wait to enter until nightfall."

Nightfall? But that would mean... Delvan's head twisted, his mouth gaping. "You're *serious*, aren't you? Have you lost your mind?!"

"Wait," said Nerio, "are you suggesting—"

"That we use the khimaira as back up," cut in Delvan. "Having that *thing* tear apart a few squads of soldiers for doing their *job* is not a backup plan, Des!" His dreams being haunted by the people charging him from the gate were bad enough, their last moments permanently burned into his mind. He wasn't about to add more guilt to his conscience.

"It's better than just walking in there blind!" she shouted, her voice echoing through the valley below. "Do either of you have any ideas that won't get us killed? Thrown in prison? Because I will *die* before I let that happen again."

She's insane, he thought, rubbing his eyes. The only problem was he couldn't think of a better solution.

Blues were rare out here, more so than in Brethefen, and if the keep's occupants knew of Delvan's flight, there was a good chance they would be scrupulous of the unannounced arrival of one. Conversely, if Desnia or Nerio showed up without him—a knight of the Court—they would be detained regardless. At least until their identity could be confirmed, which wasn't helpful.

As much as he hated to admit it, some nightmarish support might be what they need.

"Fine," he conceded. "Nerio, do you think you can keep that thing from eating us? Or anyone else for that matter? We just need to scare them, not commit a massacre."

"It does seem to listen to me, strangely. If it were attacked, or someone attacked us, well, I'd be less than optimistic."

"Not what I wanted to hear, Nerio," he said, exasperated. "Losing the horses was bad enough."

"I do not think we should be so quick to judge a predator based on its natural instincts, Lord Delvan. I am saddened by the loss of our horses as well, as the ending of any life is tragic. But the perpetual cycle of nature's change is one of the few constants in our world, we must acknowledge and accept—"

"I don't believe it," cut in Desnia. "You actually *like* the thing, don't you?"

They turned in unison to stare at the blushing Nerio. "I mean, it *is* affectionate. And I believe it means well. It is, I believe, a child still, and in need of guidance. Would it not be better from me than the principal?"

"Gods help us," Delvan muttered under his breath.

"Pretty sure they don't give a shit," replied Desnia grimly. "Nerio's horrifying pet aside, we need to think of some fake names and a reason to be there. Preferably ones with bits of truth in them—they make the best lies."

Delvan looked at her sidelong. Despite knowing her history and what she'd gone through, something about her ease when switching who she was unsettled him. Perhaps it was his rigid upbringing, and how years of convention and law had governed his life. His occasional bending of the rules was child's play compared to what Desnia must have done to simply eat. Judging her felt wrong, but he caught himself doing it anyway.

"What?" she snapped.

"Nothing," he replied, eyes glancing shamefully away. Best to keep his unjustified prejudices to himself. "I can take care of the story. The army is bureaucratic enough that it'll be fairly easy to convince them of something."

"And what happens if stupid and stubborn recognize you?"

Delvan groaned, also concerned about Kolden or Orne blurting out their real names. "I'll... think of something."

"*That's* reassuring," Desnia chided.

"Like you said, it's not like we have a lot of options." The list of potential failure points in their plan dug talons into his chest. Each prickled heartbeat caused his head to swim, sweat beading on his brow despite the breeze. But this is where they needed to be—the only place Desnia thought she could find a panacea for her ailment, despite his doubts—and he had every intention of seeing it through.

"Um," said Nerio hesitantly, "assuming our identities remain undiscovered, what is it we're looking for, exactly?"

Delvan glanced at Desnia, her brow furrowed as she avoided eye contact. "I'll know it when I see it," she eventually replied.

Too many times Delvan was left wishing Desnia would treat them as partners, rather than tools. There were moments when she was genuine—vulnerable, even—and he couldn't imagine what the weight of verging on a Seer's madness could do to someone. But something told him the aggressive retorts and shielded responses would be there even in the gift's absence. It was understandable, given her past, but more than once he'd had to bite his tongue.

"If the keep comes into view," he said, "we'll pull back and wait for nightfall to approach. If all goes well, maybe Orne and Kolden will have an idea of where we can start looking."

Desnia's only response was a grunt, and Delvan felt the pulse of his heart throbbing in his neck.

The rest of the afternoon was uneventful, the sun slowly setting behind the mountains and soaking the sky with a sheet of bloody clouds. The surrounding summits felt eerie, the winds whispering like a voice in his ear. Glances over his shoulder were frequent, the sense of someone watching them ever present against the nape of his neck, standing his hair on end.

Night began to fall, and as the last of dusk's resplendent flames withdrew into the west, another source of light grew like a beacon beyond the road ahead. An hour after the onset of darkness, the Black Bastion came into view.

They pulled their horses to a stop, looking at the gargantuan structure with wide eyes and breathless gapes. Torches lined the walls, each of the towers' windows were dotted with lantern light, and what he could only assume was a fire of grand proportions in the central courtyard lit the air like a glowing sun.

Every detail was silhouetted by the blaze, the parapets and guards along them stark shadows. The light spilled out to illuminate the mountainside, the white stone reflecting a glare up the steep slope and down into the valley.

"What the fuck is going on there?" asked Desnia.

"Do you think they're expecting us?" Nerio questioned nervously.

Delvan shook his head. "No, this is excessive by any standards. Something's wrong."

"What else is new," grumbled Desnia.

He stared at the keep for a few moments longer, waiting. There was no movement, no riders sent out to pursue or detain them. "Let's go," he said, nudging his horse forward.

"What if that fire's for us?" asked Desnia, holding her reins tightly.

"They've likely already spotted us," Delvan replied. "Given that we aren't being chased or shot at, I'd say there's a good chance this doesn't have anything to do with us. We might as well see, maybe we can use it to our advantage," he said with a shrug.

Desnia scowled but begrudgingly followed. Nerio looked to the sky and scanned before also digging in his heels.

They trotted forward, gravel grinding beneath their mount's worn, iron shoes, squinting against the light. They approached the looming gate of woven iron, backlit by a massive, roaring fire. As they came to a halt a few dozen paces away, Delvan tried to shake the needles from his arm, calling out to the guards above and hoping for no small amount of luck and lost pigeons.

"Fuck!" hissed Kolden as he watched Delvan, Desnia, and Nerio reach the gate below.

They'd arrived too late, the dark hour having made the first half of their trek treacherous and agonizingly slow. Creeping along the brightly lit slope had been an endeavor as well—merely reaching the large rock he peered above had been a mess of zigs and zags to obscure them in shadow, all while watching the trio below progress towards the keep's walls, anticipating the inevitable.

"Maybe they won't open the gates, and will send them packing," said Kolden, hoping out loud.

Orne, crouching to hide his enormity behind the dusty crag's edge, looked at him with demeaning expression. "Reary?" He left out the last part of his statement, Kolden knew: *You can't be* that *stupid.*

Kolden threw his hands to his side. "What?!" he hissed. "It *could* happen."

Orne shook his head and looked back down to the road. *They won't turn a knight away, idiot,* his expression implied. *They're going to be stuck in there with those bastards.*

"Shit..." Kolden muttered. "If Del announces himself someone might make the connection between us and him." Had Kolden told anyone about Delvan? He couldn't recall doing so, but Orne might have. Either way, there was no way of knowing what information the captain had been sent regarding them or their affiliates.

Orne grunted in agreement. Their assassin guide beside them started whispering something in his native language. Kolden wasn't sure what it was, but from the urgency, he was assuming the man was telling them they needed to withdraw.

"Shut it!" snapped Kolden. Could they wait this out? Let them burn through fuel and infiltrate the bastion once it was dark and get Delvan out?

"Del wouldn't know these idiots were on our side," he said, motioning to the annoyed assassin, "until it was too late. I don't know about you, but I don't want to get accidentally roasted..."

"Mhm," his brother said, resting his hand on his sword.

Gods-damn it, he's right, thought Kolden. Delvan wasn't their only concern. If anyone realized who Desnia was—since Kolden could only assume Delvan had broken her out of prison—things could rapidly turn worse for the unsuspecting trio. There was bound to be a bounty on her head.

Orne looked at him, the glow of the keep's fires cutting shadows into his delving brow. *Yes, let's just charge in there, great idea...* Kolden glanced from him and peeked his head above their shaded hideaway once more, watching as the gate lifted and the horses began trotting through.

He aggressively rubbed his temples as he tried to consider alternatives to his brother's bull-headed plan. Instead, questions bounced around in his skull, colliding and creating a mess of new ones.

Why had Delvan sought them out? And with not one, but *two* fugitives? Most importantly, had anyone sent a message to the keep about them?

None of his messages seemed to have been delivered, but he'd been suspect of that situation for a while now. *Probably the damn captain, or Villera, tampering with the damn birds, somehow. Sending them to an intermediary, maybe?* He didn't think them clever enough to pull off a ploy like that, but he hadn't thought them capable of being successful drug dealers, either.

The sound of the gate's rattling, rusted chains ceased. His mind became more frantic.

"Fine!" he said to his brother. "But, for the record, this is a *terrible* fucking idea."

Orne's face was impassive, turning to watch the gate close with a clatter below.

He doesn't care. Not sure why I bother saying anything to the boulder-brained bear.

Kolden turned to their guide, moving a rock that had been stabbing into his knee. The man could be faking his ignorance to understanding their language, but Kolden tried anyway, making a series of hand gestures to convey their plan in a way that even a toddler could understand. "Orne and I are going in, *tonight*," he said slowly. "Go back to Phrenwa and tell him to meet us where he and I escaped."

There was no small amount of frustrated confusion on the man's face as he began speaking back to the brothers in that strange tongue.

"Stop!" Kolden pointed up the hill from where they'd come. "Go! *Bring. Phrenwa. Here.*"

The man stared at them for a second, and Kolden began to wonder if he would need to draw a picture. Finally, he spat out some curses—*those* he recognized from their journey to the keep—and then turned and swiftly climbed back up the hillside, silently keeping to the shadows all the while.

Kolden turned and peered back down over the stone barrier. "Gods, I hope Delvan doesn't do anything too stupid."

"Hmph," was his brother's only reply.

"Yeah, I know." He shook his head. "Probably too much to ask for."

The racking chains and subsequent din of the mass of iron slamming down made their horses buck and shuffle on the wide stone pavers. Twenty paces beyond, Delvan could see the conflagration that raged in the courtyard's center, a heap of tinder composed of what looked to be chairs, desks, and even a few doors. The blunt heat that assaulted them was enough for even Delvan to lean back, the snaps of the flames' whipping ends rising above the surrounding wall's walkway.

Several guards stood before them, fully adorned in armor and hands gripped tightly around the shafts of spears and hilts of swords. They had not leveled a glinting point towards the group yet, but Delvan could see the itch in their eyes, a nervousness that turned everything unknown into a threat.

"I already don't like this," he heard Desnia whisper from beside him. A quick glance revealed the pallor of Nerio's normally dark skin.

Alright, he thought uneasily, ignoring his heart hammering against his sternum, *project confidence and they'll believe you. Just like Hilbrun used to say.* He wasn't nearly as charismatic as his old partner, but with their escape route closed off, he didn't have much of a choice. *Here goes nothing.* "My name is Lord Hilbrun al Portaine, knight of the Sapphiric Court," he announced, holding his head high and horse steady, hoping that if Orne or Kolden were in earshot they would have heard the false name. "I am here on behalf of Lord General Rosethorn, and demand to speak with the ranking officer."

The soldiers looked at each other, uneasy and quiet. The bright, crackling backdrop kept their faces in shadow, leaving Delvan to imagine what expressions they bore. A pain began to swell in his jaw, unseen pins digging into his leg and arm. His breathing became rapid, but he did his best to hold a straight face nonetheless, praying they wouldn't see the nerves behind the façade.

Movement to his right brought his attention to a small group walking around the massive courtyard's edge. Delvan turned his horse to face the approaching men and women, a heavyset, graying man bearing a captain's insignia central among them.

"Are you the commander of this bastion?" Delvan called out as they neared, hoping the tremor in his voice did not climb higher than the fire's roar.

"Aye," said the baggy-eyed captain. Delvan noticed his armor was pitted and rusting, the once polished steel now tarnished and stained. "And who might you be?"

He repeated the false name and rank, watching the man's eyes intently. There was a faint surprise in them, but that could have been for any number of reasons.

"And what," the captain asked, "does the Lord General hope to gain from this unannounced visit?"

"Spot check," Delvan said quickly. "Captain, can you tell me why you're burning what appears to be the entire flammable contents of the keep?"

The captain turned to face the fire, as if it were his first time noticing it. "Oh, that?" he asked. "Termites, my Lord. Infested the whole place. Doing our best to get rid of the pesky insects before they spread."

He heard Desnia snort but kept his focus ahead. "Termites?" he asked flatly. "Out here?"

"Aye, you'd be surprised where ya can get an infestation. I know we were.

Buggers seem to be multiplying, too."

"Right..." said Delvan, looking at the man's gleaming eyes. Something about the dreary, unkempt face left him unsettled, but he dared only push his lie to where he needed, and there were still questions unanswered. "We'll need rooms—preferably ones without any *infestation*. And I'll need to speak to your lieutenants, get a sense for how things are run here."

"Uh huh," said the captain, hawking up a wad of phlegm and spitting it to the side. "We can manage that. Villera here is my lieutenant, he can answer your questions."

Delvan looked to the tall, burly man, also overweight, though not nearly as obese as the captain. "I was under the impression you had three officers here," he said, wondering why the captain had omitted Orne and Kolden.

"Oh, them. Of course," the captain said. Delvan narrowed his eyes. "They're out on patrols for the night; never know what vermin you might find in the hills here. They should be back tomorrow."

"Do you always send your keep's blacksmith on patrols?" Delvan asked.

The captain shrugged, his lieutenant wearing a faintly masked sneer. "He volunteered," was the only explanation offered.

Kolden, volunteering for patrols? I doubt that. "We'll talk to them in the morning then, I suppose. Now, if you wouldn't mind," he said, dismounting his horse. "I'd like you to show us to our rooms. It's been a long ride."

"I didn't catch the name of your companions here," the captain said as Nerio and Desnia also slid from their saddles. "Are they also going to be performing this spot check?"

He heard Nerio behind him. "We are—"

"Introductions in the morning, Captain," Delvan quickly cut in. "When your other lieutenants are here."

The captain's visage flicked with a scowl, before returning to the slimy smile he'd been wearing. Delvan waited, fingers rubbing together as he forced his hands to stay at his side. He caught himself holding his breath, and forced a short, shallow lungful of air through his nose.

"Aye, will do, Sire," the captain finally said. He barked a few orders, and their horses were guided beyond the flames and towards the stables. "Villera here will take care of ya," he said, thumbing to the tall, quiet lieutenant. As they were being led away, Delvan heard the captain call out to them over the fire. "Sleep well and try not to get bit!"

Sleep, he expected, would not find him this night. *None of this makes any sense. What's* actually *happened to Orne and Kolden?*

He pulled Desnia's arm and began whispering in her ear. There were mysteries to solve, and he suspected she would be up for the task.

Chapter
Fifty-Eight

Given your assessment and the defensible nature of the city, the Court will not condone the substantial loss a headlong attack would incur, leaving one viable option. A siege.

Desnia paced in her room, waiting for the ruckus from the courtyard two stories below to fade as the night drew near its apex. The central opening's beacon steadily beamed light through her window, and she could hear the spray of sparks each time another cabinet or workbench was heaved onto it. She walked past the cot, which was the lonely room's sole furniture, and checked the long, manual bolt on the door's interior face for the third time.

Satisfied that it wasn't going to budge for any of those scumbags outside, she pressed her ear to the faded wood, hearing the creaks of boards as the hallway's guard shifted his weight.

"Is he going to stand there all night?" she whispered to herself.

Probably, chimed her ever-constant eavesdropper. *You know, for someone who abhors prisons, you seem to find yourself in them quite often.*

"I can leave whenever I want," she replied. "At least in here I still have a weapon." She patted the double-edged dagger at her side and glanced at the longer, decorated hilt on the one opposite.

I know you told Lord Delvan that no one would see you sneaking about, but at some point, you should probably get on with it.

"Don't fucking tell me how to do my job," she said. "Now shut it, I hear something out there."

The dull *thumps* of footsteps on thick wooden planks reached her ear. A voice began talking quietly, only letting her catch a few words. "...boss wants...the walls...thought we saw...could be coming..."

Desnia closed her eyes, straining to hear what they were saying. The guard posted near her door replied more audibly, "Right, just give me a sec to take care of this one."

Her eyes sprang open. Instinctively, she drew the plain dagger and tucked herself against the wall by the door's hinges. "*Fuck*! I *knew* this was a terrible idea," she whispered, her muscles tightening as she readied herself to pounce. One well-placed stab was all she would need.

Heavy boots grew louder in their steady cadence until coming to stop outside her door. The interior bolt was a thick bar of steel, sliding into the stone jamb and usable only by the room's occupant. Among people not worth their rations in a castle this old, however, she wouldn't be surprised if the sturdy-looking bolt were rigged somehow.

It's what she would've done.

The sound of scraping metal resounded from the doorway's keyhole. There was the familiar grind of a turning cylinder, followed by the weighty *click* of a bolt falling into place.

Her muscles relaxed as the footsteps faded into the distance, the recently arrived pair joining it. Desnia stared at the lock, dumbstruck.

Did they just, uh, lock us in? Masini asked.

"Assholes," she said, looking at the keyhole. Walking over and pulling out the long, steel bar mounted to the door, she tried turning the handle and opening it, only to find her suspicions correct, cursing as she rattled the door. She gave up after a moment.

Now, uh, might be a good time to put your skills to use. But it's only a suggestion, I don't want to tell you how to do your job or anything.

She rolled her eyes and adjusted her grip on the narrow-pointed dagger, digging the point into the keyhole. Pressure and rotation were applied until she felt the bolt in the ancient mechanism begin to retract. Her movements were slow and steady, feeling the metal creep out of its socket until there was a satisfying *clank*.

She slowly pulled the door ajar, the hinges squeaking like a rat in a hawk's talons. *Gods, I wish I had my old tools*, she thought with a grimace—they had included oil for nuisances like this.

With a single eye, she searched for any remaining guards through the cracked door. Observing an empty hallway beyond, she readjusted her silk hair tie and jerked the door partially open to avoid the drawn-out groan of grinding metal.

She slipped into the corridor and pulled the door shut behind her, keeping her body tight to the wall as she crept down the passage.

"So, do you mind telling me what I should be looking for again?" she whispered.

Hmm? Oh, right, said Masini. *Aren't you going to get Lord Delvan and the priest first?*

"His name is Nerio," she said, carefully peeking around a corner, "and no. Not yet anyway."

Uh, why?

"*Because,*" she said, "they'll have guards too. No need to attract more attention just yet and towing them along will just make searching more difficult. Besides, Delvan can take care of himself and Nerio has his... *pet* nearby."

The acid-vomiting death machine, I almost forgot.

The corridors remained quiet, the only sounds while slinking through the stone halls of her own making.

"So?"

So, what?

"What am I looking for?!" she hissed.

Sorry, I got a little distracted thinking about my potential, um, I mean definite *reunion.* He sounded jittery, his normal, casual confidence eroding away. *A cave, that's where it'll be. The entry will be protected by a seal that's impossible to miss.*

Desnia paused, waiting for more information as she listened for footsteps. "Care to elaborate?!"

Uh, big, circular slab of stone, covered in purple lines against a wall. It'll be standing vertically, like a wheel, at least as tall as the walls outside.

"Was that so hard?" she muttered. *If it's in a cave,* she thought, *then I'm going to need to head towards the basement.* Not that she knew what she would do once she found it.

Getting through the castle was going to be painstakingly slow with all the lamps burning and every courtyard-facing window brightly illuminated. Hopefully most of the guards would be on wall duty, though why there was such heavy security was still a mystery. That fat fuck of a captain had obviously been lying, and she could've sworn the flickering of the fire had given his smile a yellow shine, almost like it was full of gold—

The scuff of a boot spun her head with a flash of blonde hair. Nearly inaudible patters of feet were approaching, forcing her heart into her throat. She looked around, desperate for a place to hide.

She dashed on her toes to one of the wall's many alcoves, empty of armor, banners, or other ornaments—removed, in all likelihood, for burning outside. She pressed her back firmly against the cold stone, pulling in her stomach and holding her breath.

The footfalls drew nearer, the muffled clatter of padded armor now falling upon her ears. She gripped her dagger's leather hilt, carefully removing it from the sheath with a whisper as it stropped against leather. Shadows loomed along the walls as bodies walked in front of torches, and Desnia silently cursed. She was obscured, but not fully hidden; one person might miss her, but an entire patrol? The odds were decidedly not in her favor.

There was nothing she could do but motionlessly wait, and hope.

There was a muffled *thump* as Kolden raised his foot and stomped on the wide rock. The solid mass of dense, muted inanite defied him, retaliating against his measly kick by sending a wave of agony through his leg. "Gods-damn it!" This was the eighth rock he'd painfully dug his heel into, trying to determine which stone was the false door he and Phrenwa had emerged from.

In the dull hue of firelight shining from over the nearby ridge, he saw Orne with one hand pressed to his side, feeling at another oversized boulder. "How foo you nof rememfer?" he asked through the headwrap's bindings.

"Wow, Orne, I don't know. Maybe because I'm looking for a *rock* on the side of a *mountain* in the fucking *dark*!"

His brother just shook his head, an expression of disappointment and vexation congealing to say: *Why am I not surprised?*

"Oh, fuck off," he replied. "Phrenwa will be here any minute. Or he should be—been waiting here half the night."

They were in the right area—*that* much he could recall from when they fled the castle. He could have waited for Phrenwa or his men to arrive, but the longer they'd sat, the more impatient both brothers had become.

The sound of sliding scree turned Kolden's head, and from the patches of darkness along the slope to their side, he saw two dozen men—the full company of assassins—climbing down the hillside in their ghostly quiet. One among them hobbled along, leg straight from the splint holding it tight and a staff in his hand for support.

"You decided to join us, Phrenwa?" Kolden asked.

"Afouf fime," grated his brother.

The injured man reached the base of the slope before them, giving them a humble bow. How he was able to be that spry with an injured leg was impressive—Kolden knew that if *his* knee had been bent the wrong way, he'd be chair-ridden for a month. Minimum.

"This one says there was no persuading you to wait. If you truly intend to go tonight, we will be at your side, but I must ask, why not tomorrow? Do you believe your friend's in danger?"

Kolden could hear Orne's teeth mashing together, readying a string of muffled curses, no doubt.

"If the captain or Villera realizes who they are," Kolden said, "they'll use them as bait for us and you. Give them time to dig in their heels, and it will only give them a greater advantage. If we go in *now* and can get Del, well, he's worth a hundred in a fight on his own."

Phrenwa's face grew concerned. "Knights, they are not invincible, you know."

"We're all too aware," he replied, remembering Ferrand's body swimming in a pool of his own violet blood. "But we stand a better chance with him, regardless."

"Lef's fo alreafy," grumbled Orne. "I wanf my halferd." Kolden rolled his eyes.

The master assassin looked from them to the glowing light in the distance, pensive. After a moment he nodded. "These friends of yours, I hope what you say is true about their skill."

"I don't know if I'd call the other two 'friends,'" he said with a glance to his brother. "More like acquaintances." Phrenwa gave him an inquisitive stare. "Whatever, let's just get in there, there's only a few hours till dawn."

Phrenwa dispelled the gaze and motioned an order to someone nearby. The man, dressed in black wrappings that tightly clung to his body, walked to the stone Kolden had most recently plowed his boot into and grabbed a lip at the base. With a groaning heft, he lifted the hidden door, the stone facia swinging and placed gently down on the other side of the dark opening.

Orne looked at Kolden, his face saying: *Really?*

"You didn't find it either, mooseknuckle," he said with a sneer.

The group began filing into the black passage, a lantern being lit once they were a few paces within. The stale air was as Kolden remembered it, the same, familiar sense of urgency bearing down on him as they moved their way down the tunnel. Orne had to constantly duck his head, each of the leaning motions leaving him flinching at the pain in his side.

Kolden gnawed at his lip. Despite their circumstances, it felt like their hand was being forced. In his gut he knew they were on a path of fate's—or whatever you wanted to call it—choosing, and there was little they could do now besides follow it.

Not for the first time. And probably not the last...

Chapter
Fifty-Nine

With the underground aquifers to supply them, we will need to become creative, which is partially why we are sending several legions to join you in Tennefen, along with half a regiment of knights.

A rat rounded her alcove's corner, sniffing. It picked up a crumb, rolling it between its tiny digits and tasting it, indifferent to Desnia's presence. Her eyes flicked between it and the wall's shadows, threatening to manifest at any moment.

She suppressed the urge to kick it as it hungrily roamed closer. Instead, she remained perfectly still as the vermin crawled over one foot, then the other, as the first dark form appeared before her.

Walking in a crouch on moccasins that fell silently upon the stone, the figure was garbed in black from head to toe. The head wrapping's narrow gap looked to have charcoal smeared on the skin, turning the ensemble into the embodiment of light's absence save for the whites of the eyes.

The rat dug its diminutive claws into the fabric of her pants, climbing to her knee as another shape slipped by, blending with the night's shadows. A third silently crossed her path, keeping their head blessedly forward, ignorant of her hidden position.

Desnia felt the rat begin steadily climbing her leg. Her lips pressed together, sweat squeezing from her skin as it reached her thigh.

Another silent infiltrator padded by, the sound of heavier, dully rattling armor fast approaching. It took all her restraint not to squirm, not to breathe. The clanking footsteps were nearly to her. Another minute and the last of them would be gone.

The rat pulled at the base of her shirt, untucking it and dragging its greasy fur across the skin of her hip. Her face cringed as muscles tensed. With each scratch of a claw, it climbed higher, the sounds of heavy boots practically on top of her.

There was a sharp, pinching pain in her side as the rodent sunk its voracious teeth into her skin, tasting the salty sweat.

Desnia involuntarily wriggled and released a grunt, sending the filthy creature to the floor with a squeak. Curses clashed in angry dissonance in her mind, fear gripping her as a domineering figure suddenly filled the alcove's opening. Before she could flee, a sword was pressed to her throat, its wavy black point scratching her skin with a hunger little different than the rat's.

Her eyes slowly rose, climbing the darksteel armor and eventually locking with its wearer's. The towering man's face was wrapped tightly in haphazardly applied bandages, the scruff of a beard poking scraggly through in misshapen patches.

Despite the bandages, she recognized the ogre.

"*You?*" she said. Another one of the dark-clad operatives, his leg stiffly braced, came to a stop behind him, along with the giant's brother, his arm in a sling.

Well, isn't that a stroke, said Masini. *Of luck, I mean, not, you know...*

"Fifures, the thief if sneafing arounf," Orne said in a voice too distorted to understand, lowering the sword.

"What?" she asked.

"Never mind him," said Kolden, adjusting a crossbow in his free arm. "He's just grumpy cause his halberd wasn't where he left it. Where're the others?"

Desnia slid her dagger back into its sheath and stepped forward into the dim torch light. "They split us up. Who the fuck are these people you're with? What happened—"

She cut off as the man between Orne and Kolden suddenly drew his blade, the curved edge scratching against her throat in a blink.

"Woah!" said Kolden. Orne's head swiveled between the man holding the sword and Desnia, looking confused, which, to her, mostly made him look angry. "I know she's a bit abrasive, but you can trust her."

"*I'm* abrasive?" she asked through gritted teeth, tense eyes flicking between the sword and its wielder. "Fucking hypocrite. The rat that just bit me is probably looking for a mate, if you hurry you might catch it."

There was a snort from both Orne and Masini.

"On second thought," Kolden said, "maybe you have the right idea, Phrenwa."

"Oh, fuck you—"

"That dagger," the man Kolden called Phrenwa said from behind his face wrappings, nodding to the hooked blade at her side. "Tell me where you acquired this one."

"I'm not telling you *shit* while you have a sword at my throat, asshole."

Kolden attempted to placate once again. "Ok, her trash mouth aside, she's not—"

The blade pressed slightly harder, her head drawing back as the pressure threatened to break the skin. "I will not ask again, and if either of you interfere," he said with quick glances, "I will fell her before you have a chance.

"The blade. Where did it come from?"

Desnia sneered. The dumbfounded look on Kolden's face, along with Orne's apparent indifference, told her neither would be of help—not that she doubted the man's claims. His eyes were cold as the steel against her pulsing neck, and her defiance was clearly not going to change the situation. "It was given to me."

"Explain."

Her throat clenched, refusing to let the word escape her lips. If she said it aloud, then it would all become real—the escape, this strange bond she felt, the kiss, the... abandonment. She'd tried ignoring it, dodging the thoughts, burying the feelings, hiding from the memories. It was overbearing at a time when she was at the point of breaking—beyond it, even. But now it was being forced from her in an icy plunge that stole her breath and dragged her into the frigid depths.

The word she released was rasped, forced through a choking throat. "Mithya."

The hand of defiance which had held her heart together released its grip, letting it fall to pieces. It felt like her chest was caving in, waves of emotions lapping over her like water on a beach. Fear, elation, grief, confusion—they rolled over her in an assault she was defenseless against. Her body remained still, frozen by the blade's edge held to it, but within there was a clash that shook her world, causing her legs to tremble, making her wish she could go back to being numb to it all.

The man's hard gaze narrowed, his grip on the hilt shifting. "I do not believe you," he said, ignoring the brothers at his side as even Orne made to step forward. "If you have harmed her in any—"

"By the blood of my ancestors," Desnia croaked, her mouth somehow forming the words.

Eyes grew wide and soft, and she felt the sword fall away. She remained fixed, still unable to breathe as her inner turmoil continued. "What has happened to her?" the man asked.

Desnia forced her face into the hardest stone façade she could manage. Her lips were thin, downturned lines as she looked away from Phrenwa's gaze. "I-I don't know. She was injured, and she chose to stay behind so we could..." She gulped as she tried to swallow, unable to finish the story.

Phrenwa's eyes glistened as sadness filled them, pain streaking through the thin triangles of white and into the brown centers. "I wish to know what happened."

Desnia shifted uncomfortably, her head swimming. She opened her mouth, but words failed her, then Kolden spoke up.

"Listen, storytelling is going to have to come later. We still have to find Del and the cadentite, preferably without getting killed."

What did he say? asked a startled Masini.

"Anf fill the cafain," said Orne, his face a deeply chiseled scowl. "Anf the offer one."

"You don't have to kill *everyone*, you big—"

"Nerio's here too," Desnia said, rubbing her head and battling the emotions that threatened to shatter her fragile mind. "And his pet is—Wait, did you say 'cadentite?'"

Uh, Des, I needn't remind you where that ca-ca-ca-fucking glowing rock! probably came from. But if... Oh, well that's interesting.

"Yeah, there's a stockpile of it here somewhere," Kolden replied, motioning for her to join them as they walked. Phrenwa thankfully seemed willing to drop his line of inquiry, but she felt his eyes remain glued to her. "Fuckers are using it to grow iguan, the whole castle is in on it—which we had the pleasure of discovering as they tried to kill Orne and I. Mostly Orne though. And we'll find the priest, I guess, although I don't—"

"Where is it?" she asked, stopping in the hall. The others halted mid-stride and turned to her, both the brothers looking annoyed. There were now a dozen shadowy infiltrators around them, spread throughout the corridor. All remained quiet, looking to the thin-eyed Phrenwa, his gaze fixed on her.

"Walk and talk!" hissed Kolden. She crossed her arms and stood firm, ignoring the looks. The walking tree mumbled something as he shook his head. Kolden rolled his eyes. "There's a door off the courtyard; our best guess is that it leads into a—"

"Basement?"

He looked at her, face and voice incredulous. "Yeah... How did you know that?"

"Long story," she said as she strode between the two of them. "But I think it's why we're here. Let's go, we don't have time to waste."

She didn't look back as she heard Orne mumble behind her, "I fonf life thif."

"Speaking of which, why are you here?" Kolden asked. She ignored him. "Ugh, fine, be that way. As long as I can get my cadentite—"

"—anf fill thofe fuffers—"

"—I don't care. Do you have any idea where the others are?" he asked.

Desnia shrugged. Phrenwa suddenly chimed in. "I believe the knight is directly above us. Maybe they put you all in this wing on different levels?"

She tilted her head. *Was that an educated guess?* she wondered. *Or something else?* There was little time to ponder, as the group turned in unison and began to stalk down the corridor.

Delvan's room was easy to find, his sapphire burning her senses. She couldn't help but groan as she heard the noble threatening a bunch of bureaucratic nonsense as his fist beat against the wood. *Was Phrenwa able to hear that from downstairs?* she wondered.

Something about the look in his eyes... *If he knew Mithya, could he know why I'm here?* She didn't dare bring the subject up, lest she reveal something he didn't know.

The guard in Delvan's hallway had also left his post. "Have you seen anyone in the other passages?" she quietly asked as she approached Delvan's clattering door.

"No," replied Kolden. "It seems like they have everyone on the walls."

"I'm assuming that fire is for you, then?" she asked, inspecting the lock. She drew her dagger, slipping it's point into the keyhole—right as Delvan threw his fist against it in another round of beratement. "Would you *stop!*" she whispered as loud as she dared. "It's me!"

The pounding ceased. It was unclear if he'd heard her command or had just puttered out. She wasted no time slipping the point directly up into the slot, tapping the pommel as Kolden answered from over her shoulder.

"It's for Phrenwa's men, which I guess includes us now, so—Hey! Where did you get that knife?"

"What?" she asked, trying to concentrate.

"That dagger, I gave it to Delvan."

"He said *you* wanted me to have it," she said, feeling the point dig deeper and move the mechanism a fraction of an inch at a time. "You going to try and take it back or something? Tell me I owe you?" *Wouldn't that be typical...*

"Oh, no, I don't really give a shit."

"Then why..." she sighed and went back to the lock.

"He'f feird," said Orne.

That she understood. "'Weird' is an understatement." Before the rabid badger went off on a tirade, she felt the lock *pop* and release, the door swinging ajar.

Delvan was inside, his face flushed and sword in hand. It looked as though he were about to explode in fury until his eyes set on Desnia and the brothers, transforming into exultant surprise.

"I found these two fuckwits roaming the halls," she said.

His eyes glanced at their injuries. "What happened to you two?! And who are they?"

"Long story," said Kolden. "We'll tell you later, but in the meantime, want to help us kill some traitors and maybe get some cadentite? Orne's sad they made his face pretty and would like you to fix it."

"Fuff you," Orne cursed through the bandages.

Delvan smiled, and there was a brief flash of disdain in her chest. She hated admitting it, but she was *jealous* seeing him happy. As if it were that easy to ignore the pain and dire circumstances and just... *enjoy* the moment.

"We need to go," Desnia said sternly. "These two might know where to find what we're looking for, and we still have to get Nerio."

"And what is it," asked Phrenwa, quietly enough that only she heard him, "you're looking for?"

She glanced at him, sidelong, remaining silent.

"You should get your armor on, Del," Kolden said. "We're expecting trouble from these fuckers."

"It's kind of... torched," he said rubbing the back of his neck. "I'll just have to stand behind Orne."

The walking wall grunted.

The smile stuck to Delvan's face a few more moments as they all walked down the hall. Some of their darkly dressed party members fanned out, searching for Nerio's room. Phrenwa's step appeared firmer as he walked near Delvan and the others—whispering their story of the castle's corruption and its infestation of addiction. Desnia found little of it surprising. People in power abused it, that was as common as drunks in a bar. Delvan, however, was completely taken aback, as if it was some outlandish phenomenon.

She rolled her eyes, returning her gaze to those of Phrenwa's company with a cautious eye. *What happens when they get whatever it is they want?* she wondered. She might need to ensure they became separated before venturing too far.

They found Nerio's room on the floor below hers, his lock also pedestrian and his hallway abandoned. When she opened the door, he was elated, his visage coming alight upon seeing the others. "Lords Orne and Kolden! It's such a pleasure to—"

Desnia grabbed him by the arm and dragged him from the room, incapable of listening to the insufferably glee oozing from him. It reminded her to take a swig of the medicine. She patted at her sides, realizing with a wrenching gut that the bladder wasn't hanging from her waist.

She let out a groan. It was still back in her room. *How long before the shadows start talking?* she wondered. With a paled face, she debated going back, but too much time had already been wasted. What they needed was close, she could feel the overbearing presence hovering over this place, incomprehensibly drawing her forward.

As they spiraled down the tower's stone treads, their accompanying night-time stalkers slipped down the halls of separate levels, leaving the group without instruction, deftly aware of whatever their responsibilities were.

"Where are they going?" Desnia asked as they descended farther.

"To the walls, sleeping quarters, wherever they will be most useful," replied Phrenwa as he impressively limped down the stairs. "If we are to cross the courtyard with the brazen flame at its center, we will need a distraction."

"We might have one of our own," said Delvan.

"Oh, no," stuttered Nerio, "I don't think we, uh, well, I hope, um, maybe we don't—"

"Do you think you can get rid of the flames, Del?" asked Kolden.

"Not really how it works," he muttered.

Hmm, he's more ignorant than I imagined, said Masini. *It's simply a matter of... Uh, how can I say this without stumbling like a drunken sailor? Uh, he—*

"You underestimate yourself," Phrenwa uttered from beside him. Desnia looked at him, curious again as to this mysterious companion they had picked up.

Is he going to be an aid, she wondered, *or a leech?*

"I don't have time to explain why that wouldn't work," Delvan said. "But there *is* something else I can do, it'll just take a lot of effort."

Desnia hoped for all their sake he could do something. The courtyard was enormous, and every cranny was lit as though the sun itself shined into it. It would be a dash—hopefully a short one given Phrenwa's splinted leg, regardless of how uncannily quick he was now moving on it—to get to the passage Kolden had described.

The six of them reached the stairs' base and followed a long hall running along the courtyard's perimeter. They crept low as they reached a doorway with crisply lit windows adjacent. They cautiously peered out, seeing a suspiciously vacant, flame-filled courtyard beyond.

Desnia crouched at the back of the group, wondering what lay beyond the blinding tendrils and why—

Phrenwa's hand gripped her arm, firmer than she would've expected, and pulled her back from the others. In an instinctual motion she drew the dagger from her side and spun, but her wrist was caught effortlessly by the enigmatic man. She glared at him, the musty air flowing from her nostrils in torrents, ready to scream for the others.

He quickly released her arms, looking apologetic. "I must speak with you," he whispered.

She looked over her shoulder, the dagger gripped tightly in her hands, as the others tried to observe their route. "What?" she spat.

"The one you call Mithya, she would not have reclaimed that weapon and then given it to you unless she trusted you deeply. And now, you are here, searching for something. I must know, what is it you're truly here for?"

There was an honest curiosity emanating from him, but it was overpowered by a deep, powerful concern. "Why," Desnia asked, cursing her lack of muted inanite and Delvan's proximity. "What's she to you?"

He hesitated, eyes drifting before he finally responded, his words forced. "She's my... what's the word for this one? Twin?"

Desnia's attempted to keep a straight face. Nothing about what she felt from him indicated he was lying, but she'd known a few too many liars talented enough to get by even her acute senses. "If that's the case," she whispered back, "then tell me where you're from."

Again, the man hesitated. Fighting the instincts of secrecy was a battle unto itself, she was all too aware, but he eventually answered. "Trethefen. Both of us, we're here on behalf of our country, of this place, searching."

She glanced over her shoulder. Delvan had noticed their conversation and was watching them with a furrowed brow. An urge pushed her to trust the veiled man before her—one that was becoming far too *familiar.*

"I'm here looking for someone no one else can find," she said. "Mithya knew who, it's why she helped ensure our escape. Give me that name, show me that you're really who you say, and I'll consider trusting you."

He held her gaze for a protracted moment. "Asta."

"And now you know why I'm here."

He appeared disturbed. "Why do you believe they are here? All that we know is there is cadentite, nothing more."

"Because *you're* here. And so are they," she replied, thumbing over her shoulder. "This isn't some grand coincidence. I swear, she gets off on playing with people's lives..."

His eyes went wide, and she could guess what drivel he was going to say next.

"To have their blessing... It gives me a great feeling about what is to come, with them watching over—"

"Stop," she said, raising her hand. "I've had enough of the religious pandering. She can't help us now, trust me. The entrance to her, I don't know, *prison*, is here, probably in a cave through the basement. So, are you going to help us get there or not?" She tried to look stern, like a firm negotiator, but inside she was being buried in anxiety.

"I swear on my life, you will reach that entrance."

Desnia felt the tension in her neck drain away. With a nod, she turned around and crept to rejoin the others.

Delvan hadn't removed his gaze from her. "Everything good?"

"Yeah," she replied. He glanced to Phrenwa and back to her, then turned his attention back out the nearby window.

"I can't see anyone out there," Kolden said, squinting.

"I fonf life if," said Orne.

"Me neither," said Delvan, "But we can't wait here forever. Are your men going to act as soon as they reach the walkways?" he asked Phrenwa.

"Yes," he replied. "They should have easily reached them by now."

"Then we should go." He grabbed the door handle and slowly opened it, creeping outside as the others followed him.

The central blaze was now more coals than inferno, the heat less oppressive than when they'd first arrived. Desnia scanned the wall's walkways, searching for guards as their group skirted the edge of the central opening. The crackling embers were a persistent mask to sounds in the distance, but she could faintly hear the clash of steel and far off screams.

Or was that just in her head?

She shook off the doubt, focusing on what was in front of her while the heat poured over her like the steam of Brethefen's baths. The lack of soldiers was disquieting, and she felt as though her mind was playing tricks.

Kolden motioned to an arch in the wall on the mountain-facing side of the keep thirty yards distant.

Half a dozen soldiers emerged from it, including the obese toad of a captain. His lieutenant stood at his side, a smug expression on his face.

They stopped, holding their drawn weapons tightly.

Oh, we can take them, she heard Masini say. *One big fireball and* poof, *they're done... for... oh, fuck.*

There was a synchronized rustle of leather, mail, and armor as the empty walls suddenly populated with archers, strings to their faces. The clatter of armor behind them spun her head, revealing a score of soldiers approaching from a door.

All sights were on them as the captain smiled, gold dripping from between his teeth. Desnia blinked, now seeing a mouthful of rotted, disgusting yellow.

"Goin' somewhere boys?" the captain asked in his mumbled jargon. He ignored the muffled curses from Orne and continued. "I knew yas wasn't gonna be able to stay away, some of the boys even saw you comin', hulking around out on the mountain. And then when the bait showed up, well, I knew an opportunity when I sees it."

Desnia snarled, looking around, desperate to find a way out. She saw Nerio's face, and it was all she could do to keep herself together. His dark skin had taken on a tan parlor, eyes wide and hands shaking. She wouldn't let him or any of the others die here, not when they'd come this far.

The captain and his sycophants took a few steps closer. "You, pyro, we know who ya are, and if I see a finger twitch then you'll be stuck with twenty arrows, understand? Y'all die like the rest of us if we stick ya enough. The rest of ya, we gots a job for you, down below." He revealed the yellowed teeth once more as he dug into his pocket and pulled out a chunk of cadentite twice the size of his fist.

The glow of the purple stone was vibrant enough to overpower the fire's luminance, throwing streaks of the rock's swirling color on his face.

Her eyes went wide, and Delvan's and Kolden's face came alight. The chunk was larger than even the gate's key had been.

Oh, there's only one way to get a piece that big, said Masini. *They shattered the seal, somehow. Des, that means the way through is open, we just need to get down there.*

Desnia muttered a curse. *One problem solved,* she thought, *and a few score more to deal with.*

"Y'all's gonna be mining this for us," said the captain. "Since you destroyed our crop, you gonna work until you pay back what you owe, you hear? Now, let's get a move on shall we?"

The group remained motionless, their feet planted firmly.

The captain scratched his scraggly beard, his face contemptuous. "Listen, yer friends are all locked up in the towers, if ya think they're coming for ya. This place still has some ol' prison chains that'll get put to use soon enough. I'm looking to get some work out of ya, before I let Villera here deal with ya, but he's itching for a piece now. Want me to let him have it? No? Good, put down yer weapons and move along. And don't think of tryin' nothin', we moved all the loose stuff," he said shaking the cadentite in his hand, "and you won't be finding it if you run off."

Desnia's heart was leaping into her throat as her unblinking eyes searched for anything they could do, anywhere they could run. She doubted the archaic locks in this place would hold Phrenwa's men for long—they seemed too competent for that—but it still took time.

The captain grunted angrily. "Enough of this. You," he said, looking to a bowman at his side, "shoot that one, he don't look like he can hold a hammer anyway." He motioned to Nerio, and the man drew the string to his cheek.

"No!" screamed Desnia. "Wait, I'll—"

She cut off as a roar suffused the air. Everyone's eyes rose up towards the beating of wings trailing the tremendous bleat. A shape emerged from the shadows, skimming along one of the walls and abruptly ending the wild screams of its occupants with fang and claw. The khimaira landed, hidden from view behind the battlements as unnerving shrills filled the air.

There was a cresting flash of gold as it leapt, a *crunch* that turned Desnia's stomach immediately following. With a forceful pounce, it was airborne again, its maw stained in blood and full of a dangling corpse. It dropped its prey directly into the flames with a spray of sparks, letting out another earth-shaking roar as it circled again.

"What the *fuck* is that!" cried Kolden, lifting his crossbow in a panic.

Desnia put a hand on it, pointing it downward. "It's with us," she hissed, looking at the fright that now consumed everyone around them like a plague. "*Don't* piss it off, and it will leave you alone."

That only made his eyes wider, which she supposed was understandable.

"Shoot it! Shoot it!" screamed the captain and his lieutenant.

The arrows that had been aimed at them were suddenly averted and loosed at the winged demon, a few finding their mark, and sending it into a more ferocious fury. Archers screamed with their last breaths, some jumping from the wall and crashing to the courtyard several stories below to escape its dagger-like teeth.

Shadows caught her eye, flitting between gaps in the battlements. *Looks like Phrenwa's men got out,* she thought. "Nerio," she said, grabbing his arm, "tell it not to attack the ones dressed in black!"

"*How*?!" he asked, his face a mold of terror.

"I don't know! Just—"

She cut off as a wave of heat crashed over her. The central fire had violently engorged itself, burning brighter and taller than even when they'd first arrived. She looked between the crook of her elbow, having guarded her face with her arm from the sudden blast, and watched as the shimmering flames twisted and burnt white. Then, like a sail taken by a gust, they were suddenly flung to the side.

The wall of flames slammed into the score of men behind them, setting them ablaze with shrieks that could shatter glass. The fire charred the wall as it spilled upon it like liquid, dripping and streaking down the wide, smooth stone while clinging to the wall's face.

Little more than coals remained in the square's center, small flickers of light popping out as a few defiant embers tried to reignite themselves. She twisted to see Delvan, drenched in sweat, his arm falling back to his side as he panted and wobbled atop a stone he had turned snowy. She dashed over, slinging his arm around her neck. "Get up, don't you fucking dare pass out on me again."

"I'm good," he gasped as she helped him stand straight. She questioned that, but they had other prob—

Des, look out! cried Masini.

The lieutenant was shouting orders at men charging towards them, the archers of the group drawing back their bows. Kolden let a bolt fly from his crossbow, driving deep into the chest of a bowman, sending his arrow harmlessly into the sky. Orne stepped forward, using his armor to take the brunt of a spear's blow and cutting down one of the attackers with a parry and cresting slash of his sword, cutting through the neck and digging into the spine.

Delvan raised his hand, taking a step onto a flagstone and pressing more of his weight onto her shoulders. His face wrinkled as he strained to eject a jet of molten heat towards the attackers.

She watched as men screamed and crumbled into sizzling mounds, their comrades hesitantly listening to the shouted orders of the captain and taking cautious steps forward. "Attack, you stupid curs! Or else none of ya are getting yer iguan rations! Anyone who brings one of 'em down gets a week's worth!"

Desnia heard a whistle and the scrape of steel on stone. She looked up, seeing that a few of the wall's archers were now ignoring the attack from the other fronts to launch their arrows at her and the others, apparently hearing the captain's offer.

Another arrow pierced the air near her head, and she struggled to put the mountain of darksteel that was the armored Orne between them and the bowmen. Delvan had engulfed half their number in a blazing flood before he let out a gasping scream.

An arrow had found its mark, sinking into the top of his leg. The limb gave out and nearly dragged both of them to the ground as his full weight fell upon her.

She strained to keep them upright, looking back to the closing group ahead of them, the captain's words having filled their eyes with the light of insatiable desire. Their greed would drive them to any length, she'd seen it before.

With their loudest cries, the fiends gripped their weapons tighter and charged.

Chapter Sixty

Many of these Blues will take up permanent residence once the city has been reclaimed. Too long has that desert been parched of the King's right hands.

They came at him, like sheep eager for slaughter.

Orne butchered each that dared rush within his darksteel sword's reach. A hard strike broke a man's blade in half, which Orne followed with a punch from a gauntleted hand. His recovery swing slashed into the bone of the man's back, making light work of the dry, fragile leather armor.

The wound in his side had opened. The warmth surrounding it and creeping towards his hip told him the bleeding was profuse. It didn't matter; he just had to cut them all down first. The ones that had abused his trust, mutinied, and turned Helona against him.

His only concern was whether that flying monstrosity would beat him to it.

A spear's point glanced off his chest plate. He smacked it down, lifting his boot and snapping the shaft. The man stumbled forward, his neck falling onto Orne's waiting sword.

Bowman launched their feathered projectiles at him, the heads deflecting off his armor—the drug-addled idiots unable to aim worth a damn. He noticed the thief at his side holding up a spent Delvan, his face white and sickly with exhaustion, blood gushing down his leg. Part of Orne knew he should help, but there was something he needed, an overwhelming lust that focused all his ire on the person he wanted most.

Villera.

The rat-fucker was standing there, two spearmen flanking him and a staunch lackey with a shield and sword guarding his front.

He did not look as scared as he should be.

Ignoring the thief's cries about getting to the basement, he strode forward, noticing Phrenwa help Kolden load his crossbow at his side. Villera stared at him and had the gall to smile.

"Too afraid to fight me yourself?!" Orne boomed. His words were muffled and distorted, but he understood them just fine. He wasn't sure why others had such a hard time, but Villera seemed to get the point.

"So you can do to me what you did to Steddus and Helona—"

"Get her name out of your gods-damned mouth!"

Villera eyed him, a sly grin on his face. "Oh, were you... Huh, you *were*. Well, don't worry, you weren't missing much, trust me."

"Fuck you!" Orne took a long stride, twisting as one of the lances was thrust towards his head. He parried it, then kicked the shield before him with all the strength he had left. Pain exploded in his side from the motion, and his vision briefly blurred. He bit down hard and felt the burning oil in his veins flush his face and steady him as the shield-bearer stumbled back and toppled the lieutenant, falling on top of the man.

Both the spearmen at Villera's sides stared at Orne from beneath rusted helms, knees bent and ready to strike. He grunted and braced himself.

There was a *click* from behind him as a fletched bolt drove into one of their eyes. The man's head was thrown back, dropping him and his spear to the ground with a clatter, Kolden's quarrel sticking through the back of his malformed helm.

The man's partner turned his head, looking at his fallen comrade with a distracted look of horror. Orne seized the opportunity, grabbing the preoccupied soldier's spear shaft and tugging it forward. As expected, the inept fucker held on tight.

Why did they never let go?

Orne's sword whirled through the air, arcing down from above and cutting through chainmail—the brittle metal popping in a spray of tarnished silver—and gouging deeply into his neck, sending a dark splatter across the stones.

The man with the shield was still struggling to get off of his commanding officer as he clumsily rotated side to side, pinning Villera to the ground. Orne took the dead man's spear and thrust it—wincing from the growing pain in his side and the dizziness that swirled in his head—just under the shield-bearer's ribs and deep into his abdomen.

He keened and writhed but quickly ceased as his body went limp. Villera strained frantically beneath the dead weight, trying to push the man off with a face that was becoming more pallid with each of Orne's approaching steps.

Standing over him, Orne was deaf to the curses Villera shouted as spit flew from his lips. He stepped on the arm that was reaching for the fallen soldier's sword, feeling a sense of satisfaction at the man's grimacing visage. The shouts continued, but he didn't care.

No amount of bartering, pleading, or beratement would change what he'd done.

He stared down at the pathetic manipulator, the edges of his vision burning red.

Begging. The bastard was begging as he struggled. The coward had reverted to his true form—dishonorable swine that took pleasure in the power he held over people that he didn't earn but had stolen, just like he'd stolen from Orne. Part of him wanted the weak, little man to live in this abject horror of impending death for eternity, but the vengeful desire of Orne's heart couldn't wait that long.

Villera must have seen the rage in Orne's eyes, because he began letting out chaotic shrills that drowned even the din of the surrounding battle.

Orne stood above the wailing head.

He pointed his sword downward.

He planted his feet wide.

And plunged the blade through Villera's face until the tip bit into stone, the *crack* of his splitting skull pealing through the bloody air. The man went still. Orne grunted as he yanked the blade free, scowling.

It was still there, the knife of betrayal, lodged deep into his chest. It should be gone. Sneering, he plunged the sword down again. Yet the wound remained. Retribution should be more than this. He stabbed again. And again.

He repeated the motion until his arms ached.

Why wasn't it going away?

He screamed before eventually stumbling, unsure of how many times he'd sunk his blade into the bloody carnage that had once been Villera. Catching himself, barely managing to remain standing, he heard another cry beyond his own. He surveyed his surroundings, glaring at the blood and bodies, until he saw the thief screaming, her face pleading as she wrestled with Delvan's weight, his face whiter than the mountain's slopes and eyelids drooping low.

Forcing himself upright and flicking his sword to the side to rid it of that filth's blood, he trudged over to help. As he did, he looked around, ignoring the skitter of arrows and the cries of that heinous creature up on the walls.

Where had his brother gone? And where the *fuck* was his halberd?

Kolden lowered his crossbow, watching as his brother rampaged. Orne's blows had abandoned their normally surgical, precise grace for a wild frenzy, cleaving apart anything in his path.

"Should we help him?" asked Phrenwa from his side.

"I'm not going anywhere *near* him," he replied. "Besides, there's other things that we need to do, c'mon!" He drew the long dagger from his side, holding it awkwardly in his left hand as he ran past two smoldering corpses, their skin crisped a deep black. The stink of burning hair and flesh filled the air with a putrid odor he could almost taste.

Still shouting orders and sending men towards them—several of which Phrenwa deftly struck down, standing stronger on his leg than Kolden would've imagined possible—was the waddling captain. His expression had begun to change as his men were being slaughtered and burned, twisting as the archers on the walls continued to miss their mark as that abomination tore them limb from limb.

"What is this you're doing?" asked Phrenwa as he hobbled behind Kolden.

"That lard-ass has the only piece of cadentite around here," he said over his shoulder, flinching as an arrow struck uncomfortably close. "We're going to get it and have him tell us where the rest is."

The captain's eyes grew wide, and he began gasping between shouts. Seeing Phrenwa and Kolden rapidly approaching, he shoved forward a soldier with a wide broadsword.

The man stumbled and tripped, encumbered by the unfamiliar mail suit. He attempted to catch himself with his sword, but the patinaed, ancient blade snapped under his weight, and the scrawny bag of bones landed hard on his face, becoming still.

Probably should've spent more time practicing instead of getting high, thought Kolden as they hurried past the motionless figure.

A door to one of the towers fifty strides away burst open, another score of the captain's men pouring out of it, climbing over each other as they struggled to fit through the stone arch. The captain spun his head, globs of sweat flying off his face, looking from Kolden to his men, and began running—or whatever his sorry excuse for haste was—calling out to the new arrivals.

No, not fucking happening, thought Kolden as he switched his grip on the blade in his hand, pointing the tip downward. He sprinted, his arm flopping in the sling at his side as he left Phrenwa behind, to close the ten-pace gap between him and Mathin's limping lurches.

His feet pounded the ground as he reached the corpulent fuck. Raising the dagger high, he drove it with all his strength into the man's soft back, feeling it scrape bone and delve between ribs. Kolden felt as though he were gripping the saddle of a bucking horse as he struggled to maintain his grip on the blade as the sleazy captain tripped and surged towards the ground.

With *smack* the captain toppled onto the pavers. A raspy gasp expelled from his lungs. Kolden was dragged forward with him, his grip tight on the handle of the darksteel blade.

So much for getting him to talk, he thought, laying on the dying man's back. The captain's reinforcements were drawing nearer, and as much as he hated the idea of the location of the other cadentite going to the grave with him, he decided to make sure no one else would be able to find it, either.

He pushed himself up and then dropped his good shoulder and all his weight onto the blade's pommel, sinking it to the guard.

Mathin's corpse released a twitching spasm as Kolden pulled himself upright, hearing the scrape of Phrenwa's leg coming up behind him. He glanced up, seeing the shock on the faces of the men that had been charging at him as they skidded to a halt, looking confused as their leader lay motionless on the ground.

Their attention was quickly ripped away, however, as a discordant surge of screams rang out. Kolden's eyes drifted to the door they'd barged out of, seeing a handful of Phrenwa's assassins filing out and cutting down soldiers at the back of the group.

Knowing that the distraction wouldn't last long, Kolden jerked the knife free and hastily shoved it back into its sheath. Using his lone, good hand, he began fishing through the dead captain's pockets.

Where is it, where is it, where is it... he thought as he frantically fumbled through the few places large enough to fit the stone. Finally, his fingers felt something hard and rectangular underneath the body's excess flab. He gripped the stone and, using his foot as leverage, pried it from the man's front coat pocket.

It released suddenly, sending him careening to land on flagstones. He was ignorant to the pain, engrossed and mesmerized by the treasure in his hands. The two ends were jagged, like they'd been broken by a hammer's strike. The other four sides were smoothly polished and perfectly flat, like it had once been part of a long strip or square beam. The swirling shades of purple entranced, an unknown energy held within the object the size of his mallet.

The possibilities...

A hand fell on his shoulder, pulling him from his stupor. Phrenwa was looking at him, concern on his face—and perhaps the smallest amount of envy. "We must hurry back to the others!" the assassin said.

Kolden glanced back at their assailers, no longer distracted. Their focus was clear and all consuming. A dozen or more pairs of eyes were welded to the stone in his hand, looking starved and ready to abandon everything for the chance at a meal.

"Yep," Kolden replied. "Hurry back. Good plan."

Desnia let Orne take the brunt of Delvan's limping weight, ushering them both to the arched passage that led to the basement door. Kolden and Phrenwa were rushing back towards them, a massive chunk of cadentite in the stubby one's hand, a mob at their back calling for blood.

The residual embers of the fire soaked the pursuing throng in crimson, transforming them into horned demons, black sockets where eyes should be, breathing a haze of smoke.

They needed to get out of here.

Wait, she thought, panicked, *where's Nerio?*

In the tumult of the battle, she'd lost track of the priest, her focus being keeping Delvan standing, not to mention alive. Spinning around, she searched the pools of blood beneath laughing shadows, rubbing her eyes as Orne and Delvan shuffled away. There were corpses everywhere, some little more than singed, blackened remnants, others in their last throes as they expelled their rattles.

Their faces blended together, their anguish seeping into her and making her knees quake and buckle. She pushed through the suffocating turmoil, sifting the real from imaginary as she forcefully kept herself upright.

A huddled form, covered in sprays of blood that she hoped wasn't his, was pressed against the nearby wall, shaking with his head between his knees. Desnia stepped over to him, carefully avoiding the slain, their gore, and phantoms.

"Nerio!" she said worriedly, shaking his shoulder.

His stare was distant and unresponsive, and his eyes were... *black?* Dots of light speckled them, clouds of color like the clearest of night skies within. Desnia blinked, and she was once again looking into his brown, white-encircled globes. Putting the image out of her mind, she pulled at his arm, dragging him to his feet—

A screech, terrible and heart-stopping, rent the night from above. Nerio gasped out of his trance, his gaze focusing upward as his face became somehow more terrified.

Atop the battlements, struggling to flap its wings, was the khimaira, studded with more arrows than she could count, green blood dripping down its fur and scales. It managed to lift itself into the air, a handful of archers continuing to launch missiles at it. Its flight was erratic as it fled into the night, its cries echoing through the valley as the darkness swallowed it.

"No!" called out Nerio, tears running down his cheeks.

The creature leaving was a problem, as much as Desnia hated to admit it. The archers not engaged with Phrenwa's men were now returning their attention to Desnia and the others—the ones left alive, anyway.

"We have to go," said Desnia, pulling the priest's reluctant weight along.

Nerio regained his senses—partially—and began sprinting behind Desnia as arrows ricocheted off the pavers around them. They reached the archway at the same time as Kolden and Phrenwa, nearly colliding with them as they all turned to race down the stone tunnel.

Phrenwa hurled a spear he had picked up at the horde chasing them, tossing a man off his feet as it struck his chest. Orne and Delvan were already at the door, the behemoth wrenching the handle like it had personally violated his honor.

Desnia skidded to a halt, shoving them to the side. If the door was anything like the others, getting through it should be—

"What the hell?!" she said, seeing a mutilated lock, the keyhole a gaping mess of tangled steel. "I can't get through this!"

"If's bolfed from the infide," grunted Orne.

Kolden grimaced. "Huh, weird. It's like something got stuck in there. I mean, I would imagine..."

"Move," said Phrenwa as he forced his way between all of them, barely limping. The stone archway now clamored with the sounds of mayhem, the mob almost on top of them.

The assassin grabbed the door's iron handle and slammed his shoulder into it. A burst of splinters flew as the door's planks cracked to expose fresh, yellow timber. It was thrown open, bits of the wooden brace scattered across the floor beyond.

They funneled into the wide, spacious storage area, Desnia giving a inquisitive glance to the entry's shambles. Phrenwa slammed the door closed behind them, bracing his shoulder against it as bludgeoning fists and weapons caused it to jar and clatter.

"Why the hell didn't you do that the last time you were here?" asked Kolden, exasperated.

"No strength then," he replied, vibrations rattling both him and the hinges.

"I loofened if," grumbled Orne.

"The fuck you did," said Kolden. "And that doesn't make any—"

"Orne!" Phrenwa said, drowning out Kolden's voice, his face wrinkled and strained, "help me barricade—"

An ax head broke through the door a few inches from Phrenwa's face. Orne—looking pale—put his shoulder against a storage rack and heaved it with a loud *scrape* across the floor to block the entrance. Phrenwa wedged the broken door's brace against the handle and then began finding other items to obstruct the frenzy that was chipping through the wooden barrier.

Nerio was kneeling at Delvan's side, inspecting the wound in his leg—with an expression that did *not* settle Desnia's nerves. "I need bandages, or a belt!"

Orne dropped a crate on the ground, leaning heavily on it with a pallid, dripping face. He reached into a pouch at his side, tossing a few rolls of white linen at the priest before resuming the barricade's construction.

While Nerio was cinching a tourniquet and pressing bandages around the arrow, Desnia turned to Kolden. "Bring that cadentite here, before he bleeds out!"

Kolden glanced from the glowing stone to the barely lucid Delvan, his face distraught.

"Now!" Desnia bellowed from Delvan's side.

"But... I... Fuck!" said Kolden with a stomp of his foot. "Phrenwa, give me your headwrap!"

The assassin begrudgingly unfurled his head, throwing the black wrapping to the floor as he scrambled around the room to aid Orne. He looked... older than Desnia had expected.

"What are you doing?!" Desnia hissed as Kolden scurried to grab the long linens before hurrying to Delvan's side.

"I'm *not* having him use all of it again," Kolden said, wrapping half the cadentite block with the black fabric—likely dyed with inanite. "If he draws too much, then I'll block him by wrapping the rest of it."

Her jaw dropped open. "You're a selfish prick. You know that, right?"

"I'm not going to let him *die*, I'm just making sure he doesn't use more than he needs to. Gods..."

Desnia shook her head, looking down at Delvan, his lowered eyelids fluttering. "Del," she said, shaking him, "we need you to heal yourself, do you hear me?"

His only response was a groggy rasp.

"Gods-damn it," she spat, unsure of what to do.

They knelt there, Kolden with the glowing stone outstretched, Nerio adding more bandages to the violet mound around the arrow, and Desnia, helpless. Shadows began dancing around Delvan's writhing figure, and it took all her restraint to not swat at them.

"Why's nothing happening?" asked Kolden, his voice frantic.

"Masini, I could *really* use some fucking insight right now," she said.

Uh, he might not be conscious enough to heal on instinct, said Masini, his voice shaken. *There's... No, no you're not—*

Thundering bashes against the door broke it to splinters. The detritus leaning against it began to topple and drag across the stone as the many-headed monster's arms reached through the door, its villainous faces jeering. The twisted, horrid sight made her mouth go dry, and she had to force herself to look away.

"We must go," said Phrenwa, picking up Delvan's enervated body.

Desnia didn't argue as they all crossed the room and descended a cramped, dark stairwell. She watched Delvan's head bob in Phrenwa's arms, a sinking feeling dragging her heart to the floor.

"There *has* to be something we can do," she muttered. "Do you think"—*gods, I hate even considering being in* her *debt*—"Asta could help?"

I'm, uh, not sure, said Masini. *Healing isn't one of her 'gifts,' as the Blue would say.*

"I need *something*, damn you!" Her shout turned heads in the confined staircase, but she didn't care.

Well, our best option will only delay the wound from getting worse. But it's the safest option, relatively speaking.

"Which is?!"

Get him through the entrance to Asta's prison. Once he's in there, he will be, uh, suspended, I guess you could say.

"But he won't get better?"

...No. I'm sorry.

Desnia's hands curled into shaking fists, a tear forcing its way from her eye's corner. He had come here for *her*, he had come to rescue *her*, and because of this gods-damned curse, *he* had to pay the price? No, she wouldn't allow it.

They needed to find this entrance, before Delvan lost any more blood.

They emerged into a damp, musty cellar. Masonry walls butted roughly hewn stone as foundation met bedrock to create the capacious room. A single brazier burned in its center, casting a dull light on the dark walls. To Desnia's dismay, it appeared to be a dead end.

"Enough frunning," wheezed Orne. "Lef's funnel them through the sfair-well, we fan holf here and fill each and efery one of the fuffers. Then I fan get my halferb back—"

"Listen, you thick-skulled fuck," Desnia said, finger jabbing into his chest, "if we don't get Del to where they found the cadentite, he's going to *die*. Understand? Are you just going to leave him so you can get yourself killed too? You can barely *stand*!"

The domineering man sneered—almost pouting—but remained silent.

"Desnia," Nerio said, inspecting Delvan's wound closer, "we need to hurry. I think his artery's been struck."

Desnia's heart was hammering as her eyes darted along the nooks and crannies of the room's limits. There was a flicker, a light that didn't match the wavering pattern of the brazier's dim fingers. Desnia jogged over to it, her breath held in desperation and found a crack in the wall.

By appearances, the stone—a wide vein of white, muted inanite—had eroded slowly over time, a leak from the foundation above trickling water that ran along the vertical slit in bedrock. Gravel and rocky debris littered the puddled area, the loose, crumbling stone above the opening's peak cracked and precarious all the way to the ceiling. The entrance had only been recently exposed, by her guess.

Those idiots, she thought, putting her hand on the single, wooden post jammed in the center of the narrow opening. *Mines have collapsed from less.*

"Through here!" Desnia called out to the others. This was it, she could feel it through that crevasse, calling to her.

"How do we know what's down here will help Del? This is insane..." said Kolden as he approached, eyeing the post and narrow gap. There was a crash from the stairwell. "But then, so are they. Fuck it." He climbed through the opening, vanishing as he turned a corner in the faintly lit passage.

Phrenwa handed Delvan to Orne, the giant taking the Blue in his oversized arms.

"What're you doing?" Desnia asked.

"Go," he said like it was an order. Orne didn't need to be told twice, turning and carrying Delvan despite the exertion that was clear on his face. Nerio followed close behind, pressing on Delvan's wound as they gingerly moved around the support column.

Phrenwa turned to face Desnia. "Nothing is more important than finding

Asta. Not your friend, not the others, not me."

"I swear," Desnia grated, "if you're about to give me the same fucking speech as your sister, I *will* stab you."

"I say this in case I do not—"

"Shut up. You're coming with us."

He pressed his lips into a thin line, looking over his shoulder at the stairs, the commotion growing as the light of torches grew brighter. "I will stall for you and then follow. I swear."

"You'd better—" She cut off as a shadow moved on the wall to their side. Others danced, changing and moving as she blinked, but this one seemed... different, less ephemeral. It stalked closer, hidden in the dark behind the mess of crates filling the room.

A thought popped into her head, a question that she would have asked herself had her mind not been filled with this haze of specters. The door to the room above... it had been barred from the *inside*.

Who had locked it?

She gasped as the creeping shadow suddenly lunged forward, the point of the spear in its hand aimed directly at her chest. Phrenwa turned, seeing what was happening. With speed that defied reason, he outstretched his hand and shoved her backward. She tumbled back into the cave's mouth, sprawling on the ground while gasping shallowly.

There was a glint of steel where she'd been standing, the assailer stumbling forward as his lunge pierced nothing but air. Phrenwa moved like a viper, his sword slashing the man as he passed in front of him, his bodyweight carrying him forward.

Directly into the support column.

The post dislodged and bounced off the stone. The grind of shifting rock shook the floor as gravel fell upon it and chunks of ceiling dislodged. She locked eyes with Phrenwa, who went to run into the tunnel to join her.

"Stop!" she screamed, holding up a hand, knowing full well he wouldn't make it. He halted mid-stride—right as the cavern's narrow entrance filled with tumbling stone and dust in a violent quake, debris getting tossed into the air and the loose scree sliding out to her outstretched feet.

The dust choked her lungs, forcing her to cough as pain flared in her ribs. *Those are probably broken. Again...*

Nerio and Kolden appeared from around a corner.

"What happened?!" exclaimed Kolden. "Where's Phrenwa?"

"He's alive." Speaking was a struggle. "On the other side."

"Are you alright?" asked Nerio.

She nodded, pulling herself to her feet with his help.

"At least we don't need to worry about anyone following us," Kolden said, indifferent to her pain and clutching the glowing cadentite tightly.

"Aren't you worried about Phrenwa?" she asked.

"Of course, but he's a scrappy bastard if ever I did meet one. Besides, this tunnel is long, and we don't have time to try to dig *that* out, assuming we even could. Not with Del looking even worse." The words were the first real inflection she'd heard in his voice. *At least he's capable of caring about* something.

That she was leaving another person behind was not lost on her. After one last look at the dense, tightly packed stone that filled the space where the cave's mouth had been, she turned and followed the aloof bastard and Nerio to where Orne was standing with Delvan in his arms.

They followed the cave's narrow corridor until it opened into a larger, wider cavern. She grabbed one of the sporadically spaced torches from its stand and lifted it high. The light didn't reach the top but highlighted a few stalactite tips hanging low.

"Gods," said Kolden from her side, "you could probably fit the bastion in here."

Well, we did need the space, said Masini casually. She didn't dare ask what for.

It was a wending path. As they descended further into what she could only assume was the heart of the mountain, she glanced over to Delvan, Nerio doing his best to attend to him without interrupting Orne's excessive strides.

Nerio suddenly started moving his arms in quick, hasty motions, pressing his fingers to Delvan's neck. "Nonono... Stop!"

"What is it?" she asked, her throat choking as Orne rested Delvan on the ground, Nerio hovering over him.

"His pulse," Nerio said, his face stricken, "it's so faint I can barely feel it. Des, I don't think I can... He doesn't have much time."

"How close are we?" she asked.

Not close enough...

"Fuck!" she hissed, pacing back and forth, fingers pulling at her hair. "Masini, earlier, you were about to say something, another option besides getting him through the entrance."

Hmm, nope, I don't seem to recall—

"Tell me!"

Are you trying to die, too? Because you're more likely to kill him—and yourself in the process—than you are to save him. Without experience your soul could be pulled in, leaving your body behind—and being noncorporeal is not as glamorous as I make it seem. We're better off hoping his own healing will outpace the wound's bleeding, trust me.

Delvan's pallor seeded doubt in that notion.

There wasn't a single word Masini said she liked. And there were several parts she didn't understand. *But the idiot would do it for me.* "Too bad. Now tell me what to do."

If this doesn't work, I just want you to know... I'll be really sad there's no one to appreciate my sophisticated vulgarity.

She rolled her eyes, hearing Kolden whispering to Nerio as she knelt at Delvan's side. "Who is she talking to?"

"Her ring, I believe," Nerio whispered back.

The brothers gave each other a slow, long look. She ignored them.

"Alright, so what am I doing?"

First, take the glowing rock. Put it near you, you needn't hold it.

"Cadentite!" she said reaching out her arm.

Kolden looked from her to the swirls of color in his hands, and then at Delvan. "Fine, just don't—"

"Use it all, yeah I know," she said, snagging it from his hand and resting it by her knees.

Good, now... This is going to be hard to explain given my, uh, impediment, said Masini.

"Now is *not* a good time to be short for words, Masini."

Right, right. You're going to need to reach into him. Now, I know what you're about to say, between all the curses, and no, I can't tell you more specifics. What I can tell you is this: his soul, like yours or mine—well, mine might be a bad example, but I digress—is tethered to his living body. Once it's not, it goes, um, someplace else. Someplace special that you have the ability to go to, with said glowing rock.

"Special? What're you talking about?" she said, exasperated. "You make it sound like I can do it, just like that."

Obviously. I hoped I wouldn't need more detail, since you've done it before.

"I think I would fucking remember *that*."

Strange that you'd forget being stabbed in the chest. Or, more specifically, being stabbed twice. *Do you really think it takes two strikes from a ksat-ksat-ksat-testicle fiddler! one of my kind, to kill you?*

Desnia froze, remembering. That helpless feeling, on the ground when they were at the gate, the mage clad in black scales plunging his glowing sword into her chest.

And feeling nothing.

Then he'd removed the blade, the markings on it glowing white hot and...

She rubbed where Delvan had healed her, the pain endured difficult to forget.

"You're saying, what, I went somewhere else when he did that? Then why did the second strike work when the first didn't?"

Well, you made a tiny part of your body transition over, out of instinct to protect it, and the sword hit, uh, nothing, more or less. Kind of. Honestly, if a sapphire had been closer, you might have vanished entirely, which would be impressive, but bad for someone inexperienced. As to how he managed to pierce the veil, so to say, he has a very special weapon that you don't want to be on the wrong end of. As you're well aware.

There was a hive of questions buzzing in her head. She glanced at Delvan's gem, wondering what mysterious curse its proximity could unlock.

"So, when you said my soul could be pulled out of me..."

I meant there are forces that won't be happy about your actions and could basically rip your soul into a different part of existence for all eternity, thus leaving you to roam endlessly until you lost your mind with part or all your body left here. Basically. It's complicated. And takes practice you don't have.

Her face suddenly felt icy, the sweat like frost. "Alright, well, before I lose my nerve, or Delvan, tell me what to do here."

The brothers were watching with incredulous looks, and for the first time she saw the familial resemblance in their scowls. Nerio was biting his nails while his body fidgeted.

Rest your hand on his chest. Excellent. Now, close your eyes. Ignore the visions, they're the other half of your abilities, and not what you need right now. Focus instead on the warm, glowing rock. It's a good rock. The best rock. Make it your favorite rock. Now do you feel anything?

"Besides annoyed?" she asked.

Focus, think of it as... picking a lock.

That was actually... good advice. A lock was a thing she could understand, a collection of moving parts that made up a whole. With the right touch, one could sense the most miniscule detail, sensing each component with a touch. She tried that now, attempting to ignore the shadows and their cackles, and instead feeling the stone radiating like a hearth beside her.

There was a tingling sensation in her fingers, and the darkness seemed to glimmer and change like a curtain being pulled back. Through closed eyelids, she swore she could *see*.

"There's... lights," she said, awe floating in her voice. "Like lanterns in the night, or stars. They're *everywhere*."

Good! Good! I mean, ehem, try not to get too excited. Do you see any right in front of you? His voice sounded like it was directly behind her, speaking over her shoulder.

"Yes, there's three. And another one that's... faint, like it's far away. Where's yours?"

No distractions. Focus, we still have the hard part left. Now, the faint one, that's Lord Delvan's. I'm going to need you to grab it, and fight.

"What do you mean?"

It's the natural way of things, Des. People die, and when they do, their... essence wants to leave their bodies and move on. You have to take hold and wrestle it back, while it still remembers its body and before the gua-gua-gua-fucking things on the other side fully sink their teeth in. Otherwise, you need to get creative...

"What if it's stronger than me?" She was no fool, strength had never been her asset. Getting around fights had been a hard lesson learned young, using her other skills to survive instead. Could she win in a fight against Delvan's *soul?* Or whatever else was over there?

Then it pulls your own, uh, essence into its world with it. You can move in and out of here, Des, assuming you have the, uh, glowing rock and a nearby sapphire. But touching another person's essence while crossed over is dangerous. Forces will see it as theft, or worse, an intrusion. Fighting death and what follows isn't easy, and if you lose—being this inexperienced—you could be separated from your physical body, and then the whole, you know, eternity thing.

"Have you ever done this before?"

...No. I've seen it attempted twice, and only once was it successful, by someone with a few thousand years more experience than you. Not to pressure you or anything.

She frowned. None of that was reassuring. "Who did it," she asked, staring through closed eyes at the faintly pulsing light where Delvan's chest was. The question was a way to procrastinate, the new world around her daunting enough to give her pause.

My friend, on yours truly. But he had to put me into the ring, since I'd been dead *dead. This... half of your gift is not something many of my kind practice. Frankly we were both lucky to survive. Or, well, end up eternally shiny, at least.*

"And if I manage to pull him back, he'll be healed?"

By the Greats, no. He'll just wake up for a short time in a massive *amount of pain. The healing he will need to take care of, which he should do instinctually. Hopefully. Now, not to rush you, but you're running out of time.*

Desnia took a deep breath. She could do this, she *had* to do this. Keeping her focus on the flickering candle flame before her, she reached down and felt her hand and arm sinking into what felt like a cold mountain stream.

There were gasps. She cracked an eye, wondering what had caused them, and saw her arm.

It had turned into a misty, black smog up past her elbow—and was completely buried *in* Delvan's chest.

It was all she could do to not make her own shocked exclamation. Instead, she pinched her eyes shut once more, trying not to think about what she was doing, and grabbed the dim light tightly.

It felt like it was... diffusing, slowly burning away and floating into the nothing that surrounded her. She was hit with an epiphany, a moment of clarity where her mind transcended to become a part of her new surroundings, a guiding hand at her back. In that brief moment she knew what she needed to do. So, she squeezed.

Hard.

The light fought her, along with... something else. She could feel it, trying to drain and pull her into the blackness with what remained of Delvan, a pair of red dots glowing menacingly behind his dim soul. She gripped tighter than she'd ever done before, feeling that it wasn't her physical strength that mattered here, but her will.

And she was *not* going to succumb.

She resisted with all the energy she could muster, a low growl escaping her gritted teeth. The dimming slowed, and then began to reverse, yielding to her command. It brightened, faster and faster, until the light in his chest became a beacon that outshone all around it. She felt the last of his soul slip back through her fingers. Something—no, *someone*—told her to let go, that she had done what she could, the burning, red eyes fast approaching.

Her hand opened and she pulled her arm from Delvan's chest. Only once she knew it was well away did she dare open her eyes, seeing her normal, solid appendage once more.

Delvan's eyes popped open, red and veiny, as he released a scream of agony that echoed in the damp cavern.

Green light manifested in waving wisps around them, the glow of the cadentite beside her—which had hardly dimmed from her efforts—quickly fading as the waving aurora grew brighter and filled the voluminous cave. It only took a few seconds for the edges of the cadentite block to turn black, prompting Kolden to spring to her side and swiftly wrap the block's exposed segment.

Desnia, pulling her eyes from the entrancing sight, looked to Kolden, ready to rip his head from his shoulders. Before she could get a word out, however, the verdant display shimmered and gravitated to each of them, vanishing as it was magnetically drawn inside their bodies.

Desnia glanced at the shaft protruding from Delvan's hip, the blood still soaking his pants and leg. Her cheeks puffed out as she slowly exhaled, hating that she needed to do this. "Sorry, Del," she said as she gripped the arrow and, in a single motion, ripped it from his leg.

There was a spurt of violet blood as a raspy sound was released from Delvan's throat. His back arched and Desnia grimaced.

As the shifting glow settled and its vapors extinguished, her body became *invigorated*. Ever-persistent aches that had rooted themselves into her muscles since the beatings in the Asylum vanished. She saw Orne stand straighter, removing his facial bandage to reveal an unscarred visage. Kolden—despite how much she wished he could remain invalid—was rotating his arm freely.

There was a moan from Delvan, and Desnia looked down to see him rubbing his sweaty face. He sat up, gingerly feeling where the wound in his hip had been. Kolden peeked under the cadentite's black covering to expose a sliver of purple luminance that glimmered in his eye, letting out a breath of relief.

"What happened?" Delvan groaned.

Ha! said Masini. *I knew you could do it. Never doubted. Pupils of mine are clearly superior, thanks to my wise and unique teaching methods.*

She shook her head, avoiding the easy retort. Delvan, on the other hand, deserved a response, one that was exceedingly difficult to explain.

"It's... complicated."

Chapter Sixty-One

Know that we possess the utmost respect for you and your years of loyal service. The court has, however, ultimately voted upon your demotion as consequence for this loss. This action weighed heavily on us, but you of all people must understand that discipline in this matter cannot be avoided.

Dripping water could be heard over their footsteps as the group wandered deeper into the cave. The air was stale, and the surface of the stone looked to be covered in some form of black char.

Even with his extensive experience around Blues, it had been difficult to explain to Delvan what she'd done—she barely understood it herself. Then there were the lurking shadows, waiting just out of sight. She tried to ignore them, but the paranoia itching under her skin made her skittish—and easily frustrated over annoying sounds.

"We should head back," Orne said for the third time. "We can dig out the tunnel and finish them off. Then I can get my halberd back."

"If it gets you to stop fucking complaining, then be my guest," Desnia said. "But I'm going to keep going." They were too close, and the hauntings too vivid, for her to turn back now.

"I'm going with Des," said Delvan, making the ogre grumble.

"Where does this lead, anyway?" asked Kolden, who'd been twisting his head and scurrying around like a rodent looking for more of his precious cadentite. She kept her mouth shut, having no answer to his question.

Desnia noticed a light ahead, faint against the flicker of their torch, but visible, nonetheless. A steady glow amongst the dark.

A *purple* glow.

"It leads to *that*," she answered, picking up her pace and rounding the massive bend.

A sight that brought her jog to a crawl came into view. Filling the height of the cavern was a circular opening, a tunnel with smooth, symmetrical walls, far more intentional than the rest of the cave. Encompassing the interior of the towering corridor was a web of cadentite lines, arranged in neat, complex patterns that stretched into the mountain's core.

And there, undulating like a pool of black oil, was the peak's black heart.

Desnia stared at the rippling substance, defying gravity and stretching like an empty void to block the tunnel's end. It mutely reflected the bright, purple luminance around it, captivating in a way that horrified, but also filled her with wonder. It called to her, like the sea to a sailor—full of danger, yet, also, freedom.

Rubble surrounded them, their path previously cleared through the boulders and loose stone. Some of the larger blocks had cavities in the flat, polished faces—lines where pieces of cadentite like the one Kolden carried would have fit perfectly.

Ah, just the way I remembered it, said Masini. *Minus the seal that closed it, which is now all around us. I feel bad for whoever the poor bastard was that busted it apart. The explosion must have shaken the castle above.*

"How?" she said, still enthralled by the vertical pond of shimmering black.

What, break the seal? Well, I left a nice little flaw in it, as I've told you. Wouldn't take more than a good chisel swing in the perfect spot, though I'm surprised the idiots managed—

"What... Is... *That*?!" exclaimed Kolden, abandoning caution and running towards the tunnel's entrance.

"By the gods..." whispered Nerio. Delvan moved beside her, his gaze fixed on the otherworldly portal. Orne—blessedly—was lost for words.

"What is it?" asked Delvan.

"I... I'm not sure," she replied. "I'm still waiting on Masini to get around to explaining."

Well, it's an entrance, obviously.

Rolling her eyes, she said, "No, asshole, where does it lead?"

Ah, right. What are your thoughts on hell?

Desnia's stomach twisted into a knot. "It... It can't lead *there*."

Oh, no. What you call 'hell' doesn't exist. Desnia let out a breath, her shoulders slumping. *But this would be sort of the equivalent, maybe worse. For the living, anyway.*

Worse?

Through the fear that was drenching her, she felt the boiling furnace of anger come alight, causing her to tremble.

"You NEVER thought to mention this?!" The heads of the others turned to face her, concern painted on their faces.

Hell. He had brought her to literal hell, the crass bastard, and there was no other way to go? She'd never wished more that he had a body—so she could strangle him.

By the Greats, no. Why do you think me and the other, uh, ones like me didn't go in there? We'll be fine, though, with you to navigate us through.

"And how," she glowered, "do you expect me to do *that*?"

Because you just did it. With Lord Delvan.

"What..." Did he mean the place with lights, the one that had felt so strangely... comfortable? "*That* was, uh," she looked at the others, "that place?"

Mhm, deceiving, I know. But I assure you it's as dangerous as dipping your testicles into a cannibal's mouth. I can explain more once you head through. About where it goes, that is, not the cannibal thing; what I wouldn't do to forget—

"Wait," she said, face scrunching. "I thought you said I could get pulled in, for all *eternity*?"

Only if you try to steal the, uh, lights, or souls, or whatever. Or get caught. Definitely don't get caught.

What was he talking about? "Caught by wh—"

Also, this entrance is different from what you just did, Masini continued. She ground her teeth. *You leave a* tiny *bit of yourself here when you, uh, sneak in with the glowing rock, making it easier for your body to be separated from your 'essence'. This is more like a door, open to anyone, and fully submerges you. It's safer. Actually, safer may be a poor word choice.*

Anyway, at least this time you don't need to rely on the glowing rock to get there and come back. That's a way in, which leads to the way out—or, you know, the prison of a demigod who might want to kill yours truly.

"How do you know about this path?"

Mostly because I put it there. Listen, I can't explain more yet, but there is *a path for you to follow. You're probably the only one who can.*

Desnia's mind drifted as she stared into the abyss that reached out and touched her heart. She glanced at the others, wondering what they were thinking. Whether they were having second thoughts. Despite knowing she would lose everything if she turned back now, she couldn't help but admit that she was having some of her own.

"What about the others?" she asked quietly.

If they're either brave or stupid enough to follow you, you're going to need to help and guide them. They don't have the same 'gifts' you do and will end up wishing they were dead enough to join those around them if you're unable to find them.

It was all on her, then. Did she tell the others? Reveal that in helping her they were risking their own lives—their *souls*? She had little choice, but to the hulk's credit, they stood a chance—albeit a small one—of surviving were they to go dig the tunnel entrance out.

They deserved to know. They were probably going to turn back, abandon her like everyone else, but they should know, all the same.

"I'm going through *that*," she said, pointing at the tunnel's amorphous end. "It's dangerous; to an extent that's beyond me to say or understand, but if I don't..." The shadows on the walls were watching her, their laughter quiet. "If you want to turn back, I'll understand." The last syllables choked her, and she couldn't bring herself to look at their faces.

"Are you fucking insane?" asked Orne. He seemed to have forgotten about his stupid polearm.

"Not yet..." she muttered, glancing around. *Not far off, though.*

Nerio's visage was one of deep consternation. He shuffled his feet, looking like he wanted to say something. Finally, he spoke up with a wavering voice. "Des, I must ask. Does this lead to..." He struggled with the words, each one like a personal betrayal, "your *god*?"

"I'm sorry, *what*?" said Kolden from the tunnel entrance, his focus turning back to them for the first time since they'd found the opening.

Desnia ran her fingers through her hair, debating what to tell them. "Fuck it," she cursed. "Some of you already know part of this, but the High Realm—the mages like Jerdine, the ones that built the gate—locked away a god. One that I've had the displeasure of hearing for well over half my life. That," she said, pointing, "is the entrance to her prison. And I'm going to help free her."

Kolden turned and looked from the twisting lines of cadentite back to them, taking a few cautious steps away from the entrance after being unable to loosen any of the glowing stone. "Normally, I'd have called you sane as a Seer," she and Delvan glared at him, "*but*, I also saw someone have their soul sucked out recently, so let's say, for a second, that I believe you." His tone was incredulous, but the worried expression said differently. "Do you happen to know *why* they locked this 'god' away? I don't like the maniacal priest either, but maybe they had a very good reason."

Aside from them being all powerful and threatening our existence? asked Masini. *Hmm, that's a long story.* She could hear a... *sadness* in his voice.

"Because they were scared of them," Desnia said, making her own inference. When you're the toughest one on the street and someone bigger and meaner shows up, you do whatever you can to get rid of them. Those in power held onto it, no matter the costs.

There was a presence, hovering behind her. Massive and domineering, it filled her with a comforting determination and nudged her to encourage those around her. "She's made promises, if we help free her."

"What kind of promises?" Orne asked skeptically.

"And what do you mean 'we?'" asked Kolden.

She glanced at Delvan, afraid to hold his gaze, worried that he was reconsidering, despite everything. But he just stood there, quiet, understanding. Resolute. *Nothing I say is going to change his mind, is it?* Part of her wanted to chastise him for blindly believing in her. Another part, however, felt a warmth that helped mend some of the cracks.

"She's been locked away a long time," Desnia said. "So, I don't know how much stock to put in what she told me, but she said that she would give us—all of us—'gifts' for helping her now, and in the future."

Nerio looked like he was ready to faint, and the brothers both shifted, exchanging glances that always seemed to say more than she could recognize.

"What kind of 'gifts?'" asked Kolden. *Gods, why does he always have so many fucking questions.*

"I don't know," said Desnia with a shrug, "something about 'the power to turn us into legends.' Or 'that which we don't know we want.'" *Vague and open to interpretations. Couldn't you have been more specific, just once?* "Honestly, I don't want to trust that it could be that easy, who knows what she'd say to get us to help." *But there had better have been some honesty to it, because I swear, you bitch, if you lied about my salvation, I will give my last, sane breath to ensure you remain locked up and no one* ever *finds you.*

"If we have to go through *that*," said Kolden, looking at the seething black mass, "I wouldn't say it'll be 'easy.'"

Orne's brow had furrowed, making him look angry. Or, *angrier*. Frankly, she couldn't recall a time when he *wasn't* scowling. After a few quiet moments of brooding, he spoke. "I'll do it."

What?

Desnia was too shocked to speak. His brother, however, was verbose as ever. "What?! Have you lost your gods-damned mind? Are you even thinking?"

"Mhm," the giant grunted. "I'm thinking if a god offers to make you a legend, it's worth the risk. I'm tired of being put wherever it's 'safe' because mother can't handle the risk. We're never going to get out from under father's shadow if we don't do something. I'm not going to let mediocrity erase my name from time."

That was actually... coherent. She didn't realize the oaf had it in him.

"That's... I don't..." Kolden sputtered, finally at a loss for words.

"They might have more of your stupid rock," Orne said. "Or answers to your annoying fucking questions. Also, you're making me another halberd." Desnia couldn't help but snort.

Kolden's face turned red as he began to pace. He pulled the wrapped stone from his pocket and took a resplendent peek, chewing on his thoughts. "Fine!" he announced. "But I think this is a *terrible* idea."

"You say that about any idea that isn't your own," grumbled Orne.

He had a valid point. Maybe she hadn't given the oversized sword stand enough credit.

Nerio was rubbing his hands together, glancing back from whence they'd come. Desnia felt her heart sink. She needed him, more than she'd ever confess. There was concern, one that made her think he couldn't make it on his own, not with his disposition and what he'd so recently endured. But could she force him to follow this path?

"Please," she whispered to him.

"I..." his head hung low, his voice quiet, "I have already been abandoned by the gods, Des. To enter their domain after being cast aside? I dare not think of the consequences, nor do I much wish to speak to them."

The events of Brethefen had left him deluded, and she knew that he blamed himself. But she couldn't listen to this fountain of self-pity. As much as she wanted to keep Nerio safe, he needed to understand that his actions were his own.

She burst into a diatribe. "Your gods don't *exist*, Nerio! They never did! Why is it that when you succeed, you thank them for *your* efforts? When you fail you wonder how you disappointed them, instead of asking how *you* could be better. *They* didn't get you out from under Jerdine's thumb, you did that yourself. How can you think they watched that happen to you and think they cared? How can you love something that has let you be hurt all your life?!"

There was a pervading silence, unbroken by even the dripping of water as the cave and its inhabitants held their collective breath.

"How can you?" he asked solemnly.

"I *don't*." There was no love between her and Asta, she'd made that clear. "She has something I need. This is an exchange, we both get what we want. But don't think for a second that I worship her."

Delvan spoke up from over her shoulder. "I don't think he was talking about your god, Des."

She spun, eyes wide. "What did you tell him?" He looked back at her, silent, speaking only with his expression: *Nothing he didn't deserve to know.*

Mithya. Nerio knew—thanks to Delvan's mouth, apparently—and he'd used it to throw her own argument back in her face. That more people were aware of *her* pain, regardless of who they were, filled her with a bleak numbness. She didn't want it shared with the world that she was capable of hurting, exposing her to be weak, like everyone else.

But, if anyone could understand that pain, it was Nerio. The person capable of always doing right, regardless of the tremendous wrong he'd endured.

She turned back to Nerio, his eyes on the floor. "Maybe... Maybe that wasn't the best argument. But, Nerio, you have to know, there is *something* on the other side of that tunnel, and it's offering you the strength to *fight back*. Stop running and come with us. With me."

Nerio glanced at her with reddened eyes—a depth to them that eerily reminded her of the vision in the courtyard. "I'll... I'll go," he conceded. "But I do not yet know if I will accept this 'gift.'"

She put her hand on his shoulder, letting out a breath of relief. "Thank you."

Facing the tunnel, she felt frozen, the responsibility of others now on her shoulders. There wasn't enough space in her head for all of the questions, doubts, and fears that expanded within it.

Someone sidled up beside her. "You're not going to ask me?" Delvan said with a smirk.

"Gods, no," she scoffed. "I *know* you're stupid enough to follow me. Besides, I'm pretty sure we're back to you owing me one."

He laughed. A walk through hell awaited them, and he *laughed*. She supposed if he could manage that, she could take a few more steps forward.

As they neared the tunnel and approached the entrance into the vast unknown, Desnia thought to give them one last warning.

"Whatever you do, don't touch anything."

They stepped forward and were enveloped by darkness.

Chapter Sixty-Two

As a knight commander, you will assist in the retaking of the city, but under the command of another who the Court has deemed worth pulling from the Southern War.

Desnia blinked, her eyes opening to a captivating world of stars.

Floating in the distance, the glimmers pricked the shroud of black in every direction, distorted only by intermittent, nebulous swirls of color. From all around her came a breeze that did not pull at her hair or cool her face. Instead, it was like this place was sensing for something as it subtly invaded and groped her spirit.

The thin sheet of water she stood on reached endlessly outward, reflecting the dome above until it met the dim horizon's edge. At her feet, diminutive ripples cascaded out from her shifting boots, disturbing the unknown expanse.

"I wouldn't recommend doing too much of that," came a voice from behind her.

She spun, her feet splashing and sending an echo to accompany the waves. A man, square jawed and a few inches taller than her, stood there, smiling stupidly between long locks of curly brown hair.

I know that voice, she thought as she looked him up and down, taking in the well-tailored garbs.

"*Masini?*"

"In the flesh!" he said, outstretching his arms. "Well, sort of."

"You're... here? You seem so..." she said, stepping closer.

"Unpolished? Mhm, indeed. But far more distally inclined." He held out his arms and fingers, wiggling them.

"You're saying, what? I could *touch* you?" she asked, her tone curious and disbelieving.

An insinuating smile tugged at his face. "Don't tempt me with a good time."

Another few steps brought her closer, mere inches from his chest. She looked up into his eyes, the grinning confidence faltering as she said, "There's always been *something* I wanted to do."

"Well, Des, I mean," he said with a nervous laugh, pulling his head back, "I appreciate our relationship, and I know how magnetizing I can be, but I think maybe it would be best if we kept things platonic. You're not really my—"

In a swift, violent motion, she jerked her knee upward—directly into his crotch.

Breath left his lungs in a long, wheezing rasp, his body folding in on itself as he collapsed to the ground. Watching him writhe, his hands clutching his groin, she couldn't help but grin.

"*Gods*, did that feel good," she said.

"Yep," he said, his voice an octave higher. "I should've seen that coming."

"Men," she said with disdain. "Always thinking it's about you. Now, are you going to tell me where the fuck we are?"

It took a few minutes of whimpering and deep, shaky breaths, but Masini eventually forced himself to his feet, his clothes strangely dry despite the roll on the watery ground. Had he made any splashes?

His hands remained on his knees as he answered. "Welcome, to the Astral Plane."

Why did that term sound familiar? "I think... I think Asta mentioned something about this place. What is it?"

"Not surprising, considering it's basically their domain," he said between breaths. "It was once described to me as the natural world's opposite—a counter to its unforgiving, unbiased, and indifferent disposition. It's overlaid onto everything that surrounds us, ephemeral, yet permanent, and made entirely of matter's opposite, the thing that gives souls their, uh, substance, I guess."

"Which is?"

He grimaced as he stood straight. "Emotion, for lack of a better term. Without it we're no more than furniture—which is good for couches because I have done some *nasty* things—"

"Focus, or I'll happily knee you again."

"Right, right. By the Greats, you're violent. Anyway, the lights you see around you are souls, off in the distance. Some living and still tethered to their bodies on the other plane, some attempting to overcome their trials, and the rest heading to peace—or whatever, I don't know what happens at that point, and I'm happy to remain ignorant."

Souls? Trials? Desnia looked around, wishing she had a place to sit to try and process everything. Using the cadentite to look in had been like dipping her arm through the surface of a lake. Now that she was fully submerged, how completely alien this place was truly settled in.

There was, however, a faint familiarity. The part of her that tinged her blood the wrong color felt at home here. But her human side, and its survival instincts, were telling her to run and escape while she still could. But she had the others to worry about and needed to trudge through her discomfort.

Wait, she realized. "Where's everyone else?!"

Masini held up a hand, finally catching his breath. "Don't worry too much, they're not going anywhere—although I can almost guarantee they're not having much fun at the moment." She glared at him, fury digging her brow low. "I think we have some time," he said hurriedly, "and we can't have you running off blindly. I need to explain some things first."

She tightly flexed her jaw but kept quiet. The world around her was more foreign than any she'd ever visited, each direction similar to the other, with nothing to guide her way. She needed to know more—although, what he'd already explained was leaving her feeling more confused than confident.

A sickening trepidation, deep in her gut, told her she didn't have much time, regardless of what Masini said.

"Hold on," she said as something registered, "how are you able to talk about this? You haven't stuttered once."

"I *know*. It's great! I manifest as my true self here and am not bound by that damned contract spell." He smiled, looking to the sky—if you could call it that—and spouted off a litany of nonsense. "Vidut! High Realm! Sylvain, you old cunt! And Protorus, you annoying, pragmatic bastard!"

"Uh, what?" she asked, wondering which of them was verging on insanity. Perhaps she already had lost her mind and didn't know it. Was her own psyche cruel enough to lock her away with Masini for the rest of her days?

She tried not to vomit.

"When I died," he said, beaming, "Protorus attempted to do the same thing you did to Lord Delvan. He and I both have a bit of experience here, in the Astral Plane, and I'd managed—being the wily, handsome bastard I am—to evade the guardians long enough for him to find me—"

"'Guardians?'" She felt her heart begin to race, eyes flitting.

"—and then he tethered my soul to the ring, as my body was too far gone—necromancy is grisly business. And gross. Anyway, I think the jewelry had been his own backup plan. Adroit bastard always had one. Not perfect, but better than death.

"However, once the old stoic somehow got annoyed at my prolific, eloquent company—and began wondering what would happen to me if *he* were to die—he restricted what I could say through the ring. Here, though, I'm free to say what I want!"

Not liking the sound of whatever these "guardians" were, her dread was steadily building. "Wonderful," she said dryly. "Now, freely explain how I get to the others."

Masini's expression fell flat. "I divulge some of the most complex workings of the Astral Plane, and it's like you don't even care. Youth these days..."

She stood there, glowering at him as she waited, tapping her foot. Masini looked down at the waves spreading into the distance. "There's some dangers you should know about first. Also, you might, uh, want to not—"

"*Now,*" she interjected.

The corner of his mouth pulled straight back, turning his expression as dry as his voice. "Fine, heedlessly charge forward, that's worked out for you so well thus far."

"Masini, I swear—"

"*Shh*, lessons are about to begin. Close your eyes." Her brow furrowed, wondering what he was playing at. *He's an ass, but he wouldn't jeopardize the others*, she conceded. She sighed and let her eyelids drop.

"Good," he said. "Next, I want you to picture one of the others in your mind. Specifically, what you *feel* about them. Whether you can see it or not, that's the connection we have with the people in our lives. Emotion is the ultimate influence, and it leaves a thread to all those affected and entangled with your own. Find it and use it to bring you directly to the person you're thinking about." Then he grumbled, "Reckless as it might be..."

"What about you?" she asked, her eyes still closed.

"I am connected to the ring hanging around your neck. Where you go, I will follow."

"Not sure if that's a blessing or a curse," she said under her breath. She stretched her neck to the sides, trying to follow the ambiguous instructions. *Just 'feel' for them. That's like asking a fish to walk...*

She pictured Delvan. Images came to her mind—of him over her after being stabbed, of him collapsing as he burned down Brethefen's gate. There were emotions tied to each; relief, elation, worry. But they were *hers*, not Delvan's. When had she shared his feelings? What was the most vivid recollection she had?

Calentine. Yes, she could almost feel the heat of the flames as the Merchants' Guild burned, its glass windows shattering. She remembered waking and feeling his pain, guilt, and grief, long before she'd groggily realized he was there. Those emotions had clung to him for far too long...

Gods-damn it, Del, why do you have to be so disgustingly noble all the time?

They had torn him apart, she knew, changing who he was at his core. His guilt was an agony that no amount of liquor could extinguish, and even after he'd stopped blaming himself, the permanent need to cope remained—or maybe it had been dormant, waiting.

Reliving his anguish felt *wrong*—a heinous invasion of privacy on her part. She felt a shiver and opened her eyes with a shaking head. "How the fuck is this supposed to work? I can't do this if you don't tell me more than 'feel' for them," she said to Masini, who was still standing in front of her amongst the starry backdrop.

The mage cocked an eyebrow. "So that's definitely *not* Lord Delvan, then?"

Desnia's breath caught, spinning around. There, kneeling on the strange, shallow water twenty paces away, was Delvan.

And he did not look good.

His face was pallid and sweat-soaked. Every muscle was frozen, and short, staggered breaths were attempting to force their way into his lungs while his hand clutched his chest.

The ghastly demeanor was nothing, however, compared to the horror that stood before him.

Desnia gasped, taking in the impossible sight that had brought Delvan to his knees. An armor-clad Blue, eyes sprouting fire and mouth drooling violet blood, stood above Delvan. The shaft of a crossbow's short bolt protruded from just under his chest plate, and from it oozed a black puss, turning into a vapor that swirled around the crumbled knight.

The apparition was someone she recognized, a man long dead—Delvan's old partner, Hilbrun.

"Delvan!" she screamed, lurching forward to go to his aid.

A hand fell on her shoulder. "Wait!" said Masini as he spun her back around. Mithya's dagger was suddenly in her hand, the waved blade pointed at Masini.

"The guardians can't hurt the living!" he said frantically, putting his hands up. She narrowed her eyes, slowly lowering the weapon.

So, this was a guardian. It hadn't even glanced in their direction since their arrival, its focus completely on the struggling Blue. She scowled, the periphery of Delvan's pain chipping away at her. "Really?! Because it seems to me that he's in a lot of *pain*, Masini!"

"They can haunt," Masini said, trying to calm her agitation, "but they *can't* touch him, not without breaking the rules. I know it doesn't look pleasant—because it's assuredly not—but he's safe. Mostly."

"Mostly?!"

"Des, let me explain before you decide to start swinging that thing around and carving up my magnificent features, alright?"

She let the blade come down fully to her side, grip remaining tight. "Explain."

"I know it seems like he's enveloped by his own worst fears, which is because he is—"

"That is *not* helping your case against mutilation."

"—but they *won't* physically harm him. And—this bit is important—he has *you*. The dead at least are given a chance to conquer these tests of character; the living can do nothing. Which is where you come in. Assuming you don't do something monumentally stupid, that is, which I can only assume you were about to do, getting us both killed in the process."

With a sneer, she looked back over her shoulder, seeing Delvan's gaze transfixed on the wraith before him, unaware of them a few paces away. "If I'm doing something stupid, it's because *someone* hasn't explained what's going on!"

"Right, because you've given me so many opportunities..." Masini's deadpan expression didn't flinch as she felt her face turn red. He sighed.

"Look, when someone dies," he said, "they face the Astral Plane's guardians—like that fire-eyed... *thing*. They're different for everyone, and manifest as whatever your own worst failings, or fears, or personal haunts might be. Could be guilt, or envy, or a few thousand jaded ex-lovers... Anyway, if you overcome them—twelve bouts of them, mind you—you move on, but if you don't, they'll torment you until you do, which some never accomplish. Hence, 'hell.'"

"So then let me go help him!" she said, the pain of Delvan's guilt beginning to stab at her own heart.

"Nonono, you missed the critical part. I said they do that if someone *dies*. Lord Delvan is very much alive."

"No shit," she retorted. She said the words, but in this place everything felt *different*. To confidently say that Delvan, or even she, was still alive here was a distinct contrast from feeling it. But her own doubts and the incomprehensible garble aside, she'd, annoyingly, yet to hear a reason not to go help her tormented friend. "What's your point?"

"If someone *living* comes here—a place meant for the dead—they're unable to resist because they're not meant to move on yet. They could *try*—be it cutting, stabbing, punching—but nothing would happen, much as the guardians can't actually harm them. But you," he said pointing at her and shaking a finger like she was a child, giving her the urge to break it, "you are part of this place, and it's part of you. *You*—and the demigod you share a pair of aspects with—bend the rules here."

She stared at him, confused. "What do you mean, 'part of this place?'"

"Since I know you have the patience of an unpaid pimp, I won't get into the specifics of how aspects work. But, elementarily speaking, if you went and tried to hack at that guardian, you—unlike Lord Delvan—could actually cause harm."

That sounded like a solution, not a problem. "Good," she said, turning and strutting towards Delvan. The dagger's weight felt heavy yet comfortable in her hands, as though its burden was one of the loss she associated with it. She gripped it tighter.

Masini ran to stand in front of her. "Woah, just take a breath and calm—"

"Get *out* of my way," she said, pointing the polished blade at him.

"By the Greats, do you need to learn patience." He ran his fingers through his hair, trying to hide that he was rolling his eyes. Skewering him had never been this enticing. "Look, right now, to that fire-eyed demon, you are one of its own: an emotion made manifest—which it *will* ignore. But the whole part about you being able to hurt him? It goes *both* ways. The dead have twelve guardians to overcome. You would have *infinite*."

That sounded... unappealing. Her lip curled up, barring her teeth. Every second she stood here, Delvan was left feeling the pain of his worst days—pain that she could feel as if it were her own. It was crippling, the only thing keeping her moving forward was the ire it stoked.

She'd been helpless before. It wouldn't happen again, not willingly.

"All you've done is tell me what I *can't* do," she grated. "Tell me what I *can* do or something a lot sharper than a knee is going to find its way between your legs."

"Normally, talk like that would be a turn on, *but*," he said as the dagger twitched in her hand, "I think I might have a solution."

"Finally."

"Don't get mad at me over your own impatience. My thought is this: if you go over there and stand directly between the guardian and Lord Delvan—just do not, and, um, let me repeat that, *do not*, attack it—I think it'll see you as the next guardian, and leave."

"You *think*?"

His face and shoulders both shrugged. "I mean, it sounds reasonable, wouldn't you say?"

"Why are you asking me?! I thought you said you had experience here!" she hissed.

"More than the majority of mages, including those haughty ksatsimtri. But, technically, *any* experience is greater than zero." Her eyes went wide with a mixture of fury and fear.

"Why am I even listening to you, then?!"

"Because I was taught by one of the only people to ever claim mastery over the Plane. And *that* handed down knowledge tells me this place will only allow someone aspected to it to pass through. You've already found Lord Delvan, a feat that most mages would struggle for centuries to do. That alone is reason to believe you can trick that guardian—because this place already sees you as one."

That was actually... reassuring. Desnia still wanted to punch Masini in the throat, but the explanation helped her understand why part of her felt at home here, though she was far from feeling like a native. Especially when the natives had fire billowing from their eyes.

She walked past Masini and took a few steps closer to the guardian, testing if it would turn its attention to her. Its only focus, however, was Delvan, as if she didn't exist. "If these things are meant to test the dead, why are they bothering with the living?"

"They come to every soul that fully enters, like flies to carrion. Like the buzzing pests, however, they're not exceptionally bright. Takes them a few proverbial chomps to realize that their new guests are not in fact permanent residents."

That posed a question she almost didn't want to ask, making her mouth go dry. "And when they finally realize they're not?"

"We'd best be gone. Far. But I believe we have some time, assuming we don't agitate the locals too much."

Desnia sneered as she looked at Delvan, hating every second of his torment. She felt used. Again. Why did it *always* have to be her? And not only had her own life been put in danger, but now all the people that she cared about.

Masini had told her there was a risk, but this far exceeded even her grim expectations.

The thousand questions and accusations that swarmed her would have to wait, the sight of Delvan too much to endure. She thrust the dagger back into its sheath on her belt and strode into the haze of agony.

As she approached Delvan, all started quiet, nothing but the ripples of waterless waves and the glimmer of distant souls to disrupt the empty abyss. But with each step closer, the whimpering of Delvan's voice and the comparative thunder of the guardian's aura grew louder.

There were no words from the ethereal being, only impressions—feelings, images; torturous, one and all—which shook Desnia's core. Delvan was whispering, his mouth moving as he repeated, "It wasn't my fault," under his breath. To have overcome something, and then have its worst horrors forced back upon you with no way to thwart them... She could see why calling it hell might be an understatement.

As she arrived at Delvan's side, the guardian slowly turned its burning gaze towards her. She pursed her lips into a thin line, her heart jumping in her chest. It stared down at her with its unnerving visage. She could feel the same prodding, the invasive touch which had encompassed when she first arrived.

She took a defiant step forward all the same, putting herself between it and Delvan.

Gritting her teeth, she stood her ground, staring down this being of eternity. She refused to allow it to take that which didn't belong to it, that which she'd fought to save.

The tension hung there, palpable as the moment dragged on.

Then, the strange sensation fell away, and with a shimmering wisp of color, the guardian evaporated into the nothing, joining the undulating mists of distant hues.

There was a splash from behind her. Delvan had fallen forward onto all fours, back arching as he took deep, ragged breaths. Desnia knelt at his side, hand on his shoulder. "Del, it's me, are you alright?"

"Des?" he said, his dripping hair shifting as he turned to look at her. "What... what was that?"

"Something we need to avoid," she said. "And that we need to rescue the others from. Here, can you stand?"

He nodded, leaning heavily on his knee as Desnia helped lift him up. "That was... I couldn't..."

"I know," she said, well aware of what he'd endured. "But it's gone now."

"I'd like to get out of here," he said, "before whatever the hell it was comes back."

"Brilliant idea," chimed Masini. "And please, try not to splash too—"

Desnia scowled and stomped her way over to him, shoving him hard and sending him sprawling to the ground. "I'm tired of being *used*, Masini! And now you've dragged them into this? If I had known what this place was—"

"You *did* know, and came regardless," said the mage, pulling himself to his feet. "And so did they. There are dangers for all of us in this endeavor, me included, but regardless of the reason, we all agreed to take them."

"But why *ME*?!" she said, wiping her eyes as she heard Delvan step beside her. "Why couldn't you or the one who put you in that fucking ring do this instead? Or why not ask another gods-damned Seer?!"

Masini adjusted his shirt and tossed aside the curls of hair in his face. "Because a Seer—even one with an underdeveloped aspect—is exponentially more capable in this place than I am. High Realm mages avoid the Astral Plane because most who explore it don't return. It's daunting, even to us.

"But Blues, well you're something special, nothing like you in all the realms. I could spend an eternity in here and never find Asta, and I'm the one who put the damned door in. Then Sylvain would get what she wants." He shuddered, the first look of disdain she'd seen from him carving deeply into his face. "As far as why we didn't use another Seer, well, that's simple: they're crazier than a dry-docked sailor."

"There must be others, like me," Desnia said. She wasn't special, there were plenty who had been in the same situation as her. More than any would care to admit.

"Well, as Lord Delvan here can attest, Seers are almost as rare as he is." Desnia looked over her shoulder. Delvan gave a half nod while keeping a curious eye on Masini. "The balance between being aspected enough to navigate this place, and not so aspected that you're nuttier than a squirrel, is one that is nearly impossible to achieve—believe me, we've tried."

"What's that supposed to mean?" asked Delvan, brow angling down.

"Nothing as nefarious as you seem to think, I assure you. Needless to say, it has taken us thousands of years to find someone meeting those exact parameters. And when we heard of a former canary turned thief, whose old mine co-workers said complained of nightmares and visions, well, we became rather interested."

Every word had brought the taste of bile to Desnia's throat. All the effort to hide, to keep the knowledge of what she was to herself, and it had been for naught. *What choice do I have, though?* she wondered. *I'm only getting worse, I have been for years, long before I met Masini.*

It didn't make being manipulated any less demeaning.

Desnia huffed and turned away, running her fingers through her hair. She stood there, trying to suppress the boiling tumult inside of her.

Delvan's voice sounded distant as the surrounding stars when he asked, "So, you're Masini?"

"Iored Langiomasini, Pinnacle Mage of the High Realm" he said with a small bow. "Also, holder of the titular title of Twisted Tongue Tantalizer throughout the realm's greatest brothels."

"Uh, what?"

"Just ignore him," Desnia said, turning back to face them, calming herself enough to speak. "It's what I do—or attempt, anyway."

"I've grown on her," said Masini.

"Like a fungus," she sneered. "I'm ready to be done with this fucking place. How do we find the others without losing Delvan?"

"Touching him should be enough."

"Should?" asked Delvan.

"Don't bother with him," Desnia said. "Come here." She put her hand on his shoulder—a bewildered expression plastered onto his face—and closed her eyes. If she did lose him, she'd have another reason to knee Masini, and her confidence about being able to find him again was growing stronger.

Nerio was the next person she envisioned. His emotional tie was clearer, easier to capture and hold than when she'd tried with Delvan. Whether it was the practice or their particular shared experiences, she couldn't say. But with a few moments of thought—disregarding the way the perverse intrusion made her feel—she opened her eyes to find Masini and Delvan at her side, Nerio a few yards away.

The sight was not one she could have foreseen.

She had expected to find Jerdine—an illusion of him, anyway—tormenting Nerio. Instead, she saw him kneeling, and praying...

The landscape of gleaming dots and shifting shades had been transformed. She and the others found themselves in the center of the Devapuram, the polished stone of the dome's central, cylindrical chamber reaching up to the sky around them. Of the encircling pantheon's alters, three stood empty, the last, towering above Nerio, held a statue with its back turned to the young priest.

Leaving Nerio to beg for its attention.

Delvan's voice was shaken as he said, "Gods..."

"Stay here," she said. The last thing she needed was another guardian turning its attention back onto the Blue. As it was, she needed to hope that this one saw Delvan as still being under her influence.

She walked to Nerio, hearing the lapping of water from her feet despite stepping on what appeared to be stone. Trickling down from the disparaging effigy was a vine of black, inky smoke, wrapping around the young priest. The empty, hollow loneliness that gushed from him could have filled an ocean, and it was all she could to swim forward.

Repeating what she'd done with Delvan, she stood between the sculpture and Nerio, staring up as eyes of marble appeared on the back of its head. She stared into those vacant, white reliefs, challenging them until they vanished, along with the Devapuram's illusion.

"D-Des?" she heard a voice from behind her say.

"I got you," she said, turning around and helping Nerio to his shaking feet.

Red eyes crowned soaked, blanched cheeks as he said, "I didn't realize this place..."

"Believe me, none of us did," she said glaring at Masini.

Nerio followed her gaze, his eyes resting on the mage. They seemed to grow wide with awe as he hesitantly asked, "A-Are you..."

"You can call me Masini," the mage said, nodding his head.

"Oh," said Nerio, disappointed.

Masini stood there, blinking silently. "Were you... expecting something different?"

"No," said Nerio, suddenly looking abashed. "I just thought... Desnia said we were going to meet her god and... This place, how we got here, it's a wonder of the divine..."

"Ah!" said Masini, relieved. "Well, I *have* been called—"

"She's not here," interjected Desnia. "We have to get through this place first." Desnia scratched her head. "Actually, why *isn't* Asta here?" Considering the circumstances of their last encounter, she was certain that this is where she'd met the god, face to face.

"Hmm?" said Masini. "Oh, are you bothering to listen to me now? In that case, the answer to your question is that they are. Slightly."

"It didn't seem *slight* when I died," said Desnia. Nerio and Delvan both turned to look at her, bewildered.

"Compared to what it could be, trust me, it is. At full power, they govern this place and all of the emotional charge within it—whether amidst the living, dead, or those moving on. But, given the literal and proverbial shackles we put them in, their power has been reduced to a trickle—which is still more than we'd expected."

"Then why aren't they stopping those... *things*?" asked Delvan.

"Excellent question, I'm glad *someone* is capable of asking them in a non-derisive manner." Desnia rolled her eyes. "This place is as old as time—*far* older than Asta—and that means they're bound by the same rules as everything else here."

"None of that answers our questions, Masini," said Desnia, wishing he would get to the point.

"I'm getting there. Think of Asta as the guardians' champion, but still a guardian—incapable of directly communing with the living when in here. Although they have *some* ability to bend the Plane to their will."

Desnia shook her head. She'd been dead, granted, but she'd *spoken* to Asta. Then there were all the dreams and their communications. She now regretted dismissing his conversation about how her and the other Seers' slumber slightly brought them into this place.

Other parts of Masini's explanation were difficult to reconcile, especially if Asta had as much influence as Masini was implying. "Why doesn't she show herself at least?" she asked. "Guide our way somehow."

"Mhm, I suspect they can only get a sliver of themselves in here, given their weakened state. Similar to your arm, Des, when you reached into Lord Delvan. Except in their case, it's more like half a strand of hair."

Desnia ground her teeth, loathing her lack of understanding of this place's rules. "Those other guardians have all appeared! I've *seen* her, she's spoken to me for half my life. Why is it that now, when we need it most, she can't send a sign, a shadow, *anything*? It seems that she's done *nothing*," she retorted.

"Who said they're doing nothing?" asked Masini.

Before Desnia could argue further, Delvan spoke up. "Listen, this is all very interesting, but Orne and Kolden are still trapped with these 'guardians.' Can we get them and focus on the details after we figure a way out of here?"

In her opinion, the brothers could use a little bit of time with some self-reflection. But Delvan's concern was fervent, and she knew, regardless of how annoying she found them, they didn't deserve whatever torment they were enduring. "Fine," she said. She would do this on her own, as she always had.

She had Nerio and Delvan put their hands on her shoulder, trying not to squirm at the touch. Picturing Kolden was easier than even Nerio, her annoyance still peaked and the act of traversing this place becoming unnervingly natural.

Strangely, they found him alone, not even the stars to spatter the backdrop. Aside from his own form being visible as though in daylight, he was otherwise engulfed in a jet-black cloud. He was pacing, fingernails digging into his scalp as he manically stared at the floor.

"What the hell?" asked Delvan.

Desnia approached, looking around and seeing the dark curl of smoke drifting down like a fog, overfilling him with... angst. The shared experience nearly drove *her* to madness—an all too familiar malaise. She grabbed the ragged looking man on the shoulder, battling for his attention as the pitch of the veil eventually forfeited its hold and lifted, the night sky reappearing in the background.

"What. The. *FUCK*?!" exclaimed Kolden, looking around wildly. "Where-Where did you all come from?"

"Your personal hell is *nothing*?" Desnia asked.

"Is *that* what this place is? You know, if you'd mentioned that prior, I would've stayed back at the cave," said Kolden, rubbing his face and slowly collecting himself. "Wait, where's Orne? And who the fuck are you?"

"Masini—"

"A pain in my ass," said Desnia, ready to be rid of this place as the guardian's turmoil sluggishly subsided. "Now, come here."

"You know," Masini said to her, "there's this plant, on the southern continent, that when mixed with tea indulges you in the most blissful calm."

"What of it?" asked Desnia, having the others put their hands on her outstretched arms.

"At some point, we should sail there. Then you should purchase a *plantation* of it."

She threw up a rude gesture with her fingers, and then closed her eyes, picturing the obtuse ogre and the rage that she had felt emanating from him not long prior. A terrifying amount of fury filled her, the dilution of a betrayal that dug into one's heart and left it destitute—a feeling she wished was less known to her.

The sound of splashing and grunting exertion told her she was in the right place, long before she opened her eyes. A stone-walled pit surrounded them, a column in its center rising above the rim. On it stood a large, domineering figure, almost as tall as Orne, with shoulders that splayed somehow wider.

Cheering could be heard in the distance, a crowd hidden beyond the pit's edge, and there, before them, swinging his sword with reckless abandon, was Orne.

He was trying to chop the podium's pillar down with the broadsword, but each wild stroke sliced through it as if it were formed of mere colored mist, offering no resistance to his enraged swings.

"Gods," said Kolden at her side, "that's our *father*." He was looking up at the figure on the pedestal, his jaw gaping. Desnia, however, continued watching Orne intently.

"How," she asked, "am I supposed to get near him when he's swinging that fucking thing around?"

"You might want to do it fast," said Masini. "Must he be so raucous? Look at all the ripples."

"I could go over there," offered Delvan.

"No," said Desnia. "You'd risk being trapped in it with him by the guardian." *Gods, if I get too close, he could swing around and chop me in half.* What would happen to her then? *I wonder what the rules are around the living dying in—*

Before she'd had a chance to act, the guardian and its illusion suddenly vanished. Delvan looked at her, curious. "It wasn't me," she said. "I think, anyway."

Masini had gone quiet, his eyes darting around in a way that deeply unsettled Desnia.

"...Orne?" said Kolden, taking a few cautious steps toward his brother.

Still wild-eyed and jumpy, the dominating man spun around, sword in hand. "Kolden? Del? You won't believe what just—"

"Oh, we do," said Kolden. "Des apparently forgot to mention this place likes to construct custom hellscapes for each person in it."

The man's brow dug deeply into his nose, face turning red as he looked back to where the guardian had been, now a sparkle-spotted curtain. He turned back to them, angrier—if that were possible. "And you got me *last*?"

Desnia rolled her eyes. "Oh, get over yourself. Chopping down a stone column is a lot less petrifying than what some of the others had."

"Except maybe Kolden's," said Delvan. "His was just black... nothingness."

Orne looked at his brother, letting out a snort after a second of thought. "He hates being bored."

"Shut up, you overgrown—"

"Could you all please close your respective holes for a second?" said Masini, his visage disconcerted.

"Who the fuck are you?" grunted Orne.

"He's the mage in my ring," said Desnia, not bothering to explain further. "What's wrong?" she asked Masini.

"Well, since it doesn't appear you were responsible for dispatching this guardian, then I think that something else may have, uh, scared it away."

Scared?

"Asta?" she asked hesitantly. It was a hope, but based on Masini's expression, a false one.

"Sure," said Masini, giving her a hint of relief. "If Asta were a custodian that had come to cleanse its dominion of intruders."

Their faces turned white, not a single disturbance rippling from their frozen statues of fear. Nerio quietly spoke, his voice hoarse. "...Does that mean—"

"Us?" said Masini. "No, I'm sure it's here for the other random group of living souls that happened to stumble into the land of the dead."

Desnia reached over and grabbed the mage by the collar. "*Why* didn't you mention this sooner?" she hissed.

"Because I didn't think we'd run into one. Obviously."

"How is that *obvious*?!" She gave him a push, forcing him a step back, noticing his feet didn't splash.

"Normally," said Masini, pulling his shirt straight, "they arrive the second you disturb the Plane, like spiders on a web. Since they didn't, however, I figured it was safe to assume that Asta was providing us some level of protection."

"Clearly not," spat Desnia.

"I told you; they're limited here. It's probably taken all the vidut she can muster to keep them from us. Therefore, I would say that we've likely overstayed our welcome."

"Is there any way," Desnia asked, knowing she'd never be that lucky, "that they'll see me and do what the guardians did?"

"Mhm... no. Custodians are very territorial and devour anything invasive. They're also far more intelligent than guardians, in a strange sort of way."

"D-Devour?" she heard Nerio stutter.

"Oh, no, not actually eating us. I just wanted to make sure I got the point across," said Masini.

"What do they do then?" asked Desnia.

"I have no idea."

Desnia drew the long dagger from her side, ready to cut him to pieces.

"I thought you said the living couldn't be hurt here?" asked Delvan, looking around.

"By the *guardians*," corrected Masini. "Taking care of the living who come here is the sole purview of the custodians. At full strength, Asta could command them to ignore you, or mask you as something else—which I'm assuming she's been doing. On the bright side, Des, they will probably disregard you. Maybe."

"What about *them*?!" she asked, pointing with the blade.

"Doomed. Most definitely."

"Can we stop fucking arguing about the details and just get out of here?!" asked Kolden.

A roll like distant thunder reverberated through the ground and into their bodies. A portion of the horizon was drained by an absence of light, a pit in the endless expanse. Within it flashed black lightning, fringed red, that raised their hair on end. Two deep crimson lights formed, burning like distant coals. They became a gaze; one whose predatory sight fixed upon them.

The air began to warm. Desnia could hear the chattering of teeth from someone beside her. Steel shifted in their trembling hands as roiling black-ness—stained red like smoke-enveloped flame—transformed into a snarl that stole their collective breath.

What slithered from the darkness was a creation no nightmare could fath-om. Desnia's mouth was sandpaper, her heart drumming in her ears as the outline of a midnight, serpentine head emerged. She could *feel* its insatiable hunger, its dripping fangs seeking only punishment. The sinuous muscles beneath scales that followed exuded pure disgust, the burning of the being's core glowing and sparking between its scales.

"S-S-Snake..." Desnia rasped, sick to her stomach.

"It's just a suggestion," said Masini, "but we should probably leave."

"Where?!" cried Delvan.

Desnia spun, looking, hoping against all the odds that she was being watched over. *Come on, you bitch, if there was ever a time to lend a hand...*

A light sparked.

The speck became a blinding beam, beckoning her and illuminating their vehement pursuer, causing it to flinch. Desnia didn't bother to take a last look at the hissing fangs as she pointed to the light and screamed, "*RUN!*"

They broke into a sprint, the water splashing wildly. There was a delay in their pursuit, the demon behind them seemingly overpowered or distracted. But then the Plane shook as the beast overcame the interference, winding its way forward as it quickly leaned into the chase.

Her legs felt short and slow as it gained on them, the diminutive lead they'd been giving rapidly vanishing. Ahead, Desnia saw the colorless floor fade to become swaths of different hues—yellows, reds, blues—all mixing and blending in a current of vibrancy, the signaling flare just beyond it.

"When we get there, jump!" yelled Masini.

Desnia didn't have time to question what he was talking about as Nerio, Delvan, and the brothers suddenly fell forward and vanished through the floor's thin veil of cover.

Skidding to a halt, Desnia flung and waved her arms to catch her bal-ance—finding herself teetering on the edge of a plunging spectrum which tumbled down over the lip her toes now dangled over.

She couldn't see the others as she looked down into the rainbowed abyss, making her throat choke. She righted herself, finding a pallid Masini beside her as she glanced back, the charnel beast almost on top of them.

"Des, jump!" begged Masini.

Frozen, Desnia watched as the monster slowed, its slither ceasing and coming to a halt. It curled itself up, revealing fangs as it licked the air with a vile, forked tongue, trying to discern what she was as she slowly rotated to face it. Masini was right in that she should have leaped, but something about this horrid entity felt... connected to her.

Its hesitation—and their connection—however, was brief. It lowered itself, coiling like a spring, maw unhinging and opening wide to expose its rows of long, pointed teeth, black and hungry.

Oh, fuck.

Desnia didn't look as she propelled herself backwards over the precipice, Masini pulled along with her as if by an unseen rope. The custodian sprung with excoriated fangs, and out of blind instinct, she slashed with the gleaming dagger still in her hands as it tried to swallow her.

There was a crack, like lightning had struck at her feet, as steel met darkness. She felt it cut, gouging deep—into what, she couldn't say—and felt an emotion that buried into her marrow, a feeling that could drive one to the ends of the world, exuded like a scream from this custodian of smoldering black.

Hate.

Before the beast could retaliate and seek its vengeance, the resplendent waterfall of color vanished in a blink, and she went from falling to hurtling sideways. She landed hard on stone, the curved dagger slipping from her hands and skittering across the floor as she rolled. Her tumbling body eventually hit something hard—which groaned.

Aches and pains covered her like a blanket as she moaned and sat upright. Blinking away the dizziness, she looked around, seeing the others doing much the same, her back against Orne's armor.

They were in a tunnel identical to the one they'd entered through, aglow with lines of cadentite. But rather than a dark, dimly lit passage beyond, Desnia could see a glow, purple and unwavering beyond the tunnel's enormous mouth, beaming in from where it bent ahead.

"Did we make it?" asked Delvan as he stood and rubbed his head.

Oh, by the Greats, I can't believe you did that, Des. You almost got my shiny ass eaten! That was—

"Quiet," said Desnia, looking around. It was a demand, and an observation. Everything around her was... silent. Delvan's sapphire was exposed, and yet she couldn't sense any of the others' emotions—which they made clear with their symphony of stringed curses.

She slowly stepped forward as the others collected themselves. This place gave her the strangest sense of recognition. It took her a few moments, but she realized that she'd been here. Many terrible, torturous nights had delivered her to this very ground, each leaving her begging for normalcy, for a night's rest where she wasn't terrified of going into the one place worse than the cruel streets of Calentine's Lower Valley.

Her dreams.

And like her sleeping ventures, *it* came to her, prodigious and indomitable.

The quiet was shattered.

WELCOME, DAUGHTER.

Chapter
Sixty-Three

Assist in retaking the city, and your command shall be reinstated, your mistakes pardoned. King and His grace upon you.

Lord Demrand ce Saffstar
Regent of the King's Sapphiric Court

S he's here," Desnia whispered.

Heh, you know, said Masini nervously, *I knew it was coming, and it's still a shock. Up until now, I could hope by some miracle they weren't, and I wouldn't have to worry about their revenge, or my death—again.*

She stood, motionless, eyes fixed on the corridor's end. After years of struggle and torment, hiding what and who she was, she'd arrived at the source—and the cure. A triumph she'd never believed was achievable. The capture of the elusive victory, however, now blossomed doubt.

In her experience, there was never success without cost.

The thought of that toll weighed on her now, preventing her from moving forward. Was this all another manipulation? She was almost certain of it, but the despair of expectation wasn't enough to smother the ember of hope burning in her chest.

Only the next step forward—the revelation of which future would become reality—could do that.

While she remained fixed in place, staring off into the distance, the others collected themselves, grunting and working bruised limbs as they stood. Their voices were a dull drone in the back of her mind.

"I vote to never do that again," said Kolden, grimacing.

Footsteps approached, stopping beside her. Their muffled voice sounded distant, but a hand on her shoulder pulled Desnia from her daze, making her jump with a start.

"Sorry," said Delvan. "You dropped this." He held out Mithya's dagger. Desnia blinked away the haze and looked from Delvan's face to the blade. Aside from the shape, the darksteel weapon was almost unrecognizable.

It no longer reflected light, the metal completely matte and far blacker than the expensive steel normally was. A starless night had been captured in the sharpened metal, pulling in the light around it, and it felt... out of place.

She examined the shorter, plainer darksteel dagger at her hip, finding it looking as it did when they entered the Astral Plane. Was this a result of her attacking the custodian with the weapon?

"Mine doesn't look like that either," said Delvan. "Not sure what you did."

Neither am I... grumbled Masini.

She took the blade, careful to touch only the handle.

"Does this place," asked Delvan, fiddling with his sapphire, "feel, I don't know, *dead* to you?"

"Quiet," she said, still in a stupor. "It feels quiet."

Delvan held out his hand, palm facing up. She glanced at it, then him, wondering what he was doing. "Last time I lost it," he said, "it was all in my head..."

His sapphire won't work in here, said Masini, *on account of the whole, imprisoning a god, thing.*

After repeating the words in a whisper back to him, he nodded, as if it were the answer he was expecting.

"Hey!" boomed Orne. Desnia turned to look at him, absently sheathing the dagger at her waist. "Is there another way out of here besides *that*?" he asked, pointing to the vertical pool of oscillating black they had all just fallen through, identical to the other entrance.

Yes, thankfully. Besides, that, uh, doorway is omnidirectional. Couldn't leave an exit big enough for Asta, after all.

"Sounds like we can't go that way," she replied, happy to avoid the Plane, but curious about Masini's comment. She asked him, "How *do* we get out? Is Asta going to help us?"

'We' as in I'm still around and not destroyed by the vengeful entity? Then yes, there is a way out for 'us,' he confirmed.

The others joined her, staring down the enormous corridor towards the steady hum of purple at its end. None of them seemed willing to edge closer, hovering at her shoulders.

Except one.

"Are we going to fucking get going?" asked Orne as he barged forward before looking over his shoulder. "Well?!"

Delvan looked at her. There was an understanding in his eyes, his voice calming. "It's a lot easier to face other people's nightmares than it is your own."

Observant bastard.

"What if..." She struggled to say the words, her throat tight. "What if it was all for nothing? What if this doesn't... *fix* me?"

Delvan shrugged. "Then we'll deal with it. Not facing it won't make it better, though."

Desnia scoffed but felt some of the trepidation melt away. "Gods, I hate you sometimes, you know that?"

"Only sometimes?" he asked. She almost laughed.

How could he be calm in a situation like this? Didn't he, or any of the others, realize the significance of what they were about to do? Question the consequences of their actions? The only one who seemed to hold the same disquiet in their heart was Nerio, his visage burdened with fear and doubt.

"What about you, Nerio?" she asked.

He looked at her, wiping sweat from his brow and swallowing loudly. Words escaped him, but he nodded, his motions jittery. *After everything he's gone through, he's still willing to go on...*

Taking a deep, shaky breath, Desnia lifted her leaden foot and took her first sluggish stride towards joining Orne, who was tapping his boot and staring at them. Her heart was jumping into her throat. Around that corner laid her possible salvation, or condemnation, depending on one's perspective.

Kolden piped up from the back of the group, his feet dragging. "Let's ask everyone but me. 'Kolden, what do you think?' 'Thanks for asking! I think you're all insane!' It's fine, I don't mind being excluded. Nope, not one bit..."

Desnia tried to ignore him as they shuffled forward, his voice like a pin in her ear. The tunnel was longer than its counterpart. Eventually, the bend drew near enough to see around, more coming into view with each progressive stride.

The sight beyond the tunnel's end was one Desnia recognized but still invoked awe upon seeing in person.

A domed cavern, soaring to a height untouchable by an arrow from the strongest bow, rose before them. The perfectly flat floor was broad enough for a large village to fit within, and netting every inch of visible, white stone were streaks of luminescent cadentite.

Bold and heavy lines overlaid thinner, delicate ones, forming mesmerizing patterns that wove together in vibrant artistry. Patterns—almost floral in their cyclical nature—intertwined, making it impossible to distinguish one from another in their symmetry of magic.

Desnia's eyes wandered down from the ceiling's crown, until her eyes rested upon a sight well known to her. Chains. Mounted to the floor, each link was twice her height in length and covered in the same, continuous lines of glowing cadentite.

Chest heaving, she traced the bindings to the room's center, where a massive white shroud stood. It was as if a mountain's pinnacle had been set to rest amongst the twisting lines, its surface jutting in odd directions and angles. Desnia thought it was perhaps a dilapidated tent or building—one form or another of a temple that had begun collapsing.

There was a deep rumble.

And the structure *moved.*

Dust slid to the floor and choked the air. Mouth gaping and ignoring the taste of grime, Desnia watched as the mass unfurled and swelled.

Draped curtains of white she'd mistaken to be the shape's exterior pulled back. Stretching like canvas on boney limbs, they expanded to fill the colossal lair's breadth. Desnia registered what they were, but struggled to comprehend, nonetheless.

Wings.

Their magnitude defied nature itself, like everything else her eyes attempted to take in. A tail of matching proportions, dragging with immense weight, uncurled like a twisting tree. As it swept over the floor, it revealed a body whose hide reflected the chamber's radiance with a shimmering, pearl iridescence. Desnia realized the reflective white covering the creature from end to end wasn't skin or fur, but scales. An armor more lustrous than gold.

From the corner of her eye, she saw Delvan take a step back, his face white as snow.

Huh, are they bigger than what I remember? asked Masini. *Or have I just gotten smaller?*

Desnia was frozen, bound by the ropes beneath her skin like every torturous nightmare that had taken her to this place. Her muscles were her own here, unlike her mind's previous visits. But fear was a restraint, its hold as strong as any garish dream.

Somehow the leviathan before her was more imposing than the ominous, overwhelming voice that had left her in pain all those mornings. Those conversations, the commands that tore her apart, she now realized had been mere *whispers.* For what rose before her was power's purest embodiment.

A deafening rattle echoed as four taloned claws dragged the enormous chains by the shackles around its legs. Like a bear awakening from hibernation, its motions were slow but fluid as it righted itself, rising ever higher as the true scale of its enormity was revealed. Desnia gulped. What had she brought everyone to?

From the body that shook away an eon's worth of solitude, a long, muscular neck drew upward. Spikes, pointed and menacing, ran along its spine. And mounted atop of it was a head that made the Astral Plane seem timid.

Its maw, long and fanged like a wolf's, could swallow a building with ease. Eyes, taller than her, captivated. They burned with such intense, brilliant blue, the azure orbs appeared to glow. *The depths to them...* Desnia thought, as it craned its head down. They held within them the world, the future.

YOUR FEAR IS UNWARRANTED, a voice—Asta's voice—said, heard from within her mind, booming yet... tolerable, perhaps for the first time. *I AM NOT THE EXPECTED, BUT NEITHER AM I THE TERROR YOU BELIEVE. NOT TO YOU.*

She heard Masini let out a diminutive squeak.

"D-Did you guys just hear that?" rasped Kolden.

Blonde hair spun as Desnia looked from him to the others, who nodded with eyes fixed ahead. They... They could *hear* her. All of them.

WHILE THIS CAGE RESTRICTS ME, THERE ARE PARTS OF MY ASPECTS THAT FUNCTION WITHIN ITS WALLS, she said—although Desnia was now questioning if "she" was appropriate.

"What... What are you?" Delvan choked out.

NAMES FOR US ABOUNDED IN OUR SHORT REIGN, she communicated, blinking slowly. *THE ONE WE REFER TO OURSELVES BY, BESTOWED BY OUR MOTHER, IS HOW I WOULD CHOOSE FOR YOU TO KNOW US.* Asta stared down at them with her slit pupil, a guttural rumble resonating from deep in her chest.

DRAGON.

The others shifted uncomfortably, unsure of what to do in the shadow of this towering being. Nerio fell to his knees, and Desnia saw tears welling in his eyes.

DO NOT PROSTRATE, I SEEK NO WORSHIP. INDEED, IT IS I WHO MUST ASK OF YOU.

The glowing manacles rattled once more as the dragon shifted her weight. Desnia glanced at the restraints, remembering her own incarceration and how the isolation twisted her thoughts. Was a god whose domain was the cumulation of the realms' emotions above such fallibility? Or more prone to it?

"What do you want?" asked Orne, his voice wavering for the first time she could recall.

FREEDOM.

"And what else?" asked Desnia. The others looked at her, concern on their faces.

A QUESTION OF MERIT, DAUGHTER. TO ANSWER I MUST ASK ONE IN RETURN. WHAT HAS IORED TOLD YOU OF HOW MY IMPRISONMENT CAME TO BE?

Oh, you know, broad strokes, said Masini nervously. *I'm a bit, uh, 'restricted' myself.*

AND OF YOUR PART IN IT?

She expected a quip or retort, but Masini was despondently silent. After a few moments Desnia spoke, her neck aching as she looked up into Asta's eyes. "You were a threat to the High Realm and their power. So, they locked you away and tossed the key. That about sum it up?"

MHM, SUCCINCT, BUT LACKING. YOUR ANSWER THEN, SHALL BE THAT WHICH HAS BEEN ALL BUT ERASED FROM THE HISTORIES, REMAINING ONLY IN THE MEMORIES OF THE FEW WHO WITNESSED IT, OMISSIVE AS THEY MAY BE.

The others were rapt by the words and sight before them. Desnia crossed her arms. "I came here for a cure, not a history lesson. Are you going to explain what you want from us, or are you stalling because you can't actually give us anything in return?"

IN TIME. TO DO WHAT I ASK, YOU MUST FIRST UNDERSTAND THE RISK. THE DANGERS WILL CLAIM YOU, SHOULD YOU REMAIN UNPREPARED.

Desnia looked at everyone gawking at her. Maybe if they'd had to deal with Asta since childhood, they too would be a little less mesmerized and slightly more cautious. She was trapped by her own need, however, and begrudgingly nodded.

PATIENCE, DAUGHTER, AS I INGEMINATE AN ORIGIN ERODED BY TIME.

ONCE, THIS REALM WAS DEEMED BARREN AND INHOSPITABLE BY THOSE IGNORANT OF ITS POTENTIAL. LITTLE DID ANY BUT THE INHABITANTS REALIZE THE LIFE THAT THRIVED HERE, THEIR BIASED ASSUMPTIONS BLINDING THEM.

EXCEPT FOR ONE. AND IT WAS SHE WHO WOULD SINGLY CHANGE ITS FATE.

OUR CREATOR. OUR MOTHER.

It was hard to picture anything that could give birth to such a creature, but Desnia held her tongue. Still, it raised disconcerting questions.

POSSESSING A SINGULAR INTELLECT, HER GENIUS LED HER DOWN A ROAD OF DISCOVERY. NOT ONLY OF THIS REALM'S HIDDEN WEALTH, BUT OF A POSSIBILITY NEVER BEFORE CONSIDERED. ONE SHE DECIDED TO TEST—THE SUCCESS OF SAID EXPERIMENT EXCEEDING HER OWN EXPECTATIONS.

THUS, WE WERE CREATED, TO RULE WHERE OTHERS COULD NOT. WITHIN EACH OF US SHE IMBUED THE DISTILLED PURITY OF AN ASPECT PAIR, AN ACT SEEN BY HER FELLOWS AS AN IMPOSSIBLE MERGER OF CHAOS. THIS TAMING THROUGH LIMITATION AWARDED POWER UNMATCHED, AND THE TRUE VALUE OF THE REALM WAS REALIZED. AT LEAST BY HER.

"Wait, did you say 'we?'" asked Kolden from behind her.

YES. THOSE TO WHICH I AM BONDED BY BLOOD. MY SIBLINGS.

Desnia's face became cold and numb. There were *more* dragons?

"Where are they?" asked Delvan, speaking her same question after regaining some of his calm courage. Or did he—like her, despite everything—feel an inexplicable kinship to Asta?

THEY ARE HIDDEN, EVEN FROM ME, THEIR PRISONS LOCKED BY THE SOULS OF A THOUSAND MAGES. MINE ALONE IS ACCESSIBLE, HENCE IORED'S DECISION TO BRING YOU HERE.

"And your need for me," Desnia said bitterly.

YES.

Desnia sneered. She wanted to spout blame and voice her anger. But she knew what the desperation of imprisonment could do, what parts of your will it would bend and even break.

Understanding held her beratement, but not her tongue. "So, what, the High Realm wanted to control you, use your power for themselves, and you refused? That clearly worked out well."

THE OPPOSITE, Asta said with a hint of disdain. *WE HEEDED THEIR EVERY COMMAND.*

"*You* obeyed those fucks?" asked Orne, becoming more bewildered. Desnia couldn't help but find herself agreeing with the sentiment.

YOU SHOULD KNOW BETTER THAN ANY, DENYING A PARENT IS A FEAT NOT EASILY ACCOMPLISHED.

Parent? she thought, eyes going wide. "*What?!*" she blurted. "You mean the one that created you was—"

A HIGH REALM MAGE. ALONG WITH HER CHOSEN SIRE, THE LEADER OF THEIR ELITE, THE KSATSIMTRI.

"You... You mean..." she stumbled. Were those fuckers responsible, then, for everything? For what she'd gone through? "Masini never told me that!"

It's not a subject I much enjoy, his voice was quiet, distant. *Besides, it doesn't change what needs to happen. No one knows how she did it, so coming here was the only choice we had.*

"Did you not think to ask her?!" blurted Desnia.

WOULD THAT HE COULD.

"What's that supposed to mean?" asked Delvan.

The dragon's pupil widened, and within the gleaming blue Desnia saw the deepest wells of anguish imaginable, a despair that could crush a world under its weight. *THE HIGH REALM... EXECUTED HER.*

Masini had no response. She found herself craving an explanation from him—and how he was involved.

The others seemed equally disturbed by this revelation. Nerio had been unable to rise from the floor, and the brothers were sharing their uninterpretable glances. It was only Delvan who spoke up, his curiosity matching his boldness—or stupidity. "Why would they do that?"

Asta closed her radiant eyes and hung her head low, the great wings atop her back pulling in and rustling like billowing sails.

SHE WAS ONE OF THEIR GREATEST, Asta said slowly. *THEIR HIGH COUNCIL LAUDED HER CREATION, AT FIRST, USING US TO RULE OUR BIRTH REALM. SAMRA, THEY CALLED IT. LIKE YOU, HOWEVER, WE ONLY KNEW IT AS HOME.*

THE HIGH REALM WAS CRUEL TO YOUR ANCESTORS, FORCING THEM INTO SLAVERY, COMMITTING OTHER UNTOLD ATROCITIES. NEWLY BORN AND STILL LEARNING OF THE WORLD, WE DID NOT THINK TO QUESTION, NOT THEN. OUR MOTHER WAS PROTECTING US, I LATER REALIZED. FOR IF OUR PURPOSE WAS NOT ALIGNED WITH THEIRS, THEN WE WOULD BE SEEN AS THREATS. THEIR OWN HUBRIS PREVENTED THAT FOR YEARS, BY ALL BUT A FEW.

Desnia stepped closer. Part of her wanted to question everything, wondering if this was a con of some kind by Asta to lure them into helping her. But somewhere, deep down, she could feel the honesty in the words, and the torment associated with them, drawing her in.

BUT FOR EVERY MOUNTAIN, THERE IS A SHADOW—AND THOSE THAT RESIDE IN IT.

OUR MOTHER HAD A SISTER, WHO WAS ALWAYS ENVIOUS, BUT OF MIDDLING SKILL. HER CUNNING, HOWEVER, WAS UNRIVALED. HER OTHER MALEFICENT BETRAYALS ASIDE, SHE PLANTED SEEDS OF JEALOUS DOUBT IN THE EAR OF OUR SIRE, BRINGING OUR LOYALTY INTO QUES-

TION.

WITH OUR POWER OUTSTRIPPING THEIR OWN LEGIONS', IT WAS NOT LONG BEFORE HER WORDS FESTERED IN HIS MIND. HE SOON BECAME CONVINCED THAT WE WERE A DANGER TO THEIR STRANGLEHOLD ON THE REALMS, RATHER THAN THEIR AID IN IT.

UNBEKNOWNST TO HER, HE INVITED OUR ELDEST BROTHER TO THE HIGH REALM UNDER FALSE PRETENSES, AND WAS ATTENDED BY HIS UN-SUSPECTING, DUTIFUL CHILD. OUR SIRE'S—AND EVERY MAGE'S—POW-ER IS AT ITS PEAK ON THEIR HOME REALM, WHEREAS OUR BROTHER WOULD BE WEAKENED BY HIS SEPARATION FROM US, ALTHOUGH HIS POWER REMAINED FORMIDABLE.

Desnia could guess where this was going. Too often had she seen others fall into the same trap, taken somewhere by someone they trust, who claimed to be their friend or partner, only to end up with stones tied to their feet at the bottom of the river. "He killed his own child," she said quietly.

CITIES WERE RAZED. HE WAS LEFT GRAVELY WOUNDED EVEN AFTER CALLING ON THE OTHER KSATSIMTRI, BUT YES. AND WITH HIS FILICIDE, WE WERE DIMINISHED, FOR WITHOUT ONE, WE ARE NOT WHOLE.

Delvan was rubbing his sapphire between his finger and thumb, pensive. Desnia, despite her predilection to avoid lectures such as this, found ques-tions raising in her mind. But Kolden found his voice before she did.

"Did he come after the rest of you, then?"

WHILE IT WAS LIKELY HIS INTENT, THE HIGH REALM SOON REALIZED THEY COULD NOT KILL US, NOT WHILE WE REMAINED IN OUR NATIVE SAMRA. AND AFTER THE DESTRUCTION WROUGHT BY THE BATTLE BE-TWEEN OUR FATHER AND THE FIRST, THEY DARED NOT BRING ANOTHER OF US TO THE HIGH REALM.

"Challenging your own father..." whispered Delvan. The brothers' eye-brows raised at the comment.

MANY OF US WISHED TO BUT WERE NEVER AFFORDED THE OPPORTU-NITY.

OUR MOTHER, IN A FIT OF RAGE OVER HER CHILD'S MURDER, KILLED HIM.

There was a sorrowful retribution in Asta's voice, and Desnia wondered if it was disappointment in the dragon's lack of contribution, or that so much loss had stemmed from the single, resentful deception of a lone family member.

BLINDED BY OUR OWN GRIEF AND VENGEANCE, said Asta, a monstrous lip pulling back to reveal the tips of black fangs, *WE WAGED WAR WITH THE HIGH REALM, ATTEMPTING TO REMOVE THEIR BLIGHT FROM SAM-*

RA. THEIR ARMIES WERE SUNDERED, THEIR MAGES DECIMATED, AND IN OUR FURY, DESTRUCTION RAINED UPON OUR HOME. UNTIL...

The dragon's eyes closed, her wings sagging.

"Your mother," Desnia said.

THEY CONDEMNED HER, she said, raising her head, a growl reverberating the air. *THEY BROUGHT HER HERE, TORTURING HER AND THREATENING HER EXECUTION UNLESS WE GAVE IN TO THEIR DEMANDS. THE SPELLS THEY USED WERE INDESCRIBABLE, HEINOUS MONSTROSITIES THAT EVEN WE WERE HELPLESS TO DEFUSE, NOT BEFORE SHE WERE TO SUCCUMB.*

WE COULD NOT BEAR THE THOUGHT OF LOSING HER, TOO, AND ACCEPTED.

THEY BOUND US IN THESE CHAINS, she said, shifting the heavy shackles, *AND LOCKED US AWAY IN THESE CELLS, SWEARING TO NEVER RETURN. THEIR FINAL, INEFFABLE ACT ONCE WE WERE TRAPPED, DISREGARDING THEIR PROMISES, WAS TO TAKE OUR MOTHER'S LIFE. INSURANCE, TO PREVENT DRAGONS FROM EVER BEING BORN TO THE REALMS ONCE MORE, AND PUNISHMENT FOR THE CASUALTIES OF OUR WAR.*

Desnia felt her heart sink. "Masini?" she whispered.

I didn't think they would kill her, he said somberly. *She was my mentor, my friend, but the death toll... We had already lost and didn't think they would stop at simply exiling us from here.*

"*Don't* tell me you didn't think it would happen!" she hissed. She'd *trusted* him. Through all the quips and jokes and prods, she grown close to him, leaning on his voice in her times of greatest need. She was abrasive towards the mage, true, but beneath the surface there was a quality of character there that she thought she knew. How could she have been so mistaken?

You weren't there, Des! The fact there is still life in this... place, is a small miracle. Don't pretend to know what it's like to make decisions in war, knowing both options are terrible. I thought it was the right thing; I was protecting my home.

But after it happened... Well, my perspective changed. Enough for me to leave a flaw in the seal, a last resort. I tried to do what I could to continue protecting my home, preventing change from here that I suspected would happen, but hoped wouldn't. It was futile, and it has brought me here.

But don't, for one second, think that what happened doesn't still haunt me, Des.

She ground her teeth, wondering who this was she thought she'd come to know. What was stopping him from betraying her? Letting her guard down seemed stupid, in hindsight.

Glancing to her side, she noticed the others looking at her, even Nerio. Had they heard what Masini said? Had Asta granted them that?

TIME HAS CHANGED MANY PERSPECTIVES, IORED. KNOW I DO NOT HARBOR ILL WILL, AND YOU SHOULD NOT EITHER, DAUGHTER. FOR NEW PERILS ARE ON THE HORIZON.

I HAVE BROUGHT YOU HERE BECAUSE IORED SPEAKS TRUE. THE ONE WHO WAS THE CATALYST OF OUR DEMISE, THE WHISPERED MALEVO-LENCE, HAS COME TO POWER IN THE HIGH REALM. SHE SEEKS THAT WHICH NO ONE WAS ABLE TO DISCOVER: HOW HER SISTER WAS ABLE TO CREATE US. AND SHE BELIEVES THOSE SECRETS LIE HERE, ALONG WITH THEIR ASSOCIATED POWER.

There was a long pause. Desnia wanted to be irate, feeling a stab of betrayal from Masini. She'd shared secrets with him, but he'd kept *this*? There were secrets still her own, but still.

Kolden had a look of consternation on his face while he scratched his head. "Hold on, did you say, 'brought *us*?' What's that supposed to mean?"

Desnia knew the answer before Asta spoke, having been exploited for far too long. *ONE OF MY ASPECT PAIR INCLUDES THE ABILITY TO... MODU-LATE EMOTIONS. THE OTHER ALLOWS ME TO STARE ACROSS THE ASTRAL PLANE AND SEE THE FUTURE'S POSSIBILITIES BASED ON SAID PASSIONS, FOR THEY ARE WHAT DRIVE US, AT OUR CORE.*

A NUDGE AT A HORSE'S THIRST TO SEND THEM IN A DIFFERENT DI-RECTION, PLACING ITS RIDER WHERE THEY NEEDED TO BE. A CURIOSITY ABOUT AN UNSEEN OBJECT, AMPLIFIED ENOUGH TO STEAL IT. A SENSE OF CALM TO PREVENT THE RASH. OCCASIONAL ADJUSTMENTS TO EN-SURE THE SINGULAR FUTURE WHICH BRINGS SAFETY TO THE REALM.

The others looked angry, rightfully so. Except Nerio, whose head now hung even lower. His silence was beginning to concern her.

"You *played* us?" growled Orne.

YES. IF I HAD NOT, YOU WOULD HAVE ALREADY BEEN INVADED, AND WITH US LOCKED AWAY, YOU WOULD HAVE FALLEN.

SO, TO ANSWER YOUR QUESTION, DAUGHTER, WHAT I SEEK, ASIDE FROM MY FREEDOM, IS THE PROTECTION OF THIS REALM AND THOSE WITHIN IT. ESPECIALLY THOSE WHO SHARE MY BLOOD, PRESENT AND FUTURE.

"How do you plan to accomplish that?" she asked.

THAT IS A FUTURE TOO DIFFICULT TO SEE, AND DEPENDENT ON THE HIGH REALM AND THEIR NEW LEADER. THE POSSIBILITIES ARE ENDLESS. BUT I WILL FIGHT.

Desnia narrowed her eyes. For the first time during the conversation, she had the suspicion that Asta had lied. Their incarceration was unjust, and she could empathize with that. But if the last war with the High Realm was as destructive as Masini claimed...

"Does this leader have a name?" asked Delvan.

Fangs, pointed and black, emerged from snarled jowls as the dragon spoke. Desnia watched its claws curl, scraping along the floor in a motion that sent vibrations through her feet.

SYLVAIN.

'*Protection,*' Desnia thought warily. *Doesn't seem the most appropriate word...* Could she, however, leave Asta here, chained and forgotten by all but the mad? She had scolded Masini for his decisions, but now, faced with one that could change everything she knew, she realized the plight of his—and her—choice.

"*If* we agree to help you," Desnia said, "how would we get these chains off?"

YOU CANNOT.

What? Her gut somersaulted and she saw heads turning in confusion.

NOT IN YOUR CURRENT STATE. MY REQUEST IS THEREFORE INTER-TWINED WITH MY OFFER.

"Which is?" Desnia asked hesitantly.

I WILL GRANT EACH OF YOU A BOON, IMBUING YOU WITH A PAIR OF ASPECTS, OR GREATLY AMPLIFYING THE ONES YOU ALREADY POSSESS. WITH THEM, YOU CAN ACQUIRE WHAT IS NEEDED TO BREAK THESE BINDINGS.

Delvan's jaw dropped with understanding. "You're offering to make them *Blues...*"

BEYOND THAT. YOUR CAPABILITIES ARE SCANT SHADOWS OF THEIR POTENTIAL. I OFFER YOU POWER, SUCCEEDED ONLY BY MY OWN.

"How?" he asked. Desnia looked at him, still trying to process the words. They weren't... Something was *wrong*.

With a shift of the immense links that echoed through the chamber, the dragon lifted a bound foot and slid a talon beneath a scale on its other leg. It dug the black, razor-pointed claw into the flesh under the iridescent armor without a flinch.

When the talon emerged, she saw it glistened, wet atop the black point.

DRINK OF MY BLOOD, AND IT SHALL BE YOURS.

Desnia didn't squirm like some at the sight, her mind drifting as it fished for the answer laying beneath the murky haze.

Delvan's brow furrowed. "You want us to *what*?"

HMM, Asta said, curiously, looking at Delvan more closely. *I WOULD EX-*

PECT YOU TO BE LEAST AFFRONTED OF ALL.

"Why?" he asked.

BECAUSE YOU ALREADY WEAR THE BLOOD OF MY KIN AROUND YOUR NECK.

Desnia's head snapped up. *Wait, she can't mean... His sapphire?*

She twisted to find Delvan gaping, clutching his gem tightly. "That's... That's not—"

WHAT DO YOU THINK WAS DONE WITH OUR BROTHER'S CORPSE? THE HIGH REALM REFUSED TO KEEP IT WITHIN THEIR BORDERS. THEY COULD SENSE THE VIDUT—WEAKENED THOUGH IT WAS WITHIN HIS DECEASED, PHYSICAL FORM—FROM HIS STILLED HEART AND THOUGHT THAT HE POSED A THREAT FROM BEYOND. THEY DID NOT UNDERSTAND WE ARE ETERNAL, FOREVER TIED TO SAMRA. EVEN IN DEATH, WE REFUSE THE ASTRAL PLANE.

IN THEIR FEAR AND MISUNDERSTANDING, THEY BROUGHT HIS BODY HERE AND BURIED IT. BUT HE WAS MIGHTY, NOT ONLY IN PROWESS, BUT MAGNITUDE, AND HIS SEPULCHER WAS OF A SIZE UNPRECEDENTED.

OVER MILLENNIA, HIS BODY DECAYED, BUT THE VIDUT WITHIN HIM REMAINED, TRAPPED WITHIN HIS HEART, SUFFUSING HIS BLOOD. ITS PILFERING HAS BROUGHT ABOUT A NEW ERA OF OUR CHIL-DREN—SHADES THOUGH THEY MAY BE.

SO, YOU SEE, YOUNG NEPHEW, YOUR HOME IS NO MERE MOUNTAIN.
IT IS A TOMB.

Delvan staggered a step back, hand still firmly grasping the sapphire around his neck. He had turned paler than the others, all of them looking from Delvan to the dragon.

Had she spent her childhood roving through the carcass of one of these things? She shuttered, remembering all the times she reached a young, tiny arm into the crevasses, grabbing—

"Wait!" she suddenly shouted, glaring at Asta. The thought that had been eluding her, buried beneath the revelations that twisted her understanding of their world, suddenly came to her. How had it taken her this long to realize? "You said you had a *cure*! That's not what the fuck this is! How is making *this* worse," she said, tapping her head, "going to make me *better*?!"

The massive eye turned to her, the dragon's head lowering near the floor. The words that were spoken, Desnia somehow knew, were only addressed to her.

I TOLD YOU THAT YOU WOULD ALWAYS BE A PART OF ME, THAT THERE WAS NO REVERSAL FOR WHAT YOU ARE. THERE IS NO CHANGING THAT.

Desnia's heart sank to the floor. Everything she'd hoped for, the motivation for her long journey here, was suddenly swept from beneath her feet. How had she allowed herself to grasp such childish ideas?

She didn't give a fuck about the masses, and now she was being asked to sacrifice *more* for them? They'd never done anything for her. The last time she'd tried to help, she'd landed in prison.

YOU MUST LOOK FURTHER THAN THE IMMEDIATE FUTURE, THAN YOUR IMMEDIATE DESIRES, DAUGHTER. IN TIMES OF NEED, THE EASIER SOLUTION MAY SEEM THE SHORTEST PATH, BUT IT IS OFTEN THE MOST COSTLY. SUCCESS DESPITE DISTANCE, THAT IS OUR GOAL. THE GREAT ACHIEVEMENT. TAKING THE HARD PATH TO FIND IT BECOMES A ROAD TO REWARD IS WHAT THOSE WILLING TO SUFFER THROUGH ITS OBSTACLES AND THORNS AND RISKS FIND. AND THOSE WHO DARED NOT RISK, HURT, OR STRUGGLE, DISCOVER TOO LATE THE CONSEQUENCES OF THEIR IN-DOLENCE.

KNOW THIS BOON WILL NOT AFFLICT YOU BUT ELEVATE YOU TO THE DIVINE.

THE OTHERS DID NOT LOSE THEIR MINDS BECAUSE THEY HAD TOO MUCH OF MY BLOOD WITHIN THEM. ON THE CONTRARY, THE CHANGES BROUGHT BY MY SIBLING'S REMNANTS ARE POWERFUL, BUT LIMITED.

THE ASTRAL PLANE IS NOT A FORGIVING PLACE, AS YOU KNOW. THE CRACKS IN YOUR MIND ARE ALLOWING MORE OF IT IN, AND WITHOUT STRENGTH TO REBUFF IT, YOU WILL YIELD TO THEIR FATE. I AM OFFER-ING YOU A WAY TO NOT ONLY RESIST BUT TO BEND IT TO YOUR WILL. THROUGH TRAILS YOU WILL CONQUER A MASTERY SELDOM ACHIEVED.

There were whispers coming from the others, all likely having their own private conversations, encouraging them to take on a fight they barely understood, let alone could win.

She dug her fingers through her hair. It could never be simple. Why had she considered otherwise? To pass through this storm she had to delve deeper into it.

Idiots, she thought. *All of us.*

Nerio's knees ached, the floor cold and lifeless despite the shimmering color.

Was there a god above manipulation? One who did not work for their own gain? *Or are they like men, one and all?* he wondered. *Using the tools at their disposal to benefit none but themselves?*

Divinity rose before him in a hulking mass; beautiful, yet terrifying. He had begun to think, in his abandonment, he would never commune with another. That he'd been used to their ends and then dismissed, forgotten.

Turns out, the day a deity revealed itself was the same he realized they were all the same.

YOU MUSTN'T FRET.

"How can I not?" he whispered.

YOU HAVE FACED THE ODDS AND REMAINED TRUE TO YOUR HEART. WHERE MOST ARE WITHERED, BROKEN, OR JADED, YOU REMAIN AFFA-BLE. WITHOUT YOU, MANY WOULD BE DEAD.

"Because of me, many *are*."

BRETHEFEN WAS FRAGILE, IT WOULD'VE SHATTERED REGARDLESS OF YOUR ACTIONS. MANY SOULS STILL LIGHT THE PLANE BECAUSE OF YOUR ACTIONS.

Nerio thought of Captain Gernbard, and the sacrifice he'd made as he defended a truth that was not whole. "I don't know if... if I can find that faith again. What you offer, it could hurt so many. I've seen what can happen when you give people hope to which they can aspire."

AS HAVE I. YET WE PERSEVERE. I AM NOT LOOKING FOR YOU TO PLACE YOUR FAITH IN ME, BUT TO FIND IT ONCE MORE INSIDE YOURSELF. PEO-PLE WILL PERISH, A GIFT LIKE THIS DOES NOT COME WITHOUT CONSE-QUENCE, TO YOUR POINT.

There it was, the concern at the forefront of his mind, voiced by a god. He didn't want more tragedy, or the weight of those souls on his conscience. It was suffocating there enough already.

THE CHOICE I HAVE PRESENTED YOU IS NOT AN EASY ONE, A CROSS-ROAD WHERE ALL DIRECTIONS LEAD TO DEATH. YOU'VE SOUGHT A GUIDE YOUR ENTIRE LIFE, ONE WHOSE VOICE COULD LEAD YOU FROM THE HARM YOU'VE ENDURED.

I COULD TELL YOU THAT I'D BE THAT GUIDE, BE THE HAND WHICH DIRECTS YOU. BUT I DON'T NEED TO.

BECAUSE YOU DO NOT NEED IT.

YOUR DECISIONS ARE YOUR OWN TO MAKE, AND WHILE IT MAY SEEM IMPOSSIBLE, YOU ARE CAPABLE OF MAKING THE RIGHT ONE.

He slowly lifted his head, feeling as though it were some form of sin to look upon the divine entity before him. But the fear of decision was a burden that could easily distract from sacrilege.

Desnia was standing to his side, looking stern as always, contesting wherever she could, no doubt. How she found strength was a mystery he wished he could solve. There would be no choice for her—which explained the scowling—not if she wished to avoid the fate of the other Seers. She would continue should he refuse, into a life he struggled to see fitting himself into.

"She would be better off without me."

SHE WOULD NOT BE HERE WITHOUT YOU.

He took a deep breath, staring back at the floor. "If I were to diverge from this path she walks, would harm come to her?"

MUST YOU ASK THAT WHICH YOU ALREADY KNOW THE ANSWER?

The deaths of thousands, or the death of one—could he stand to have either plague his soul?

The gem's facets dug sharply into Delvan's hand.

What this creature, this *dragon*, was saying couldn't be true, could it? If it was, what did that make him?

He found himself trembling as he looked up into the cerulean discs that stared down at him, a knowledge to them that made him feel ignorant of all he'd previously claimed to know. Yet, at the same time, he felt as though he was home, in Calentine, surrounded by other Blues and familiar granite.

YOU'RE A KINDRED SPIRIT TO MY FALLEN SIBLING. HE, TOO, WAS EN-AMORED BY DUTY YET CONFLICTED BY QUESTIONS OF ITS NATURE.

"Duty..." Delvan said, voicing his hidden thoughts aloud. "To whom am I supposed to owe my allegiance? I had thought for a while that, someday, I could return to Calentine. The rational part of my mind knew that was a fallacy, I guess, but it was a hope all the same.

"Then I tried to forge my own way. I chose helping Des over my old ambitions because it felt right, like it was what I was *meant* to do. But now... I feel as if my entire life has been a lie. Are any of us capable of escaping fate?"

DESPITE WHAT YOU MAY BELIEVE, NOT ALL THAT COMES TO PASS IS WRITTEN. EVEN I AM CAPABLE OF BEING SURPRISED, A LESSON LEARNED IN MY YOUTH WHICH LED TO OUR IMPRISONMENT. THE ARRIVAL OF THIS PARTY WAS A STRONG POSSIBILITY BEFORE MY INVOLVEMENT. I MERELY ASSISTED ITS FINALITY, BUT IT COULD NOT HAVE COME TO PASS JUST AS EASILY.

That such a being could be wrong or fail to foresee its own binding terrified him. It seemed so powerful. Could it possess such human failings? Or was fate's magnetism as fickle as this creature even the High Realm feared claimed?

He remembered Hilbrun's rantings, his belief that a more potent magic laid hidden somewhere in the ruins of the past. Delvan had recently come to believe that meant the mages, but maybe, unbeknownst to even his friend, *this* is the dormant power he'd sought.

An enhanced gift wasn't what Delvan coveted. A small part of him was enticed, but too much destruction followed him as it was. His abilities, amplified, could cause untold destruction, and he questioned whether he'd be able to control it.

"How would death from my hands differ from theirs?" he asked, the faces of those who perished in his fire flashing in his mind.

I OFTEN WISH MORE OF US BESIDES THE FIRST PROFFERED THAT QUESTION EARLIER. PERHAPS THEN THE TWELVE OF US WOULD STILL BE TOGETHER.

"...Twelve?"

YES, THE NUMBER CORRESPONDING WITH THE BLUE VARIETALS IS NO COINCIDENCE, FOR YOU EACH INHERIT THE ASPECT PAIR FROM ONE OF US. I AM THE EIGHTH BORN, AND DESNIA IS MY DESCENDANT. YOU ARE OF THE FIRST'S KIN.

Delvan's hand slowly opened, the gem's imprints leaving red lines on his skin. He stared at the crystalline blue and once again was reminded of his late friend's words. "I had no choice in this," he said solemnly. "Not in who I became, the gift I received, who I served, none of it. Now you leave me with the illusion of another? Serve, or face the annihilation of everything I know?"

I AM NOT ASKING FOR YOUR SERVICE TO ME. THE CHOICE THAT YOU FACE IS AN UNFAIR ONE, BUT IT IS YOURS.

YOU HAVE, HOWEVER, MADE MORE DECISIONS THAN YOU GIVE YOURSELF CREDIT FOR. YOUR ALLEGIANCE HAS BEEN GIVEN—TO DESNIA AND THOSE THAT SURROUND YOU. AN UNSPOKEN OATH THAT YOU COMMITTED TO, REGARDLESS OF THE COST.

I AM ASKING YOU NOT TO ALIGN YOURSELF WITH ME, BUT WITH OUR HOME, A PLACE I KNOW YOU WISH TO PROTECT. THE OTHERS WILL NEED YOUR EXPERTISE, YOUR GUIDANCE, IN THE TIME TO COME. MOST OF ALL, THEY WILL NEED YOUR VOICE OF REASON AND VIRTUE.

WE DID NOT HEED OUR BROTHER, AS OUR FAITH IN OUR PARENTS WAS ABSOLUTE. DO NOT LET THEM REPEAT OUR MISTAKES.

Slowly turning his head, Delvan looked at the others, each enthralled by what stood before them—and the future it represented. Would he be able to live with himself were he to abandon them to the risk ahead? Or would his presence be the source of their demise?

The familiar claws of shadow dug into his chest, sending pains through his side and ice through his veins.

How, he wondered, *can I help them when I can barely help myself?*

There was wisdom in the dragon's words. Within his power was a choice, the ability to decide whom he shared the branching path of fate's possibilities. Could it be that helping himself wasn't possible, and it was the others that would help *him.* What could he do in return but offer the same?

Perhaps that is more important than the road traveled, or where it leads. That is a meaning to this life I could make my own.

A giant, white monster. Of *course* that's what a deity looked like. How stupid to think it could be anything else. Oh, and don't forget the teeth. And wings.

And ability to talk *inside* of his head.

Fuck, thought Kolden, *maybe this has all been a nightmare?* No, nightmare was too pleasant a word. Hellmare? That wasn't a word, was it? It should be, in his opinion.

Wait, he thought, a lump forming in his throat, *if I can hear its thoughts, can it hear mine?* Wouldn't that be embarrassing. What would it do? The thing probably hadn't eaten in a few thousand years. Maybe his diminutive size would be to his benefit for once, and he'd be seen as too small for a snack. Nothing but a sac of bones to get stuck in between those massive fangs.

A MIND OF RACING QUESTIONS YET YOU DO NOT ASK THOSE WHICH BROUGHT YOU HERE.

Yep, he was definitely going to start using "hellmare" from now on. Assuming he lived through this.

"You know, I've been kind of distracted by, uh, a few things. Sort of forgot to ask."

YOU NEEDN'T FEAR ME.

"That is *so* much easier said than done..."

I AM, AND SHALL ALWAYS BE, AN ALLY.

"Says the, uh, dragon that schemed to bring us all here." Kolden cringed. He shouldn't have said that. Stupid mouth.

WOULD YOU RATHER STILL BE IN DRUNT, BENEATH A MASTER WHO CLAIMS CREDIT FOR YOUR WORK? FORCED TO REMAIN IN THE DREDGES

OF NOTABILITY WITH A MASTERY UNAPPRECIATED? DO YOU THINK YOU'D EVER BE SATISFIED?

Shit... The hellmare had a point. He blinked, shaking his head. "Mhm, nope. I can see what you're doing. In my experience, an offer that seems too good to be true often is."

IF YOU BELIEVE THAT, THEN YOU DO NOT UNDERSTAND THE JEOPARDY YOU SHALL BE IN WHEN YOU ACCEPT.

"I thought you were trying to convince me, not make me more apprehensive."

I ALREADY HAVE. I'M JUST WAITING FOR YOU TO REALIZE IT.

Kolden's face scrunched, his eyes narrowing. "I'm beginning to think I might not like you..."

THEN YOU MAY COMMISERATE WITH MY DAUGHTER.

What was this game? He made his own choices, obviously. Sure, they were influenced by an incessant desire to *know*, but that didn't mean he was inherently prone to wanting to accept this insane offer. Although, if he didn't, what opportunities for understanding would he miss?

He felt at the cadentite weighing down his pocket. "You're saying that you can give me answers? Ones that will explain this stone, how it all works."

ALONG WITH—

"Dangers. Yes, you made that abundantly clear. I want to know how that gate worked, and the sword that one fucker had, or how it ties to all of us. And how we can *use* it."

There was a guttural roll from the dragon's throat, its eyes narrowing slightly. *THEY WILL COME TO YOU. AND FROM THEM, DISCOVERIES OF YOUR OWN—ONES THAT WILL PLACE YOU IN INFAMY AND WITHOUT PEER.*

Kolden's lips turned into a thin line. Why should he expect straight answers to straight questions? *No wonder all those Seers went insane, having to deal with this.* He should try to keep ideas like that to himself, though how do you hide inside of your own head? And did the dragon's eyes just start looking... annoyed?

Kolden released an audible *gulp.*

Yep, he thought with a nod of his head, *hellmare should* definitely *be a word.*

"I'll do it," said Orne, clenching his teeth and standing tall.

WERE YOU TO SEE THE POSSIBILITIES THAT I DO, YOU MAY NOT BE SO EAGER.

"You can turn us into the ones they write songs about?" he asked gruffly.

YES.

"And we will be at the forefront of the fight when those bastards attack?"

YES.

"Then why are you fucking arguing with me? Isn't this what you wanted?"

There was a quiet moment, fraying Orne's patience. He'd gone through hell to get here, chasing a dream that he'd tried relentlessly to forge into a reality. Now the one that offered it was, what, reconsidering? The thought alone was enough to make his face burn with anger.

WHAT I WANT IS FOR YOU TO UNDERSTAND. THE CHANGE THAT I'M OFFERING WILL NOT BE MERELY PHYSICAL, BUT ONE OF CHARACTER. TELL ME, WHERE DO YOU PLACE FAULT FOR THE BETRAYAL OF THOSE SWORN TO SERVE YOU? THOSE YOU THOUGHT YOU COULD TRUST, OR EVEN LOVE?

Orne responded through barred teeth. "They cared more about that stupid plant than they did about me! They didn't know what it was to respect command, let alone me. They can all rot."

RESPECT IS COMMANDED BY THOSE WILLING TO GIVE IT.

"Bullshit," he grated. "They weren't capable of it; they were rejects, dissenters, every one."

OR PERHAPS THEY WERE JUST IN NEED OF THE RIGHT LEADER.

What was this thing saying? That *he* was the problem? Wasn't it supposed to be all-knowing or something?

"There's nothing wrong with my leadership!"

YOU CANNOT DRIVE A GROUP WITH THE WHIP AND EXPECT LOYALTY. A FIRM HAND MAY BE REQUIRED FROM TIME TO TIME, BUT A FIST WILL NEVER BE ABLE TO HOLD MORE THAN ITS OWN IRE. YOU WOULD BE WISE TO REMEMBER THIS IN THE TIMES TO COME, OTHERWISE THE LEGEND YOU CARVE MAY NOT BE ONE OF YOUR LIKING.

That didn't even make sense. Damned metaphors. "What do you mean?" he demanded.

WOULD YOU BE THIS KEEN TO TAKE MY OFFER WERE YOU TO KNOW THAT IT COULD LEAD TO THE DEATH OF YOUR BROTHER OR DELVAN?

"I would never do that!" This thing was lying, it had to be.

INTENTIONALLY, NO. THE LOSS OF A SIBLING IS A CRIPPLING PAIN, AND SHOULD YOU NOT SEEK TO ADDRESS MISTAKES OF OLD, MORE THAN SIMPLE MUTINY MAY BE IN YOUR FUTURE.

Orne's hand curled into a tightly bound fist as he stepped forward and made a curt gesture. "I will *NOT* be the reason they die! I will be the reason they *survive.*"

THEN PROVE IT.

Desnia looked upon the creature that consumed her periphery, feeling defeated. The accomplishment of escaping prison, navigating the Astral Plane, defying that swine and closing his gate, all felt moot in the face of a choice which only had one option.

The others bore a jumble of emotions—more than one appearing to hold at least a shadow of the animosity she felt. That made her feel *slightly* better.

"What is it you want us to do?" she practically shouted. This was the part she was familiar with, when the scope of their responsibilities was laid out and one got to discover how deep a hole you'd dug yourself into. She was reminded of the bulbous Mixton and his greasy smile. Hopefully, someone had worked up the gall to slit his throat by now.

WITH THE POWER I SHALL VEST INTO YOU, I WISH FOR YOU TO GET THE ONE SOURCE OF VIDUT STRONG ENOUGH TO BREAK THESE CHAINS. ONLY WITH IT, AND YOUR COMBINED EFFORT, WILL IT BE POSSIBLE TO FREE ME OF THIS CONFINEMENT.

"And what is that?" asked Delvan.

Nothing easy, she thought, *that's for sure...*

A SOURCE OF POWER. THE LAST OF ITS KIND STILL UNBOUND IN THE REALM.

MY BROTHER'S HEART.

Ohh, said Masini, *that should be... interesting.*

"Why?" she asked in a quiet tone. She wasn't the only one with questions, however.

"Could you be a little more specific?" asked Kolden.

"If it was in Calentine with the sapphires," said Delvan with a furrowed brow, "then it would make sense that it was among the other gems. But that would mean... Oh, no, it can't possibly be—"

YES. YOU ALL KNOW OF ITS EXISTENCE, BUT BY A DIFFERENT NAME—THE KING'S JEWEL.

Desnia's jaw dropped. *The* King's Jewel? It suddenly made perfect sense—in the most terrible of ways.

"Hold up just a second," said Kolden, voicing a concern that had crept into each of their faces. "When you say 'King,' you don't happen to mean the immortal one that sits in a big tower in Calentine, do you? The same one who has wiped entire cities from the map? The one who rules over *all* the Blues and armies in the empire? That would be ridiculous... Right?"

THE SAME.

"Fuck," Orne grumbled.

"Kolden's right," said Delvan. "We don't stand a chance against the King."

IT WILL POSE CHALLENGES, BUT WITH THE POWER I SHALL BESTOW, YOUR COMBINED MIGHT SHALL RIVAL THEIRS.

"So," said Desnia, "we'll have to potentially fight our own armies, as well as the High Realm's if they manage to get here before we grab the gem. Fantastic..."

That made them all shift uncomfortably, quietly contemplating. She'd always found the King to be more legend than monarch, but even she thought of the stories she'd heard, the devastation he'd brought to enemies of the empire, or ones he wished to conquer. If there was a shred of truth to any of them...

This could be more daunting of a challenge than she thought.

There was a small part of her that considered a different route, one which involved her taking the dragon's "gift" and then absconding. Running to the ends of the world and hiding away.

She immediately dismissed the notion. She could never hide from this creature, not with her ailments—and most certainly not with them amplified. This was to be a full commitment, then. A contract of service that she'd be bound to until complete.

How disgustingly familiar.

Asta reached its talon forward, the links stirring dust that dried Desnia's tongue. The massive, black point reached forward like a finger, many times her height in length. The wet blood at its end glistened, and she suddenly tasted bile at the back of her throat.

DO YOU ACCEPT?

She couldn't help but stare, her mind racing as it tried to comprehend what now lay before her. She resented her lack of choice, but was there a way to make the most of it? What would the others do?

Orne stepped forward, stomping his foot down. "Yes, I accept."

She saw Kolden's hand playing with the lump in his pocket, eyes glancing from his brother to the dragon. After a moment he let out a begrudging sigh and strode next to his brother. "Well, I'm not going to let this idiot do it on his own. I'll do it." She swore his face turned a faint shade of green.

Delvan was still fidgeting with the sapphire on his chest. He looked at her, a concern in his eyes that was buried in conflict. He looked at the brothers, and to Nerio, kneeling on the floor. Finally, he nodded.

She felt the weight of a giant, blue eye turn to her. She met it, her face hard as stone. "Oh, fuck off. You know my answer already."

Nerio was the last. His chin dug into his chest, and he seemed deaf to everyone around him. He slowly turned his head to look at her, and a sense of dread spread through her core like a rot.

Would he decline?

The thought of him leaving tore her apart. She cared about him, deeply. Could she do this without him?

"Please," she found herself mouthing silently. His face grimaced, dipping low once more, but after a pause, he nodded.

HOLD OUT YOUR HANDS.

They each extended their arms, hands cupped together. With finesse that defied its size, the dragon pointed the immense claw downward and put a droplet large enough to spill over their fingers into the waiting, makeshift vessels.

Desnia stared at the pure-blue mixture, swirling in her hands with a radiating energy. It seemed endless as the sky's heights, deep as the ocean's current, and breathtaking as the greatest treasure. In all her time thieving, never had a stash of riches made her heart flutter as it did now.

Orne wasted no time, pressing his cupped hands to his lips and drinking it down with dribbles running through his beard. Kolden scowled, then closed his eyes and did the same. Delvan took a deep breath, bracing himself, and then drank deeply.

Desnia looked back at her hands, trying not to be revolted. *Fuck it,* she thought, pressing it to her lips and guzzling it as fast as she could. It was warm—burning in her chest like tea on a hot day. Once it was downed, she pressed her arm to her lips, doing her best to keep her stomach's contents where they belonged.

Looking over, she saw Nerio, who had watched her solemnly. With a last, distraught look at the churning blue liquid, he finally pressed it to his lips and slowly drank.

THROUGH THE BACK OF THIS CHAMBER IS AN EXIT. TAKE IT AND RE-TURN ONCE YOU HAVE MY BROTHER'S HEART. AND IORED...

Uh, yes? he asked, his voice shaking.

THEY WILL REQUIRE TEACHING. BE SURE THEY ACQUIRE IT, OR I SHALL

FIND THE REMNANTS OF YOUR SOUL ON THE PLANE AND USE WHATEVER ENERGY I MUST TO ENSURE YOU LIVE A LONG, TORMENTED LIFE.

Right, right. I'll, uh, do what I can, as that sounds very fair, and extremely unpleasant.

GO. I WILL WATCH OVER YOU WHEN I CAN. TRUST EACH OTHER, AND PREPARE FOR THE FIGHT AHEAD.

Keeping a wide berth from the dragon, the group slowly worked their way around the large chamber, watched by that great, pervasive gaze. There was a small hallway in the back, hardly wider than Desnia's shoulders and not much taller than she was. Orne had to duck and squeeze his way through.

Desnia took one last look back into the enormous chamber, taking in the sight of the winged dragon among the lines of glowing cadentite. She'd found the cure she'd sought for most of her life—as well as the debt incurred.

She didn't say anything as she turned and followed the others through the narrow corridor, but she knew that despite leaving the god behind, its eyes were still on her.

The tunnel was long and lit only by twisting lines of purple cadentite. When it eventually ended, they found themselves in a small room, with a pattern on the floor resembling the gate that had been beneath Brethefen.

"What's this?" she asked.

A miniature ga-ga-ga-fuck! That's so annoying. A 'door', said Masini, confirming her suspicions. *You needn't do much but stand on it, and it will take you outside.*

"Seems risky, your people putting a gate here, so close to Asta."

The others looked at her, and she assumed that they could no longer hear Masini. *It, like the entrance, is omnidirectional. It can only go out. It's also a one-time use in case anyone accidentally got stuck in here. Plus, not sure if you saw the hallway, but there's no way Asta could use this, and even if they clawed their way in here, it's intentionally made too small for them to fit.*

"You guys didn't fuck around with your prisons..."

No, we thought it prudent to ensure what was locked away, stayed locked away. Now, it's going to be cramped, but you all need to stand in the central ring. It should recognize me and send us on our way.

"Should?!" She was tiring of hearing that word from him.

Mhm, well, only one way to find out. The urge to kick him in the crotch again grew stronger by the second.

She repeated the instructions to the others, who begrudgingly stepped into the pattern's central ring. It was tight, their bodies pressed against one another. She stood there, uncomfortable, waiting.

And waiting.

"Masini, I swear on the gods, if—"

There was a flash of light, white and disorienting. There was nothing but the engulfing feeling of cold, a ringing peal in her ears.

Then, as fast as it came, it was gone, and they found themselves standing on the slope of a mountain. Scree was loose beneath her feet, and a frigid wind cut through her clothes. She clutched herself, looking around.

"None of these mountains look familiar," she said.

The gate is designed to take you far from its origin.

"Well, fuck," she said.

Before she could brood on the concern about their newfound location, a pain in her head dropped her to her knees. The others looked at her, but were soon clutching their stomachs, their faces turning pale and ill. Only Delvan was hale enough to come to their aid. He did what he could for the others—which amounted to little as they began to writhe and moan—before coming to her side and resting a hand on her shoulder.

She didn't even notice his sapphire, the chill she normally felt from it instead emanating from her gut like ice.

The pain came in waves, and between the crests she looked with watery eyes at Delvan, his face somber and still stained with azure blood.

"I don't know what's happening to them," he said. "Can you stand? I need your help."

She shook her head, doubling over as her gut twisted.

Between surges of agony, she caught a glimpse of what was to come. Spoken not of words in a foreign tongue, she was left with the impression that this had been but a small step in a long climb, the most treacherous paths still ahead.

"Idiots," she hissed between barred teeth. "Every one of us."

END PART 4

EPILOGUE

J erdine couldn't help but cringe, knowing what the colossal tower before him stood atop.

"It is impressive," said Valander from beside him. "I did not think such a building could be constructed in these people's short lives."

"Took them several," grumbled Jerdine. He hated Calentine and its streets, permeated with the radiant energy of tainted blood. Those damned knights were everywhere here, bearing a power they had no right to. The Hunter had liked it because there was more vidut to harvest, but the man's predilections had been distasteful.

"More impressive, then." Valander was stretching his neck, gazing up at the carved reliefs that soared along the gargantuan structure, rising like a spike from the ground and disappearing to a point at the summit of the escarpment it rested against.

This man and his damned adoration. "Come, our meeting awaits," he said, eager to be free of this city.

They strode through the arched, embellished doors, walking past the temple that was suffused with the tinted light from stained glass. They walked towards a set of curved stairs that had gem-bearing guards at either side.

It had taken countless threats, bribes, and promises to arrange this meeting. Valander was wearing the illusion of the formal attire of a military man. Jerdine had opted to purchase actual clothing that met the status of such council, though the self-declared "king" of these lands was little more than a barbarian atop a mound of excrement. Nonetheless, they needed to deal with him.

Jerdine had opted to use some of his precious vidut to create an illusion, masking his face as to not draw unwanted attention. Besides, people of the southern continent had skin that was tinged reddish, and they needed to look the part of the dignitaries they claimed to be.

Through bespoke halls of polished granite and engraved elements, they were led to the meeting chambers several stories up. They were shown to a door, cut of opulent wood and masterfully carved but... *smaller* than what Jerdine had expected.

"In here," one of their armed guides said, opening the door.

Jerdine followed behind the stately stride of Valander as they were ushered into a well-lit room, tinted orange by the tall, stained window. Furniture of comfort and thick carpets lined the lavish space, cases of books climbing the walls.

Near the back of the extravagant, sprawling office was a wide desk, two chairs sitting before it. At its back, sitting squarely and writing, was a dignified looking man with a greying, well-groomed beard and a thick head of waving hair.

Pinned to his ornate garment's lapel was a shining sapphire.

Jerdine tried not to quiver as the energy pressed against him, feeling amplified in the room for some reason.

"Please, take a seat," the man said, putting down his quill.

Valander strode over and gave a modest tip of his head before sitting. Jerdine, however, was less inclined, and already irate, which he tried to cleanse from his voice as he spoke. "I was under the impression that we were to meet with the King," he said.

The man behind the desk wasn't even gracious enough to offer a forced smile. "You must understand, no one meets with the King, not even in your circumstances. I am able to speak on his behalf, however, and will be negotiating terms. I am Lord Demrand ce Saffstar, Regent of the King's Sapphiric Court."

Jerdine had heard of the man. Apart from his affiliation with the boy who had upended his plans in Brethefen, he was one of the few living First Borns, if memory served, and most said it was him who held the true power in the empire.

It would have to suffice.

"I am Dracnic, of the Kingdom of Arglinipy," said Jerdine. The false name was one of import in the tiny kingdom—which he essentially owned—on the southern continent. Their production of gold was unmatched, and they currently held a strategic position in the Calentinian's war on the far-off continent.

They cannot even present us a feast. Arrogant, puny fools thinking they already own the place. Damn them and the egos their accursed gems bestow.

"And this," he continued, trying not to grit his teeth, "is General Valander, our newly appointed military commander." It was easier to utilize a name no one here would recognize.

"I understand," said Demrand, "that you are here to offer terms of surrender."

"Terms of..." gaped Jerdine. "No, you misunderstand. We are here to present an *offer*. One that would benefit both of our kingdoms."

"While we have a King, I might remind you it is merely a title that has been upheld over time. We are an empire, one which is not above conquering. And it is proper to use 'my Lord' when addressing me."

Great, another one of those... "Well, *my Lord*, while we're aware of your empire's... tendencies, you must be aware of the trade and gold that have kept you wealthy and fed on the southern continent. Our country may be a small one, but it is highly defensible with the mountains and jungle, as you're no doubt aware." *You pompous prick.*

Demrand leaned back in his chair, although he still looked rigid. Men like this needed to indulge more, in his opinion. "What is it you're offering?" he asked.

"A percentage, of all gold mined in our borders," Jerdine said, feeling a stab in his gut. Valander had forced his hand and somehow known more about his holdings than he'd ever intended. Proffering such sums of money made him writhe. "And we will supply safe harbor for any of your wounded."

"What do you ask in return?" the stern man asked, his voice wary.

Valander finally broke his stoic silence. "Spirit Walkers." The ridiculous name for the bastard children of the Fifth.

A grey eyebrow rose on the regent's face. "That is quite the price. How many and under what conditions?"

Yes, everything was for sale, for the right price. One thing that was no different here from the High Realm was the politics.

"At least a dozen," said Valander. "Preferably twenty."

"That's a significant amount."

"Yes," said Jerdine, "but so is our offer. We require their services for two years"—*hopefully less, given Valander's patience*—"and in that time ten percent of the mine's gross output shall be tithed to Calentine." It was ten percent less than Valander had directed him to offer, and he could feel the man's eyes turn to him, but he refused to give away more than that.

"Quite the proposal," Demrand said after a thoughtful moment. "What do you need them for?"

"Searching for additional caverns in the mountains. We know more gold is there but need to find it." It was partial truth, not that Valander cared. But, if they were going to be stuck in this forsaken realm any longer, he refused to be poor while stranded here.

"Make it twenty percent," the regent countered.

Is he insane?! Jerdine wanted to cut the man down for such a request—that was enough to pay an army for decades worth of service. Instead, he stuck with their original plan, not wanting to further incur the wrath of the ksat-simtri by his side. "Ten percent, and there is more for us to offer." The regent steepled his fingers before him, waiting. "We have texts, long hidden among our people, which describe an additional gift the Spirit Walkers may have. One that could profit us both."

Demrand gave a dismissive shake of his head. "Myths. And ones I've heard countless times before. We are not interested."

"Does the instantaneous transportation of troops across great distances not appeal, my Lord?" Jerdine asked.

"It does... But I am not naïve enough to believe it will work. Test it if you wish, but we shall take profits that are actually tangible. Fifteen percent, for the next *five* years."

Three extra years? You conniving shrew. "Twelve percent," grated Jerdine, knowing that he couldn't deny the deal. Not without repercussions.

"Agreed. I can offer fifteen Spirit Walkers, possibly more in a few months' time, if we can take some from assignment."

Ah yes, removing spies takes time. What a waste of an aspect... "Excellent, we look forward to it."

"One last thing," Demrand said. "We're sending two legions west. You may accompany them—and the Spirit Walkers—and travel south from there once we have completed some... *punitive* tasks. I understand it will add some months to your journey, but Spirit Walkers are scouts difficult to part with, as I'm sure you're aware, and the second legion will be joining the war front and can provide escort for you."

Retaking Brethefen, are you? Jerdine forced a smile. "Of course."

The regent stood, prompting them to do the same. "I have another meeting, but a formal contract will be drawn and delivered to you. The legions will march in a few weeks' time. Feel free to make yourself comfortable on the Upper Tier until then. We'll be in touch."

They both gave modest bows and left the room, their guides bringing them from whence they came.

"You did well," said Valander in a rare compliment. "We will begin their training immediately."

"We will need to be discrete," said Jerdine. "They're highly resistant to our aspects' powers."

"We only need them to open one portal, long enough for a few mages to come through with a prefabricated gate. Even a small one will be enough to begin."

Yes, and then he could be free of this benign rock and back to where power truly resided. This couldn't come fast enough.

Demrand watched the doors close behind the pair.

"Gallus," he said.

A man bearing a sapphire, wearing a blue, orange-lined uniform appeared beside him, his gift disabled and allowing him to be seen again. "Yes, my Lord."

"Follow them," he said, touching his chest. He could feel the other gem there, wrapped and hidden beneath layers of muted inanite-dyed fabric underneath his coat. The orange jewel burned with a fire only matched by the sun's, and even in this disguised state, it constantly flooded him with a power that was much more... potent. "They're not who they seem, and I would like to know more."

"I felt it, too, Sire." Gallus was a perceptive one; if only all his sons could live up to such expectations. "It was... strange."

"What it is, is foreign," he replied. "I would know their hidden intent, and where their interests truly lie."

Afterword

You made it!

This book has been a lot of work in the making, the culmination of several years of effort. Fun fact, the end of this book was originally part of the very first draft of a story which covered Of Gems and Stone, this book, and more.

That book was trash.

But taken from the proverbial dumpster were ideas that drove me to refine and expand this world and its events. This was a vast improvement upon those chapters I wrote what feels like forever ago, and I hope you've enjoyed reading it as much as I enjoyed writing and refining it.

If you did enjoy it, I would implore you to leave a rating on Amazon or similar sites. As an indie author, my visibility is dependent on ratings, reviews, and the kind words of my readers. Without them, this book is unlikely to go further than your hands. I post updates on Facebook and my website lambertsbooks.com if you're interested on finding out the status of the next book or days that I am doing free promotions.

At the end of the day, however, I write and publish stories that I would want to read, and I'm elated that you were enthralled enough to finish this one. I hope that you continue to follow Desnia, Delvan, and the rest of the gang along in their journey.

On to the next!